SUMERFORD'S AUTUMN

HISTORICAL MYSTERIES COLLECTION

BARBARA GASKELL DENVIL

ALSO BY BARBARA GASKELL DENVIL

Fair Weather

Dark Weather

<u>Time Travel Mysteries</u>

Future Tense

<u>BANNISTER'S MUSTER</u>

(*A MIDDLE GRADE TIME TRAVEL ADVENTURE*)

SNAP

SNAKES & LADDERS

BLIND MAN'S BUFF

DOMINOES

LEAPFROG

HIDE & SEEK

HOPSCOTCH

HISTORICAL FOREWORD

When I started writing some years ago, I set my books during the medieval period, and quite quickly made the choice to translate my books into modern English. "Thou art a scoundrel," just didn't appeal, and no one would have wanted to read it. I certainly wouldn't have wanted to write it. However, this leaves the author with a difficulty. Do I use entirely modern words, including slang, or do I create an atmosphere of the past by introducing accurate 15th century words and situations.

I made the choice which I continue to follow in all my historical books. I have been extremely strict concerning historical accuracy in all cases where I describe the background or activities. I do not, on any page, compromise the truth regarding history.

Wording, however, is another matter. For instance, all men (without titles) were addressed as "Master ----" But this sounds odd to our ears now. Only young boys are called master now. So I have adopted modern usage. 'Mr. Brown," has taken over from 'Master Brown". It's just easier to read. I have used some old words (Medick instead of doctor for instance) but on the whole my books remain historically accurate, but with wording mostly translated to modern terminology, which can be understood today, and hopefully allow for a more enjoyable read.

I was once criticised for saying that something had been bleached. (I didn't imply that they went to the local supermarket and bought a plastic bottle of the stuff, paying on credit card). But yes, in that age bleaching was a common practise. They used various methods including sunshine and urine. But it was bleaching all the same.

Indeed, nowadays most writers of historical fiction follow this same methodology.

Also a quick word of warning... Most of my books do contain small amounts of sexual content. As with all elements of my writing, I try to make them as realistic as I can, and as such have chosen to included this aspect of relationships too. If you choose to skim over these parts, there are not too many, and I hope you can still enjoy the rest of the story.

Regards

Barbara Gaskell Denvil

For
Gill
& Flo

CHAPTER ONE

The boy died at once, one quick smash to the skull, another to the chest. His bones caved in, his life went out. An hour after the boy was killed, they found the bramble thorns; one spike still wedged up hard into the horse's hoof. Another had been kicked free and was found later in the straw.

Ned and the under groom were sweeping up bloody shards of bone as the late September warmth oozed like melted butter over the hills beyond the castle turrets. But the dew still seemed to bleed where the broom had missed.

Just ten days out from the skirmish at Exeter with Turvey only back in his stable since last night, orders had been relayed for the old charger to be treated with reverence, scrubbed down and well fed. Instead the horse had taken to his huge hind legs, bared tooth and gums, thundered like Prince Harry in a tantrum, and kicked the new stable boy into splinters.

"Turvey's a war horse," the earl objected afterwards. "The damned animal's trained to kick and gouge. Am I expected to ride a damned palfrey into battle? I assume the groom was an inexperienced fool."

"The new apprentice. Little more than a child."

"He will therefore not be missed. Go and make sure Turvey's

1

settled. Give him mashed apple in his grain and if he frets, set him up with a mare."

"And the dead boy, my lord?"

"I've spent two years training Turvey. He anticipates every command I give on the field. That's worth more than gold. A peasant boy has no value at all."

The horse, mountainous mottled grey, rolled huge eyes and shivered like a baby. The chief groom held the bridle hard to the bit and wedged his heels against what was left of the stable door, holding firm. Little scarlet beads sprigged the straw. The boy's corpse was dragged away. It took four strong men to control a rearing destrier, and the apprentice should never have stood so close. A kick from both front legs had crushed the boy's skull like a tin cup. Flecks of brain pooled in the sunshine.

At first the incident had been reported to Lady Sumerford, the yellowing bruise across her left temple and cheekbone another reminder of his lordship's return, the horse normally less irascible than the master. Her ladyship said, "Hamnet, get the remains cleaned up and take the body back to its parents. I presume it had parents? Tell them the Sumerford estate will pay for the coffin and the priest. And you'd better take a purse. Give them a sovereign. A little generosity is better than encouraging back stairs gossip."

"Indeed, my lady. But I have been informed – his lordship's personal groom is convinced, my lady – that the horse was purposefully enraged." Hamnet's voice faded; a murmur as unconvincing as the story. "Even tortured. Thorns inserted into the hooves, my lady."

The lady laughed. "What nonsense. Who could get close enough? Who would want to get close enough? They are lying, to cover their own ineptitude." She clicked her fingers. "Hamnet, do we employ anyone else from the same family?"

The steward didn't think so, but a recent attack of the gout hindered memory.

"Hamnet," barked the countess, "don't gawp. Go and find out."

The household, pausing in its bustling, muttered at rumours and thrived on gossip. The apprentice's death became a welcome diversion, replacing drab routine with a satisfying and bloody mystery and even a hint of murder.

"Were a nice enough lad," muttered Ned. "Had no enemies far as I could tell, and no warranting of them. All the horses took to him kindly till Turvey come back. But I seen them thorns myself, and they was spiked up intentional."

"Bramble thorns? That'll sting right enough. Sounds like they aimed on hurting the horse more'n the boy," said Alan Purvis, small master of the dairies.

Red haired Remi, youngest of the castle pages, hugged his knees. "Just a weasely groomsboy and I don't care if he was done in or not. Besides, probably some girl from the village did it. Jealous females, my Pa says, being worse than them Swiss pikers."

"No young miss hammered thorns up Turvey's hooves," sneered Ned. "There's no female as could get near that horse."

"Lived out with them weird old spell-makers in the forest, didn't he?" remembered the dairymaster.

Ned snorted. "Bugger off, Purvis. Ain't no one under no spell in this castle 'cept the Lord Humphrey hisself. But I'm telling you, that horse were thorn spiked – and been done deliberate."

Outside the rosy dawn quickly paled and the rising sun turned sullen. The dust speckled sunbeams sank and the clouds hinted at afternoon rain.

"Who was the child anyway?" demanded Sumerford's youngest son, eyeing the ruined stable door.

"My lord, just some insignificant lad old Ned was training for a groom."

"None too well, it seems."

Hamnet acknowledged the implied criticism without bowing low enough to exacerbate the gout. "His lordship's battle charger was in a fury, sir. Ned informs me the creature had been spooked. Thorns, my lord."

"Rubbish," said Ludovic.

"Whatever you say, my lord. I must now carry out your lady mother's instructions sir, and arrange the return of the body to its parents. A coffin has been ordered from the jobbing carpenter. He's

3

nailing it up now in the small courtyard before starting work on the stable doors. I'll send the porter's two lads with the cart."

"I shall go with them," said Ludovic.

Hamnet hesitated. "To some outlying hovel? My lord, his lordship your father will object."

"He objects to everything I do on principle," said his lordship's youngest son. "So I shan't tell him." Ludovic paused momentarily, eyeing his father's steward. "And nor will you."

"Naturally not, my lord."

"And Hamnet. Three sovereigns."

The staff, aware that since completing his knight's apprenticeship in the south some years past the earl's younger son fostered lofty pretensions to an idealistically high standard of justice, considered he would doubtless soon grow out of it.

Hamnet's hunched shoulders shuddered imperceptibly. "And does your lordship require me to accompany the cart, sir?"

"Certainly not, Hamnet, what conceivable use would you be?" Ludovic shook his head. His hair caught the last sheen of light, gold on gold, as the sun now huddled behind the clouds. "Just find out where the child's family lives and give the direction to the porter's boys. I'll ride beside the cart and deliver the purse myself. You can stay here and keep your mouth shut."

"As your lordship wishes."

It was raining as promised and a silver drizzle spun through the cart's churning wheels. The youngest Sumerford pulled his hat low over his forehead and followed the cart ruts through the mud. It was a longer journey than he had expected. He shook his head, spraying raindrops from his feathers.

The cart stopped. The cottage was no more than a croft hidden under the autumn leafed beeches, its single thatch sodden and caved, losing its bindings. One tiny window below, another above, and a threshold of dirt. Ludovic dismounted, boots to the slush and last year's fallen leaf. The small door looked as though it would break if he knocked upon it. In any case they should have heard the trundling of the cart, though the rain was heavy enough to muffle sound. His fist was raised to knock after all when the door swung inward to shadow. A dark apron shuffled into a curtsey, vague movements within obscurity. Ludovic peered into the deep shade. The woman had browless eyes squashed vacant over a beaked nose; pigeon faced. The darkness behind her smelled of urine and grime but her apron was clean and the blotches on her skin were only the leathering of age.

"My lord?" She was frightened and hesitant. Ludovic strode into the lightless interior, following the bobbing shadows. His eyes adapted slowly. The stench thickened, heady and nauseous.

He did not know the boy's name and had never asked. "There has been an unfortunate accident, madam. My father's stable apprentice; your son I presume. The Earl of Sumerford's sympathy of course, goes without saying." A lie his father would dismiss with blank indifference. "His lordship will naturally pay all expenses. I need to speak with the boy's father."

"The boy's father is long gone, my lord." Whispers, in case her words might seem somehow discourteous or unwelcome. "Killed fighting for the king years past, my lord."

"At Bosworth?"

She shook her head and her starched cap dropped pins. "At Bosworth field, the good man fought for King Richard, and even though the king was killed, my master lived on. But he was killed ten years past at Stoke, fighting for the new king, Henry Tudor."

"You're the boy's only parent then."

"I was the babe's nurse, sir. Then with the poor mites being left orphans, I brought them here to my brother's house. Now he's gone too. There was the Sweating Sickness, my lord."

He could barely hear her respectful and nervous murmurings, and saw only shrinking shadows. "So who is the guardian of the boy training at the Sumerford stables?"

"There is none, my lord." She stepped back timidly. "Since young Gamel is fourteen years now and the man of the house. But I've looked after him, best as I was able, most of his young life." She paused, gazing earnestly.

5

"Gamel?"

The woman curtsied. "Gamel, sir. As went to apprentice at the castle stables a month gone, my lord."

"Gamel then." Ludovic sighed. "I must inform you that the earl my father returned last night from the siege at Exeter. A fractious war horse is murderous in a temper. Your boy came too close. My sympathies. The cart is outside with the coffin, the body washed and sewn. I can order it taken on to the church immediately, if you've a wish to accompany the cart."

The woman sniffed, eyes wide and moist, struggling to keep a respectful silence. It was from behind him that the voice said, "I'll go with my brother."

Turning from the dingy interior and half blinded by the incoming light, Ludovic watched the small shape emerging from its damp glistening aura. Another child, a girl in long skirts with black hair to her waist. Ludovic was surrounded by whispers; the misery of the frightened woman, the drip of rain on leaf, the breeze amongst the trees. Now he spoke only to a silhouette. "As you wish. I'll instruct the boys to drive straight to St. Edmund's. You may ride on the cart." He held out the purse, soft leather and heavy with its three sovereigns. She did not take it. "This will cover the priest and grave diggers, and keep your family for a few months." Ludovic placed the purse, cords untied, on the stool beside the empty hearth.

The girl came from the doorway into the cottage and stood before him. He saw only the intensity of her eyes for no candle was lit and the shadows hung dark. The entering swirl of soiled skirts reignited the inherent stench; damp soot, rancid goose grease and stale cabbage water, but the rain in her hair smelled suddenly sweet.

She said at once, "My brother was killed by a horse? How? Were you present? Did you see what happened, sir? Gamel was – good – with animals. He loved horses."

Ludovic raised an eyebrow. "I was not present, no. I did not witness the accident, nor do the daily routines of my father's stables ever inspire me to conjecture. However, I have been apprised of the events and am sorry for them, but they are not my concern. Now your brother's remains have been prepared for the grave, and if you wish to

6

accompany the coffin to the church, I will make the appropriate arrangements."

He thought the girl blushed, but the shadows remained unresponsive. She said, low voiced, "I didn't mean to question your word, my lord. I only wondered if Gamel had time to love – the horse that killed him."

Ludovic stared at her. She did not look up or meet his gaze. He asked, "Do you pay rent or tithes here? Without your brother, do you have other means of support?"

The girl paused, then shook her head, still intent upon her toes.

He turned on his heel. "Come to the castle tomorrow," he said over his shoulder. His velvets were steaming. His body, warmed from the ride, was chilling quickly. "I'll leave orders for the steward to put you into service. Tell him I sent you." He strode back outside and gave instructions to the porter's lads. The sumpter, bedraggled in the rain, tossed its mane. Ludovic spoke briefly to the horse, calming it, then turned again to the girl at the doorway.

The old woman had draped a threadbare kersey shawl around the girl's thin shoulders. Now reaching to clutch at her apron skirts was a younger boy, as skinny as his sister, who had appeared from the upstairs chamber.

The girl pulled the shawl over her head and came back out into the rain. Together in the drear of drizzling daylight, Ludovic watched her, now seeing her clearly. She was a little older than he had at first imagined. Her eyes were large like huge hazel bruises, stark against pale skin. She was gazing at the box on the cart. Ludovic would not normally choose to touch some village brat, but, without thought, reached out his hand to her. "The boys will take you to the church."

The girl did not curtsey. She moved back and did not take his hand. Ludovic stepped forwards and put both palms to the girl's waist, hoisting her up impatiently. He felt the coarse shapelessness of her gown between his hands, the slippery veneer of old grime, and beneath it the warmth of her small body. His fingers brushed the narrow curvature of her hips. Avoiding intimacy, he moved and caught instead the sleek wet coils of her hair. He looked up suddenly, read her expression and was startled. The girl looked neither grateful

7

nor melancholy. The bitter, smouldering fury in her eyes matched that of any war horse. He bumped her down onto the cart's wide bench. Her wooden shoes thumped against the boards and she tugged down the frayed hem of her skirts. There were flea bites on the bare protruding bones of her ankles.

She did not thank him. Ludovic turned, looking back over his shoulder to the cottage. The elderly woman had sunk into a deep curtsey, stiffened knees painfully bent. She was thanking him profusely. "Oh so incredibly gracious, my lord. And the purse – so very generous."

He looked up again to the cart bench where the girl sat hunched. She had bundled her skirts around her feet, and her face was dark beneath the shadows of her hair and her shawl. He still felt grease on the palms of his hands from the decrepitude of her clothes. Her anger and contempt were in some way equally defiling.

Ludovic nodded to the porter's lads to drive on. He wiped his hands on the damp velvet of his coat, turned, mounted his own horse, and rode back through the rain to Sumerford castle. He rode slowly, curbing impatience. His thoughts seemed more burdensome than usual.

CHAPTER TWO

Gerald cleared his throat, made sure his father was not present somewhere beyond the immediate visibility of the firelight, and said, "I know exactly who he is."

"We know who you think he is," said Ludovic. "And it's a damned unwise opinion."

The great hall was ablaze with candlelight, the dizzying brilliance of a hundred tiny flames from sconce, table and chandelier, outmatched by the thunderous dance of leaping carmine from the hearth. Yet Gerald sat, knees to chin, in the shadows. "I don't think it. I know it. If you weren't all cowards, you'd know it too. Our gentle Tudor monarch certainly knows it."

"Our gentle Tudor monarch," said Brice, "has already separated several pretty heads from their bodies because of this particular conspiracy. I intend staying as firmly attached to my head as is humanly possible."

Gerald scowled from his corner. "If you're all terrified of the bastard Henry, then I pity you."

Ludovic smiled. "No need to fear him, my dear. Our esteemed father will find out and murder you long before the king gets his hands on you."

"Cowards," repeated Gerald. "Abysmal cowards and traitors to the

Yorkist cause."

"Ludovic's right," said Brice softly. "He may be a supercilious little peacock, but he's still right. Forget the damned king. It's our beloved papa will tear your head from your shoulders if he smells the taint of treachery."

"And be careful for Humphrey," added Ludovic, crossing to the long table beneath the chandelier. "I've no wish to make unjust assumptions, but Humphrey enjoys carrying tales to Father."

Gerald sniggered. "Humphrey? He wouldn't understand a plot if I explained it to him. Poor sot doesn't know his prick from his toe."

Brice shook his head. "The only two things our most elegant brother does recognise, my dear," he said. "He's mighty fond of both. Sucks one and cuddles the other. No doubt he'd like to suck his prick too, but he can't reach it. I've watched him try. He's mighty jealous of the hounds, I'm sure."

Ludovic filled three pewter cups from the big earthenware wine jug, took one for himself, presented another to Gerald and indicated the third for Brice to collect for himself. "But does it matter?" he objected. "Even if this Perkin Warbeck creature is the true Duke of York, what difference does it make? The king now has him in custody, so there's an end of it. And besides, fourteen years ago the whole country accepted proof that old King Edward's boys were the result of a bigamous marriage. They're bastards, and have no more right to rule than damned Henry Tudor himself."

"Everyone in England has more right to rule than Henry Tudor," muttered Gerald. "Besides, it was Tudor himself who repealed the law turning King Edward's children out of the succession, and making them legitimate again."

"Only so he could marry one of them to bolster his own miserable claims," grinned Brice. "So let's have an end to this. I'd always assumed those boys were done to death in the Tower a decade back. And if not, so what? Whether this Warbeck is the real heir to the throne or simply some idiot low-born impostor from Flanders, matters not one wit now he's finally the king's prisoner. Drink up and be merry, little brothers."

"Merry? With the true king taken?" Gerald buried his nose in the wine cup. His shirt cuff showed a rip, well darned. "And me without a shilling to my name. So if you're feeling merry, big brother, then you've a good smug reason for it since I see you're dripping more cloth of gold and silk damask than damned Stanley himself. You're as much a younger son as I am, so how do you generate such enviable wealth? You're not one of Tudor's darlings."

"Heaven forbid," shuddered Brice. "I hold my life and limbs too valuable to associate with kings. I'm merely careful with my allowances, little one, with no wish to throw away my small purse on lost causes."

Ludovic frowned at Gerald. "You've been sending money to these conspirators?"

Gerald nodded at once. "How could I do anything else? I know it as a true cause, and I wish Tudor dead. So every penny I can find goes to help."

"I'll not be lending you money for a new shirt then," said Ludovic. His own doublet, well-padded against the castle's draughts, was of fine purpura deep dyed in mahogany and trimmed in sable, worn over a linen shirt thick laced in silver thread.

Gerald eyed him with sudden suspicion. "And you Lu, you're the damned baby of the family, so how do you dress like a duke? We've an alarmingly expensive mother and a father more parsimonious than the bastard king. So, what am I missing?"

"Missing loyalty and familial duty by the sounds of things," Brice pointed out. "We younger sons must all do what we can, my beloved, and it won't be something I ever discuss with you. You may be shameless in revealing your secret transgressions, but I am not. What humble means I can contrive to constitute a decent living, is my business alone. Now, have you finished explaining your treasons, little brother? Or have you more shocking opinions to confess?"

Gerald turned away, retreating again into the contemplation of his wine. "You two think only of self-indulgence. Clearly our father's sons, both of you, as selfish as he and not much better than Humphrey. Hoarding your own secret treasures, and hiding the way of it. What, are you both turned to robbery on the highway? Certainly you've neither the sensitivity nor the altruism for noble causes."

"For lost causes, no."

"Cheer up my dears." Brice stroked his miniver trimmings. "We'll all have a new purse for Humphrey's nuptials. Mother will insist on it. With a real heiress beguiled into the family, will she risk the noble sons of the house appearing in darned hose? Never. Mother'll steal from father's coffers to deck us out like maypoles, I promise."

"Humphrey's imminent wedding," brooded Gerald, "is as shameful as every other damned affair arranged by our gallant father. How dare he drag some poor innocent female into this family, with Humphrey the way he is? Do you think they've warned the bride's family that her groom is a depraved loon with the brain of an infant?"

"Why should I lament?" objected Brice. "What bride ever really knows what she's getting? Do they care? The woman's gaining the heir to the Sumerford title and estate, isn't that enough?"

"Humphrey doesn't know what he's getting either," said Ludovic, refilling his cup. "She might be a termagant. Presumably she's bringing a deal of land and property as her dowry, and will end up a countess. It's a fair deal."

"You think being married to Humphrey a fair deal?" demanded Gerald, shocked.

"You're a fool, my dearest beloved," Brice smiled. "A sad collector of sentimental and inane causes. Who do you sympathise with most? The future bride of our handsome big brother, or this impostor Perkin Warbeck, feigned prince of the realm?"

Gerald stood abruptly, emerging from the shadows of the alcove. "I don't know this woman. None of us do. But I know I wouldn't care to see any innocent female married to a dribbling lunatic, and that's more or less what poor Humphrey is. How can you bear to think of her sharing his bed? Required to produce a Sumerford heir? For God's sake, I shared Humphrey's bed as a small boy and he was a damned uncomfortable companion then, with sticky fingers groping just where I didn't want them. Thank the Lord they soon moved him into his own separate quarters in the opposite tower. As for the true Duke of York, he's a man I love and admire as the rightful king of England. I know where my loyalties lie."

"In a bog, my dear, stuck in a bog," Brice said. "Forget princes.

Loyalty should remain close to the heart, concentrated only on oneself. There are dangers enough in this sweet wide world, without choosing to antagonise the powerful. What interest should I have in loyalties, my pet, when they surely do nothing but enrage some other warring faction?"

Ludovic drained his cup. "Yet self-interest turns boring if permanently unchallenged. And we're well enough accustomed to antagonising the powerful in this household, since our beloved parents have breathed out hatred and vice ever since we were born."

"Indeed," Brice sniggered. "After nigh on twenty five years of spasmodic acquaintanceship with our noble sires, I have learned the value of self-interest. And how do you imagine we were ever born, my sweet? Can we contemplate visions of dearest Papa making passionate love to our esteemed Mamma? Certainly not. An absurdity. My conception was no doubt achieved in some more sombre manner as yet unknown to me."

"He presumably beat her into submission," Gerald muttered. He sat again, and was chewing his lip. "Poor Humphrey was clearly begat by violence."

Ludovic again poured the wine. "Can Humphrey be brutal?" he mused. "He has a child's temper, but seems tame enough. Yet he has a propensity – against animals – he once killed a hunting bitch. And he stamped on the barnyard kittens when Father refused to take him to court. Perhaps – thorns in a horse's hooves for instance – would he be capable do you think?"

Gerald looked up. "I had a particular groom once when I was young. Goran Spittiswood. My first horse and my first groom. I liked them both."

Brice clapped his hands. "Enough, little ones, enough. First we are embroiled in treachery and false pretenders, and now in the idle comparisons of servants." He stood abruptly, swinging back the long skirts of his surcoat. "I cannot abide the contemplation of the contemptible. I shall leave you to your absurdities, my beloveds, before I expire of tedium."

"Nobody could spook Turvey," Gerald muttered, watching his brother's departure slant across the candlelight. "You can't think that damned giant of a horse would stand meek and mild and let someone hammer spikes into his feet. Go to bed, Lu, and think of gentler things while I dream of Richard Plantagenet and the future victories of our true king."

The tallest turrets of the Sumerford castle, on a bright clear day, might see across the tree tops to the velvet hills around Taunton where the young man named Perkin Warbeck by the king, but who called himself Richard Plantagenet and claimed to be the true Duke of York and prince of the realm, had last breathed freedom. But as the autumn wind whistled its bitter ghosts one midnight, the young man's wife had whispered her warnings, and Richard had taken her advice, and left. He had crept from the camp, unable to face the morrow's battle which he knew he must lose. Exactly as Henry Tudor had done before the Battle of Bosworth twelve years earlier, the inexperienced boy had listened to the night terrors echoing across the moors, and in abject misery had deserted those who followed him. Henry Tudor had also fled, but being an older man, had attended to his advisors and returned by the morning's light. Richard Plantagenet did not, his advisors were as inexperienced as he was himself and his battle was never fought. Now, having surrendered to his enemy in return for the promised safe keeping of his wife and son and the lives of his men, he rode under guard to Westminster. His claim to the throne was over.

Autumn russets shimmered, staining Somerset's vales and flickering through the forests like little flames fanned by breeze. Across the fields and pastures of the Sumerford estate and flanked by the shadows of the castle, the tenant farmers deep ploughed their yardlands for winter crops. The martins were flocking high in the sun dipped azure beneath the clouds, massing for migration, and a heron was picking along the waterline, long toes fastidious amongst the squabbling gulls. The Abbey's bees were returning to their hives, fat with clover, as echoes of the Abbey choir were interrupted by bird calls.

The evening hazed into blues, shedding warmth. And in a small croft just inside the borders of the forest, an old woman huddled weeping while a dark haired girl, on her knees in the straw and ashes, laid twigs and lit a flicker of fire to warm the damp corners. The girl brushed away her own tears, the back of her hand wiping streaks of soot across her face. She owned no kerchief so sniffed, keeping her head down, her hair in her eyes, eyes stinging from salt tears and smoke and the sharp tang of mouse piss. The next morning she would start at dawn and walk to the castle to claim the position promised her. It would doubtless be scrubbing and sweeping and labour she despised, but she would be fed and earn a few pennies for sending back to the croft, so keeping all of them alive. Gamel was dead but the rest of them could live.

Finally within the castle stables Turvey snorted, nodded and slept, his huge head slumped to his chest as his grooms settled down into the hay, scratched their noses and prepared for their own sleep. The long day sank further and the sun dipped its colours into the ocean, spreading a haze of cerise across the small cold waves, while beyond the barns and the scrabble of rats, the strange piping song of the little quail gathered his friends for their night's escape to a warmer south.

Each day swelled, swam and ebbed. Weeks passed within the small safe promise of an ordered life, the routines of the seasons, the melodies of the countryside, secured and watched over by the great castle in whose shadow each man lived, and hoped, and struggled, and finally slept deep in his cot, snoring with a forgetful and untroubled conscience.

It was the eve of the wedding, and the family had guests.

In the great hall the table was set for the supper feast. The silver flashed in the high perfumed candlelight, the well bleached linen was edged with the Sumerford arms embroidered in scarlet silk, and the huge stone walls, swathed in massive tapestries, absorbed the skittering draughts. Wedged into a minstrel's gallery with its boards creaking in time to the fiddle, the Sumerford players kept the pace as cheerful as determination rather than talent permitted, while the earl led the prospective bride to her place. The bugle announced the first course and the platters were borne in. The roast venison steamed, on its nest of galantine, dates in compost and marchpane leaves. Humphrey began with pickled eggs and frumenty, baked porpoise and blandesoure. He had dropped his napkin, wiped his fingers on the tablecloth and had to be reminded by his mother not to belch. His father sat on his other side, and beyond him, the bride. The Lady Jennine, heiress from the north, neither spoke nor ate, but drank liberally from her wine cup and gazed with faint dismay at the bleeding porpoise, central upon its mighty silver stage. Her napkin, neat folded across her shoulder, was the same colour as her face.

Since her parents were deceased, the Lady Jennine was accompanied by her brother, a boisterous gentleman who appreciated the wines on offer, and sat opposite his sister with his wife at his side, making bawdy jokes with his mouth full. His wife was cautious of his elbows.

Brice tittered. He wore white damask and rose velvet, courtesy of his mother's insistence on the family's best appearance, and his new clothes inspired his good humour. Gerald, who also wore new clothes, looked as though he might be on the verge of tears. Ludovic, as the least important member of the immediate household, sat at the end of the table and kept his eyes on his platter. It was he, however, who first became aware of the interruption.

Hamnet's voice was only a murmur, heard beyond the screen to the corridor, his words lost beneath the players' pibcorn and rebec. Then the steward's voice was raised, a woman's shrill insistence answered. There was a scuffle, Hamnet began shouting, and three women pushed into the hall. The oldest and tallest was forcibly dragging the other two, and set herself forwards before the great table. The music faltered, the feasting paused. Only Humphrey, unperturbed, continued to eat. The earl stood in silent fury, his lady screeched, flinging down her napkin, and Brice began to laugh. Only Ludovic recognised two of the intruders.

"Throw them out," spat the earl. He sat again abruptly as the countess stood.

She said, "I shall deal with them outside." The steward began to manipulate the clump of unruly women backwards past the long screen.

Brice jumped up at once. "I'll come with you," he said, ignoring his father's glare. "An utterly fascinating distraction, don't you think?"

Humphrey chose two powdered chicken pastries from their dish, and put both into his mouth at the same time. Without a word Ludovic put down his napkin, scraped back his stool and followed the growing commotion in its enforced retreat from the hall. The earl began a hurried discussion with the intended bride concerning her bride clothes, her preference for fresh flowers rather than beads in spite of the difficulties of the season, and the necessarily placid temperament of the chapel priest who would officiate at the nuptials. The earl would not countenance a chaplain who preached hellfire. The marriage blessing would be a calm and unquestioned affair.

Hamnet had detached the more officious of the entering women from her grip on the other two, and was hauling her towards the front doors. The countess, rigid backed, addressed the other elderly woman who stood close, dishevelled and seemingly terrified. The countess demanded an explanation.

Ludovic turned to the third, little more than a child, who was standing silent in the shadows. "The meaning?" Ludovic raised an eyebrow.

The girl stared at the continuing turmoil beside her. "I didn't want to come. I knew it would serve no purpose."

"I didn't inquire as to either your wishes or expectations." Ludovic smelled the familiar dreary aroma of dejection and stale poverty. "But I require an adequate explanation for your unwarranted presence, and that of your relatives."

She stared down at her clogs. "They aren't my relatives. One is my nurse Ilara. You met her before. The other is Dulce, her brother's widow. She insisted we come here."

Village brats living in dirt and squalor did not have nurses. Ludovic sighed. "Nor did I ask for a summary of your family tree."

The girl said, "I told you. They're not my family."

Ludovic watched her with growing impatience. She had neither curtsied, nor did she address him with respect. "You are impertinent. More than likely her ladyship will have you beaten. Do you now work within the castle, as I arranged more than a sennight past?"

The girl nodded, still not looking up. "Yes, sir. In the dairies outside."

The woman Dulce was struggling to remain on the doorstep. Hamnet thrust her out into the dark. Her boots squelched as she hit the mud. Ilara, twisting her fingers in her apron, sidled to the open doorway. The young girl began to follow. Ludovic put out an arm, blocking her way. He said, "I am still awaiting an explanation. Is this about your brother's death? The family considers that matter closed."

With both her chaperones now outside, the girl stopped suddenly before Ludovic's outstretched arm and turned to face him, looking up directly into his scowl. Her expression was unexpectedly fierce with an open and vibrant contempt. Ludovic stared into the girl's green eyes, flecked like quartz crystals. Her pupils reflected the candlelight and Ludovic's equal fury. He felt as though he looked into his own eyes. The girl said, her voice an angry whisper, "What difference does it make? You won't care. You won't be interested."

"It will make a deal of difference to you, if not to me," Ludovic said. He wondered why, on all that was holy, he was choosing to persist. "It will either mean you are thrashed, turned off from your employment here and cast out, or merely ejected peaceably. Now, for the last time. Why did you come here?"

The other two women having now been removed, the doors were closed. The steward put his back to the handles in case of repeated assaults. Noises from outside subsided. Brice had taken his mother's arm and they stood behind Ludovic, who spoke briefly to them over his shoulder. "Leave this with me. Go back and amuse our guests."

"I imagine they're already mightily amused," spat the countess. "What a delightful impression of our family they must now have."

Brice nodded cheerfully. "But especially of our dear Humphrey, don't you think?" and led his mother back into the hall.

Ludovic dismissed Hamnet and turned again to the girl who remained silent. "You have told me everyone else's name," he said. "But not your own."

18

"Do you need to know the names of all your dairy maids? But your steward could have told you. I'm Alysson Welles. And you don't need to cast me off. I'll willingly leave your employ."

"But since I've no intention of letting you go just yet," Ludovic said, "no doubt you will at some time answer my question. I have considerable patience, but it is running out. You and your companions barged in here in the middle of a social gathering with my brother's affianced bride and her family in attendance. Your behaviour is insufferable. I am still waiting for a suitable explanation and an unequivocal apology."

"We embarrassed you? How – unfortunate." The girl leaned back against the wall, Ludovic's arm still between her and the doors. She smiled. "My abject apologies of course, my lord. We should never importune our noble masters."

Ludovic clenched and unclenched his fingers. "And the reason for this – importunity?"

"Simply that your brother attacked me. He tried to rape me. He hurt me. Badly. The dairy master refused to interfere. He told me I should be flattered. He said it was a lord's business to do whatever he wished. I ran home." She glared up at Ludovic. "Ilara was frightened and told me to go back to work. Dulce isn't so easily cowed and considers herself my protector. It's a long walk from the house to the castle, as you know having been there. Otherwise we should not have arrived so late in the day. And if your steward hadn't attempted to throw us out and refused even to speak quietly to her ladyship and tell her we desired a private word, there wouldn't have been this ridiculous commotion. That's the full story. May I leave now?"

Ludovic paused, again unclenching his fist. "Which brother?" he demanded.

"The eldest. Your fine Lord Humphrey. And it doesn't matter if you don't believe me. I don't care if I'm thought a liar, and I certainly don't care about your opinion of me." The girl dodged suddenly beneath Ludovic's arm, thrust herself at the great double doors, tugged one open, squeezed through and was gone into the night.

CHAPTER THREE

The servant held out the swathes of crimson silk, assisting his master into his doublet, stepping back to comb out the trailing sleeves, then forwards again to turn up the small tight neckline and pat the baudekyn smooth across his lordship's shoulders. Ludovic was dressing for Humphrey's bridal Mass, but he did not bother to look into the mirror before him. There were quite other matters on his mind.

Of the two women who filled his thoughts, one was about to become his sister-in-law but it was not as a sister that he thought of her. She was deliciously ripe, round breasted, small waisted, and full lipped. She was not a woman he wished to imagine gripped between his eldest brother's fumbling fingers. He imagined her instead within his own embrace, naked and sweating against his pillows. He imagined the slender softness of those legs now so well hidden beneath her skirts, his hands sliding their length up to where they joined. He imagined his mouth on hers, and his kisses exploring lower. She was not a woman you could see without imagining illicit romping.

Another shadow strained at the edge of his thoughts, an irritation rather than a temptation. A small boned skinny brat, with thick black hair and eyes vivid with anger. Ludovic did not imagine her within his embrace or in his bed. She smelled of sullen exhaustion and years of weary toil. She smelled of dirt. But his considerable dislike of her rooted in another reason altogether, in that she clearly disliked him even more. He had not yet understood why. The question itched liked the flea bites he had seen on her ankles. The girl was angular, common and rude. But her eyes stayed with him, even against his will, and haunted his dreams.

His manservant knelt and buckled his shoes. Ludovic sighed, nodded, and sent the dresser away. He tightened his belt and strolled down to the principal hall. The bridal party was already waiting. The bride was sumptuously shimmering, her satins as rosy pink as her cheeks and the full rise of her breasts from their cleavage. Ludovic forgot the black haired village waif and returned to other sweeter contemplations.

The union between the Lord Humphrey, heir to the Sumerford title and estates and his intended the Lady Jennine, heiress of two northern merchants' fortunes, was to be celebrated within the porch of St. Edmund's, the village church. The heiress, although exhibiting no evidence of marital joy, showed no signs of hesitancy. Her new husband's behaviour seemed to leave her unmoved, while the carefully planned luxury of her wedding arrangements appeared to please.

An early October frost had spliced the stained glass windows with tiny white studs, like diamonds set amongst the saint's haloes. The oak leaves were falling as the final words were read. The elderly priest bobbed, Humphrey beamed and patted him benignly on his tonsure. "If this couple be rightfully trothed and there be no impediment hereby declared," the priest announced as loudly as he dared, "then in the name of the Father – ," drenched the ring in holy water and held it out to Humphrey.

Humphrey, being not quite sure what to do with it, passed the ring to his mother. "Stand up straight and breathe in, Humphrey," his mother reminded him.

Her eldest son shook his head. His hair, uncapped for the ceremony, frizzed in the breeze as the bright red curls turned to fire in the sudden sun. "Can't," he explained simply. "Belt will fall down."

Ludovic, taking one quiet step forward, swung back the huge looped and fur lined openings of his baudekyn sleeves, and took his elder brother's hand in his. Humphrey's plump palms were frigid in the cold air. Ludovic rubbed them gently, bringing back circulation, then, carefully controlling each movement, brought Humphrey's fingertips around the bridal ring. The Lady Jennine held out her hand. The ring was slipped on each of her finger in turn; "In Nomine Patris, Filii et Spiritus Sancti," and the gold band finally encircled her wedding finger and rested there.

Ludovic nodded and moved back. Humphrey grinned, pleased with himself. "Well done, well done. Is that it, then? It's bloody cold. Can we go home now? Is there more food?"

"The wedding feast," Ludovic reminded him.

"Oh, excellent! Come on then. Let's hurry."

Autumns at Sumerford tended to blaze. The fires were lit huge, jugs of steaming hippocras crowded the tables, the candles' beeswax sweated. The feasting done, Lady Jennine sat meekly by the fireside, back straight and feet together, her hands clasped in her pink satin lap, her gaze concentrated on the equal brilliance of her wedding ring. Humphrey, partially distracted by the dance of flames, sat beside her. He had finally remembered his bride's name and repeated it carefully to himself several times, in case he forgot again. His mother, the Lady Gertrude, Countess of Sumerford, spoke at length and for once found her conversation politely uninterrupted. Her three younger sons lounged together far across the hall, cups in hand and shoulders to the tapestried wall. They eyed the bridal pair through the steam of their well spiced wine.

"She's certainly gorgeous," admitted Brice. "But drinks a lot for a lady, you must admit."

"Poor soul." Gerald sighed. "Faced with Humphrey across the church porch, what would you do? She needs to drink for courage."

"Besides, she's not a lady," Ludovic reminded them. "She's a rich merchant's daughter with sobriety neither an expectation nor a duty."

"Mother's a lady." Brice smirked into his velvets. "And she drinks a lot."

"Naturally – since she's married to Father," said Ludovic. "I doubt she'd find any advantage in staying sober. She drinks, she keeps out of the way, and she hides her bruises."

He watched the young bride under discussion as she lifted her cup. The Lady Jennine met his gaze over the brim, blinked twice and smiled slowly. "The woman flirts," noticed Brice. "Perhaps not as innocent as we supposed, my dears."

"Any female quite that – beautiful," murmured Ludovic, "would find staying virtuous somewhat challenging, I imagine."

"You're both shameless," Gerald said, low voiced. "This is our good-sister, entitled to our support and respect. You've no right to discuss her personal attributes, nor slander her reputation. It's atrocious behaviour. You shouldn't even be –"

"Thinking what we are all undoubtedly thinking," smiled Brice. "Hereby speaks the saintly watchdog of our moral scruples, restorer of my conscience, noble traitor of the realm, conspirator and rabble-rouser. What would I do without you, little brother?"

Gerald blushed. "I admit the lady's quite delectable. I could hardly deny it."

Ludovic drained his cup. "Unexpectedly beautiful. And beautifully unexpected. She shows no sign of – disgust – in contemplation of her bridegroom. I admit I expected neither her elegance nor her manners. Perhaps she was warned after all. But with one briefest glance at the gown she is barely wearing, one can hardly accuse her of an excess of modesty."

"Oh, pooh, my dears." Brice tossed his russet curls. "Have you never seen the ladies of the royal court? They walk virtually bare breasted. Fashion demands it."

"We live in a rural backwater and fashion be damned," Ludovic pointed out. "A woman naked in my arms is always a pleasure. One walking near naked in company is a little more startling. But I do not complain. And I wish Humphrey joy with her. I am fond of Humphrey. He's never done me injury, and I consider him harmless. So I have absolutely no intention of interfering in his marriage. But I shall keep out of his way as usual, relish my own solitary company, and remind you that my thoughts are my own."

"Humphrey – utterly harmless?" Gerald turned his back on the group by the fire. "Didn't you suspect him of torturing horses just a few days back? I don't believe he did, but I'm not so sure what he's capable of. Perhaps none of us are entirely – innocent."

"Blood of our esteemed paternal great-grandfather, you think?" Ludovic laughed. "We are all capable of murder, no doubt, if it suited us. But I've none planned as yet. Nor plans to seduce my sister-in-law."

Yet the Lady Jennine's place in his thoughts remained warm, and although only imagined, her touch was warmer. Her fingers hovered short and dainty, the palm narrow, the nails gleamed. She appeared discreetly polished. Her white gossamer headdress did not wilt in the heat from the fire, her brow did not perspire and her nose did not scorch or glow. No sweat collected in the deep fold of her cleavage, and she spoke always softly, and with deference. She was entirely controlled and entirely harmonious. Her pretty blue eyes, pink mouth and little pointed chin were perfectly proportioned, her brows plucked, her forehead shaved. She breathed perfume.

The vision remained welcome and clear in his mind the following day when Ludovic strolled out to the dairies and demanded to see the Master. It was another bright cold morning and the autumn leaves were dropping fast. The dairies were housed in barns kept distant from the kitchens, though the butter churns overlooked the herb garden. The larger sheds smelled rank, of cow dung and sour milk. Huge vats ranged the walls and the master was skimming the warm creamy froth. "My lord?" For fifteen years Alan Purvis had barely seen the noble family for whom he worked, yet had now spoken with several of their lordships in the space of just a few days. He bowed very low. "The girl? Dismissed, my lord. On her ladyship's direct orders. Dismissed yesterday, my lord, without pay."

"I see. Purvis, tell me exactly what happened when the girl complained of being attacked. What, if anything, did you see?"

The dairy master set down the huge wooden skimmer and wiped his hands on his apron. His experience with the Sumerford estates prompted diplomacy. "My lord, I witnessed nothing. Nothing at all, with respect my lord. The girl was unskilled, and not so quick to learn. Oh, I admit she was willing enough to try, my lord, but had no aptitude and couldn't tell a yearling from a twelve year old. So I set her to the goats' cheese instead. But she showed no more talent with that, nor even understood the cooling of the tubs nor the slowing of the starters till I showed her full twice over."

Ludovic stared at the master with considerable distaste. "My good man, are you daring to give me a lecture on dairy farming? Let me tell you I consider it a disgusting process. And does no one intend giving a straightforward answer to a straightforward question any longer? I do not wish to discuss cows, goats or udders. I require only information regarding the girl Alysson Welles who was recently employed here until attacked on, I believe, the twelfth day of October."

"Forgive me my lord." The small man chewed his lower lip. "I found the wench one morning, my lord, in a huddle by the ripening vats. Crying, she was, late in the afternoon close to sundown. I gave her a kick and ordered her back to work, but she said as how she'd been hurt, and needed time to get her breath back. True, she was bleeding around the mouth and was bad bruised where her gown was torn. When I demanded the reason for it, she gave blame to the Lord Humphrey, though I beg you forgive me for the repeating of it my lord, and said as how she was attacked but fought him off. I didn't believe a word of it. I gave her a slap and a scold and threatened to send her to Master Hamnet for a whupping. But she ran off, sir. It wasn't till yesterday when she comes a trailing back, but her ladyship told me to cast the wench off without a penny and tell her not to return. I was only too pleased to obey her ladyship's orders, my lord. The girl was a liar and a trouble-maker."

"Late in the afternoon, you say? And she claimed to have fought her assailant off?"

"She did, my lord. As if a weak female creature could manage any such thing. I knew it for a lie."

Ludovic scowled and stomped back to the castle, to his brothers, the blazing fires and warmed hippocras. There were overripe curds

25

stuck to the soles of his shoes and the stench of sour whey lingered in his nostrils.

"I've no interest whatsoever in the unpleasant complications of this family's myriad failures," objected Brice. It was his bedchamber, the shutters closed against the gusting wind. The fire, disturbed by the chimney's downdraught, flared across the hearth and smoke filled the room, collecting up amongst the ceiling beams. Brice had sent his manservant away and the shadows held only himself and his two younger brothers. "I happily admit being utterly unconcerned by our lady mother's ambitious machinations, our father's filthy moods, Humphrey's marital bliss, any perversely favoured activities concerning thorns and horses, and his possible ravishing of dairymaids. Nor do I care about the looming and well deserved execution of our beloved Gerald when he gets discovered up to his pimpled chin in royal treachery. I have important business tomorrow, and I'm leaving for a few weeks. I shall be glad to see the last of you all."

"I'm off too," admitted Gerald. "I've – matters to attend to. Far more important matters than you two with your petty little games."

"My petty little games pay me rather well, as it happens," grinned Brice. "And don't pretend you're not interested, because I know you're curious. But I'm not telling."

"At least my – games – are honourable." Gerald scowled. "I doubt if yours are, since you keep so secretive." He turned to Ludovic. "As for spying on poor Humphrey's wife –"

"My interest in our dear sister-in-law is purely brotherly," interrupted Ludovic. "And I'm not spying on Humphrey either. I was merely trying to remember where he was and what he was doing on the afternoon of the twelfth, day before the Eve of Wedding feast."

"He was with mother," said Gerald promptly. "Trying to learn his coming role in the wedding off by heart. Which he then forgot anyway, but that's where he was all day. No time to wander the dairy sheds, steal cream or grope the cows, I promise."

Ludovic frowned. "And hasn't since appeared, somehow without my noticing, covered in scratches or nursing a kicked groin?"

"Don't be absurd, Lu," said Brice. "You know it's a pack of lies, and who cares anyway? Why do my two little brothers immerse themselves in such demeaning irrelevancies?"

"I imagine," Ludovic spoke more to himself than to the others, "she hoped to revenge the death of her brother."

"I imagine," said Brice, "she just hoped to make trouble. Angling to be bought off perhaps. But since I wouldn't recognise a dairy maid if I saw one, I've no interest in this tedious rigmarole. Besides, if I remember rightly Lu, you've not been averse to playing with servant wenches yourself in the past."

Ludovic raised an eyebrow. "Peeping, were you, my dear? But whoever I've played with in the past was extremely willing I assure you. Enough of that. So, you're both off on your private concerns tomorrow, kindly leaving the Lady Jennine to me. Unfortunately Father's organised a hunt. His hunting parties are always so damned dreary since he and Humphrey slaughter everything on sight. Gerald, your precious pretender is a prisoner now anyway. Why not stay at home with me a few days longer?"

Gerald shook his head. "I've received word that I'm wanted. It's true the Duke of York is a prisoner, but it's not that simple. Do you realise, this has been Henry Tudor's greatest nightmare for six long years of struggle. Our miserable king has spent more money on espionage and propaganda concerning this so called fraud and impostor, than he has on any other single thing since his own struggle for the throne. Since before Stoke he's sweated and wept, executed his friends and relatives, locked his mother-in-law away until her death, and made himself ill with worry. Yet now he finally has the boy after all this time and effort, he's terrified of actually doing anything bloody. Clearly he knows he's dealing with true royalty, and he's frightened of condemning the Duke of York to death and then facing some sudden incontrovertible proof that this was his own wife's brother and the rightful king all along. So he dallies and fidgets, keeps the young man confined to court, shows him off to ambassadors and disbelievers, tries to humiliate him, but pays him and his wife an

27

allowance as if they're courtiers instead of prisoners. It's as clear as daylight."

"It's as clear as mud."

"The king knows the Duke of York to be genuine. I know it. He knows it. Most of European royalty knows it. But Tudor certainly isn't about to give up his crown, rightful heir or not. So he's playing games, wasting time, buying allies, and building up a false story as full of un-darned holes as any muddled fabrication could be, to try and convince people the Duke of York is simply a common peasant from Flanders. Who would believe it when the young man speaks better English and Latin than Tudor does, and has court manners more elegantly perfect than half the court themselves?"

"They say the late King Richard's sister tutored him, simply to challenge the Tudor dynasty. The Duchess Margaret hates Henry Tudor since he killed her brother and stole the throne from the Plantagenets. You know that. Now she sits on half the power of Burgundy, so she's set up a conspiracy and a fraud, just to pull our new king down."

"In a few short months she manages to tutor a lumbering peasant brat speaking only Flemish, to convincingly impersonate an English prince?" Gerald stamped impatiently on the worn Turkey rug before the fire. "What idiotic slander." The vibration sent sparks up the chimney.

"Must I listen to all this?" Brice sighed, flinging himself across the thick velvet coverlet of his bed. "And when they catch you and clap you in irons, just remember to tell them your big brother Brice had no part in this nonsense. I'm fond of my head and would like to keep it. Besides, I don't give a damn who sits on England's crumbling throne. They all demand the same taxes."

"But how endearing," mused Ludovic, "that you trust us so completely, Gerald my dear. Brice will tell us nothing of his suspicious dealings away from home, yet you so openly admit your most dangerous involvements – conspiracies which could so easily cost you your life."

"If I can't trust my own brothers - ?"

"Brice doesn't."

"Nor you, beloved." Brice, leaning back against the pillows, grinned across at Ludovic. "You're as circumspect as me, little brother. You should be more destitute than the rest of us. So how do you demonstrate such wealth, my boy?"

"I've neither wealth nor secrets to disclose," smiled Ludovic. "Enough sovereigns for a new doublet occasionally. Begging pennies and favours from Mamma. Where's the duplicity is that?"

Gerald snorted. "What lies, Lu. You wouldn't lick anyone's feet if your own life depended upon it. You're more arrogant than our dear father, more supercilious than Brice, more proud than mother and more clandestine than the lot of us. I believe you even conceal yourself when you go to the privy."

Ludovic laughed, "So evidently I'm also more stupid than Humphrey. What a charming family."

"But I'm still leaving tomorrow," said Gerald. "And I wouldn't save you from being dragged off hunting by father anyway, even if I stayed. Go take out your bad temper on the deer."

The hunting party departed the castle shortly before dawn. The first hint of the rising sun breathed a tentative pink haze up from the eastern horizon but the sweeping sky above remained black, moonless and cold. Ludovic yawned and mounted his bay. Humphrey, an excellent rider who enjoyed the hunt more than most other things apart from the anticipation of food, was already briskly cheerful. His new bride was not. She regarded the small palfrey with a nervous dislike, but she had already suggested staying at home and been immediately refused. Humphrey expected company. Already two of his brothers had deserted him in his favoured entertainment. "Oh pooh," Humphrey told her. "Amazed you don't ride already. Doesn't everyone? Most odd. You'll have to learn to ride at full tilt soon, you know. It's what I like above everything. You'll soon like it too. We shoot lots of animals. Big red deer and hares and partridge and wild pigs. If I miss anything, father finishes them off. It's great fun."

The Lady Jennine sniffed, curtsied obediently, and allowed her brother to assist her in mounting the little palfrey. The brother snorted humorous derision, hands to his sister's rump. His own wife giggled and winked. With a heave, the Lady Jennine, reaching nervously, was hoist towards the saddle. As she clutched her skirts, her brother grinned widely and surreptitiously pinched her bottom. "Come on, Jenny. Be a good girl. For now, anyway!"

Ludovic watched with some curiosity. He had been on the point of offering to stay at the castle himself, purely to keep the bride company of course, should she wish to miss the hunt. But since he had little expectation of agreement, and now there was something else altogether on his mind, he said nothing but followed some way behind. His new sister's behaviour and the extreme vulgarity of her brother had begun to interest him. He was therefore distracted, dawdling at some considerable distance from the main party, and quite alone when the attack came.

CHAPTER FOUR

The forest was loamy and wet. With most of the trees already winter bare, the pale dazzle of dawning sun slipped easily through the open branches, dancing across the dew strewn undergrowth beneath. The season's first mushrooms were sprouting little brown roofs for beetle and ant. But beyond the first creek and the light canopies of scattered aspen and hazel, the older trees drew in darkly; oak and willow and a tangle of holly. The deer were rutting.

Some miles from the castle, the ruins of the lonely watch tower were shadow dank under ivy and heaped stone. Dating back to the ancient Normans and unused for three hundred years, it sheltered only pigs and rats. The tower was not safe. Twice lightning had struck and stones often hurtled from the shattered turrets. A broken stair clung treacherously to one remaining outer wall, winding ever upwards to a windswept view across the tree tops to the sea. Being half open to storm, the tower was useless for anything except a smuggler's storage, and where it remained enclosed, it stank of mould.

Ludovic rode along the small hilltop, skirting the tower's tumbled rubble before heading his horse down again into the little valley. He was alone. He could no longer hear the others, the brisk vibration of hooves, the giggles of the women and Humphrey's hearty eagerness.

From trot to amble, Ludovic finally stopped, still high on the crest, letting his mount graze and his mind wander.

The Lady Jennine's face floated pleasantly through his thoughts. He wondered, irreverently, if his brother had yet managed to bed her. He wondered whether, as Gerald insisted, the caresses of a halfwit would seem particularly vile, or if, to a woman of virtue, the touch of her wedded husband would be always acceptable, since sanctioned by the Church. Ludovic considered her brother unexpectedly coarse and his attentions remarkably unbrotherly, but the behaviour of northern tradesmen were another world to him. He then wondered if her sly and watchful expressions were truly signs of flirtation as they seemed, or merely the innocent friendliness of a good woman.

His thoughts undressed her slowly, unpinning the starched chiffon from her hair, slipping the gauze fichu from her breasts and the satin from her shoulders, discovering the pink velvet compliancy of flesh, the swell of her nipples and the soft scents of her body. Then the first arrow struck him.

He felt it screech like flame through his upper arm muscle just below the shoulder. He swayed in the saddle and caught quickly at the reins, tightening his knees and whirling around towards the direction of the shot. The second arrow pierced his thigh and he felt himself fall.

He opened his eyes on soaring stone and one slanting beam of light. Pain hit, like a pestle to the mortar. He made no immediate attempt to rise. He doubted if his body would support him. Then someone said, "So I haven't killed you. What a shame."

He turned his head and saw skirts. Dark blue broadcloth, frayed hems over wooden clogs, and a thin kersey cloak, faded brown and threadbare. There was a familiar smell of goose grease and unwashed depression. Ludovic sighed, attempting to wedge himself up on one elbow. The other arm was bleeding heavily. His new lampas silk brocade coat was no doubt already ruined. "I may still be alive," he said faintly, "but it seems you have just signed your own death warrant."

She looked away. "But you killed my brother Gamel. Now I think you've killed my little brother Pagan as well. Why not me too?"

Ludovic lay back. The ground was wet and hard. His eyes burned, he could not think clearly and his body seemed surly, incapable of either defence or attack. The pain of the two arrow wounds was immense but it was the back of his head that hurt most. The dizziness and nausea increased. He recognised the arches of the old watch tower. He had been dragged under the shelter of the broken stairwell and a glitter of sunshine from the window slits striped his face, momentarily blinding him. "You are clearly insane," Ludovic murmured. "But since you presumably aimed to kill, not such a bad shot. Can you tell, am I badly hurt?"

Alysson Welles sat down cross legged beside him with a bump, and regarded him carefully. He saw the fear in her eyes, and watched her control it. Then he saw the sudden flash of light catch the steel in her hand at the same moment as she raised the blade. With faint alarm, he recognised his own knife. He wondered if she had sufficient skill to dispatch him quickly and painlessly. He slowly closed his eyes. After a moment he opened them again. The girl was cutting down his coat sleeve and the doublet beneath it. The knife caught in the heavy weave, wrenching against the injury, and Ludovic bit his lip.

"Go ahead, yell if you want to," said the girl, concentrating on her work. "It won't worry me. I really don't care if you pretend to be brave or not."

"Whatever I do or do not do," said Ludovic with some asperity, "is not out of consideration for your opinion, I assure you." He felt the cold air on his arm as the sleeve fell away. "I assume the arrow head is imbedded?"

"Looks like it," Alysson agreed. "Do you want me to dig it out? Your knife seems fairly sharp. But it'll hurt."

"I imagine it will. It will presumably hurt a good deal more if left in and allowed to fester. I prefer you to remove it, if you will. Have you any experience in this sort of thing?"

"If you mean, am I in the habit of shooting people and then nursing them back to health," said Alysson, "then no. Surprisingly, you're the first. But my father was an archer and he taught me to shoot when I was little. And Ilara is quite clever with medicines and she taught me too. I've just never had the chance to use any of it before."

"Then you clearly need practice," said Ludovic. "I am glad to be of service."

She seemed already prepared, and an earthenware bowl filled with stream water was set on the ground beside them. There were also piled bandages, apparently torn from a chemise. The fine stitching of a hem and the tucked folds where a waistband had once been, were still apparent. Then Alysson began to remove the arrow. The shaft was broken off well past the fletching, but the heavy steel point remained deep within the muscle. She was careful and deft fingered but the pain was considerable as she used the tip of the knife to ease the arrow head loose. It took a deal of time.

Eventually, keeping his voice steady, Ludovic said, "Since you are going to some trouble to keep me alive, even apparently to cause no more pain than inevitable, I presume you did not actually try to kill me after all."

"Of course not," said Alysson scathingly. "Or I would have."

After a short pause as Ludovic watched the blood pour renewed from his upper arm, he continued, "Another reason then? You merely wished to get to know me better perhaps? You find aiming at inanimate targets a shocking bore? Or you simply wanted to pass the morning in some more enterprising manner than sewing samplers?"

"Lie still," Alysson commanded. "You're already bleeding like a stuck pig, so don't wriggle." She held her breath and the metal head sprang free, flipping out like a rotten tooth pulled by the barber.

Ludovic disguised the sigh of relief. He moved his arm experimentally, and winced. "Much better," he said weakly.

"If you must know," Alysson, attentive and studious, began to wash the gaping hole in his arm, "I'm not such a good archer really. Actually I'm a bit surprised at how bad my aim was. You probably won't believe me, but I just wanted to scare you. I aimed over your head."

"I am a fairly large and prominent target," Ludovic pointed out. "And I was sitting quite still at the time."

"Just as well," said Alysson, unwinding the first bandage, "but you were uphill and I was in the valley. I shot high, but the sun was in my eyes – and I'm sorry, if that makes you feel any better, which of course it won't. I just wanted you to fall off your horse. To get your attention. And to see you hurt for a change."

"You were remarkably successful in that at least," said Ludovic. "I hope you enjoyed the spectacle. Where is my horse, by the way?"

"Run off," said Alysson, knotting the bandage around his arm, "galloped away at once and never looked back. Not very loyal or loving. Evidently even your trained animals don't like you."

"And how is it exactly," demanded Ludovic, stung, "that I've earned such vehement hatred? I cannot remember doing anything at all to injure you. Indeed, I've gone out of my way to make some recompense for your losses, and ease your situation."

Alison sat back, staring at him, bemused. Her fingers were stained with his blood. "Pompous – arrogant and blind," she said. "You come marching into my home, curtly informing me that my beloved brother is killed by fault of his own carelessness, as if your horses have every right to trample to death anyone they please. You throw money at me as if a few pennies could buy the life of the person I loved most in all the world. You don't even say you're sorry. Then I'm nearly raped by your horrid brother and you and your staff seem to think I should have welcomed it. I'm cast off without my pay, though I worked very hard for nearly two weeks. Now you've stolen away my little brother too. What have you done with him?"

Ludovic gazed up at her in amazement. "I beg your pardon?"

"You should," said the girl. "But it's Pagan, my little brother, I care about. He was only twelve, and small, poor mite, since he never had proper food. He followed us when Dulce made me come to the castle to complain that night. But I haven't seen him since. None of us have. We've all searched everywhere, endlessly. So where is Pagan? Is he hurt? Still alive? What has happened to him?"

Ludovic watched her tears glisten suddenly in the glancing sunlight. "My good girl, I haven't the slightest idea what you're talking about," he said. "Do you take us for kidnappers? Procurers for Southwark's molly houses? Cannibals?"

"Since you thought my beautiful Gamel's life was worth just a few pennies -"

"Three sovereigns."

"Do you think I'd sell my brother for three hundred sovereigns? He was such a good boy. Both my brothers are – were – so kind and loving and clever. I suppose you think people like us can't possibly be good or clever." She was increasingly distracted, constantly rinsing her fingers in the bowl of bloody water, then pushing them through the thick coils of her hair. "But I don't understand. Pagan followed us that day, I know he did. And none of us have seen him since."

Ludovic watched her as she struggled not to cry. "Whether or not you meant to kill me," he said quietly, "you've still taken a dreadful risk. You must realise that if I choose to make this public, you'll be hanged without question. Were you that desperate?" Alysson nodded, silent. "But how can you possibly imagine," he continued, "that my family has some sort of absurd vendetta against yours, and wishes to annihilate you one by one? For what conceivable reason would anyone have stolen away your younger brother?"

"I don't know." She hung her head. "But within two weeks I've lost both my brothers. You see, since the great battle when my father was killed, life has been so very wretched. We all dreamed of – a turn of luck. When Gamel was taken on as apprentice at your stables, it seemed as though perhaps things would improve at last. And then –"

Ludovic had wedged himself up against the old lichened wall and was sitting supported, nursing his arm as it bled profusely through the bandage. "I'm sorry," he said. "Genuinely sorry. But boy apprentices are killed sometimes. Chargers are notoriously dangerous, being trained to battle and bred for strength and temper. They have sometimes been known to kill their own riders, and will certainly kill on the battle field. It's a hazard all grooms face, especially the young trainees. And it may not seem much in my family's favour, but in fact the three sovereigns compensation I gave was considerably more than usually paid under such circumstances. And I delivered the purse myself, believing an official appearance by one of the Sumerfords was warranted instead of simply sending the coffin unaccompanied and barely explained. And I am sorry if I seemed arrogant. That was – unintentional." He smiled slightly. "It is, perhaps, my natural manner."

"I suppose I would have known all that," Alysson said to her lap and to her fingers fidgeting with the remaining bandages. "And you did arrange for me to get work at the castle, even after I was rude to you. And my being rude was – intentional."

"But," Ludovic continued, "Perhaps we should now consider a more practical programme. You have still lost your younger brother, and I am without a horse and unable to walk."

Alysson looked at him dubiously. "And you've still got one of my arrows sticking out of your leg."

"Something I have hardly overlooked," Ludovic admitted. "But I don't need your medical skills for that. I can deal with it myself. Some clean water, and the rest of those bandages might be helpful."

She tipped the twisted strips of torn linen into his hands, and scrambled up. "I'll get the water. It'll take a minute. The stream's down the bottom of the rise."

The second arrow had pierced Ludovic's left leg, deep into the outer thigh muscle. As soon as the girl had trudged out of sight, he ripped open the unravelling wool of his hose and began to ease out the arrow shaft, widening the wound and loosening the imbedded passage of the metal. Gently and slowly the arrow, remaining intact, released its grip and was drawn free. It emerged thick with dark blood and engorged with small worms of flesh and sinew. Ludovic regarded it a moment, then lay back against the damp stone with a sigh. His leg throbbed unceasingly, but the worst of the pain was ebbing.

The girl came back, a little breathless. "I suppose," Ludovic said faintly, indicating the arrow and its dripping point, "I should just be glad you didn't use a broadhead. But this is a bodkin, and far too lethal for peacetime use – or poaching – which I presume is what you originally intended doing."

Alysson set down the bowl beside him. "These were my father's arrows," she said. "Gamel kept them for practising. And it was Gamel who always – well, I shouldn't say any more."

"Don't be absurd," said Ludovic, losing patience. "Putting him on

37

trial for stealing his master's livestock would seem singularly pointless under the circumstances. Now," and he proceeded to wash and then bandage his thigh as Alysson watched. As he tied the final knot, he looked up at her again. "And you needn't worry. I don't intend hauling you before a jury for attempted murder. Not that you don't deserve it."

"Does it hurt very much?" inquired Alysson sympathetically.

"Of course it does," Ludovic said tersely. "And should at least be stitched if not cauterised, none of which is possible here. You're a confounded nuisance. And just how was knocking me unconscious going to help get your little brother back anyway?"

Alysson shook her head. "Having you weak and confused, for me to ask questions. Besides, I wanted to humiliate you. Though it wasn't planned. I was out looking for pheasant when you rode by."

"How convenient for you." Ludovic flexed his thigh muscle and winced. "Unfortunately I doubt I can make it back to the castle just yet. It's a damned long walk, probably three or four hours even without a limp. And I can't send you there for a spare horse. They'd arrest you on the spot. So you might as well run home. Once I'm able to stand, I'll make my way somehow. And tomorrow I'll see if I can trace your brother."

"That's silly." Alysson shook her head again. "You can't stay here alone in the wet. It'll be ages and ages before you can walk that far, it could even be days. It'll be freezing cold tonight. You could die. I don't want to get blamed for that. And if you do walk, it'll just make the wound worse and you'll end up having to have your leg cut off or something. Besides, there might be wild boar. And robbers. People use this old tower for hiding out, you know. That's why I found this bowl here, and sometimes other things are left here too."

Ludovic smiled suddenly, evidently amused by something he did not explain. "But surely not ready supplied with bandages for possible accidents?"

"Actually, you're wearing half my shift and now you've bled all over it anyway. Which is a shame really, because I only had the one."

Ludovic laughed. "I suppose I should buy you another one. But the castle apothecary will find it highly suspicious that I present my injuries already bandaged with a woman's intimate apparel."

"Can you," Alysson wondered, frowning, "think of a possible excuse for all this? I mean, will you try? I suppose in the end you'll think it's easier just to tell the truth and haul me off to the magistrate after all."

"Since I am not in the habit of expecting sudden attacks to my person while peaceably riding my own lands, I have no plausible excuse ready at hand." He continued smiling. "But I shall think of something. For reasons which escape me, I have no intention of having you arrested over this. Now, before it gets any later and I change my mind, you should get off home."

"I'll have to stay with you," Alysson decided. "When you fell off your horse, you hit your head on the stones and you were unconscious for ages. I dragged you in here, which wasn't quick because you're dreadfully heavy, and then I even had time to tear up my shift for bandages and fetch water too, and when I got back you were still cully-headed. Actually you look rather bosky-eyed even now."

He felt it. "My apologies for being so dreadfully heavy," he murmured, "and also for appearing bosky-eyed, whatever that entails. I gather you also had time to search me for weapons, and steal my knife."

"Well, otherwise you might have woken up and tried to kill me." She paused, blushing slightly. "I wouldn't have blamed you really. I suppose you still have a right to be angry. Actually, considering everything, you're being awfully polite."

Ludovic grinned suddenly. "Apart from the ruination of my good clothes," he said, "I confess I'm finding it all rather interesting. Mind you – having my arm and leg amputated sometime next week might spoil my humour somewhat. As for you staying here with me, that's entirely unnecessary. Sooner or later someone from my dastardly family will no doubt miss me and come looking."

"Will they guess where you are, do you think?"

Ludovic thought a moment. "No," he said. The hunting party had taken an entirely different direction.

"Well then," said Alysson. "Stop being annoying, and just put up with me."

CHAPTER FIVE

On waking, Ludovic was surprised to realise he had slept. He was even more surprised to find a girl in his arms. Her dark hair, a little damp, tickled his nose. Her head was nestled against his uninjured shoulder, and she was still sleeping.

Ludovic lay quiet, careful not to wake her, but also careful of his own body. Every bone stabbed in a hundred places but pain was concentrated around his left arm, his left thigh and the back of his head. The hard wet stone beneath him was unpleasant, but the girl's warmth had kept the extremes of cold at a distance. He breathed slow and shallow, attempting to clear his head. His memories were vague, and he did not know how much time might have passed since his fall. Under shelter of the curved stone stairwell he could not see the sky, but a general darkness enclosed him and no daylight entered from the high window slits. October nights fell early, but he hoped it was not yet so late. He shifted a little to ease the pain in his shoulder, and discovered the girl's green gaze intent on his face.

In the deepening gloom Ludovic saw the pearlised sheen of tears along her lashes, and the damp reflections on her cheeks. She was shivering. Instinctively he drew her close. "What hour is it?" he asked.

She thought a moment. "I don't know."

Ludovic had no idea which one had first embraced the other,

or even whether more than the simple need for warmth had inspired it. But the cold was bitter and their closeness imperative. He smoothed one finger beneath her eyes, wiping away the recent tears. Her skin felt chilled and very soft. "You shouldn't be here." He smiled into the shadows. "You should be safe at home. If you stay here much longer, you'll lose more than the comfort of a good night's sleep. You'll lose all reputation. You must know that."

She sniffed. "Don't be silly. I have no reputation. No one knows I'm with you and no one cares. I'm not much liked in the village. They call me foreigner, because I wasn't born in Somerset. But Ilara and Dulce will be dreadfully worried. After losing Gamel and now Pagan too, they'll be terrified, not knowing what's happened to me. I should go back to them. Can you walk yet?"

He had been wondering exactly that himself. Alysson tentatively moved away and the icy freeze struck immediately with the loss of her closeness. The torn ruins of his clothes clung damp to his chest, and where the bloody bandages were knotted around his arm and leg, the bitter cold bit. He caught his breath, willing the pain away. Then he began to crawl himself up backwards against the stone wall, taking his weight on both feet and straightening his legs.

He tumbled sideways, gasping, gulping ice. For a moment he saw nothing. Blind and gagging, a dreadful dizzying nausea paralysed him. Alysson knelt at once, peering down. He spoke softly into the utter darkness. "Are your father's arrow heads by chance bound with copper glue? Do you know?"

She didn't know. "Does it matter? I think Papa would have made his arrows in the usual manner, whatever that is. Those he left at home were alike to all the others."

"Copper glue then." Ludovic sat again, forcing back the bile in his throat. "It generally poisons the injuries it makes. But the wounds were well washed, and they've since bled enough to cleanse them again. I'll be dizzy and nauseous for a few hours, but I hope no more than that." He looked up into the girl's worried frowns. "Now run home and confess to your nurse or whoever she is, what an idiot you've been. If I survive my own journey home, I'll put out a search for your brother some time tomorrow. In the meantime, you'd best leave me in peace."

"Will you really look for Pagan?" Alysson peered at him through the lengthening dark. "Will you promise?"

"Good God girl," Ludovic sighed. "I'm not in the habit of having my word questioned by village brats, nor required to make promises regarding my behaviour. Nor, come to think of it, constantly being told I'm silly by someone who has just nearly killed me. I suggest you hurry off home before I become suitably arrogant again."

Alysson giggled. "Then I'd better leave you my cloak. Otherwise you'll freeze."

Ludovic regarded her thin brown rags with amusement. "Very chivalrous," he said. "But I am wearing three layers of thickly padded materials, including a fully fur lined coat. Now stop hovering over me and go away before I spew in your lap."

He listened to the patter of her feet through the damp mulch, the scurry of pebbles and the sound of her hurried breathing as she scrambled down the hillside and was gone. Then he did vomit, and was unable to move away from the smell of it for some time. The cold wind blustered in, surrounding him and whining amongst the ancient stones. It occurred to Ludovic that he should have offered his own coat to the girl, but was thankful he had not thought of it. Eventually he managed to crawl deeper under the half shelter of the winding steps where the ground was harder but dryer, and the stink of his own regurgitations only a distant reminder.

The steps above his head were worn and many had crumbled, breaking into sudden holes and cracks, their dust spinning into a haze of grit as the wind gusted. The tower, missing its internal wall and retaining only a remnant of roof, was increasingly unsteady and where the hoar frost ate at the plaster between the stones, it continued to loosen, whispering of collapse. The clambering ivy further threatened its stability, but still standing after four hundred years, Ludovic assumed it would survive one more night and himself with it. He pulled the fur lining of his coat around him, attempting to ignore the drifting misery of pain. Then, for a little while, he slept.

Two women interrupted his dreams, floating, enticing, disturbing his rest. One, high browed and light haired, gazed with azure eyes and pale fluttering lashes. She was heavy breasted and white skinned, swirling satins and soft fox trimmings. She wore emerald earrings and a wedding ring which he had put on her finger himself, though it denoted her marriage to his brother. She smiled, simpering, and held out her small hand and led him to the heaped feathers of her bed.

But when he followed her, and stripping off his doublet climbed willingly between the bed curtains, he found there a small girl with a green eyed glare. Tiny breasted and smelling of unwashed beggary, she pushed back great waxy coils of dark hair and curled, sobbing, against the pillows. Her lashes were long and black and sparkled with tears like a necklace of diamonds. He leaned over her but she raised a knife and thrust it into his arm. He woke to sudden alarm, looked for the girl, but knew he was alone.

He could see nothing but between the huge shadows of night crept a whisper, as insistent as the wind.

The cold intensified, like a sudden plunge through ice. The whisper clarified. "Why?" it begged, sibilant and perplexed. "Why?" The sound circled, repeated and repeating. It oozed like liquid amongst the stones. Its echo trailed into hidden corners, hesitant and fearful. Then, between opening fringes of deepest shadow, a tiny dome of light moved and came forward. No flickering torch but a blue pennant, star like, it travelled slowly, disembodied and unsupported, using neither staircase nor bracket nor plinth, floating first to the open heights of the central tower and then down again, resting at a short distance from his face. Ludovic stared, quite unable to move.

"Why?" the light whispered.

He watched the encircling exploration, an enchanted thing searching and discovering no rest. It rose again, sweeping up then down, and once more finding him, hovered before his gaze. Ludovic reached out his arm, answering softly, even while not believing what he saw. "What are you? What are you asking?" His finger touched only air, but the cold burned.

The light swung away, swooping as if winged, fast now, hurtling into sudden invisibility. Ludovic stared upwards into unrelenting dark.

"Why me? Who am I? Who are you?" whispered the breeze from above. For a moment the night was unchallenged. Then the light returned abruptly. A minute hollowness filled with luminosity, a blue aura and a tiny bitter glow; the light then grew and took strength. From the point of a star, it blazed into the star itself.

Ludovic said, his own whisper no louder than the question he answered and his own pains forgotten, "I don't know who or what you are. Where are you from?"

"Why did it happen?" moaned the star. "How have I lost myself?"

The light went out. Blackness moved in, becoming absolute. The cold became the normal chill of a starkly rimed night. The glimpses of sky remained starless. There was no moon, no sheen of reflection nor entering glow of anticipated dawn. The silence was as complete as the dark. Ludovic sighed. His breath curled in damp wisps before him and he breathed its warmth back into himself, but saw nothing. He leaned back, shivering. He was unused to the sensation of fear, but the flying lantern had been unnatural and the whisper surely unholy.

He did not sleep again, and kept his eyes open. Nothing happened. He did not know the passage of time, but when he heard a scuffle and the rattle of pebbles, he jumped as though struck. The girl whispered, but a good deal louder than the bewitching murmur. "What's the matter? Are you all right?"

His extreme relief annoyed him. Ludovic said, "What are you doing back here? Of course I'm all right."

"Are you always this bad tempered in the middle of the night?" said Alysson. "I only came back to try and help."

"I'll have you know I'm an exceedingly benign and good humoured person under normal circumstances," Ludovic said with feeling. "I'm only this bad tempered when stuck full of arrows while placidly minding my own business, struck unconscious, insidiously poisoned, and forced to sleep out in the open on frigid damp stone during a particularly freezing night. So go away."

"I brought blankets from home, and dried biscuit and a flask of ale and a spare cloak." She sniffed. "It was Gamel's. It's not as thick as your coat, but it's dry." She clambered under the stairwell beside him and unpacked her bundle. "I'd have been back quicker, but I tried looking for your horse. I couldn't see it though. I suppose it ran all the way back to the castle. And I thought the forest would be full of your noisy people searching everywhere for you, but they must have gone in another direction. Or perhaps they just don't care. Perhaps no one really wants to find you. It would hardly be surprising."

Ludovic relented. He shuffled back against the wall, edging himself up until sitting, shaking his head clear of doubts, pain and sleep. "You have an irritating sense of humour, but you're a good girl. You should be fast asleep in bed, but thank you. I'll take the ale first."

"I thought you'd be thirsty." She handed him the small leather flask and a handful of broken biscuit crumbs. She was brisk and reassuring. "It'll be dawn soon. I hope you slept. Can you walk yet?"

The pale lilac of a tentative sunrise tipped the reaching tree branches as Alysson supported Ludovic on his stumble down the little hill and into the damp shelter of the forest. They travelled very slowly. Ludovic forced his left leg to move, but could take little weight upon it. He leaned far more than he would have liked on the thin shoulder of the girl beside him. He could feel her narrow bones, but also her warmth. Once again her hair tickled his nose. There was an owl, plaintive in disturbance, and the clinging dewy fingers of a spider's web. The wind had dropped and the chill decreased.

The wound in his leg was weeping heavily again, the bloody warmth strangely comforting down his thigh. "Can you see in this wretched murk?" Ludovic said. "Are we near yet?"

"Very close, I promise." Alysson was wrapped half beneath his huge wealth of sable lining. She adjusted her pace, quickening a little. "I know this part of the woods, even in the dark. After all, I've lived here for ten years. Do you feel any better?"

"Sufficiently. But I doubt I could walk again for some time after this. I'll need to appreciate your hospitality until I'm strong enough to get back to the castle, or until the Sumerford troops discover me."

Alysson nodded. "That's all right. Ilara's expecting you. She's preparing hot food. Dulce's ashamed of her house and thinks you won't want to sleep there. But I said you wouldn't care. Will you?"

Ludovic smiled. "I shall be only too glad of warm shelter. I dream of a decent cup of wine, but I doubt if you can supply that. My own flask was attached to my horse's saddle beside my sword, now gone. I expect not to disturb you for long, nor cause too much inconvenience. Though it's simple retaliation, of course, for your murderous impulses."

She sniffed. "I am sorry. I've said that lots of times and I do mean it. But it's not all me, remember. You've offered to search for Pagan, for which I thank God and you too, but you don't seem at all troubled by your horrid brother's attack. He was much more murderous than I am. And I certainly didn't do anything to provoke that."

Ludovic hesitated a moment before replying, then said softly, "There's no need to press that story, you know. I know it to be a lie. You achieve nothing by an accusation which cannot be true."

Alysson stopped abruptly and Ludovic nearly fell over. He gripped her shoulder, steadying himself, and felt her wince. "You know it's a lie?" she demanded. "How can you know? Why should I lie?"

"I have an idea why, and sympathise a little," Ludovic said, low voiced. "But any more is better left unsaid. I hold no grievance and Humphrey is not here to answer for himself. Let's agree not to pursue the subject."

After a moment Alysson began walking again. She stayed silent.

The familiar sagging thatch caught the early sun between the trees, and the woman Ilara, peering out, stood at the open doorway. A small fire of twigs smouldered damply on the hearth, and was the only light or heat. Alysson helped Ludovic inside and he collapsed on a stool, drawn close to the flames. He was given ale and the fluttering apologies of the two elderly women, agonising over the behaviour of their protégée and nervous for the failings of their home. Alysson immediately shooed them back upstairs, and back to bed.

She sat curled on the ground beside Ludovic's stool as he watched the fire smoulder into soot and drank his ale from a wooden bowl. "That's Gamel and Pagan's pallet under the window," Alysson said. "You'd better sleep there. It's only straw but it's quite soft and dry. I sleep upstairs with my nurse and Dulce. They wouldn't normally be in bed this late, but they were up all night, first worrying about me, and then talking to me for ages when I got back. Being weak, you should sleep easily too. Besides, there's clearly no point us talking."

Ludovic leaned back thankfully against the thin unplastered wall behind him and gazed down sleepily at the girl by his feet. A cooking pot swung over the flames and the faint scent of simmering pottage smothered the older smells of dirt and urine. The fire's warmth was fitful, but the relief of sitting again, and of enjoying something more sheltered than the filthy freeze of the old watch tower, felt glorious. He finished the ale. "My dear Alysson," he said, "talking seems the least of my problems. I am utterly lame and half dead. I shall probably have to hobble around like some old gout ridden grandfather for the next few days, and watch as my leg is lanced of blood and pus at regular intervals. I've already become engaged in the most unappetising proceedings simply because of you, such as talking to obtuse and vindictive dairymen in the vicinity of farting cows and rumbling vats, while unwillingly instructed in the vile business of cheese making. I have been forced to undergo a winter's night away from the comfort of my own bed, and will have to think up a whole pack of completely unbelievable falsehoods in order to keep you out of gaol. Is there anything more you intend inflicting on me?"

"Probably food," said Alysson. "I think you need strength."

CHAPTER SIX

L udovic regarded the sliced turnip with faint suspicion, politely dipping his spoon into the pottage. He had never tasted turnip before, and sincerely trusted he would never be required to do so again. He chewed slowly, with a studious concentration of manners, and gradually the look of startled indignation faded, replaced by resignation. He hoped, without much conviction, that what he felt moving in his mouth was the natural swill of the pottage, and not live maggots.

He was equally aware that the two women Ilara and Dulce were paying far more attention to him than they were to their needlework, so Ludovic continued eating and, with a valiant attempt at an expression of satisfaction, finished everything on his platter. He looked hopefully for a napkin, found none, and drew out his own very damp and bloodied kerchief with which to wipe his mouth and fingers. "Delicious. You are very kind and I thank you," he said faintly.

"There is a little remaining in the cauldron, my lord," whispered Ilara, "should you wish for more, my lord."

Ludovic smiled. "I assure you, I could not eat another thing. However, I do appreciate the offer." He was acutely aware of the probable cost of their generosity, and the likelihood that he had just, however unwillingly, eaten the whole family's food for the entire day. "Just a little ale – if that's possible."

Dulce leapt from the tiny table, holding tight to her cambric cap as it spilled pins, and scooped up a cup from beside the fire. She brought it, curtsying deeply, back to the table. Ludovic drank, clearing the sour taste from his throat. Alysson watched her two protectors' over anxious discomfort and stood up abruptly. "Dulce dear, isn't it market day? Do go. In fact, you'll be late. And perhaps, Ilara, you'd like to go as well."

"But my dear, what of our guest?" whispered Ilara, curtsying nervously to the air. "It would hardly be polite –"

"On the contrary," said Ludovic at once, "I should be extremely disturbed at the thought of interrupting your usual routine. Besides, I need to talk to your – young protégé. She'll be quite safe with me, I give my word."

"Oh my lord," breathed Ilara, "as if we would imagine anything else. And if you're quite sure my lord, and would prefer to be left private -"

"He would," said Alysson briskly.

After a few moments bustling, Ludovic held the door open for the two women to scurry out. "And since," he said, "I expect to have gone before your return, I must thank you now for your great help and consideration. I shall not forget it."

"Oh, my lord," breathed Ilara, as Alysson quickly pushed the door shut on her departing shadow.

It occurred to him, somewhat vaguely, that since these people kept neither scullion nor maidservant, it might be common manners for guests to offer some sort of assistance themselves, such as helping to clear up or even wash the trenchers. However, since he hadn't the slightest idea how to do such things, he said nothing about it. "And now," he said instead, "will you explain to me, without unnecessary prevarication or false pride, just what source of income your household currently has? I don't wish to appear ungrateful, but I could hardly avoid seeing there was little meat in your pottage except some scraps of bacon, which frankly seemed less than well salted or preserved."

"Oh dear," said Alysson faintly, "maggots again?"

"Irrelevant," Ludovic smiled slightly. "The only matter now relevant, is whatever you will all manage to eat for the next few days. I have no money on me, though this heap of silk and sable should bring in a pound or two." Something was biting him under the arm and he scratched absently as he pulled off his ruined coat, vaguely hoping that not every cranny of his body was now indelibly infested with lice.

Alysson frowned at his proffered coat. "Don't be absurd," she sniffed, "and sit down before you fall."

Ludovic sat, immediately and heavily, on the nearest stool. "Perhaps," he admitted, "I am not quite ready yet for travelling. But I am certainly able to interest myself in your survival, in spite of your wish to curtail my own."

The fire had lapsed into soot and the cauldron hung there, forlorn upon its chains, the cheerful sounds of a simmering breakfast doused. Alysson hung her head. "We manage. We pick berries and herbs. There's nettles and roots and acorns to collect. The mushrooms are coming through now, and occasionally we catch duck and quail. You know already, so there's no harm in admitting we used to go poaching, but Gamel was a much better archer than me. I don't catch much. Occasionally Dulce manages to sell the surplus at market. When it doesn't rain too much, we can gather wood and sell faggots too, but most local people come into the forest to find whatever they want themselves. Sometimes we find gall knots on the forest oaks and make ink for the Abbey. I used to make reed mats, but your people drained the marshes in the estuary, so there's no reeds anymore. Then we kept geese, with fresh eggs and feathers for fletching. But the last one died a year ago. We finished eating it in the summer. Now we've started beachcombing. Though eating isn't as important as finding Pagan."

"Starving is unlikely to help find your brother," Ludovic said. "On return to Sumerford I can send you money, but I can hardly finance you forever. I have another suggestion. I'll arrange a position as personal maid to the new lady at the castle, my brother's wife, the Lady Jennine. She brought little in the way of female staff with her, and since we're a household of men, we've not much to supply."

"For Ilara you mean?" Alysson hesitated. "But she's elderly now and she was never used to the nobility. You've seen how nervous she is."

Ludovic raised an eyebrow. "I meant you."

Alysson screwed up her nose. "They won't want me. I doubt your mother would even allow me inside your walls. Besides – there's – your brother."

Ludovic regarded the girl with considerable impatience. "I see no point in your persisting with that accusation," he said curtly. "It no longer serves your interests."

Alysson glared. "It never did serve my – interests." She stood with a sniff and began clearing away the wooden spoons and platters in a swirl of angry skirts. The smells of rancid goose grease reasserted. "Do you take me for a trollop, or a beggar's brat, to tell lies and bear false witness?"

"It wasn't Humphrey," Ludovic frowned. "Someone else perhaps. I've no intention of discussing my brother's private business with you, but frankly, he's not capable. Besides, he was otherwise engaged on that day. Perhaps you mistook him."

"I may not have been born in Somerset, but no one can stay around here for long without knowing all your family very well indeed," Alysson objected crossly. "Your Humphrey is very large with a gut like a pregnant sow. He has a huge fuzzy red beard, a fuzzy red moustache and lots of bright red hair. How could I possibly mistake that?"

Ludovic sighed. "Then perhaps I should explain that my brother and his new wife have entirely separate quarters, and even in a comparatively small castle such as Sumerford, there's little reason why you should ever come into close contact with any member of my family apart from the lady you'll serve. And even if my brother does happen to lumber across you, there can hardly be any safer place than under his own wife's protection." He watched Alysson, the high colour in her cheeks fading. "As for my mother," he continued, "I'll deal with her. In the meantime I'll send money for a new chemise and a better gown, and you can present yourself at the main house in a few days." He paused again, deciding against the additional insult, then changed

52

his mind and said it anyway. "But first I must suggest," he said cautiously, "that you make some attempt at a good scrub. At present you'd make – let us say – a dubious impression."

He thought she was going to hit him over the head with the spoon she had retrieved, but instead she sat abruptly and stared into her lap. "Is it that bad?" she whispered. "I suppose you really do think I'm a trollop and a beggar. But I do wash, quite often even when it's horribly cold, down in the stream. We can't buy good soap anymore of course, but it's mainly the clothes you see, they're hard to wash when you haven't got anything else to change into. And in the winter, well, it's not easy being naked or wearing wet clothes, and then you can never be sure who might be fishing in the stream, or looking for herbs along the bank. Then the cooking smells hang around for so long and seep into the clothes, the house being very small, and especially when it's cold with all the windows shut. And I'm afraid there's fleas in the straw too and they're so hard to get rid of. We used to try and smoke them out, and we used clover and wild lavender over and over, but they always came back. I mean, when there's nothing you can do about things, it's easier not to worry about them. I never knew it was so bad."

Ludovic got up and hobbled over to her. His leg throbbed, but he bent, and put his sound arm around her. She turned her head to his rich velvet stomacher and sniffed. Ludovic combed his fingers through her hair, caressing as he would a distraught puppy. Her thick curls felt cool and pleasant, and he smiled. "I should not have spoken," he said. "But when arriving for a position as lady's maid, the first appearance would seem to be of some importance, even if an agreement is already arranged. I can make sure you're employed child, but in all decency I should not force my sister-in-law into anything she might find unappealing, or be reluctant to accept. You must do your part. I'll send money for new clothes, and that should help."

She peeped up at him, wondering reluctantly whether she should pull away, but finding the unaccustomed security of masculine comfort unexpectedly pleasant, she stayed. "I didn't always live like this," she said, her voice muffled against him. He knew she blushed, ashamed of her excuses, but the pressure of her face held firm to his chest seemed surprisingly natural also to him. "My father was the Mayor of Canterbury for many terms," Alysson went on softly, half lost in memories. "He was a barrister before he was an alderman. He was also a great archer, and – utterly loyal to the king. It was King Richard back then of course. We had a beautiful big house, and servants, and lots of nice clothes, and a real wooden tub we could bring out into the kitchen for proper baths. Real baths, every month, and my turn was always after Mamma so the water was still almost hot. Ilara was my nursemaid ever since I was born. She used to wash my back with a real sea sponge, and tie up my hair in ribbons, and I had clean linen and gowns all brushed and pressed. But then my father fought for King Richard at Bosworth. Afterwards, everything got much worse. With this new Tudor king hating everyone who'd fought against him, our home was taken away. We were fined huge taxes and people were frightened to help us in case they got into trouble themselves, so we took a little cottage down by the Kent marshes. Ilara came with us but of course all the other servants had to be sent away. Then my father tried to get back into favour by fighting for the new king at Stoke, and he was killed there. With Papa gone, Mamma and I worked harder but the Kent fens are alive with biting mosquitoes, and my mother got sick with the ague. Mal-aria they called it; bad air; and so it was for she died too. I was only nine and my brothers were little more than babies. It was Ilara who gathered us up and brought us here to her brother's house. We had nothing left, and have had nothing since, so maybe I'm truly a beggar now. I'll be glad to go back and work at the castle again – if you can arrange it. But your mother won't want me."

"Silly puss. She'll have nothing to do with it," Ludovic said. His fingers slipped down, both his arms embracing her closely, lifting her a little against him; his own promise of reassurance. Her eyes, deep green in the shadowed angles, gazed up beneath moist lashes. Her body, thin and shivering, seemed absurdly vulnerable, a fledgling bird in his arms. Through the shapeless broadcloth of her gown, he touched the prominent rise of her backbone and ribs. Without thinking he bent and put his mouth to hers, and kissed her. For a moment it was little more than comfort, but then something changed

54

and became imperative, and what had been buried then surfaced. Her lips parted to his, and Ludovic felt an immense and passionate relief, as if everything he had ever wanted was about to be answered.

The kiss deepened. He tasted her breath, heated and surprised, against his tongue. She neither pulled away nor reacted with anger, yet did not return his ardency, as if she had no notion exactly how to react. Ludovic wondered fleetingly whether she accepted him because she wanted to, or simply as the local lord with every right to do with her as he wished. So he held her tighter, abandoning caution.

"If," said the voice behind him, "you wish to indulge in these sordid little assignations, I wish you'd leave word at the house and avoid having the entire household alerted to search for you. Our dearly beloved father is near dead of heart failure, and I've been dragged back with the expectation of attending your funeral."

Ludovic whirled around and stumbled, nearly falling, gripping the table for support. The girl remained crushed within half an embrace. "Damnation. What now?"

"Behold – probable damnation indeed, my dear," said Brice. "And I really must object, little brother, to your choice of venue. This place stinks of rancid bacon and piss."

CHAPTER SEVEN

"Naturally, you may do as you wish," the earl said with deliberation. "I have never interfered with my sons' intimate appetites. I simply desire to know if this was a genuine attack, or a badly disguised tryst. Every guard, constable, soldier and servant has been scouring the countryside for you, night and day. I have been unable to sleep and your mother has driven me to distraction. And you were then discovered in bed with a trollop? The same trollop who, I am told, was previously involved with Humphrey, and has since attempted to cause trouble by accusing him of raptus." The earl played with his large ruby thumb ring, staring beyond it towards his youngest son. "I must inform you, Ludovic, I am not well pleased."

Ludovic bowed slightly. "My apologies, sir. But you are mistaken on several counts." He was standing, slightly bent and in considerable pain, before his father's high backed chair. The earl sprawled comfortably, legs stretched to the fire. Ludovic regarded him with polite contempt. "The attack was indeed genuine and there was no tryst, disguised or otherwise," he continued quietly. "In fact, I was ambushed. Presumably by outlaws. I had allowed myself to become somewhat detached from your hunting party since I do not enjoy your riotous slaughters, as you well know. The – attackers – used battle honed bodkin points and since I was obviously not wearing armour, these did considerably more damage than an ordinary hunting arrow. I was unhorsed and knocked unconscious by the fall."

"And where, may I ask," interrupted his lordship, "did this astonishingly fearsome and daring robbery take place? Did your murderous assailants follow up on their attack? Bludgeon you into disclosing your purse? Presumably strip you of your furs, horse and weapons?"

"As I am quite sure you know perfectly well, sir, my horse galloped off and made its own way back to its stable," said Ludovic patiently. "Its riderless return was no doubt the initial indication of alarm to the household. Anything of value was in my saddle bags, and so remained safe from theft. Luckily, the men seemed uninterested in my clothes and boots. I was left unconscious but alive."

"How – fortunate," smiled the earl.

"On opening my eyes, I crawled to the shelter of the watch tower, which was nearby," Ludovic continued. "I was able to abstract the arrow from my leg, but nothing else. And I can only say, if all your people were already searching for me by this time, sir, they did a very poor job."

"Remarkable," murmured his lordship. "I never realised we had such inept outlaws in my forests, nor in fact, any outlaws at all. Nor such inadequate, blind and feeble minded servants and sheriffs. Indeed, it seems I am surrounded by a whole county of astonishing incompetents. But forgive my interruptions. Naturally you interest me. Do go on, my boy."

"Indeed." Ludovic swayed slightly, but rebalanced himself. He had not yet seen the apothecary. The summons from his father had pre-empted surgery. "It was pure luck," he said, increasingly faint, "that the girl, sister of the apprentice groom lately killed by your destrier, was searching for mushrooms and – heard me."

"Heard you?" The earl smiled slightly. "You were presumably moaning piteously. My condolences."

"She was able to offer some medical assistance and later on she returned with blankets and ale," said Ludovic with fading patience. "Once I was able to walk, being nearly dawn by then, she helped me back to her own home, which was comparatively close by. I was still there when Brice discovered me."

"Your brother has already informed me of the exact circumstances under which he found you, Ludovic." The earl nodded. "You need not dissimulate."

"I have no need to do so," Ludovic said. "The girl and her guardians fed me and treated my injuries. They are poor people, more so since the death of the boy, but they were kind. I have frequently received less generosity from those of my own class, and I was grateful. I was certainly not discovered in bed, either alone or in company. The kiss Brice witnessed was simply in gratitude for the girl's generosity."

"Generous indeed," murmured his father.

Ludovic straightened his back. "This girl, as you obviously know, was previously employed here at the castle. Her accusation of assault by Humphrey appears to have been an innocent mistake. She was certainly never illicitly involved with him yet was unjustly dismissed from her employment here. It is possible that I now owe her my life. I have promised to find her work in the castle again."

The earl raised an eyebrow. "Indeed? Because she is your mistress?"

"Respectfully sir, that is utterly absurd. I hardly know the girl." Ludovic glared. His father did not seem particularly intimidated. "I merely intend fulfilling an obligation. The family is destitute, and the girl saved me."

"Well my son, you had better go and get yourself attended by the mediks," decided his lordship, stretching comfortably. "Otherwise it seems you may expire at my feet. And since your young female is no longer present to salvage your life and limb, you might even breathe your last and ruin my new Turkey rug. Unfortunately, I am far too tired to exert myself or help you in any particular manner, having been kept up all night with fruitless worry."

Ludovic was put to bed, objected strongly to being bled having already lost a good portion of whatever quantity of blood he usually enjoyed, refused to answer the doctor's astonished questions on unravelling the strips of chemise bandages, and demanded a continuous and plentiful supply of spiced wine. He then told Brice what he thought of him.

"To carry tales to our father!" Ludovic said in fury. "I would have thought better of you than that."

"Calm yourself, little brother." Brice sat on the edge of the bed, smiling gently through the shadows. "I carried no tales, I only passed on information. Indeed, I considered it amusing. I cannot be held accountable simply because our dear papa has no sense of humour."

"That may sound benign." Ludovic sank his head back thankfully on the heaped pillows. "Yet you were dragged away from whatever secret business you were engaged in at the time. It seems more likely you reacted in temper and spite. You know perfectly well that our beloved lord and master has no sense of humour whatsoever, and never in his life laughed at anything except someone else's misfortune."

"Not dragged back, my dearest. Came willingly." Brice patted his brother's hand lying limp on the thick squirrel fur coverlet. "I returned home to find the place in an uproar, with my little brother believed dead and dismembered by ravening beasts. I dutifully set out to discover the corpse, and instead found you in dalliance with a strumpet. Quite a disappointment, as I'm sure you must realise. A gory death would have been so much more interesting. Boredom, you know, is my ever-conquering foe."

Ludovic smiled. "I shall attempt to entertain you more extravagantly next time. But not a strumpet, big brother. Kindly get your facts right and refrain from exaggeration. She's a perfectly respectable young woman, quite personable under the circumstances, and – extremely good natured. I believe she saved my life."

"A saint then. I revise my opinion."

Over the following four days, Ludovic gradually attempted to organise his three promised charitable operations into some slow and hesitant progress. The success of these ventures was, however, unsatisfying, and his lordship was in no position to either check on results or instigate the necessary next steps.

During this time he lay in bed, was barely able to rise or stagger as far as the garderobe, and quickly developed a worsening fever. The apothecary prescribed vervain, comfrey and rosemary boiled in hemp-water. This appeared to do no good whatsoever, although it was properly distilled during the night of the full moon and stirred thoroughly while Jupiter was at its zenith.

The chief medik declared himself deeply concerned, begged to bleed his lordship once again, dodged the candlestick promptly flung in his direction, and departed with his fleam. He reappeared that evening in order to redress and re-stitch the injury to Ludovic's thigh, and discovered it to be swollen and infected. He lanced the wound and inserted a small rod, keeping it open for prolonged drainage. Ludovic became slightly delirious. He was vaguely aware of a continuous avalanche including a few family visitors, scurrying servants and dutiful doctors, all more or less eager to pat his sweating brow and listen to the nonsense he was unaware of speaking. He slept very badly and drenched his bed in perspiration.

His mother clasped his hand with dutiful if limp affection. Ludovic noticed that her lip was swollen and her jaw bruised, and decided that his father's mood had not improved. He told his mother of his need to find employment for the girl who had saved his life, and asked her ladyship to speak to his sister-in-law Jennine on the subject. His mother did not seem to understand a word he was saying. Always uncomfortable with sickness and possible infectious miasmas, she kept rigidly distant and left soon after.

Ludovic next spoke to Humphrey, who was a more regular visitor. "Alysson. Good girl," muttered Ludovic. "Like her. Need to do something. Ask Jennine."

Humphrey smiled widely. "Yes, Jenny's a good girl. Glad you noticed. Glad you like her. Nice and plump and pink. Mother said I'd be pleased with her. Didn't believe it at first. But she's right. Pleased as cockle shells. Mean to keep her."

Ludovic sighed. "But she has only one female to wait on her, Humph. Must need more."

"I don't want ladies waiting around," decided the Lord Humphrey. "Got a wife now. Happy with her. Just been trying to explain it to you. You're not listening properly, Lu. You want ladies, you go find your own. Besides, Papa says you've got more than you should have already."

The invalid received few other useful visitors. The Lady Jennine naturally did not make improper visits to her brother-in-law's bedside, her brother and his wife had departed north, and Brice's secret business now reassembled. Brice promptly departed. He left word that he would be gone for a month or so, expecting to return only for the Christmas season. Gerald also remained absent and was assumed to be in London.

Twice Ludovic awoke from dark dreams with a whispering perplexity in his ears, and a hovering light that danced before his eyes. Haunted by memory, by yearning and by fever, it seemed only natural to be haunted also by wraiths. He could and would not answer, and closed his mind against such visions.

After some days, Ludovic was still confined to his bed. "Another week, at least, my lord, or I cannot answer for the consequences," whispered the castle medik. "Indeed, far longer may be necessary. A month perhaps."

"You are obviously quite insane," Ludovic informed him. "Any more than a few more days is absolutely inconceivable. Do whatever you have to, short of amputating my limbs or bleeding me empty, but get me back on my feet."

Through the distinctly unwilling services of the steward, Ludovic managed to send a purse to the cottage in the forest. Without present access to his own far larger and far more secluded coffers, he was able to send only two sovereigns, but was confident this would be sufficient to buy several new gowns and shifts, and additionally feed the girl and her nurses for some considerable time to come. Ludovic could barely hold the quill and the accompanying message was of necessity vague. "Injuries deteriorated. Unable to come myself. Will organise employment soon. L.S." Besides, Ludovic was not at all sure if the girl could read. He therefore added only a brief post-script. "No sign yet of your brother."

The search party sent to look for the small Pagan Welles was complicated by even greater confusion. No one, including Ludovic himself, knew exactly who they were looking for, nor why.

From temporary lucidity, Ludovic lapsed into fever again as his wounds continued to fester. The shutters in his chamber were kept constantly closed and the windows fastened tight against the insidious danger of entering atmospheric airs or autumn freeze. A blazing log fire was lit across the wide stone hearth, and kept consistently fierce. Troops of pages were sent to ensure the heat was contained and that no treacherous draughts were permitted to enter. The heavy bed curtains were also kept drawn, and within their deep sweltering shade, his lordship sweated copiously. The newly weaned alaunt puppies were excluded from the chamber as the promised week of further inactivity became ten days.

His father, although an infrequent visitor, was the only one who seemed edified by the inarticulate nonsense inspired by his youngest son's delirium. Indeed, although he considered himself far too busy to spend time dawdling at the sickbed, the earl appeared quite pleasantly entertained each time he left the chamber, smiling contentedly but secretively to himself, in spite of the fact that Ludovic lay partially unconscious.

Sumerford's autumn turned towards winter and the last leaves fell.

In the meantime, to his considerable regret, Ludovic's own private and well concealed business affairs were inevitably left utterly unattended. His previously arranged appointments were either entirely forgotten or unable to be fulfilled, and he had access to no one at all he could trust to take a message. What was more, the passage of the days became increasingly confused in his mind and one heated hour blurred into consecutive fevered nights. He did not know either day or time. He once asked the doctor what the date was, but was told he must not worry himself on matters of irrelevance while his life was in danger. The doctor further suggested that the priest be called, but Ludovic suggested that the doctor and priest could both go to hell together.

Under such circumstances, it was therefore not surprising that a particular stout gentleman of dubious appearance remained lurking, in spite of the bitter weather and inclement season, in considerable discomfort and nervous agitation beyond the huge shadows of the castle walls. The gentleman often peered surreptitiously past the great gates and raised portcullis to the outer courtyards and their well-guarded Keep, and trod the less well patrolled confines of the extended gardens, all in the hopes of seeing Sumerford's youngest lord before being discovered and hustled away to gaol himself.

The meeting which had previously been arranged, had been missed, which was unprecedented. His lordship had not come. Nor did he come the following day. He did not appear at all, and no message was sent.

Captain Clarence Kenelm regarded his very short and pugnacious companion, and spoke softly but distinctly. "You'll have to be the one to do it, lad," he said, shaking his head. "Can't be me, you'll see that I reckon. Gotta be you. Wait till full dark, but be quick about it, and if they sets them hounds on you, don't tell them it was me as sent you."

The boy stared back in blatant disgust. "Oh yeah, I see that all right. Clear as a lateen sail in a bloody gale," he objected. "Sounds proper fair, don't it! Can't be you 'cos you might get caught. Don't matter if I'm caught. So you reckon I'm wittol-headed? Well, I got news for you mister. I ain't that stupid. And I ain't going."

The larger man cuffed the boy soundly around both ears. "Snivelling little brat," he muttered. "Chuck you overboard one day, I will."

"Might as well," sniffed the boy. "Don't do me no bloody good slaving for you, that's for sure. And now without his bloody lordship, we can't even catch the bloody morning tide."

"Which is why you gotta get into that there nasty cold castle, stupid little bugger," persisted the captain. "We got sheepskins stinking out the bilges, and rats chewing their teeth flat as a gallows noose on the bloody ropes, but no coin at all for supplies. And now half the crew's threatening to hop it. We needs his lordship. 'Tis bloody urgent. So bloody get in there and tell him."

"It's you as must have buggered up the days," the boy accused, increasingly sullen. "His lordship don't never forget nuffin and don't never get befuddled neither. You've gone and got your bloody meetings stirred backwards, I reckon. So you go and sort it out. And see if you likes getting your arse chewed by them great big dogs."

"Listen to me, you snivelling little doxy-prick," seethed the captain through the gaps between his teeth, "If you don't go, I shall have your bollocks boiled with onions for my supper. And what's more, you'll sleep up top of the mizzen mast all the way cross the bloody German Ocean till we gets to Flanders, and I hopes the gulls shit in your hair. An' I hopes we has bloody raging thunder storms, too. So you're pissing scared of them great big dogs, is you? Just you wait and see what I does to your arse, if you don't obey my orders. You'll be proper sorry your mother ever put you to her tits, you will."

"No need to get bloody personal," muttered the boy, staring down at his bare toes squelching through the mud. "I s'pose I'll have ter go. But happen you'll be proper sorry how you treated me when I'm dead."

CHAPTER EIGHT

"What is it?" demanded his lordship with deep suspicion.

"My lord, a new potion, something a little different. The usual concoctions, as your lordship is sadly aware, have not benefited the infection as they should. But if you would drink this –"

"Does nobody in this damned country answer simple questions anymore?" objected Ludovic. "I asked for the recipe, not a series of your damned pathetic excuses."

The small man bowed apologetically. "There is tincture of marigold, my lord, and a little hyssop and some rue. I have also added penny royal, and tansy, and a touch of poplar bark for the pain."

"Good God man," Ludovic regarded his apothecary with incredulous outrage. "Do you think I have a disorder of the womb? Or need an abortion? Take this filth away. You can take that milky pap away too, which the damned medik gives me in place of food. It's a damned insult. I want wine and some decent meat."

The apothecary bowed again with a hasty step backwards. "As your lordship wishes. I must say, with the greatest of pleasure, it does appear that your lordship is somewhat recovered this evening."

"I've been imprisoned here for an interminable length of time," said Ludovic firmly. "It must be at least next year by now. So I intend getting up, and you're going to help. I'm heartily sick of this wretched bed and I'm going downstairs." The apothecary opened his mouth. "Without argument," added Ludovic, swinging both legs from the sheets. He groped for leverage and steadied himself. His feet found solid ground and after a moment, appeared to hold him upright. He straightened his knees. He did not fall over. He felt a little nauseous and distinctly dizzy but he remained standing for a few deep breaths and then tested one leg in front of the other. Rather to his own surprise, it seemed to work. "Shirt, hose, and bedrobe," he commanded. "And hurry, before I collapse."

He was welcomed into the great hall with obvious pleasure by the bored gathering of females beside the fire, who scurried to make a place for him and help him to a chair. Ludovic sat thankfully, stretched his legs to the flames, his bedrobe firmly wrapped around him, and sighed with relief. His mother at once clapped her hands for Hamnet and sent for hippocras, then summoned a page to inform his lordship the earl of their son's sudden and unexpected recovery. The Lady Jennine then laid down her embroidery and leaned forward to smile reassuringly at the invalid. The other lady present, her silent female companion, carefully retrieved the rather haphazard embroidered sampler.

Ludovic's sister-in-law said, "My lord, what a great pleasure to have you up and about again. With the coming of winter making it quite impossible to take afternoon walks, I confess we ladies have found life a little dull lately. We had almost given up hope of seeing you before Christmastide."

"Probably given up hope of ever seeing me at all," grinned Ludovic. "So had I, as it happens." In spite of feeling a little faint, he could not avoid noticing that his new sister's smile was oddly lascivious and the manner in which she licked her lips, particularly inviting. The candlelight shadowed her deepened cleavage, the curve of her shoulders almost bare. As she leaned towards him, her breasts strained against their satin confines. Ludovic had undressed her in his mind many times in the past, but now, strangely enough, he discovered that he no longer cared.

Her ladyship the countess nodded. "I hope your appearance is not precipitous, Ludovic," she said, "but no doubt whatever I say will not make the slightest difference, as usual."

The steward brought spiced wine and Ludovic drained the cup and held it out for more. "Best medicine in two weeks," he said.

"Three weeks," interrupted the earl, striding into the firelight. He stood before the hearth, and peered down at his youngest son. "You have been quite ill, my boy."

Ludovic raised an eyebrow. "Kind of you to notice, sir," he murmured.

"I invariably notice when the smooth running of my home is thrown into utter disruption and every servant set to making putrid toniks and gruel instead of roasting venison," said his father. "And naturally, I have already sent troops of guards to scour the forests for outlaws and armed criminals. No doubt you'll be pleased to learn that your assailants will soon be brought to justice, or slaughtered in their lairs."

Ludovic blinked. "And – has anyone yet been discovered, sir?" he asked carefully.

The earl narrowed his eyes. "Surprisingly not," he said. "It seems you should be more careful with whom you associate, my boy."

"And what's that supposed to mean?" demanded Ludovic.

"Merely that I am not entirely in my dotage yet, nor taken leave of my senses," said his lordship. "And also that occasionally invalids, although seemingly unconscious, have sometimes, in fevered delirium, been known to make unintended references, alluding to matters they might otherwise not have cared to mention."

Ludovic had not yet thought of an answer when his father, sweeping a full length of French gorget beneath bliaut, and lined in gorgeous lettice to his boots, smiled with a certain smug satisfaction and strode again from the hall.

The countess regarded her affronted son. "It appears your father knows something we do not, Ludovic."

"My damned father," said Ludovic with feeling, "frequently deceives himself."

His mother sighed. "And others," she said faintly.

The fireside gathering discovered sufficient conversation for several more hours, but eventually the countess excused herself, declaring she was exhausted and ready to retire. The Lady Jennine was therefore obliged to follow, and her female companion with her, still trailing embroidery silks. Ludovic preferred to stay awhile and was content to sit alone, while the contemplation of being again confined to his bed seemed altogether depressing. He lounged in the well cushioned chair, demanded more wine and stared into the fire's embers, deep in his own thoughts. Two candles had been left alight, one massive marbled tower of beeswax upon the great slab of the mantle, and a smaller stub in the adjacent sconce. Hamnet had snuffed the candles of the chandelier himself, and the two pages had removed the rest. The earl did not like expensive candles wasted after nine of the clock, and Ludovic was happy with the long fluttering shadows. Barely able to walk, however, he was ill prepared for intruders.

He was not at first surprised to hear the surreptitious movements and sounds of careful entrance to the hall behind him. Many people moved around the castle even at that late hour, muffling their footsteps so as not to disturb their masters, while the outer confines of bailey and moat were patrolled day and night. But the sudden voice startled Ludovic considerably.

"Beg pardon, m'lor," whispered the boy, hands behind his back, "but you didn't come. Left us proper worritt, it did. In the shit, you might say."

"Good God, Clovis," exclaimed his lordship, remembering to keep his voice low. "What are you doing here, brat? Where's the captain? You'll get yourself clapped in irons, and me with you."

"Sorry m'lor," said the boy unconvincingly, "but the captin's pissing toadstools and we'll miss the tide again. Can't just bob about off the cliffs without being seen and the custom's boats sent out fer us. Waited a week already we have, and them hides is stinkin'. Tis your fault. You didn't ort 'ave forgot."

Ludovic accepted this criticism with grace. "It's my fault indeed," he said, "but I've been bedridden and mostly out of my mind. More than I realised, it seems. I'm exceedingly sorry for missing our appointments, but I'd no one to send with explanations or money, nor even knew the passing of time or what appointments I might have missed. Wait here, and I'll get the coinage for you now. If you hear someone coming, hide over there. If you get caught, say – well just say – well, think of something. You usually do."

"Long as you keeps them bloody big dogs locked up," said Clovis gloomily, moving nearer the fire for warmth.

Ludovic grinned. "They'll be in their kennels, except for my father's mastiffs which keep to his rooms at night, and my mother's absurd spaniels which are probably already smothered under her bedcover by now. Stay here, and don't be rude to anyone."

"'Cept you, you mean," sniggered the boy.

"Naturally," agreed Ludovic. Clovis promptly sat, curling himself into the big padded chair that Ludovic had just left. "And don't wipe your nose on the cushions." Ludovic, gripping chair backs and table tops as he passed, stumbled from the hall towards the stairs. He reached for the lower balustrade and hoisted himself slowly up towards the upper floor. Within the depths of gloom at the top and already gasping for breath, he staggered into the corridor leading to the west tower and his own quarters. Already regretting having offered to fetch the funds required, he leaned back a moment against the wall, gasping for breath and stability. He became immediately aware of the second intruder.

Creeping up the backstairs from the castle kitchens, she had found herself in a maze of upper corridors and locked doors. The darkness was complete. The small figure was now lost and extremely frightened. She had finally spied the main staircase leading down to the great hall, promising escape, and was aiming for it. Keeping stealthily to the shadows, she was considerably more startled than he was when she bumped into Ludovic. "Good God," he said in a hoarse whisper, "has the whole world gone mad? Is everybody attempting clandestine admittance to this miserable place? What are you doing here?"

"Thank the heavens," sighed Alysson in extreme relief. "I thought you were one of them."

Ludovic grabbed her wrist. "Come with me," he commanded, "and keep utterly silent."

Alysson found herself dragged into a large and almost lightless chamber, and was shoved unceremoniously towards a low wooden settle. Ludovic closed the door firmly behind her. She sat obediently and watched as he hobbled over to the hearth and kicked the smouldering logs into a fitful flame. "Now," he said, turning back to her with a scowl, "explain yourself. This is remarkable folly, and could get you dismissed again."

"Dismissed?" objected Alysson. "I'm still waiting for employment. I'm still waiting for something. You promised, and I believed you, but you've done nothing at all. You said you never broke your word and I trusted you."

Ludovic frowned. The only light came from the fire, a pale pinkish flare that rose and fell, leaping into momentary brilliance. He sat heavily on a chair facing the settle, and stared at the girl opposite. "I don't break my word," he said. "Except when absurd females shoot me full of arrows and send me into weeks of fever. I've been damned ill, and this is my first day out of the sickbed. Frankly, I thought I'd made some attempt to fulfil my promises. Clearly my orders were misunderstood. But I did send money."

She shook her head. "We never got it."

Ludovic raised an eyebrow. "I wonder who did," he said. "But never mind that now. Come and make yourself useful. I need help, since I can barely lift my own feet from the ground. You'll have to carry something downstairs for me. It'll be heavy, but I think you'll manage." He stood, a little shakily, and went towards the open archway at the far end of the room. Alysson followed him. Beyond the archway was the bedchamber, a massive room which seemed to her dark and intimidating. The window alcoves were fully shuttered, the fire had sunk to embers, and the hesitant light illuminated only the soaring posts of a great curtained bed, rumpled beneath heaped furs and linens and shaded by a canopied tester. Ludovic was standing by the window seats, indicating the padded turkey cushions. "Remove that," he said, "and lift out the chest you'll find inside. There are several, take the smallest, which will be on top. Carry it over to the hearth." It was a wooden coffer, carved and solid, and although very small, was heavier than she had expected. She heaved it from its place and took it across to the firelight, setting it there on the rug. "Very well," Ludovic nodded. "Have you the strength to carry this downstairs?"

"Money?" decided Alysson.

"Naturally," said Ludovic. "Now follow me and keep quiet."

Their appearance at the bottom of the staircase within the hall, sent Clovis scurrying beneath the long table. Alysson dropped the little coffer in front of the fire, where Ludovic sat again with a deep sigh. "How tedious it is," he said, "having neither energy nor strength, and being surrounded by idiots. Clovis, come out and don't be a fool. This is not one of the large dogs you fear, but a friend of mine, name of Alysson. We have your funds."

Clovis reappeared on his hands and knees. "You said hide," he reminded Ludovic, aggrieved, "if anyone was to come in. 'Sides, it's bloody dark, and you took ages."

Ludovic ignored him, leaned down and opened the chest by a series of interlocking braces, each unleashed in careful order and so releasing the final clasp. He lifted the lid. Piles of silver coins gleamed, full to the top. Ludovic nodded to the boy. Clovis had crawled closer and now sat cross legged beside hearth and treasure. "Bloody cock-shit," he said, awed.

"First you will mind your language, remembering the female present," said Ludovic. "And then you will carry this, most carefully so as to drop nothing and not be seen or caught as you leave, and take it out to Captain Kenelm. Naturally you will make no attempt to steal anything, as doubtless the captain will promptly search your every cranny and throw you to the sharks if he finds one coin hidden under your tongue or up your arse. The Fair Rouncie will then catch the morning tide, and I hope not to see any of you again for a very long time."

"'Sif I'd try nicking anyfing off you, m'lor," said Clovis, deeply insulted.

He watched as Ludovic first helped himself to a handful of coins from the chest, then closed the lid again and passed it to the boy. "Be off," Ludovic said, dropping the pile of silver he had retrieved onto the rug. "Hurry, before the tide turns." Clovis grabbed the little chest, embracing it with fervour, and trotted off. The main doors of the great hall, secluding their draughts behind the screen, squeaked as the boy squeezed through and disappeared. Ludovic turned to Alysson. He indicated the money on the floor. "Take that," he told her, "and buy whatever you need. I sent sufficient before, but I've an idea my father may have intercepted the message. This is considerably more, and should keep you all for some time. Soon I'll be able to organise the employment I promised, but may need a day or two. I'll send word when you should present yourself. Buy some clean clothes and anything else you need, and in the meantime you'll tell no one, no one at all do you understand, about what you've just witnessed. Nor will you ask any questions. What happened is certainly not your business, and you will now forget it."

Alysson was standing before him, outlined meekly against the firelight. She nodded. "Just one question, if I may. Have you – looked for Pagan?"

"I gave orders while I was ill, but it's possible that little was done, since I was not around either to explain or to ensure results." Ludovic watched her, his gaze shifting from her face to her toes. Beneath the bedraggled hem of her old blue broadcloth skirts, her feet were bare and muddy. "Tomorrow I shall give further orders, and make sure a proper search is carried out," he said quietly. "But it must now be at least a month that your brother is missing. Can you still believe in his return?"

Alysson swallowed, clasping her fingers tight. "Yes. No. That is, anything might be possible. But even if he is – dead – I should wish to know it."

"Very well." Ludovic paused, before saying, "Your feet are bleeding, child. What became of your shoes?"

"It doesn't matter," she murmured. "It's only Pagan that matters."

Ludovic sighed. "You should not hold out too much hope," he said. "But I'll do what I can. In the meantime, buy proper shoes and a gown, and get some decent food. Once you're allotted a position here you'll be given the usual livery, but you should have your own linen and a change of clothes. I apologise for the delay, it will not happen again. Now – pick up your money."

Alysson sat on the rug, carefully tucking her toes beneath her skirts, and began gathering the loose coins. She looked up, frowning. "There's too much," she said. "You should take some back."

He laughed. "Don't be absurd. You saw how much I gave the boy. Take what I've given you, keep what you need and give the rest to your nurses."

"I know nothing about the boy because you told me to forget him, so I have." Alysson clutched the handful of coins against her, peering up at Ludovic through the growing shadows. "Besides, that's different, since it's obviously business of some kind. Which I've forgotten."

He laughed again, reaching out his hand to help her up from the ground. "Silly puss. Come here." He pulled her roughly onto his lap, and put both arms firmly around her. "Listen, little one. It seems our castle boundaries are so badly guarded that all and sundry can walk in here as and when they wish, but once again you've taken a great risk. You shouldn't have come, and if you're caught here with me, then there'll be no conceivable way I can talk anyone into hiring you as a maid. And stop sniffing into my bedrobe. It's most improper."

"It was improper coming here. I knew that," she admitted. "But I was desperate." She wriggled from his lap and stood, her feet leaving little smudges of blood on the polished boards. "We haven't been – eating. I had to sell my shoes. And I would never have come here, not otherwise. I don't want to beg for charity. But you'd promised, and because of what you said – and did – I believed you. Then I couldn't understand why nothing came - not even a message. I never thought it might be my own fault, because I made you ill."

The weight of her small body against his legs had seemed somehow comforting, the thin rigidity of her bones strangely pleasant. Now she had climbed free, he felt suddenly cold. "I'm clearly a more fragile creature than you supposed," he said. "I had not expected to be so incapacitated myself."

"I'm sorry," she murmured. "About everything. And thank you. I'll go now."

"But for pity's sake," he said quietly, "don't get caught. If you're found leaving with a purseful of silver and at this time of night, there'll be only two possible explanations and neither of them at all respectable. And once I'm found here still awake, I can say what I like about it and no one will believe a word I say. So hurry off, and I'll let you know when I've arranged your employment. But I doubt I'll see you again child, for I've no normal contact with the ladies' personal female staff. I'll try and check on you from time to time if I can, and I'll set a search for your brother as I promised. Goodbye Alysson, and look after yourself."

She smiled, and leaning over abruptly, kissed him lightly on the cheek. Then she quickly left the hall. He did not hear the doors close behind her.

CHAPTER NINE

"We have no choice in the matter," said his lordship. "You will therefore comply with a good grace, Ludovic, and observe some rare filial obedience."

"As the youngest son, I've no place being at court, sir," objected Ludovic with no noticeable shift towards filial obedience. "Take Brice. Take Gerald."

"You are not about to suggest I take Humphrey, I trust? No, I am relieved." The earl studied the reflections in the large ruby set into his thumb ring, and gave it a quick polish. "And it may have escaped your notice, Ludovic, since you are so clearly immersed in your, let us say – clandestine – affairs – but neither of your other brothers is presently at home. Nor, since they show about as much proper respect as you do, do I know how to contact either of them. It would therefore be somewhat difficult, even for me, to demand they accompany me to court. Besides, I doubt it would be wise to take Gerald too close to the dangers of the Tudor shadow."

Ludovic frowned. He had not suspected his father of knowing about Gerald's opinion of the Tudor king, and sincerely hoped he knew nothing of his actual activities. He was equally uncomfortable regarding his father's hints concerning his own secret business, possibly divulged during delirium. "I never indulge in clandestine affairs," he said with dignity. "But if we've been summoned to court, I suppose we have to go. At least her ladyship should be pleased."

"No doubt," said the earl. "That eventuality hardly concerns me. We leave the morning of St. Nicholas. You will not disappear, discover distractions of any kind, or fall conveniently ill in the meantime. I do not believe in relapses. Do I make myself clear?"

Ludovic stood on the long grassy slopes curving away from the towering grey stones. He gazed across the partial moat, sluggish and cold within the shade from the castle walls. The portcullis beyond was cranked fully open as it always was. No Welsh wars or foreign invasions threatened the countryside and the portcullis had not been lowered for years, nor the drawbridge raised. The way was clear into the sunny courtyard within, with its guarded gatehouse and the smell of the stables beyond. But Ludovic looked down into the pallid waters and drifting reflections, wondering if they hid the body of a young boy, bare bones sunk to the mud as his flesh was eaten by the fishes and little crabs. After more than two months, Pagan Welles had never been found.

He then looked briefly up at the high portion of the eastern tower where the old existing windows had been enlarged and the glass set in leaded diamonds. That was the Lady Jennine's quarters, at some distance from Humphrey's and, close only to the countess's larger apartments. He knew Alysson Welles now worked there, and through his own endeavours had been taken on as a personal maid to his sister-in-law. He had not seen her since and was unlikely to do so, but he had ridden out once to the small cottage at the edge of the forest where the women Dulce and Ilara lived, and had spoken to them at some length. He had learned that Alysson was content with her new position. He learned that her little brother had never returned, and he reported the failure of his own several organised searches. So Alysson grieved, as they all did, without explanation for the child's disappearance. And Ludovic learned that the money he had supplied had seemed gloriously extravagant to them, had bought the clothes

Alysson needed, would pay for fresh straw, candles, livestock and repairs to the cottage, while also keeping them in food for a year or more.

Ludovic had returned to full health, though a small scar on his left arm, centred on the muscle just below the shoulder, and a far larger scar on the turn of his left thigh, both occasionally reminded him of the previous month when he had lain ill, and spoken too much, it seemed, during his fever. His father had never told him exactly what had been said, and Ludovic did not ask.

But he had no desire to go to court.

It was a week's interminable journey from the Somerset coast to Sheen, with the trundle of the piled litters and the snorting of the sumpters. During his more secret journeys, Gerald no doubt rode the eastern hills, taking the Fosse Way towards London and arriving in three days. But Gerald did not travel with a wearisome rumble of endless baggage, nor did he take his mother along with him. The countess and her ladies did not appreciate either the jolting of the litter over the bumps and holes of the roads, nor the constant disembarking before the fording of rivers. Speed was impossible. It would be a cold, wet ride and relentlessly tedious.

Humphrey had seen them off. He had been plaintive. "I could come," he'd said. "After all, I'm the heir. I am the heir, aren't I, Papa? You said I was."

"Indeed. And therefore the only one I can leave in charge during my absence, my boy," said the earl with careful gentleness. "One day this castle will be yours. You must learn to be its guardian."

"But Jenny would like court, wouldn't you Jenny?" Humphrey turned up his fur trimmings. It had started to rain. "It's fun, with lots of food and we don't even have to pay. The king pays for everything so papa doesn't complain about extravagance or waste, and we can eat whatever we like. People wear their best clothes, and go hunting. Lots of hunting and killing things. I only ever went to court once, but I liked it lots. I'd like to go again."

The lady had tucked her arm through her husband's, and now peeped up, smiling at him. Her face was a little flushed with the cold and the increasing rain spangled her eyelashes. Her lips, swollen pink with the warmth of her rising breath, looked unusually kissable. Ludovic frowned. He wondered if she was happy with her new maid, and whether they were on equable terms, or whether the lady was a harsh mistress in private. It would certainly be impossible to ask. Ludovic banished the absurd thoughts, and waited on his brother's final goodbyes. He was already mounted and, kept too long inactive in the cold, his horse was becoming fretful.

The earl had ridden off a short distance and was supervising the loading of his countess and her small retinue in the larger litter, well rugged and cushioned. Now alone with Humphrey, Ludovic still watching, the Lady Jennine giggled. "Sweetheart, I shall keep you entertained while the family are away, never fear. I would much sooner be alone with you, my dearest, than go to some boring old palace. You'll see how much fun we can have. I'll let you do all those things you enjoy so much, my pet. And you shall teach me to ride again. Only without the horse. And without clothes either. I hate real horses, but you have a saddle I like very much. Like last week, remember?"

Ludovic frowned. This was somewhat more explicit than he was used to hearing from gently brought up females, and he wondered if he had misunderstood. He looked down at his brother again, who was nodding eagerly. Ludovic, then suddenly aware that his good-sister no longer simpered at her husband but up at him, saw her dip into a slow and deliberate curtsey, and, quite as deliberate, close one sweep of pale eyelashes, and wink.

"Do come along, Ludovic," the countess called from her padded chariot. "It is frightfully cold and I insist on being at Salisbury before dusk."

"Highly unlikely," Ludovic sighed, turning his horse towards his mother. He bowed briefly to the Lady Jennine, and waving to Humphrey, followed the train. The steadying sleet swept into his face, he pulled his hat low over his eyes, tightened his knees, quickening his horse to a trot, and wished himself somewhere else entirely.

The Palace at Sheen was over full and groaning with Christmas celebration. The mummings had already begun, the first miracles staged, the minstrels and jugglers so energetic that no corridor remained empty and no tray of jugs and cups was safe from spillage. Quarters being allocated according to hierarchy, Ludovic found himself in what he promptly called an alcove, adjoining his father's only slightly larger chamber. A small solar then led to the countess's larger and more airy bedroom, but since she had cluttered this with the furniture and comforts brought with her and shared it with her two ladies and three maids, few separate servants' quarters being made available except for the grooms, the atmosphere turned quickly claustrophobic. The earl's personal dresser slept on the truckle bed in his room, and his page on a pallet under the tiny window. Ludovic had brought no personal staff, being content to use his father's manservant, and thought this just as well. Aristocracy from such unfashionable places as Somerset were not considered worthy of the very best chambers, but after the problems at Exeter, those loyal to the king were expected to receive some measure of additional royal favour. The Earl of Sumerford had certainly been loyal to his king. He was therefore invited to court.

Edward, Earl of Sumerford, quietly suspected another more surreptitious motive apart from simple gratitude and favour. After four days, he knew he was right.

The great halls of the palace were garlanded in holly, with plaited ivy twined over the ante-chamber's lower beams. The hearths and sconces were draped with winter-greens and mistletoe kissing boughs were hung below the iron braces of the candle bright chandeliers. A terrifying swelter, reminiscent, Ludovic thought, of his past sickbed, invaded every corner. The nobles wore their ermine and sables as a matter of imperative display but then sweated in considerable discomfort, drooping moustaches and soaking their silks. The ladies wore small pools of sour smelling perspiration in each cleavage, their starched gauzes quickly damp and limp. The servants scurried, flushed a vibrant pink above their livery. No one saw the king, and the queen, it was said, had not yet arrived.

There was incessant gossip, more popular even than feasting, but it made use mainly of coded hint and double meaning for Henry Tudor employed spies. The king's fear for his crown had always governed his temper ever since his first unexpected and precarious grip on its golden circlet, but lately that fear had grown and multiplied. He was increasingly dangerous to cross, and his suspicions of other men's intrigues had become inexorable. Even his favourites were said to fear him now, and the great palace at the Tower on the river had become a place of dread instead of the centre for politics and for pleasurable celebration as it had once been.

But celebration at Christmas was obligatory, so the music was high pitched and continuous, while the many miracle and mystery plays were consistently well attended as the king kept court. The food and wine were not quite as plentiful as Humphrey had remembered and the candles allotted to each apartment were counted, for the king was famously parsimonious. But his majesty, although making allowance for the huge sums he had paid over the past six years on foreign espionage and bribing his allies, could not be seen to celebrate the holy birth in any less style than his predecessors.

Ludovic saw him for the first time on the second day. The king was not a small man, but his hunched and narrow shoulders diminished his stature. His mouth was clenched and thin lipped, but his evident lack of humour was not, they said, entirely his own fault. "The king has only four teeth left, and wishes to preserve them," said the young Earl of Berkhamstead. "And his breath is known to smell of the graveyard. Quite dreadful I believe, though I'm rarely close enough to corroborate."

Ludovic swung around, surprised. "I understood it was unwise to speak ill of his majesty."

"I make it a practice to be unwise," said the young man. "But I have an advantage, being a close relationship to the Woodvilles. It is amazing what an aunt or two in the right places can do for a man. Not that it did the king's mother-in-law any good, poor lady."

"My father," said Ludovic carefully, "is most loyal to the king."

"Aren't we all," smiled the advantaged earl. "I certainly avoid slander at all times, speaking only the truth. Indeed, without my

Woodville aunts, I'd also avoid the truth. Sycophantic flattery is so much more practical with kings."

"I doubt if I'll have any occasion to speak to his majesty," said Ludovic. "I should have nothing to say to him, nor him to me. I have few friends at court, and intend leaving immediately after epiphany."

"If you need another friend, sir," nodded the young man, "I should be happy to oblige. May I introduce myself? I am Will Grey, second Earl of Berkhamstead, often unwise, rarely sober, but always – intentionally – alert."

"I'm not entirely sure what you mean, my lord," said Ludovic, raising one eyebrow.

"Oh, you will soon," he smiled. "You see, I already know your brother."

"Damnation," said Ludovic to his bedchamber walls, sometime after midnight.

His father was lounging against the open doorway which united his own chamber to his son's. "You are becoming obtuse, Ludovic," said the earl. "Am I to understand you disapprove of something in particular, or of everything in general?"

"Both," said Ludovic. "It seems impossible to have any normal conversation without risk of slander, and I haven't the slightest interest in who copulates with whose wife, mother or daughter, nor who has buggered his page or acquired a new mistress. I don't care in the slightest about these men's struggles for land, the argument over widow's rights, inconvenient enfeofments, heir's entailments, new or existing attainders or the past or future legal or illegal seizing of property. It seems the reprehensible behaviour of my great grandfather was not so rare after all."

"My respected grandfather," said the earl with an unblinking stare, "was a nobleman of peculiar courage. His perfectly legal acquisition of the castle which now houses you, should not be belittled."

"Perhaps I take after him," said Ludovic. "At any rate, I'm damned sick of being constantly polite. It's not in my nature to be continuously careful of what I say. I have no idea who most of these people are, and don't want to. It's the damnedest Christmas I've spent since Humphrey fell in the moat. All these idiots think about is how to bribe or threaten their way onto the king's council, or simply the latest fashion in hosiery."

"Codpieces," nodded the earl.

"Is that a suggestion, or just an observation, sir?" Ludovic asked politely. "Are you simply cursing or perhaps reminding yourself of something you had forgotten to fasten?"

The earl did not deign to smile. "Fashion becomes increasingly important at court, my son," he said. "One must stand out from the crowd in some way, but one must not be noticed for any behaviour which might seem ill advised or dangerous. One must be noticed for something innocuous. Fashion is the answer."

"I shall attempt to take codpieces to heart, sir," said Ludovic. "Though should I wish to draw attention to myself, it would not be the groin I'd choose to make prominent. In the meantime, do you know an Earl of Berkhamstead? William Grey, I believe, a Woodville relative."

His father frowned. "Not personally. Only by repute. He is not important."

"His codpiece," said Ludovic, "is presumably too small."

The earl ignored this remark. "Make friends with whom you please, Ludovic. As long as it is no one on the verge of being arrested, though I gather there are plenty of them around. As long as you remain diplomatic and use some semblance of whatever small intelligence you have inherited from me, I am not interested in the dreary identities of your chosen companions."

"You are exceedingly obliging, sir," smiled Ludovic. "I shall keep your disinterest in mind."

It snowed. A fine white crust layered the city, drifted upriver across the rising floodwaters of the winter Thames, and found a brief safe home on the palace's lower window ledges, the angles between the towering chimneys, and the curled ironwork above the doorways where the blustering winds did not reach. There was no hearth in Ludovic's small chamber, but fires were lit in his parents' rooms, keeping most of the draughts at bay. Then the snow flurried out and the weather built quickly into a squall. Early morning mass was held at the adjacent chapel, and the short walk back to the palace through its gardens became a wonderland gallop as gentlemen clutched their surcoats tight and ladies clung to their veiled hats. The gentle snow was now a pelting sleet, bouncing back off the pathways to soak every silken hem, and transforming the grass into a muddy sludge.

Ludovic, walking alone and not caring to hurry, felt his arm grasped from behind. He turned around in surprise and discovered his friend of the day before, William of Berkhamstead, crinkled brown eyes and a soaked partridge feather nodding to his nose.

"You look amazed to see me," said the young man. "Did you think my conversation yesterday so casual that I'd not bother to find you again?"

Ludovic paused a moment, allowing the heavy rain to find its path down the back of his neck. "I am not my brother," he said quietly.

"Which is a shame," said Will, "since I admire him and would not object to another the same. But he speaks well of you."

Ludovic did not smile. "Which brother?" he asked.

CHAPTER TEN

H is majesty was not a handsome man, nor even a noteworthy one. But even to those who did not know him and had never before seen him, it was immediately apparent who he was. Only the king sat.

Yet at some distance across the great hall stood a far younger and smaller man, sweet faced, too pretty for an experienced courtier, too gentle and too quiet, but who seemed to attract as much notice as the Tudor king, and possibly more. A young woman of great beauty stood close at his side, yet they seemed somehow incongruous as a pair for she was dressed in luxury and great fashion in a gown of saffron silk, fox trimmed with draped sleeves of green sarsenet, their fur linings sweeping the boards, while the man at whom she looked so lovingly was attired in plain wool doublet and a short coat of dark worsted. He looked more like a servant yet fulfilled no obvious duties, and was greeted and addressed with curiosity by many, with mockery by some, and with courtesy and respect by most.

"We call him Piers, Perkin or Peter Warbeck," said a voice at Ludovic's shoulder. "We are ordered to use that name and no other, though the young man will not acknowledge it."

Ludovic turned slowly. "And if permitted," he asked, "what name would you prefer to use?"

"That is a dangerous question to ask," smiled William of Berkhamstead. "But since it is your brother Gerald whom I consider my closest friend and confidant, you might guess the answer, and not choose it to be spoken aloud."

"And the lady?"

"His wife, Katherine." William smiled. "She clearly loves her husband, but they are forced apart and forbidden to share their quarters, day or night. The Lady Katherine is Scottish nobility and now waits upon her majesty the queen. She sleeps in state, whereas he, poor young man, is constantly watched and sleeps tight squashed between two minders within the chambers of the king's Wardrobe. Yet her majesty, perhaps not to the king's liking, releases the lady Katherine each day to be at her husband's side. Who knows what is reported each evening on the lady's return to her mistress."

"If this pretender's claims are correct," said Ludovic, watching the presumed servant smile, and bow, and display his courtly manners, "he would be full brother to the queen."

"Indeed," smiled William. "Absurd is it not? But even during the Christmas celebrations, her majesty and this young man are carefully kept apart. The queen arrived yesterday but has not yet entered the great hall, and will not be permitted I am sure while he is present."

"Even more absurd," said Ludovic, impatient. "The queen kept from her own palace because of a servant who might be recognised as something more? Why is he not kept away, which would be simpler?"

"This is a king who does not know how to do the simple thing," murmured William. "He is a man of machinations and manipulations, and has always been this since he was a pretender in exile himself. Now for ten long years he has chased this – claimant to the throne. The rumours have long haunted him and although in public he has dismissed the affair as laughable and too clearly false to merit serious action, in private he has been constantly terrified and taken every action possible.'

Beneath the clamour, laughter and the music, they kept their voices low. Ludovic said, "I am little more than a country bumpkin, my lord. Beyond the relentless gossip and my brother's tales, I know little of the facts."

"The rumours first arose in Portugal in '87, and suddenly his majesty, with never a thought for Portugal before, sent every courtier he could spare to Lisbon, spies one after the other and then spies paid to spy upon the spies. It cost our thrifty Tudor king a fortune and he has been paying ever since, while worrying himself into decrepitude. They say he has been so ill at times the royal doctors have feared for his life. This – Peter Warbeck – may be the death of him yet, without the need to wage any war. But now at last the king has captured him. So he must be shown off. He must be humiliated and paraded as proof of Tudor's mercy and further proof of this fraudulent pretender's falsity. In comparison to the king displaying his ultimate success after ten ruinous years of panic and dread, her majesty the queen is of small significance indeed." The young man smiled. "Indeed, her majesty has always been that, while overshadowed by the king's mother, and kept away from matters of state."

Ludovic sighed, looking across the heads of the crowd to the mismatched pair, bored and uncomfortable and glued to their places, politely acknowledging the interminable platitudes. "As I have said before," Ludovic answered carefully, "my brother is free to make his own judgements, but my father is loyal to the crown. And I am his majesty's guest."

"Ah yes, your noble father." William of Berkhamstead smiled widely. "And a summons to court after so long an absence. Royal favour at last perhaps? Or perhaps because your father, in his youth I believe, was a regular at the Plantagenet court during the late King Edward's reign, and was, I am told, acquainted with his younger son, the Duke of York."

Ludovic raised an eyebrow. "Which is relevant because?"

"Because, dear Gerald's brother," Will continued to smile, "all those who can corroborate, most wisely and diplomatically, that this young man Warbeck bears no resemblance to that Duke of York, are now suddenly being encouraged to attend at court. They are being encouraged to speak loudly – as long as they say exactly what the king wishes – declaring that this Flemish impostor carries no likeness whatsoever to the old King Edward's sons. They must bear witness

86

that this common prisoner, so well treated by the king's merciful grace, is clearly a fraud perpetrated by the Duchess Margaret of Burgundy. In other words, your father is here to play his part."

"He has not mentioned it to me," said Ludovic.

"But he will know," William said. "I promise, he will know."

Aimlessly treading the hall's outskirts, Ludovic eventually joined his mother at her request and was quickly introduced to a hundred noble mothers of unmarried daughters. Discovering excuses, he escaped for fresh air. The air was not noticeably fresh, but it cleared the senses and the candle smoke from his eyes. Outside the palace, interrupted by the intermittent boom of the church bells, the rain had ceased but the gardens remained empty. The paths were still wet and the frigid cold bit hard. Eight of the clock, the evening moon was already bright in an uncluttered sky and the adjacent music of the Thames, now tamed by an ebbing tide, was gentle and pleasant. Ludovic leaned against the low hedge and contemplated the dangers of ambition, being the driving force, both plough and thresher, of the court. He had escaped the sweated heat, the unsubtle intentions of his mother and the spite of gossip and persistent slander, though Ludovic was sure William of Berkhamstead would find him soon, to utilise the advantages of rare privacy. But someone else found him first.

The small boy was running hard and already out of breath. About seven years of age, clearly well fed and well bolstered against the dangers of the weather, he appeared almost round in layers of rose pink silk and cerise velvet, far better dressed than most aristocratic sons his age. His face, from exertion, matched his clothes. He skidded, soft shoes wet, and landed almost at Ludovic's feet. Ludovic picked him up.

"Don't," yelled the child in fury. "Get out of my way." Ludovic promptly let him go, and the child tumbled again. Ludovic smiled and helped him brush the mud from his knees. "Are they following?" insisted the child. "Can you see them?"

Ludovic could not. "I imagine you are evading your nurses," he said, regarding the angrily bobbing head at his waist. "Isn't it rather cold for night time escapades?"

The tousled curls shook. "Of course not. I'm sick of those stupid women. I won't be told what to do and it's Christmas and I'll go to bed when I want."

"I can remember thinking something similar at your age," said Ludovic. "But I never achieved it. It never worked."

"What I want has to work." The boy stamped his foot and the mud squelched. "And if they don't obey, I shall tell Papa and he'll cut all their heads off."

"Ah." Ludovic smiled faintly. "Then I have an idea who you must be."

"I'm a prince," said the prince. "I'm Harry and this is my palace and I'll do what I want."

"I'm pleased to meet you," said Ludovic. "And I wish you luck with getting your own way. It never worked with me, but no doubt it will with you."

"You're supposed to call me your highness, and bow very low," the prince informed him.

"It's much too cold for that," Ludovic said. "Let's walk down by the river. Your nurses are less likely to find you and it's also too cold for standing still."

The king's youngest son grinned. "All right. And then you'll get the blame if anyone sees me."

The royal gardens sloped directly to the floating piers where gilded barges were tied beneath their bright heraldic awnings. The king's personal yeomen of the guard patrolled the paths, but no one stopped the two quiet figures strolling in the shadows, the man and the boy. Then, standing close in the clarity of the moonlight, the boy lifted his face, and Ludovic suddenly realised the remarkable similarity of the pretty child to the unfortunate young man he had watched being paraded within the hall. For one moment, Ludovic held his breath.

The man was perhaps twenty four years of age, the young prince was seven. But the resemblance was unmistakable. Piers Warbeck, son of an obscure Flanders boat builder, adventurer and vile impostor, illiterate peasant and dupe of the power-hungry, looked near close as a brother to Prince Henry of England, grandson of the late King Edward IV. But if Piers Warbeck was after all who he said he was, then he was actually the son of King Edward IV, and uncle to this prancing prince. Now both called themselves Duke of York, which was impossible, but who had the greater right was no longer so clear.

Prince Harry said, "You're not talking. You should entertain me."

Ludovic laughed. "I was thinking. About you, as it happens. I hear they say you're the image of your grandfather."

The boy nodded eagerly. "He was a king. My mother's father. She was a princess and now she's a queen. And I've got a brother. He's a prince too. We're all extremely important."

"I am naturally impressed," said Ludovic. "But you have not mentioned your father."

"Well, you must be stupid," said the prince. "Everyone knows he's the king. But actually I don't see him very often. Anyway, his father wasn't a king. I don't think his father was anyone at all, but he's dead so it doesn't matter."

"Dead ancestors are the most convenient," agreed Ludovic. "Most of my ancestors are safely dead, which I consider thoughtful of them. But I was particularly interested in your maternal grandfather, also dead of course, but who you are said to resemble most closely."

The boy nodded vigorously again. "They all say it. Though my hair is red. I like being red. They say it's fiery. I've got a fiery temper too. Sometimes they say that's good and sometimes they say that's bad, but I like it." He paused momentarily. "You've got fair hair too. But it's yellow, not red."

"Indeed." Ludovic, having retreated from the confines of the palace, wore no hat.

"And my mother says I have a mouth like a little pink rosebud," the prince announced with pride. "She says her papa had a mouth like a rosebud too. I like my mother best out of everybody. Besides, she's the queen."

"An advantage," admitted Ludovic. He had noticed movement behind him and the bustle of servants hurrying the paths and peering over the low clipped hedges. "But I think," he said, "you are about to be recaptured."

"Oh well." The prince opened his pink rosebud lips and managed to smile. "I don't care anymore. At least I got away and made them hunt everywhere. I expect they're really worried and frightened and they'll get really told off for losing me. They might even get beaten. So I don't mind going back now. Besides, it's horribly cold by the river. That's your fault. You said to come down here."

"It is undoubtedly my fault, and I apologise." Ludovic had signalled to the first of the scurrying nurses, who was running over. "But our conversation was – particularly interesting."

"That's because I'm a prince," insisted the child as he was swept up into a tall woman's arms. He called back over her shoulder. "And I won't tell them it was your idea to walk in the cold and I'll tell Papa not to cut your head off."

"I'm much obliged to you," murmured Ludovic, already out of earshot. "Who knows? It seems one day I might need salvation after all."

It was not the prince who heard, but someone else. The Earl of Berkhamstead smiled. "I see you've met our royal brat. They call him the Duke of York, having been so titled by his father. Not admitting at the time that the existent Duke of York is still very much alive. I gather you noted the likeness."

"It could hardly be missed."

"Then perhaps I shall now call you friend with more justification."

Ludovic smiled. "The resemblance might simply mean the Burgundian duchess has chosen well."

"To discover such a mirror image amongst the foul slums of Tournai? I doubt any wise man could believe in such a chance. Could you?"

"I imagine it would be wise not to believe anything else."

"But I have told you already," nodded William, "I do not choose to be wise." He reached out, taking Ludovic's elbow. "Will you walk with me along the river side? I can at least tell you something more of what I know. It is not treachery just to listen."

"On the contrary," Ludovic said. "I imagine it is. But I will certainly listen, for all that."

CHAPTER ELEVEN

The calls of fire came bursting like the flames themselves through the corridors. It was the feast of St. Thomas and the supper tables had been well laden, three full courses of twelve dishes each, and twelve roast swan set with steel wire to curve their white re-feathered necks, mimicking the living birds. It was an evening feast rather than midday dinner, but in spite of the traditional alms giving and the feeding of the beggars entitling the charitable to good fortune and the Lord's blessings, the night was lit not with heaven's stars but with flames.

It started in the rambling chambers of the king's Wardrobe.

The elegant young captive known as Peter Warbeck did not attend feasts or sit amongst the nobles. This night he had been instructed to present the gilded wine cup to his majesty, kneeling to serve him personally. The king was gracious, thanking his servant before dismissing him, but the intended humiliation was clearly apparent. Nor did the Lady Katherine his wife sit at supper, for she was closeted with the queen in her own quarters. Master Warbeck was therefore back in bed and tucked tight when the fire started at around nine of the clock.

No one knew how it had started, but the first frantic orders were not to douse the flames, but to ensure the continued safe custody of the prisoner.

A multitude of candles, dripping chandeliers, huge open fires and the proximity of torches flaring amongst the drying greenery of the Christmas decorations, constituted a thousand daily opportunities for fire. Guards were alert to the constant danger and small ignitions were common enough. Yet this was a virulent blaze, and its specific beginning was lost in smoke. Alarm spread, guards and servants running, the squealing of the ladies clutching their trains and the sudden hurtle of the hounds rushing from the smell of danger. After three long expensive hours it was finally doused, though the stench lingered, drifting in sooty fingers to the high beams, while many of his majesty's most precious possessions, housed within those cramped and cluttered chambers, were burned and lost.

Excuses were demanded, and given. The stewards and assistant stewards offered reassurance, and apologies. "But it is thoroughly extinguished, my lords. There is no danger, I assure you. We are accustomed to such problems. Such matters are always efficiently and speedily dealt with."

But some members of the court, disturbed from their beds, were not easily appeased. "Not so speedily this time, it seems. Evidently this was far larger than usual. And started in the vicinity of the royal Wardrobes, I hear?"

"True, my lord. But is of no significance, except that naturally the stacks of thick hangings and closets of materials led to the more rapid spreading of the fire."

"Unless it began in that young man's chamber. You know who I mean. That's where he sleeps, isn't it? Perhaps he started it himself. As a diversion. An attempt at escape."

"I am assured not, my lord. There can be no question of such a thing. I beg you will not consider it. This was an accident and no malice. There is no need for distress."

"I'm not in the least distressed, my good man. But don't tell me it's a coincidence, for I won't believe it."

Few believed it. Gossip and rumour spread as fast as the flames. Ludovic immediately looked to hear William of Berkhamstead's opinion, but the young earl had remained inexplicably absent for the entire evening, even at supper before the fire started, when Ludovic sat alone and wondering.

It was late. No curfew was kept at Sheen and in any case, the fire naturally disrupted all quiet dispersal of courtly merrymaking and the usual retirement of noblemen with their own, or someone else's wife, strolling to their chambers for the further pleasures of bed. Ludovic avoided the still clamorous fire fighters and aimed for the quiet shadows of more deserted corridors leading to the chapel and the inner, private courtyards. Even here the smutty smells of burning velvets and singed tapestries lingered, carried by the tongues of draught through the stairways and beneath the doors. Ludovic, with no clear idea where he headed, kept walking.

"Not each endeavour can be successful," whispered the voice from the darkness, hidden around the next corner. "This came close. The next attempt will succeed."

Ludovic stopped. It was not the hint of conspiracy that alarmed him. It was the familiarity of the voice.

Another voice, now almost as familiar. "But not too soon. The duke will be even closer watched. This has set us back three months at least."

The shadows moved, restless echoes of figures streaking through the gloom. What lay around the corner sent out its own foretelling. A man's long legged shade paced, then paused, then marched again.

"This was a perfect plan. Are we such fools, to fail and fail again?"

A third voice, less familiar. "His grace remains safe. While the king fears to execute him, we have not failed. We are all free to try again."

"But Tudor will guess this was no accident. Will he send the duke to the Tower?"

And again extreme familiarity. "In the midst of his own Christmas celebrations? I doubt it. Tudor would be humiliated. He's desperate to prove how insignificant this pretender is, to belittle him, not to admit he's still plotting and on the verge of success."

Ludovic walked abruptly around the corner and faced the startled silence of three men. He looked long at his brother, turned to the Earl of Berkhamstead, and then back again to Gerald. "What if I had been

94

someone else?" he said. "It would not be your precious Duke of York sent to the Tower, it would be you."

The sighs of relief could have put out the fire. "Thank God, Lu," Gerald said. "But everything we do is a risk. You know that."

No one carried a candle or torch, but the darkness was split. The moonlight slanted pale through the rows of narrow windows, a pearlised spy peeping intermittent, windswept clouds announcing rain in the night. The rain would be welcome, dousing the fire's last embers.

"How much did you hear?" demanded the Earl of Berkhamstead. The men's faces in the pale glimmer became more ghostly and fearful.

"Enough," said Ludovic, "but nothing I didn't already know or guess. Is there nowhere more private to discuss this business?"

"Because you intend joining us?" asked Gerald at once.

Ludovic shook his head. "No. Simply because I don't want to attend your execution. Nor my own. But I admit I've a growing sympathy for this Duke of York you all follow."

"I've taken a room in a hostelry by the river," Gerald said. "Come to the Swan and Cygnet in the morning if you can get away. Is Father with you?"

"Of course. Did you think I'd voluntarily join this miserable rabble of a court unless dragged? But I go my own way. He won't be watching me."

William smiled. "I'll be riding to the hostelry myself early tomorrow while the court sets out to hunt. Perhaps you'll accompany me?"

The wet night turned to a bright dawn and the rising sun burnished the land. Wet palace stone gleamed and now the nearby forests themselves became glittering palaces. The nobles were already in their saddles, trumpets strident as the hunt moved forward. The Earl of Sumerford was hardly surprised when his son refused to join him, knowing his youngest boy as a surly and unwilling huntsman. But Ludovic and William were also mounted, though turning their horses away from the woods they trotted quickly down towards the sluggish ribbon of the open banked river.

The Swan and Cygnet was a quiet tavern, sufficiently far from the king's palaces to be little used except by travellers, and its upper chambers were small though comfortable. On the table stood a large jug of ale and another of mulled wine. Four men sat around the table, the rumpled bed left in the shadow of its curtains. They were drinking and talking softly. Although unlikely to be overheard, some conversations are best kept low. Gerald said, "Very well. You won't agree to join us. But you accept who he is then?"

Ludovic smiled, stretching his legs, and drank his ale slowly. "Yes, I accept it. I've seen the likeness, and the manners, and the elegance. And I've judged the absurdity of our Tudor king's present desperate ambiguity."

Gerald leaned forwards across the table. "Exactly. Tudor consistently tries to humiliate the duke, yet instead only proves his own fears. This enemy has twice led armed forces against the king and instigated rebellion both from abroad and within England, claiming nothing less than the throne itself. Dammit, he's been officially crowned King Richard IV in Ireland. Any other leader would execute such an enemy immediately on capture. And Tudor is not known for his mercy. He tortured, hung and quartered twenty miserable rebels outside Exeter less than two months back. Yet he fears to execute the very man who led the rebels. Tudor proclaims this – Perkin Warbeck – a folly and a fraud, a lowly, piteous joke – yet instead treats him as a noble prize. Clearly, he knows full well who he is."

Ludovic drained his cup. "And if your plots succeed and you set him free, what then? We have insurrection and the country split again by civil war. For what?"

There were four men around the table, their faces scorched by the blazing logs stacked along the hearth. The fourth man was known to Ludovic as Gerald's squire and principal servant Roland, who now interrupted. "My lord, few will follow the Tudor king once they know a genuine alternative has risen. The king may claim loyalty through fear, but he is much hated through all of England. The lords will turn against him."

"They've already proved otherwise," Ludovic said, terse. "England may not love her Tudor king but he's grown in power since '85. His retaliations are famously severe and few lords will risk their necks following a foolish young man without experience or any taste for battle. Besides, it's nearly fifteen years since this Duke of York was pronounced illegitimate and barred from succession. Do we know his story between then and now?"

"Indeed." William sat back, chin to his chest and finger tips tented. "I told you some of it after you'd seen the likeness to Tudor's son Henry the other day. King Edward IV's two sons were housed in the royal apartments at the Tower after his death, but when proof was brought of their father's bigamous marriage, they were set aside and Edward's brother Richard was elected king in their place. But there were rebellions and risings from the boys' Woodville family and their supporters. So constituting a danger and a focus for disruption and treachery, these illegitimate princes were closeted away, and few knew what had happened to them. Some assumed them quietly disposed of, murdered perhaps, and Tudor announced as much though had no way of knowing. Probably he hoped it, since they stood more in the way of his own claim than as any hindrance to the reigning King Richard. Some gossip spread though the public cared little. But the truth was quietly confided to the boys' mother, the queen dowager Elizabeth, now Tudor's mother-in-law. Discovering that her boys were safe, she came suddenly out of sanctuary and supported King Richard until the battle that deposed him."

"Every man knows what happened at Bosworth," Ludovic said. "Enough of past history. I was a child, but my family fought for King Richard. Which is why they've been so carefully loyal to Tudor ever since, in order to protect their interests after threat of attainder." He smiled at Gerald. "All except my stubborn brother, that is. But now to the present. What of these murdered princes?"

"Never murdered of course. I've spoken at some length with the Duke of York," William said. "He remembers being smuggled out of the Tower and down to the river one night, wrapped tight, taken

97

aboard a ship, hustled below and ordered to stay quiet. His elder brother, having originally expected to be King Edward V and now indignant at his treatment, was taken aboard a different vessel, a grand carvel which sailed off first. Both ships and both boys were taken to Burgundy and put into the secret care of their aunt. The Duchess Margaret supervised their education, their health and their few careful companions, but all in private. The Duke of York was bare ten years of age, and remembers little else but confusion. He'd lost both parents and all the life he knew, first closeted in the Tower and then abroad. But his aunt informed him that his exile from England was to forestall plots either to return the boys to the throne, or instead to murder them. Hence the secrecy, which continued."

Gerald nodded fiercely. "It was King Richard's most trusted servants who travelled frequently to Burgundy, being paid to ensure the boys' wellbeing and safety. Francis Lovell of course, Sir Edward Brampton and in particular, Sir James Tyrell. But when the king was killed in battle and Henry Tudor sadly gained the throne, the danger to the young princes was considered far greater. The announcement of their bastardy being destroyed by Tudor, so the elder, now being the actual heir to the crown, supported and financed by Burgundy and others, returned here, via Ireland, to fight and gain back his country."

"The Battle of Stoke? Yet if that was truly Edward V, why come under an assumed name? In Ireland they say he was crowned not as Edward V, but as Clarence's son, in spite of knowing Clarence's son to be in Tudor's custody for years. Indeed, the poor wretch is still imprisoned in the Tower where he's been held for years." Ludovic shook his head. "The battle of Stoke was nearly won I gather, but to what avail?"

"The prince's true identity was known to most, and in the end, to all." William smiled. "Perhaps an incognito not so well designed, but a little subterfuge seemed a necessary protection in the beginning. Even the dowager queen knew it was her son who marched on her son-in-law, and she backed him with all her heart and all her money. Which is why she was quickly closeted invisible and penniless in a convent and permitted neither regular visitors nor correspondence.

Poor lady. Henry Tudor does not forgive easily, not even his own wife's mother."

"Yet cannot bring himself to execute this latest prisoner, who is the greatest enemy of all."

"Tudor was successful not only at the Battle of Stoke, though it was his lords who fought, and as at Bosworth, never lifted a sword himself, but was also successful with his propaganda afterwards. When informed that Prince Edward was dead, having been slaughtered during battle, he set up a child impostor, this Lambert Simnel, and claimed it was him all along and never any noble lord at all. Most of the common people believed it."

"My father believed it," said Ludovic.

"Of course he didn't," Gerald said at once. "He knew, as all the lords did, but could say nothing. They wished to say nothing, for since the true prince was dead – what point rebellion? But no lord believed that the royal houses of Burgundy, the dowager queen herself, and half the most powerful nobles of England, would risk their lives to fight for a little foolish boy, a ragamuffin scullion child set up to impersonate a prince. Of course Lambert Simnel was never the focus of any claim at all. He was Henry Tudor's dupe, to make the failed rebels seem foolish, and belittle their cause forever. Which is why Lambert Simnel went unpunished, simply sent to work in the royal kitchens as a pot boy. For that, quite simply, is what he always was. The king has since promoted him – did you know? Now Simnel's one of the king's chief falconers. You credit the king with the grace to promote an enemy so powerfully supported that he nearly took the throne, and was the death of half the nobility of England? Of course not. The boy was an innocent lad, set up in secret by Tudor's council to hide the truth."

"I'm less interested in a dead prince," Ludovic said. "Tell me about the living one."

"You have seen the living prince yourself," said his brother. "He is a gentle man, courageous and gracious."

"But unhappily, no war monger," said William, shaking his head. "On the first campaign in company with King James of Scotland, this prince we call Duke of York refused to continue while the Scots ravaged the land, stealing crops and assaulting any townsfolk who refused to supply free bed and supper. 'I will not be party to my own people robbed and harried,' he told them. 'This is my England and I am their true king. I will not have them suffer for the passing of their own lord's troops.' Is that the natural response of an ignorant foreigner, of some peasant boy from Flanders?"

"And he stuck to his word, and the Scots turned back," said Squire Roland. "But it was a shame, for it meant there was no invasion, and few admired him for what they called his weakness."

"He dislikes the shedding of blood," said Gerald.

"Both of others, and of his own, I gather," said Ludovic. "I hear he deserted his own troops after the failure at Exeter. His loyal followers were hung, drawn and quartered. He abandoned them."

Gerald hung his head, as if taking the shame on himself. "He is young and inexperienced. He could not face the terror and misery of leading his poor followers to certain slaughter, and also had his wife and son to consider. But he shows courage now. He suffers every humiliation set upon him, but remains always polite. He is never rude and has not one word of recrimination for all those scoffing lords who come to insult him, calling him Perkin and accusing him of treachery, ingratitude and lies. He smiles like the prince he is, simply turning his head graciously away, remaining always amicable. He is unstintingly charming. That is true courage, while his heart weeps within."

"As I see it," Ludovic smiled, "he has no choice. After surrendering in exchange for his life, he's been forced to sign a series of ridiculous, humiliating and contradictory confessions, all presumably prepared by Tudor's council and each more unbelievable than the one before. He signs 'Warbeck' as instructed, though knowing the signatures mean nothing of course, not being his own name. Yet he sold his pride to keep his head, and at least is now enjoying some small measure of comfort into the bargain."

Gerald scowled. "Comfort? Are you mad? His lawful wife is taken from him, and addressed now always by her maiden name. His beloved son has been smuggled away, no one knows where. Is that comfort? And to walk the entire breadth of the city while the crowds jeered, peering down from their windows to spit; while the duke, a walking spectacle but head held high, was forced to deliver his own friend into the royal prison for the king's cruel revenge."

"I pity them both." Ludovic stretched, refilling his cup. "It must be a misery I can barely comprehend. But he risked worse, coming to challenge a king known for inclemency and vengeance. Yet your duke is still, unaccountably, alive."

William nodded. "With his bastardy now officially denied, he is the true Plantagenet heir, whether or not he is ready for kingship. He would learn quickly, with help and experience. And instead of a cold, hard and hated man, as meagre with his love as he is with money as he taxes and slaughters our countrymen, we would have a sweet natured king, a kind and pleasant man, who would love his people."

"Then he'd be called a weak king," said Ludovic, "by the very people enjoying his kindness."

"I'd sooner have a weak king than a loathsome one without a drop of royal blood," Gerald spat, also reaching for the ale jug. "This Tudor usurper is a much loathed creature. Can you imagine what sort of kings his children will make after him? And they say young Arthur is sickly. What if we have another Henry, this second son, the spoiled golden brat Harry? A Henry VIII to fear, I promise."

"Harry? The people love him, because he's the image of his grandfather, Edward IV."

"And so is Richard, the Duke of York. For Edward IV was his father."

Ludovic stood, crossing briefly to the fire. The hostelry's casement windows were rattling, a squall blowing up from the river. He turned, facing the three men at the table. "I believe your Duke of York is who he says he is, but I will not join your conspiracies," he said. "I've no wish to hurl this country back into war, and in any case, Tudor is too strong and would certainly be victorious as he was at Stoke. I like your Duke of York, and pity him. He's a gentle man, and sweet natured, and perhaps even courageous in his own way. But if you push him into further insurrections, he will die young. I wish you luck, and him most of all. But I will not risk my neck for a cause I feel no passion for, nor put my life on the block because I pity a good man."

Gerald sighed. "Then just remember, you haven't seen me, Lu. Especially as far as Father is concerned. I beg you to say nothing. I have not been here."

"Don't be a fool," said Ludovic.

With their prince remaining captive in spite of the successful distraction of a widespread fire, three of the men still had much to discuss in seclusion. Ludovic rode back to Sheen Palace alone.

The sleet, furious and persistent, sped down the river's valley, whistling sibilant through the wind. But Ludovic remained oblivious of the weather. He was thinking of Gerald, and the wretched young Duke of York whom the king had labelled foreigner and peasant. And he thought of the probable future and the various disasters which would likely follow the situation as he understood it. He was now also thinking, with an awful urgency, of what his other brother's secret missions might entail. Secret monies and secret missions were the currency of Henry Tudor and his fears and suspicions. Ludovic wondered whether Brice was also involved in plots and spying, but just perhaps - since he clearly did not ally himself with Gerald - not against, but for the Tudor side.

CHAPTER TWELVE

Returning from the tavern to the palace, a haze of swirling dirty mist engulfed the rain. The river carried its own weathers, and a clear day over the country could fade quickly into foggy ghosts over the sluggish polluted water. The bite of ocean gales swept up from the estuary, the bleak wetlands and submerged marshes with their wailing water birds and the heave of the tides. So the Thames and its banks slunk into a vague and threatening murk, a clutching invisibility lined with a bitter damp cold.

Ludovic, although not well used to London or its surrounding hamlets and suburbs, had always lived close to the seashore and the vagaries of the coastal cliffs. Never intimidated by cold, he now rode slowly back to Sheen, thinking of his brothers, and his king, and the madness of all men. The rain became silver filigree and the haze closed in.

When whispers formed in the mist, he knew at once what they meant. He had heard them before. He sighed, tightening his clasp on the reins.

"Will you find me?" whispered the wind, soft murmurs and insubstantial suggestion. Ludovic turned, staring across the Thames into nothingness. He turned again. The land loomed in blurred shadows like the scattering of ashes after the fire is out. The river was lost in thick fog. Ludovic shook his head, cleared nothing, and rode on. The whispering wove like threads through the haze. "Why?" it breathed. "I am so alone. Will you find me?"

Ludovic stopped. He could see little in front of him now, only his mount's ears pricked forwards, alert and nervous. The cold had intensified. Then the horse's ears snapped back, lying flat against its head in terror. It stood still, shivering, and would not move. Ludovic turned up the fur trimming of his coat and peered ahead. He had heard of men drowned when London's river surged in flood, the mist disguising the danger. But the Thames had been at low tide and even the heavier rain had not threatened it slipping its banks. Ludovic listened for the insidious slurp of water but heard only whispers.

"They have all left me," moaned the breeze. "Everyone I love has forgotten me. Why won't they come?" Ludovic calmed his horse, bending low over its neck and speaking softly. The horse rolled its eyes and shuddered. From the outer corner of his eye, Ludovic watched the light swoop towards him, growing as it closed. It came, a small blue flame tinier than a candle, and hovered before his face. "Why?" it pleaded. "I have done nothing wrong. Why won't they come?" Ludovic held his breath as the light moved, fluttering like a heartbeat. It encircled his face, searching for recognition, blinking out and then reappearing, perplexed.

The light suddenly elongated like a candle flame almost extinguished by the wind. Again it came close. "I will be good," it promised. "I swear to be good. Why does no one come for me?"

Ludovic spoke, not caring if someone beyond the mist heard. He spoke to the star and its small, lonely voice. "Who are you?" he asked softly. "What is your name?"

The silence lengthened. Then the whisper replied. "I do not know. I have no name. I am no one. I am lost and do not know myself. Will you tell me who I am?"

Ludovic shook his head. "Are the dead always so alone?"

"I wasn't – before," the voice was slow, as if the wandering consciousness was capable of memory. "I was loved once. But now I am not loved anymore."

"You are not of my world," Ludovic answered gently, his own

whisper as soft as the shadows. "I cannot welcome ghosts or phantoms into my life. Have you no place to go, no path to follow? Why do you come to me?"

There was no reply but a gentle sobbing, a bleak misery in the mist. The light blanked out. Ludovic sat very still and stared, but nothing returned, no candle, no star and no breeze, only weeping in the dark. Ludovic sat there for a very long time. Eventually there was silence. The fog did not lift, but Ludovic rode on. "I think," he said to his horse, "I am going mad."

It was past dinner when he arrived back at court.

On Christmas Eve, the Lady Jennine sent her personal maid home. "Pin up my hair first dear, in curls as I showed you," she said. "Then go down to the kitchens, tell them I sent you and ask for all the cold venison left over from supper to be parcelled up for you. Then go on off to your nurses for your own celebrations. You needn't come back until St. Stephens. I shall save you some roast boar and some quince pastries from Christmas dinner, and you shall have those for your St. Stephen's supper in my chamber."

Alysson curtsied. "You're – very kind, my lady."

"Oh, pooh," said her ladyship. "You know, when my good brother asked me to hire you, I was not entirely pleased. Ludovic's a very good looking young man, and I – well, I had no idea who you were and why he so specifically wanted you to work here. He warned me you weren't even experienced. It seemed rather unusual. Perhaps – you understand of course – I tend to think the worst in such situations. I have my – reasons, as you know. But now I'm delighted I agreed to take you on. You're quite the favourite lady's maid I've ever had."

Alysson grinned. "Since I'm the first and only."

The Lady Jennine winked. "Now, you won't be telling that to anyone else, I hope. And especially your young man when he comes back."

"Ludovic – his lordship – is not my young man," said Alysson with a quick scowl. "I'm – well, I'm just nobody. But he's a lord and very arrogant so he'd hate you saying that. Besides, I don't even like him."

"Well, I do," said the lady. "But we won't discuss that yet. Now – take two days off and I order you to enjoy your celebrations. I shall certainly enjoy mine."

Alysson dropped the combs and hair pins in less than perfect order and began to untie her apron strings. "Then I'll go now, my lady or I'll arrive too late to enjoy anything but bed. It's already dark."

"I always liked walking at night, but that's another story," smiled the lady. "I suppose the dark bothers some. Or are you still frightened of my husband creeping up on you, silly girl? I shall keep him far too busy for that, I assure you."

First through the principal bailey and long courtyards, the heady smells of the smithy furnace and the stables with their scents of soft dry hay and fresh manure, on past the high Keep and the lounging guards, Alysson hurried, keeping her cape over her head and her nose down. Over the drawbridge and the spit, spit, spit of rain pattering onto the moat below. She skirted the outlying farms, the pastures lying fallow and the huge barns, winter snug with the cattle snorting in the straw. No cows to milk these days, and no dairy master threatening to beat her. Alysson hoisted up her parcel of food and began to run. She did not pass through the snuggled village with its watching windows and the church steeple pointing hopefully to its God. The unpaved pathways wound to the market square and an unnecessary deviation. So she kept to the empty lanes, hidden between hedges.

The light rain dulled the stars but the clouds were parted by the sharp night breezes and a sickle moon peeped cold between the trees. Finally she came to the edges of the forest. With still an hour to walk to Dulce's house if she cut through the thickly wooded paths, or two hours if she took the wide road around the forest outskirts, Alysson again chose the quicker way, pulled her shawl tighter, blessed Ludovic for her little warm boots, and ducked her head below the willow boughs. The branches were bare, leafless and stark. Silhouetted against the thin paring of moon, they were blacker than the night. Something rustled, small animals active while the world slept, and an owl hooted soft, searching for the life in the undergrowth.

Alysson slipped deeper into the forest. The moonglow hovered low in the breeze. The cold became ice.

At Sheen Palace the yuletide feast was extravagant. The high table, raised on its royal dais and sheltered by a huge heraldic awning, was crowded not with people but with food. His majesty sat central, a little hunched in his carved chair, regarding his court spread at their separate tables below, watching intently but eating little. His diet was strict for his health had worsened, and for the entire year he had pleaded exemption from the rigors enforced by Lent, Easter Friday and all religious abstinence. To his left sat his queen, a rare appearance. She smiled to those who bowed to her, but did not seem inclined to speak. To the king's right sat his mother, severe in her dark robes. The Lady Margaret had been born an heiress with some claim to eminence but no title of her own, though within the royal family she appeared to outrank everyone else, bar her son. And sometimes, in private, even him. Her husband Lord Stanley, Earl of Derby, quite ignored, sat beside the queen and attended to his stomach. He had never been known as a quiet man, but after his brother's recent execution over the damnable Warbeck affair, he had become morose. Beyond the Lady Margaret, Prince Arthur sat, glorious in purple. Now back from Ludlow and affianced to the Spanish princess, he was considered of an appropriate maturity to share his father's table, but he looked to his grandmother with studious care and was not talkative. Although now eleven years of age and conscious of his status and his pride, the Tudor heir to the throne was perfectly aware that his grandmother must, in all things, be regarded as paramount. At least he was content that his little brother Harry had been confined to the nursery and did not sit amongst the adults. Christmas, for whatever rank, came only once a year, and it mattered most of all for proving precedence.

The great roast boar, glazed in mustard and its tusks shaved to points, was borne in by six men including the chief cook, who beamed at the applause and stayed to carve. The other tables welcomed their smaller platters, forty roast goose stuffed with forcemeat, and eight dozen partridge all carried in rows upon their roasting irons. There was venison on beds of flaming Seville oranges, heavily spiced sheep's testicles, tripe stuffed with boiled onions and saffron, jellies drizzled with syrup, and huge subtleties shaped as the manger, each complete with a haloed infant. Plum porridge, Christmas pie and a variety of custards completed the first course. The trumpet calls faded and the minstrels began to play.

The lowly and insignificant servant addressed as Peter Warbeck, or, when wishing in particular to insult, the diminutive form Perkin, did not wait on his sovereign at table this day, nor partake of the feast in any manner. But his wife, without doubt the most beautiful at the higher ladies' table, was present throughout. She answered now to her maiden name of Lady Katherine Gordon, but had, to his majesty's surprise and irritation, refused to accept an annulment of her marriage on the grounds of her husband's false pretences and fraudulent identity. She was not permitted to sleep with the man she loved, but she remained adamantly married to him.

Ludovic, youngest son to a countrified earl out of favour since Bosworth, sat at a different table to either his father or William of Berkhamstead, and at a considerable distance from the royal dais. This pleased him. It was the only thing which did, though the food was excellent and the wine plentiful. He was thinking of other things altogether. He wondered what was happening at home, what his three brothers were up to in their varied and troublesome ways, and whether he believed in phantasms, spirits, and visitations of the dead. Most of all he wondered about the green eyed girl who walked so softly through his dreams, perpetually present even while he considered it unlikely he would ever see her again.

Three days later on the anniversary of the Holy Innocents, he was still suffering from mild indigestion. The headache had passed, but whether it had been caused by too much wine, too much food, or too much thought, Ludovic had no intention of repeating the experience. He welcomed the holy day's enforced abstinence and avoided both food and wine. He also avoided Lord William of Berkhamstead and even kept his mother company at cards.

It was snowing on the fourth day when he set out alone for Ludgate and the city. He retrieved his sword from the gatekeeper and fastened his baldric beneath his coat. His horse, well rested, was avid for exercise and they made good speed along the river side as far as the Strand.

Most of the grand houses' occupants were away attending court, and a gloomy silence hung beneath the gentle hush of snowflakes. It was busy at the Ludgate however, with queues in both directions. Ludovic, impatient, pushed through; his clothes, his manner and his horse finding a path. Then he was in London, the iniquitous heart of every countrified gentleman's antipathy. In fact Ludovic enjoyed the Capital although he was not well acquainted with it.

But he knew his way to the docks. He rode the breadth of the city through the paved and unpaved streets where the captured Duke of York had been paraded day after day before Christmas. As a cheat or forger is put in the stocks to humble and expose his fraud to the public, so the son of Edward IV was humiliated and forced to act the groom, though chin held high and eyes straight ahead as the crowds jeered. Treated as the peasant the king claimed him to be, the young man then led his own friends to their death and disgrace in the Tower. He would not be well liked in the city, especially around the docks, for this so called pretender was the cause of a great embargo on trade which had meant the looming ruin of many English merchants. Burgundy's unfailing support and refusal to abandon the boy or admit his imposture, had led to Tudor's eventual sanctions on all things pertaining to Flanders and Burgundy and the Holy Roman Emperor. Antwerp no longer enjoyed uninterrupted commerce. Their ships were refused permission to sail into English ports, their exports were forbidden to land on English soil, and their citizens of all ranks were promptly sent back home. Even the Hanseatic League was denied their usual business. Within England, all matters Burgundian ceased. Maximillian had quickly responded in kind. He banned all English trade. Fortunes were lost.

Cutting away from the river and shadowed by Baynard's Castle and then the mighty warehouses, Ludovic eventually skirted the Tower, frosted in white like the Christmas subtleties. He felt well rimed himself, his coat wet and its fur trimmings ice studded, his hat drooping and snowflakes collecting on his shoulders, knees and boots. He plodded slow now, though his horse snorted and shook its mane, jingling its harness, eager to quicken its pace. But wet cobbles were treacherous and the Tower threatened all travellers passing its looming stone.

Beyond the Tower, St. Katherine's dockyard swelled with noise. The great wooden cranes swung and clanked, the customs men were yelling across the forests of masts and a jam of barges raced off to help unload. There was a tumult of business surrounding all those fine carracks too tall to sail past the Bridge to the smaller wharves within city limits. Lying mid river, recently arrived, double banked and waiting for its place at the quay, was a tall masted carvel, streaming salt water from flush planks and the crusts of old barnacles. The decks were busy, the crew hauling down the last sail and straining on the ropes.

Ludovic stopped beside the water's edge, away from the cranes and the main bustle, and peered through the drifting snow. He brushed off his hat, clamped it back on his head, and cursing quietly at the freezing conditions, waited. It was the hectic activity on the carvel's decks that Ludovic watched; the ship's master bribing the custom's officers, a quick search, the papers signed, and then the slow tug towards land with the masts creaking and the boards groaning. Finally the ship docked with a thud as ropes were thrown and fastened. At last, amongst the scurry of the crew pushing ashore, Ludovic stepped on board.

The decks rocked gently, sluicing the slime of the German Ocean from their planks. Ludovic balanced, adjusting his stance. The master shouted his last order and strolled over. "My lord."

"Done?"

"The regular cargo will go ashore when the first crane comes ready, my lord. Then we'll offload your special shipment after dark. 'Tis done, and exactly as we like it. Ship shape, you might say, and mighty profitable too, my lord."

"Both that end – and this?"

"That end most of all, my lord. I've the coded papers in my cabin. But this end will do us fine too, I reckon, once transactions are complete. You'll have no complaints, my lord, I promise. And might I ask, my lord, about our other – concern? The Fair Rouncie, and the good Captain Kenelm?"

Ludovic nodded. "She's still in transit, Hussey. There was an unaccountable delay to her setting off. But she sailed over a month back and I expect to hear some time soon. She'll not return to London of course. Kenelm will put in somewhere on the Southwest coast early next year."

The stout captain nodded. "Indeed. The Rouncie carries a greater danger than we do, and could hardly risk the London customs. But we take a risk ourselves, my lord, and I reckon it's a touch too public for payment just yet if you don't mind."

Ludovic shook his head. "Don't be a fool, I'm hardly likely to demand ready coin in full daylight with the customs men at less than spitting distance, and all the world looking on. On the contrary. I've come to arrange payment, but not here. I want the full amount taken to a hostelry by the river near Sheen, name of The Swan and Cygnet. Ask for Sir Gerald Sumerford. Give the money directly to him, and no one else."

"A relative of yours, my lord?"

"Of a sort. But I don't want him informed that the coin comes from me. It must be handed over as a donation – for the matter in hand." Ludovic smiled. "Do you understand?"

The ship's master tapped his nose with a conspiratorial wink. The snowflakes already attached to his short beard flew free and fluttered into the river's breeze. "Certainly, my lord. I'll send Isak and two of the best and biggest from the crew. It'll be a large sum, so will need guarding."

"Oh, and Hussey, no mistakes. I shall know if anything goes missing."

"There'll be no mistakes, my lord, I swear. It's hardly worth my living to defraud you, which you must know sir, since I owe that very living to you. It shall be attended to exactly as you say sir, tomorrow after dark. The full sum shall be deposited, but quiet like, and only to the person of Sir Gerald."

"And remember the message," Ludovic added.

"I will sir," said the captain with a small bow. "The name of the donor is to be kept secret, but the full moneys passed over as a donation for the matter in hand."

CHAPTER THIRTEEN

"I am honoured, Ludovic," said his father. "It is rare these days that you even acknowledge my presence. I must thank you for deigning to notice me at all."

"Since you sent for me, sir."

"Did I? Perhaps I did. I wonder why." It had continued snowing and from the earl's small chamber window, the palace gardens appeared spread in a silent wonderland. A robin was singing from the branch of a holly bush, but the Earl of Sumerford was not attending to matters beyond the window. "No doubt I had a reason," he murmured. "You are aware, I imagine, this being the day marked as Epiphany, we leave court early tomorrow?"

"I am naturally aware of that, sir," Ludovic said, frowning down at his father. "I hardly think you sent out three pages to search for me only to inform me of the date."

The earl was seated before the fire, legs stretched. He watched the dance of the flames and did not look up at his son as he spoke. "It is relevant, none the less," he said. "As you are hopefully also aware, my son, politics no longer interest me. I avoid the watchful eye of kings, and of this king in particular since my estates in Somerset aid in keeping a safe distance between my family and royal disapproval. Nor do I not seek approval. I supported Henry Tudor at Exeter against the rebels, since it was in my neighbourhood, in my interests, and impolitic to refuse. Now this Christmas I attend court at his majesty's command and have fulfilled what was required of me. But tomorrow we leave. There is no further reason to tempt the hand of fortune."

Ludovic nodded, still frowning. "I understand, sir. With only one day left, you wish me to be circumspect. It is reasonable advice sir, under the circumstances, but I cannot see why you feel it necessary to warn me. I don't believe I've shown any particular inclination towards wild behaviour, either here at court or previously. In fact, not since leaving the nursery. But I shall keep your words in mind, and trust you will not be disappointed."

"You sound remarkably pompous, Ludovic." The earl sighed. "Your mother's example, I'm sure. The fact remains that my specific meaning appears to have escaped your notice. Even your small attention span should have alerted you to the principal political hazard of the moment. Yet I have twice seen you speaking to that young man generally known as Peter or Perkin Warbeck. Since his status is that of a palace servant, although admittedly an unusual one, there is absolutely no need for you to address this person at any time. Frankly, it is unwise to do so. You will not do so again."

Ludovic lifted an eyebrow. "You clearly suspect more than is strictly accurate, Father. I simply indulge in occasional curiosity, as do most of the court."

"Indeed?" The earl turned suddenly to face his son, his eyes narrowed. "I had not previously considered you so frivolous, my boy. However, you will indulge me in this, and refrain from idle curiosity for this final day. I hope you understand me?"

"Perfectly, sir." Ludovic smiled. "I shall be glad to leave court tomorrow, as it happens. You know I never wished to come."

The earl ignored this remark. "You asked me, shortly after our arrival, if I knew anything of the young Earl of Berkhamstead." Ludovic nodded. "I seem to remember saying I considered him unimportant," continued the earl. "I was wrong. I am never wrong, but this time I admit to having been unaware of certain facts. William of Berkhamstead is not unimportant. You will avoid this Perkin

Warbeck, and you will avoid the Earl of Berkhamstead. I trust I have made myself sufficiently clear?"

"Succinctly, sir." Ludovic bowed slightly, and turned to go.

"Oh, and Ludovic," Ludovic turned back reluctantly, "give your brother my regards when you see him later today," said the earl. "I would ask you to pass on the same warning I have given you, but it would be quite pointless."

Ludovic, considerably startled, carefully kept his expression blank. "I am at a loss sir. Which brother do you mean?"

"Why Gerald, of course," smiled his father. "Who else?"

The Epiphany midday dinner was sumptuous but Ludovic left immediately afterwards and rode the short miles to the Swan and Cygnet. Gerald, his squire Roland and the Earl of Berkhamstead were waiting in the small private chamber upstairs. The fire had guttered and Roland was kneeling, resetting the logs. Ludovic closed the door behind him and William marched over quickly to lock it. Ludovic turned to his brother. "He knows," he said.

Gerald blanched. "Who knows? The king?"

Ludovic laughed. "Good God no, I hope not. Our father knows. He asked me to give you his regards."

Gerald sank down onto a stool with relief. "That's a damned predicament, certainly," he said, "but at least if it's not Tudor himself or his filthy council –" Gerald sat up again, staring at his younger brother. "But how does he know? Who told him? Did you?"

Ludovic stared back. "I shan't dignify that question with an answer, my dear. In fact, Father's made a few vague allusions to your activities before, but never as obvious as he was this morning. He's also forbidden me to speak to William, or to the Duke of York again. It never occurred to me he was even watching. He said he's done what the king asked of him, though was not forthcoming on exactly what that was. Then he asked me to pass you his regards. I've no idea how he knew I was coming here today. The man's abnormal."

Gerald nodded. "I shall keep out of his way for a few weeks. Besides, I've no intention of coming home just yet. There's too much to do here."

William filled four cups from the jug and then passed around the wine. He spoke to Ludovic. "So you've spoken to the duke again, since I introduced you several days ago? I wasn't aware of it. May I ask what was said?"

Ludovic drank, and took a chair beside the newly blazing fire. "Not a great deal. We were not private. But he spoke a little of his past, his travels in Portugal with Sir Edward Brampton and others, acting as a page, and learning about life. He has a melancholy about him which I find touching. He said he has never owned his own life, and in that respect these days are little different. Only that in the past, when he was subject to the desires of others, those desires were invariably kind, whereas they are no longer."

"Now they are sinister," William interrupted. "Every order, every passing moment, is designed to humiliate. The duke sleeps on straw, so tight stuffed between his two guards that they barely manage to move an elbow without giving the other a black eye, or scratch a flea bite without causing a major disturbance. The Wardrobes are a cramped and stuffy place of bad smells, the sweat and stains of other men's clothes, a hundred snoring servants and irritable tempers."

"I imagine there are worse things than a night's sleep interrupted by snoring," smiled Ludovic. "The entire loss of any future would, I imagine, be the worst of his grace's present problems. He knows he'll never be free again, and will probably end his life by execution."

"He's spoken to me of it," Gerald said. "He has no fear of death, he says, if living means nothing more than this. He misses his son, you know, just a year old and snatched from him. And most of all he misses his wife."

"He told me he intends taking up his music again, if permitted," said Ludovic. "Evidently he was tutored in the lute when he was still a prince and his father was the king. He had some talent for it, he says, and it will help lighten these interminable empty hours, if allowed. But for a man who once led an army, it must be tedious now to beg for everything."

"He gets his way in some things," William nodded. "The king needs him to keep up this ludicrous pretence of being a Flemish boatman's boy, and the bargain relies on compliance from both sides."

"And I believe his sister the queen intercedes occasionally," Gerald added. "But I presume she must be careful not to take too obvious an interest. She's never been officially allowed to meet the duke, but messages are passed by the Lady Katherine. Her majesty knows this Perkin Warbeck is in truth her young brother."

Ludovic snorted. "She knows? Then she should move herself to have him acknowledged and set free."

"Too dangerous," William sighed. "This is not a powerful queen. Her own mother was virtually imprisoned after supporting the first of the princes to challenge Tudor. The royal mother-in-law was immediately beggared, shut away in a convent without access to friends, family or society. Only her essential board was paid. Now the queen fears the same could happen to her."

"So she'll see her own brother executed instead?"

"Other queens have suffered the death of their unwanted relatives in the past, and besides, she has no power to alter anything the king decides. The only female with power in this land is the king's own mother. And think, should the queen support a brother who would take the throne not only from her husband – but also from her son?" Gerald looked across sharply at his brother. "But you suddenly take a deal of interest Lu. You refused to join us, yet it seems you've changed your mind."

Ludovic stood abruptly, shaking his head and placing his empty cup back on the table. "An interest perhaps, but no more than that," he said. "I like the boy. I pity him. But he's too nice a man to make a good king, and in any case, I've no appetite for conspiracies. I only came to say goodbye. We leave court tomorrow at first light."

The squire Roland had returned to the hearth, once again on his knees, sparking the logs with the poker. He looked up as Ludovic crossed towards the door. "Forgive me, my lord," he said quietly, "but I believe we have more to thank you for than that. Their lordships do not agree with me, but I think I know the truth. You see, a few days ago we came into a very large sum of money, mysteriously donated towards our efforts. There are many who wish us well. Our group of conspirators, as you call us, is not so limited and many others are involved at a distance. It is a – web, you might say – of secret planning. But since all foreign royalty has retired from financing the cause a year back, we have never received such a huge though anonymous donation. I believe we have to thank you, my lord."

Ludovic looked down at the square young man, the poker still in his hands. "I won't insult your intelligence by denying it," he said. "But it's not something I want broadcast, and I've no idea how you guessed."

Gerald grinned. "Roland acts as my squire for convenience," he said, "but in truth he's a great deal more than that. We all consider ourselves equal in this matter. In fact, when he insisted it was you who'd sent the money, I told him he was wrong. I said it was nonsense. But how in God's name did you get such a sum?"

"A private business." Ludovic stretched out his hand and began to unlock the door. "But there won't be any more donations. So don't waste it."

"Forgive me for delaying you, my lord," said the squire hurriedly, scrambling to his feet, "but there is one more small thing. We happen to have heard, should it be of interest to you my lord, Philip the Fair is now negotiating for the renewal of free trade between his Flemish traders and our English. Since the Duke of York is captured, Duke Philip has abandoned his support. The embargo is about to end, my lord. Regular trade will begin again. I thought – just perhaps – you might wish to know."

Ludovic paused, his hand on the door handle. "Indeed? Philip the Unfair, in fact. You are certainly astute, Master Roland."

Collecting his horse from the stables, Ludovic pulled down the brim of his hat. No wailing whispers or haunting lights interrupted his ride back to court and he arrived in time for a light supper. The epiphany gifts were exchanged afterwards. Those who had spent large, chose to give in public. Others, including the Sumerford family, kept private. The earl, even when his estate had basked in royal favour under the previous monarchy, had never believed in wasting resources and did not indulge in gift-giving. Ludovic, torn between not wishing to follow his father's example in anything, and the problem of not exhibiting too much inexplicable wealth, presented his mother with three lengths of silver tissue, and his father with one of the recently printed books, which he was quite sure would never be read. The countess gave her youngest son a small hand scripted Book of Hours, in the hope of his finally absorbing some religious morality, and a silver candle stand to her husband, in the hope of his becoming more generous in the allowance of candlelight permitted at home.

The journey was accomplished in slow stages, and during the sluggish monotony it was his brother's wife and that lady's new green eyed chamber maid who hovered in Ludovic's mind, haunting his thoughts as surely as the whispering ghost of weeks past. But there were other considerations that troubled him. Ludovic had obeyed his father, and did not again communicate with the unfortunate servant Peter Warbeck before departure. But during one of the many river crossings between Sheen and Sumerford, he drew his horse alongside his father's as they sat watching the turbulence of an inconveniently swollen ford.

"You happened to mention yesterday," said Ludovic, slightly slumped in the saddle, "that you came to court in order to fulfil some particular request of his majesty's." When his father did not answer, Ludovic continued. "You did not choose to explain what that requirement was, sir. However, if you'd be so obliging, I should like to know."

"I am never obliging," said the earl.

"Was it, by any chance," Ludovic persisted, "to corroborate the impossibility of – the pretender – bearing any resemblance to the late Duke of York? I gather you knew the young prince many years ago. And I understand that his majesty has called on many of the previous Plantagenet court to publicly and loudly denounce the likelihood of the one being the other. I imagine most have complied."

The Earl of Sumerford paused, as if deciding not to answer. Then he sighed. "You are, for once, correct Ludovic. But the matter is settled and I see no profit in discussing it further."

"I should simply like to know the answer, sir," Ludovic said softly. The sounds of the rushing water almost drowned out his words. "Not the answer you gave the king, which I can guess. But the real answer. The prince you once knew, and this Peter Warbeck? Could one truly be the other?"

They were interrupted. The grooms had discovered a better place to ford upstream. The horses turned aside, plodding through the squelch of muddy banks. Ludovic expected his father to use the interruption as an excuse to ignore his question. He was surprised when the earl spoke again. "I knew the young Prince Richard many years ago," he said, his voice also more quiet than usual. "Edward IV was still alive, and the court was a very different affair to that of this Tudor usurper. But it is difficult to remember one small blonde child with a high pitched laugh and pink cheeks, chasing his puppy down the corridors. I cannot easily liken a child to a grown man."

"I have never before heard you refer to the Tudor king as a usurper, sir. You – interest me."

Their slow progress through the mud was followed, with a horrendous slurping and squeaking, by six mounted men, two horse drawn litters and three heavily laden carts. The earl sighed again. "I shall say this only once, my boy, and you will then forget what I have told you, for it will not be mentioned again. As a pragmatist, I am a loyal supporter of the new regime. For the sake of diplomacy, having no intention of losing either my title or my lands and with no wish to drag my family name into destitution, I will continue to fight for Tudor if it is required of me. For this reason, I informed the king and his council, as has everyone, that the prisoner Peter Warbeck bears no possible resemblance to the prince he claims to be. The truth is – that I do not know. In almost seventeen years, I cannot recognise a twenty four year old man as the seven year old boy I once knew. Prince Richard was an exceptionally pretty child. This – Warbeck – is sweet faced too, though not as much. But what I will say, is that he greatly resembles the old king Edward. He could even be – let us speculate – his son."

Ludovic smiled. "I understand you, sir. Thank you."

They had come to the easier crossing. Here the ford's slabs and rocks were sufficiently high above water to support boards laid for the carts and litters to pass. The baggage cart crossed first, testing safety, led by the chief groom. The earl prepared to follow, gently walking his horse down the slope. He turned once, before fording the river. "But do not leap to erratic or unwise conclusions, Ludovic. And do not assume that I am interested in the truth of this matter. I am neither sure, nor will I permit the question to trouble my nights. I once presumed the prince dead, and the probability did not disturb me then, as his possible resurrection does not disturb me now. He is, in any case, a bastard and never born to rule. His existence and identity has haunted Tudor for six years or more. It will not haunt me. Direct your mind to other matters, Ludovic. You are not your brother."

CHAPTER FOURTEEN

A young woman was waiting in the great castle's hall. Her looks and her bearing seemed immediately remarkable. Ludovic had never seen her before and was intrigued.

With the cavalcade bustling from the bailey to the great doors and eager to be back in the warm after a journey of unremitting tedium and discomfort, Ludovic was one of the last to enter. A bluster and flurry of wind slammed the doors behind him, dislodging the snow from the window ledges. His mother, stripping off her gloves and loudly complaining of the unnecessarily freezing weather, the disgusting state of the roads and the appalling discomfort of all travel, was already mounting the main staircase. The Lady Jennine, solicitous, stayed close at her side. Humphrey was speaking to the earl. He was attempting to explain the various complicated and ingenious endeavours at estate management which he had invented and operated during his father's absence. The earl was attempting, with a faint shudder, not to listen.

"But nobody's tending properly to the land, Father. It's not right. So I sent for the overseer. I ordered him to start ploughing something."

"I imagine Famington was – delighted with your remarkable insight, my boy," murmured his lordship. "But perhaps, since the land is clearly frozen hard at present, ploughing may not be an entirely practical solution."

Humphrey frowned. "Do you think so Papa? I don't see why not. The horses need to be whipped to plough harder, that's all. And it wasn't even snowing last week. You said I had to look after everything while you were away, and I've worked very hard at it. But it's not easy. Even the hens have stopped laying enough eggs."

His father sighed. "The reproductive habits of domestic fowl have never been my main area of concern, Humphrey. But I believe, in general practise, all hens lay rarely during the winter months. The females of most species, I have noticed, tend to achieve even less during the colder seasons. We must be patient, and wait for spring."

"Well, it had better hurry up," objected the Sumerford heir, sucking the ends of his moustache. "I miss Master Shore's eggy custards."

"I shall ask your mother to have a word with the cook," said the earl, disengaging himself from his son's earnest clasp. "In the meantime, you might speak to our esteemed chaplain regarding the usual expectations of the seasons. Spring is invariably apt to arrive in March or April. See if Father Dorne will consider bringing it forward, with a timely word to the Almighty on the subject. But for the moment, my boy, I am weary. My excessive age, you know. No doubt I shall see you at suppertime, or hopefully later still. I may have a private supper brought to me in my chambers. In fact, you can report the priest's reaction to me some time tomorrow. Though come to think of it, I may sleep in. Indeed, I may decide to sleep forever. And if you happen to see your mother, kindly inform her that I am not to be disturbed for any reason whatsoever. Indeed, not for the foreseeable future."

The earl disappeared into the upstairs shadows, leaving Humphrey perplexed. He shook his head and wandered off to search for his wife.

With his lordship's return, the servants were in uproar, scampering from the kitchens to the hall and from the hearth to the stairs. There were fires to light in the bedchambers, the main fire in the hall to build higher and more candles lit, hippocras heated and jugs filled, extra provisions for a huge homecoming dinner to be brought in from the pantries, ale taken out to the grooms now unsaddling the horses and dragging away the carts, and a mountain of baggage to unpack. Ludovic, in the midst of the noise and disorder, threw his gloves and wet coat to Hamnet, ordered wine, and strode to the warmth of the hearth. Hands behind his back, he stamped the mud from his boots and turned to face the disruption. The unknown young woman he had noticed previously, still stood at the bottom of the staircase, as though waiting for something or someone. She was watching him as he watched her, and seeing his regard, curtsied very low.

Ludovic smiled. She was not dressed either as a servant or in the plain green serge beneath white Holland aprons of his mother's female attendants. Nor did she appear to be a guest, since no one had acknowledged her or showed surprise at her presence. Her curtsey was too low for any lady of rank considering herself his match, but he welcomed it, since its depth showed off her cleavage to remarkable advantage. As she looked up again, her smile was certainly not obsequious or even entirely proper for a subordinate.

The lady was very dark. Her hair was pulled severely back from an elegant and high plucked forehead, then glowed thick around her ears, and was pinned into a small headdress of white gauze. She wore expensive silks, powder blue over pleated white, and the low neckline was trimmed in otter against the swelling curves of her breasts. Her sleeves were not as ostentatiously flowing as fashion dictated, nor swept the floorboards as a lady of the court would have ensured, but they were embroidered in deep blue and trimmed in sleek grey fur. Her stomacher, wide and stiff, further accentuated her breasts, and her skin in the candlelight was soft and creamy with a faint glow of reflection. She was not, perhaps, as classically beautiful as the Lady Jennine, but her face was charming and full of character with a remarkably kissable mouth. Her narrow hips and full breasts were distinctly alluring. Then, peeping up at him, she rose from her curtsey and Ludovic saw her eyes.

"Good God," he said.

"You didn't even recognise me, did you?" said Alysson, skipping over. "Admit it."

"No." Ludovic laughed, taking her hand as she practised her

curtsey again at close quarters. "I've been away a month, and didn't see you for more than a month before that. In two months you've changed a good deal."

"Good food, and a good mistress," Alysson nodded.

He held her at a slight distance, looking her over. "Are kindness and sustenance so miraculous?"

She grinned. "Miraculous? Did I look that bad before?"

It was a challenge Ludovic chose not to accept. "Is my sister-in-law spending all her inheritance on your clothes, or have you stolen one of her gowns for the day?"

"Her things don't fit me." Alysson shook her head. "We tried once but she's much bigger than me in all sorts of places, and I just looked silly. So she had this made especially for me and gave it to me for Epiphany. I chose the pale blue to make my hair seem blacker. Do I look nice? Do you like it?"

"A most improper question," smiled Ludovic. "But you look delightful."

"Improper? Is it so different now I work in the household? I suppose I'm respectable now, and you can't just – well, not the way you did before."

Ludovic smiled, but did not answer her questions specifically. He murmured, "You have a great deal to thank your mistress for."

"To thank you for," said Alysson. "So that's what I wanted to say. I don't usually come down here, but I had to see you. To say I'm sorry, and I'm grateful, and if I don't see you ever again, I hope you're – happy. It's funny living in the same house as other people but never seeing half of them. At home we could even recognise the beetles, we saw them so often. Here I can't remember most people's names."

"I presume you remember my name."

"Don't be silly." The firelight reflected the lights in her eyes, making them dance. "And I hope your shoulder doesn't hurt anymore, and your leg is all healed up. Should I speak about men's legs? Probably not, but I hope it's better anyway. And I hope you're – enjoying – things. Did you have fun at court?"

Ludovic regarded her for a moment. "No," he said.

"Oh. Well, Christmas was really nice here. My lady sent me home for two whole days, with meat and pies." Ludovic kept his attention firmly on her face and tried not to let his gaze slip to her cleavage. "Didn't you have big feasts and meet interesting people?" she continued. "Mistress Tenby is positive that everything wonderful instantly happens at court."

Ludovic laughed again. "And who is Mistress Tenby? Another of your strange collection of nurses?"

"You ought to know who she is," Alysson informed him reprovingly. "She's worked for you for years. Mistress Tenby is manager of all the female staff, even the dairymaids and the wash-girls. But she's not more important than me, not anymore. I've been promoted."

"I'm naturally impressed." Ludovic snapped his gaze back up again from the depths of her neckline. "Though I must apologise if I'm a little vague about hierarchy. I'm afraid I have no idea about staff promotions."

"I started as a common maid. Bottom of the midden heap," Alysson explained. "Latest come, lowest in rank. Now in just two and a half months I'm the highest; the principal lady's maid and personally in charge of all the Lady Jennine's private possessions. I suppose that doesn't mean much to you. I expect it sounds – rather pathetic. But it's awfully nice for me."

"My congratulations," Ludovic murmured. "I can guess the likely benefits."

"And you must appreciate my dress too," noticed Alysson happily, "since you keep peering at the trimming. It's real otter you know, and very soft, and these skirts are so nice to walk in. This is the first time since I was very young that I've worn a gown anything like this and it feels very special. I suppose you wouldn't know how wonderful it feels to walk in silk skirts, but it makes a big difference."

Ludovic reluctantly snapped his attention back up to her eyes with a grin. "I've always been partial to – otter trimmings," he said with a slight bow. "And though my experience of skirts may be somewhat limited, my imagination is not. I'm glad you enjoyed your Christmas."

"Well," Alysson frowned momentarily and hung her head, "apart from missing my brothers. But – I know you tried to help about that too." She smiled again; golden veins in hazel green depths. "Now I'd better get back to my duties, but – thank you for everything. And if I don't ever actually see you again, I hope you always have good luck."

Ludovic raised an eyebrow. "As it happens," he said very softly, "I think I shall ensure that we do meet again. It would – please me. I might arrange something."

"What did he say?" demanded the lady.

Alysson began to unpin her hair. She sat at the huge mirror, a candle mounted either side; the pale scattering of light washing her reflection from wan to flushed. She shook her head and the black curls tumbled free. "He liked the dress. He said I looked – delightful. That's an interesting word to use, isn't it? I don't think he was just being polite. People don't say delightful unless they mean it."

"Silly child. Of course he meant it. Why would he not?" The Lady Jennine, wearing only a chemise so fine it was almost transparent, stretched across her own bed. She curled her bare feet beneath the coverlet. The chamber was stifling, the flames roaring up the chimney, a fire huge enough for a hall. Propped by pillows, she watched the nervous intensity of her personal maid. "Now, be precise. What did he look at most?"

Alysson turned to gaze at her mistress, slightly perplexed. "I don't understand. He looked at me."

Jennine sighed. "What part of you, ignorant brat?"

Alysson thought a moment. "He said he'd always liked otter trimmings," she admitted. "I thought that was an odd thing to say, but it must have been true, because he kept looking at the fur around my neckline. I like otter too."

Her mistress giggled. "This is never going to work, my dear, unless I explain a few things and you listen to me carefully. Did your mother teach you nothing?"

Alysson coloured. "My mamma died when I was still very young, my lady. I was brought up by my nurse, and she's extremely timid. I suppose I'm very – ignorant."

127

"You're a positive freak," decided the lady. "Now, take off that good gown and hang it on the peg before the silk becomes too creased. Delicate materials should never be brushed or steamed too often, it ruins the colours. You can fold it back into the chest later. Now – where was I? Oh yes, witless ignorance, bashfulness and breasts. You need an education, my girl, and though I say it myself, I am positively the very best person in the world to give it to you. But I shall be frank. And you must not be embarrassed."

Alysson stood bare toed beneath her shift, reaching for the dark green broadcloth of her work gown. "I expect I shall be embarrassed," she said. She slipped the fine pleated shift off over her head and quickly pulled on the more practical linen. "And to be honest, I'm not sure I want to do this at all. I don't think it'll work. And I don't think I want it to work. It feels rather shameful, and even dishonest." She came back and stood, a plain maid again, before her lady's bed.

"Stupid child." Jennine sat up and leaned forwards, speaking crossly. "What other future do you have? Can a woman ride to battle and come back a hero, cloaked in glory, expecting to be knighted by her king? Can a woman study science and write books on astronomy, or invent a printing press? Can a woman preach and become a famous bishop, or a king's Chamberlain? Can a woman travel the world, have adventures and discover new lands? All we can do is decline into obedient old age in a convent, or marry a powerful man. But you can't do either of these things, and you know it. You are a nobody, an orphan, and the daughter of a man who fought for the wrong king. You don't even have brothers to look after your interests anymore or arrange a respectable marriage for you. As for the convent, you'd shrivel up and die in a year. So this, my girl, is your only option. Don't be so squeamish."

Alysson sat and tugged on her stockings, fastened her garters, pulled her skirts back down and began to re pin her hair. No gauze this time, but a neat white cap with every sleek black curl severely hidden away. Aware of being watched, she blushed slightly. "I'll be a bad pupil. I'll let you down, I'm sure. It's horribly frightening. And of course, it's terribly kind of you to try and help, but I can't at all see why you're doing so much for me."

"Because I want to," said the lady. "And my motives are my own business, but I have my reasons, and they seem good to me. So don't argue. Do you want a miserable future in abject poverty? Or do you think working for me all your life to be a fine ambition?"

Alysson stood up again, neat, tidy and invisible. "Well my lady, it seems all my family die young. Perhaps I will too. I have very little respect for life anymore."

"Pooh." Jennine stretched, becoming bored. "And stop calling me 'my lady'. It's quite irritating. You know who I am."

"If I call you Jenny in private," Alysson objected, "I might forget and do it in public." She bobbed a curtsey, smiling suddenly. "So you're my lady, and you've told me nothing about your past." She rebounded from the curtsey with a small skip, and sat abruptly on the side of the bed beside her mistress. "So I believe you're a grand heiress, daughter of a merchanting family from the north, and utterly, utterly respectable."

The lady sniggered. "And if I truly was all that, I certainly wouldn't be able to keep my dear Humphrey in check. Keeping him quiet is what I'm here for, and I'm very well qualified. Otherwise he'd be chasing you again, my dear, or something far worse. But my qualifications make me an excellent teacher as well, which is just what you need. Trust me."

Alysson stood again and crossed to the window. The Lady Jennine's quarters were high in the eastern tower, looking down across the main courtyard to the cold grey moat, and the sloping farmlands beyond. She stared out, eyes blurred with memories. "Of course I trust you. But as if anyone would look at me, when you're there."

"I sometimes think," Jennine lay back again, crossing her legs, hands behind her head, "you must be blind, my dear, as well as ignorant. I may be more voluptuous, which works well with most men, but you are a good deal younger and almost as pretty when you smile, which you don't do often enough. Your eyes are quite remarkable, and your mouth is positively adorable. I am twenty nine years old and well past my first blush. I am ageing. No, don't try to deny it, I've no illusions and I have a well silvered mirror. My skin is tired and I need ever more honey and paint to hide the marks. You are the future, my pet, and prettier every day. And now I shall teach you how to use it."

"I don't want to learn how to – flirt."

"Flirting wouldn't work with that young man," frowned Jennine. "I tried it when I first arrived, but he saw through me as clear as water. He's far too experienced. He is also mightily arrogant, and way too confident. But I know more subtle tricks to pull him down."

Alysson turned in a hurry. "That sounds horrid."

"You already do it without even realising." Jennine pursed her lips. "You think he admired your otter trimmings? How absurd. He was staring at your breasts, my dear, and spent half an hour undressing you in his mind." She kicked her legs from the bed and stood, strolling over to Alysson's side at the window. The brittle icicles still frosted the glass outside. Jennine put her arm around her maid's shoulders. "It's a shame I can't have you hide behind a screen and watch what I do with Humphrey. You'd learn a great deal."

Alysson pulled away at once. "You couldn't. I couldn't."

"I know," Jennine said, somewhat wistfully. "Never mind. I shall find another way to teach you. I've tutored others in the past, far less beautiful and far more stupid. You'll be a joy to educate, my pet."

Alysson had walked away, sitting again on the rumpled bed. The bed curtains, half pulled, hid her blushes. "But I'm still not sure I want to be anyone's mistress, Jenny," she said. "I'm not like you. I'm not the type to be someone's lover."

"Even his?"

Alysson shook her head, starched cap primly in place. "Especially his."

CHAPTER FIFTEEN

The cabin was suffocating. Although ice was forming on the mizzen mast and the poop deck was slippery with salt sprigged snow, below decks it was airless. Ludovic sat on the low straw mattress, boots up on the desk, head back against the wall. The space allowed little movement, the desk the only other furniture apart from the bed and one tiny stool. Two paces in either direction would have met with walls or door. The candle was a stub and it smoked. The stench was stale and heady with reminders of untanned hides, unwashed wool, untreated canvas, boiled cabbage, vomit and urine. The sour smells mixed with brine and sweat, and Ludovic found it increasingly hard to breathe.

Captain Kenelm had managed to squash himself onto the stool and was regarding his business partner with complacent affection. "Welcome aboard, my lord, but then, seeing as this ship is more yourn than mine, you knows you're always right welcome, and this time as much and more. T'were a mighty profitable trip, my lord. Best ever, p'raps. I'm right sorry if it must be the last."

"Legal trade already recommences, I'm afraid Kenelm," Ludovic sighed. "We righteous smugglers must abandon our more lucrative commerce and turn tediously honest once more."

"Don't know wot the country's coming to my lord," objected the captain. "Nuffing left for a decent sailor to earn his keep no more, 'cept suffer them piratical attacks and risk our miserable lives for a few rotten pence."

"I hope we shall make a little more than a few pence, Kenelm," said his lordship. "But certainly the wealth we've amassed over the last couple of years is likely to be at an end. I'll still finance your next trip to Flanders of course, though it'll be a normal cargo, and no need to bribe the customs. But I'll reduce my profit percentage if you're nervous of pirates."

"Them dirty little buggers is always around, specially through the Narrow Sea," said the captain sadly. "But I ain't scared of them. I knows how to handle mesell. We'd a bit o'trouble on this trip, as it happens, and aboard my own cog it was, which is wot I don't expect nor don't allow. Not pirates this time, but one bastard in my crew picks a fight just six mile out of Antwerp, and murders one of my best men. I was proper peeved, as you might imagine."

"With less space than it takes to squash lice, I'm surprised you don't have more fights onboard," Ludovic said. "Forced to travel like this, I might end murdering the entire crew. What did you do with him?"

"The usual," muttered the captain. "Roped him alive to the bugger he knifed, and chucked them both overboard. Give them crabs and fishes a proper feast."

"A charming thought," sighed Ludovic. "Is that every captain's method of justice at sea?"

"For those as is fair minded like me, and more merciful than some," Kenelm nodded.

He was interrupted. The door, a little uneven on its hinges, swung open suddenly, kicked by a small boot. Clovis, grasping a jug and a tray with two sliding cups, burst inside and slammed both cups and jug on the table. "Wine," he announced, seemingly affronted at something. "An' don't ast fer no more, cos it ain't coming."

Ludovic smiled. "I appear to have offended you, brat. But no doubt I can dispense with the wine, since it's likely an evil brew. And I'll willingly dispense with your company at the same time, I think."

"Other people," remarked Clovis, glaring at the captain and

ignoring his lordship, "gets let off once we makes port. Specially when it ain't even a proper port. Other people gets treated fair. But some members of the crew, 'cluding those as is more loyal and hardworking than others, gets told to stay behind and serve stupid drinks."

"Filthy little urchin," objected the captain. "Rope you up to a rock and chuck you overboard next trip, I will. Learn some respect, and 'pologise to his lordship."

Clovis nodded to Ludovic as he backed from the cabin. "Not your fault, m'lor," he admitted. "Having got in with this nasty old bugger, don't reckon there's much you can do about it now. But I warn you, bit of chewed old sinew he is, and not a fair bone rests beneath 'is smelly old hide."

The door closed; the cabin shook. Captain Kenelm sighed. "Forgive the little bastard, my lord. Brought up bad, he was. I'd have him whupped, but he's my nevvy and my sister'd whup me if she found out I'd done ought. And the little bugger would tell her, that he would." The captain shook his head, smiled again and remembered business. He poured two cups of dark wine. "And now, my lord, since you knows these politckals and such like, and the ways of trading both proper and – them other ways – more advantageous, as you might say – so tell me my lord, be there a chance of another blockage soon? A nice big embargo to cover half o' France, Spain and the rest 'o them. That's what I'd like."

Ludovic grinned. "I like the idea myself, but it won't happen Kenelm. The reason for sanctions is sadly over, the wretched young rebel is captive, and Flanders and Burgundy have professed undying friendship with England once more. And there'll be no more disagreements, for Spain will see to it. It's Spanish royalty who insisted on Tudor making a truce with everyone, for they refused to unite their daughter in marriage with Tudor's heir unless there was a secure peace both here and with our neighbours. And Tudor wants this marriage."

"You mean we've lost our living just for the sake of some fool brat to wed, and occupy his shaft in some female's bilges? I don't reckon that's decent."

"There was pressure from the other side as well," said Ludovic.

"Maximilian was pushed into abandoning his support for the Duke of York so he might encourage England to join the Holy League against France. France, you see, is attempting to pillage and plunder all nearby countries at will and must be stopped from swallowing the world." Ludovic smiled at the captain's grimace. "As you know, my friend, the English loathe foreigners on our shores and suspect them all of theft and forgery. What they do not realise is that foreign policy rules our land more surely than the king."

"Not that I understand all that, nor rightly care," said Captain Kenelm. "But tell me, wot's the Duke 'o York got to do with this? Just a little lad, he is, and a right pretty one too they say."

Ludovic paused. "That is a long story, which I have no desire to tell. Suffice it to say he was the reason for the embargo, and a great deal else besides. Not Tudor's younger son, but the youngest of the old King Edward's sons, sent away from England in secret under King Richard. The boy has been in Burgundy ever since, kept safe there by the Duchess and others. He was encouraged by them to come to England and claim his crown. He has failed."

The captain grunted. "Them little boys was bastards," he remembered. "And wot's them got to do with this Perkin Warbeck the king speaks of?"

"They are one and the same," said Ludovic softly. "Or so I guess, for none of us can be sure. You have believed Tudor's propaganda, my friend, as has most of the country. And not for the first time. It seems we are all willing to be Tudor's dupes, and so on and on into the future."

"I ain't no irrit," objected the captain. "The lad done signed a confession. That's proof enough fer me."

"He signed a confession in order to keep his wife safe, his son alive, and his own head on his shoulders, as would most of us," said Ludovic, draining his cup and standing up abruptly. "Though the confessions, for anyone with sufficient interest to actually read them, are as absurd and clearly false as most romances. I'd as soon believe in the knights of Camelot."

Kenelm watched his benefactor stride to the door and pause there, palm on the handle. "But them's true too, my lord," he objected.

"Which is why our king has named his lad Arthur, so we knows there'll be a noble and prosperous England promised to come. Now you've got me proper confused, my lord."

"I apologise, Kenelm," Ludovic smiled, pushing open the low door and ducking through. "Certainly Tudor may try to impress the people by claiming descent from myth and legend if he wishes, since he has no claim to any descent more respectable. But none of this matters. Now I'm going ashore before the insidious aromas of our sturdy cog drive me to return my dinner onto your bed. In the meantime, if we must now contemplate a more honest trade, I suggest you consider alum. You've been doing your best business with merchants of illegally exported wool and leather, and dying those cloths is the next necessary step. Alum is the essential basis for dying, and with the Vatican creating its own embargo in order to keep all alum profits for itself, perhaps a little smuggling might be attempted after all. Some legal imports, let us say, with a few extra casks hidden in the hold."

"Well now, my lord," grinned the captain. "I knows nuffing wotso'hever 'bout alum. But I reckon that's about to change. Maybe we've a bright future ahead of us after all sir, King bloody Arthur or otherwise."

"Tighter," insisted the Lady Jennine. "Are you frightened of a little minor discomfort, girl? What woman fears pain when her looks are the stake? Breathe in, and thrust the starched folds well up beneath your breasts. Like this."

Alysson wrinkled her nose. "I shall probably crack my ribs. And that won't be attractive at all."

"Stupid child. How will you ever achieve childbirth, if you can hardly bear a tight stomacher? Not that women of our profession usually encourage childbirth, but avoiding it can be difficult. It happens."

Alysson sat abruptly on the cushioned window seat. A shy lemon sun halloed the spun black silk of her unpinned hair, hiding her scowl in shadow. "You want to get pregnant now," she pointed out.

Jennine smiled, her mood quickly switching from impatient to confiding. She sat next to Alysson and took her hand into her lap. "This is a secret, my love, but I think perhaps it's happened already. You'll tell none of the other servants of course, not until I've informed her ladyship. I need a little more time to be absolutely sure, but I think it's done."

"I'm pleased for you." Alysson frowned, reclaiming her fingers. "I know it's required, but it seems such a risk. What if the child is – like – Humphrey?"

The lady giggled. "Highly unlikely, as it happens." She stood, crossing to the large standing mirror, smiling widely at her reflection. "But it's what I'm here for, we all know that. A wife is a breeding mare, chosen for the width of her hips and the regularity of her monthly bleeding. She must come from a rich and powerful family with a large dower and excellent contacts, but her greatest value is her belly. We are cattle, my dear. Your position is less humiliating in fact, for a mistress is neither sow nor mare. She is a pretty trifle, and her value is her beauty. She will learn all her lover's secrets, which his wife will never do."

Alysson sighed. "I can't imagine Ludovic having a – wife. But I suppose he will have to marry one day."

Jennine nodded. "It will be expected of him, naturally. These Sumerford sons have been allowed their independence far too long already. You know, after the battle of Bosworth many of their lands were snatched by the crown, and they might have lost everything if the earl hadn't bent his knee to Tudor. The countess managed to save her dower properties, and these are to be parcelled out to the younger boys, so Ludovic will have a small share. I can't remember where. But with the greater estates left to Humphrey, of course he needed to be married off first. He's a good age now, but my dearest husband was no easy match as you can imagine. And their lordships considered it of prime importance to discover a lady capable of keeping their heir – under control, let us say. Highly unlikely from some aristocratic young virgin. Better a mature female of the comfortable middle classes. My real identity is my own business of course, but I do my job. And now, especially if I am with child, his

136

lordship will look around and find suitable wives for his other sons."

Alysson put her legs up on the window seat, cuddled her knees and stared out to the moat. The water caught the sunlight and turned silver. It was early March and the first birds were returning from their warmer winters. The wheeling flocks spun patterns across the sky. Cloud splattered, it threatened rain. Alysson watched a kestrel swoop from the long trees in the east, parting the flocks, hunting on the wing. She spoke to the sun. "I know you're being kind, Jenny. I could never have expected such understanding treatment. But I don't want to do this, and if I try, I'll fail."

Jennine stamped her foot. "Nonsense, child. I've not wasted my time and money for you to turn chaste now. You'll practise what I tell you, and study like an obedient child at school."

Alysson glowered. "I can already read. My father taught me years ago. And I am chaste."

"Don't sulk," ordered the lady, "or I shall slap you. Your mouth turns down and you look like a duck. Certainly being chaste is an excellent beginning. Men like to be the first. No doubt the poor souls dread being compared to some previous lover with better equipment. But chastity is simply that – a beginning. A whore may charge a higher price for her hymen, but once done, there are few who will trouble to sew it back. That's an Eastern trick, where the men have absurdly particular demands. Our English prefer a little cheerful corruption between the sheets."

"So what happens when I grow ancient?" Alysson demanded. "You're only twenty nine years and you call yourself old. I shall have no family, no friends and no home of my own. I shall be even more destitute and pathetic than I am now."

Jennine shook her head. "Would marriage be better? An ageing wife is ignored while the husband, however decrepit and wrinkled, looks for a younger replacement to flatter him. The wife will die in childbirth, or become widowed and retire to a convent, or stay lonely and bully her sons."

"As the Countess of Sumerford does."

"None of her sons allow her to bully them," smiled the lady. "But she is bullied by her husband. Haven't you noticed the bruises, the scars and bloodied lips? No mistress would permit such a thing. A mistress is never beaten by her lover."

"No. She's discarded, while he finds another."

"Only if she's untrained, and weak."

"You may call the countess weak," insisted Alysson, "but she has some rights. And I cannot bear to imagine what she'd do if she found out who you really are, and what I am planning to do. She dismissed me when I was just a dairymaid. Now she would have me thrashed half to death."

The Lady Jennine's smile seemed smugly satisfied, as if she smiled more to herself than to another. "We all have our particular reasons and secrets," she said quietly. "But at least you now admit you're planning to do this. It's the only wise choice of course, so less mawkish timidity if you please, and let us get back to work."

Alysson stood obediently, breathing in for the fastening of the stomacher. "It doesn't matter anyway," she said softly. "He said he wanted to see me again but that was a month ago. He's never come to get me, or looked for me at all."

Jennine raised her severely plucked eyebrows. "Absurd. Do you expect a lord of Sumerford to tramp his own castle corridors, searching for a servant girl closeted in my private apartments? He will send for you child, when he wishes. And it won't be long now. He's already made sure you're still here."

Alysson was startled. "You know that? How?"

"One of the pages, sent a week back to inquire if I meant to join the hunt the following morning. You were sitting there by the window as you often do. Don't you remember? The boy kept looking at you, surreptitious but attentive, matching you with your description." The lady laughed. "But no one needs to question my intentions, since Humphrey insists I always hunt, however much I dislike it. And it wasn't one of Humphrey's pages. I knew exactly who had sent the boy, and why."

"It could have been anything. You can't be sure."

"I'm fairly sure I recognised Ludovic's page boy, and have more experience in these matters than you seem to guess, in spite of all my confessions, my dear." Jennine took Alysson's hand and led her to the mirror. "And you must be ready. Learning the use of belladonna and rosewater, how to dress, to simper, to smile and be artful. But that is not enough. Once you have the man prone in bed, there are far more essential matters to remember."

Alysson shook her head. "I can't."

"Well." The lady considered, turning Alysson to left and to right before the mirror. "Perhaps not the first time. We don't want to make you look professional. I shall teach you a few things, but not too much until later."

"All he will care about is whether I've – bathed."

Jennine laughed. "But you do, my pet. You wash all the time. But of course many men have peculiarities. Perhaps your charming prince lusts over bathwater, or soap, or sponges maybe? You've never told me this little detail before."

"He hasn't any strange – lusts – not as far as I know." Alysson reverted to the scowl. It reflected dark in the mirror. "It was just that I never used to be able – that is, living in the cottage. Well, never mind. It doesn't matter anymore. I wish I was back there sometimes. And I hate this game."

"It is not a game," said the lady, eyes suddenly cold. "Your future depends upon it, and you will do exactly as you are told."

CHAPTER SIXTEEN

Brice came home with a partially healed sword cut across his wrist and an inflamed graze on his left cheekbone. The countess, who was wearing a matching bruise on her right cheekbone, greeted him with disapproval. "I do not see," she said, "why my sons insist on indulging such rough behaviour. Fighting in peacetime is perfectly unnecessary in this civilised country. First Ludovic was wounded before Christmas, and now you. I am disappointed in you Brice. I always considered you the least contentious of my sons."

Brice grinned and kissed his mother. "Indeed, I am a gentle soul, Mamma, as you well know. Fighting is certainly to be avoided at all times. It risks spoiling my new doublet, and can do shocking damage to a pair of fine silk hose. But sometimes, regrettably, it cannot be avoided. Footpads, Mamma. Sadly I travelled unguarded. And one solitary gentleman, beautifully dressed and bejewelled in the latest fashion, is a target for ruffians, even within the boundaries of our own lands it seems. I was outnumbered of course, though naturally defended myself most honourably."

Ludovic had strolled over to the main doors, now flung open with the sunshine slanting bright across the polished boards. "The same desperate outlaws perhaps," he suggested, smiling as his mother bustled off to arrange a welcome home dinner, "that attacked me last year in the forests?"

Brice chuckled. "Indubitably, little brother. The world is becoming a hideous place. But I hear I escaped an even worse fate. Christmas at court. I hope you kissed the king's hand?"

"His feet," nodded Ludovic.

Brice's smile broadened. "How unlike you, Lu. And did they smell of the privy, or the sewer?"

"The executioner's block," said Ludovic.

He turned to walk off but Brice put out an arm, restraining him. "And this new diversion? This Perkin Warbeck? Did you kiss his feet too, my beloved?"

Ludovic's eyes narrowed, and he paused. "I saw him," he said briefly, turned at once and strolled back upstairs.

Brice crossed to the fire but he called after his brother. "Surely such an intriguing subject, my loved one." Ludovic did not answer and Brice raised his voice. "Tonight, after supper, come to my chamber, or I shall come to yours. I should like to discover more of dear Gerald's obsession with this fascinating new pretender, and perhaps learn something of your own opinion."

Ludovic stopped and looked over the balustrade. "An intriguing subject indeed, but not one I'd have expected you to adopt, my dear. Besides, you should ask Gerald, not me. And let me point out that you're in danger of becoming beguilingly eccentric, since the two minor injuries you appear to have suffered are clearly not of recent acquisition at all, and therefore cannot have been provoked within our boundaries. An equally intriguing subject, don't you think? Which of these so stimulating secrets should we discuss first, do you think? "

Brice sniggered into his new sables. "My beloved boy, I can hardly humiliate myself by always telling dearest Mamma the truth, now can I? How tedious that would be. Come to my room tonight. We shall drink the best Burgundy now that trade is resumed, and I shall tell you everything."

Ludovic appeared already lost in the upper shadows but his voice answered quite clearly. "I doubt you would ever tell me everything, my dear." The diminishing words faded into the depths of the corridor, floating back like an echo. "And in any case, not tonight, big brother. Perhaps tomorrow. Tonight I shall be busy. Very busy indeed."

⋯✦⋯

"He has been surprisingly gracious," frowned the lady. "I would have expected a brief summons, as is usual in these matters. A cursory nod is often considered sufficient. This Ludovic is perhaps a more – sensitive – and gentle man than I realised."

"I have no idea what you're talking about," said Alysson with a scowl and a marked lack of respect.

"I have received a message," continued Jennine patiently, "sent via his lordship's personal secretary James Parton, who bowed low and politely requested, should it be convenient to myself and to the lady in question, that Mistress Alysson Welles be so kind as to partake of a light supper with Lord Ludovic in his chambers at six of the clock this evening. It was further suggested, that should both myself and Mistress Alysson be agreeable to the arrangement, his lordship will send a page to escort the lady to the afore mentioned chambers. I naturally informed Master Parton that the invitation was perfectly acceptable, both to myself and to Mistress Alysson."

Alysson glared. She said, "I feel sick."

"It's a very nobly staged assignation," said Jennine with a sigh. "Evidently he means to do the thing properly, starting early with food and conversation. Your prospective amourette is doing you considerably more honour than you seem to be doing him, my dear."

"He wants to get me into bed," muttered Alysson. "That's seduction, and is not in the least bit honourable. It's – sordid."

"It's life," said the lady. "You'll go, you'll remember all your lessons, and you'll tell me everything tomorrow morning."

Alysson gasped. "You mean, I might have to stay all night?"

"Well, that depends," said Jennine. "If you do everything I've taught you, then probably yes. He'll want you to. But some men don't like a woman to stay too long. He may do his business and then tell you to leave. So on the way there, you'd better take note so as to remember the way back in the dark."

"This is ghastly," gulped Alysson. "I shall probably spew all over the bed."

"Well, you'll certainly make an impression if you do that," said Jennine. "But I doubt he'd ask you to stay all night afterwards. You'd better take a large kerchief." She giggled. "Now, come here and let me dress you."

"You don't need to pluck my eyebrows again, I hope," Alysson said, both eyebrows lowered in a frown. "It hurts, and it goes all pink and sore. Last time I had little spots of blood. Why are eyebrows considered so wicked anyway?"

"They are shockingly unfashionable, stupid girl." Jennine stripped the thick green broadcloth from Alysson's small figure, and regarded her for a long and intense moment. "Yes, very pretty. You will do nicely and if he undresses you himself, it will work beautifully. However, if he expects you to undress yourself, it may be less successful. You are still hopelessly ungraceful."

"That's because I'm embarrassed," Alysson mumbled. "I'll just tell him I want to keep my clothes on."

"You will do no such thing," said Jennine, aghast. "Now, we'll have to use the pale blue silk again. After all, we can hardly let the dear boy think you've somehow acquired a royal wardrobe. It's a shame, though. I'd have liked to put you into something new, perhaps a little more transparent. But no matter. This is quite alluring. The colour goes beautifully with your hair and makes you seem sweet and innocent."

"Except for the neckline," Alysson shuddered. "I thought he really liked otter trimmings, until you spoiled it all by telling me he wasn't looking at the fur at all."

Jennine giggled again. "Well, it seems he likes you for your ridiculous ignorance, child, which might explain why he didn't fall for my own early attempts. Perhaps he's one of those who particularly enjoys ravishing innocence. Some do, you know. I just hope it doesn't mean he'll drop you after the first time. That would be a dreadful waste after all my work. But I think not, since he's waited this long and is going to so much trouble himself. Supper indeed!" She began to lace up the blue silk beneath Alysson's arm, tucking the soft curved neckline down a little. "And don't hitch that up again as soon as I'm out of sight," she ordered. "Remember everything I've told you. Be mysterious if you can. And if he hurts you, just take a deep breath. It shouldn't hurt too much, unless he wants it to."

Alysson turned abruptly, the stomacher still taut between her fingers. "If he tries to hurt me, I shall hurt him."

Jennine sighed. "That would be quite impossible as well as utterly unthinkable. You will be naked, prone, and locked in his bedchamber. What possible harm could you do him? But who knows, he might want you to struggle. I shall give no more advice. If my tutoring brings good results, I shall be well satisfied. If not – at least I have tried. But for pity's sake child, try not to scowl."

The page bowed low; exceedingly polite. Silently brisk and torch flaring, Alysson followed the boy through the interminable corridors. She knew she'd never be able to remember her way back in the dark and decided that, if thrown from Ludovic's chambers after the dreadful deed was finished, she'd simply have to curl up outside his door and wait for daylight. She wondered if she'd have the courage to ask him for a blanket. Her stomach heaved and she felt sick. She was shivering but knew her cheeks were hot flushed. As they passed other servants in the shadows and on the stairs, Alysson kept her eyes down, flushing deeper. She would, she supposed, look like a trussed chicken by the time she arrived, sure that the Lady Jennine's efforts at instilling her with grace and beauty had all, assuredly, been quite useless. Which was probably just as well.

Ludovic was reading. He stood at once as she entered, and took her hand. She thought he appeared remarkably unembarrassed, as if he arranged these sorts of trysts on regular occasions, which annoyed her. He smiled, looking at her for a few moments, then led her to a chair by the hearth. She hoped the heat of the flames would give some excuse for her face looking scorched.

He leaned one elbow to the mantle, looking down on her. She heard her own heartbeat like a bellows, but said nothing. Finally he said, "I really rather expected you'd refuse to come. But at least you haven't lost the scowl. I'm delighted to see you haven't changed too much after all."

Alysson took a deep breath and glared up at him. "I have changed. But last time when you'd just got home after Christmas, I was really pleased to see you. I was happy and I wanted to say thank you. This time is different. It's – humiliating."

Ludovic grinned. "It seems you are jumping to conclusions, Mistress Alysson."

Alysson felt her blushes creep higher. "I'm not stupid," she mumbled. "I do know what's proper, and this isn't. I shouldn't be here alone with you whoever I was, and it's worse and it's disparaging of you to pretend anything different. I do know my place, even if I don't like keeping to it."

"I can remember a time," said Ludovic, amusement irritatingly fixed, "when you went out of your way to try and prove your own value. You also once told me that your reputation was of no interest to you whatsoever. However, I take your point. Naturally, you've now assumed your charms have grown sufficiently to tempt me into immoral invitations. Hence your permanent scowl. You're clearly expecting imminent rape, wholesale ravishment, or at least some iniquitous attempt at seduction." He paused a moment, watching as her fury mounted. "What would you do, I wonder," he murmured, "if I leapt on you now and carried you off to my bed."

Alysson gulped. "Bite you, probably," she said.

Ludovic chuckled. "But you've neither admitted nor denied my accusations."

Alysson took a deep breath. "Well, I certainly don't have any faith in my – charms, as you so rudely put it," she said. "Though I know I look better than I did, and I'm not so skinny, and it's a nice dress." She was staring into her lap, fingers knotting and re-knotting. "And I have bathed." She knew her face to be flushed, right up to her plucked eyebrows and beyond. "I like bathing," she continued, voice wooden. "And I'm not expecting all those – horrid things you just said. Not in the slightest."

"Don't lie," said Ludovic.

Her head jerked up and she glared at him again. "Very well. I am expecting it. But I don't want you to."

"Well, that's all right then," said Ludovic. "Because I don't intend to." He took a chair opposite her, stretching his legs. "Tell me, did you practise this particular introduction to the evening, or was it ex tempore? Not many women react to a supper invitation by immediately launching into insults and bad temper. But then, I always have found you – delightfully unique."

"You started with the insults," said Alysson crossly. "You tease me on purpose, you know you do." She felt her blushes begin to fade, and looked up at him with an immediately more pleasant expression. "Do you really not – that is, you didn't mean – and you don't want to?"

He chuckled again. "I didn't say I don't want to. Simply that I don't intend to. Not yet anyway. I have invited you to a late but quite innocent supper, because I wish to talk to you in private."

"Even if it's not the proper thing to do? Which you know it isn't?"

Ludovic nodded. "I am not famed for being proper, my child." His smile appeared permanent. "And our meetings have hardly been convenable in the past. After all, you've been in this chamber alone with me once before, and you even know where my secret coffers are kept hidden. I had the pleasure of kissing you – long ago – and I seem to remember, though admittedly I took you by surprise, you neither bit nor dissuaded me. Nor did I think your remarkably tolerant mistress would be shocked. She seems to me to be a lady of some experience herself, and probably unshockable."

"Oh well." Alysson relaxed noticeably. "In that case, thank you for the invitation. I was terribly worried you know. I – well I imagined all sorts of terrifying things and it was really humiliating."

His eyes narrowed. "My dear girl, would you really be so

distressed to learn some man desired you, and found you sufficiently attractive to approach you with – improper intentions?"

"Probably." Alysson looked at her lap again. "But especially you."

Ludovic appeared momentarily startled. "Especially me?"

"Yes of course," said Alysson. "Because I trust you and you're a friend. And with anyone else I'd kick them, but with you I suppose I couldn't. Well, actually I might anyway, but I'd feel really guilty after all you've done for me. And it would be extra embarrassing, whether I tried to fight back or whether I just – put up with it. "

"And do you consider," asked Ludovic casually, "that any man's advances, and evidently my own in particular, would prove so excessively unwelcome?"

She nodded vigorously. "That's a silly question. Naturally I'd hate it. Who wouldn't?"

Ludovic paused a moment. "I have noted – in the past – on occasion," he murmured, "that a subtle approach to seduction, under certain circumstances, does not always seem entirely unacceptable to everyone."

Alysson abruptly thought of the Lady Jennine and her own two months of careful tutoring, now virtually abandoned, and hiccupped. "Well," she said cheerfully, "I'm just glad that doesn't apply to you – or to me."

"Of course not," smiled Ludovic. "So perhaps we had better change the subject, and enjoy our supper instead."

Only one course was spread, and the dishes, although varied, were limited to those served easily and privately to only two people. Ludovic ate very little, watching as Alysson ate a very great deal. After a while he signalled for the three pages who had brought the meal, to leave. He then served Alysson himself.

"Gingered chicken breast?" he suggested. Alysson was aware that his eyes were on her own breasts, though clearly ungingered, so sat up straighter and shook her head in a fluster. It had been easier when the pages had done the waiting and Ludovic had kept the conversation inane. "A shame," he said. "I believe Master Shore prepares it particularly well. Perhaps some smoked eels in burned cream instead?

The Exe is quite clogged with eels this time of year you know. We should do our best to use them up."

Alyson quickly found his concentration too intense and felt herself flushing scarlet again. "Now, I wonder why you're blushing." Ludovic smiled. "I see nothing particularly reprehensible or embarrassing about eels. Unless, of course, you have a very marked sense of word play, which I rather think you have not. Or do you simply find the room too hot?"

"Very hot," said Alysson quickly. "And I think I've eaten enough thank you." She pushed her chair back from the small table and Ludovic nodded. He reached for her cup and poured the wine. She shook her head at that too. "I'm not used to it. I really shouldn't drink too much."

"That is precisely why you should," Ludovic informed her. "You are still ridiculously nervous, in spite of my protestations earlier. And I want to talk to you properly, without you crouching there like a fox at bay." He grinned suddenly. "There now. You are scowling again, and after all my efforts too. Evidently you believe your pride is injured once more, and guess I am either laughing at you, or insulting you. As it happens, I am doing neither."

"How do you know what my scowl means?" Alysson objected.

"I know perfectly well," said Ludovic. "You scowl frequently, and always for precisely the same reasons. The scowl stands for wounded pride, the glare for defence. Now, drink your wine like a good girl. Remembering what you said – that I am a friend – and that you trust me."

"I do trust you."

"Then unhunch," Ludovic said. "After all, we have eaten together before, and this meal is, I believe, somewhat more palatable than the last. Which is not an insult – merely an observation." Having filled both their cups, he led her away from the small table and back to her chair by the fire. "And the room is not too hot," he continued, "it is only your discomfort that makes you think it. And the only cooler place I have to offer you is my bedchamber, to which you would no doubt object. Now," he sat opposite her again, "tell me, without subterfuge or embarrassment, how you are. Clearly your mistress

148

treats you well, but you were not born to a servant's life. So, are you happy enough?"

Alysson sipped her wine. "I'm not sure how much happiness is enough. But probably I have more than enough. Certainly more than I expected. That's why I wanted to thank you – last time."

Ludovic paused a moment. "The Lady Jennine is clearly – an unusual woman," he said at last. "But I don't ask you to speak about your mistress behind her back, and have no interest in her private affairs. When I arranged to have you placed in her service, I'm afraid it was simply a matter of convenience. I wanted you well cared for, and some sort of financial aid made available. But we are a household of men, and do not employ many women. I doubted my mother would take you on after the previous misunderstanding. There remained only my sister-in-law. But now I wonder whether living permanently in her quarters is – entirely suitable – for you after all."

Alysson looked up in surprise. "She's kind."

"I never suggested otherwise." Ludovic sounded impatient, then shook his head. "Very well, then. Let it rest. As long as you're content."

Alysson remembered all the things which had lately troubled her, and how they had all, in one unexpected evening, been put to sleep. "I'm certainly content and thank you, very much, for everything. And being a maid doesn't seem so hard. After all, I was only ever an alderman's daughter. I was never – any more than that."

"My dear girl," Ludovic drained his cup. "What exactly do you think aristocracy entails? Forget the holy anointing of kings and the sacred rights of nobility. Does Henry Tudor seem like God's merciful gift to all Englishmen? Is he somehow more righteous than the decent man whose throne he usurped? It is not the lord or the bishop, but the tradesman and the alderman who found the solid honesty of our towns, and the farmer who supplies the food, keeping England prosperous. There is corruption at every level, but it is the mighty of the land with the greatest power who despise honesty the most. Believe me, child, I speak from long experience of such things. How many wealthy men, do you suppose, gain profit from helping others? And this rabble of barons and earls, knighted for slaughtering their king's enemies on the battlefield, or for secretly conspiring to further the injustices of those already in power. Do they seem somehow more entitled, more deserving? Minor donations come to charity, with the foundation of a church or an alms house perhaps, but simply to ensure a rich man's own blessed benefits after death." Ludovic refilled his cup to the brim, and in spite of her refusal, refilled Alysson's as well. "Let me tell you a story," he said.

CHAPTER SEVENTEEN

Ludovic crossed his ankles on the wrought iron grate, his boots a
little scuffed and part smeared with ashes. A log tumbled within
the hearth and the fire sparked. The chamber had been bright before
supper with a dozen tall perfumed candles lit, but now three had
gutted and another hissed, the wick sinking into liquid beeswax in its
dish. Long shadows began to fill the room.

The ceiling beams were painted deep red with scrolls of carved
ivy, and though they were high, almost high enough to disappear into
the gloom, Alysson was impressed to notice there were no hanging
streamers of dust or corners woven in cobwebs. The room was well
tended, every angle polished by a diligent staff. But even higher,
invisible between the ceilings and the great tiled roofs leading across
to the castle turrets, came faint squeakings and the scampering of rats.

Within the chamber, the fire reflected across the rich magenta
surface of the wine and over the faces of the two people sitting close,
springing demons in their eyes. The words Ludovic spoke were
echoed in the leaping flames, stories equally alive, one dancing to the
rhythms of the other.

"My father's grandfather," Ludovic began softly, "was the first Earl
of Sumerford, but he did not live here as a child. I never saw him of
course. I did not even know my grandfather. But I know our family

history, as do all those born on these estates. But my father's grandfather Lionel was born far north from here, in Yorkshire near Hull. Of ancient Norwegian and pagan lineage, he was flame haired with a brutal temper. His father was John Pownsey, a seafarer, part pirate part fisherman and no gentleman. The mother was a third cousin once removed to the noble Sumerfords, barons of Somerset, a wisp of a woman without fortune but with a temper worse than her husband's. How they met and married I have no idea but it was surely mutual attraction, since their disparate circumstances should have kept them apart. Certainly she had claim to neither title nor riches, but her descent was far better than his. This seagoing man, my great, great grandfather, then fought at Agincourt for the Lancastrian king and came home blind in one eye and popular. Brute courage and luck made him a great fighter, and common sense made him loyal. He was too lowly to be knighted, but the king saw him and remembered his name.

"This castle, secure beneath the blessed sun of splendid aristocracy, lay far distant and never even seen by the lowly brine seasoned Pownseys. It did not enter their dreams. But when the Baron of Sumerford died of wounds taken at Agincourt, the heir to the title expired with the dysentery soon after, his three sons dead of the pestilence, one cousin of the yellow pox and another suddenly stabbed in a brawl, Lionel's ambitious Sumerford mother leapt to claim inheritance. It was of course denied. Mistress Pownsey was not direct in line, and although the male heirs had mostly been wiped out within the space of two years, a daughter remained. So one young woman, just twelve years old and sickly, stood adamantly between my ancestors and the power of the Sumerford estates.

"His parents told Lionel what to do. I doubt he needed telling twice. He was their only surviving son after many infant deaths, and their one hope. He rode to Somerset. He entered across the drawbridge without challenge, being a relative and simply desiring courtesy and conversation with the heiress and her advisors. He charmed the advisors, the stewards, the tutors and the secretaries, and asked to meet the girl. I have no idea if Lady Edith was frightened or suspicious. She was simply a child and accustomed to obedience.

Lionel abducted her at once. Killing the astonished guards in his path, he dragged her to her own quarters, those occupied now by the Lady Jennine incidentally, and locked her in with himself. He then proceeded as you might expect.

"He eventually freed the girl, I imagine there was need for food and water at the very least, now claiming her as his wife. They had exchanged oaths already, he said. Perhaps she had genuinely accepted him during those terrifying days in his power. Perhaps he had charmed her too. I imagine it was initially rape, but afterwards best accepted and quickly interpreted as legal. She was very young, even a little younger than the Beaufort heiress when the ignoble Edmund Tudor got her pregnant with our noble Tudor king. And the Lady Edith Sumerford was also with child. A new Sumerford heir was born in the autumn.

"So Lionel Pownsey was not immediately arrested for his violent impudence, and instead took up residence in the castle, lord of the estate and husband of the lady. Naturally, on hearing of the outrage, many others in the family objected and appealed to the king for justice. But the noble King Henry V remembered the name of John Pownsey from the battle at Agincourt, and therefore honoured the son Lionel, awarding him the lands he now claimed, and creating him first Earl of Sumerford. Evidently it was the rape of a little girl that now fitted the lowly Pownsey boy for aristocracy. The king had no interest in a twelve-year-old made to bear the child of abuse. My family title was assured.

"Edith Sumerford died in childbirth but my grandfather Lionel, son of Lionel, was born healthy, with red hair and the foul temper of his line. After Henry V's youthful death, the Sumerford estates continued to prosper, but the new earls also followed the salt tides surging through their blood. They took to piracy along the Somerset coast. They were as ruthless and brutal as piracy demands, and their newly claimed aristocracy kept them safe from the law. It was shortly after my father's birth, welcomed as the next son and heir, that the second earl was killed at sea. My father was consequently brought up by his mother, and so escaped, just a little perhaps, the influences of his birth. But he is not a man to be crossed, and my mother knows it.

"My father is mightily proud of his title and ancestral heritage. I find it unpleasant, but that is my family, and though I am the youngest born and will claim nothing of the estates, I have the same blood in my veins. Do you consider me more noble then? Am I more deserving of respect than the daughter of an alderman?"

He paused, one eyebrow raised. Alysson, her pale blue silks still neat, sat in silence. The candle in the sconce behind her gave her a halo, the firelight on her face a deeper glow. Eventually she said, "I have no idea who my great, great grandparents were, or their parents before them. Perhaps they were pirates, perhaps they were dung raykers. Farmers I expect. They were certainly not earls or barons, but who knows? I don't care. Why should you care about your ancestors?"

Ludovic smiled. "Care? No, I don't care, child. I am who I am, and have not the slightest interest in any other's man's opinion, nor of who I am, of why I live here, or the reasons I might claim aristocratic privilege. I am often accused of arrogance and I have no care for that either. I am telling you something quite different. I am telling you that nobility is not sent by God or the angels, is neither blessing nor curse, and matters no more than the wind that blows the wheel of fortune, or the strength of one man's determination." He paused, looking across at her. "I am simply telling you that I give nothing for pretensions of title or power, and that when I invite you to dine with me, it is the request of a friend to a friend, and you are free to refuse."

Alysson smiled but shook her head. "No one else in this house would agree with you. But I understand and I'm really very happy to see you again. Of course my reputation's unlikely to be ruined anyway, even if it mattered, which it doesn't. It was only the – assumption – of why you wanted to meet me – that was upsetting. The Lady Jennine, you know, is extraordinarily kind to me but her opinion of men isn't entirely – trusting. She wouldn't be at all shocked by your grandfathers. She told me – in detail – what to expect from you – and exactly what I should do in return. But you haven't done what she said at all."

Ludovic had seemed morose, sitting deep back in his chair and speaking softly, like the faint chanting of the monks from the distant monastery. Now his face brightened and he chuckled. "I should be fascinated to know exactly how you were tutored to respond to my evil advances," he said. "Presumably not by shooting me in the leg or knocking me unconscious."

Alysson scowled again. "You seem to think it's all a game. You don't even seem very surprised at my lady's assumptions."

"I'd wager you weren't told to scowl and insult me either," Ludovic grinned. "Perhaps I should point out that nothing the Lady Jennine does would surprise me in the slightest. I have my own assumptions regarding her character, and it's an opinion she might choose not to hear. But no matter. It's you I'm interested in, child. I placed you in this position, and am now not at all sure I acted wisely. I hold myself - responsible."

"Responsible?" She was still scowling. "Well, you're not. I've thanked you for getting me the position, and it's helped me a great deal. But now I'm responsible for myself."

"Nevertheless, my sense of responsibility has been alerted, and now refuses to sleep." Ludovic had removed his feet from the hearth. He now sat forwards a moment to watch the glow of the dying flames. "Though it seems high time," he said, "that you stopped thanking me, or it will soon become abysmally tedious." He stood and placed another small log far back amongst the charred ashes. He watched it take the heat, sparking into tiny flames along its length, the satisfying smell of burning wood again bursting rich and musty into the chamber. Finally Ludovic wandered over to the table and refilled both cups from the wine jug. His back was to Alysson when he said, quite casually, "But to return to the Lady Jennine's assumptions. Tell me, how were you meant to react, child, to my supposed seductions? Can a mistress want her maid compromised?"

He didn't see her blushes, but knew they would be there. Alysson watched his back, tall, lean and muscular, as he moved quietly around the deep shadowed chamber. His hose, tight knitted silk and close hugging, outlined each movement, and his doublet, half unlaced over a plain linen shirt, was short and revealing. She sighed. "My lady sees the world for what it surely is. She accepts what seems most probable, and tells me to respond for my own benefit."

"Which would be?" Ludovic sauntered back, bringing the wine.

Alysson relaxed and smiled suddenly. "You want me to say horrid things. But I won't. I'm just so glad you didn't do – what she thought you would. And anyway, she just told me to – do whatever you wanted."

"Indeed? Most interesting. And an enchanting proposition. But when, I wonder, have you ever come remotely close to doing exactly what I want of you?" He returned her refilled cup to her and again sat opposite, legs stretched to the hearth. "You may inform your mistress, my child, that I do not expect either slavish agreement or strict obedience from the women in my life, and least of all from you." He paused before continuing. "Or did she, perhaps, tutor you in the more interesting arts of elusive temptation, role playing and subtle arousal? And in how to fulfil my desires, however – unattractively capricious – they might prove to be?"

Alysson blushed roundly and the scowl reappeared. These were exactly the matters the Lady Jennine had spoken about. "Certainly not," she said with a gulp.

Ludovic laughed. "Yet it seems the lady is openly encouraging her own personal maid to succumb to the improper advances of her brother-in-law, teaching her to become his mistress. An interesting and highly unusual situation. Which I would guess has troubled you for some time." She refused to meet his eye and stared adamantly into her lap. "No need to answer me, child," he continued gently. "I read your face and know your answer. But I can promise you this. I make my own decisions, and do not require the help of the Lady Jennine. I do not respond to the manipulations of others, or allow them to pressure me in any way. Nor will I attempt to compel you." He leaned forwards suddenly and took her hand. She was startled but he laughed at her. "When I first brought you to the castle and put you into your mistress's care," he said softly, "I was well aware of both your innocence and your ignorance. I would be ashamed if you lost both because of me."

She let him hold her hand, loose and pleasantly cool, but she shook her head, taking courage. "I might have been – innocent. At least – in the way you mean, I was. I am. But I'm not stupid. I might know a lot more now, but I wasn't ever ignorant." She looked up, accepting his gaze and his intensity. "It was you anyway. So you can be ashamed if you want. Before I ever met you, it was you – cured my ignorance."

Ludovic raised both eyebrows, momentarily amazed. "Impossible," he said. "My memory's certainly not that reprehensible."

"Not with me, stupid." She tried not to scowl. "It was in the forest one day. Two summers ago, and the sun was bright and hot. I was collecting herbs. Then I heard you laughing and talking, and one of the village girls with you. I should have run away but of course I knew who you were. I was – curious, so I hid and watched."

"Good Lord." Ludovic burst out laughing. "You watched me? What did I do? Though I suppose I can guess."

"Well, actually," Alysson looked back down into her lap where Ludovic's clasp on her hand had tightened slightly. "I didn't see anything – embarrassing. You had your back to me and you leaned the girl against a tree, and started undressing her. You got about half way, but you didn't bother to undress yourself at all. Then you just started breathing fast and sort of pushed a lot. It was very boring. After a few minutes you stopped and the girl made funny noises, and then you just turned away, getting your breath back and adjusting your clothing or something – I couldn't see. I wondered what all the fuss was about. It was quite disappointing. Just a waste of time really."

Ludovic appeared to be choking on something. Alysson retrieved her hand, since he was squashing her fingers. She wished she hadn't said anything, but his assumptions of her ignorance and his own pompous sense of responsibility had annoyed her. Now she glared at him.

He was, inexplicably, finding speech difficult. "I apologise," he said at last. "Most profusely. In particular for proving myself such a sadly inept lover, and also for starting your education in such an unpropitious manner. But this is a subject which inevitably leads directly into temptation, so before I risk offending you again by offering a tutorship with considerably more illuminating results, and be tempted to prove myself somewhat less inadequate than you suppose, I shall attempt to make amends in quite another fashion." He stood, stretching and grinning. "Therefore, before this conversation plunges into more dangerous topics, as it is surely about to do, I shall instead prove my manners and escort you back to your chamber. It is quite late, I believe. Finish your wine, it will help you sleep. Then, when you're ready -"

Alysson looked up, surprised. "You'll take me back yourself?"

"I believe I owe you a little gallantry, and am still quite capable of walking," he said, grinning widely. "Or were you expecting to stay here for the night?"

The Lady Jennine had scalded her when she had suggested otherwise. "Of course not," she said. "I just thought you'd send for a page. Or probably expect me to find my own way."

"Dear, dear," murmured Ludovic. "Throw you bodily from my bed I suppose, ordering you to get dressed quickly and be off, and not to disturb me on your way out. Is that what your lady led you to expect?"

Alysson giggled. "She warned me that you might. I knew I'd get lost, so I was going to ask you for a blanket, and then try to sleep outside in the corridor until morning light."

Ludovic seemed to be choking again. "My dear child," he said finally, "I beg you not to let your mistress's experience of men lead you into a similar distrust, at least not of myself. I am not my great grandfather." She had risen, and he took her hand, tucking her fingers inside the crook of his arm, nestled inside the bend of his elbow. "And though I cannot always swear to treat you quite so – monkishly," he said, one hand resting across hers, "I shall certainly always treat you with respect." He began leading her to the door, looking down at her upturned face at his shoulder. "I shall never order you either into – or out of my bed, my dear. And I'd be obliged if you tell the Lady Jennine exactly that."

CHAPTER EIGHTEEN

He had not expected to be assaulted by spectres in his own home.

Resisting all other temptations and one in particular, Ludovic had ridden to the borders of Bedfordshire. He had spent the last of a bedraggled and soggy spring on his mother's dower lands, one of those few remaining properties of her own personal inheritance, having announced her intention of bestowing these Bedfordshire pastures upon her youngest son subsequent to her own eventual demise. "It is all I have left," she had first informed the family, her left temple newly grazed, the marks part obscured by a starched gauze veil. "At present they bring me a small income, my only private means and sadly insufficient at that. But poor Ludovic should inherit something, and this is little enough to give. Brice will receive those substantial Kentish estates, awarded by our late beloved King Edward to the Sumerfords after Towton. Small profit goes with them and little else but a bleak sea wind, but no doubt Brice will know how to expand given time and the capital he appears inexplicably to generate. Then Gerald will have the small holdings outside Nottingham, King Richard's gift after the Hastings conspiracies. I believe they are barely prosperous, though my dear boy will surely know how to increase the dues. Everything else goes to darling Humphrey of course, and to his own precious heirs after him."

The expected heir had been loudly proclaimed. The Lady Jennine was with child. The castle doctor had predicted an October birth, though such matters were notoriously unreliable and the lady smiled, supposing an earlier date. Although the weather was not much improved, the lady walked in the castle gardens each afternoon and refused to be closeted indoors as the doctors recommended. Her personal maid accompanied her at all times, both well wrapped against the April winds, orchard blossoms in their faces and arms linked more as friends than mistress and servant. But Ludovic was not there to see. He remained in Bedfordshire, becoming acquainted with his future tenants and studying how the yield of the land might be improved for a more prosperous living.

It was late May when he returned and the apple and cherry blossoms had long since blown. Brice had left once again, but Gerald was back home when Ludovic rode up. After sending his steward, his secretary and the four outriders to the stables, Ludovic strode alone into the hall. Gerald was also alone and regarding the empty hearth, but looked up as his younger brother's footsteps echoed. "By the holy blood, Lu," he said, "I don't see why it's thought so damned obligatory to clean out the fires and fill the hearths with these absurd jugs of greenery just because summer's officially expected. I'm freezing. It's been frosty as hell all morning."

"Hell is generally considered to be particularly warm," Ludovic said, stripping off gloves, hat and surcoat. "There's no frost in Hell. I have it on the best of authority. In fact, I recommend it as a pleasant option. Not that I need to tell you. No doubt it's precisely where you're already expected."

Gerald smiled. "As a traitor to the crown, or as an ungrateful brother?" he said. "Both apply, I suppose."

Ludovic stretched himself into the chair beside the spreading willow boughs in their pottery jug. He pointed his legs towards the non-existent fire. "Gratitude? Not to me, surely?"

"You appear to have forgotten you recently gave a very large sum of money into my keeping."

160

"Oh, that." He hadn't forgotten. "I've made plenty more since that. Have you wasted it all already?"

Gerald shook his head. "As it happens, no. In a month or before, we may see just how useful it's been."

"You'd better not tell me anymore." The open road was never comfortable and the weather had been foul, but there were other reasons he was pleased to be home. He sighed. "I've heard the court gossip. Bedfordshire's closer to London, and the slander arrives there first. So I know little has changed, though they say trade is prospering again after the embargos were lifted."

"Who cares about trade?" objected Gerald. "Tudor deserves no credit for England's growth, and in fact, he's increasing taxes again. The rural communities are complaining of dreadful poverty, and London's slums are certainly seeing no benefit from Tudor's rule. In fact, our sweet natured monarch has proclaimed loudly that if he can't be loved, since Heaven help us, who would condescend to love such a creature, – then he aims to be feared. And that's one thing he's been successful at achieving, I assure you. But other more important matters are about to change, though I won't tell you if you don't want to know."

"I don't want to know." Ludovic sunk his chin into the thick fur of his doublet. The draught, creeping down the empty chimney and fluttering the willow boughs, still found his neck. "Tell me instead, how's the rest of the family?"

"Mother has a split lip, and Father's out hunting."

Ludovic frowned. "Can you really imagine I want to know about them? No, tell me about Brice. Is he still astonishing us lesser mortals with his burgeoning wealth and its unknown source? And what of our beloved Humphrey? Is he excited about the imminent arrival of the fruit of his loins? Or is he like mad Henry VI, seeing the arrival of his own infant as far less believable than visions of the saints in the chapel?"

Gerald looked away. "Brice is gone off on mysteriously profitable business again. Humphrey's out hunting with Father. Seems to think of a child of his own as a welcome new playmate."

"Personally," murmured Ludovic, "I'd never considered him

161

capable of producing one, but perhaps I was wrong. No one, including himself, ever believed Henry VI sired his own heir either, but who can ever be sure? In such issues the father remains always the dupe and only the woman can tell." He looked up suddenly, catching Gerald's eye. "And the lady in question? Does her condition keep her tucked away, or does she continue to present her increasing charms?"

"Keeps regular company and looks fine as ever." Gerald gazed with severity at the turkey rug beneath his feet. "I've never had anything to do with women in delicate conditions before. Frankly, this one seems ever more beautiful. Is that normal? I hadn't expected it. I admit it's distracting."

"Any distractions, brother dear, should be welcome." Ludovic nodded. "Let us hope they keep you from the block." He paused, as if deciding to say nothing more. Then he sighed, and said, "And the lady's personal maid? You may remember that I know her. Is she still employed here?"

"Oh yes." Gerald wrinkled his very fine nose. "Father made some disparaging remark about your particular predilection for servants and chamber maids just yesterday. Appears to think she's your secret trollop or some such. But the girl walks with her mistress every day. You'll see her."

"Father's indelicate opinions rarely interest me," said Ludovic. "As long as he doesn't personally insult the girl."

"Father? Speak directly to a chamber maid?" Gerald grinned suddenly. "You must be mad. He'd never demean himself. No – he was rude enough about your supposed taste for the gutter, but even ruder to me. Says I've never even approached a woman to his knowledge, and can't achieve anything more than pollutiones nocturnas. Probably thinks I'm into buggering my page. In the meantime, he's arranging a decent marriage for Brice."

"About time, I suppose. And Brice says?"

Gerald shook his head. "Brice smiled, stroked his new baudekyn and sables, and rode off without a word. But he won't object. She's rich."

"It'll be your turn next, my sweet."

"I don't have time for women," said Gerald at once. "And it's not

162

because I'm a pederast. I've far more important matters to consider, and you know exactly what they are."

But Ludovic did not see either the Lady Jennine or her personal maid that day, for a fine sleet dampened the afternoon and the lady's dinner was served to her in her chambers. Nor did she appear at supper. A minor stomach upset kept her in bed, and the doctor was called. He announced later, to an interested audience, that the complaint was caused by a chill in the digestive system, but since he could not administer a purge due to the lady's delicate condition, he had ordered her to remain indoors for at least a week. The unborn infant, however, seemed to have suffered no adverse effects and remained decidedly active.

That evening the moon presented its crescent horns through a mist of diminishing drizzle. A silver sheen caressed the grass, drifting like cobwebs across the moat. Ludovic was walking. Hat pulled low against the damp, he wandered down to the outer courtyard, nodded to the lounging guards and strolled over the drawbridge. The castle slept. He looked up to the high windows of the Lady Jennine's quarters and saw neither the pale luminosity of flickering candle light nor the deeper glow of a fire lit to warm the chambers. He had been gone more than two months and wondered, amused at himself, if he had been missed. But there were other considerations, more urgent. The probable paternity of Humphrey's child did not bother him, and Brice's further activities were of no greater concern. But he wondered just how much danger Gerald was in.

He was not expecting the assault. He did not at first recognise it. There were footsteps, soft as a child running through mud. Ludovic, briefly irritated and surprised at anyone approaching him in the small cold hours of the night, wished to be alone and intended avoiding all interruptions. He turned. But there was no one there.

Confusion, once quite unknown to him, had recently become a more frequent companion. Ludovic smiled to the moon and returned to his own thoughts.

Then the whispers came, an interruption he could not command away. "Can no one find me? Will no one look?" Ludovic turned, pivoting, almost unbalanced. The blue light hovered one breath's space from his eyes.

Accepting the unbelievable, his own whispers as soft, Ludovic breathed one deep breath. "I think perhaps I know who you are," he murmured. "But why do you come to me? Or do you search this place for anyone who will listen?"

The light floated, tiny within the mist. "I am drawn to you," it said. "Don't you want me? Does no one want me anymore?"

Ludovic focused more clearly. "The living do not usually seek the company of the dead. Do the dead seek the living then?"

The light remained still, as if considering. "Am I dead? Is it sure?"

Ludovic smiled. "I have never known a living soul travel in such a way. I believe you are dead."

"How did I die?" whispered the voice. "And why am I so lost? Does no God tend to His Heaven? Are there no angels to mind the wandering departed?"

Ludovic, sighing, shook his head. "I am no priest nor do I know where you are, either dead or living. But I will promise you this. Tomorrow I shall begin a search for your body."

"You know me then?" The light blinked, then reasserted. "Will you tell me my name," it begged.

"I cannot be sure." Ludovic answered softly. "Are you drawn to others besides myself? Has no one else called you by name?"

The whisper intensified, as if excited. "I feel others, perhaps people I knew once. I search for anyone who will listen and who might care. There was a woman. She was old, and sad, and sat alone in silence. I thought she was my mother. But when I went to her, she cried. I cannot bear the misery of others, when I feel such misery myself."

Ludovic nodded. "And others? Did you have a sister?"

The voice faded, perplexed, as if remembering. "Yes. I remember a sister. And there's a man, but he fears me. He turns away and hides. Only you answer me, though give me no name."

"I will continue to answer, though I cannot say I welcome the ghosts of the mists." Ludovic looked back towards the moat. "And tomorrow I shall begin to search. Is that what you want from me? Someone who cares, and will look for you?"

The light flickered, streaming its own small aura along the grass. "I want many things. To remember what it was like to be loved. To be with those who care for me and find the brightness and the warmth. To be safe again, instead of always lost."

"It may be difficult. You must be patient. But I'll try and discover where you are," Ludovic said. "Perhaps if I find where you died, you'll be free to move on to your place in the Heavens. At least rest assured I care, and am looking."

CHAPTER NINETEEN

"H e's back," said the lady.

"I don't care," said her maid. "Besides, I already know. And anyway, it was much better while he was away." He had not told her he was going, nor said goodbye. It had been two days before she had actually discovered his absence. Nor had he sent word on his return. From the window she had seen him ride in, and felt her heartbeat stop. She had then waited for some message, but received nothing. And although she was learning not to scowl, she was disappointed.

"You used to be so polite," sighed the Lady Jennine. "If he does send for you, you'll frighten him off with that horrid temper of yours. I've told you a hundred times, stupid girl. Mistresses must always be pleasant, light hearted, and help the man forget his worries and his nagging wife."

"I'm never going to be his mistress," Alysson objected. "He told me – and I told you. He doesn't think of me that way. He says we're friends."

"No man between the ages of eight and eighty sees a beautiful woman simply as a friend. Unless of course – but never mind about that – your education can absorb only one important matter at a time. This young man wants you in his bed, however much he may choose to deny it, and for whatever capricious arrogance of his own making.

And neither he nor you will spoil my plans my dear. I have never allowed such a thing. When I decide something, it must be done. Now, we will practise your next meeting with him. Change that frown to a smile, and repeat what I've been teaching you."

Alysson was staring at her fingers, tightly clasped in her lap. "Am I really beautiful?" she asked.

"My dear child, you are becoming tiresome." The lady leaned forwards, tipping Alysson's chin up with her finger. "You'll do, which I've told you before. Dark hair is not fashionable, but with regular combing and smoothing with silk, at least it gleams. It's thick and frames your face prettily. Your nose is well shaped and your mouth has a charming curl when you smile, though that's rare enough. Your eyebrows are too thick and hard to pluck, but your chin is neat and your neck is long and smooth. Your skin takes colour too readily, and there are dangerous signs of old weathering from rough living, but of course your figure has improved vastly. Now it's swelling in just the right places, though you persist in this ridiculous modesty and wear your necklines too high. But your eyes, my dear! Yes, your eyes are truly beautiful. And once a man looks into your eyes, he will believe that everything else about you is perfect too. Which is why you suit my purposes very well, if only you'd be less petulant and self-willed."

Alysson wrinkled her nose. "I don't understand when you talk about your purposes. Why do you care if I end up as Ludovic's mistress? You're very kind, and I don't mean to sound rude. But it's all very odd."

Jennine smiled. "Because I care for you, silly child, and this is the only answer which will suit. I am far too experienced to mistake your feelings for him, and I've no wish to see you lonely, simply because you're too shy and ignorant to get what you secretly want. Besides, your foolish young man has almost exactly the same eyes himself, which must surely prove a connection of sorts. Now, fetch me the new pink gown and I shall help you brush out the creases. He'll send for you today, I'm sure of it."

The message came shortly after dinner. The page, bowing low, addressed the Lady Jennine. "My lady. Lord Ludovic begs permission to invite Mistress Alysson Welles to walk with him today, at three of the clock this afternoon in the castle grounds, weather permitting. With respect, my lady, should you be gracious enough to agree, I shall return at the appointed hour to escort Mistress Alysson to the hall."

"See?" insisted the lady after the page had been sent off. "I knew it. I am always right."

"And I'm right too," said Alysson, struggling into the pink camelot and trying not to catch her hair in the laces. "Daytime, not night time. And walking in the garden, he said. Not romping in the bed."

"I admit," Jennine admitted, "he is keeping unusually circumspect. I've never known a man to be so patient. Perhaps he isn't quite as aroused as I imagined. We shall have to work on that. Don't worry, he'll be as eager as a falcon for a mouse once I've finished with you."

Alysson looked up, the scowl reappearing. "I'm not a mouse. And I don't want –"

"Oh for goodness sake, Alysson," sighed the lady. "Just get those sleeves fastened while I do your hair. And keep quiet for once."

Ludovic was waiting for her at the foot of the staircase, leaning on the turn of the great wooden balustrade. He watched her careful descent, each footstep hesitant since she wore new shoes and was frightened of slipping. The page's narrow back hid Ludovic's smiles. He took her hand as she reached flat boards, and led her over to the main doors.

"It may be chilly outside," Ludovic said. "Will you be warm enough?"

She wore a light wrap over the pink camelot, but knew she would freeze. The Lady Jennine had refused to countenance enclosing her in coarse wool, and a fur cape would seem incongruous on a chamber maid. Alysson nodded cheerfully. "I'm never cold. Especially if we walk fast."

They walked together through the smaller and then the larger courtyards into the bailey, skirting the long stable block and heading out beneath the massive iron portcullis across the drawbridge. The moat was sluggish as always, its dank surface algae slimed and stagnant where the banks rose shallow into muddy grass, but choppy and impatient where the huge stone walls rose sheer from its dark waters. Ludovic led Alysson beyond the sight of her own quarters, amongst the low hedges, the holly bushes and blackberry thorns, and on into the orchard where the thick trees hid even their shadows. No one could now see them from anywhere within the castle and only the long rows of the kitchen gardens, sloping down towards the farm pastures beyond, stood between them and the horizon. Then finally Ludovic stopped, and turned. He shrugged out of his own thick fur lined surcoat and slipped it around her shoulders. "Now stop shivering," he said, "and listen to me."

Alysson thankfully snuggled into the luxurious furs and velvet. "You'll get cold now."

"Then our wearisome doctor will insist on confining me to bed for a week, and I shall blame you," smiled Ludovic. "It would hardly be the first time in my sick bed due to your reprehensible behaviour." He took her hand. "But I need to talk about matters somewhat less – frivolous. Sadly, I must be serious, and risk reminding you of things you may prefer to forget." He was watching her expression, and paused a moment before continuing. "I need to talk about your brother," he said.

She was startled. "Pagan?"

"You may think me quite mad," Ludovic said, "and indeed, I have thought it myself at times. But I believe your brother calls to me. There's a voice, lost and searching, and I can put no other name to it. Do you know anything of him, since he disappeared?"

Although she was well wrapped and now quite warm, Alysson was shivering again. She peeped up through the sables. "No. And I don't understand why he'd choose you to call to. But he cannot possibly be alive after all this time. He wouldn't have run away like some boys, not run off to the city to make his fortune or anything like that. He was very young, and a little frail. I believe he died though I don't know how. Near here, perhaps, since this was where I last saw him."

Ludovic nodded, watching her closely. "I promised the voice to begin a new search for the remains," he said. "Though frankly, I've little hope of success."

She shook her head. "It would help." Her fingers now gripped his, hoping for reassurance. "I'd hoped, being so young and quite innocent you know, that Pagan was at peace. It's helped me, believing he was in

169

a happier place – with Gamel and our parents. Knowing there was nothing I could do to help him anymore. But now, if you say he calls – then is he miserable? Is purgatory so lonely then? He should be safe with the angels."

"I've no answers to such questions," Ludovic said. "I'm no priest, and rarely believe what the priests tell me since I doubt they know any more than the rest of us. But I promised this – apparition – to look for the child's body. And I shall do that. Though I suspect he fell victim to the moat as others have before him, and no one can see beneath those waters. If he's there, he'll stay there and no one can find him. Nor do I understand why he comes to me. I'm not the master of this estate, nor hold final authority. I had no hand in his death, nor knew him when alive. It seems strange."

"Aren't ghosts always strange? Or messengers from Hell?" Alysson sniffed and tried not to let wisps of sable tickle her nose. She had forgotten her kerchief. "I've missed Pagan so much. And I was still grieving for Gamel when Pagan went missing. But it would be a great kindness to find his body, so he could be given a proper Christian burial. Perhaps that's why he isn't at rest."

Ludovic watched her tears, small silver smears descending to his mahogany velvet. He smiled and put his arm around her, holding her face to his shoulder. "Don't cry, little one. The world is full of sadness and we must all die eventually. In the meantime, I shall do my best." He curled his fingers to the back of her head, where her net caul failed to contain the coiled weight of her hair. A pale sunshine was exploring the apple trees but a chilly wind blew directly in from the sea and the echoes of the gulls blew with it. "But he's your brother and I know nothing of him," Ludovic continued gently, "so I believed you should know what I intend doing, and why. And I wanted to ask if you have any further knowledge, or guess where he might lie."

She was crying properly now, though squashed to his chest and trying to stifle the sound. "I know nothing," she mumbled. "Nothing at all."

His fingers curled further into the thick coils of her hair, detaching the caul and its pins. His other hand held her close. "Don't cry, little one," he murmured, "or I shall be impelled to do something you would probably not like."

She stopped crying at once and looked up, wet lashed in surprise. "Why? You've been very kind. But I haven't got a kerchief and the Lady Jennine will slap me if I wipe my nose on the sleeve of this dress. So why would you do what I wouldn't like?"

He pulled his own kerchief from the depths of his doublet and handed it to her. "Wipe your face," he commanded, "and salvage both your sleeves and my coat." He watched as she blew her nose with defiance.

"I shouldn't cry. I know it's silly after all this time." She handed the damp linen back to him. "It's a very pretty kerchief," she said with a sniff. "Thank you."

"The Sumerford arms," Ludovic smiled, regarding the damply crumpled remains. "You had better keep it."

She blew her nose a second time and tucked the embroidered kerchief carefully inside her cuff. "I'm sorry, but I can't help it," she mumbled. "I loved Pagan and Gamel so very much. So I don't see why you feel - impelled to do something - horrid."

Ludovic's smile widened. "Not precisely horrid, child, though perhaps unwise." He looked down on her face muffled by his own furs, her cheeks and his sable both bright with her tears. Then he bent his head to the damp softness and kissed her long and hard.

He felt her gasp, inhaling, surprised, drawing in the breath from his own mouth. She wriggled, suddenly nervous and then taut beneath the pressure of his hand, but neither pressing closer nor pulling away. His fingers gently caressed the knots of her spine, his other hand tight in her hair. He explored the fullness of her lips, watching her wet lashes flicker and her eyes close. Then he felt her breath against his tongue, sweet and warm and unhurried. When finally he released her, straightening reluctantly, he still held her cradled to his chest. Her own hands remained trapped within the great swathes of his coat, but her face nestled willingly against him and she sighed.

"And was it – so horrid, little one?" he murmured.

She swallowed, paused a moment, then shook her head.

He chuckled. "Bereft of argument? How unlike you. But you're quite safe. I won't attack you further. I was simply – as explained – impelled."

Since she still found no words, he eventually turned and began to walk with her slowly back towards the castle. His arm remained around her shoulders, cuddled a little beneath his surcoat and guiding her, and though they came within sight of Sumerford scrutiny and the castle's many hundred gazing windows, he removed neither his arm nor his velvets. He brought her across the drawbridge and to the doors of the great hall, swung wide to the courtyard air. Then he reclaimed his coat, taking it back and folding it casually over his arm. He stood a moment looking at her, rearranged her light wrap around her and the caul about her hair, reattaching its loosened pins. "There now," he said with a grin, "you look adequately respectable again." He nodded to a page standing by the outer doorway. "Take Mistress Alysson back to the Lady Jennine's quarters," he said. Then leaned forwards, and kissed her very lightly on the tip of her still damp nose. "I shall keep you informed," he promised, "of what I do, and whether I discover your brother." Then he turned again and strode back into the pale sunshine.

Alysson watched him disappear into the haze, sighed deep, and began to follow the small red haired page up the main stairs.

Each step was striped in light with the slanting shade from the balustrade and huge carved banisters, no dust beams but a dithering sheen. The rows of tall windows were well polished, the afternoon sun only slightly diffused by the thick glass. The hall and stairs were bathed bright but at the top of the staircase in the long upper corridor, windowless with its wide locked doors on either side, the shadows leapt suddenly huge. The page reached up and took a small torch from one of the sconces. The air was still, the flames did not flare, though flickered as they walked. It was darker still as they reached the curve turning into the next steps upwards, a chilly dank black.

Then, with a burst of draught into total darkness, the torch was blown out. The page squeaked as if struck and then silenced. Alysson

172

stood quite still and heard only her heart thump. Then she felt the damp hand around her neck.

The fingers were thick and soft, the palm wide, the flesh sweaty. More fingers crept with eager determination into the neat neckline of her gown. They forced quickly deeper and over the hoarse panting breath of her assailant, she heard the gauze tear. But she was already screaming louder than all other sounds. Then the other hand, fisted, swung to her jaw, and she was silenced too.

Pain jarred, ramming against all her senses, and from two directions. Her jaw throbbed with an incessant, reeling insistence. And into her cleavage and around one nipple, was the pain of scratched, oozing flesh. Alysson struggled, searching for the breath to scream again, but the hand around her neck tightened and her throat was squeezed shut.

Then a sudden rush, someone hurtling past her, grabbing at the creature's hands, forcing them, finger by finger, away from her. She discovered breath again, and with the points of her new shoes, kicked first at the shin, then knee up to the groin. She remembered Gamel's voice. "This is where, Alysson. If some bastard ever tries to hurt you, you kick them here. Right here. Understood?" And she did what he had told her, and aimed right there. She heard the answering grunt.

She had defended herself once before, and now she tried to scratch and bite as she had then. But it had been sunny in the dairies, and now everything was hidden, and strange, and terrifying. There seemed to be two shadows struggling together, one large and one small. A strangled voice, guttural and very faint, "Not now. Not yet. Take me instead. Take me." She turned from them and ran into blackness.

She fell onto the lower stone of the narrow winding steps leading to her own quarters, felt with both hands and scrambled up. Then a torch in a high alcove, a timid light growing, brought back her sight. Alysson found her breath. She stood shaking on the landing, gripping her shawl, forcing herself to think. Eventually, with both hands clenched and a heave of deeper breath, she turned and ran back the way she had come, clattering down the stone steps. "Get away," she shouted, as loudly as her sore throat permitted. "Let the child go and get away whoever you are."

The silence rebounded in echoes. Where she had been attacked and had then left two shadows merged and struggling, there was no one now. She leaned back gasping against the wall. It was wet with condensation. It felt like tears. Finally, shoulders hunched, she remounted the stairs, pushed open the door and hurried into the warmth and comfort of the Lady Jennine's solar.

The lady was dozing in her bedchamber, the bed curtains drawn shut and the windows tight shuttered against insidious draughts. Alysson crept in, feeling the gloom increasingly morbid. The other two maids had been sent away and Jennine was alone. Alysson did not wish to wake her, the lady had been persistently kind but she could be sharp when irritated, and besides, her rest and afternoon sleeps had been advised by the doctor. The pregnancy was growing large. Its pressure on the lady's lungs was constant. Alysson heard her Sertorius breathing behind the curtains, like a little child's snores.

She tiptoed into the garderobe and sat in the dark on the latrine, eyes closed, forehead in her hands. She felt sick.

"And what," demanded the voice, "is this all about?" Alysson looked up and gulped. Jennine was peering at her. "I need the jakes, silly girl. What's the matter with you?"

Alysson jumped up in a hurry. "Nothing." Then thought better of it. "I was attacked. There's a monster in the castle," she gasped in a rush. "A creature, some dreadful thing that leapt on me and tried to strangle me."

Jennine laughed. "What absurd nonsense is this? I'm not interested in your ridiculous imagination, girl. Go and make up my bed, I shall be out in a moment." Alysson had straightened the bedcover but was sitting on it when the lady reappeared, holding her belly in discomfort. "Damned infant. This wretched business certainly proves our good Lord is a man. In the past I always managed – but never mind about that. Dammit, don't just sit there, Alysson. Help me lie down, and rub my back. And now tell me about Ludovic. What did he want, this patient lover of yours?"

Alysson shook her head, bending to massage her mistress's shoulders. "He – he was kind. He's going to look for my little brother again. You remember, don't you? Pagan, who disappeared. Ludovic is going to search for Pagan's body, so he can be properly buried." She paused, and sighed. "That's all. Then he sent a page to bring me back here but at the bottom of the top steps, something attacked me. It's not a silly story. Look at the marks on my neck."

Jennine gazed up with a giggle. "So Ludovic decided to take you at last, did he? Don't tell me you pushed him off and made him angry?"

Alysson glared. She could feel the bruises, the pressure of fingertips like huge burns around her throat. She tugged down the neck of her dress where the little gauze fichu had been torn. Peering down at herself she could see three long scratches, dark with dried blood across her breast, and another bruise turning dark around the nipple. "Of course not. And I'm not making it up. Why would I? Look."

"I see," the lady still smiled. "Some men like it rough, of course. You'll have to accept it my dear. And to tell the truth I'm hardly surprised, for it's those that pretend to play the gentleman who turn nasty when they're aroused. Don't be ashamed. Look, I'll help you wash and put a little salve on the scratches. I think it best not to involve the doctor, my dear, but I shall look after you, don't worry. At least we know Ludovic is finally a fish to the hook as we've wanted for so long." Jennine struggled to sit up again against the bolster, and patted the bed beside her, indicating Alysson to sit. "Now we can take our plans further."

Alysson held her breath. "I don't lie. It wasn't him."

The lady frowned. "Don't be tiresome, Alysson. And don't make me cross. You know how exhausted I get these days. If Ludovic enjoys rough rutting, then we shall think of new ways to excite him."

"It was dark. I couldn't see who it was. But it wasn't him. His hands are quite different – slim and long fingered. These hands were – sweaty – and podgy."

"And mine," said the Lady Jennine, cold eyed, "are surprisingly hard when I find someone odiously annoying. So be quiet, Alysson, and stop making a fuss about a few tiny scratches. Now I shall tell you what you need to practise for a man who likes to mix sweetness with pain."

CHAPTER TWENTY

On the 9th day of June the royal kitchens at Westminster Palace were in turmoil. Every cook, assistant cook, pastry maker, baker, clerk of the spicery and carver of subtleties was shouting at every scullion, and every pot boy was whimpering. The turnspits were burning their fingers, the Marshall of the great hall was in a fury and the brewsters were sliding across wet floors, for there was the Trinity Sunday feast to prepare for his majesty and the entire court in residence. The over laden tables were creaking and even the ceilings were steaming and dripping condensation. Meanwhile Sir Gerald Sumerford, his squire following close, linked his arm through that of his friend Lord William Grey, Earl of Berkhamstead, and wandered the palace grounds as if he had every right to be there, while casually watching the flocking of the swallows in the bright blue sky above, and bending to smell the new planted roses amongst the hedges at his side. Although he was not in fact at present a member of court, no guard assumed reason to object or question his identity. The Earl of Berkhamstead at least was certainly well known. There was nothing suspicious, the weather was sumptuous, and the holy day was nearing its midday.

The nearby Abbey bells chimed for the twelve o'clock None service, but the three men did not enter the great hall of Westminster for dinner, instead continuing to wander the gardens, sauntering down towards the river and its summer sparkle, where they happened to encounter three other young men, plainer dressed, but still of quality. No one was stopped.

It was much later and nearing a star-glistened midnight when the captive known as Perkin Warbeck escaped. Eluding his two permanent guards, the young man somehow climbed from an upper window and was immediately gone into the shadows.

His absence was discovered within the hour.

Panic ensued, messengers sent galloping to every port, troops of guards scrambling down along the river banks, others marching up river and into the great forests of St. James, up the Westbyrne Brook to the monastery grounds of the Hyde park, and out to the surrounding villages and the gravel pits of Kensington before doubling back towards the jousting grounds at Smithfields. The city gates were locked and guarded, so no one had entered London's alleys through the Ludgate, but the summertime river could be swum, and in the night's shadows nobody could trace the passage taken.

The king, it was said, was quite unperturbed. When finally given the news, he called it a minor matter and of less significance than the bellyache sustained from dinnertime's plentiful smoked trout and lobster in creamed garlic. "This pathetic feigned lad," his majesty yawned, "is little more than a lowly simpleton, and not worth the loss of my well-deserved rest. No doubt Warbeck will be found again one day, God willing."

Yet strangely, in spite of the king's casual disinterest displayed in public, the massive rush of armed guards sent on the business of recapture was immediate, well prepared and well disciplined, and told at all costs not to return without the prisoner.

The court, cheerfully sensing renewed scandal, gossip and conjecture, was delighted to be disturbed. It was generally decided that the creature Warbeck had shown great ingratitude since his treatment had been merciful to the extreme. Not only allowed to live, but given warmth, food and even the occasional glimpse of his wife, he had thrown away such gracious generosity for stubborn wilfulness and a foolhardy risk. It simply proved how ignoble and uncourtly the man really was.

Those who felt differently chose to say little, and the opinions of the Lady Katherine his wife, her majesty the queen, and far away the busy courts in Burgundy and Flanders, were never sought.

On a muddy bank between great clumps of rushes, three men sat close together, their black clothes merging into the darkness, weaving them virtually invisible amongst the reeds. The frogs were calling and star shine reflected tiny pools of silver within the marsh, but the men avoided the light.

One, although the smallest of the three, was clearly the more respected. "Thank you, but you must leave me now," he said quietly. "You've done enough, and the rest is up to me. I refuse to cause the death of more of my friends."

"Your grace," said another, voice no louder than the gentle swirl of the water beside them, "we will see you at least as far as sanctuary."

"No my dear Gerald," said the first man, "it's become too dangerous. Tudor is notoriously tricky and I feel his hand in this, more perhaps than our own."

The third man nodded. "I'm suspicious too, your grace. It should never have been so easy. Half our plans weren't even needed, as if every step was already expected, and paths opened for us before we even looked for them. You know what they say."

"They say as William said," murmured the Duke of York. "That Tudor has been too long trapped by his own need to appear merciful, and by his fear to execute someone he knows should be sitting on the throne he stole. At first, keeping me a menial at court served to belittle my claims, as if of so little importance that even my death was irrelevant. But it has gone on too long, and foreign powers still rattle Tudor's insecurities. Now he can't send me to the Tower and be finally rid of me without some obvious cause to keep his reputation clean. Flanders would grumble, Burgundy would petition. Even the Pope would complain. Meantime Spain wants her daughter safe. An

England while I still live and breathe is not considered safe. So Tudor needed me to escape. And I obliged."

"Then we've done you a great disservice, my lord," Gerald sighed, "and have led you not to freedom, but to death."

The man the king called Perkin Warbeck smiled. He was sitting thigh deep in mud, but his good temper remained. "Our plans were excellent and your loyalty's helped bring me sanity these long months. But this wretched false king of yours is no fool. Did we underestimate him?"

The squire Roland had draped his own thick kersey coat around the Duke of York's shoulders. A balmy June night, but the marshy water was cold and a wind crept through the reeds from down river. Roland said, "Underestimated or not, we had no choice, your grace. We'd set our plans for this night, and had to carry them through or risk immediate capture. I believe we were betrayed."

"But I should have realised. Almost, I knew." The youngest son of the late King Edward, continued to smile. "The fault is entirely mine. Two guards have watched me each minute of my life since I was first captured, yet tonight, the very night planned for my escape, Rob went off happily to fetch wine, and Will Smith, who has been the most determined and unflagging guard of all, suddenly sleeps as deep and sound as a drunken hedgehog, though he's barely touched his ale for a week. The window was unshuttered and unlatched, though the vines outside are as easy to climb as a ladder, so why change my chamber to that one? Truly the fault is mine, and if I'd been less frantic, less eager, less nervous, I'd have called the whole plan off. I'll accept the consequences, but I'll not accept you two sharing them. That's an order. So leave me now."

Roland shook his head. "With all respect, I'll obey your orders once you're on the throne, your grace, and I can bend my knee to you instead of bending it in mud. You're free now, and I'll happily risk my life to keep it that way. I'm no loss to the kingdom, your grace, but you are."

"Perhaps I'm not either." Richard of York pulled the woollen coat around him. The night wind was blowing colder. "I'm neither experienced nor ruthless. Perhaps Tudor's the best king for England after all." He sounded morose and the smile, for the first time, had faded.

"We've time for neither recriminations nor regrets now, your grace." Gerald Sumerford pulled his hat low across the back of his neck where the wind bit. "But I'd like to know who betrayed us. Who knew?"

"My lord," Roland sat closer, voice like the rustling of the reeds where the frogs continued to call. "Only we knew. One of us is a traitor."

"Of late there have been only seven of us," said the duke. "I trust every one, and have done from the beginning, with my life."

"But more than seven at a distance," said Gerald at once. "For instance, my brother financed this particular attempt. But he'd never have betrayed me, for that would risk my life as well as yours, your grace. But others – at the tavern – within the court."

"No matter." The duke shook his head, the soft smile returning. "Luck may be out, but it's unutterably good to breathe freedom again, even just for a little while. It's cold and wet, but tastes as sweet as marchpane. So, I was betrayed. Hardly the first time. Meanwhile Tudor has long decided the game was stale, and wanted to change tactics. He was waiting for just such an opportunity, needing only an excuse. Now I've given him the perfect excuse and if I'm captured, it'll be the Tower and the gallows. At least an end to vitriolic humiliations, so I won't complain."

Gerald shivered. "You have to get away. To Scotland again. Or Ireland. Both will shelter you."

"Scotland's made peace with Tudor."

"They break every treaty, and always have. They can break another one."

"Gentlemen, enough." This time the duke had retained his smile. "I remember the Tower, and have been there before, it holds few terrors. Maybe I was born to humiliation after all. It's my destiny perhaps. From prince to proclaimed bastard, smuggled abroad, put up as page to an adventurer, a child without parents, family or country, a wanderer, finally led to the life of pretender. But from the semblance of honourable captive at his court, a position I negotiated with Tudor

180

when I surrendered at Beaulieu, now the king treats me as a servant. For all the roles I've played in my life, cleaning a man's privy is not one I intend to adopt. They say life's a wheel of fortune. Well, let the wheel form full circle and roll me back in the Tower. I've lost all those I love and although my aunt in Burgundy insists otherwise, I doubt I'm fitted for kingship."

"It's blood and birth that fit a man for sovereignty, your grace." Roland shook his head. "You have both, while Tudor has neither. And England needs her rightful king to save us from this hateful usurper, this foul creature of black moods and greed, bleeding the country wizened and dry with his vengeance and his taxes."

"And I must warn you, my lord," Gerald sighed. "The Tower's not the same place you remember. As a child you were housed in the royal apartments before King Richard had you moved, but the quarters were still rich and spacious. You were treated with honour. Now the Tower's a place of dread, and with more prisoners each day since Bosworth, Tudor has bare space to squash a man into a stone cubicle."

Roland stood, shivering, the mud sticking to his doublet and hose. "Forgive me, but there's no time for this, my lords. We've not gone far enough and they'll be after us within the hour. For his own reasons, Tudor may have wanted you to escape, but he'll not want you lost for good. He'll want you recaptured, and quick."

Richard Plantagenet also stood. His plain clothes were thick with marsh mud and the threads of weeds and rushes. "You're right, my friend, I've got my breath back and now I'll be off. But alone, as I've told you."

"Not without me," Roland said. He turned quickly to Gerald. "Get back to Lord William, my lord. You need to present a fair face to any who suspect you of conspiracy and if we're betrayed, you need to see how far the treachery's gone. I'll stay with his grace." He turned again to the duke. "Forgive me for disobedience. But I won't leave you. You must not be alone. And since they'll expect us to escape down towards the sea, we'll keep to the plan and head upstream. If your leg is recovered now, your grace? And you have the strength to run again?"

Ludovic Sumerford moved the girl's face to the side, exposing the pale curve of her neck down to the turn of her shoulder. He flicked the short veil away. The marks around her throat were quite distinct, as if painted with rouge. Large finger tips, flattened and strong, had spread their darkening bruises. Ludovic, surprised, inhaled deeply. "Who? How?" he demanded.

Alysson pulled away. "So – servants often get beaten. Why should you care? And anyway, you weren't supposed to notice. Isn't this what women always do? Hide their necks and stiffen their veils more than usual?"

Ludovic shook his head. "Exactly as my mother does. I'm too well experienced to miss the signs. But this wasn't done by Jennine. So who?"

"Oh dear." Alysson sat down abruptly and the long cushioned settle in Ludovic's outer chamber creaked. "I don't know who it was. It was dark and I couldn't see and he didn't speak. It was the same day I saw you last, after we walked in the orchard – and when you – well, you know."

He smiled. "I kissed you."

She continued in a hurry. "You sent me back with a page boy. Someone jumped us both. I don't know what happened to the boy. This is what happened to me."

"You fought the man off? You got away? What else was done to you?" Ludovic seemed somehow angry. His annoyance confused her.

"Nothing. Yes, I fought, and I don't see why you're cross. There are scratches as well, big nasty scratches that bled for ages, and more bruises too. But I got away. Then I went back to help the page, but he'd gone. Everyone had gone."

"Show me the other injuries. Have they been properly treated? Did Jennine send for the doctor?"

"I can't show you," objected Alysson. "They're in – difficult places. And Jenny helped me with ointments, but she didn't want to call the doctor." Alysson looked down at her lap, blushing slightly. "She didn't believe me when I said it wasn't you who did it all."

"Good lord. A fine reputation I shall have." Ludovic bent over her, one finger beneath Alysson's chin returning her gaze to his. "But it doesn't smell right. There's something more to this. What else did your intriguing mistress say?"

"Nothing." Alysson looked away again, misty eyed.

"Since now you call your mistress Jenny, I've an idea you know a good deal about her, and probably a good deal I'd like to know." Ludovic frowned, again examining the five purpled bruises. "But I won't ask. And I'm not cross with you, child, but with this whole damned situation. Only what has given Jennine the impression I'm into brutal seductions? I'm damn sure she was after me herself when she first arrived at Sumerford."

Alysson sniffed. "That's very – conceited of you. And anyway, she has a very nice relationship with the Lord Humphrey. It's quite – touching."

"Damned sure it is. Touching in more ways and more places." Ludovic scrutinised his guest with deep suspicion. "And conceited I may be, impudent brat, but I'm neither blind nor stupid. I know exactly what a woman's expressions invariably mean, and I know the difference between a lady and a whore. The two overlap often enough to cause confusion, but your mistress is as plain as starch to a codpiece."

Alysson gulped. "I don't want to say -"

"You've no need to say anything," Ludovic interrupted. "I didn't expect you to respond. But I placed you in that damned woman's service in the first place, and now I'll make damned sure you stay as safe as my own protection can keep you. Which clearly hasn't been secure enough. I only invited you here this afternoon to let you know how my search for your brother has progressed, but now it's evidently a whole different type of search I need to initiate."

"And did you find -?"

He shook his head. "I've had men out searching as far as the forests, every farm and right through the village. I had my own groom ride the bucket down the full depth of the main well, and there's nothing. The smaller wells don't permit a man's descent, but we've done our best with torches. This is a fairly difficult castle to explore and doubtless there's corners I've never seen myself, but the staff have dug every herb plot and peered into every shadow from turrets to pantries. Even the cellars have been scrubbed out." He laughed. "Frightened off whole colonies of rats, indignant to have their domains invaded. Two of the boys ended up with bites and one nearly lost a finger. But there's been no sign of your brother. I haven't given up yet, but I fear it's the moat has claimed him. If there's nothing else left to do, I shall send in swimmers but the waters are thick. No one can see under there, nor swallow without catching some foul disease."

"Then you'd better not." Ludovic was still bending over her, his foot now on the edge of the settle where she sat, his elbow supported by his knee, his face intent. She found the scrutiny disturbing, and his voice, now more impelling than usual, still seemed to hide anger. "And I am grateful, in case you think I'm not," she sniffed, trying to maintain dignity, "but perhaps it seems like an imposition – so you're cross, and as for the other – business – I know it wasn't you, and I promise I told Jenny it wasn't."

Ludovic watched her for a moment, pausing without lowering his regard. "If you cry," he said very softly, "I warn you, I shall be obliged to kiss you again."

Alysson fumbled for her kerchief, discovered it and blew her nose. She had a headache.

The invitation to visit Ludovic in his chambers at the respectable hour of two in the afternoon, had arrived at an inopportune moment. The Lady Jennine had been lecturing her personal maid about the incongruity of avoiding a man's rough love-making. "Men," said the lady, "are trained to battle after all. Do you have any idea, Alysson, what battle must be like? A welter of blood and gore so vile it clogs the nostrils. Yet you expect a creature capable of such cruel brutality, to gently kiss your finger tips and sigh with unrequited desire?"

"Chivalry," muttered Alysson.

The Lady Jennine had sniggered rather rudely. "What a fool you are, child. Chivalry is simply a children's story, and a rule of law which used to keep the lords from slaughtering each other, taking hostages for vast profit instead, while satisfying their blood lust with the wholesale dismemberment of the common man."

Then the page had entered, announcing Lord Ludovic's request to meet with Mistress Alysson. Jennine had bundled her into the blue silk with otter trimmings, had allowed her to hitch the neckline higher since that hid the partially healed scratches, and had arranged the little veiled cap herself. "Not that it matters," she had said, "since the dear boy obviously made these bruises himself."

"He did not." Alysson had resisted the urge to stamp her foot.

Now her head throbbed and she felt hot tears blur her eyes. She blew her nose again. "I'm not crying. I'm just – tired."

"Then perhaps," murmured Ludovic with a faint smile, "I should take you to bed."

"Oh dear." Alysson fidgeted with her kerchief. "That's very – silly. And you shouldn't tease people at horridly uncomfortable moments. It's not fair."

"You may remember," smiled Ludovic, "that you've slept in my arms once already. But now, if you're quite so horridly uncomfortable, perhaps I can help." Moving forwards, he sat abruptly at her side, half facing her. The dimensions of the little cushioned settle pressed them close. Unless she stood to run, Alysson had no escape. She blushed, squeezing away. Ludovic removed the damp kerchief from her grasp, tucked it neatly up her sleeve, and grasping both her shoulders, held her firm, forcing her to face him. Then he leaned over, and kissed her.

Involuntarily her fingers clutched at the front of his doublet, she leaned back as he pressed against her, and relaxed, relinquishing control. He released her only when she gasped for breath. "Open your eyes," he demanded. "And look at me." She obeyed with a gulp and blinked, gazing up at him. She thought his eyes glittered green, looking somehow demonic. "I'd take you as my mistress this minute, my sweet," he said very softly, "but it would be to please myself and bring you little benefit. So I will not do it, or at least, not yet. But the time will come, Alysson, when you consent."

Baffled and suddenly intimidated, Alysson glared. "Am I at the end of the list then? How many other chamber maids regularly fall in and out of your bed?"

Ludovic laughed. "As it happens," he said, "I don't make a habit of tumbling the castle staff. I've never been fool enough. The village girls in the past perhaps, but not my own family servants, and I've never brought any girl back here to my own rooms. Nor – strangely enough

– am I used to the chamber maids informing me I'm silly, conceited, and promiscuous. You are, my dear, quite unique. Not last on the list, but first." He still had a firm hold on her shoulders, forbidding her to pull away. "And my motives are clear enough, I'd have thought. My sister-in-law is playing a mighty strange game, and I won't risk your safety by playing along until I understand the rules. Nor will I make use of my own power or Jennine's pressure to intimidate you into something against your will. Yes, I desire you, and I want you to know that. But I care in many ways, which means I also want to protect you. I'm fully aware that you neither despise nor fear me. Yet it seems you fear any intimacy beyond kissing, so I doubt you're ready for anything else, and I've more honour than that. So I'm waiting."

"You're waiting? Because I don't want you, or to satisfy your honour?"

"Both." He grinned. "Nor will I demean you by indulging in a stream of sordid assignations under my parent's roof while you're still employed by them as a servant. There's a good deal I can't explain yet, but in the meantime you need looking after." Ludovic frowned suddenly, looking down. His hands on her shoulders had disturbed the wide fur neckline of her gown, and across the partially uncovered rise of one breast, the tips of dark scratches had become visible. "What in heaven's name?" he demanded. "Are these the other wounds you spoke of?"

Without hesitation, Ludovic grasped the soft otter trimmings and tugged the open neckline down. He touched one finger gently to the long ragged marks. "Don't," she whispered. "It's almost better."

"Better be damned," murmured Ludovic. "They're healing badly. You'll have scars, but thank the saints there's no infection." His hands were against her skin, her breasts were almost uncovered and Alysson shivered. "You should have demanded the apothecary or the doctor," Ludovic told her.

"Demand?" glared Alysson, pulling away and tugging up her gown. "How can I demand anything? I'm a servant, remember. And Jenny thought you'd done it, and the doctor would have just asked awkward questions." The pain of the wounds had long faded but now she tingled where Ludovic had touched her.

At once Ludovic leaned forwards and put his arm around her, drawing her close. This time his kiss was more urgent, she felt crushed, opening her mouth to his insistence. Her hands crept around his shoulders, gently savouring the rich velvet, her fingertips deep in softness, feeling the warmth of his body beneath. The thick silk of his hair brushed against the back of her hand. She reached up, exploring. Immediately she felt his own hands move, one grasping her tight, the other crawling around to her breast. His fingers were warm and dry and hard, and avoiding her injuries, tucked purposefully into her neckline, pushing towards the nipple.

"My lord," the voice was calling outside, footsteps running, the door pushed open, the draught like sudden ice. Ludovic lurched backwards, startled and looking around. "My lord," the page bowed hurriedly, distracted and desperate. "His lordship the earl – at once, my lord – you must go to him at once. It's our lord Gerald, sir. He's been arrested – for treason."

CHAPTER TWENTY-ONE

"I t's orders, Mistress." The boy clasped his hands behind his back, very grubby fingers tightly entwined. He planted his feet wide, stuck out his stomach, and glowered. "And I does as is ordered, wevver I likes it or doesn't. Nor won't say which. His lordship done told me personal. So that's that."

"I remember you," Alysson glared back. "You're that odd little boy that hid under the table months ago. So why did Ludovic send you to me?"

"His lordship," Clovis informed her, "trusts me."

"Well I don't," said Alysson flatly. "I've no idea who you are. And what am I supposed to do with you anyway?"

"You'll not do nothing wiv me," declared Clovis, straightening to assert dignity. "His lordship – wot's not here no more, so's there's no bloody arguments no how – 'as been and done and made me his page. Working for his lordship mind – and for a whole penny a day wot's more – to do wot he says. Not wot you nor nobody else says. And wot he says is to watch you, Mistress. And see wot goes on, being as he ain't here to do it hisself."

Alysson listened with some impatience. "Watch me do what?"

The boy wore a somewhat mismatched assortment of clothes. He so obviously did not resemble a page of the Sumerford estates that Alysson hoped he would not make himself too evident. A grimy and salt encrusted shirt showed little more than a coarse and unbleached neckline beneath a doublet so worn and rubbed that it wore a sheen more resembling satin than the untreated wool it truly was. The colour was indeterminate, but the outer surcoat, trimmed with moth-eaten sheepskin, was a virulent green, reminiscent of verdigris. The hose were knitted blue, with holes in both knees and ladders disappearing beneath the doublet's ragged unhemmed peplum. His ankle boots were tough brown leather, badly scuffed and brine stained. He had doffed his small orange cap, complete with wilted partridge feather, and had stuffed this through an old leather belt lying rather loose about his middle. He was clearly wearing his best.

Their lordships were all absent. Within only two hours of the terrible news being relayed by the galloping, sweating, and exhausted messenger, his lordship the Earl of Sumerford, his second eldest son Brice, and his youngest son Ludovic, had all left the castle at full speed. Apart from one saddle bag apiece, they took neither luggage nor escort, but were accompanied by a groom and two of the castle guards. They had swirled out through the stables and across the drawbridge as if the devil himself was on their heels and the echoes of their departure remained hanging like great black clouds beneath the portcullis.

Alysson stood staring at the unwelcome child, and presumed that the only three remaining Sumerfords, being the countess, Humphrey and Jennine, would view this newly come apparition with considerable distrust. She sighed. "And how will I explain you to everyone else?"

"You'll not be asked to do no such fing," announced Clovis with growing animosity. "I knows my place and will do wot I does best. I've introduced myself to you, wot his lordship done asked me to, just being polite as is proper. And now that's done, I'll be off quicker'n spit. You won't be seeing much of me from now on, Mistress, and them others, well, they won't be seeing me at all. But I shall see them, and I shall see you, sure as piss in the privy." He bowed rigid from the waist, turned to leave, but managed one last complaint over his shoulder. "Nor I ain't so little neither, nor you ain't so mighty big, Mistress. I reckon there's a fair bit o' respeck due both sides." Alysson watched his affronted departure and wondered, not for the first time, just what Ludovic was up to.

※◇※

Many miles away, Ludovic was leaning, damp shouldered, against cold stone, and the slap of the moat against the outside wall echoed within. The Tower was a place of icy shadows, even in summer.

Gerald was sitting. He was not shackled and his pallet, where he slumped, was well padded. But there was little else in the room except condensation, with neither window nor brazier, but one guttering candle stub on a shelf made the shadows dance. "So Father got you in," Gerald sighed. "But wasn't interested in coming himself."

"Father's still with the king," said Ludovic. "He's more interested in getting you out than getting me in. Assurances of family loyalty, reminders of proven valour at Exeter. It was Brice got me in, truth be told. Seems Brice has some influence, having evidently met the king before."

Gerald looked up, surprised. "How? Brice always avoids court, even avoids London. Too busy on secret business."

"Which, being secret, we have no idea what or where. Perhaps it brings him to London, perhaps to court. Who knows?"

Gerald shook his head. "No matter. It's his grace, and poor Roland I cry for. Not myself."

Ludovic paused, watching his brother's expression. When he finally spoke again, it was very softly. "Roland is in Newgate, my dear, and will stay there until his execution. We can do nothing for him, which you know. You must not try, or it will bring your own immediate death. I am sorry for it, but he knew the risks he took. In the meantime, we believe we can ensure your pardon and release within the week, but you must try a little diplomacy, and remember we speak of Piers Warbeck, not of his grace the Duke of York. You gain nothing by obstinacy, and help neither yourself nor your family

190

who will all sink under royal suspicion. Perhaps more importantly for you, you do not help Master Warbeck. He is here in the Tower you know, and will remain. He has lost his freedom forever, but he has not yet lost his life. Tudor still prevaricates. But now any overt support for Warbeck's claims from England's nobility will send the boy to the gallows, not to the throne."

"They put him in the stocks, after he was captured this time." Gerald's eyes were bloodshot and it was clear he had not slept. Apart from his own discomfort, Richard Plantagenet's misery had kept him awake. "The stocks, Lu. The rightful King of England, chained and hauled up on public view as a trickster, first at Westminster, and then, God save him, at Cheapside like any common criminal claiming false charms, devaluing his customers or selling rotten meat. His grace stood there with as much regal dignity as he always shows, head bent as the wooden frame was locked around his neck. Said not a word when they announced his crime to the crowd, and they say he never spoke during all six hours he was kept standing there. The people jeered him, ignorant fools. They believe Tudor's lies and stories. Don't they remember how Tudor stole the throne? It's Tudor should be chained in the stocks."

"Dear God." Ludovic sighed. "Use your head while you still have it. Your words can be heard here, my dear, we are in royal custody and the guards constantly patrol the corridors outside. What good will it do your Richard of York if you die for him now? He's already been taken from the stocks and is imprisoned in the Tower, in the Lanthorn I've been told. So comfortably housed, at least, which is more than can be said for you."

"Yes, another absurdity." Gerald glared at Henry Tudor's invisible shadow. "I'd be better housed if I'd paid, but my coin's all spent. My prince has not a farthing either, and he's being called a fraudster and counterfeiter of false identities, a lowly boatman's son from Flanders who's had the gall to name himself a long lost prince and claim the throne of England. Yet dragged to the Tower itself, he's not slung in some dungeon cell as any common born traitor would be, but royally housed, I hear, just like the prince he says he is. These are double standards indeed."

"Enough." Ludovic heard the rattling of the keys outside. "Time's up. But we've paid for a week's comfortable board and expect a warrant for your release before Saturday next. I doubt I'll be back for they won't allow it, but I'll be here to meet you and bring your horse as soon as you're freed. Keep cheerful if you can."

"Cheerful? I hear the lions roaring from the menagerie as I close my eyes at night. It's a bizarre world, Lu. What does Richard Plantagenet hear? And Roland, chained in Newgate and facing imminent death?"

The door creaked open and the gaoler poked his nose around the iron braces. "One hears the tides of the Thames," Ludovic said softly, turning to leave. "And the other is courageous enough to listen to his own heartbeat in peace. A man with confidence in his righteousness, must be confident also of the glory awaiting him after death."

"I may not be freed in time to visit Roland," Gerald whispered, one eye on the open door and the gaoler now waiting out in the corridor. "But he must have some comfort before the end. He'll be hung as a traitor, and you know what that means." He dropped his voice lower. "Lu, I beg you. You – understood – before. See Roland and do what you can for him. Pay for some ale, some meat and a blanket. He'll be chained in the pits, no doubt. See him for me, at least once – before it's too late."

"You ask me to openly visit a condemned traitor?" Ludovic stared down at his brother, their faces diminished by the lightless gloom. "Do you realise what you're asking, Gerald?"

Gerald hung his head. "I'm desperate, or I wouldn't ask. Roland was the bravest of us all, you know. But there's no wife to visit him, no father to pay his keep in prison. He's penniless and alone."

Ludovic paused one moment, staring. Then nodded in silence, turned and strode from the tiny room. His boots echoed on the damp stone as the cell door clanged shut behind him, the key grating in the old iron lock.

Outside Ludovic collected his horse and his weapons and rode out through the mighty gates of the Byward Tower and across the drawbridge. A strong wind swept up the river, agitating the surface of the moat. The sky was grey clouded and a spit of rain hung in the air.

Ludovic twitched up the trim of his surcoat, and headed into London's cluttered streets. The stench of sewerage, steaming with a summer's warmth however cold the wind, clogged the gutters. Ludovic turned from the riverside, avoiding the wharfs where his usual business lay, and aimed instead for the cheaps. It was sleeting when he arrived at The Poultry. The bloody gizzards and intestines were heaped beneath the stalls like battle strewn remains, awaiting the ravens, the dogs and the scrummaging rats. He rode on. With the rain now sliming the cobbles and the markets busy and crowded, there was no possibility of speed. It took two hours to pick through the Shambles and reach the Newgate portcullis. Ludovic sighed, and dismounted.

"Your business, my lord," demanded the gaoler, eyeing Ludovic's sable lined coat and his fine impatient horse.

Ludovic held out his purse. "I've coin both for the man I intend visiting, and for the man who opens the door for me, but no sealed appointment," he said. "Take your choice."

"You'd better come in, my lord," said the gaoler, bowing at once. "The rain's getting mighty bad, and 'tis warmer inside."

"I doubt it," said Ludovic.

Five days later they met in an upstairs private solar at the Rose Tavern, set back in fashionable Leadenhall Street, as the sun was shining through the wide unshuttered windows. His lordship the Earl of Sumerford sat facing his son Gerald. Behind him stood Brice. Ludovic sat to one side, taking no part in the conversation. He was looking out through the windows over London's uneven tiled rooftops. He appeared almost absent, but he was listening.

The Earl of Sumerford spoke directly to Gerald. He sat at ease, his legs stretched to the slanting sunbeams, but his eyes remained cold. "You will receive no second chances from this king," said the earl, "for he is not a man of mercy. He has pardoned you once, but would not do so again. Tomorrow morning you will therefore retire immediately into silent seclusion in Somerset, and you will not leave the castle nor take part in any manner of public action for many years, unless it is in support of your anointed monarch. If you are obedient until the end of the season when I imagine this business will be concluded, I shall then endeavour to settle your marriage. Perhaps watching the inevitable misdemeanours of your own wife and children will satisfy your yearnings for danger. Until then, my son, your behaviour will be at all times circumspect, loyal and diplomatic. Otherwise his majesty will find no need to arrange your execution for I will have you imprisoned under guard myself. The dungeons at Sumerford are less spacious than those at the Tower, but will suffice, I believe."

Gerald stared back at his father. "Tudor pardoned me," he said, teeth clenched. "How gracious. But there was no evidence against me, and no crime for which I could be pardoned. When the Duke of York was dragged out of sanctuary by Tudor's guards, Roland was arrested with him. This placed me under immediate suspicion. Roland has long been my squire, but in truth he is more friend than servant. Each of us has played a part and he chose that of my squire. But nothing is known against me personally, nothing can be proved and my own arrest was utterly unsupported."

The earl regarded his son with contempt. "Does the king need evidence? He executed his own Lord Chamberlain, his mother's own brother-in-law, on evidence of little more than rumour. The king will fabricate evidence if he wishes, or will choose to overlook its requirement entirely. Have you no more sense than to seethe about justice when speaking of kings? Do I have a son who can do no more than rave and ramble against his fate? Or will you remember your responsibility to the Sumerford name, and swear loyalty to your family, if not to your king?"

Gerald nodded, looking first away, then up at Brice. "The Sumerford pride? Yes, I'll swear. I know exactly what I owe to my name and title. A title and estates stolen from their rightful owners, just as Tudor stole his. And you, big brother? Do you know what's due to our family pride?"

"Me?" Brice laughed, hands to the back of the tall chair where his father sat. "Yes, I understand very well, my beloved. Very well indeed.

194

I helped in your release from the executioner's block, though you don't seem particularly grateful. A little bribery, even in royal circles, is mighty useful if well-handled and cleverly directed. And bribery, you know, has always been my forte for I also understand the love of money so – remarkably well."

"Then I am naturally grateful, and naturally I thank you." Gerald sat rigid, his face expressionless. "With bribery? But enough left over, I see, for a new surcoat. Cadmium muslin damask, lined in black marten. How lucky there was sufficient remaining from the – business of bribery."

"Indeed." Brice smiled extravagantly wide. "But then, I am invariably lucky in such matters. A particularly beautiful coat, I hope you agree. And you may not have noticed, but the shirt is fresh tailored, with a neckline cut in the new lace cutworks. And I hesitate to brag, my beloved, seeing the sad state of your old boots, but my shoes are also new, and the latest Italian fashion."

Gerald blinked. "Indeed, you must have impressed the king," he said quietly, "when you helped arrange my release, and the permission for Ludovic to visit in the Tower. How fortunate that you had such beautiful new clothes for such an occasion."

"I always have new clothes, beloved." Brice dimpled, his smile remaining benign. "And I am always fortunate. But then, I have always chosen such innocent pastimes, and make my coin without recourse to conspiracies, or by dabbling in treason."

Gerald started to rise, his eyes narrowed. The earl interrupted. "No further immaturity Gerald, I beg you, the youthful belligerence of your nature already exhausts me. Having clearly inherited your mother's facile banality, you are now doubtless unlikely to remember either your duty or your dignity, so informing you how much you have to thank me for would now appear pointless. But in my presence at least, we will indulge in no petty squabbles. Kindly contain your simplistic naiveté a little longer, my son. I intend resting before dinner, and retiring early to bed since we have a long ride tomorrow. Brice, you had better come with me. Ludovic, you will keep Gerald company and ensure his utter and complete obedience to my requirements."

Ludovic remained sitting as his father and Brice left the room. He was watching, morose and unblinking, the plunge of a hunting kite, the squirm of abandoned kittens in a rubbish dump below, the kite's claws piercing the wriggling scrap of fur, then the flash of feathers disappearing into the bright blue distance.

Gerald said, "Did you go?"

Ludovic turned reluctantly. "I went."

"Won't you tell me? Is it so bad?"

Ludovic sighed. "It's a message I would sooner not carry. But a dying man has a right to be heard, and his last wishes respected." Ludovic stood and came slowly over to sit where his father had sat before, facing Gerald. "I went to Newgate," he said quietly. "I paid for Roland to have food, ale and blankets supplied for the week, but all requests to unshackle him or move him to a better position were refused. He is reckoned a dangerous prisoner of some consequence, and there were orders to keep him securely chained in the depths of the limboes. I could not change that, however much I paid the guards."

"What did he say?" whispered Gerald.

"That he has no fear of death. That he believes what he did was right, and that he obeyed God's will, even though he failed. That he prays for the Duke of York, and for you, every day. That he loves you both, and will gladly die for you."

Gerald nodded, blinking back tears. "Go on."

Ludovic paused a moment before continuing. Then shook his head and said, "He asked only, if you were free to do so, you would come to witness his death. To show yourself to him, so that he knows you are free, and alive. And that amongst a jeering crowd he will see one loving face before he sees only his own blood."

"Dear God. When?"

"If you intend fulfilling this last request," Ludovic said very softly, "then I believe we have a little over one hour."

Gerald jumped up. "You mean this morning? And you'll come with me?"

"He asked me to," said Ludovic, "and I will go, though I would sooner go alone. If you are recognised by anyone in authority, you may be arrested again, and then if I am not arrested myself, Father will certainly kill me."

"Of course I have to go." Gerald's words faded into whispers. "And is it the full penalty, do you know, Lu? Or has it been commuted to – a lesser sentence?"

"The full penalty," said Ludovic softly. "A traitor's death. And we have an hour to get to Tyburn."

CHAPTER TWENTY-TWO

T he prisoner was lashed to a light wooden hurdle, dragged by two horses from Newgate to Tyburn, its boards scraping the cobbles. It was not a cold day and a gentle sun smiled as if all was right with the world, but it had rained in the night and the stretcher's open frame was bespattered with the softened mud and muck London collected in her gutters. The prisoner's face and body were soon clogged with the slime of animal piss and the garbage of a thousand emptied chamber pots, the bloody slops washed down from the Shambles, and the steaming excrement of the horses pulling ahead. Roland's eyes were closed, the sunshine gleaming on the streaks of filth and lines of pain.

He wore only an unbleached shirt reaching to his knees. Beneath it, his legs were bare, and the neckline, ready for the noose, was pulled well open and a little torn.

Dragged without wheels, the stretcher jolted, bumped and shuddered across the cobbles. The prisoner swung with each movement and was slung to both sides, though his ties did not loosen nor his shackles fall as they clanked, rubbing tight to his ankles. Some folk watched from the roadside. Thieves and ruffians were often cheered, but this was a prisoner who confused the crowd. They watched in silence, or turned away.

The scaffold was set high, with only one noose of the three available spaces being needed today for only one prisoner, and the hangman waiting beside his ladder, patient in the sun. No priest accompanied him, for this traitor did not warrant the chance to repent, nor earn a place at Heaven's gates. The rope was already slung over the cross bar, and the boards already laid below for the quartering. A group of guards was chattering at the base of the scaffold, another two stood bored on the platform.

As the horses drew up, the guards came forward and Roland was untied from the stretcher, his hands released and the shackled unlocked. Though shaking and weak from the hurdle, he was pushed forwards at once to climb the ladder. He stumbled, the ladder swayed, he clung a moment and then climbed again.

Gerald and Ludovic stood directly before the scaffold, gazing up. There were others around them, but no great crowd. This was no famous offender nor popular local. But a traitor's death held charm for some and a few had gathered. Roland looked down, saw the two men standing prominent, and smiled. Gerald's eyes were filled with tears but he smiled back, barely seeing his friend's face. "He has seen us," said Ludovic, "and has the answer he wanted." And, briefly removing his hat, Ludovic stepped forward, looked up at the man on the platform above him, and bowed.

The hangman had climbed the crossbar and now placed the noose around Roland's neck, arranging the knot to the back where it pushed against the top of the spine. The captain of the guard held up his parchment, loudly proclaiming the charge. "One Roland Fiddington found guilty of heinous treason as charged, and condemned herewith to death. To be hanged, disembowelled and quartered, and his head to be placed on the Bridge as a warning to all traitors. The sentence to be carried out forthwith."

The guard who still held the prisoner, muttered, pushing at him. "Your last chance to speak now, lad. Confess your crime, and plead for the good Lord's mercy."

Roland smiled but his voice was a little lost, cracked by thirst and exhaustion. "I confess only to loving my true king," he said, speaking directly to Gerald and Ludovic, who now stood very still, gazing back.

"My king is Richard IV, held at present as a prisoner in the Tower. I have committed no crime, as he has not, nor am I ashamed of anything I have done, except failing to bring the rightful king to power."

The guards grinned, shaking their heads. A condemned man was entitled to his last words, but they'd be reported back, and would not please the king. One nodded to the hangman. He tested his rope again, repositioned it slightly, and with a quick glance up, pulled away the ladder. It fell clattering to the platform, and the prisoner dropped, and swung.

Roland's face, deeply flushed, began to swell and his eyes, although closed, seemed to protrude. His legs kicked a little, though feebly, and his body contorted. He made the gulping involuntary sounds of slow strangulation, the gurgle from the constricted gullet and escaping air from the lungs. Then, streaking through the filth already coating his bare legs, the trickles of hot urine dripped as his bladder lost control. The guards and the hangman watched, counting time. Finally the captain nodded again, and the hangman leaned forwards, caught Roland's body and stilled its relentless swing. Then he reached up and cut the rope. The body fell slack into his arms.

Roland heaved, gulping in new breath. He rolled over as if reclaiming life and force, but the guard bent down and held him firm.

"Oh don't, my dear friend, don't try to breathe," Gerald whispered. Ludovic put one arm around his brother's shoulders, saying nothing.

One guard held Roland's ankles, stretching them apart and strapping them firmly to the board on which he now lay. Another caught his flailing wrists, and lashed them to either side. The hangman flung up the filthy shirt, exposing the prisoner part naked. One of the guards was lighting a small fire, a few inches from the board beside the prisoner's head. Without wind, the sparks spat little, one flame rising suddenly, painting Roland's face vivid. The hangman leaned between Roland's legs. He held the curved metal pincers used to geld horses, reached forwards, and clipped. Roland screamed.

The hangman threw the wedge of dark bloody flesh onto the fire. The flames sizzled, almost extinguished, then flared. The hangman laid down the gelding irons, and took up the knife. He waited for a count of three, then put the point to Roland's belly, just above centre. He pressed, and the skin split and parted. He ripped downwards and the body opened.

Roland had stopped screaming. As he was eviscerated, his intestines cut from his belly, thrown to the fire and burned, the prisoner made only one small choking sound, for he had fainted. Spared the final pain, he did not see his own entrails coil amongst the flames and turn to soot and stench. He was dead before they sliced him further.

"Come away now, my dear," said Ludovic softly. "He has no further need of us."

Gerald was staring, unable to move. He still watched as Roland's body was sawn into quarters and his head hacked from his neck. The blood poured out across the boards to the heaped sawdust below. The hangman, his sleeves rolled up, was bloody to the elbows. The man neither smiled nor frowned, brisk in his work, eager to prove efficient, and be done.

Ludovic pulled Gerald away. Gerald turned, bent over, and vomited in the gutter, heaving and sobbing. "Hush, hush my dear," Ludovic said softly. "We are too conspicuous, and must be gone. There is nothing more we can do here."

Gerald wiped his mouth, stumbling forwards. He looked up at his brother, red eyed. "How does any man bear a torture like that, Ludovic? How can a good man be made to suffer such a death?"

The rest of the small crowd still stood watching. Ludovic pushed past. "He fainted. He felt only the first cut," Ludovic said. "And was dead long before the end. They say a hanged man will dangle alive for near to an hour, if unlucky. This was far quicker and perhaps there's some mercy in that. Now he's in God's hands, and will be healed, the pain forgotten. And we must hurry."

Gerald gulped. "You don't mean to get back to the inn for dinner? Surely not, for pity's sake, not to eat?"

Ludovic shook his head, pushing Gerald onwards and into the shadows. "I doubt I'll be eating anything for several days. But I mean to keep you alive, my dear. Both of us if possible. And that means away from here before attention moves from the entertainment to the spectators."

The alleys took them into the warmth of the darkness, quick steps back to where their horses were left saddled. Ludovic kept one hand to the hilt of his sword, the other clasping his brother tight. Within the hour they were back at The Rose.

Ludovic did not see Brice until the evening.

He was standing alone in the small courtyard that enclosed the stable block, and was staring up at the stars as if expecting answers there. Ludovic had avoided both dinner and supper, both his father and his brothers. He had not travelled to the wharves to oversee his business as he was apt to do when in London. Instead he had kept strictly solitary, and his thoughts in check.

Now Brice came behind, his hand hard on his brother's shoulder. Ludovic jumped. "Escaping, my beloved?" Brice said. "I imagine you did not enjoy the spectacle this morning?"

Ludovic frowned. "You've an uncanny knowledge of what goes on these days, my dear. How is it, I wonder, when your previous acquaintance with the city, with court practice, and with politics, was always proclaimed to be – so disdainfully slight. Have you changed professions, perhaps? Or maybe, nothing has changed at all."

"Too subtle for me, my beloved," Brice said. "Or are you implying, I wonder, that my secret supply of wealth has more to do with our glorious king, and less to do with my own ingenuity?" He yawned, shaking his head a little. "I am saddened, my dear, to discover you as obtuse as the rest of the family after all. I had always considered you just a touch – not much you understand – but just slightly – more intelligent. Indeed, I am now quite bored by the prospect. I think I shall go to bed."

But he made no move back towards the tavern doors, and Ludovic stood a moment, watching him closely. Then Ludovic said, "Gerald, for all the danger of his questionable choices, was always honest with us. He told us his beliefs and his business. You never have. Will you tell me now?"

Brice chuckled. "Why? For you to scald and criticise? I do now what I have always done, my beloved, a profession I took up when I was bare seventeen years of age, just back from the knight's apprenticeship, and wearily impatient to go my own way. But you don't tell your own source of riches either, little brother. Why expect such honourable verity from me, my love, when you keep your own improprieties close?"

"Oh, mine are dull enough. I'm into trade, with some small evasion of the customs when possible. When the embargoes were in full force, life was profitable. Wool out and wine back. Now my ships bring me less, but risk less too." Ludovic smiled. "But I've an idea you knew all this already, big brother. I've an idea you know it all."

"I'm hardly invincible, beloved." Brice nodded, smiling back. He stood close though being somewhat shorter than Ludovic, looked up. "But perhaps I knew, or perhaps I simply guessed. No matter. I don't delve into our family secrets as you think I do, having my own interests to absorb me. But your other improprieties are even more evident, little brother, and perhaps even less salubrious."

Ludovic blinked. "You imagine me involved in Gerald's conspiracies perhaps, because I went to see a brave man unjustly slaughtered this morning?"

"Oh, no, my beloved, hardly that." Brice laughed. "You are far too self-important to endanger your hide for a false claimant to the throne, and far too pragmatic to put your ideals before your comfort. I meant your little scullion back at the castle. Improprieties galore. I envy you your hedonistic indulgences, little brother."

"You'll not tempt me into angry denials," Ludovic said. "I believe you know the truth of that business as well, and if you care to slander both myself and the girl, then it's your own dignity you wound." He turned, hiding his temper, and began to cross the courtyard again, striding back towards the light at the open tavern doors. He turned back only once, speaking half over his shoulder. "And this from a man who has already sired his own brother's heir? Your own self-indulgences, big brother, seem far less salubrious than mine."

Ludovic heard Brice's chuckle behind him as he swung back indoors, quickly climbing the stairs up to his own chamber. He shared it with Gerald and Gerald appeared to be asleep. Ludovic was quite, quite sure that Gerald was fully awake, and would remain so most of the night, but he had no wish to talk or to relive the morning's hideous events. Ludovic climbed part dressed into bed and closed his eyes to the shadows.

CHAPTER TWENTY-THREE

A lysson had been awake for some time. She was not sure how late it might be, but knowing she had already slept, though remaining sleepy and a little heavy headed, believed it must be the small hours, so turned, pulling up the counterpane, hoping to sleep again. Then she realised what had awoken her and opened her eyes at once. The sounds were over her head, repeated and persistent. Footsteps, forwards six paces, then back. A tapping, then roused to banging. Then silence. Then beginning again.

It was not Alysson's usual bed, though she had no place specifically her own. Sometimes, especially since her mistress's pregnancy had progressed, she slept in the huge curtained bed with Jennine snuggled close, for the lady liked her back and shoulders rubbed when she was disturbed by the child moving, or when troubled by other pains. However Alysson usually slept in the truckle bed in Jennine's chamber. It was narrow and low to the ground, but it was a proper place for a lady's maid.

If she was out of favour, and her mistress was angry with her which now occurred more often, Alysson slept on a hastily made up pallet in the garderobe. This was the least pleasant option, and one she avoided.

However, when the Lord Humphrey instead of sending for his

wife came instead to her rooms at night, Alysson was bundled onto another mattress dragged into the lady's outer solar. Here she was sleeping now, although Humphrey had not come. It seemed Jennine had been expecting him and, in any case, this was Alysson's favourite bed. Not so deep, not so soft, but gloriously private, and it was here that she slept best. Though not tonight.

Alysson knew exactly who her mistress was. The secrets had been divulged, not all at once, but not reluctantly. And now nearly nine months after her wedding, the lady, huge with child, seemed more friend than mistress except when she was angry. But Humphrey was a subject Alysson refused to discuss. When he occupied Jennine's bedchamber, Alysson closed her ears. The walls were massive stone, thicker than her thighs, and only a little sound crept through with the draughts.

This time the sound travelled. Not silenced by stone, but echoing through wooden floorboards, the noises were heavy and pronounced. Alysson had not even realised there was a chamber above. The winding staircase that led to the Lady Jennine's apartments stopped at her own door and appeared to go no further up. Alysson pulled the counterpane back over her ears. The disturbance continued for a long time. Footsteps in one direction, always six. Then in the opposite direction. Tapping. A furious banging and then silence. And then, as Alysson sighed, preparing to sleep, they would start again.

Discovering his new page curled up cheerfully beneath the sunny window in his own bedchamber, Ludovic threw his gloves, hat and surcoat at him and scowled. "Fine job you're doing, brat. I haven't employed you to keep my cushions warm."

Clovis made no attempt to rise. He received his master's clothes and rolled them into an unceremonious bundle in his arms. He grinned over the top of them, chin resting on the soft tan leather of the riding gloves. "Got plenty for the telling, though," he said. "Bin busy, right inuff."

"I have ridden all day," Ludovic frowned. "I need a hot bath before anything else. No doubt it will surprise you to learn that as my page, arranging this is one of your duties. When I am submerged to my shoulders in extremely hot water, I will listen to your stories. Just tell me this first. Is she well?"

"Oh, yes," said Clovis, hopping down from the cushioned seat and dumping Ludovic's clothes in a heap on the bed. "Fair, fine and fancy, I reckon. Though I don't rightly know wot you sees in the wench, meself. Bloody bad tempered bissom, she is."

Ludovic smiled faintly. "You are quite right, she is. However, you will not say so again, either in my hearing or out of it. Now go and see to the bath."

Within a little less than half an hour, he was naked and sitting not quite to his shoulders in the simmering water required. The small chamber on the lower floor, reinforced beneath to support the weight of water, held little else beside the standing bathtub. Not the usual barrel shape but both wider and longer, this was cooper built in thick wood, braced with copper rings and lined in soft linen. It took a deal of filling and scullions with buckets of water boiled over the kitchen fire, had been known to spill half their burdens before arriving at the proper place.

Ludovic rested complacent in the luxury he had been dreaming of all day. He leaned his head on the shaped backrest, cushioned in wads of linen, and closed his eyes. Steam spiralled above him into a soggy haze, the upper ceiling beams dripped with condensation, and Clovis, perched upon the chest of linen and towels, complained about both damp and heat. "If you persist in being irritating, my urchin," Ludovic said, "I shall make you wash my back. Now, instead tell me what you have discovered."

"I ain't washing no one nor nuffin," objected Clovis. "Would make me well nigh wet as you, and barves is wot I don't hold wiv. Besides, you can prance round nekkid if you wants, but I ain't touching your nekkid bits, so forget it."

Ludovic sighed. "Naked or not, brat, I shall leave this bath and thrash you if you persist in annoying me. Now – the news – or the thrashing. Take your pick."

"Well, don't look like I'm gonna get no gratitude," sniffed Clovis.

"But might as well tell it, now I've gone and got it." He paused for affect, but receiving no answer except a faint splash of the sponge, continued his story. "For a start, your Mistress Wotsit don't leave them chambers much, so it's mighty hard to know wot she's up to. Does the odd errand, and is mighty friendly wiv her mistress, but not much else to say. An' won't talk to me, just gives shitty looks when I sees her. Mind you, I followed her when she got a day off, and she never seen me at all."

Ludovic raised an eyebrow. "You were supposed to be watching her for her own protection, not simply for the purposes of spying."

"An' how's I expected to do one wivvout the other?" demanded Clovis, much aggrieved. "You listening or just griping?"

But the point at which Ludovic began to answer was interrupted by the sudden thump of heavy footsteps in the corridor outside, and the sounds of at least five pairs of boots running from the kitchens towards the back staircase. Then as the footsteps receded, other noises intervened. Shouting, the imperious summons of his mother's familiar voice, and then a great banging and clattering. Finally the door was thrust open and Brice strode in, looking first at the small and disreputable figure sitting on the chest, and then down at his brother. Brice regarded Ludovic with some amusement.

"Attended by a winsome cherub, instead of the sweet Aphrodite of your dreams, my beloved? How sad. The trollop Aphrodite, is of course, at present otherwise engaged."

Ludovic frowned and started to emerge from the water. "What now?"

Brice, leaning momentarily against the open door, arms crossed, shook his head. "Yes, yes, I know little brother. You must of course defend her name and reputation. But there's no time, my beloved, for the infant you appear to believe I have sired myself – my own name and reputation evidently being beyond repair and naturally not meriting defence – chooses to enter our gentle world this very evening. Inopportune of course, as all Sumerfords tend to be, since we lords and masters are barely returned from our travels and are instead ready for our beds, alone or otherwise. But the future heir of our glorious title is announcing its arrival at this moment. Excitement is rife. But since the said brat is not seed of my loins, my loins being far too precious to me to entrust to the machinations of a woman I wholeheartedly distrust, I feel sadly unexcited, and will now retire. I leave the spreading of family congratulations to you, little brother." He nodded, moving back into the cold shadowed corridor, pulling the door closed behind him. As the door snapped shut, he called, "Good night, beloved. Enjoy your cherub, by all means. I shall say nothing of it, I swear."

Silence followed his departure. The rush of servants and the calls for water, for towels, for the doctor and the apothecary, had ceased. "Well now," said Clovis. "Seems like it's gonna be a busy night."

Doubled over, squatting first on a stool and then stumbling to her bed, the Lady Jennine was attended by her maid Alysson, Mistress Purvis the dairy master's wife, Mistress Barnes the principal brewster, Mistress Beatrice Shore, the head cook's eldest daughter, and the impressive Mistress Tenby, madam of all the castle's female staff. At first they encouraged Jennine to walk, dragging her feet interminably around the room. But as the labour became dangerously prolonged without noticeable progress, they backed away, frowning to each other, disagreeing as to the most suitable advice and how best to proceed, and bickering, as quietly as possible, about who amongst them should take precedence.

"But has someone sent for the midwife?" demanded Mistress Beatrice under her breath.

"Midwife? What midwife?" scoffed Mistress Tenby. "The nearest woman is a day's ride away, and is no doubt already called out somewhere else. At the castle, we have always managed everything ourselves."

The evening blackened into night and finally the night dawned into a new day without any signs of the child's birth being evident. Jennine no longer accepted guidance from the bustling women around her, but lay on the great bed, her knees drawn up and her head bent down. The windows were tight shuttered and although it was early July and pleasantly warm outside, a huge fire had been lit in the hearth, its logs flaming so high that the chimney caught the heat rising and the wind descending, and roared, as if in sympathy. Steam rose from the two cauldrons set with water to boil, and as the sweaty dampness increased, it smelled stale, desultory and tired. The chamber dripped and heaved, tight shut around the moaning and the pain.

The door was kept closed when possible, and the gap beneath it stuffed with rags. No draught was permitted, and only the firelight and the flicker from one small candle beside the bed shuffled the shadows around the room. Neither cold nor any bright lights, being those two most proven dangers to a woman in the throes of birthing, were permitted to enter.

In the outer solar the castle medik, the elderly surgeon and the apothecary waited, alert for the sudden sounds of an infant crying as they discussed herbal cures and stirred the medicines they had prepared. Now they frowned and predicted disaster. The perfumes of fenugreek water, pressed cherries, willow bark and dittany were strong at first, then mellowed and finally faded. The mixtures were cooling in the cups, ready to be passed to the first woman who dared stick her head around the door.

The expectant father, though normally also waiting in the vicinity at such a time, was not present. Nor were any of the Sumerfords except for the countess. She stood wringing her long fingers, a little hesitant, before entering the birth chamber.

Jennine wore only her chemise, its skirts pulled up to her waist. She had begun to cry, choking sobs that seemed to hurt her, and was curled on the bed, gripping the hand of her personal maid who crouched beside her. When the countess entered, Jennine looked up, then turned away. "It won't come," she said, half whisper. "It knows. It knows the truth and refuses to be born. It doesn't want me, any more than I want it."

The countess walked immediately to the bed. She pushed Alysson away, and took Jennine's hand tight, wrenching at it. "Listen, foolish girl. This is the Sumerford heir about to be born. You are honoured to

210

be mother to this child. Stop thinking only of yourself - and push, girl, push."

Jennine rolled away, snatching back her hand and calling for Alysson. Beatrice Shore, the cook's daughter, whispered urgently in the countess's ear. "My lady, I've helped my mother give birth to eight little sisters and two brothers, and only one ever died. I know what I'm talking about my lady, and this is going on too long. She's going to die, I know it, unless we do something."

"Do something?" demanded the countess. "What can we do?"

Beatrice whispered, "Time, I believe, to send for the midwife, my lady."

Her ladyship shook her little headdress with a sniff. "There's a woman in Exeter who smells of pisspots but I have no faith in such a female." She stood again, leaving the bed and crossing to the fire. The chamber seethed, sizzling in its darkened swelter. Mistress Tenby kicked at the logs and the fire rose higher, spitting anew. The countess took Mistress Shore's arm. "Well, girl? Tell me quietly. Do we cut her open, to save the child?"

Beatrice shuddered. "I don't know how to do such a thing, my lady. And it would surely kill her."

The countess lowered her voice. "It's the child that matters. In such a case, what else can we do?"

Beatrice stared around, eyes wide. Sweat had polished her face and her skin reflected the glistening fire. "I believe the baby's upside down, my lady," she whispered. "I've seen its little foot poke out more than once. But the child won't turn. Perhaps if I could grab its legs, and pull, I might save both their lives."

The countess thought a moment. "Try it. Do you need her tied down?" She gazed across at the rumpled bed. It had been covered with old blankets to keep it from becoming soiled or blood soaked, but now every cover was in turmoil. Jennine tossed, rolling to one side and then the other. She had begun to scream, but a weak sickly sound, without strength or breath. Alysson had run again to her side, and was holding her, rocking her in her arms. Mistress Purvis continued to stoke the fire and watch the water boiling. Mistress Tenby had hurried outside to collect medicines.

"No, don't hold her down," said Beatrice. "She might panic and do herself more harm. I'll try my best. Will you help, my lady?"

The countess backed towards the darkened window. "No." She shook her head again. "I gave birth to six children," she said softly. "Six boys, but the first two died. All that pain and misery for those tangled bloody shapeless things without breath or heartbeat. So much for midwives. The next time I dispensed with the wretched woman and was attended by my sister and my mother-in-law, and neither knew much. But in my day, you see, there was less knowledge. When the next four lived, I could barely believe it. And every child a boy, and his lordship was – grateful. For me the memories are not so sweet. So I will stay here, but I cannot help. I cannot – touch."

Alysson looked up as Beatrice came to the bedside. "She's bleeding heavily," Alysson whispered. "What do you plan to do?"

Beatrice shook her head. "The child's lying the wrong way up," she said. "I'm sure of it. But I've no experience of such a thing. I think I know what to do, but I'm only guessing."

"The others?" Alysson looked around. The other women were watching, but no one else came forward.

"They've less experience than me," Beatrice said. "Mistress Tenby is unmarried, though she says she attended her mother once. But the child died, and so did her mother. Mistress Purvis, well she's only experienced with cows. But they pull the calves out, don't they, if they don't come natural? Well, Mistress Barnes knows a little more having helped birth her sister's babies, but that was many years ago. And her ladyship, well perhaps she knows more than the rest of us, but she's frightened to get involved. They should have called some woman in from the village. There's plenty there have helped bring a dozen infants into the world, and know far more than me."

"Well, I don't know anything either," sighed Alysson. "I watched my two little brothers birthed, though I was very young and only did what the midwife told me. But I'll help."

Night had led to another day. It was gone dinner time and a bright summer's morning had clouded into a dreary afternoon. But neither sun nor cloud entered the birthing chamber and it remained constantly closeted in its sweltering darkness. The Lady Jennine was almost silent and almost unmoving. Sometimes she cried a little, and when the pains gripped her too deeply, she moaned and struggled. Alysson held her tight. They had brought her chicken gruel and a cup of strong beer, but although these were known as the best tonic for the pangs of birthing, Jennine had felt too ill to eat or drink. She had three times taken the medicines she was given, but this had done no good.

"When I was young," said Mistress Tenby, leaning over the bed attempting to serve the chicken gruel, "there were special charms spoken continuously over the bed, and herbs burned on the fire. Now they say these things are old fashioned, and even harmful. I don't believe it. If I knew the charms, I'd pronounce them myself."

"We don't need charms, we need prayers," muttered Mistress Barnes.

"Then who has a rosary? There must be a Bible in the castle? Does the lady have her own Book of Hours? Your ladyship, will you send for the priest?"

"For pity's sake," muttered Alysson, "no priest. Jennine will think he's come to read the final penance before she dies."

"Perhaps we should be prepared for that very thing."

"Hush, she'll hear you."

"Besides, it would be most improper having a man in this chamber now. And what's more, a man without any understanding of a woman."

"So he says."

It was close to supper time. Mistress Tenby drank the gruel prepared for Jennine. "Then do we save her ladyship, or the child? Do we call for the surgeon?"

Beatrice kneeled beside the expectant mother, bending over, her voice soft. "My lady, do you hear me? If you try to lie still, I think I can help. But there are risks, and it will hurt, maybe quite a lot. Will you let me try?"

"For pity's sake, do you think it doesn't hurt now?" Jennine stared up, bloodshot eyes and her mouth dry, lips split. "Do anything. Cut it out."

Alysson clasped her from behind, whispering in her ear. "Jenny, the baby's trying to come out feet first. But Beatrice may be able to pull it out anyway. Open your legs my dear, shut your eyes, breathe very deep, and pray."

"Shit praying," Jennine gasped, teeth clenched. "It's that bastard that did this to me. But I'll breathe till my breathing stops forever. Then look after the child for me if it lives. Promise me you will, dearest?"

"I promise. Try to push now, Jenny."

"One last thing, before it kills me." Jennine's voice faded, so faint Alysson barely heard. But she knew what was said. "Once I'm gone, my dear – be careful. Beware Humphrey."

Edward Sumerford was born just before ten of the clock on a hot summer's night in July, and from his first breath, yelled his fury at the indignities of birth. His two fat feet were red with pulling. He had finally emerged backwards, crushed toes first, and sucking his thumb. He was plunged into warm water, hurriedly washed, and then wrapped in the linen newly warmed by the fire. The cord at his navel was cut long and tied tight, the proper procedure for a boy. A wide strip of linen was bound around his middle to keep the knot in place, a padded bonnet was tied around his small squalling face to protect the fontanel and keep the brain warm. He was then shown briefly to the exhausted mother and was finally bustled into the countess's arms.

Her ladyship held her grandson and agreed, with faint surprise, that he was a fine size, his masculine equipment was impressive, his voice was lusty and he was undoubtedly handsome. "The tenth day of July. Excellent. A Sumerford should be born in the summer." She then quickly handed him back to Mistress Tenby, who swaddled him in more linen and laid him in the family crib.

"It's time to send for the wet nurse," Mistress Tenby announced. "I believe she's been waiting outside since first light today."

Beatrice and Alysson stayed beside the Lady Jennine. Beneath her eyes swelled purple bruises of exhaustion. She was bleeding heavily and becoming weaker, while the bedding, already ruined, would have to be changed right down to the mattress. The faint coppery smell of blood drifted through the sour stench of overheated sweat and the mustier perfumes of burning logs. But the relief was sublime. "I'm still alive," Jennine smiled, thick tongued, words tumbling. "Maybe only just. But breathing."

"You won't die now," said Alysson. "Probably never. You managed to live through all that, so now I imagine you can live through anything."

CHAPTER TWENTY-FOUR

"This is an honour indeed, my lord." Ilara curtsied lower than her joints normally permitted. "We were not expecting – we had no idea -"

"An honour beyond all expectations, and far beyond our merits, my lord." Dulce had recently returned from market, and still wore her cloak. Ludovic recognised the threadbare kersey Alysson had once worn. "But I pray there's nothing wrong, begging your pardon my lord?"

Ludovic frowned. "There's no occasion for concern. I came for only two reasons. Firstly, to be reassured as to your financial security. Secondly, regarding my search for the younger boy, Pagan." He took the stool offered but refused the cup of ale. "I've discovered no signs of the child, but before abandoning the search, I need to know whatever you remember of his disappearance."

Ilara fumbled with her apron. "My lord, almost nothing. We left," she blushed, unwilling now to repeat the circumstances, "in a hurry, as it were, to come to the castle with Alysson. Dulce told Pagan to stay here in the cottage. But I looked around and saw him following. I called, telling him to go home."

"But he didn't want to stay in the house on his own," Dulce said.

"Never did. Hated to be alone, poor lad. He was always timid. Not – the brightest of boys, you understand."

"When we came to the castle, I saw him run off into the shadows," Ilara continued. "It was late by then, and dark. I called out to him again but he didn't answer."

Dulce nodded. "We didn't want to be stopped by the guards, so we couldn't go after him. But I called once, before we crossed the moat. I told him to wait there for us, and then we'd all go home together."

"We never saw him again," whispered Ilara.

Ludovic sighed. "No help then. I have sent out men in every direction, and throughout both the castle itself, its grounds, and its surrounding estates. Now I believe the child will never be found. It seems likely he drowned. The banks of the moat can be dangerous, especially in the dark. I am sorry for it, but I see no further solution."

Ilara curtsied again, hesitating, unsure of her words. "It is – so personal of you, my lord – so untoward – and truly wonderful of your lordship to look at all, and to bother yourself with our affairs. The boy was a good child and sweet natured, and we loved him. But to you it must be of such insignificance. And now of course, so much time has passed."

"And as for ourselves, my lord," said Dulce, "we have never – not even when my dear husband was alive – been so comfortable. We have everything we need, and a good deal saved for the future. We have our own chickens, three geese, and two goats for milk and cheese. Now when I go to market, I go to buy and not to sell. What we make, we keep for our own necessities for we've no need of extra coin, which seems quite marvellous to us. The cottage is fully repaired, we have a new bed with a real mattress upstairs and a store of candles, pots and linen. Indeed, we consider ourselves quite wealthy with everything you supplied my lord, and now young Alysson's salary as well. She brings it to us each month on her day off, since she says she has no need of it herself, but secretly we save it for her. The new bed has more than one use, my lord, for we keep the extra coin under the mattress. It's a mighty good feeling, and all thanks to your lordship's great kindness and generosity."

"And now to come visiting us," murmured Ilara, overcome. "So wonderfully condescending, my lord. We are deeply honoured. And especially at a time such as this."

Ludovic looked blank. "At a time such as this?"

"Why, the birth of your precious little nephew, my lord. So exciting. It's a long time since a Sumerford was born at the castle. A boy too, a new heir indeed, and the whole village is speaking of it. The market was all a bustle this morning, and the folk are so excited."

"Good Lord," said Ludovic.

"And the little darling," Ilara nodded eagerly, "will you tell us, my lord, what is he like?"

"I haven't the faintest idea," said Ludovic in some amazement, "though I imagine he has the usual count of arms, legs and fingers, since no one has mentioned different. I have not personally seen the child."

The ladies looked disappointed. "Not seen him? Not sickly, I trust, my lord? Not kept away from folk?"

Ludovic shook his head, smiling faintly. "I believe he is decidedly robust, but I'm afraid it did not occur to me to look. Don't they all appear alike? Mistress Alysson will no doubt be able to satisfy your curiosity better when next she visits. I, on the other hand, have more absorbing interests and unless you have further questions, I shall now return to them."

He had come alone, riding briskly through the forest edges, thick in their summer leaf. He had almost expected to see the small blue light and hear the mournful whispers, but no ghosts followed him and he had neither seen nor heard it for some time. Ludovic, assuming that the search for the child's body, although it had failed, had been sufficient to send the soul on into its proper resting place, rode home satisfied.

Wild ducks had settled on the moat, casting no reflections in the torpid murk. No one had thought to shoot them since the castle stores were summer high and the pantries were full already of carcasses hung in their cool stone alcoves; venison, partridge, pheasant, swan and boar. So the ducks were permitted to live, bottoms up and heads down in sudden dark ripples, then flat footed and dabbling on the sun dried banks while preening their scrubby feathers.

Rising from the dull waters, the castle was ancient. Its massive stone, once pale, was now dark stained by the centuries. Across merlon and crenel, thick black streaks from turrets down to portcullis marked the passage of a thousand storms, then baked by four hundred summers. From the moat upwards crawled the moss and algae; green slime rising, black decay descending, pocked by gale and brine. There were two entrances. At the main entrance, guarded by gatehouses, the drawbridge crossed where the moat lay narrow, then ran beneath the rusted iron portcullis with its chains now too pitted to easily turn.

Once more, as often, Ludovic stopped first on the far bank, looking up to the Lady Jennine's quarters in the high eastern tower, blind windows echoing the passing clouds. His own chambers lay in the lower level of the western tower, but high enough to watch the sun sink its daily passions across the sea. It was Brice who inhabited the apartment above him. Those chambers could not be seen from the drawbridge or from the great outer courtyard and its stables. The western tower stood at the back, linked to the battlements built out over the escarpment, and far above the straggling beach and tumbling cliffs.

The moat's waters did not encircle the back, for here the castle rose direct from the rocks from which its stones had been cut, and instead of water and ditch, was protected by height. But to the north, east and south the moat widened, a sluggish defender, rich in the smells of stagnant waste, mildew and the decay of old forgotten creatures. It had once served as sewer as well as fish pond, but in past years a vast cess pit had been dug out at the back where rock met earth, and where the second entrance stood in narrow shadows. The fish and crabs caught from the moat however, though they were plentiful, were still served only to the staff and not to the carefully fastidious lords themselves.

Ludovic watched the ducks dip down to hunt beneath the surface, wondering what else the waters hid. Then he tightened his knees, rode across the drawbridge and was home. Back in his own chambers, he called for Clovis.

"This one last errand before I send you back to your uncle, brat. I doubt I need you any longer after this, but if I do, I can call for you."

"If I'm available to the call, that is," objected Clovis. "Might be at sea. Might be too busy."

Ludovic grinned. "In which case, I shall be out of luck. But no doubt I'll survive. Your usefulness is nearly over, urchin."

Clovis glowered. "That there penny a day were mighty useful, though."

Ludovic threw him a small leather purse, its strings tied tight. "I cannot imagine what for. You are somewhat young for strong liquors or wenching."

Clovis, neatly catching the thrown purse, turned his scowl to a snigger. "Just shows you don't know everyfing, don't it," he said. "But I ain't staying where I ain't wanted. So, till you finds out how much you miss me, m'lor, I'll bugger orf."

"I shall attempt not to miss you too soon," said Ludovic, "since I can now protect the lady myself, and to considerably more affect. Your information was helpful, however, hence the additional purse." He smiled, stretching his legs and crossing his ankles up on the low table before the hearth. "In the meantime, tell your uncle I'll finance one more trip before the winter sets in, and ask him to come and see me this evening for the usual arrangements."

"Taking risks, ain't we?" observed Clovis. "Having me, and now old Uncle Kenelm come open faced into your high and mighty castle, rubbing shoulders wiv nobility. Wot if he gets seen?"

"Unfortunately our business is fairly legal these days," said Ludovic. "Little need now for secrecy, which in any case has become too much of a Sumerford habit. I couldn't care less whether the good captain is seen or not. You, however, are another matter, since no one in his right mind would employ such an impudent whelp, and I've no desire to be thought insane. You have your coin now, so off with you. First bring the boy to me as instructed, then you can go home and give my message to your uncle."

"Cherubs," muttered Clovis on his way out. "Whole bloody family's moon-raved if you 'ast me."

The pageboy Clovis brought to Ludovic's solar, appeared indignant. Ludovic nodded for him to enter, and sent Clovis away. The boy, neat in his livery, bowed and stood before the empty hearth, awaiting orders. His bright red hair lay well combed across his small forehead. "Is it right, my lord that you wished to see me? Begging your pardon, but have I done something wrong, my lord?"

Ludovic looked him over. Not remarkable; a page like any other. Ten or twelve years perhaps, smart in a plain uniform kept scrupulously clean, his eyes respectfully lowered.

"Your name?"

"Remi, at your service, my lord."

"Very well," Ludovic said. "You are the boy I ordered to take Mistress Alysson back to the Lady Jennine's quarters a little more than a month back?"

"My lord?" The page, unsure, bowed again. He kept his gaze on the Turkey rug and his polished brown shoes. "It's a long time ago, sir. I remember doing so once. I hope – no one – has complained of me, my lord. I did nothing wrong."

Ludovic regarded him in patient silence. "No one has complained," Ludovic finally said. "On the contrary. Mistress Alysson has informed me that she was attacked. You distracted her attacker. She is – particularly grateful." He paused, watching the page hang his head, not daring to look up. "Tell me," Ludovic continued, very quiet, "who attacked Mistress Alysson and yourself?"

The boy bowed again, shoulders slumped. "No one, my lord. That is, I couldn't see. It was dark. Very dark, my lord. He – the person ran off. I don't know who he was."

"But you know this no one was a man?"

"My lord, surely so?" The page glanced up, saw the cold anger in Ludovic's eyes, and stared back again at his toes. "Forgive me, my lord. I do not know. I was not hurt. No one was hurt, I swear."

"Come here," said Ludovic softly. He went.

Ludovic swung his legs to the ground and sat forwards. "Kneel. And undo your shirt," he commanded. The child bent on one knee beside him and unlaced the little starched opening of his broadcloth doublet. Beneath it, his shirt was open at the neck. The long scars still gleamed pale, curling up from the child's chest and around the shoulder, then almost to the chin. "It would seem," murmured Ludovic, "that this nobody hurt you indeed."

The boy slumped down, relacing his shirt. "I had forgotten, my lord."

"Indeed? Is it such a common occurrence, you can forget injuries which still leave their marks after a month?

"Forgive me, my lord. I – I'll report to Master Hamnet for punishment, my lord."

Ludovic raised an eyebrow. "You have lied to me and are lying still, but I do not intend to punish you." He leaned forward, stretching one long finger to the boy's chin. "Look at me. Now, why lie? Who are you protecting?"

"No one, my lord. I beg you, I cannot say, my lord."

With a sigh, Ludovic leaned back. "Relax, child. If you've been ordered to silence by someone whose authority exceeds my own, I cannot hold you to blame. Mistress Alysson informs me you attempted to protect her, taking the assault meant for her. You should be rewarded, not punished. But I should like to know the truth."

The boy hung his head again, saying nothing.

Ludovic dismissed him and went at once to find the earl. The occasions on which he purposefully sought out his father being rare, the Earl of Sumerford was somewhat taken aback. He was inspecting the new coat his tailor had presented for examination before the final trimmings, and turned from the mirror, regarding his youngest son with mild surprise.

"Ludovic, is it not?" he said, shrugging out of the wealth of damask and passing the coat to the tailor, who departed hurriedly. "Yes, you seem vaguely familiar. My son, I believe. Though of course, one can never be sure."

Ludovic bowed, a little stiff. "Since, of all your sons, I resemble you the most, I imagine you can rest assured of my parentage, sir, if not my character."

"Sadly, sadly." The earl leaned against the window, elbow to the small ledge, his deep golden hair lit by sunbeams. "But since I imagine the wearisome journey from your quarters to mine cannot have been undertaken on a mere whim, I await news of the disaster which is undoubtedly about to befall us."

Ludovic, although not invited, sat on the nearest uncushioned chair. He stretched his legs and looked up at his father. "I see you are preparing for the morrow's baptism, sir. Have you seen the child?"

The earl's eyes narrowed. "I am beginning to fear for your sanity, my boy. Clearly your unsavoury cavorting with chamber maids has addled what little brain remains to you. But yes, the infant has been presented to me, briefly, which I considered more than sufficient. Since you are undoubtedly too cautious to risk setting eyes on the new Sumerford heir yourself, I can inform you that the child undeniably has two eyes, an unappealing bump of a nose and a very large mouth of absurd proportions. The noise it makes is, I am assured against all evidence, quite normal. I imagine it has all the other usual accoutrements, but since it was wrapped like a pupae in the cocoon, I cannot guarantee anything further. Are you satisfied, my son?"

Ludovic smiled. "A fully witnessed description was not quite what I had in mind, sir. No doubt I shall see the infant eventually, and in the meantime I can, I believe, control my natural curiosity. In fact, it was Humphrey I wished to talk about. I intended to lead the conversation from – child to father."

The earl raised an eyebrow. "Unnecessary, Ludovic. Although my age is admittedly considerable, I believe I can still tell the difference."

"In which case," continued Ludovic, unperturbed, "perhaps you can satisfy my curiosity regarding the father, rather than the son. I have not seen Humphrey since we returned from London, which in itself is unusual. Is he well, sir?"

The earl sighed. "Undoubtedly Sumerford is a castle of many corridors and passages, my son, which tend to remain unlit. Naturally I sympathise. Clearly you have forgotten the way to your elder brother's apartments, or perhaps you are simply nervous concerning the hidden corners. I shall send a page to escort you in safety to Humphrey's chambers and assist your ailing memory."

"You know," sighed Ludovic, "it is quite exhausting talking to you sometimes, sir." He paused, but his father said nothing, so he continued. "Admittedly I might have made a more personal inquiry as to Humphrey's health. But I am accustomed to seeing him over the dinner table at least, and the fact that he's been so long absent somewhat escaped my notice. If anything, it seemed an advantage. However, I thought you might know something of his present situation. No matter. Presumably he will be present at his own son's baptism, and I shall see him tomorrow."

"I am edified, my boy," said his father. "I presume this means you've the intention of gracing the occasion yourself. I did, I remember, command your attendance, but compliance is never a natural assumption with any of my offspring." The earl sat abruptly and heavily on the window seat beside him. "It may be of some interest to you, Ludovic, since you appear to be so particularly concerned for your family at present, to know that I always considered myself fortunate to have sired sons. I was naturally prepared, especially considering your mother's predisposition at all times to ignore my known wishes, for the disappointing responsibility of siring only daughters. But your mother showed unusual perspicacity and eventually produced not only the required male heir, but three other sons, these latter being of at least average intelligence. However, over the years I have had occasion to regret the very circumstances which once pleased me. A daughter, although of little interest in all other ways, would have been remarkably convenient for forming alliances through marriage, and although the business of the dower would certainly have been a disadvantage, I feel the gaining of powerful allies would have proved an acceptable compensation. And daughters are, if nothing else, obedient. Certainly, if they are not, there is an easy solution." The earl sighed, clasping his hands on his velvet lap. "Instead, my eldest son, perhaps too long in the womb and therefore tarnished with his mother's woeful lack of brains, is hardly the heir I had anticipated. My second son now shows a complete disinterest in my exhausting efforts to find him a suitable wife, and disappears as frequently as he may, on business which he refuses to disclose. My third son is dangerously loose witted and

224

threatens to bring the entire family to the block for treason. What is more, I suspect him of being either pederast or buffoon. My fourth son is, to the shame of the Sumerford dignity, entangled with loose women from the gutter, and shows neither sense of duty to his father, nor common sense of any other kind. At least, I am led to believe, he has temporarily refrained from the business of dangerous and illegal smuggling."

Ludovic jumped. "I beg your pardon, sir?"

"Pardons are the currency of priests and kings, my boy, as you should know." The earl yawned. "I have never seen fit to exonerate either the errant or the plaintive, and have no intention of starting now. In the meantime, I can inform you that your eldest brother has indeed been somewhat unwell. The usual complaint, but exacerbated by the family's absence, the warnings of royal displeasure, and the matter of his unborn child. Now that the infant is birthed, living and robust, with his wife promising to return to health in the immediate future, dear Humphrey is beginning to feel somewhat recovered. I expect him to attend his son's baptism tomorrow."

Everything that Ludovic had intended saying had gone. He nodded, rose, and with a slight bow, left his father's chambers.

CHAPTER TWENTY-FIVE

"The last of them entered the chapel a few moments ago," said Alysson, running in breathless and slamming the door behind her. "There's the whole family in there now."

"Well, I should hope so," Jennine objected. "Going through all that horror for a child no one was interested in, would have driven me either to murder or suicide. At least the brat is wanted by somebody."

"But it seems a shame you can't be part of the celebrations yourself," said Alysson. "How mean, when the mother can't hold her own child at its Christening."

Jennine giggled. "Forty days until I'm permitted to enter sanctified premises. Still thirty-seven to go. The holy portals are barred to the unclean, and a bleeding woman must by all means be restrained from polluting the shrines. As if I care. Ecclesiastics all have dirty minds."

"I always felt it so unfair," Alysson nodded, "for God to design us this way, and then call us unclean for being like it."

"It's the men, my dear. Priests are terrified of women. Frankly, I've always believed my bodily functions to be purely my own business, but bishops dislike anyone having business they can't poke their noses into. If I ever meet up with God, which seems somewhat unlikely, I shall pass on your complaints and ask Him to consider changing things." Jennine smiled. "But I expect it'll be Lucifer I curl up with forever in the hereafter, who I'm sure will take us exactly as we are, without objections. And what's more, if I'm considered too wicked for the resurrection, then that's fine with me too. What's there to come back for?"

"At least you do seem to feel considerably better now," Alysson observed. "Three days ago I thought you might – well never – be the same again."

"I am not the same again," said Jennine. "My body has been ravaged, my breasts are sore and swollen, I'm constantly exhausted, there's usually a squalling brat in some adjacent chamber reminding me of my ordeal, my belly sags and is creased with vile pink marks – and I am bleeding and therefore considered unclean. I always knew childbirth would be death of me, and I was nearly right."

"He's very sweet," said Alysson.

"He's a screwed up little turd," said Jennine. "At least, thank God for one small mercy, I am not expected to have much to do with the child. You like him – you take him."

"One day he'll inherit everything. All the wealth, the castle, the lands, and the title too. Doesn't that make you feel proud?"

"As long as I'm still around and can encourage him to spend most of it on me. But no doubt the brat will take after his father. When he grows up a little and shows some character, I shall see. If he inherits my character instead, then maybe I shall start to take an interest."

Alysson shook her head. "You can't tell things like that for years and years. Unless – forgive me – but if the child is a little simple – like his father – then I suppose that will show itself early."

"You are becoming sadly simple yourself, my dear," said Jennine, hitching herself up against the heaped pillows behind her. "You cannot really think –," she paused, watching Alysson's expression, then smiled again, "– no, perhaps not so simple after all." She laughed. "You know, don't you, my pet?"

"You more or less told me long ago," admitted Alysson. "So – whose son is he?"

"No, no, my love." Jennine reached out for the cup of warmed hippocras beside the bed and regarded her maid through the steam. "That's something I intend keeping to myself and even the father doesn't know for sure, though he may guess of course. But no matter. Rest assured, the child will grow up with a family likeness and flaming hair. But not dear Humphrey's brains."

"It – wasn't," Alysson lowered her gaze, "Ludovic? Was it?"

"It should have been." Jennine's smile widened. "I chose him first, but he didn't come to the lure." She drained her cup and waved it at Alysson for refilling. "Jealous, my dear?"

"Why should I be?"

"He liked me that was clear enough. I chose him at once as the best looking of them all and I'm perfectly positive he wanted me, was avid in fact, for I saw all the signs. I know men and read them easily. Dear Ludovic was almost hooked. But something stopped him."

"Decency," suggested Alysson. "Honesty. You were affianced to his brother."

"What a little simpleton you are after all, my dear." Jennine turned away, irritated. "No one in this family has any understanding of decency, honesty, kindness or restraint. Which is why I fit here so comfortably. Ludovic was suspicious, perhaps. I do not care, and have not bothered to analyse his motives. But rest assured, decency did not enter his mind."

Alysson scowled. "He's being – decent – with me."

"You mean, he's not called to see you, not enquired after your health, made no contact at all since his rushed departure a month ago, and has not even sent a message of congratulations regarding this wretched child." Jennine tittered. "Decency, my dear? I believe complacent disinterest nearer the mark. And you – for all your denials – feel neglected, unattractive, are pining with your silly tail between your silly thighs, and dream each night of passion, even though you've not the slightest understanding of the word."

"I know exactly what it means. And I don't want it. I want caring and kindness. And decency."

"Put in a little effort for once, and try attracting the man you want. Then perhaps passion will eventually lead to kindness."

Alysson shrugged. "How? I never even see him. He doesn't want me."

Jennine sat forward, once more irritated. Her shoulders ached. "Alysson, I swear I shall slap you if you persist in this nonsense. I've told you already what to do, and in some detail too. First of all the simple things that most women manage, like biting your lips to make them look pink and swollen. Dampening your shift so your skirts cling to your thighs and hips. Pinching your nipples to make them stand out tight and push up through your clothes. I've even bought you the finest linen chemise and an expensive silk gown, exactly the softest materials to show off your breasts. And all you do is hitch up the neckline, like some silly miss keeping herself pure for the convent. Do what I tell you, and I'll give you all the time off you need for wandering these damned cold corridors until you bump into your boring Sir Galahad. I shall send you on errands into the main hall, give you messages to take to the steward, anything to make sure you meet the man. But you have to show him you're available. Which you are, if only you'd admit it. You're a bitch on heat, with no mutt to sniff at your rump."

Alysson opened her mouth, decided the words would be unwise, and flounced off to tidy up the garderobe. Confined interminably to her bed, Jennine remained fractious, her body sore and throbbing. Sometimes Alysson avoided her, sometimes, since she was the only one capable of such endeavours, strived to cheer her up.

Two days after the Christening the infant settled into the nursery wing below with the wet nurse, three day nurses and two night nurses. Washed, swaddled, well fed and fast asleep, the small Edward was carried upstairs to his mother's bedside each evening for a brief inspection. Jennine smiled with carefully practised motherly condescension, patted the child's head until warned not to do so for fear of the infant's cranial vulnerability, pronounced herself thoroughly satisfied, and sent it quickly away again. Humphrey, it was murmured, visited the nursery far more often, greatly intrigued by his son. He liked to poke, liked to hear the small whuffling noises which he claimed to understand ("He likes me") and was eager with questions. In particular he wished to know when the child would be able to play with him. He seemed a little disappointed by the answer, but continued to visit. He also began again to visit his wife. The forty days church enforced abstention evidently did not occur to either of them.

It was raining when Humphrey came early to Jennine's quarters, clutching a handful of wet daisies and grasses he had picked from between the stable cobbles. He beamed, first at Alysson and then at his wife. Jennine was lying on the bed, though uncovered, her chemise hitched to her knees and low across her breasts as she talked to her maid. Humphrey presented her with his bouquet. Jennine sat up, waving at Alysson. "My dear, you can go. I shall be busy, it seems." She regarded the wilted weeds with appropriate delight. "How sweet. How considerate. Humphrey darling, just wait one moment." And again to Alysson. "Take the day off and go visit your funny old nurses. Come back tomorrow morning but don't be late. Hurry now, off, off. It's a hot day and no need for a cloak."

"It's raining."

"Oh, very well, go get your cloak. Now away with you, until tomorrow."

Alysson wandered across the great open courtyard towards the drawbridge. She wore her tippet up to cover her little headdress, but the rain was just a sparkle, barely strong enough to wet her shoulders. Some of the horses were being led from their stables by their grooms; trotting on their lead reins across the cobbles. The earl's massive grey destrier stopped suddenly, hooves solid to the stone. Alysson paused, watching, breathing the hot sour smell of fresh manure, listening to the snorting of the horses, bridles jingling and the grooms laughing. But Turvey had no intention of exercising in the rain. The groom leading the beast was immediately nervous, coaxing but no longer insisting. Then Turvey was led carefully back to his stall. Alysson watched the departing rump, the flick of the long plaited tail, the twitch of the haunches tall as the groom's shoulder, and the hooves, thick fringed in coarse white hair, the hooves that had killed her brother.

She did not look back at the castle once she had left its great spreading shadow, hurrying into the sunshine and the bright grassy slopes. She headed south towards the forest. Gazing back at the south tower, domain of the countess, would show her only the casement windows long since enlarged from the original arrow slits, with no glimpse of the western tower behind, where Ludovic's apartments looked away across the sea.

A rainbow arched half way over the first forest beeches, indistinct in its plush pastels with the sky shining through. Alysson ducked beneath the low branches. The perfumes of growth replaced the tired castle smells of stables and old soot, damp, dirt, kitchens and scrubbing, stagnant waters and close living. The forest smelled of hope and happiness, loam, leaf and flower. The ground was a little muddy and the rain drops spattered, caught first on greenery before collecting weight, rolling from twig to frond and then collapsing to the soggy mulch below. The branches were open, beryl leaf flutter letting through the light.

Alysson, enjoying freedom, did not hurry. Then she heard the footsteps. The faint squelch of someone following, surreptitious and very quiet, but the softened undergrowth made little noise and Alysson's own steps were almost soundless too. She looked around but saw no one. Many people wandered the woods, collecting faggots, wild herbs and berries in season, or grazing their animals. She continued, and the echo kept pace. When she stopped, curious and staring back through the trees, the other steps ceased too.

Then whispers; breath turned into unknown words. A voice of threat without meaning. More footsteps crackling on dead leaf, the slurp of mud and a low laugh.

She hurried at once, half skipping, soft shoes slipping where the mud was thicker, her hems splattered with flecks of wet earth, careful not to tear her livery on thorns or trip on creepers, but suddenly frightened and eager to get far away. But whoever followed could go as fast, and did, the sounds increasing with less need for secrecy and no more care for caution.

Skirting the forest edges back to her own cottage would take longer. Yet crossing directly through the trees to shorten the distance, would bring her into thicker shade and further from help should she need it. Alysson paused again. The following crunch of feet in the undergrowth stopped abruptly. She held her breath although she was already breathless, and called, challenging. The answer came at once.

"You know who, girl. Who you have met already before."

She did not recognise the voice, which was gruff, and somehow clumsy. "Why not give a name?" She backed a little, ready to turn and run.

"Ain't it considered unlucky to name the devil?" Half a laugh, half smothered, as if disguising its owner. "Or call me destiny, come to claim my victim."

Alysson ran. The arm came around her neck, hauling her back. She tripped over large boots and fell face down in the mud. It felt as though the wetness came up to meet her and swallow her. A huge weight sank onto her back, someone sitting astride her and bending his face to her ear. Her ribs, pressed into the yielding ground, felt smashed, knocked breathless. "Well little fawn, it's been a good hunt. Now let's get you ready for the pot."

Large sweaty hands grabbed her flailing arms, wrenching contrary to the joints of her elbows and forcing her hands hard up behind her neck. Alysson felt something snap, and screamed. "Too rough, little doe? Never mind. That won't matter in the end."

If she lost consciousness, she thought quickly, she would be unable to fight. Her mind raced. She stopped struggling, saving breath, and slumped, eyes shut. Then she waited for her captor to relax. Her wrists were caught in only one of his hands. The other began to roam. He felt down her back, ranging across her hips and buttocks, slipping down over the coarse broadcloth of her gown, feeling her thighs beneath, stretching to the hem of her skirts, ready to raise them. Busy, abstracted, assuming she had fainted, his hold on her hands had loosened.

She flung herself sideways, hands free, then rolled and kicked with all her force. Her assailant fell, tumbling and losing his grip in surprise. Alysson raked, ten little square nails down the face in front of her. He roared, swung one fist and knocked her back. She rebounded and bit, her teeth snapping tight on his nose. She gagged on coarse damp skin, but held on. The man roared again and lurched away, striking her with his fist once more across the side of her head. Her ear rang, hollowed echoes and then suddenly deaf. She kicked, aimed for his groin, caught his knee instead, and as he yelped, sprang up and tried to run.

He was much taller and twice as fast. Her scrambling legs wobbled. Again his arm came around her neck, forcing her hard back against his chest. He wore leather, not velvet, but she had recognised Humphrey, his beard a huge red brush and his eyes pale blue glass. She brought her leg back between his own and this time found his groin.

Roaring, he let her go, and kicked. His boots were huge, and he continued kicking. Winded and prone now on the wet ground, she saw her own blood ooze across her eyes, smelled it in her nostrils and tasted it thick and hot in her mouth. Different pains merged into one violent agony. As he bent over her again, she grabbed for his moustache, gripping the thick red curls. She clutched a handful of frizz as he wrenched away, cursing, and kicked her once more. The toe of his boot cracked against her ribs. She yelped. She had no breath left for larger sounds.

Alysson was losing consciousness when she heard his last words. Still partially deafened, the voice sounded strangely distant and lost within its own smudged echoes, but she knew what he said as he strode off through the trees, stamping on brambles and twigs and muttering to himself. "Too much of a mess now. It won't do no use no more. But next time, slut, I'll have you. Just wait. For there'll be a next time."

The little dithering silver rain continued to fall, and the sunshine pooled over the grass between the leaf shadows, sparkling into a thousand refracted reflections within a thousand tiny raindrops. Alysson lay on her side, knees curled up to her belly, but the pain seemed to belong to a body far away and quite removed from her own. She could not feel herself, or know what injuries she had sustained, but she watched her own blood wash past her eyes before she closed them.

CHAPTER TWENTY-SIX

It was black night when she opened her eyes, and winced, breathing shallow. The pain took her by surprise and it was a long time, confused and rummaging in her memory for explanations, before she realised what had happened and where she was.

As memory returned, the pains which circulated throughout her body concentrated in three specific places. Worst was her head and face, then just below one elbow where she thought her arm might be broken. Lastly her ribs on one side, surely cracked. She also realised no one would be looking for her. Jennine had dismissed her for the night, while, since this was not her regular monthly day off, Ilara and Dulce would not be expecting her. She would have to crawl to the cottage, and hoped she might arrive by dawn. Her nurses were far closer now than the castle was, and the comfort they would surely offer was far more enticing. They would be unable to protect her should that become necessary, but Humphrey himself would be back at the castle.

At first she was unable to rise, but eventually, crawling with both knees and one hand, she began to find her way through the trees. The night was dark but a sliver of moon puddled its silent silver across leaf and ground, and Alysson had lived too long beside these woods not to know her path. She stopped frequently, sitting back to catch her breath and clear her head. The pain came like the tides, rolling in from some unknown and distant shore, swamping her entirely before ebbing. When the tides receded a little, sinking back into memory, then she crawled on.

Dulce found her curled unconscious on the doorstep as first dawn peeped up behind the trees. Her screeches brought Ilara rushing out, and Alysson opened her eyes. The two women half carried her inside, and eventually, with difficulty, took her upstairs to the grand new bed they had recently bought. Alysson collapsed onto the softly yielding feather mattress, closed her eyes again with a small moan, and went to sleep.

The Lady Jennine was annoyed when her favoured maid did not return in the morning as instructed. With little idea of where Alysson lived, Jennine waited. By dinner time she was furious, while quietly wondering if her own moods and demands had antagonised too far, and if Alysson had left for good. She inquired of her other staff but no one knew or cared where the spoiled personal maid had gone. The three older women were secretly glad, for it left more opportunities for them. Luxurious clothes, closeted discussions, private walks and special treats had only been enjoyed by Alysson in the past, but in her absence might now be shared amongst many.

Jennine summoned a page to discover Alysson's home, ready to send a message of bitter dismissal, then a concerned inquiry as to the reasons for the disappearance, and finally a plea to return. But she changed her mind on each, deciding it more dignified to ignore the whole situation. She would not care. Her personal maid was no longer employed, and if she ever dared return, would be thrashed and sent running. In the meantime the lady kept silent, and seethed.

Then three days later a message came from Ludovic. An invitation for Mistress Alysson to visit his quarters at two of the clock that afternoon, once more a respectable time, with a request to discuss matters of interest to them both. Jennine hopped out of bed, regarded the page with imperious anger, and stamped her foot.

She sent her own message back to the youngest Sumerford. Mistress Alysson was no longer in her employ. The girl had chosen to take a prolonged and unauthorised absence without even an explanation or excuse. She would never be accepted back. The subject was closed.

Ludovic received this news with considerable surprise. He reflected a moment, and then promptly changed his clothes for riding gear. Hat in hand and buckling on his short sword, he strode down to the stables and ordered his courser saddled. Within an hour of discovering Alysson's disappearance, he was deep within the forest shade. It was a bright and early morning but the summer foliage was thick and the sunbeams found fewer open angles. The bird song, busy and insistent, continued from somewhere beyond the green canopy.

Someone else's horse was already tethered outside the cottage by the time Ludovic arrived and the small door had been left slightly open. He walked in, announcing himself clearly, but remained unheard. There was a good deal of noisy chatter coming from above so he found the stairs, a creaking set of uneven wooden steps crouched in the back shadows, unbanistered and unstable. He strode up them.

With the only other two items of furniture being a small crooked stool and a large wooden coffer, the bed took most of the floor space, an ancient palliasse, its tester proudly striped in blue and green and tasselled in pink. The counterpane was dishevelled. Alysson, half prone in the bed, slumped against an assortment of lumpy bolsters and pillows at her back. To one side, candle in hand, stood a man Ludovic vaguely recognised as the only practising local medik. Dulce and Ilara stood at the bed head. The window, being small, let in limited light but the candle flared and showed Alysson's face as flushed, feverish and strangely marked. She turned at once as Ludovic appeared at the top of the stairs, but then turned away.

"What exactly," Ludovic said, one eyebrow raised, "is going on?"

"Oh, my lord," said the young man with evident relief, "I am most particularly pleased to see you, my lord. If somewhat surprised, begging your pardon. May I have the honour to speak to your lordship for a moment downstairs?"

Ludovic nodded, but continued watching Alysson. "Well, child," he said quietly, "will you tell me yourself?"

Alysson gulped, voice faint. "Afterwards. Talk to the doctor first, if you will."

Downstairs again in the one cramped chamber, light streaming in through the open door, Ludovic questioned the village doctor. "But the women will not explain, my lord," the young man said, blowing out the candle and setting the stub on the table. "And in spite of my insistence, no one will inform me how the accident occurred. They refuse to answer my questions, but it was a brutal attack, I am sure of it, since no ordinary tumble could have produced such injuries. The young woman has a broken arm, at least three ribs also broken, as you have seen she is much bruised and cut about, and there may yet prove to be internal damage. I have straightened and strapped her arm, while the women have washed and bandaged her other wounds and applied some ointments of their own. I have prescribed a tonick of willow bark for the pain, and have taken blood once, but am loth to do so again since the young woman is very weak. She is being fed a nutritious milk diet, and will surely recover in time. But she must stay in bed for a month at least."

"Alum, for the wounds?" inquired Ludovic.

"These are humble people, my lord, and I doubt they could afford it."

"But I could," said Ludovic. "You may now consider yourself employed by me."

"Doctor Manders at your service. I have served your esteemed father from time to time in the past, my lord."

"Well Doctor Manders, you will now hurry to the village apothecary and order a supply of alum salves. As it happens, I have very good reason to know the man's recently taken in a new supply. You will also obtain anything else you prescribe as appropriate, without consideration for cost. You will return here promptly. Tomorrow I may arrange to have Mistress Alysson transferred to the castle for further treatment, but in the meantime you will visit her here. I expect her to be cured as soon as possible."

The doctor frowned. "Broken bones, my lord – it is not usually -"

"Cured," said Ludovic curtly. "As soon as possible." He then turned his back on the doctor and once again climbed the stairs.

Dulce and Ilara were attempting to tidy the bedcovers, tucking Alysson's small lumps and bumps into a neat and invisible confinement. Ludovic smiled at them. "If you will allow the impropriety," he said, "I wish to speak to Mistress Alysson alone. The doctor will probably return within the hour, and I shall be down before that to discuss the situation with you. But perhaps, first -?"

With much curtsying they scuttled downstairs while Alysson and Ludovic stared warily at each other. Ludovic abruptly sat on the edge of the bed, gazing through the gloomy shadows. "I suppose," murmured Alysson, "Jenny's furious with me, but I don't care. Ilara was going to walk all the way to the castle to explain what happened, but she's old and tired so I told her to wait till later. Jenny must be spitting daggers."

"What that woman does is of no conceivable interest to me," said Ludovic. "Now tell me, child, how did this happen?"

Alysson took a slow and deeply exhaled breath. "Once when I told you I was attacked, you didn't believe me."

"The proof this time would be rather hard to dismiss," said Ludovic. "And stop turning away. If you imagine I'm squeamish about a few lacerations and bruises, then you underestimate me as usual." He smiled and took her hand in his, resting on the old woollen counterpane. Her other hand was concealed within a large sling, her arm heavily bandaged. "Now, while I concede it to be no specific business of mine, I should like an explanation," he continued. "How did this happen? How serious are the injuries? How do you feel? And who was it?"

The covers were pulled up almost to Alysson's chin, although the day was exceedingly warm, but what was visible seemed almost entirely disguised. Her head was thickly bandaged around the top of her skull, as though she wore a round white turban. Her hair, bedraggled and partly pulled back, did not quite hide the huge weals and scratches around her neck. Without the doctor's candle, the light was poor, but Ludovic could clearly see the destruction of Alysson's face. One eye was swollen, the lid closed and darkened. Beneath the eye a series of scars ran open down her face, though smudged with layers of ointment. The cheekbone was blackened with bruises, and the right side of her mouth was cut, the lips blood caked and puffy. Her nose was also swollen and deeply marked with small grazes and cuts, the nostrils ripped on both sides. Her left cheekbone bore another huge bruise, yellowing through the purple. She appeared to find breathing difficult and her voice lapsed into gasps, indicating a throat too sore to speak. The one small hand that Ludovic held was roughened and cut across the back and fingers, and he knew her other arm was broken. He said nothing and waited for her reply.

Eventually she shook her head, though that seemed to hurt her. "I did see who he was. But you won't believe me."

"Because I disbelieved you before? You think it was Humphrey?"

"I pulled out a handful of his hair. I couldn't mistake him."

Ludovic said, "So as before, you tried to defend yourself? You attacked him in return? Would the signs be fairly evident?"

"Yes," said Alysson at once. "I did what little I could. I scratched him a lot and pulled his hair out. I bit his nose, hard. It bled. If you saw him, you'd know."

Ludovic sighed, leaning back. "I have seen him. For the past three days, Humphrey has been quite evident at all times. He is fat and complacent as usual, delighted with his son, and pleased to spend time again with his once more restructured wife. He eats, he belches, he sings the infant lullabies. He shows not a mark nor a bruise. He is completely unscathed."

Alysson stared. "That's not possible."

"Answer my other questions," Ludovic said. "How did this happen?"

Alysson's perplexity turned to scowl, exacerbated by bruises. "I feel wonderful. Nothing is in the least serious. I tripped over a twig and fell down on my way here three days ago. That's all. Nothing else. And I don't want to go back to the castle and I don't want to see you ever again."

Ludovic smiled widely. "How inconvenient," he said, "since I have every intention of seeing a great deal of you, and will probably arrange to take you back to the castle tomorrow."

"I won't go."

"You are hardly in a position to resist," Ludovic pointed out. "I just need to decide whether to settle you back in Jennine's apartments, or install you in mine."

Alysson gulped. "Jenny won't have me. And I don't want you."

"I could put matters right with Jennine easily enough," Ludovic pondered. "But I doubt there's a place for anyone to be properly nursed there, apart from the lady herself, with the nursery quarters below and the infant already stealing most of the attention. In fact, Jennine wouldn't welcome you until you've recovered sufficiently, which seems fair enough. On the other hand, much as I should like to keep you to myself, and my own rooms are certainly large and comfortable enough, it would set up a deal of gossip which might prove a nuisance." His smile had spread to a grin. "However, since I always imagined I'd take you as my mistress sooner or later, it might as well be sooner."

"You can't. I won't. I'll scream."

"As it happens, the western tower is quite well isolated from the rest of the personal quarters," Ludovic said. "The only ones who would hear your screams would be Brice and the seagulls. Neither would take the slightest bit of notice, I promise."

Alysson opened her mouth in fury and then paused, thinking. "You're only teasing," she decided. "I look frightful. You wouldn't want to touch me. And since you're calling me a liar, I don't want you."

"I might consider waiting for you to recover from the first attack before instigating my own."

"I don't believe you could even think about – what you're thinking about – for months and months, the way I must look."

"On the contrary," smiled Ludovic, and leaned over and kissed her lightly on her left cheek where the swelling was slight, but the bruise spread large. "I find you charmingly – different," he said. "And can quite easily contemplate – almost anything. However, although my father seems convinced I already have you regularly in my bed, it might not be the most tactful moment to establish it as the truth. I shall have to consider the options."

"I won't go to Jenny's," Alysson said. "Apart from not being wanted,

241

I won't go anywhere near Humphrey. And I'm not a parcel to stay wherever you put me."

"You would certainly need to be guarded, "Ludovic admitted. "And my own personal protection would be the best, since anything else has been sadly deficient up until now. But I'm not sure of the ideal way to achieve it." He smiled, taking up her hand again. "Perhaps I should take you to Bedfordshire."

"Good gracious," said Alysson. "Where's that?"

Ludovic shook his head. "No, I can hardly expect you to travel so far in this condition. The doctor would never allow it. But something must be done."

"I can stay here." Alysson pulled her hand away.

"But I can't," Ludovic said, "and I need you close. I need to keep you under watch, and besides, the medical attention you'll get at the castle would be far superior. I might even be able to arrange for your odd little nurses to come and help look after you, though I do wish they'd stop being so damned grateful. Each time I see them, they're so confoundedly humble and honoured, it's exhausting."

"You know," Alysson said, "apart from all the money you've showered on them, they've a very good reason to be grateful." He once again reached for her hand but she quickly tucked it away under the covers. "Now the great Ludovic Sumerford has been seen visiting here a few times, the locals are quite in awe of Ilara, and have taken her to their hearts."

Ludovic raised an eyebrow. "I'm glad to have been of service."

"More than you realise," smiled Alysson. The smile appeared distorted, her right eye remaining closed in a permanent wink, and the smile curling only at the left side of her mouth. "There's now a good deal of local gossip regarding romantic assignations and the possibility of you making Ilara an autumn bride."

Ludovic blinked in stupefaction. "Me?" he said blankly. "And your nurse?"

Alysson managed to nod. "They seem to think the nobility capable of anything. And clearly they're quite right. Of course, they believe you're all somehow next to the saints and the angels, but they never expect any of you to behave normally."

Ludovic regarded the patient with amazed suspicion. "I refuse to believe a word of it," he said. "And although your nurses may be uncomfortably over-honoured at my presence, you, brat, are not nearly honoured enough. And I warn you, once I've decided exactly what to do with you and where to put you, you will go where I say and behave with suitable obedience." He leaned over again, rearranging Alysson's pillows in a more comfortable manner and readjusting the bed cover. He saw her wince as he straightened the blanket, his hand brushing against the sling that held her right arm. "Feeling dreadful, my dear?" he said, leaning back again. "The doctor will be here with better medicines shortly, and in the meantime I shall be off to organise your return to the castle. Our tame medik there is extremely efficient, better I'm sure than any local barber." He sat a moment, watching her, then stood. "I shall be back tomorrow," he said. "Until then, little one, you'll be quite safe, I promise."

Once again downstairs he smiled at the two bobbing women, explained about the doctor and his own immediate intentions, and left quietly. He was not smiling at all as he rode slowly back to the castle.

The page in the corridor outside bowed quickly, and opened the door. Ludovic strolled in, smiled widely at the lady spread on the deep cushioned settle, feet up and head supported by pillows, and nodded briefly, the semblance of a bow. "It is of course most improper of me to visit you here alone, my lady, especially since you are – let us say – confined to your chamber after the rigours of childbirth. But I've an idea you are more than averagely unshockable."

The lady sat up hurriedly and smiled with a slight simper. "My lord. An honour."

Ludovic closed the door sharply behind him. He stood by the hearth, one elbow to the mantle and one boot to the iron grate. He took a leisurely and slightly impertinent look around the chamber before slowly returning his gaze to the lady. "I believe we have a few matters of interest to discuss," he said.

CHAPTER TWENTY-SEVEN

The countess gasped, one fluttering and outraged hand to the stiffened stomacher just below her heart. "Ludovic, you are clearly suffering from sunstroke if not a fevered dysentery. Do you seriously expect me to house a maidservant in one of the available bedchambers, as if a respected guest of the family?"

Ludovic smiled, though his eyes showed neither warmth nor compliance. "It is precisely what I expect, Madam. My suggestion may seem unprecedented, but the girl's origins are respectable enough, being the orphaned daughter of an alderman. Indeed, under the circumstances I believe some form of aid is due her from the Sumerford estate. You will no doubt remember something of her past experiences with this family. Her brother, apprenticed here as a groom, was killed by my father's battle charger. Her younger brother disappeared somewhere on these premises, presumed drowned. She herself discovered me when I was attacked in the forests last year, and was particularly instrumental in my recovery. She has been satisfactorily employed here for many months as the Lady Jennine's personal maid and my good-sister seems unusually fond of her, treating her more as friend than servant. Now she has been assaulted and seriously hurt on our estates and probably by a member of the castle staff. It would seem we owe the girl something."

There was a momentary pause, broken as the countess smiled suddenly and unexpectedly. "Oh, that girl. In which case, just perhaps -"

Ludovic raised his eyebrows. He had been prepared for a far more prolonged argument, ranging from blunt and immovable refusal to the reluctant offer of a small purse, the payment of her medical expenses and the promise to rehire the girl after her return to rudimentary health. This would have left him with only two alternatives: to take Alysson into his own apartments after all, or to revise his entire plan within a more complicated framework. Instead he regarded his mother in astonishment.

"You agree?"

"Under the circumstances, I can have no objection," said her ladyship. "Besides, I am quite sure it will annoy your father."

"But I suggest that Mistress Alysson is not installed on his lordship's side of the castle. I intend something nearer my own quarters."

The countess sniffed. "How unimaginative of you, Ludovic. But you may do as you wish of course. I am really not in the least interested in any unsavoury involvements you hope to indulge. I have sanctioned your request. You may arrange all further details with Hamnet. I presume I have no need to remind you not to house this common female too close to my own chambers?"

"Certainly not, Madam," bowed Ludovic. "That would not serve my interests in the slightest."

The younger Sumerford passed his instructions to the steward early on the following morning. There was one small and one larger adjoining room situated a few paces from the west tower, looking out from within the main building. These enjoyed wide casement windows gazing both to the right over the seashore, and to the left across the tip of the stretching forest boundaries. On a level identical to Lord Ludovic's rambling apartments, these two rooms also led to a stair up to the battlements where walks could be enjoyed on mild days, with further windy access to the western tower. The chambers were therefore adjacent to Ludovic's without being interconnected. They were frequently sun clad, usually bathed in light from the late morning on until the day sank. They were also particularly private. They could not easily be reached unseen, and they could be overlooked only from the upper level of the western tower.

"You will have both chambers aired and warmed," Ludovic informed Hamnet, "then prepared in appropriate comfort. The inner chamber will house the patient, necessitating a complete change of mattress and suitable bedding. I shall arrange the young woman's arrival for late this afternoon. She will not be joining the family at mealtimes and nor will she expect any particular personal service, but I want her kept comfortable and treated with respect. I trust you understand, Hamnet?"

Hamnet bowed, a little stiff. "Certainly my lord."

"Gossip amongst the staff does not concern me in the slightest," Ludovic continued. "But should I learn of any direct disrespect shown to my guest, I shall deal with it severely. That is all, Hamnet."

The entire family was present at the noontime dinner table, but Ludovic did not discuss his unorthodox intentions with any of them. Nor did his mother appear to remember the affair. Conversation centred on the inane, though Brice twice inquired of Gerald how his pet pretender to the throne was adjusting to life in the Tower. Gerald returned scowls and scathing expressions in silence and no other personal business was discussed. Humphrey entertained his parents and younger brothers with an accurate imitation of his two week old son's snuffles, burps and whimpers, and remained excessively cheerful due to the generous excess of eggy custards served as part of both courses and in various shapes, sizes and casings.

After dinner Ludovic set off through the forest. The two sumpters, the litter, two grooms, and the castle medik trundled at some distance behind. The path through the trees was narrow, little more than a deer track in places, and the litter therefore took the longer route around the forest's edges, expected to arrive perhaps within the hour.

Alysson was asleep and Dulce was out collecting wood for the cooking fire. Ilara led Ludovic into the cottage, whispering and indicating the need for quiet by pointing to the ceiling as she curtsied. "My lord, again such an unwarranted honour –"

"Yes, no need for all that," said Ludovic briskly, removing his hat. The house had been noticeably refurbished over previous months but sour milk, goose grease and chicken droppings had permeated the walls for too long, so the smell, now slightly enriched by the odour of bleach, remained. "I have a suggestion," Ludovic continued, discovering a small stool on which to sit at some distance from the hearth and its damp ashes, "and need only your approval. I have arranged for two rooms to be prepared at the castle, the inner as Mistress Alysson's bedchamber, and the outer being a small solar, suitable for your own sleeping quarters. I have a cushioned litter on its way here, and once it arrives I intend escorting both yourself and Mistress Alysson to the castle. My intentions with regard to her immediate future are fixed and not open for discussion, but should you decide against accompanying her, then you are free to stay here and I shall install an experienced woman from my staff to look after her instead. You and your sister can then visit the castle as you wish."

Ilara curtsied again, sat and clasped her hands in her lap. "As you mentioned something of your intentions yesterday my lord, Dulce and I have been considering the situation all evening. We've decided I should certainly come to the castle to look after Alysson, should you be so kind as to allow such a thing. Dulce must stay here to care for the house and the animals. She'll find it strange to live alone again, but perhaps I may be permitted to return and keep her company on occasion, and maybe she'll also be able to visit us sometimes. We would both be deeply honoured, my lord. That his lordship the earl and his lady have agreed to such an arrangement -"

Ludovic interrupted. "And Mistress Alysson also agrees?"

Ilara looked at her lap. "It's certainly by far the best thing for her, my lord, as we've assured her. Indeed, we've repeatedly explained the honour done her by your invitation. But she has certain doubts I'm afraid. I trust you'll be able to overcome those, my lord."

Ludovic grinned. "As it happens, I'm not used to having my intentions thwarted. But I imagine that forcibly carrying a struggling woman into my home might raise some questions. Not that it would be the first time the castle had seen such things, but we like to consider ourselves a little more civilised these days." He stood, automatically brushing down the back of his hose. "I shall go up and inform your Mistress Alysson of her fate."

Ilara also stood, hurriedly curtseying again. "I think she's asleep, my lord. If you would be so kind –"

"Rarely," smiled Ludovic, and quickly climbed the stairs.

He discovered Alysson flat on her back in bed, but her scowl was wide awake. "As if you'd care about waking me up," she said, struggling to sit. "I suppose you've come to impose your commands."

"Precisely," he said. "How are you feeling, little one?" The upstairs chamber was as usual dreary. The tiny window's polished horn allowed the passage of only a semblance of light, and the low beamed ceiling restricted it further. The bed's sagging tester, copiously layered to catch dirt, straw and any scuttling and many legged creatures which happened to fall in from the roof cavity and its limp thatch, hung low so that Alysson was almost invisible within the shadows. Ludovic sat on the side of the mattress beside her and smiled with what he hoped was an encouraging and welcoming expression. If anything, he thought she looked worse. Although obscured by the gloom, the swellings and bruises appeared more virulent, and while the other wounds were well plastered with alum salve, these large white patches glowed almost leprous. The bandages around her head were a little blood stained, her right eye was completely closed and her mouth seemed more unnaturally distorted. "You look a little better," lied Ludovic. "I hope you feel it."

Alysson sniffed. "No I don't, and there's no need to be polite," she said. "Obviously you know quite well I feel awful considering how I look, so you're just being plain silly."

"Your persistent doubts regarding my intelligence may well be correct," Ludovic said. "I've recently considered the probability of lunacy myself. Certainly most of my family would agree with you. Indeed my brother Brice named me ludicrous Ludovic when we were younger, adopted from his juvenile Latin, and a favourite definition which he thought very witty for a number of years. You have my permission to remember it. However, as far as I'm concerned, you

248

look charming as always, especially since I've no intention of quarrelling with you today. I shall save that for tomorrow. In the meantime, I must apologise ahead for the inevitable discomfort, but I'm about to gather you up and smuggle you off to my lair. Is there anything you particularly want to collect first, to bring with you?"

Alysson stared, one eyed. "You really mean it? But how can you? I'm a servant, for goodness sake. I'm – sick. I can't work, and I can't – do anything else either, in case that's what you're thinking."

"I have no idea what you're talking about," said Ludovic with the same studied smile. "But you may be pleased to know your nurse Ilara will accompany you, you will have adjoining chambers quite separate from my own, and incidentally at some distance from the Lady Jennine's. You will, I assure you, be most comfortable and well-tended. Nor will you be molested by myself or any other member of my family or staff." He took her hand, and was surprised to find it shaking. His smile faded. "What, frightened, little one? You'll be safe with me, I promise."

Two pages flung open the great hall's double doors and Hamnet stood to one side, bowing as the horses drew up on the courtyard's cobbles. Ludovic dismounted, strolled over to the litter as the leather flaps were flung up, and scooped up the principal occupant, gathering her into his arms. He carried Alysson through the waiting shadows and away from the afternoon's warmth as the castle's sudden chill closed about them.

The embrace was more distant than passionate and Ludovic was particularly careful of Alysson's broken arm and other injuries, but her small snuggled body seemed deliciously warm, almost weightless and attractively vulnerable. He was pleasantly conscious of her pliancy as he cradled her, the suggestive pressure of her rounded hip against his ribs, and her face turned tight to his chest in embarrassment as he carried her past the many servants, over to the main staircase and quickly up to the next floor. A page scurried ahead, holding a torch. Ludovic dismissed the child when he came to the allotted rooms, and the boy pushed open the door and retreated at once.

Ludovic marched in, kicked the door shut behind him, and the damp chill of the castle corridors vanished at once. The afternoon sunshine pooled over the polished boards, dancing through the window's leaded diamonds. The chamber glowed. In spite of the day's warmth, a small fire had been lit and its flames leapt, creating a second prancing fantasy of light and shade across the floor. Two walls were plastered and painted with hunting scenes, forests and flowers, and these pictures were echoed in the colourful Turkey rugs on both the floor and the main unplastered wall behind the settle. There were cushioned chairs, small tables, several chests and coffers, and an open door leading to the larger bedchamber.

Ludovic carried Alysson through, and laid her carefully on the bed. Another fire had been lit. It sizzled across the hearth, flaring up into the huge chimney space, a busy crackling presence amongst the sunbeams. The mantle was white marble and supported two huge silver candle holders, the tall beeswax candles unlit. The bed was very wide and well padded, its posts carved and its plump feather mattress recently turned, soft packed within fine bleached linen and heaped with goose down pillows. The many blankets were thick wool in a variety of colours, the billowing counterpane was chequered velvet with embroidered borders, and the fur coverlet was beaver; glowing more luxuriously than a hundred layers of silk.

The bed curtains were fully open, but they hung heavy behind her, great swirls of rich damask lined in rich lemon. The tester was tasselled, flounced, swagged and painted with enormous bouquets of exotic yellow flowers, and to either side were curled iron sconces holding more fat candles. It was a world of whispered promises and basking sunshine, and Alysson stared around, barely breathing, her hands smoothing the huge fur bedcover beneath her as she gazed in wonder.

Ludovic sat on the edge of the bed, watching her delight. In the sudden daylit brilliance, he saw her injuries and bruises quite clearly for the first time. He was disturbed, carefully rearranging his smile to disguise it. "Pleased?" he asked softly.

"Of course I am. Can this really be all for me?" Alysson sat astonished, swollen mouth a little open, one eye unblinking. "It – it's the most beautiful place I've ever seen in my entire life. It's far more gorgeous than Jenny's. Naturally she has more rooms and they're larger, but they're not nearly so – utterly – fabulous."

Ludovic laughed. "You're enchanting, my dear, and deserve a place of far greater enchantment than this. As for your Lady Jennine's quarters, I had occasion to visit them just yesterday. My mother had them newly decorated before the bride arrived, and my mother's taste is usually extravagant. But I found the chambers lacking in style and strangely gaudy. Neat and spacious of course, but quite missing the usual Sumerford luxury. Perhaps my mother was less enthusiastic about Humphrey's marriage than she claimed. However, these rooms, little one, are now yours. Left long unused, they have not been redecorated for many years and the arras and furniture are sadly old, while the wall murals are ancient. The bed, on the other hand, is made up freshly, exactly as I stipulated. You deserve a little extra comfort, I believe, and I saw no reason for thrift."

"Thrift?" echoed Alysson. "This is – positively majestic. Of course, I've seen your apartments too, although it was dark and I was frightened so I barely remember, and they're another matter altogether. Your rooms seemed more sumptuous but they're rich and much too – masculine. Besides, you're a Sumerford."

"Indeed," Ludovic chuckled, "and use my own coin for my own indulgence. But I believe you'll be well looked after here, child. In fact, I shall make sure of it. The doctor insists you be confined to bed for an age, so you've no need to face any of the rest of the family, unless Jennine chooses to visit you here. She knows you're coming. However, I've no intention of letting her see too much of you."

"I don't understand," said Alysson. "I work for her."

"Not anymore." Ludovic shook his head, still smiling. "But we'll discuss that another time. For now, your meals will be brought to you here, a page will be stationed permanently outside in the corridor so you may call for anything else you need: ale, wine, the fire lit, shutters put up and so forth. There's a truckle bed set up in your solar for Ilara, but no doubt she'll insist on sleeping in here to keep an eye on you for the first few days in case you expire of shock while she's not looking. And I, of course, will visit regularly."

Alysson had sunk back thankfully against the bolster, her shoulders and neck too long strained. But now she sat forwards again with a start. "The servants will serve me?" she frowned. "But I know lots of them. They won't like it. They all gossip like mad, you know, and squabble endlessly, and will be horribly jealous. After all, they know I'm just a servant too."

Ludovic's smile narrowed a little. "Kindly relieve yourself from any weight of unnecessary thought while here, my dear. I intend thinking for you," he said. "And the considerations of servants have never troubled me in my life, and certainly never will. They shall, as always, do precisely as ordered, and will serve and obey you as a guest of my family, which is exactly what you are."

She sighed, leaning back again. "I can't be rude to you now," she objected. "Not after all – this." She waved an appreciative hand. "But it's no good telling me not to think for myself because you know quite well I shall anyway. I really can't let you think for me or order me around, however nice you are about it." She gazed up at him, half frowning, as if too puzzled for clear expression. "And I really can't understand why you're being so – incredibly – astonishingly kind. It's like the stories of chivalry and Lancelot and Gawain." Then something else occurred to her and the frown materialised. "And just how far away," she said, "are these rooms from your chambers?"

"Not very far," Ludovic admitted, "but separated by a staircase, a large storage room and two very thick stone walls. So I promise not to climb in your windows at night, since it's an exceedingly long drop to the moat." He grinned. "Actually, not even the moat. The buried cess pit, which would be a sadly ignominious end. Speaking of which, that's the door leading to your garderobe, thoroughly cleaned and perfumed, which negates the need for stumbling around outside at night searching for a privy."

"Perhaps that's the greatest gift of all." Alyson rediscovered her smile. "Jenny sometimes used to make me sleep in her garderobe when she got cross with me, and of course poor Ilara never had one at all."

Ludovic laughed. "The castle's fairly antiquated," he said. "But we have most of the necessities. Now, are you ready for me to send Ilara in to help you undress and get you into bed? I'll arrange for your other clothes to be brought down from Jennine's chambers later on, and you can get rid of that damned livery broadcloth. In the meantime, I imagine all you need is a chemise. Once you're settled, I shall bring in the doctor."

"Bring him in?" wondered Alysson, blushing suddenly and lowering her eyes. "I know it's your place and your doctor and your decisions, but you're not going to be – here – I mean, with examinations and things – are you?" She hesitated, watching his developing grin. "It's bad enough having the doctor. I'm not used to being – poked – and looked at."

"Absurd child," said Ludovic fondly. "I promise you, I intend behaving with circumspection and suitable propriety at all times. Well, for the present, anyway. After all, in spite of my lack of interest in what others think of me, I do, I suppose, have some sort of position to maintain." He leaned forwards, abruptly taking her hand in his and lightly kissing her fingertips. He remained watching her with faint amusement, still clasping her hand. "However, if you don't want to antagonise me into undressing you and tucking you into bed myself," he continued, "I suggest you decide to trust me a little. I believe I've proved myself averagely trustworthy." He released her fingers and stood, looking down on her. "Now, lie back like a good girl and I shall collect your nurse for you. I'll see you myself a little later."

CHAPTER TWENTY-EIGHT

Pulling a chair up to the bedside, the Lady Jennine, shoulders stiff, sat and looked around her. In spite of the comfortable grandeur of the furnishings, she appeared strangely displeased, her anger rigidly controlled. "Well, my dear," she said, mouth pursed, "very nicely you've done for yourself after all. Very grand indeed. And has he declared himself?"

Newly bandaged and fur cover pulled up tight, Alysson took a deep breath. "Well, he has mentioned future – possibilities. And he's been exceptionally kind."

"He surely has," said Jennine, tight lipped. "Remarkable."

Alysson recognised her erstwhile mistress's unmistakable expression. "I know it's an unusually nice room," she said apologetically, "but of course it's just because I was so badly hurt. Well – look at me. Anyway, he's not thinking about – things – at the moment. He couldn't be. Could he?"

"Men rarely think of anything else, whatever the circumstances," said Jennine. "Certainly these injuries make you horribly unattractive at the moment, but the man has enough sense to realise they'll heal. He knows what you looked like before! So if he's planning for the future, then so must we. We must certainly take full advantage of the situation."

"Oh dear," sighed Alysson. "I don't have the energy to think about that now. I get very giddy when I try to stand up and my head hurts all the time. The doctor says this arm won't heal for weeks and weeks, and I don't even see very well. Can't these horrid plans and plots wait until later?"

"All this exceptional generosity and comfort - the man clearly feels sorry for you," Jennine decided. "At least we know he didn't attack you himself this time, but there's nothing seductive about pity. We have to start changing your image from pathetic victim to alluring temptress." She reached over, tilting Alysson's chin up with her finger. "Yes, your neck's badly marked but luckily your breasts aren't. Since you have to stay in bed in your shift anyway, that's a definite advantage. We should pull at the neckline a little like this, even rip it perhaps, so next time he comes to see you, move casually to the side and let the covers slip back as if you've not the slightest idea how revealing it is. The man obviously likes his women to appear innocent, so it must all be done as if -"

Alysson interrupted. "He'd guess. He's not such a fool as you seem to think him."

"All men are fools. And this one was frightened to come to me when I first encouraged him, so he's more of a fool than most."

The Lady Jennine was still in attendance when Ludovic strolled in. He acknowledged her presence, more of a nod than a bow, and turned at once to Alysson. "Well, little Cyclops, do you feel any better this morning?"

"Yes, a little." Alysson quickly readjusted the dipping chemise, and then the bedcover up around her shoulders. "Your doctor's medicine made me dozy last night, so I slept very well indeed. And he used a new splint and rebandaged my arm quite tightly, which feels a great deal better. And the ointments have helped too. But he says I shall be in bed for a long, long time, and that's very disappointing."

"Reluctant to stay safe wrapped after all, little one?" Ludovic wandered over to the window. It was close to dinnertime and the sun was high, sparkling on the tips of the distant waves. The gulls Ludovic could hear from his own chambers, were also calling here. He turned back and spoke first to Jennine, who was sitting forwards, watching him wide eyed and avid, her smile carefully enticing. "But I believe you are also officially confined to your bed, madam," Ludovic said. "Presumably my guest is honoured to discover you so far from your apartments on her account. However," he bowed slightly, "no doubt your own state of delicate health must remind you of the necessity to remain – let us say – within the comfort of your own bedchamber."

The lady blushed. It was positively the first time Alysson had ever seen her colour, and she was sorry for her. Jennine stood with elegance and gathered up her train. "Indeed, my lord, how thoughtful of you to remind me. I shall return there now." She turned back to Alysson. "Goodbye, my dear. I shall certainly – be capable I believe – of visiting again, before your full recovery brings you back into my service." She curtsied stiff backed to Ludovic. "My lord." And swept regally from the room.

Alysson frowned at Ludovic. "I've never known you to be intentionally rude to anyone before," she said. "Of course, you're rude most of the time anyway, but you don't mean it. At least, I don't think you do. It just seems to come naturally to you. So why don't you like Jenny? You know quite well she's only had a baby, not the pestilence. And she's been such a good friend to me."

"I have my reasons." He came and sat on the edge of the bed beside her. "I dislike her being your friend and am aware the fault is mine. I placed you in her service, but I've no intention of returning you to it."

"There you go, telling me what I have to do again." Alysson sighed. "And I know I should be grateful, and truly I am. Indeed, I can't believe how kind you're being. But I hate – being ordered around." She blinked her one eye, gazing up at the man smiling relentlessly down upon her. "And anyway," she said, "what's a Cyclops?"

Ludovic grinned. "Unimportant, my dear. I've spoken to the doctor again this morning, and I've already sent Ilara down to collect the midday meal he's prescribed – a horrendously dull diet of milk, gruel and some sort of pap not fit for an infant, but no doubt he knows what he's doing. Personally I suspect all mediks of knowing less than they claim, but since I don't trust in purges, leeches, tonics mixed according to astrology, magical charms, the miraculous effects of pilgrimage or the dubious tortures of barber-surgeons, I suppose I might be accused of being somewhat difficult to please. "

"But isn't that one of the reasons you brought me here," remembered Alysson. "Because you said your castle doctor was so efficient?"

"Merely that the others are worse."

Alysson shook her head and looked down at her fur covered lap. "But I shall get strong again sooner or later," she said quietly. "And then I'll have to – leave here. You say you don't want me going back to work for Jenny." She looked up, suddenly challenging. "But what else would I do?"

"My dear child, the possibilities are endless." Ludovic took her one hand, smiling gently at her. "Indeed, I have some very specific ideas myself, but since you dislike me ordering your life, for the moment I'll keep them to myself. And although my powers within this household are not quite as omnipotent as you seem to imagine, I can certainly guarantee the safety and comfort of one small female housed sufficiently close to my own quarters. However, should you decide to return to my sister-in-law's chambers as her maidservant, my authority ceases. You'd prefer that, perhaps. But," his smile deepened, "it seems the lady herself is eager to put you back into my arms. And as it happens, you know, you can achieve that quite simply by staying here, without the additional delay of returning to her first."

"I'm not your dear child," Alysson scowled and tugged back her hand. "I'm not a child at all. And you've been listening."

He laughed. "No. I don't need to. You've said as much before, and I've guessed the rest. In fact, I had a brief talk with your friend in private a few days ago. She admitted very little, but it left me more than ever determined not to put you back into her employ." Ludovic reached once more for Alysson's hand, clasping it reassuringly. "Though I should dearly love to know exactly what measures she's recommended to snare me," he said. "Something more devious and subtle, or the vulgarly obvious to start with? The torn neckline? The dampened chemise? Biting the lips for colour would be impossible at the moment, and belladonna eye drops most inadvisable. But in her previous life I imagine your dubious confidant made full use of those tricks, as well as honey, rouge and coal." He leaned over suddenly, lightly kissing the tip of Alysson's nose where the small scratches were already closed. "But you need no subterfuge of that sort, little one. I promise, you are quite beautiful enough without it."

Extremely indignant and highly embarrassed by the accuracy of his guesses, Alysson then discovered her temper abruptly fragmented, leaving her suddenly without words. She gazed up, and whispered, "Beautiful?"

"Undoubtedly. Don't you know it?"

She shook her head. "I know I have nice eyes, but there isn't anything else remarkable about me. My eyes are actually very like your eyes, but in other ways Jenny says I'm plain. Gamel used to say I was too skinny and dark and looked like a gypsy. You said I was dirty. You said I smelled."

"How unforgivably insulting. Forgive me. But the situation is now a little different, and you smell delightful."

Alysson sniffed. "I probably smell of ointments and medicines. And maybe I'll never even be – passable again – after this. I'll be hideous and no one will ever want to look at me at all." Her fingers tightened involuntarily on Ludovic's and her one eye began to sting, feeling suddenly blurred and watery. "That morning, immediately after – when Ilara was washing away the blood – I saw my reflection in the bowl of water. It was – dreadful. And I looked in the mirror this morning. It's no better."

"I have warned you in the past," said Ludovic very softly, "that if you cry, I am irrevocably impelled to kiss you. I fear that might hurt you, since your mouth is swollen. So I suggest you listen to me instead, and decide for once to believe me." He smiled into the puckered ruin of her small face, the dragging open sores, the darkened swellings and the puffed closure of her right eye, its lashes stuck to her bruised and wounded cheek. "I find you constantly delightful, now and always," he continued. "And certainly these injuries will all heal, most of them quickly. In time, even the deepest scars will fade. You will then feel strong enough to antagonise me again, but in the meantime I suggest you permit me to order the comfort and safety of your life within these walls, as I intend to do in any case. Once you are

258

quite better and wish to leave my protection, we can discuss your future and quarrel together about its course. For now you are my guest, and you are very welcome."

It was Gerald who discovered her first. Since his prince's recapture and Roland's death, Gerald had stayed in Somerset, speaking little and remaining often in his quarters. His four large rooms in the main building close to the north tower, which was the earl's domain, did not connect with Ludovic's. But Gerald had become restless. "Our esteemed papa is becoming more of a nightmare than ever. The damned man watches me," Gerald complained. "How do you manage to elude his notice, when everything I do is spied on?"

"I doubt he needs to spy. Our beloved father has twelve pairs of eyes, the nose of a hungry weasel, and the instincts of a fox. While you, my dear, are wilfully self-exposed. Your sins are so flagrantly conspicuous, I imagine even the rats in the roof cavities discuss your latest misdemeanours every evening over supper."

"Very amusing." Gerald did not seem particularly amused. "But you get away with openly housing your mistresses in the castle, which may not bother Brice or myself, but would be expected to send our dearly beloved parents into apoplexy."

Ludovic smiled. "Sweet papa may already be writhing in apoplectic revulsion for all I know, but he hasn't spoken to me about it. On the other hand, somewhat unexpectedly, our dearest mamma has sanctioned my – perfectly innocent by the way – injured guest's temporary presence. I don't believe you've ever made the acquaintance of the highly respectable Mistress Alysson?"

"Don't be a fool, Lu. I'm not likely to give in to moral outrage, but I'm certainly not going to formally bow to the woman."

"My family is so appallingly dull," sighed Ludovic. "And evidently has the combined imagination of a crippled flea. Can't you presume anything but the vulgar worst? In fact, Mistress Alysson is a most charming if destitute young woman, daughter of a mayor though I forget which city, and most assuredly is –– so far anyway – not my mistress, trollop, whore, bawd or wanton – or any of the other inelegant and inaccurate terms which my dreary family seems determined to assume. I cannot see how you, of all people, can claim sufficient moral high ground from which to judge. I shall find myself forced to consort with Brice instead, if you insist on becoming boring."

Gerald smiled faintly. "But such abstinence is seriously disturbing, always supposing you're telling the truth. It's not like you Lu. I thought it was me our dear father liked to accuse of buggering his page."

"Patience, my dear. Clearly you haven't seen my page."

"If you just insist on being flippant," Gerald objected, "there's no point discussing anything serious. Anyway, I only came to tell you I'm back off to London tomorrow. There's – developments. Perhaps I'll take your advice and keep my business quiet from now on – but I have to go and sort some things out first. I'll be back before Christmas at least."

Ludovic raised an eyebrow. "Christmas? Good God, Gerry, it's only August. Do you plan on informing the rest of the family, or are you hoping I'll do it for you after you've gone?"

"You can tell them. They all know what I'm up to anyway."

"Then be careful, Gerry." Ludovic frowned, his hands on his brother's shoulders. "They say it takes six strokes of the axe to lop off a head these days. The country's executioners are exhausted and the axes too worn from over-use."

"Cheerful bastard. I'll be careful. You look after your little – guest."

"Oh, I shall do that." Ludovic smiled again. "And with the greatest of pleasure."

The earl was in company with his heir and discussing the hunt when Ludovic next saw him. Autumn was falling fast, the forest already tinged with saffron. The stags guarded their harems, proud kings and hopeful courtiers, brown eyes alert through the sun flecked drizzle, antlers high, wide and crowned. Humphrey had brought down a doe and was pleased with himself. "My arrow, Papa. You saw it."

"Your arrow indeed, my boy. And undoubtedly it was that arrow, rather than any of the others, which killed the beast. When the carcass is roasted and the meat sliced upon the platter, I shall remind you of it."

Humphrey nodded earnestly, patting his belly. "Thought I'd go and see it hung. Have a look, you know, while it's upside down in the pantries. I like that."

The earl sighed. "I would rather you did not frequent the pantries or associate too freely with the kitchen staff, my son, but doubtless whatever amuses you is harmless enough. Visit your doe by all means. Perhaps next time we shall catch you a stag."

"That would be tremendous fun, Papa. Can we go tomorrow? Can we?"

"Not tomorrow, my boy. I am past the age of daily hunting forays. The following day perhaps. I shall see."

"Tomorrow would be better, but the day after is all right." Humphrey's smile, moustache bristling, narrowed into frown. "So tomorrow I'll go and visit my doe in the pantries instead. They're a bit chilly in there, but I like all that meat hanging up. It's all cut open, with bits showing inside." He sighed in cheerful contemplation before continuing. "But I don't see why you keep talking about getting old, Papa. You can't be growing up much because you don't get any taller. I've watched, and you're always the same. Ludovic is as tall as you, and he's the youngest. Brice is next oldest after me, but he's not even as tall as Gerald. And Gerald is younger than Brice. And older than Ludovic, though Ludovic is taller than Gerald. Come to think of it, Ludovic is taller than me, but I'm the oldest and he's the youngest. And I'm taller than everyone else except him. And you of course, Papa. But Brice is the shortest, except for mamma. Mamma's little, though she's old too. And Ludovic is taller than me, but I'm fatter so that makes up for it because I'm still bigger. But you're not fat. So you can't be getting older."

His lordship's eyes glazed. "I fear I get smaller every day, my son, and talking to you diminishes me further. I am tired. Go and inspect the pantries, Humphrey, if you must, and inquire as to any surplus custards while in the vicinity. Thus you will continue to grow, in one sense if not the other."

Humphrey had noticed Ludovic. The great hall was empty except for the passage of servants preparing the great table for midday dinner, but Ludovic, descending the main staircase, was now in his path. "Look Papa," said Humphrey with pleasure, extending one plump finger. "It's Ludovic. Hello Ludovic. I was talking about you to papa. Wasn't I Papa?"

"Indeed, my son," sighed his lordship. "I remember distinctly."

"How unfortunate," said Ludovic. "I far prefer to be forgotten."

"That's silly," Humphrey objected. "You're my little brother. I can't forget you. And papa is your papa, so he can't forget you either. Can you Papa? I've got a son too and I don't forget him either. At least, not very often. He's only little but he'll get bigger when he gets older. Which is what I was talking about to papa, wasn't it, Papa? You're my little brother, Lu, but you're taller than me. I'm not sure how that works."

"I may be taller, my dear," Ludovic pointed out, "but you are considerably larger in girth."

Humphrey beamed. "Just what I said. There you are, Papa. I said just that, didn't I?"

"And your hair is considerably – redder," said Ludovic, patiently sidestepping towards the doorway. "And you have a great deal more of it."

This new insight appealed to Humphrey. "Never thought of that. But you're quite right. It is. I've got a beard and I've got a moustache and my hair's really bushy. I like that, except when people make me comb it. And it's redder than anyone's. Except papa, which is all right because papa's older. Your hair is just yellow, Lu. Not red at all. And Gerald's hair is sort of gingery like the biscuits. And Brice has lots of red bits but some bits are almost brown -"

The earl interrupted. "Sadly, my boy, the unfortunate clarity of my memory still includes those relevant details of my sons' abysmal appearance, and without recourse to your inestimable descriptions. Please feel free to leave. I should like to speak with Ludovic now he is here, it being a rare enough occurrence." As Humphrey obediently trotted away, the earl turned to his youngest son. "Stop hovering hopefully in the vicinity of the doorway, Ludovic, and come here."

Ludovic bowed slightly, and approached without noticeable enthusiasm. "I feel sure there's somewhere else I'm supposed to be," he said.

"No doubt, my boy," said the earl, "but her chambers are in entirely the opposite direction."

Ludovic smiled. "I make sure not to visit the lady every day, sir. That would make my appearances seem sadly commonplace."

His lordship did not seem amused. "You are evidently without contrition, my son," he observed coldly. "I, however, have the strongest objections to such flagrant contempt regarding both Sumerford dignity and my property. To discover that a son of mine openly houses his lowborn mistress in a chamber reserved for guests of quality, exhibiting neither sufficient filial respect to beg permission for his behaviour, nor even to inform me of it and apologise for the situation once contrived, leads me to suppose that my advanced age has either led me to a greater inadequacy than I had supposed, or has so ravaged my memory that I have since forgotten your confession."

Ludovic sat rather abruptly on the nearest chair. It was clearly to be a longer interview than he had hoped. "The young woman is not my whore," he said. "This is a statement I have repeated already many times, though it would clearly seem pointless to labour the point in face of obvious disbelief. However, it happens to be the truth. Her ladyship my mother, as mistress of this house and its accommodations, recently gave permission for those rooms to be used for that exact purpose, and I saw no need to disturb you with information of obvious irrelevance. You'll have no occasion to meet Mistress Alysson since she'll not be joining the family at mealtimes or any other time, and in fact is confined to her chambers under doctor's orders."

The earl had taken the chair opposite, drawn to the empty hearth and its jug of wilting boughs. "Your opinion of what is, or is not relevant to me, Ludovic, seems to be strangely at odds with my own," he said. "And even though this female does not aspire to eat amongst her betters, I presume she requires sustenance of some type on a reasonably regular basis? And I further presume that it is the head of this family who supplies such sustenance, with recourse to his larders, his kitchens and his staff?"

"Forgive me, sir," said Ludovic with a blank stare. "I shall bring the requisite purse to your chamber before supper."

"I am naturally much obliged." The earl's gaze was equally unemotional. "I must further inform you, Ludovic, that your esteemed mamma, albeit ostensibly mistress of this castle, holds no authority superior to my own in any regard, not even with respect to the smallest detail, let alone the use of the guest bedchambers. In future you will therefore come directly to me. I require information on all aspects of life within these walls and relating to the Sumerfords, including confessions regarding your behaviour regretted or otherwise, and certainly when requesting permission to indulge in such appalling lack of taste and obvious impropriety. Do I make myself quite clear, Ludovic?"

"You do, sir." Ludovic smiled slightly. "However, I naturally assumed you'd be in favour of my arrangements regarding Mistress Alysson, considering the circumstances."

"You were wrong," stated his lordship briefly.

Ludovic shook his head, still smiling. "Perhaps you are not quite – familiar with every aspect of the situation, sir," he continued. "No doubt I should have informed you of the details at the outset. But I also assumed you would prefer not to have those circumstances broadcast."

The earl's eyes narrowed. "You become daily more like your brother Humphrey. Kindly explain yourself."

"I have naturally concluded," said Ludovic, "that your own – affairs – have been kept strictly clandestine over the years, sir, since none have ever been – let us say – openly introduced within these premises. You have clearly done as you complain I have not, and your mistresses have always been housed at a distance. But although remaining unacknowledged – it seems you have chosen to be less elusive regarding the direct although illegitimate offspring of such liaisons."

"You have clearly taken leave of your senses, Ludovic," the earl said, now seemingly more startled than baleful.

"I think you understand me perfectly well, sir," Ludovic said. "And regarding Mistress Alysson, I must inform you that while she requires urgent and prolonged medical attention, she is here as my guest, being, incidentally, a perfectly respectable young woman. She sustained severe injuries during a personal attack instigated by someone whose identity, although as yet unknown to myself, may, I believe, be particularly well known to you. Indeed, this with regard to my reference concerning – bastard offspring – of clearly Sumerford appearance. And I repeat, Mistress Alysson is not my mistress. But your own past conduct, my lord, is naturally your own business. As mine is mine."

CHAPTER TWENTY-NINE

"Lie back," Ludovic commanded. "Head against the bolster, close your eyes, and if you persist in constantly grabbing at my doublet laces in abject terror, you'll end up inadvertently undressing me. Which," he informed her, sitting inappropriately close and leaning over, enclosing her in his shadow, "might please me more than it pleases you."

"I'm not terrified. Just nervous," Alysson admitted. "And I do trust you. It's just that I don't suppose you've ever done this before."

"I haven't," Ludovic said, cradling the small bowl of warm herb scented water. "Unsurprisingly, I've never had occasion to." He dipped the soft linen cloth, squeezed it out, and carefully began to wash Alysson's right eye. "But it's hardly likely to test my abilities, nor over-excite me, and I promise not to hurt you. Now stay still."

Some of the swellings had recently subsided, several of the bruises had paled and many shallow scratches had closed into thin pink scars. But amongst the other wounds remaining, after ten days Alysson had still not been able to open her injured eye. The puffy discolouration had sunk back to normal but hardened puss still glued the long curling lashes to the lower lid like spiders' legs to a honey pot.

"So why hasn't the doctor? Surely - ?" Alysson murmured.

"Because he hasn't," said Ludovic. "And he hasn't because he's a

266

fool." He continued washing the lower lid, the warm water bathing her face and sliding to the pillow where he had laid cloths and a towel. "But the eye no longer weeps so there can be no internal infection. Whatever keeps it stuck so firmly is simply ingrained after being left untouched too long. The pus needs removing." Then with the corner tip of his own finger nail he began to prise loose the coarse grains, still sticky and clinging like sediment. Gradually each came away, slowly leaving the eyelid clean, pink and tender. Again he washed across the lid, the cloth cleansing between the long black lashes. "Try to open your eye, child," he said. "Slowly. Don't force it."

"I can't," she whispered after a moment. "It's so sore." The other eye however, was open and watching him. "Will I be blind forever, perhaps?"

"What a delightfully positive and trusting expectation of life you have, little one." Ludovic leaned over her again, bent low and gently kissed her injured eye. The tip of his tongue slid across the line between the lids, easing away the upper lashes from their long attachment to the lower, his breath warm and his tongue firm. Sitting up again, he said, "Try again."

Alysson's eyelid flickered, the wet lashes fluttering free. She peeped warily through the crack of light, making her wince. Ludovic, attentive, smiled. With one and a quarter eyes, Alysson watched the slow smile transform his natural hauteur to gentle amusement. His mouth lifted into tight tucked corners.

"I can see you," she said with awe.

"A dubious achievement." Ludovic sat back. "Now, avoiding both window and candle, try opening your eye further. And blink." He grinned, removing the damp sheen beneath her lashes with the ball of his thumb. "Courageous child. How do you find the world? If things seem blurred, I imagine that's normal."

"Not really blurred." She was delighted. "Just a little sore."

Ludovic leaned forward again, one finger smoothing the partially healed wounds which still divided her cheek like dark stripes, the scabs long and raised. "A little bloodshot perhaps. That will soon pass, as this has."

She nodded. "Am I really getting better?"

Ten days in the castle, two weeks since the attack, much had improved. Alysson no longer wore a turbaned bandage and the scratches and grazes across her forehead and temples had paled to a pebbled maze. Many bruises remained, now a sallow and dirty yellow without swelling or internal bleeding, but covering her face like a flung palette of watery and dismal paints. Her lips had quite healed, but the tiny rips on both nostrils remained scabbed and bloody, and her neck still bore the huge weals and scratches from chin down. Most obvious were the great ragged marks down her right cheek from eye to jaw, some now healing beneath dark scabs, others only pale and narrow scars, but one still wide and vicious, blood pocked and painful.

Away from Alysson's hearing, Ludovic had argued with the surgeon. "It may mark her for life. It should be stitched."

"My lord, the pain might kill her. I cannot risk sewing the wound simply for the sake of one disfiguring scar. There is no dangerous infection and the ointment keeps it safe from harm."

"And away from the air so it never closes."

"Begging your pardon, my lord," murmured the doctor with diplomatic reverence, "but I am experienced with injuries such as these, being similar to those taken in battle, and I understand my business, I assure you. If infection should creep in, I shall immediately bleed the patient. Already the worst of the injuries are past and the young woman recovers quickly."

"And the broken bones?"

"Three broken ribs, my lord, bandaged and healing adequately while Mistress Alysson refrains from all unnecessary movement as I have instructed. As for the most serious injury, the broken arm, well that will take considerably longer, my lord. Many weeks. But clearly it mends straight and shows no deformation."

"Very well. And the injured eye?"

"Must be left to heal alone and untouched, my lord. Forced open too soon, the invasion of light might cause irrevocable damage."

"Nonsense, man," Ludovic had retorted, notwithstanding his total lack of medical training. "Stuck too long, and the poor girl will never find sufficient strength to open it."

Indeed, now open, Alysson's right eye was violently blood shot, the lower lid weeping and red. But she could see. "Things seem to be pink striped," she admitted. "But I think it's me, not them. At the moment you have three pink stripes down your nose. But you don't really, do you?"

"Not to my knowledge," smiled Ludovic. He took her left hand, no longer roughened and grazed, and held it tightly. "But now I must spoil all the advantage I've gained, and probably ensure you dislike me once again. Unfortunately I need to remind you of the attack. I've a few questions I want to ask."

"Oh," she looked down at her lap, tucked within the fur bedcover. "I'm confused about some of it, you know, because I fainted. But I'll tell you whatever I can."

With deliberate care, Ludovic moved back, leaning against the heaped pillows beside her. He kicked off his shoes and swung his legs up onto the bed. Then he stretched his arm quite firmly around her shoulders and pulled Alysson into a gentle embrace. "Now, little one. Remember everything as clearly as you can, and don't be offended by whatever you imagine I'm thinking. I am probably thinking something quite different in any case. Firstly, you've informed me without hesitation that your assailant was Humphrey. I accept you see my brother sufficiently often to know his appearance well, but now describe this man again, without giving him a name. Try to remember exactly what he looked like, and also what he said."

Alysson accepted Ludovic's embrace. It felt safe and comforting. She was by now accustomed to both his brotherly and occasionally less than brotherly intimacies and welcomed them all, whether she admitted it or not. His soft velvet doublet, laced in silver cord, was padded against the cold but beneath its yielding luxury she could feel the hard solidity of the muscled body and the strength of his protection. She sighed. "It was under the trees and he came at me from behind. He strangled me. It's hard to see clearly with someone on top and all around, moving all the time, and hurting so much. He was very big. As tall as you I think, and much wider. His shoulders were huge and his neck was short and thick. He was massive and layered in fat and his hair was everywhere, frizzy and red and

269

covering most of his face. But his eyes were bright blue and cold, and he looked so furiously angry."

"Remember his clothes," Ludovic commanded.

She paused, thinking. "Leather. Thick leather, black or brown, and a white bare necked shirt. His belt was heavy buckled. When I was on the ground, he kept kicking me. His feet were enormous and he wore clumsy leather boots. I didn't really see anything else."

Ludovic nodded. "And his voice?"

"That was the only thing that didn't seem like Humphrey," Alysson said. "His voice was very gruff, and Humphrey usually has a soft, childish voice. But perhaps because he was so angry."

"Very well. And his accent? What did he say?"

Her own voice was muffled, murmuring into velvet. "The accent was slightly different as well," she said. "Coarse, though not really common. But he was so angry, it was hard to tell. And what he said was strange. I don't remember much of it now, but he said something about trussing me for the pot, and being my destiny. And he said I'd met him before, which was stupid because I've met Lord Humphrey many, many times and of course we both know I have. I asked his name before I actually saw him. He said it was unlucky to name the devil. That didn't sound like Humphrey at all. But when I saw him, it was."

"I assure you, my brother's incapable of speaking that way," Ludovic said. "And he's a good hand's breadth less tall than myself. But these things would be hard to judge under duress. So you fought back and wounded him? Tell me."

"I pulled out his hair and scratched his face. I – bit him. His nose was all bloody and I had his blood on my tongue all mixed with so much of my own, it made me feel very sick. I suppose I did little enough damage, certainly not nearly as much as I'd have liked. But some scratches must have showed afterwards."

Conveniently close to both the village church and the more respectable of the three taverns, the Kenelm household stood to the left of the market square, off the only paved street in the village of Browny and within sight of the Browny Stream, its swollen pond and boggy banks. In accordance with recent fire regulations, the house was one of the few which had deigned to comply, fitting a new tiled roof, and with a large water barrel squatting outside the door. Being several miles further away from the castle, Browny Village considered its freedom from watchful eyes an integral part of its independence, and fought against compliance on all matters ordained by its overlord.

The Kenelm cottage boasted a fully equipped kitchen, where the remains of the previous roof thatch was laid down over the beaten earth, offering useful nesting for the chickens to lay their eggs. A goat lived at the bottom of the battered stairway, tethered to the banisters. Mounting these steps was considered inadvisable unless a friendly acquaintance had already been established with the goat. For all but the Captain, his widowed sister and her son, there seemed little relevance in taking the risk.

There was a distinct smell of sour milk, mutton tallow, goose grease and poultry droppings which Ludovic found sadly familiar. He stepped over the chickens, ignored the goat, and called for the captain. A thin woman appeared, quickly wiping her hands on her apron. "My lord, forgive me. My brother is still at sea. There has not been – I pray – not bad news, my lord?"

Ludovic smiled, shaking his head. "Nothing of that kind. In fact, I've no news at all. I hoped he might have returned without informing me, or at least you'd have heard when he's expected."

"You are always the very first to know, my lord. Fair weather or tempest, my brother never forgets what he owes you, sir, nor wishes to forget it."

"And your son?"

"My boy Clovis has gone with him as usual, my lord. I expect them back before winter sets in, long as the weather keeps favourable, and he'll be docking at London till the spring. November he said, though December if there's a delay. But soon as his feet touch land, he'll finish the ship's business and come straight to you here, my lord. He's done nothing wrong, I swear it, and always follows your orders to the letter."

"I've no complaints," Ludovic said. "I trust your brother, Mistress, and the boy too. I've a particular job for them both, that's all. But it must wait."

On the ride home, it rained heavily. The wind picked up from the east, presumably excellent for speeding the sails through the German Ocean, but significantly less welcome to a solitary rider wearing a light damask coat. One hand to his hat and the other to the reins, he regarded the sudden whisper and flickering light equally unwelcome. The apparition, minute and wavering, did not seem affected by wind or rain. Like a candle flame somehow burning under water, the light swept close. Ludovic sighed. "I have tried to find you," he muttered into the sleety silence. "But I have found nothing. I have not been able to help."

"I have found no peace," whispered the light.

"Then I am sorry," Ludovic answered. "Indeed, I am sorry for many things. But unless you tell me what else I may do for you, there seems no further aid I can offer."

"No one helps. No one aids," whispered the nameless voice. "But I have no home and no rest, so I am blown where I find acknowledgment."

The rain bounced from the path, creating its own busy thrum. Ludovic shook his head. "Come where you will and when you will, since I cannot stop you," he said. "But I admit I have other matters on my mind, and others to protect."

The light shimmered, then sank, and blinked abruptly out. The drear gloom moved back. The rain closed off the countryside. Ludovic was not feeling entirely placid by the time he arrived home and called for his father's steward.

"I've an interest in someone employed here, Hamnet," he said, stripping off coat, gloves and hat and tossing all three to the page running at his side. "I require information concerning any member of staff known to work on the premises, but who does not hold an existing and adequate position within the kitchen, the stables, dairies or upstairs chambers."

Hamnet bowed. "The ladies' maids, for instance my lord?"

Ludovic's eyes narrowed. "Don't be a fool, Hamnet. I'm not

272

looking for illicit companionship, and if I was, I certainly wouldn't require your recommendations. I'm looking for a specific person, certainly male, whose name I do not yet know, who bears – let us say – a remarkable likeness to the Sumerford family. To the Lord Humphrey in particular. And who is employed here on a secretive, unexplained or irregular basis."

Hamnet bowed low. "My lord, I swear I have no idea, no idea at all my lord." His expression grew puzzled. "There exists no such person to my knowledge, nor ever has. Nothing of such a clandestine nature has ever occurred, or I would surely be the first to know. Within these walls, my lord, it would never be permitted."

Ludovic turned away, speaking softly to himself. "It seems we are all searching," he murmured. "Nameless, lost, looking for some measure of understanding consistently denied us. Whether dead or alive, we all need answers we cannot find."

It was three more days before Ludovic returned to Alysson's chamber, and found her surprisingly fractious.

"Well brat, you seem considerably better," he said, strolling in and throwing his coat to the chair. "In fact, you look very well indeed."

Both eyes bright and wide, Alysson glared at him. "As if you would care, my lord. I'm amazed you even bother to notice."

Ludovic chuckled. "Since it's the first time you've addressed me as my lord ever since knowing me, I imagine I'm in disgrace," he said. "You had better tell me what I've done."

"Nothing at all, I'm sure," said Alysson, grabbing the covers up around her neck and raising her chin over them with dignity. A small fire had been lit, though a faint haze of sunshine entered through the half shuttered windows. The chamber was therefore pleasantly warm though a little gloomy in the corners. It smelled of lavender. "Being a Sumerford, you couldn't possibly ever do anything wrong," she continued with a sniff. "And if you did, it wouldn't be considered wrong anyway. I'm simply honoured you've remembered me."

"Ah," said Ludovic. "I see. I assume three days has been too long an absence."

"Four days," said Alysson, "and I've no interest at all in how long you stay away. In fact, four days isn't nearly long enough."

Ludovic promptly sat facing her, one knee bent up on the crumpled bed covers. "I'm delighted to find you more yourself," he said, grinning at her scowl. "All this recent polite gratitude has been most unaccustomed. But I am strangely flattered. Since you've been counting the days, I presume you've missed me."

"Not in the slightest," scowled Alysson. "If you'd been listening, you'd realise I've been saying the exact opposite. I've no desire to see you at all."

"Bored?" guessed Ludovic.

"How could I possibly be bored?" demanded Alysson. "My dear Ilara is here most of the time, at least until yesterday when she went back to stay with Dulce for a few days. Then there's the doctor, who is fascinating company. And Jenny came once, and since you weren't here to be rude and frighten her away, she stayed for quite some time, which was very pleasant."

"So during a total of – what is it – four days – you've been entertained for approximately four hours." Ludovic nodded, still grinning. "I understand perfectly. Being confined to bed is damnable, as I remember perfectly well myself. I was once forced to stay in my own bed for an interminable length of time, after someone had unaccountably stuck me full of arrows while I was placidly minding my own business. Apart from the inevitable pain and suffering, I found it excessively dreary and utterly boring. So I sympathise. I apologise for abandoning you to boredom, but I've been more than usually busy. Very largely on your behalf, as it happens, but that's of no matter. I shall now make amends."

Alysson sniffed. "I don't need playing with, as if I'm a puppy," she declared. "Or do you intend sending in the minstrels? Perhaps a priest might be more appropriate."

"Well, the puppy analogy sounds quite attractive," Ludovic said, "since rolling around on the ground together suggests all sorts of possibilities. But not too helpful for broken bones and bruises. My father only hires minstrels for festivals, and most of them are deaf anyway, and as for our chapel priest, he'd be no fun at all I'm afraid. He's far too timid to entertain a young woman in bed. I, on the other hand, know exactly what to do, should you welcome the benefit of my long experience."

CHAPTER THIRTY

"My dear girl," Jennine said, drawing up a chair. "You are quite amazingly lucky, and since your own looks are nothing to rave about, you hardly merit it. Oh yes, don't sniff. I know I once told you how pretty you are, but naturally I exaggerated. Yet do you appreciate this remarkable luck? No. You are not even grateful. I despair of you, and cannot imagine why I bother visiting this drab bedside. You've become horribly dull."

"You know I like him, Jenny." Alysson sighed, staring up at the painted ceiling beams. Few of her injuries remained and even the red welts around her neck had now faded, but her broken arm still kept her under doctor's orders, and those orders included staying strictly within her bedchamber.

The Lady Jennine giggled, reaching out to pat her knee. "Like him? Silly child. You adore him and pine for him. I've been in this business too long to misjudge the signs. And from what you say, he has quite an infatuation for you too. Ride the crest, my dear. Enjoy your youth before it fades."

"But that's exactly what frightens me." Alysson closed her eyes, envisaging the future. "You've taught me what to expect. Three years at the most you say, maybe less. And afterwards discarded, and exchanged for a younger woman. Then what? I creep back to Dulce's cottage and grow old all alone? Twenty years of misery, just for three years of glory."

"Not at all," Jennine said promptly. "Three years or more – or less – pleasure is pleasure after all. Even one year is better than none at all. While he's still eager, you make him buy you a nice little house in the village. That way your reputation will quickly be forgotten, or at least diplomatically overlooked, especially by the men. Having your own freehold property will soon entice a husband from amongst the locals. You'll be able to pick and choose – and still be young enough for children, if that sort of squalid business appeals. And I shall always be here, and will remain your friend, my dear, I promise. So don't be a drab, and tell him yes."

"He hasn't actually asked me, not in so many words. He's just talking about taking me away to this other house of his in Bedfordshire, so I suppose that must be what he means."

"Exactly, silly goose. He wants you to himself, of course. No man suggests bundling a young woman off to some strange and distant place with no intention of climbing between her legs. What else would he want? A housekeeper? But forget about going to live anywhere else. Far too lonely. A man wants his mistress for an hour or so most days, and a few hours most nights. Then you'd be left utterly alone for the rest of the time, and all day while he's off on his own business. Maybe even for months when he comes back here on his father's orders. What would you do, all alone? And how horrid to be dragged off a hundred miles to some mansion he doesn't even strictly own yet. You want to be hidden away, as if he's ashamed of you? If you take my advice, you'll stay here." Jennine spoke with some urgency. "I could never visit you in Bedfordshire, you know. It wouldn't be – permitted. You must refuse to leave here. Entice him, just as I've patiently explained for nearly a year now. Goodness knows, I've tried to help. So keep him here, where I can carry on helping."

"He said going away with him was for my own protection."

"How absurd. Just some ridiculous excuse. What could be safer than this great castle with all its guards and servants? Come back into my service, my love, and I will protect you myself."

Alysson's frown was lost in shadows, for the late autumn twilight came early and the candles had not yet been lit. The fire shot dancing reflections around the chamber, but the bed curtains shielded the glare. "How nice – how kind – how unusual, to feel doubly wanted." Alysson curled back against the cushions with a sigh. "It's wonderfully reassuring, and so kind of you to want me as a friend, Jenny, even though I'm just a servant. I never really had a proper friend before. And he wants me too, at least I think he does, even if it's just for that one little thing."

"That one little thing is a woman's greatest power," Jennine nodded. "And that's the real thrill, not their silly pricks and all their false promises, but that feeling of power, of authority and command, that's what keeps a woman breathless. Listen to me, my dear, for I've managed a number of young girls as you know. I've trusted you, Alysson, since female friendship has a far greater value than any man's lust... Now you must trust me."

"I do. Honestly I do. But I admit – not frightened exactly but please tell me, Jenny – what is it – you know – actually like?"

Jennine giggled, leaning over the bed to clasp Alysson's hand. "Not too bad, though usually uncomfortable. Most of the time it's just shockingly dull. It helps if you add a little imagination and a little variety, and that was my fame, for I know all the tricks. Any rutting male becomes absurd of course, for they're laughable in bed. Sometimes they're quite grotesque but naturally you have to make sure you don't laugh at them. So all most women do is lie still and shut their eyes. That's acceptable for a wife, but it won't do for a mistress. At present you're much too shy for anything but the first lessons, but don't worry, for once the affair starts I shall teach you everything. Another reason you must stay here close to me. With my help you'll keep the man ensnared for a couple of years at least."

Alysson shuddered. The chamber's gloom seemed to swell and Alysson snuggled down further into the bed. She ached from long inactivity but her returning strength seemed more punishment than prize. She had always understood what her recovery would mean. "I don't know what I want Jenny. I don't know what to do."

"Then listen to me and do as I say. Or are you holding out for marriage, silly goose? He'll not do it, he can't my dear, and it will never even enter his head. He has a duty to his family and will accept an arranged marriage as his kind always does. You're simply a little nobody, without family, looks or property. You think because I did? But my case is unique, and could never apply to you and Ludovic, my dear. You have nothing to offer. How could you snare such a man into anything except your bed?"

Alysson turned away, blushing. "I never said I wanted marriage. Of course I don't expect it, and I know it's impossible. I just don't think I want to be any man's mistress for a few short years. Even his. But now it's hard seeing him so often, and yet -"

Jennine interrupted. "The man's remarkably handsome. The tallest in the family, by far the best looking, still young and very well built. I understand, my sweet, especially since you're so hopelessly innocent. He carries a grace and charm that appeals even to me, with a better turned thigh and calf than I've seen on any man for many a long year. Take him, silly child. But stay here where I can keep an eye on you, and help you whenever you need a friend. And you will need a friend, you know. Any woman trapped in a man's clutches needs her friends."

Alysson's eyes stung, suddenly watery. She closed them with a sniff. "I know I have to leave these chambers very soon. There'll be no more excuse to stay once the doctor says I'm better and takes the splint off my arm." In spite of the discomfort and the pain, she had begun to dread her own recovery. "So it means going back to Dulce's cottage. Or going far away with all the risks you've told me about. Or -"

"Or coming back to work for me. I won't work you too hard, I promise. I might even give you two days off a month if you like. But that's not important. It's that young man you want, and I shall help you get him."

"What if I decide I don't want him?"

Jennine pouted and slapped Alysson's hand, still clasped within her own. "How tiresome you can be, child. I know exactly what you want, and exactly what's good for you. I wish you had seen me when I was at the height of my power. I was magnificent, the most beautiful woman in the business. With just a click of my fingers every man came running." She sighed. "Of course, I was younger then. This is a woman's true misery, for although men are slaves to their pricks and far weaker than us, they stay virile for many years while a woman is withered by the time she turns thirty." She examined the back of her own hand, pinching the soft, plump skin. "Naturally I lie about my age, but time threatens, like the winter's cold winds. Already I must sit a little further from the candlelight, and not face the full glare of the fire. And producing that wretched child has ruined me even quicker. I'm a great deal more beautiful than you, my dear, but you are a great deal younger."

It was Brice who brought the message. He had been away some time, returning as November rushed in with a tempest. From All Soul's until St. Martin's the storms pelted and raged, hurtling in from the seas and painting salt crusts across the window mullions. Every door rattled, the casement frames shuddered, the wind whistled down the chimneys and across the battlements, whipped up the moat into wild grey crests, slapping its waters high and furious up against the castle walls, and oozed through gaps into pantries and cellars. Draughts rushed through every crevice and beneath every door, flapping beneath the rugs and blowing out the candles.

Brice spoke first to the earl, then finally sought out Ludovic. His information, he admitted, did not yet seem urgent, but demanded attention or Gerald would soon find himself back in the Tower.

Ludovic was aware Brice had come home, but, not expecting to be discovered so promptly, had settled in the library annex at the back of the great hall beneath the minstrel's gallery. The fire had been built high some hours back, but was now beginning to spit, more smoke than flame. A hundred years of Sumerford records, wax sealed, neatly tied and long ignored, were folded and stacked along the higher shelves, while folios, scrolls, two huge bibles and several ancient books of illuminated prayers stood on the lower. One bright polished row held a selection of the new publications from the Westminster printing press, a recent nod to civilised modernity with a collection by Chaucer and Mallory. Ludovic, slumped in the window seat with one foot up and the open book resting against his knee, appeared to be reading. He was not.

Brice strode over and stood before the fire, kicking at the dying ashes and raising dust. "Gerald," Brice said abruptly, "should be kept permanently at home, preferably locked up in the cellars."

"You have made the smoke a good deal worse," complained Ludovic. "And what has Gerald done now?"

"The same. Pamphlets. Plotting. Treason. Not yet under arrest, but certainly under watch."

Ludovic put down the book and gazed at his elder brother. "I was not aware," he said, "that you were in London."

"You are more interested in my humble self and the reasons for my whereabouts, or in our dearest brother's imminent execution?"

Ludovic sighed. "Clearly, this time he must be got out of the country," he said, standing and stretching. "Flanders, and at once. You should have arranged it while you were there instead of riding all the way back west. And since evidently you move in sufficiently powerful circles to anticipate royal intentions, you could have stayed to help counter the danger."

Brice took the seat Ludovic had left, first smoothing down his fine turquoise silk hose and stretching his legs, not to risk straining the knitted weave over a careless knee. He began idly flicking the pages of the discarded book. "What a suspicious mind you have, my beloved," he said, smiling over the leather binding. "But I hardly need our magisterial monarch to inform me of the next on his list for the axe. And I assure you, I am not, in spite of your doubts, close enough to our vengeful Tudor's cherubic ear to gain his confidence. I can influence neither royal inclinations, nor Morton's careful politics of fear and bias. But strolling the capital's streets tells its own tales. Rumours are rife. The court is abuzz. As for transporting our dearest Gerald abroad, if you know a way of carrying him bodily from one realm to another, kindly instruct me, for I do not. Our honourable brother is more stubborn than Mamma. I have seen and spoken to him. Indeed, I personally warned him of the danger he faces. He remained unmoved. I despaired, and returned to enlist family support."

Ludovic frowned, first staring down at Brice, then over his head through the window above to the courtyard cobbles and the violent swirling winds kicking up the gravel and old dead leaves, the servant girls' skirts flattened against their thighs as they ran heads down, clutching their bonnets, across to the kitchen doors. A horse neighed, the grooms were shouting. The clouds tumbled high and dark and distant tree branches flung bare arms, twisting like windmills. A sudden backdraught hurtled down the chimney and the dying fire went out with a cough and a spit. A sooty haze filled the room.

"Damnation," said Ludovic. "Does no one ever bring good news anymore? I've other plans afoot and no desire to leave here just yet. Gerald can look after himself."

"Indeed," Brice smiled. "Why not? His death would raise you one step nearer to the inheritance, my beloved."

Ludovic's eyes narrowed. "If I thought you meant that, my dear, I'd run you through now, and come nearer to the title still."

"With this new mewling infant between us all and the mighty glittering prize? No, little brother, I am teasing of course. And this wretched damp and rambling castle, one lowly countrified title and an ill favoured family reputation, hardly tempt me to dream of the heritage either. Humphrey and his dubious offspring may keep whatever miserable crumbs are due them. I have my other – far more profitable business."

"What does Father say?" asked Ludovic.

"What does dearest Papa ever say?"

Ludovic sighed. "Then it's London again, to salvage the family honour."

Turquoise and black, damask, bliaut silk and velvet, Brice nodded, rich russet hair neat clipped across turquoise shoulders. The window behind him began to thrum as the rain slanted, sleeting in steel. "And what a sweet ride it will be, my beloved, travelling east through these wild November storms. I almost envy your good fortune. How sad that I cannot accompany you."

"What precisely do you mean?" Ludovic raised one eyebrow. "Is your own – more profitable business – of so much greater importance?"

"Indeed it is, but what ignoble suspicions you have, my dear. I am distraught to discover myself so eternally distrusted." Brice stood, strolling to the far door and speaking over his shoulder. "But I am also busy on papa's business, and sadly not my own. I am instructed to brave the savage winter seas and sail to Flanders, there to build a secure nest and await dear Gerald's arrival. You, my dearest, must play the Hector with Gerald."

Ludovic glared after his elder brother. "And if I can't persuade Gerald?"

"Then we shall no doubt present a cheerful and united gathering on Tower green to witness his execution by Christmas," Brice called from half way across the hall. "In the meantime, my beloved, you had better tell your little sparrow to prepare for the season's celebrations alone. Though no doubt dearest Mamma, so famous for her tolerance to whores and trollops, will extend the family generosity and invite your lonely mistress to the Yuletide feast in your absence."

Ludovic discovered his empty wine cup, snatched it up and followed Brice, kicking the door shut on the smoky annex behind him. "Your perverse insistence on being disliked," he said softly, coming to Brice's side, "has sometimes inspired me to feel the opposite. But don't tempt me too far, my dear. I also have a temper."

Brice sniggered. "Looking for a quicker way to rid the country of sad Sumerford pride? But beware, my love. I'm not famed for my swordsmanship and you consider yourself the family champion." He bowed with elaborate elegance. "But in fact you've little idea of who I truly am and what I do away from this dreary place." His smile, eternally complacent, narrowed a little. "Perhaps – just perhaps, my sweet – I have skills you have not yet guessed."

"I am beginning to think," said Ludovic, "the entire family is utterly insane. Father and Humphrey without doubt. Gerald is certainly mad. You are clearly on the way. I await my own first signal."

"I would suggest," smiled Brice, "with your mistress ensconced in the best guest chamber, those early signals have already arrived."

"If you had ever met her," said Ludovic, returning the bow with a stiff back, "instead of choosing the slander of ignorance and supposition, you'd realise her presence here is proof not of my madness, but of my sanity and plain good taste."

CHAPTER THIRTY-ONE

Alysson stretched out her right arm, staring, unblinking, flexing the fingers and twisting her wrist. She was still charmed, almost surprised, to find her muscles obeying her, her bones knitted again as neat as a fine pair of hose. But those same muscles had shrunk and become weakened and thin. The veins seemed garish, wriggling serpentine just below the pale wrinkled flesh. Alysson extended her left arm, holding the two parallel. They no longer matched. She sighed, pulling down the sleeves of her chemise again and retightening her robe.

It was six days now since the sling had been discarded, the bandages unwound and the splint finally removed. Discovering her pallid puckered skin unshrouded and again displayed, Alysson gazed for a long time, practising her grip and the feeble strength of her fingers.

She had learned to eat with her left hand, clumsy with a spoon but nimble enough with bread, pies and food already sliced. Often it had been Ludovic who had sliced it for her, sitting beside the bed as she ate, telling her absurd stories so that she laughed and spilled her soup. At first her diet had been milk sops and gruel, but by early September Ludovic had insisted she receive proper solids, red meat and custards. He had spooned much of it for her, tying her napkin around her neck like a collar, commanding her to open her mouth, and shovelling in food as a mother bird feeds its fledgling. He had even named her as such. "Now, little squab, open. Close. Chew. Now swallow. And smile."

He had taught her chess, presenting her with his own set wrought from ebony and silver. When occasionally he failed to beat her at the game and threw down his king in surrender, Alysson scowled and called him a cheat. They had wagered at dice, with prizes of honeyed biscuits and aniseed cakes. He had told her something of his family history, not the wild stories of rape and abduction that he had recounted once before, but the quieter, sweeter tales of hard work, care for the land, character, friendship and loving. He had read to her for long hours by the lilting light of the fire, books of giants and unicorns, bloodshed and chivalry, crusade and comedy. He had read her love stories of King Arthur courting his queen, and of knights laying down their lives for their ladies.

One day, he promised, when she once more had the use of two hands, he would teach her to play the lute. "I am sadly no master," he told her, "but I can show you the chords and some simple tunes. Then I expect the pupil to surpass her instructor." But sometimes, after supper when the wind whistled and the fire flared, he would sit within the shadows, candles snuffed, and play the old melodies, fingering the strings with his eyes closed as if he played while half asleep and dreamed to the music.

On mild and sun pooled afternoons, he had taken her up onto the battlements to walk with him, stretching her legs and breathing deep. There she stood mesmerised as he held her steady against the breezes, gazing across the glistening miles of placid Somerset plains. The views peeled away in every direction, across meadows and pasture, field crops cut flat after harvest, orchards with the fruit ripening and heavy, and on over the cliffs to the sea, the raucous sea birds and the horizon's shimmering haze.

He had doctored her with the salves and ointments, changing bandages, and reassuring her as her injuries healed. Finally he had held her other hand while the surgeon removed the sling, the splint and bandages, and straightened her right arm, feeling and bending it before pronouncing his satisfaction and praising his own medical expertise. Ludovic had grinned in delight. "Well, my dear. Welcome back to health and freedom." But she had carefully not mentioned freedom herself, nor sought to leave her rooms.

Ilara had been hovering, watching just as eagerly while the doctor worked. Then, with Ludovic thrust from the chamber, she had helped Alysson into a fresh scented chemise, tied her warm blanchet around her, and brought her to the window seat. When Ludovic was permitted back into the room, Ilara had left them together and Ludovic had taken Alysson into his arms and kissed her cheek.

"Two arms indeed. I barely recognise you, little one. But you should stay here for another week at least, to fully recover your strength. The doctor will still visit daily and show you how to exercise your elbow again, and I will come as often as I can. Do you mind staying confined just a little longer? If you wish, you may come downstairs, explore the castle or sit in the hall, but it's far too cold now to walk the battlements, and I must warn you, not all my family will welcome your presence on civil terms."

"I'll stay here, I think," Alysson said. "They're beautiful rooms. I don't feel imprisoned here at all."

Now six days later Ludovic came to tell her she must move, as she knew he would. He shook his head, striding over to the cushioned settle where she sat curled in front of the fire. "Family business," he said, sitting abruptly beside her. "And I have to leave. Tomorrow morning I ride for London. But I travel alone so if you agree, you could come with me. I'd set no conditions and force no rules. There's the house in Bedfordshire I've told you about, and it's mine as near as dammit. Came into the family as part of my mother's dowry, and will come to me by deed of gift either on her death, or before if she wishes. I've been there several times recently, refurnishing, overseeing the farmlands and employing new staff. It's considerably more comfortable than the castle, though a good deal smaller of course. You might like it there."

Alysson stared at him, confused by the sudden unexpected urgency. "But I'd be left there all alone?"

He nodded. "Sadly yes, but you could bring Ilara and I'll be back, probably within the month."

Alysson stumbled over the words, unable to make any decision in one moment that already she had avoided for a great deal longer. "But I haven't – you've never even asked – and would I – or wouldn't I? I mean, what would I do? You haven't explained. Who would I be?"

Ludovic frowned, drawing her to him, one arm gentle around her shoulders, the other hand tilting up her chin to look at him. During her convalescence he had embraced her often, though always in careful friendship and never with passion. Now he kissed the tip of her nose between the two tiny silver scars that still marked each nostril. "Listen, little one. This has happened unexpectedly, and my departure brings the situation to an unfortunate climax. I meant to arrange matters in a more comfortable fashion, and ask you in a gradual and more elegant manner, certainly with a good deal more romance attached." He paused, smiling down at her. She gazed back, unsure. "I want you as my mistress, Alysson," he said. "I've made little secret of what I want, and you must have expected some sort of invitation eventually. Come with me now to Bedfordshire and I'll set you up in style. I can afford a good deal of luxury, and I swear I'll treat you well. You can have your own separate apartments and keep your privacy when you want it. You can bring Ilara with you, Dulce too if you wish it, and I'll hire other female servants for you too. Once this final business with my brother is done with, I'll live almost permanently away from Somerset. Then you can travel with me, come into London, perhaps to Flanders. I know it's abrupt, but I've hinted as much for a long time. What do you say, my love?"

"You mean right away? Tomorrow?" She swallowed, catching her breath. "And I'd be –?"

"Mistress of my house. And," he grinned down at her, "mistress of my heart."

"That's silly," she turned away with a quick scowl. "You don't even sound sincere. Just sarcastic. You never talk to me like that."

"Clearly I should have." He kissed the top of her loose curls, pulling her a little closer. "I fear your scowl is a bad sign, little one. I hoped my offer might please you. But it seems I've insulted you instead."

"Oh dear." Alysson looked down again, cuddling close to his velvet and sable warmth. "I'm not insulted. It's not as if – well it isn't – and anyway, I'm not stupid so I'm not surprised. It's not an offensive invitation, at least, I don't think it is. It's just that I'm – terrified – of making the wrong decision."

Ludovic sighed. "I'm not entirely sure what you mean, my love," he said gently. "There's nothing to be terrified about, I promise. I'll never hurt you nor abandon you. I swear I'll look after you, indeed one of the reasons I want you to come with me now instead of waiting until I return to do the thing properly, is frankly for your own protection. Don't you trust me, little one?"

"I don't think you'd want to hurt me," said Alysson miserably. "But three years is such a little time and then I'd grow old and be so lonely and probably no one would talk to me because I wouldn't be respectable anymore and the women in the market would turn away when I go shopping, and I'd have to stand all on my own in church and stay indoors cooking turnips with only the chickens for company. Is a little happiness really worth it, however lovely it would be for three years?"

Ludovic gazed at her with blank amazement. "You're giving me a three year time limit?"

"Is that too much?" Alysson sniffed, burying her head deeper into his doublet lacings. "I don't want to sound greedy, but anything less than three years would be – just – too desolate for words. A woman of thirty may be too awful for a man to contemplate but I'm still only eighteen so I don't think I'll grow old that quickly, and I promise I wouldn't do any of those other things, like asking you to buy me a house and not – that is – refusing other things – until you did. I think that's a horrid idea, even if it would be awfully useful to have a house of my own – for afterwards."

The short and startled pause was interrupted explosively. "Jennine," said Ludovic.

She shook her head. "Jenny's been really helpful, and terribly kind." Alysson extricated her newly restored right hand and wiped her eyes with the back of her knuckles. "But the trouble is, she's so much stronger than I seem to be, and she thinks I shouldn't care about the things I do."

"I should have murdered the damned woman on sight," muttered

Ludovic, bringing out his own kerchief and silently handing it to Alysson.

"It's not fair that you don't like her," Alysson insisted, taking the kerchief and blowing her nose rather violently. "All this terribly long time I've been kept in bed, all I've done is just sit here looking forward to your visits. But you didn't come every day, and sometimes you stayed away for two or even three in a row. I'm not complaining. I know you had other things to do. I know I'm not important. But sometimes I got quite demented, and Ilara just clacked about having to cheer up and appreciate my happy situation, with a few hints thrown in about keeping my virtue. At least when Jenny came she was good company, like a real friend, and she made me feel wanted."

"Good God child, I should have moved you into my own quarters from the beginning. None of my family believes anyway – but that's beside the point." Ludovic, having forgotten his regard for her injured arm, now held her very tightly so that her words were quite muffled and came in short gasps. "How can you possibly be pleased," he demanded, "feeling important to a woman who orders you to brush her clothes, make her bed and wash her back? That's servitude, not friendship, and one of the reasons I don't want you back working for her again. She may have treated you kindly in some ways, but I don't intend you to play the servant anymore. If I'd used what few brains I still have, I would never have arranged that position in the first place."

"I wanted you to."

"Because you had no options back then. Now you have. You may not like the option I'm offering, but it's worth considering, my dear. As for abandoning you after three years, that's utterly absurd. I shall do no such thing."

"What then? Five years? Do you think you could last that long?"

He laughed. "Now, listen to me," he said. "It's autumn again, so it's a year, more or less, since I first met you, and my intentions have changed a few times since then. So has my life. But now I've spent a long time being extremely careful not to upset or alarm you, and like a damned fool I've purposefully never mentioned love. A few hints – but nothing to scare you off. Since the attack, and even before, I've offered a brother's comfort and a father's protection, meaning you to know me first, and hopefully reciprocate what I personally felt. Perhaps I was wrong. Had I made myself clear from the beginning, Jennine wouldn't have been able to instil her own wretched beliefs into your head. Who is she anyway? Do you know? She's no virginal merchant's daughter, of that I'm positive."

Alysson blew her nose again, still clutching Ludovic's kerchief. "Whatever she is, she understands men. She says all men get infatuated and think it's going to last forever, but it never does. Women get old and saggy and wrinkled and men don't want them anymore. You can say you're different but you don't know until it happens. When I'm all sallow and spotty, I won't like me either. Besides, Jenny isn't trying to put me off, she thinks I should be your mistress. But she makes it sound so – unappealing."

"Dear God." Ludovic's fingers crawled up into her hair, cradling her woebegone puzzlement. "Now whatever I say and whatever I promise, that wretched woman's words will take precedence."

Her voice became little more than a whisper. "You know I – like you, Ludovic. I do – very much. You've been kind and you haven't just treated me like a peasant and dragged me off into the bushes. But I feel so confused and miserable and hopeless."

"Do I seem such an immature fool to be swayed simply by passion, only to grow cold when the hunt turns to capture?" Ludovic's embrace tightened. "Sweet heavens," he sighed, "I've experience of my own, and know women perhaps as well as my sister-in-law knows men." It was late afternoon and the first candles had been lit an hour back, but the shutters had not yet been raised and the swirling gusts of rain beat outside the glass. The fire was blazing, and in its light Ludovic gazed down at Alysson's small face turned up towards him. The reflections burnished her last remaining scars, silvered threads running like tears down her cheek. "I'll tell you," Ludovic continued softly, "why I didn't come every day to visit you, when I should have, and knew you needed me." He smiled, again kissing the tilted tip of her nose. "I should have kept you comforted and amused every day. But wanting you too much, I sometimes avoided the temptation. I longed to climb into bed with you and kiss away the misery. But I'd only have frightened you, and perhaps hurt you more." He paused, as if careful to choose his words. "I doubt I've ever been a coward before, my love. You've made me aware of many weaknesses. But I also have strengths. I can look after you, and keep you from danger. You must have realised danger might still threaten. In Bedfordshire you'll be safe, even if I can't be with you at first. And I'd not touch you until I return, when I can arrange matters more kindly and give you the happiness you deserve."

"I won't be in danger if I keep away from Humphrey. I won't walk alone anymore, and I won't do anything stupid." Alysson buried her face against Ludovic's chest with a sigh. "I don't deserve happiness any more than anyone else, and hope can be so terribly destructive." She blew her nose with deliberation. "I used to be such a hopeful little girl and I had such sunny dreams. When first my father died, and then my mother, I learned how treacherous hope can be. But I was young so I went on hoping anyway. Then life grew dark and cold and sad over the years, but there was always Gamel, and there was Pagan, and that kept hope going. Well, you know what happened next." The kerchief had become very wet. "And now there's you, but I don't want hope starting up again. I just want to be comfortable, and have enough food, and a little friendship. And it's being here, in this castle with Jenny, and you most of all that I don't want to lose. Going far away and not having anyone, that seems even more – hopeless." She had grasped his sleeve and was clutching the fur trim like a rosary between her fingers. "When you come back you might not even want me," she gulped. "In London you might meet someone more beautiful, with money and experience and no horrid scars." He started to speak but she interrupted him. "Will you – hate me, if I wait for you here, where I do feel safe? And when you come back, if you still feel this way, can you ask me again?"

Ludovic unhooked her damp fingers from his sleeve, and curling them within his palm, brought her hand to his mouth and kissed it. Then he slipped her hand inside his doublet lacings, holding it against the soft warm linen of his shirt, his heartbeat steady and deep beneath. "Yes, my sweet, if that's what you want," he said. "But however long I'm away, don't learn to doubt me, or sit here endlessly pondering on the perfidy of men and the treachery of hope. I've every intention of making you very happy indeed, my love, and the future's not so far away." He leaned back, bringing her with him, almost as if they were bedded together. "And in case you're thinking I've already proved a lack of credit by having abandoned all the women in my life so far, let me assure you I've never before asked any woman to live with me or be my mistress, nor ever spoken of love to anyone at all. Not that I imagine you'll approve, but those in my past such as the girl you once saw me with, have meant as little to me as I did to them. You're quite unique, my love, as are my feelings for you. When I return, I shall prove it."

She smiled, holding gently to the vibration of his heartbeat. "I like feeling unique," she murmured. "You won't be gone too long, will you?"

"By no means. And I'd argue with you a great deal more now if it weren't for needing to leave early in the morning, and still having preparations to complete." But he made no attempt to release her, to stand or move away from her, as if intending to stay for some time with her comfortably in his arms. "And much as I long to," he murmured, "I dare not take you to my bed now, only to leave you cold and alone afterwards. I'm not yet entirely master of my life, not here, and I have family obligations. But I can't leave you in these rooms, or trust my parents to respect any further convalescence. So if you care to go back to Jennine, then I must agree to it. But I'll have a word with my sister-in-law before I leave. I've no authority over her and can't force her hand, but I want you treated less as a servant. And I want you well protected." He smiled. "I can threaten a little perhaps, but I doubt she's a woman to intimidate easily."

Alysson nodded. "I'll be all right with Jenny."

"In one respect, I doubt that very much," he said. "But I'll try and mend whatever damage she does when I come back."

CHAPTER THIRTY-TWO

Gerald was not staying at the Swan and Cygnet, nor did Ludovic discover him at The Rose or The Bull. He asked at every inn and ale house in Crooked Lane and Fish Street, hurrying between doorways and keeping tight to the walls, rain lashing his face, hat pulled low. Only those forced to travel had come to London, for the weather was foul. Few carriers' inns were therefore fully occupied yet Gerald Sumerford was staying at none of them. Ludovic took a late dinner at The King's Head, then abandoned his exploration of the city's expensive and respectable areas and their brightly lit hostelries, moving down towards the river, the lower cheaps and finally taking a wherry south over the river to Southwark. With the wind howling and the sleet washing the gutters almost clean, Ludovic began a search of the less reputable taverns.

"He's staying at The Horn, close by the Fleet," Brice had said. "And under his own name, for the fool has no notion of the danger brewing. I myself paid for a further two week's board in a front room for him, so he'll still be safely there." But he was not.

After three tiring wet days in the saddle, Ludovic had arrived in London with Alysson's and not Gerald's face tucked immovable within his memory. He barely spoke to his bedraggled and despondent groom, and on reaching The Horn had left the man to stable the horses there, with a chamber booked and a promise to return before dark. Walking London's streets quite alone, especially for an out of city stranger, was not always wise. Southwark was considered even more dangerous. But Ludovic, hand to his sword hilt, remained distracted. He was disappointed in himself.

He had, he decided, mishandled the affair from the very beginning. He now discovered an uncomfortable but growing sympathy for his great grandfather and that gentleman's decision to forcibly abduct the woman he wanted. Instead Ludovic's care, consideration and patience had, in the end, achieved nothing except a bewildered and mutual confusion. Though the thought was unforgivably absurd, it appeared Humphrey's jovial inanity had proved the more successful approach, bringing it seemed, the only happy union within the entire family.

Unaware of how much and for how long Alysson had wept after he had left her, Ludovic remained conscious only of failure, and the urgency of an imminent and miserable departure. He had been obliged to return immediately to his own chambers, ignore the pounding headache which almost blinded him, call his personal manservant and complete his preparations for the next morning. He had, however, made time to speak to his sister-in-law.

He was grateful to find her alone. "Madam, your servant." Thankfully, such irregular visits to the lady's private quarters appeared to be accepted without the slightest embarrassment. "Family business," Ludovic explained abruptly. "And I leave at dawn tomorrow. As I'm sure you're aware under the circumstances, without my presence in the castle, Alysson cannot continue to occupy her present chambers."

Ignoring past and persistent disapproval, Jennine was gracious. "I understand, my lord. Alysson is most welcome to return here as my maid. Indeed, I shall be delighted to have her back."

"Unfortunately I've no time now to arrange matters as I'd like," Ludovic said, "but once I return, I've no intention of her remaining as a servant in this house. I'd be obliged if you'd remember that."

Jennine simpered. "I understand perfectly, my lord. It comes as no surprise."

"In the meantime, I believe she needs protection," Ludovic frowned. "I imagine you understand that too."

"The silly girl fears dear Humphrey. No such thing of course. Some village lout accosted her in the forest. But I shall keep her safe."

Ludovic stepped further into the candlelight, looking down at the woman he had once desired and now specifically disliked. His headache, increasingly severe, now restricted both patience and the luxury of manners. "I know perfectly well Humphrey was not responsible madam, but I've a remarkably good idea who was, and it was neither village lout, nor stranger. Once again, I think you understand me quite well."

"I do not, my lord. How could I?" Jennine tossed her head, almost losing her cap. "You forget, I'm virtually a stranger here myself. It is only a little over a year -"

"Then simply remember this." Ludovic stood close, speaking very softly, eyes narrowed. "If any harm, of any kind whatsoever, comes to Alysson Welles during my absence, I shall hold you personally responsible. Even if it should then be proved you are utterly innocent of all involvement, and could have done absolutely nothing to save her, I shall still hold you responsible. And I will then make my own decisions as to the consequences. I trust you continue to understand me completely?"

"You are absurd, my lord," Jennine said, mouth tight. "But knowing your reasons, I shall be pleased to overlook it. Naturally Alysson will be quite safe with me."

The Southwark alleys wound narrow and filthy down from the river to deep amongst the hovels surrounding the Clink, the bearbaiting pits and the warrens of lightless tenements. Ludovic wandered the pilgrim's way, stopping at each of the inns on both sides of the road, asking not for Gerald Sumerford, but for any traveller of his description. Gerald's description was easily given, his hair was distinctive, his manner educated, his clothes perhaps not. Ludovic found him at The Three Tuns.

"There's a Goran Spittiswood been staying here, my lord, with hair a remarkable bright red just as you say, my lord. Has taken a small room private for himself, top floor under the attics, and been with us for five days already, my lord. But I'd say would not be one as would interest such as your lordship."

"I'll be the judge of that. Is he in?"

The innkeeper led Ludovic upstairs, four dingy and creaking flights to a tiny doorway shrouded in cobwebs and shadows. The innkeeper knocked on the door. Ludovic did not wait for a reply.

Gerald leapt up, stared in blank amazement at his brother, and sank back to his bench. "Good God, Lu. How in God's name did you find me?"

Ludovic thrust the innkeeper from the room and shut the door carefully behind him. Across the desk where Gerald was sitting, were piled sheets of paper. Quill, inks, ink blots, and the hurried preparation of illicit pamphlets. Ludovic eyed the letters. "I followed the smell of treason all the way down from The Horn, where Brice originally sent me."

Gerald sighed. "He shouldn't have sent you. I'm safe enough."

Ludovic drew up a stool and sat close, keeping his voice low. "You've no notion what the word means my dear. I don't trust your idea of caution or common sense, and come to think of it, I'm not sure I trust Brice."

"Oh, Brice is all right. Pompous, arrogant and supercilious, but not as bad as Papa. And he put down a fair purse for me at The Horn where I was staying, but I claimed that back off the landlord. I bought paper and ink instead. Do you know what they charge for paper these days, Lu? It's a scandal, since the Italians produce the stuff quite easily now. Anyway, I moved in here instead. Costs less than a quarter."

"I'm not surprised. It's a slum."

"Just where I fit in, it seems." Gerald grinned, spreading out his arms. "Sold my clothes too. The poor buggers around here walk half naked, and will buy anything they can. Fine linen fetches a decent price."

Ludovic, who wore his usual damasks and sables, shook his head.

"Then I'd better watch my back. Come back to The Horn with me, Gerry. I'll pay."

"Give me the coin instead."

Ludovic was reading one of the pamphlets. "And you nail this stuff to church doors? Gerry, they'll have your head."

"I'm too long in this business to make an idiot of myself and get captured now," Gerald said, sitting back and frowning at his brother as the brazier crackled over smouldering coals at his back. "I know what I'm up to. And I owe it to the rightful king, and to poor Roland too. But if I lose my life after all, then I'll make a good speech on Tower Green before I go. I knew the risks when I started. It's his highness that matters."

"If there was the slightest chance of restoring the crown to the Plantagenets and sending Tudor scurrying back to Brittany, then I'd back you and probably finance you too." Ludovic stood and wandered over to the window. Across the grey waves, the shadows of the Tower filled the furthest horizon. "But you're no fool Gerry. You know it can't be done."

"If I can get the prince out of the country, then perhaps it can. He needs an army to back him. Burgundy and Flanders will give it to him."

"They didn't before." Ludovic turned back, eyes narrowed. "Now father's sent Brice to Flanders. He should have sailed by now and may be there preparing a place already. But it's you must leave the country, my dear. No arguments."

Gerald opened his mouth, then paused, the scowl clearing. "All right. But give me just a few more days, Lu. Then I promise I'll go peaceably." He smiled, relaxing suddenly. "Once over there, I can find a way of talking to the Duchess Margaret, and Maximilian too perhaps. They both still support Prince Richard, you know."

"Once you're there, you can do what you like." Ludovic sat again, hands to the brazier. Outside the wind blustered and the sleet rattled the window casement. "But you're not to come back to England, Gerry. I'll want that on oath."

"I'll swear to it. At least, not unless I've a fair sized army at my back."

"Or until your poor bastard prince is executed, with nothing remaining to plot about."

Ludovic took his brother back to The Horn with him, arriving shortly before curfew closed the Ludgate. The landlord remembered his previous customer, and in company with Ludovic's ostentatious finery, accepted Gerald's reduced appearance without complaint. They ordered a hot supper, a chamber with a generous hearth and a fire already lit, a jug of hippocras and another of ale, and a good bed with the linen clean and well aired. The wad of pamphlets was parcelled and hidden in the clothes chest.

Gerald slept through the long winter's night, but Ludovic, his brother's restless elbow in his ribs and his mind on other matters of equal dejection and disappointment, did not. A gale howled down the chimney and hurled the fire's hot ashes into a smoky haze. The room smelled of stale beer, soot and Gerald's long unwashed petticoat padding, hosiery and under-braies, in which he slept.

In the morning, still weary and heavy eyed, Ludovic rode down the Strand from the Fleet to Westminster. Leaving his brother scribbling out messages of hatred against the Tudor usurper, Ludovic headed for the Tudor court. Early morning, but the day was dark as the sleet persisted beneath low black clouds. He arrived shortly after breakfast, coat and hat sodden and his horse dejected. The Thames danced with rain tumbling across the sullen waves and threatening flood. Thunder echoed from over St. James and the Leper Hospice, and lightning cracked the clouds in brief overhead silver.

With little light creeping through the windows, Westminster Palace was aflame with candles, perfumes of beeswax, lavender and smoke, with a constant flaring draught from passing crowds. Now nearing the first day of the '98 Christmas season, the court was noisy. Ludovic asked for William, Earl of Berkhamstead. He was directed down one long corridor, a page running ahead with a torch. The earl was still abed.

"Married?" repeated Ludovic, surprised.

"It happens," sighed the earl, hopping naked from the bed and quickly pulling on a bedrobe, tying it tight around his recently expanding waist. "So we can't talk here. Meet me in the Maria Chapel in a few minutes."

The unknown lady, peeping over the eiderdown, looked cross. "My apologies, my lady." Ludovic bowed, then turned back to Berkhamstead. "I can wait elsewhere, if you've a mind –"

"Oh, I've finished with all that nonsense for today," said the earl. "I'll be dressed and out to meet you quick as a piss and a spit."

Leaving the earl and his new countess's allocated chambers, Ludovic headed out to the eastern courtyard and across the small paved opening to the next maze of corridors and the larger chapel beyond. It was when approaching the short sodden courtyard crossing that Ludovic glimpsed someone who did not seem keen to be seen. Dodging quickly back into the shadows was a well-dressed man, short statured but muscled beneath his brocaded coat, sleeves trimmed deep in baudekyn and then in sable, which swept the boards like a woman's train. Plumed hat tucked under his arm, the man's hair caught the sudden candle light and gleamed rich russet over an embroidered neckline. And then he was gone. A rustle of departing silken sleeves, the quick clip of boot heels, and then silence. Ludovic stood still and stared.

He reached the Maria Chapel moments before Lord William. Mass was long finished and the marbled aisles were empty of all but shimmering reflections from the votive candles. William bustled in behind. The great arched ceiling echoed and their words were less private than they were supposed to be, but no hovering priest appeared to be listening and it was too stormy to walk outside.

"Gerald's been busy. Have you met up with him lately?"

Lord William shook his head. "He sent you? I assure you I've not lost enthusiasm, and I'm as interested as ever in the cause. But," and he sighed, "my uncle insisted on marriage, and even made the match on my behalf. It's been two years he's been negotiating for me and tell the truth, I like her so I was getting impatient. He's the older generation of course, and says if I don't produce an heir, he'll be next in line to the earldom and I ought to be careful or he'll bump me off to claim the prize. Silly old fool. Told him he'd be welcome to it. It's not worth a gauze codpiece since my father gambled half the property away and the rest was confiscated after Bosworth." William genuflected as an afterthought and then wandered over to the raised pulpit, gazing up at the painted murals depicting the Madonna's expression of sublime satisfaction as she was raised to the heavens, the clouds parting generously for her ascent. "Got me a nice girl though," murmured William. "Can't complain. Gwennie's sweet, and I'm pleased to have her at last. Comes with plenty of good farm land up in Norfolk and a couple of mansions in Surrey. Nice arse too."

"I'm pleased for you," said Ludovic. "But when did you last see Gerald? Do you know what he's up to?" Berkhamstead did. Initially he had helped with the calligraphy. "And how much do you know about present rumours?" Ludovic demanded. "Do the authorities suspect? Is Gerald in immediate danger?"

"Oh no," William smiled. "Or I'd have done something. No – no. I saw some of the pamphlets on the very doors of St. Paul's a few days back, and not a thing was discovered, though of course the notes were pulled down and destroyed. Waste of good paper. Do you know how much paper costs these days?"

"I've heard," Ludovic interrupted him. "But another of my brothers, who seems to know more than he should, has the family in uproar believing Gerald's about to be arrested. You don't agree?"

William came back over, linking his arm through Ludovic's and lowering his voice. "Listen my friend. There's no specific suspicion yet as far as I know. Of course, in this game there's always danger, but it's a situation that justifies some risks. Have you ever been inside the Tower?" The thunder boomed outside, rolling like slow cart wheels around the Abbey steeple. The rain had increased. The sound of it pelting on the roof disguised William's words. "The Duke of York is housed in a small apartment in the Lanthorn, two tiny chambers and not even a privy. He's shackled, chains around his ankles attached to an iron collar on the neck. Can you imagine that? This is a king's son and the rightful monarch of this realm, but called Perkin Warbeck to his face and treated as a criminal with his legs bleeding as he shuffles around those damned damp rooms."

"He's alive," Ludovic pointed out. "After his last escape, everyone expected Tudor to order his execution. Yet he remains alive."

"Is that always such a blessing?" William leaned back against the pulpit, thumbs hooked in his belt. "Kept like that, and with no hope of improvement however long he lives? I'd as soon be dead. But listen, there's more. You remember that poor little bugger Warwick, old Clarence's son?"

Ludovic nodded. "The late King Richard's nephew. He's kept in the Tower too. I'm aware of that. It's been ten or twelve years now, poor child. There're no Plantagenets this Tudor wretch will risk allowing free."

"I understand why any new king needs keep a careful watch on the existing nobility. But Tudor's so fearful of possible threats to the throne, he treats what's left of the old royal family worse than cattle. He wants Warwick entirely forgotten by the people. After the fiasco at Stoke when the story was put about that it was Warwick claiming the throne even though he was already in custody at the time, poor little bugger, well, now Tudor's taking no risks."

"I remember. Fifteen years back King Richard sent the boy north in state to Sheriff Hutton castle with the other young Plantagenet heirs. But less than a day after claiming victory at Bosworth, Tudor sent for Warwick and put him under guard. The priorities of a usurper." Ludovic shrugged. "It stands to reason for a man terrified of any challenge to a crown he knows he doesn't wear by right."

The Earl of Berkhamstead began pacing the marble slabs. "Well, Warwick's a grown man now, poor miserable wretch. Caged all alone for many a long desolate year in the Lanthorn, but now at last has a new neighbour. They're cousins of course, and they've found a way of conversing through the floor. Over the months Warwick's scraped a crack between the stones, for he has the quarters directly above. Whispering, one with his ear to the ground, the other standing on a stool and muttering to the ceiling. They use the windows too, one above the other, and pass messages tied to cord. At least they have a semblance of company now."

"Dangerous," nodded Ludovic. "They'll be accused of plotting."

"I've been there," said Berkhamstead abruptly. "Poor bastards have no hope of escape. It's not plotting they yearn for, its friendship. Warwick has gone a little simple I'm afraid, but after twelve years in solitary confinement that's hardly surprising. He was only a child when he was taken. Yet he's a good natured boy, just desperately lonely. No Christian king would treat a pig that way let alone a young noble of the realm, guilty of no crime except his parentage." The earl shrugged. "What can I say? I'd creep in and strangle this Tudor bastard myself if I could get away with it, but all I could manage was visiting the Tower under a pretext to take books and ink, helping alleviate some of that terrible boredom."

"Good of you. But risky. Will get your name on the list of future suspects when something goes wrong."

"Nothing will go wrong. Nothing can be done to help either of them now. I got permission to visit by saying I'd sworn an oath to thank the Lord for my marriage, and this was my penance. The marriage is well worth an honest thank you, come to think of it. Sadly, she comes from a prominent Lancastrian family loyal to the Tudor cause. I don't like that, but it helps with my own security. And tell the truth, Gwennie herself doesn't know a York rose from a Lancastrian forget-me-not."

Ludovic strolled towards the chapel doors. "Well, I wish you good luck, prosperity and ten sons," he said. "But I'm getting Gerry out of the country next week, as soon as I can arrange a berth for him. No doubt I'll see you again before I set off back home."

"Give Gerald my regards," William said, following and closing the chapel doors with a grind. "Tell him to kiss Maximilian's hand for me." He grinned as Ludovic frowned. "Yes, yes, I know. That's not why or where you're sending him away, but I promise that's where he'll end up. Gerald won't give in yet, and Maximilian's still Prince Richard's strongest foreign supporter."

They separated beyond the small courtyard, Lord William hurrying back to his wife and Ludovic heading out towards the Palace stables to collect his sword and horse. It was around the last corner that Ludovic saw a familiar figure once again. The same silks, gilt on shadowed vermillion and sleeves trailing in sable glory. The same red hair. A short man, but self-assured with a firm stride and a straight back. Brice was not in Flanders yet after all.

CHAPTER THIRTY-THREE

The wharves were humming, puddled and rank. The great wooden cranes squeaked and whined in the wind, hoisting the bundles from the ship's streaming decks to the soggy land. Ludovic kept back, avoiding the scramble and heave. It had stopped raining over the two previous days but the wind still swept bitter up from the sea, and the Thames was turbulent with a threat of ice forming in the stagnant angles behind the berths and the bobbing piers.

Over the past eight days Ludovic had come five times to St. Katherine's, waiting for The Fair Rouncie to sail upriver into London with its cargo of alum and rich dyed and woven wool. But she was late. Tempests at sea accounted for many ships delayed, but tempests at sea might also mean the ship never came to port ever again.

On the ninth day Ludovic sighed with relief. He first heard the news at The Nest, the sailor's taverns always busy with information and as tight packed with gossip as with squabbles. Still with no sign of his ship, Ludovic ordered hot beer spiced and gingered, and was told, as usual, what ships had docked and which were due. "The Fair Rouncie's been sighted, my lord. 'Twas her, as you was asking of yesterday, if I remember rightly my lord."

Ludovic drank his beer and hurried outside. He recognised the single mast waiting out in the mid-river queue for docking. The old cog still had the custom's tug alongside, and Kenelm was no doubt busy bribing its officer. There would be a long wait. Ludovic wandered back into The Nest, sat down and ordered mulled wine.

He found Clovis first. The boy had been sent ashore to work out a deal with the hoistmen, and had chosen the same tavern for a quick cup of ale before business, breaking into the coin given him for bribery and barter. Ludovic saw him scamper in and, taking his own cup with him, came out of the long shadows, catching hold of the boy. Clovis wriggled, expecting trouble.

"I ain't done nuffing," Clovis complained, attempting to peer back over his shoulder at who had grabbed him, while trying not to spill his ale. "And if I done it, it ain't my fault."

Ludovic grinned. "I doubt if you have ever done nuffing in your miserable life, brat. And inevitably, most of it is assuredly your fault. However, I'm not here either to arrest or beat you, though no doubt you deserve both."

Clovis twisted around in delight. "Didn' expect you, m'lor. Fort you was back in Somerset. Captin's still onboard, he is, but we'll be docking afore sun down and he'll be as surprised to see your lordship as I is."

"It's two months I've been waiting for both of you. My original need is superseded and now there's a new plan, but the details can wait until Kenelm comes ashore." Ludovic shook his head, regarding the small urchin now beaming up at him, and smelling distinctly of brine and grime. "Are you capable of getting all the way back to Somerset on your own, child?"

Clovis frowned. "Reckon I could. Might take a week or more, though, 'pending on transport. Wot's it worth?"

"I need you back at the castle," Ludovic said. "But I'll explain everything once I see your uncle. Go finish your own business, then tell Kenelm I'm here waiting for him."

<hr />

It was a different tavern later that afternoon, sitting around a small table in the back room with two jugs of ale and the sun slipping low

305

towards a winter's early evening. "It turned out a longer trip than we meant, my lord," apologised the captain, draining his cup. "Good business, mind you, with a fair profit already done the other end, though I had to wait for it, and another expected this end. Was worth the wait. You'll be proper pleased, my lord, I can promise you that."

"But you might not be," said Ludovic, low voiced. "For I've a favour to ask, and one I expect you to grant. It's of considerable importance to me, or I'd not ask."

Kenelm beamed. Clovis, uninterested, remained nose deep in his cup. "I'd not be refusing any favour you asked of me my lord," said the captain. "And that you know."

"To go straight back out to sea," said Ludovic abruptly. "It's winter, the weather is treacherous, and you've just set foot on land after a long time away. Your family is waiting, your comfortable home and a soft warm bed. So I've an idea how wretched my request will seem, but as I say, it's important. I apologise, and you can refuse if you must, but my brother's life may depend on your answer. He must go to Flanders, no further, but within the week if possible."

Kenelm groaned. "I'd refuse you nothing, my lord, but the poor old girl needs a good scrub, and is running mighty sluggish to the windward with her arse deep crusted in barnacles and worse. I'd planned on having her careened and left here till next spring. Can your brother not wait, my lord?"

"This is not a simple matter of smuggling, Kenelm, with only putting ourselves at risk of a fine or a few months locked up in the Marshalsea waiting on trial. This is a whole different matter, my friend. My brother must be got out of the country or risks his life, nothing less. I'd have liked him gone before now, but regular trade's closed up for the winter and I can't buy an honest berth before spring. My other ship's already in Italy and Hussey's expected to lie in the dry docks at Genoa till March, so he won't be back. As for the rest of the ships plying for human cargo, my urgency looks immediately suspicious, and I've no other contacts, even for bribery. Besides, bribery has become such a normal part of business here, it no longer buys any privilege. So I need you, my friend, with no other to ask." Ludovic refilled all three cups. "I'll pay well, which you'd naturally expect, but I'll also pay in full for the hull's careening when you get back." He sighed, sipping his wine. "Meanwhile, I want the boy for something quite different," he continued. "He can't sail with you."

"Well now," smiled the captain. "Don't reckon I'll miss him. So we'd best get down to business right away, my lord, being as it's urgent. Now you tell us both exactly what it is you want."

Ludovic brought Gerald to meet Captain Kenelm that evening. It was a third tavern, this one in the north of London, intentionally well away from both the docks and the lodgings at The Horn. Gerald bubbled, almost absurdly excited. He had never travelled abroad before, and was hatching a nest of ready plans. Ludovic was simply tired. He ordered a jug of Burgundy.

"Not as fine as what we brought in ourselves during the blockade, my lord," Kenelem sniffed, tasting the wine. "Seems the legal stuff Burgundy sells us, is a right inferior sup."

"They've a lot more customers to satisfy now," Ludovic said, draining his own cup without complaint and immediately refilling it. "During the embargo we were able to pay for the best, since the Burgundian vintners had few other ways of doing business."

Gerald listened with an avid interest and a wide grin. "So that's how you make your mysterious wealth, Lu," he said. "Is Brice in it with you?"

"No, he damn well isn't," said Ludovic. "He has his own game, which I often wonder about and intend finding out one day soon. But for the moment, with the sanctions lifted, our business is back to boringly legal and far less profit."

"Except for the alum, that is," added the captain obligingly. "Papacy has a monopoly. We don't take no notice of that of course. His lordship's idea it was, since I didn't have not breath nor hide of what alum were. And a fine bugger of an idea too. Done us proud this past few months."

"Thank you, Kenelm," said Ludovic. "Please feel free to discuss all the details of our secret business with whomever you wish."

The captain coloured. "'Tis your brother, my lord. Reckon I never thought -"

"Never thought indeed," Ludovic sighed. "It's my brother's life and freedom I'm trying to preserve, but I prefer you not to ensure my own arrest while at it." He turned to Gerald. "Brice is now supposedly arranging a place for you in Flanders. The inestimable Duchess Margaret already has a court full of English refugees, so you can join them and all plot cheerfully together for all I care. The good captain will take you there, Gerry, leaving in five days' time. Unfortunately, it cannot be arranged sooner since the ship has barely docked an hour back and half the cargo is still to be unloaded." Ludovic grinned, looking to the captain and then back to his brother. "This poor man has barely had time to breathe the noxious fumes of dry land after returning from his last trip. He was dreaming of his good sister's wholesome home cooking, until I demanded he risk his life and his cog back on the chilly ocean waves yet again. I hope you appreciate the magnanimity of the situation?"

Gerald chuckled. The captain remained faintly puzzled. "Just doing a favour, as it happens," he said, hesitant. "Happy to oblige, and for a fee such as you've promised my lord, well there's not a pirate on the high seas would turn you down."

"Paying a handsome price to get rid of me, are you?" smiled Gerald. "I'd sooner you give it for the cause."

"This is my cause," said Ludovic. "I want you safe out of England and out of Tudor's grasp until all suspicions are forgotten. And once I know Kenelm is about to slip his ropes, I'll give you a fair purse to you set up your new life. Not before, so don't bother asking. I daren't even buy you a new doublet until the last moment, for fear you'll sell it."

"Your lordship is right welcome to my cabin of course," said the captain, complacent. "But it's tight for me, and I reckon you're a mite taller."

"Just pray for fair weather," smiled Ludovic.

"In December?"

"Well, ask for a bucket then, and pray for strong winds to blow you fast through the fogs and ferments."

"One thing," nodded the captain, "surely ain't likely to get becalmed."

⊶◈⊷

With a smart new hooded cape over his shoulders and a hundred promises made and repeated, Clovis set off the next morning for Sumerford. A ride in a carrier's cart all the way to Exeter was already paid for, and a small purse tied to Clovis's belt, sufficient for three days' food, a possible overnight lodging if it rained or snowed, and to allow for a lift in any other cart that happened past Exeter in the direction of Sumerford. Silently repeating the list of specific orders both for the journey and for arrival, Clovis climbed on the back of the cart, shoved the wooden crates and parcels out of the way, and unwrapped his bread and cheese.

Gerald was finishing his breakfast, feet up on the table, ankles crossed. He lurched forwards as Ludovic strode back into the chamber. "Good God, Lu, can't you announce yourself before you march in?" Gerald complained.

"You've got remarkably jumpy," Ludovic pointed out. "Do you know something you're not telling me, big brother?"

Gerald smiled. "Nothing. Well, not much. But there's been rumours of course." He finished the crumbs in his mouth with a cough. "I did think someone had seen me hammering a paper to St. Olave's doors, and had to slip away quick. But that was the advantage of Southwark you know. Not much interest in supporting the king there, and not much interest in the law either. The place is more full of criminals and cutpurses than Newgate goal."

"Berkhamstead seems to think you're in no particular danger," Ludovic nodded. "Brice thought otherwise."

"Not like Brice to make a fuss about nothing," Gerald conceded, breaking the manchet roll in two pieces. He cradled a wedge of salt pork between them, and stuffed the entirety in his mouth.

"So you know full well you're under specific suspicion?"

"I'm accepting being hustled out of the country, aren't I?"

Ludovic stretched his own legs up onto the table, and clasping his hands behind his head, leaned back with a sigh. "Four more days before you sail. Will either of us survive them? You are to promise me, Gerry, no more of these pamphlets, and no other risks until you're safe away from here."

Gerald paused, mouth full of bread and pork. "But I've half a ream of paper still, Lu, paid for and ready cut. I can't waste that. And then there's the Tower to visit."

Ludovic sat forward with a stamp and clatter, feet back to the floor in an instant. The ale jug spilled, its remaining trickle worming across the polished wood. "Gerry, try that and I swear I'll knock you out and carry you over my shoulder to the docks," he said between his teeth. "And I'll tie you up in Kenelm's cabin myself, and sit on you until the damn ship sails. How can you consider such a thing? Every visitor that poor bastard receives is noted and listed. You need permission first, and you'd never get away with a false name."

Gerald shook his head. "They check the names. I'd have to tell the truth. Besides, I got mightily tired of being called Goran Spittiswood, but it was the only name came into my head when I booked into that last place. Got it from a groom of mine I had as a boy. You might remember him."

"I don't," declared Ludovic. "And you'll not even approach the Tower, Gerry. I forbid it. You'd endanger yourself, and me too."

"William got into the Tower," Gerald objected. "He even bribed his way to a few minutes in private. Several of the guards genuinely like the prince, and it seems they're unusually sympathetic."

Ludovic raised an eyebrow. "Isn't it remarkable to allot such sympathetic guards to a shackled prisoner? I also understand there were some unlikely oversights on the night of the fire, and then more that helped the escape from Sheen. Almost as if it was all encouraged. I've a suspicion Tudor needs these escapes in order to justify his own actions. And what if the next attempt justifies an execution?"

"That won't happen. No one escapes from the Tower. Poor bloody Warwick's been kept alone in there for more than ten years, and never managed to do more than lose his mind." Gerald returned to the bread and meats, with a look of regret at the spilled ale. "Innocent of any crime except being the last king's nephew, poor little sod. But it shows how that Tudor knows full well his precious false pretender, this supposed boatman's ignorant boy from Tournai, is truly the late King Edward's son. Why else house him in that apartment in the Lanthorn, just below poor Warwick? Why call a prince a fraud and a commoner, but still treat him like a prince?"

"Listen Gerry," Ludovic leaned forwards again, gripping his brother's doublet lacings. "I no longer care. Oh very well, I now fully believe this hero of yours is the true prince, and I know Tudor's a bastard, but it's your life I'm interested in, with a fair consideration for my own. Leave it, at least until you meet up with the rest of your band of conspirators in Flanders and Burgundy."

Gerald shook him off. "And have you seen this absurd confession they've made the prince sign? It's as full of holes as my hose. So I have to finish writing out the pamphlets at least, Lu. If I agree not to go to the Tower, will you simply allow me - ?"

"You will not." Ludovic spoke softly, eyes narrowed. "Do you hear me plain, my dear? For I'll not let you out of my sight over the next four days. Not for the privy, not for sleep, and certainly not for leaving this inn. As it happens, I've given up a fair amount that matters a good deal to me, Gerry, in order to gallop up here and pack you off to safety. So until you sail, you'll do nothing more to invite danger or I'll murder you myself."

CHAPTER THIRTY-FOUR

F or three days they talked, at ease in the hostelry's peaceful comfort, fire blazing and candles lit while the gales gusted outside. The stench of the Fleet was safely locked away, the sleet and storms kept out. Even the sudden smoke from the chimney and the draught whining beneath the door barely ruined the warmth or the company. Ludovic paid for most meals to be brought to them, avoiding the clamour of the ale rooms, and at first even did as he had promised and accompanied his brother to the privy.

Over jugs of wine and steaming hippocras, they remembered old stories, the laughter of childhood and the absurd humiliations of puberty. They spoke joyfully of past glory and achievement, practise with sword and archery, the rare moments of their father's approbation, the glimpses of their mother dressed in her finery to attend the Plantagenet court. They remembered many things.

"Goran Spittiswood," said Gerald. "My groom, when I was twelve. We were almost the same age, so good friends. I had a new bay, first proper courser after riding ponies for ten years, so I went down to the stables as I did most days, keen to ask Goran how my horse was doing. Goran was flat on his face in the straw, with the back of his head kicked in. I spewed all over his back. Well, his brain was showing through wet and red and shining there in the dirt, and at twelve years old, I hadn't ever seen anything like that before. He didn't mind about the spew of course. He was dead. Old Ned was chief groom then. Said someone had hammered spikes into Angel's hooves."

Ludovic paused, staring, then broke the lengthening silence. "I remember Angel. Father's destrier before Turvey. A vicious bastard."

"Who? Father or the horse?"

"Both."

"I thought of that last year, you know, when you kept asking about that other apprentice groom that was killed."

"You didn't say. You should have."

"It would only have got you more fired up, Lu. I doubt it was true anyway. No one could have got close enough to either of those horses to go sticking spikes in their feet. They'd have been killed themselves."

"Maybe two men together, and one of them someone the horse trusted?"

"You suspect Humphrey? But who in God's good world would have helped Humphrey torture a damned great brute of a war horse?"

Another silence stretched, the fire throwing its giant shadows across their faces. Finally Ludovic sighed. "What would you say, Gerry, if I decided to marry a commoner and cause another family scandal?"

Gerald laughed. "As if I'd care. Besides, I'll be in Flanders. You mean your little maidservant? Bring her over to meet me and I'll sing at your wedding."

"I don't know," Ludovic said, half to himself. "Mother would never acknowledge her and Father would probably banish me from Somerset. But I've absolutely no ambition for power or Tudor recognition. What would it really matter to anyone, except myself?"

"Follow your heart, Lu," Gerald said, suddenly serious. "Challenging at first perhaps, ignoring a lifetime's teaching, and awkward never facing Papa or Mamma again, but who wants to? Mamma would take the Bedfordshire property back but you've your own means of support, it seems. There's no law against marrying your mistress, after all. Old King Edward got away with it twice, and the second was a commoner of sorts, though it mucked up the succession and here's me caught up in the consequences. Strange though, since you were always the most arrogant of us all. But how many of us expect happy marriages in the normal way? Not one. Arranged alliances are a bore, and the best you'll get if you're lucky is a little friendship and a few ungrateful sons. Besides, no noble father is going to hand over his heiress to a younger son, nor give you the family beauty. Now I've followed my heart. You should do the same."

"She's not my mistress," Ludovic sighed. "Though she should have been."

Gerald was intrigued. "Turn you down, did she? Good for her. You might be reckoned a handsome bugger, but you can't expect every damned woman to fall at your feet you know Lu. And you can't expect everyone in the world to like you either. Some don't. Do you good to remember it."

It was the following day and a late dawn's sullen sunshine was drying the puddles. Ludovic had a meeting with Captain Kenelm arranged; the final business of the smuggled alum and the morrow's sailing to confirm. High tide was due early, but winter curfews were strict and the Ludgate would not open until six. Ludovic therefore proposed getting his brother on board the afternoon before, but he could not leave Gerald alone in the cabin overnight, with the Tower's dark shadow looming directly over the dockyard. Too close. "Come on," Ludovic said. "We'll wander down to the ship now, finish what I need to sort out, and get back here for dinner. Then you can spend the afternoon packing before going back onboard this evening."

Gerald pulled a face. "I've nothing to pack. And walking the whole width of London three times in one day is a shameful waste, Lu. You've a damned good horse down in the stables. Leave me here while you ride over to the docks. Put what little I own in your saddle bags, save me carrying it by hand later on. It won't take you long and I'll be here waiting."

Ludovic regarded his brother with considerable suspicion. "I'd sooner walk, and take you with me."

"Don't be a fool Lu," Gerald smiled, shaking his head. "I'm off tomorrow and looking forward to it, so I'm not likely to do anything rash now and I won't put my journey in jeopardy. You go and finish business with your captain, and then gallop back here for a pie and pottage dinner. I'll be a good boy while you're gone, I promise."

Then as the early calm slunk quickly beneath raging storm clouds rushing up from the sea, the breeze turned to hearty gusts, the thunder broke and the rain tumbled in an icy dark, so the decision seemed made for them. Ludovic, wrapped in his thickest coat, brimmed hat and waxed cape, trudged down to the stables, collected his reluctant horse and rode east into the unrelenting sleet. "You are to stay here. If I see mud on the soles of your boots when I get back," he told his brother, "I shall save myself a deal of money by throwing you in the Thames and holding you down myself."

Gerald had grinned. "I could as easily drown in the wintry German Ocean on my way to Flanders."

"You wouldn't drown in the Thames anyway," Ludovic shook his head as he slammed the door on the chamber's bright warmth. "You'd be poisoned by shit before you even sank to the bottom."

Kenelm was waiting for him, the Fair Rouncie uneasy at her moorings. Once past The Bridge and sleeking towards the estuary, the tidal river swelled in the storm and the ships bit at their ropes. Ludovic climbed onboard and accepted the cup of hot mulled wine offered him. "Then we're agreed," Ludovic nodded. "You keep a half of my profits from this last trip and it's a fair price under the circumstances. I want my brother delivered safely to Antwerp and then it's up to you if you manage to pick up any cargo on the way back. I'll be in Somerset after Christmas if the weather holds. Come to the castle or send a message."

"That I will, my lord. There'll be no problems, don't you worry."

"And once I'm settled back home myself, I'll pack Clovis off to your sister." Ludovic sighed, stretching his legs to the cabin's panelled limits. "I trust the weather won't delay your embarking with tomorrow's tide?" The steady rain beat on the wooden decks over their heads, a distant echo of thunder and no promise of the storm abating.

Kenelm shook his head with a smile. "Not likely, my lord. Wet above and wet below, it don't bother me. A full gale out at sea, well that's a hiccup as can turn a man's bilges bright yellow, but a crack o' thunder and lightning matters no more than a piss."

"I am exceedingly glad," said Ludovic, "that I have no need to go to sea myself, my friend. This cabin is enough to make me bilious and we're still in port."

Kenelm's smile turned to a grin. "With your lordship doing the business on land, being your lordship's place of greatest skills as it were, and me at sea being my own proper preference, well, we makes a good team I reckon, my lord, and I trust it'll go on for many years to come, legal or otherwise. I'm a happy man since meeting you, my lord. My sister prays for you every night."

"I think," said Ludovic, "she should speak a little louder."

The captain refilled both their cups. The hippocras had cooled but the sweet smell of spices remained and Ludovic drank deep. The final arrangements now settled, a strangely pleasant sense of peace and accomplishment was returning with the wine. Alysson's smile was once again glowing in his mind, and the likelihood of having her once again in his arms within the week. He was setting his empty cup on the desk when a sudden stamping of hurried footsteps and the sound of Gerald's voice came thumping over his head, someone half sliding down the steps to the cabin, and the door swung open with two wet faces pushing into the gloom. Rainwater streamed to the cabin's boards.

Gerald was muffled inside his hooded cape and recognisable only by the sharp tip of his slightly hooked nose. It was the other man who spoke first. "Sumerford? Thank God, so this is the right ship after all," groaned the Earl of Berkhamstead. "Close your hatches man, and answer to no one."

Four men within the cabin made it impossible to move. The captain, flurried and finding no space to bow, stepped abruptly back to the bed and sat. Ludovic grabbed Gerald's shoulders and pushed off his dripping hood, peering into his face. "Gerry? What on earth?"

"They're onto us," Gerald gasped. "Tudor's armed guards came to the inn. I saw them ride up and I heard what they demanded. I had time to run, but I've an idea they saw me."

Ludovic's eyes narrowed. "You were outside already?"

William had collapsed on the bench. "We were just getting back. Two moments earlier, and we'd both have been taken."

Still holding to Gerald's shoulders, Ludovic shook him furiously. "What were you doing?"

It was William who answered again. "Came to find me," he said. "Wanted to give me his pamphlets to finish, and explain where he was going. There should have been no harm done, but someone in the king's pay knows more than they should. We weren't seen leaving court, I'm sure of that for we couldn't have been followed in this weather without me noticing. Clearly the guards were on their way to the hostelry before we left Westminster. They knew where to go, they knew the place, and they knew the name. We got away, or Gerald would already be under arrest."

Ludovic glared at his brother, cold eyed. "You deserve arrest, you fool. You promised to stay indoors and wait for me."

"I only promised not to nail up the pamphlets or to go to the Tower," Gerald spluttered. "And if I'd stayed indoors as I should, I'd be in the Tower myself by now."

"If it's urgent, I can sail tonight, my lord," interrupted Kenelm, trying to follow the discourse. "The crew's already mostly onboard, and with this storm the rest'll likely leaves the taverns within the hour."

"Right then," said Ludovic. "Tonight it is, whether the crew's drunk or sober." He turned to William. "And you, sir? Are they after you as well?"

The earl shook his head. "I don't believe so. I've been at court for an age and they could have taken me anytime over the past month if they'd wanted. I may have a few questions to answer on my return, and maybe they've looked for me, and frightened my poor little Gwen, but no – I don't believe I've any need to run just yet. Now I know you're both safe, I'll hurry back to my wife."

"Good," Ludovic nodded. "Then I'll scout outside before returning to the inn. No doubt I'll have questions to answer myself if they come looking for you again, but with luck I may be able to help allay some of the suspicion."

There was a pause. William looked at his feet. Gerald gazed upwards at his brother. "No, Lu. You can't go back," he said softly. "It was your name they gave at The Horn. The lords Ludovic and Gerald Sumerford. There's a warrant out for both of us." Ludovic stared back, each man's forced breathing and the creaking of the ship's hull the only sounds. "Your name first." Gerald's face was white in the small stub of candlelight. "I was trapped between the courtyard and the doorway, so I heard everything they said. Will and I stood there in the shadows, frightened to breathe, just listening."

"There's a warrant out for the arrest of the lords Ludovic and Gerald Sumerford for High Treason, signed in the king's name," William whispered. "Wanted for immediate questioning under close confinement. Anyone assisting their escape is also subject to arrest."

The one lantern swung gently from the ceiling beams. Its guttering candle lit Ludovic's hair in streaming flax but shadowed his face. He stood in stunned silence, swaying slightly as he balanced loosely against the gentle roll of the ship.

"So how did they know where to come?" said Gerald. "I hadn't even been at The Horn for some weeks previous. I'd moved to Southwark."

Ludovic said, "Brice. He knew you were at The Horn. He paid your shot, and sent me there to look for you. He knew exactly where we'd both be staying."

Gerald shook his head a little wildly, raindrops flying. "Don't be bloody stupid, Lu. Brice is a clever bastard, but he wouldn't do that. Not Brice."

"A clever bastard, and very rich from his very secret business. Spying for the king pays damned well I hear. And what better way to earn your fortune, with a damned naïve fool of a brother admitting his treasons freely within the family?"

"We've no time for this," William interrupted. "If you can set sail this evening, all the better. I need to get going myself before the guards hurry back to court and frighten the life out of poor Gwennie again."

Ludovic nodded, thin lipped. "Then take my horse. I'll have no more need of him, it seems."

Kenelm, having stayed diplomatically quiet for some time, now stood and came to the centre beside his own desk. "Well, my lords, if you'll forgive me, the case seems clear. 'Tis both you two young lords must come to Flanders with me and we'll set sail within the half hour, full crew or no. I shall give my orders now and set the ship to rights. We're banked in, and if I've to slip my ropes quiet like, I need a man on shore and the crew to their places. Those as needs to go must take to the land now if it pleases you my lord, and those as is staying must make themselves as comfy in here as can." He turned, bowed, and stomped off up the steps, the ill hung cabin door swinging shut behind him.

Ludovic sank down on the bed. "Damnation to hell," he muttered, though only to himself. "Well, that's a fine end to everything."

"Not an end, Lu," Gerald bent over him, still dripping from cape and hood. "I've no words to express how sorry I am, little brother. I've played you an ill trick, and would have done anything in the world to avoid it, had I realised. But they say Flanders is a grand place. You don't care about mother or papa, and no one cares about poor old Humphrey. I can't believe Brice betrayed us, but he'll not be missed one way or the other. Neither of us expected to inherit much, and maybe we can get back one day if this blows over. What's left to miss?"

"Only my life. My dreams. So to hell with hope." Ludovic stared up at him from the shadows, his green eyes glazed and as cold as the sleet. "You're a bastard fool, my dear," he said softly, "but then of course, so am I."

CHAPTER THIRTY-FIVE

Deep hidden within winter's chilly dark, the small cog slipped her moorings and sailed downriver, slowly as the yard arm was hauled up and the sail raised. Wary past the Tower's artillery, the waters parted, wavelets slapping the clinkered hull as the sail cracked against the mast, flattened, took the wind, and billowed. The drizzle hung like a cobwebbed mist in the starlight and from behind the clouds the moon's aura hinted at an eerie silver sheen. The river took the reflections, a huge black silence as they entered the battlemented shadows of the Tower, and then on towards the estuary and the open sea.

The strong wind had dropped, but in the fretful night breeze the ship picked up speed. Kenelm took the tiller, keeping his orders brisk and quiet. A crew of nearly thirty, half of them half drunk and half asleep, worked the decks, sliding quickly down the wet rigging, callused hands long accustomed. London's closed reek was gradually left behind and the breezes blew fresh.

In the small cabin below decks at the stern the two men kept their silence. Ludovic stretched prone on the bed, hands clasped behind his head and eyes firmly closed. Gerald sat. He balanced rigid, glaring at the door creaking on its uneasy hinges. An oil lamp hung suspended from the low beamed ceiling, swinging as the ship pitched. Its small flame flared out and shrank back. The shadows streaked pale, the men's faces hidden in gloom.

"Come to bed," Ludovic said softly, eyes still shut.

Gerald jumped as if slapped. "I'm all right. I'm not tired. You sleep. Besides, the bed's too narrow for two."

Ludovic opened his eyes. "Don't be a damned fool, Gerry. You intend sitting up for the next three nights, determined to wallow in guilt? It won't help either of us if you make yourself ill, my dear, and your suffering won't help me. Besides, I don't hold you responsible. Not entirely, anyway." He sat forward with a sudden grin. "And we'd better make sure we get on, since Kenelm's solution for shipboard murder is to rope the killer to the corpse and toss them both into the ocean."

"Best place for me," muttered Gerald.

Ludovic sighed. "Come to bed, for pity's sake. Let's get some sleep before we hit another storm and both end up on the floor."

"I'd best sleep on the floor anyway," Gerald said, staring blankly into the furthest corner. "I'll use my cloak as a blanket and my boots as a pillow. You take the bed."

"Dear God give me patience," said Ludovic. "Are you intending to behave like this for the whole voyage?"

The next morning, having managed to sleep together and groan into each other's ears for most of an uneasy night, Ludovic and Gerald joined the dawn queue at the prow where two heavy wooden seats were built out from the gunwales into the air, their open centres dropping straight towards the sea. Most of the thirty strong crew, muttering and complaining of a variety of headaches and belly aches occasioned mainly from their previous celebrations whilst in dock, appeared to have formed the queue already. Those already perched on the seats of ease, grunted to themselves in concentrated effort. The ship had gained speed in the night and her sail blew full, but the hull pitched forwards as she clipped each wave, tipping deep into the sea before lurching upright once more.

"I think," Gerald decided, "I shall stay constipated until Flanders."

"Queasy?" inquired Ludovic.

"Just terrified of hurtling bare arse over head off the privy and into the sea."

"An ignominious end."

But the weather stayed comparatively calm for some hours and a tepid sun seeped through the cloud cover. They saw little of Kenelm, the captain being kept busy with his ship, and after striding two circuits of the deck to clear their lungs and heads and then climbing up to the small poop deck to watch the ocean heave for a few monotonous moments, both men finally returned to the cabin.

A meagre breakfast of stale biscuits and cheese had been eaten some time back and a cold dinner was some way off. Ludovic slumped on the stool, hauled off his wet boots, tossed them to the corner and stared at his brother. Gerald stretched on the bed, stared at the low beams, and blew a small trail of dust from over his head.

"I thought I'd like being at sea," Gerald said with bleak reluctance. "I didn't know it would be like this. I had a vague idea about ships being exciting."

"Try climbing the rigging in a storm. I imagine that's sufficiently exciting." Ludovic put his feet up on the desk. "I always knew I'd hate sailing. But at least neither of us seems destined to vomit through the entire journey. Evidently some people are more liable to seasickness than others and seemingly I'm not that delicate. But I've a hearty dislike for the smell of the ocean."

"Then I can't see why you decided on a career as a merchant, dependant on braving these sickly waters," objected Gerald. "Or why you decided to keep it all so damned secret either."

"Smuggling's illegal, in case you'd forgotten," Ludovic pointed out. "And although you could never keep your mouth shut regarding your own far more illegal activities, I decided to be more cautious. Besides, it's no one's business but my own."

"Distrustful bastard." Gerald thought a moment. "So, have you forgiven me yet, little brother?"

Ludovic yawned. "It might be pleasant to believe this is anyone's fault but my own, but I can't. I've voluntarily involved myself in your business for some time now, Gerry, and I've supported your cause albeit from a careful distance. Besides, I'm lucky I've never been hauled up over my own illegalities. So – I get caught over yours instead. It was an unpleasant shock I admit, but I don't blame you in particular."

"It's because of me and you know it is." Gerald shook his head. "But how did anyone know we were at The Horn? Don't tell me Brice, for I won't believe it. Besides, you said he was already in Flanders."

"I said he was supposed to be."

"If Brice had wanted to give me over to the authorities, he could have done so a hundred times. Why now?"

"Because those same authorities are now desperate to find the traitor pinning damned stupid pamphlets to church doors, with a high price offered for information I imagine. And it's hardly the first time you've faced arrest."

"But the first time you have."

Ludovic sighed. "And that's something I don't fully understand. It may even be a mistake. But I expect my name's on someone's list ever since I visited your poor squire in prison and attended his execution."

"Poor bloody Roland." Gerald shook his head. "I'm sorry Lu, for everything and everyone. I keep saying that and it doesn't help, I know, but it's the truth. God, I really am sorry."

"At least we're not locked in the Tower, my dear." Ludovic smiled gently, gazing across at his brother. "And at least we've a few possessions with us. There's all your meagre property, and what little I'd brought of my own. We're both armed, have warm clothes, and I've plenty of money plus what Kenelm still owes me from the last profits. Shame about the rest of my gear left at the inn, for the crown will be quick to confiscate that. But just some linen, a few furs, boots and other nonsense, so no great loss. William has my horse and will no doubt make a good master."

"And my pamphlets," muttered Gerald. "When they find those, it'll seal my fate forever."

Ludovic raised an eyebrow. "I thought there was only blank paper left?"

"Oh well. A little more than that."

It was later when a ragtaggle boy brought them a meal of cold meats and more biscuit, a jug of sour ale and a message from the

323

captain. "Ca'pin says anovver storm's comin' up a few miles ahead," grinned the boy. "Black clouds on horizon. Best stay below."

Gerald regarded the cold meat and pinched one gristled wedge of unrecognisable grey flesh between his fingers. "Is this all anyone's eating, and in damned cold weather like this?" he demanded.

"Least it ain't maggoty," the boy pointed out, relentlessly cheerful. "Will be soon, if we gets delayed. An' we can't cook nuffin. Stones on deck is too wet."

"So take the stones below and dry them off," suggested Gerald with fading patience.

The boy sniggered. "Oh yeah. Start a fire below decks. That's all we needs." The amused chuckle echoed from above as the boy scampered back up the steps. Gerald stared miserably at Ludovic over the small platter of unappetising food.

"Eat," commanded Ludovic. "With another damned storm coming, we'll need our strength. Kenelm took on stores before I saw him yesterday, so the meat's fresh."

Gerald poured the ale. "I'd sooner drink and forget everything."

"Do that and I shall let you drown," Ludovic warned him. "Saving your bastard life if we capsize will be hard enough, without you being pissed. And let me warn you, the boat will probably split apart if a gale hits too hard. This ship was due for careening and re-caulking at the end of the last trip, and half the nails are rusty."

"I can't swim," said Gerald with a faint smile.

"I know," said Ludovic. "I can, but it's of no consequence. The cold will kill us both before we drown anyway."

"I'm not sure if you're trying to cheer me up or punish me for having caused all this," muttered Gerald. "In either case, I'd prefer you just ate your dinner and kept your opinions to yourself."

"I shall say no more," Ludovic grinned. "Just lash yourself to the bed. Or better still, the chamber pot."

Kenelm briefly visited his guests as they finished their meal, stomping into his lost cabin with a wet and leathered smile. "Your lordships all snug and well fed, then?" he inquired. "And slept deep, I trust? We've a spot of bad weather coming up, but nothing to worrit over and nothing I'm not used to. Might get a bit rough though, so best keep below."

"I've no wish to sound ungrateful," said Gerald, "but you wouldn't get me on deck if you paid me."

"Well, 'tis yous paying me, so's can go where you wish, my lord." The captain bowed, his grin fixed. "But it's a nasty squall by the looks of the clouds, and I doubt we'll get through it afore evening's done. Either of your lordships feel a mite shitty, then best stay in here and spew in the pot. And it ain't no shame on you neither, for there's seasoned sailors will heave up their guts in a storm. The hold will be awash wi' it by nightfall."

Ludovic smiled. "Thank you, my friend. We will endeavour to survive. I didn't expect calm seas, being December. I've trusted you for five years now, and you've always come through."

"And will again, my lord," Kenelm said. "Never yet met a storm as would frighten me. And she may be old, but the Rouncie's as strong a ship as ever sailed the German Sea. Try and get some sleep, my lord, and I'll come visit again in the morning wi' the sun."

The gale hit within the hour. They heard it first and felt it immediately after. The wind roared and the ship hurtled sideways, rolling so deep that the crashing boom of wood against water was momentarily deafening and every plank shuddered. Gerald tipped from the bed and sat gasping on the floor. Ludovic laughed and hung on to the stool.

For the first hour the sounds from above vibrated below, the thunder of running feet as loud as that from the sky, the screaming of Kenelm's orders over the wind, the answering shouts of the crew. The yardarm had been lowered well before the storm hit and the sail remained lashed to the deck, but there seemed many other duties needed to secure the ship and Kenelm's voice continued to echo. Then the storm hurtled into even greater force, and the men became strangely quiet, all their efforts concentrated in hanging on or staggering to greater safety, with little else to do except bail until the tempest passed.

Neither Ludovic nor Gerald said much. Crouched below, they could barely hear each other, and there was nothing to say. Gerald clasped tight to the chamber pot, vomiting until weak, when he rolled onto the bed, knees clamped to his belly. Ludovic slumped down and wedged his feet to the immovable base of the desk. He breathed deep, keeping his stomach controlled. The lantern went out in the wind from the slamming door and a slime of black water leaked down the steps from above, swamping the boards ankle deep. There was no counting time. They were kept blind below, but could have seen no more on deck. The night swept in, but it was already furiously dark from gale, cloud and rain.

Then the wind dropped. The ship lurched a little, swung between waves, righted itself and floated free. Released quite suddenly from threat and disaster, The Fair Rouncie bobbed peacefully, slapped by the last of the floundering waves. The noise ceased completely. The sky cleared to a fine night and a fat pearly slice of moon stared down at her own peacefully rippled reflection.

Gerald groaned and sat up. Ludovic blinked and smiled. "Still afloat," he murmured. "Quite a surprise." He explored the strength of his legs and waded through dirty water to the swinging door and the steps beyond. He peered up. Without light he could guess little and did not trust his feet to the stairway, but the faint moaning of men staggering upright and returning to their posts sounded like a ghostly chorus on its way through Purgatory. "I think," he said, returning tentatively to the stool, "the crew lives. Though we'll surely have been swept off course, so God knows where we are now."

"In the damned ocean," muttered Gerald.

Ludovic sat again, rather heavily. "This water is ice. But it's growing no deeper. I doubt we're sinking."

"What a boringly practical soul you are," complained Gerald. "Is there anything left to drink? A candle to light? A dry tinder box? And anywhere to empty this stinking chamber pot?"

"Practical questions indeed, my dear, but why ask me?" Ludovic stretched, pushing his fingers through the knots of his hair. "This ship may be half my own, but I've not the slightest idea where anything is. Certainly the ale jug and the cups are somewhere on the floor and floating in filthy water, and I suggest the pot needs emptying over the gunwales." He stood once more and slopped through the muck over to the bed. Finding the high wooden edge by feel, he rolled himself onto the mattress and curled into a position of acceptable comfort. "Move up, my dear. I am utterly exhausted and now we seem destined to stay afloat, I intend sleeping."

"How can you?" Gerald objected. "After that?"

"The smell from that chamber pot isn't helping I admit," said Ludovic. "But if you try throwing its contents overboard now, you'll probably fall over after it. I therefore suggest it waits until morning. In the meantime, I hope to dream of sweeter things." He closed his eyes and pulled the blanket to his ears.

Gerald struggled back against the wall at bed's edge, wiping his mouth on his sleeve. "Well, I suppose there's nothing else we can do, so we ought to sleep if we can. But I've a foul headache, my whole body aches, my guts feel punched, my eyes sting and my ears are buzzing. How in purgatory can you sleep so easily?"

"A guilt-free conscience and a thick skin," murmured Ludovic. "I trust our good captain to do whatever is necessary, and he'll hardly need any assistance from me. So goodnight, my dear. And if another storm rolls in, I have no desire to hear about it. Let me die quietly in my sleep."

CHAPTER THIRTY-SIX

"Well nigh back to the English coast, my lords," said Kenelm. "But time lost is time gained, when you thinks about it." Since neither of their lordships appeared to appreciate the meaning of this obscure insight and shook their heads, Kenelm patiently explained. "What I means, my lords, is best off closer to the coast when a storm gets a touch above itself, so being blowed back done us a favour. I reckon we've ended a touch too far to the south, but once I've made sure exactly where we is, we'll set sail north east."

"And no serious damage to the ship?" inquired Ludovic.

"We took on water," Kenelm admitted, "but 'tis all shipshape now. T'would be a terrible thing to capsize the first time ever in my life, being the first time your lordship were ever onboard." He grinned with a brief bow. "Mind you, I've an idea you'd be coping with the situation whatever happened, my lord, and no doubt you'd be a'rescuing of me."

Gerald laughed. "Nice to know someone has such faith in you, little brother."

"Luckily it won't be put to the test," said Ludovic, pulling his boots back on as a bright frosty sunshine dazzled through the open doorway. The captain was halfway back up to the deck when the call came.

"Carvel sighted due south, ca'pin. Flying no flag and coming hard at us."

"Shit," muttered Kenelm and ran the last steps.

Gerald peered at Ludovic over his cup. "And what's that supposed to mean?"

"I've no idea." Ludovic quickly drained his own cup and stood. "Some other vessel needing help after the storm perhaps. But Kenelm didn't seem well pleased." He went to the door, looking up.

"Best stay here. We don't want to be in the way," said Gerald.

"But arm yourself in case, Gerry," Ludovic said, quickly buckling on his own sword. "This time we carry nothing except ourselves, but there's no way of telling that from a distance since I imagine we've a hold full of storm water. We'll be lying low as though heavy with cargo."

Gerald at once reached for his sword, tucking his knife into his belt. "What do you suspect, Lu? Pirates?"

Ludovic nodded. "Something I know very little about, but Kenelm's mentioned the danger from time to time. Breton pirates are thick on the south coast in summer and haunt the Narrow Sea spring to autumn. But we're not in the Narrow Sea, and this is winter."

"I'd sooner fight for my life than lie rolling and spewing down here in some filthy storm," Gerald said. "And escaping Tudor was necessary policy, but the idea of running away never appealed. Instead I'll kill a few bastard pirates before they kill me, and die happier than on the executioner's block."

Ludovic sighed. "Up until two days ago, I'd no notion of dying in any manner whatsoever. And I always knew I'd hate going to sea."

Knife ready, he took the first two stairs up to the deck. The usual sound of wind, the crack of the sail and the creaking of wood, hurried footsteps and voices, were all muted beneath the noises of the sea; heaving water and waves slamming the ship's sides. Gerald was close behind him. "I'm coming with you, little brother. You'll not get all the fun to yourself this time."

The morning was bright and cold. A fair breeze and a choppy sea made for good sailing weather. But the lack of noise had been misleading. The great shadow of a carvel, a three masted ship much larger than their own, blocked the horizon at a bare few minutes distance. She carried heavy artillery and the barrels of four cannon protruded towards them from her side. The deck was crowded, the crew ill matched and heavily armed, gap toothed grins wide in the sunshine. Ludovic stopped in surprise, balancing himself behind Kenelm. The captain kept his eyes steady on the approaching carvel, speaking cautiously from the corner of his mouth. "Pirates, my lord. 'Tis mighty unfortunate, but we carry nothing worth stealing and I hope to bargain our way clear."

"Bargain with what?" demanded Ludovic. "The only thing you have to bargain with, my friend, is us. Two hostages for ransom."

Kenelm shook his head. "Leave it to me, my lord, and stay below I beg you."

"I'd prefer to be protecting my own ship and my own skin," Ludovic said.

"'Tis up to you, my lord. But pirates is nasty buggers, and they'll not be fighting fair. Those cannon could blow the Rouncie to splinters, and our shot's soaked through. So I'd sooner not be worriting over yous, my lord."

The ships closed, spray dancing between. "I shall keep back under cover unless I see I'm needed," Ludovic said. He stepped away, keeping beneath the poop deck's low shadows, Gerald quickly following. Knives loose at their sides, they stood quiet and alert.

Someone was shouting from the pirate ship. "Have you ort to declare, my fine friend? We've four to your one, the powder boy's on his toes and my crew ready to fire. If you've any wish to save your miserable lives, give your cargo over, and we'll be off."

"Not Bretons then," muttered Gerald. "Are English pirates any less savage, do you think?"

"They sound Cornish," Ludovic answered. "And no."

The carvel's eager crew leaned over their gunwales, peering down at the smaller ship below them, close enough now to spit. Kenelm stood firm and shouted up to the man above. "Captain Kenelm at your service," he cried. "And you'd be welcome to my cargo, but I carry naught." His voice was blown back as the carvel's sails slapped hard against the mast.

The waves danced in icy spray between the ships. The Rouncie was caught in surging eddies, the wind springing her forwards while the larger boat blocked the open current. No one answered Kenelm and he sighed deep as thick ropes hurtled through the sudden glitter of sun on sea, iron clamps ripping over the gunwales and hooking ship to ship with a huge shuddering boom. The wind whistled in the rigging overhead and clasped unevenly together, each planked keel creaked and strained to find its balance, lurching to the pull of the waves and the confines of the embrace. The cog's sails flapped hollow and sank. The decks rocked again as eleven men slid down the ropes, landing wide legged and grinning on the Rouncie's narrow boards.

The largest stood facing Kenelm. "No need to show us around." He waved to his waiting men. "I reckon we'll find our own way, thanking you kindly."

"I'll molest no peaceable visitor," Kenelm roared, keeping well back. "But you'll see we've no cargo to steal."

The pirate captain appeared to find this amusing. "Ain't never met a man admitting to what he had, lest he had some well hid," the man said.

"I'm hiding naught," Kenelm insisted, showing empty hands. "And won't hardly lie, not with a host of cannon staring me in the face."

"And no seafaring gent is stupid enough to reckon on cannon fire once hard up hull tight on hull." The other man was still grinning, hands to his belt where his crossed blades were catching the sun. "Fire on you," he said, "and we'd blow a bigger hole in our own sides, and well you know it. So ten men it is to search, and eighty others watching close, bows aimed with arrows to the nock, and ready to jump over and help if there's one word from me."

Kenelm made no move to draw his own steel. "I'll not try and stop you," he muttered. "I told the truth and we've no cargo or I'd hand it over. We're a small ship and I ain't after trouble. We've played fair, and I reckon on getting the same from you."

Back in the chill shadows beneath the poop deck, Ludovic and Gerald stayed quiet, poised and waiting. Fingers impatient to their blades, they watched as the pirates scattered. Five of them rounded up Kenelm's glum and glaring crew, searching them for weapons and pulling the few knives found from their belts. The other pirates ran down to the storage deck, the solitary cabin and the hold. Every thump of boots vibrated across the decks as the little cog swayed on her tethers, every footstep rebounding as their steps and shouts echoed back up from below. "'Tis right. There's naught here but swill and wet hammocks. A rubbish haul, it is."

The sun slid over the wet wood above as the Rouncie's crew stood sullen, staring up at the other ship's huge rolling threat and its dark shadow swallowing their own light. Then one man came up amidships, Ludovic's sable trimmed coat over his arm. "But reckon there's sommit we've not bin told. A cabin wi' fine clothes, and signs o' someone sleeping there 'part from this scruffy little shit arsed captin o' theirs."

"That's my cabin, and my coat," objected Kenelm.

"Fucking liar," grinned the man carrying the furs. "This be a gennleman's gear, an' would only fit you wiv anovver bleeder sitting on your fucking shoulders. An' more stuff down there, there is, though naught else so fine. So, maybe you got no cargo but I reckon you got some fancy fucking passenger well hid."

"Which," interrupted the pirate captain, grinning down into Kenelm's glare, "means a high fare already paid, so plenty of coin somewhere on board. So do I have my men ripping your planks apart to search for it, or do you tell me where it's hid? Come now, my friend, I thought we were playing fair?"

From the deeper shadows Ludovic stepped immediately forwards, knife back in his boot and sword in its scabbard. "I think," he said softly, "it would be me you are looking for."

The pirate captain turned quickly. He looked Ludovic over carefully. Ludovic stared back, eyes narrowed against the wind. The captain said, "So, my beauty! A decent cargo after all, it seems. You've a name and title?"

Ludovic remained expressionless. He spoke softly, his words almost drowned by the crack and groan of water against wood and the whine of the pull on the ropes. "And money," he said, "though not much. The fare paid in full remains with the ship's owner back in London, but I've a purse on me and you're welcome to it in exchange for my life, and that of the captain here and his crew. My name's Goran Spittiswood and sadly I've no title. I'm on my way to Flanders, with a business to set up in trade, Bruges dyes to buy in exchange for the coin I carry and other merchants to see for future backing."

Kenelm and his crew stood watching and listening, wary and silent, still under threat. The pirate captain faced Ludovic. Slowly he drew one blade from his belt, and stretched out his arm, sword point to Ludovic's chest. They were of a similar height but the other man was considerably older, dark bearded and leather skinned, his hair straggling in dirty ringlets well past his shoulders. He frowned. "Spittiswood's no gentleman's name, sir, but a gentleman you clearly are. As for your purse, I'll take it whether freely given or no, so your bargain hardly interests me. But pointless bloodshed won't interest me neither, and this ship's too small to be worth commandeering. Little more than a pigeon's egg, and the crew a timid rabble." His sword point moved up, now hovering at Ludovic's throat. His men crowded around.

Kenelm, suddenly released, did not move. "Master Spittiswood's word is true enough," he said loudly. "I've knowed him for some months and has always dealt honest and fair wi' me."

The pirate ignored him. He took Ludovic's coat and swung it around his own shoulders. The thick crimson taffeta, trimmed and lined in fur with a swirl of drifting sleeves, seemed incongruous on the other man, too rich over dun broadcloth and dirty serge. The pirate's doublet was black leather, his shirt and sleeves were blood stained and brine caked, his hose ill-fitting grimed kersey. Not a man interested in ostentation, and over his own broadcloth surcoat, Ludovic's finery seemed colourfully absurd. The pirate laughed, spread out the coat's skirts one handed, kept his sword raised, and bowed. "Captain Naseby, Black Baldwin at your service." He straightened, the smile glazed, his eyes cold. "I'll keep your coat, I'll take your purse, and I'll take you too, sir. I've an idea I'll get a tidy ransom if I can find out your real name. For I'd swear you've a rich father in London or maybe a rich wife in Kent. Something of the kind, at any rate. And I've interesting and well-practised ways of discovering the truth."

333

Ludovic untied his purse strings and dropped the small leather bundle onto the pirate's palm. "Thinking of torture?" He smiled. "I'm not enamoured of physical suffering, and will no doubt be overpowered easily enough. But I warn you, I've no wealthy father, nor any wife at all. My coat came from my own earnings, I've a small holding with the Lombards in London, and a rented property in Cheapside. You may choose to ruin my ambitions, but I've nothing more to offer."

Naseby turned to Captain Kenelm. "I've naught against an honest sailor and will let you go. But I'll be taking this gentleman with me, with any of your men as wish to volunteer for a more profitable life than you've been offering them, and a couple more if you please, as use for leverage on Master Spittiswood here. Choose two for sacrifice, captain, or I shall choose them myself."

Gerald walked out from the crowd of reluctant and muttering crew, coming to stand by Ludovic. "Take me," he said. "I'm Master Spittiswood's friend, and I'll come with him willingly."

Ludovic sighed. "This is no friend of mine," he said. "Send him away. He's simply my servant. And I've no use for him."

Captain Naseby smiled and shook his head. "Maybe not, sir, but I have. He can carry the message back once I find out who your father damned well is." The pirate stopped, looking his second hostage over more closely. Gerald was dressed in rough clothes and appeared more the servant than the lord, with only his hair bright red in the sunlight to stand him out from any crowd. Naseby was staring at Gerald's hair. The breezes reasserted, whipping Gerald's hair into his eyes. He squinted, pushing it back. Naseby peered, seeming momentarily uneasy. "And what's your name, boy? And where did you say you came from?" His outstretched blade quivered from one neck to the other.

"I didn't say," Gerald replied. "But it's Yorkshire originally, same as my master. I'm his manservant Gerald Pownsey. I'll accompany my master onboard your ship, but he's telling the truth and there's no one to pay a ransom."

Naseby turned again to Kenelm. "Chosen your other discard yet, my friend? You'll not be seeing him again, so choose careful. I'll take whatever one as will scream loudest, and persuade your cautious

Master Spittiswood here to divulge his real name." Then he looked over Kenelm's head to the crew. "Any of you bastards care to join me in a better life, and come a pirating? We've better food, better wine, and better prospects." No one stepped forwards and Naseby grinned. "Bunch of miserable cowards. But I'll take the skinny urchin there as my leverage. Between him and that poppy top servant, I'll peel back the sympathies easy enough on Master Spittiswood."

The thin boy who had twice delivered Gerald and Ludovic's meals to their cabin, was dragged forward. His rough wooden heels scraped across the wet decks as he stared around in wide eyed terror. "I ain't done nuffing," he yelped. "I don't know these gents, nor their rotten names. I'm Cap'in Kenelm's new cabin boy, that's all, mister."

"And now," grinned Naseby, "you've the honour to be my new sacrifice." He turned to his own crew. "Chuck the brat up to the Cock's Crest, lads," he said. "We'll bring these others along with us." Two of the pirates grabbed the boy and swung him, hurtling him up high to the carvel's gunwales. The child's body twisted midair and slammed hard against the planks, but several men leaning over the side grabbed his flailing arms and hauled him aboard. He disappeared with a squeal.

Gerald's hand twitched towards the hilt of his sword. The crew had already been disarmed, though few of them had carried more than a knife. Kenelm's sword had been taken, though Ludovic still wore his. But leaning along the gunwales of the carvel the waiting pirate crew stared down, near on a hundred men and all heavily armed. Many had bows drawn and arrows nocked, their aim steady on Kenelm, Ludovic and the other men. Naseby carried steel enough for ten. His baldrics crossed over a wide barrel chest, a long sword at his left, a short sword at the right hip. Through the cords of his doublet, the straps of his baldrics and the thick leather of his belt, a half dozen knife hilts protruded, a bristling bombast of confident threat. Gerald carefully controlled the impulse to attack, clasped his hands before him and looked down at his boots.

Ludovic was watching Naseby. He said, "The child you intend to use against me, is unknown to me. But naturally I dislike the idea of any other soul suffering torture on my account. I've told you my

335

name. Release the boy. But as I've also told you, I've some money kept in trust with the Lombards in London. Send my servant back with Kenelm here, and he'll fetch it for you. It should be sufficient to pay my ransom."

"You've admitted to that, which means you've got more, my friend. Too easy." The pirate grinned. "We'll see what we get out of you over the next few hours onboard my own ship." He lunged suddenly forwards, his sword pricking Ludovic's arm.

Ludovic's reflexes obeyed instinct. Unsheathing his sword in one fluid sweep, he slashed upwards, knocking Naseby's steel from his grip. The pirate's blade spun up, then clattered to the deck. Six of Naseby's men grabbed Ludovic as Gerald was held forcibly back. One wrenched both Ludovic's arms up behind him, another took the sword. A third searched his body, running huge callused palms inside his doublet and shirt, smoothing down his groin and hose, but found no other weapon. The fourth pirate, one foot shoved between Ludovic's legs to unbalance him, swung the hilt of his own sword to the side of Ludovic's head with considerable force. He slumped at once, both his arm and his head bleeding heavily. "Unwise, my young friend," said Naseby with evident delight. "You've proved yourself no country trader. You're a fighter and a knight exactly as I thought. And I shall have my fun with you, I promise, before selling you back to your kin."

Ludovic heard nothing. Brine and blood smeared together across his face, he was dragged unconscious to the side of the ship and a rope was looped beneath his armpits and around his body. Kenelm and Gerald watched as he was hoisted up towards the carvel's gunwales. For a brief moment he swung limp, circling mid-air, head drooping down and face hidden by the windswept swirl of shaggy black hair.

He was quickly hauled in.

CHAPTER THIRTY-SEVEN

When he returned to an uneasy and unsteady world, Ludovic thought at first he lay again in Kenelm's cabin. But it was a larger cabin, dirtier, cluttered and smelling of piss. A pain ramming through the back of his head reminded him of what had happened, but some confusion remained. He was alone and uncomfortably prone on someone else's bed.

He sat up carefully. With slow patience, he examined himself for injuries and found little. His arm stung but the slight wound had closed beneath its own dried blood. No one had washed or bandaged the cut, leaving it to the possibility of infection. It meant, more than anything else, that Gerald had been kept away from him.

The greater hurt was to his head, but Ludovic did not think it serious. The pain outweighed the injury. More serious was the removal of his boots. Someone had tugged them off before throwing him to the bed. Now the boots lay on the floor, one close, the other by the far wall so his knife, hidden down the cuff of his left boot, had clearly been found and taken. He had been searched thoroughly while unconscious. His doublet was unlaced, his hose loosened and the codpiece part unhooked, his shirt was pulled open and his sleeves were ripped wide. Ludovic sighed and swung his legs to the floor. He pulled his boots back on, redressed himself and, holding to the furniture, managed to reach the door. It was locked.

Ludovic returned to the bed and lay down. It was stained with memories of varied abuse, smelled of tired sweat and years of salt caked filth. The bolster was thin from age and only part filled with lumps of damp wool. He clasped his hands behind his head, and wondered. The ship rolled, a gently rhythmic sway like the rocking of a cradle. They were therefore not, he decided, under sail. They were at anchor somewhere off the English coast. Nearer to home, but a fact that was unlikely to help him in the least.

It seemed a long time later when the door opened. Ludovic's eyes were closed but he heard the key in the lock. It was Alysson's face, and her voice, which had kept him sane in the dreary hours. Now he was loath to think of anything more malicious. He did not look up. "Get 'im up," someone said. "Walk 'im if 'e's able. If not, drag 'im."

"I shall walk," said Ludovic.

"Nice ter see yer awake, yer honour," sniggered someone else. "Pleasant dreams, was it?"

"Shurrup," said the first voice. "Capin's waiting larboard. Get this bastard up there, smart."

One leading, one behind up the few steps, Ludovic was marched from cabin to daylight. The sun cut his eyes, the glitter on the water's surface a sudden affront. He breathed deep, clearing the fug, drawing in the fresh briny tang. The crew lounged along the decks, weapon heavy and staring, curious as he passed. Crossing larboard, Ludovic saw Captain Naseby, and behind him the long haze of a distantly purpled coastline. Through the haze cliffs rose, almost white in the bright daylight. Ludovic blinked, regaining both his sight and the clarity of his thoughts.

The captain turned, hearing his approach. "Ah, Master Spittiswood. Welcome aboard the Cock's Crest. There's few I allow onto my ship, and fewer still gets to see my cabin. A mighty rare pleasure you've had. But I'm afraid you'll not be staying long."

"I'm desolated," said Ludovic, "but will hopefully – survive - the disappointment. And what have you done with my servant? I need him."

"Trussed up in the hold with the brat," Naseby said. "You'll see them soon enough. In the meantime, my friend, I've a few matters to explain." He leaned back, elbows to the gunwales, grinning into the sunshine. Through the long knotted curls of his hair, things crawled. He scratched absently. "First, I'm a man of my word. What I says, you'd better believe, which is more than I can say of you. And what I says is this. It's a good few years I've been in this game, and am not easy fooled. You've a knight's training. Whether with a title or no, a gentleman you surely are, my friend, with money behind you. I'll sell you back to your family in one piece, or I'll chop you up small enough to feed the fishes when I throws you overboard. Your man Pownsey'll carry my demands to wherever you comes from. But if he's not back with all the coin in a week, then first I has my fun, and then my men does. Last of all, the fishes gets the pleasure."

Ludovic smiled. "And if Pownsey grabs the chance of freedom, and runs?"

Naseby shook his head. "Oh, he'll not be going alone, never fear. That little poppy top tries to run, he'll have his tongue ripped out and his prick lopped off, and they'll be carried back to me for my dinner afore I chucks you to the sharks."

"Has it not occurred to you," Ludovic said, "that we might be telling the truth? It seems you will go to a great deal of trouble, three of us will die to no avail, and your journey will be delayed for no reason whatsoever." His head hurt. He leaned against the mizzen mast. The lateen sail, neatly folded, lay roped on the deck. The ship was far cleaner above than below.

"Well now, I'll take that risk. Got naught else to do as it happens," said Naseby, gap-toothed grinning. "Bin poor pickings this past month, for shipping's lean in winter. Happen I'll get me a ransom from your lordship fine enough to buy me a comfy cottage in Mevagissey and settle down for the cold months. You'd like to know your coin is well spent, no doubt."

"I need to see my servant," Ludovic repeated. "Is he unhurt?"

"Let me see." The captain scratched his groin. "A mite squashed, maybe, but no more than that I reckon. So far, anyways. The little lad, though, well there was a few of my men couldn't resist."

Ludovic frowned. "What has been done to him?"

"Ain't none o' your business, as it happens," grinned the captain. "Not your servant, is he? If 'tis true you was a paying passenger aboard the other ship, and the brat the cabin boy – well then, he's naught to do with you. But just to be friendly, one gentleman to another, I'll tell you anyways. Thing is, you see," Naseby scratched again, "we've a problem with women. There being none."

"It's hardly surprising. None would want you," said Ludovic. "But I'd have assumed you'd not be averse to using force?"

Naseby shook his head cheerfully. "Not in the slightest, my friend. Pleases us no end. But we spend many a long month at sea, and females is bad luck on board. Now that little lad were too skinny for me, but there was plenty others took a turn. One arse is as good as another for most. But me, well, I reckon you'd suit me better."

"I'm flattered. But now," said Ludovic, "I still wish to see my servant."

Naseby nodded to one of the men who scurried off. "You can, as it happens," he said. "For it's both of you I wants to speak to. Reckon I've given you a fair idea of what will happen if you'd don't co-operate. Now we'll get down to business, my friend."

Gerald's hands were tied tightly behind him but he was clearly unhurt and unmolested. Seeing Ludovic, he smiled. "How's the boy?" asked Ludovic.

Gerald shook his head. "Not good."

Kenelm's cabin boy was brought up over one of the men's shoulders. He was tied wrists and ankles, had been crying until sick, and was deeply cowed. Vomit streaked his shirt, he was bare legged and bruised. The pirate slung him down on the deck at Naseby's feet. Naseby stared across, glazed eyed, at Ludovic. "Now you've power over three lives, my young friend, and 'tis time to decide. You'll stand there and watch while I carve up the urchin here, and have his skin off him like I peels a Seville orange, starting at them little pink toes. If you've not spoken by the time I gets to his scalp, I'll start on you. One ear maybe, or a finger. Or face down on the deck in the boy's blood, with your hose round your ankles."

Ludovic smiled. "What a lurid imagination the Cornish do have," he said. "But of course, under the circumstances, I will tell you whatever you wish to know. First, however, I should like to hear exactly what you intend doing to each one of us afterwards."

"You gets to go home," Naseby grinned. "And your servant with you, once he's back with my coin in full. And like I told you. What I says, I does. I'm an honest man, I am. You'll get no more than that from me."

"And the boy?" Ludovic indicated the barely breathing child near his feet.

"We'll keep him," Naseby said. "And alive. He'll join the crew. One ship's alike another, and he'll be cabin boy here instead. But wi' us, he'll get his share of the loot like all the crew does. Maybe he'll have a few other duties, and my cook has taken a rare fancy to him, but he'll get used to that too in time. Might end up a pirate captain hisself in time."

The boy made no response to this information and Ludovic was unsure as to whether he was conscious. "Then my name's – Lionel," Ludovic said at last. "Younger brother to William, Earl of Berkhamstead. At present he's at court for the Christmas season, but my servant knows him and can find his way there easily enough. My father's long dead, but my brother William is head of the family and will, reluctantly I imagine, pay the ransom. But the family's neither powerful nor wealthy, as you can find out easily enough yourself. What will you ask?"

"An earldom, eh?" Naseby scratched inside his shirt. "Good news, that is. I'm obliged to you, my friend. And though I were looking forward to a little pig sticking, it keeps the decks cleaner this way. Flaying can leave a nasty mess. Besides, that poor little bugger is bleeding a fair bit already, and my cook wants the chance to clean him up sweet again. Now then," he turned to those of his crew who were crowding around. "Reckon we'll sail tighter to shore and then row these two in to land. I'll keep his pretty lordship in the usual place up at the big house, whilst a couple of you hold the servant's hands nice

341

and tight and trot him off to London." He turned back to Ludovic. "I'll give your Pownsey six days. If they's not back with the ransom before that, I shall be true to my word. Fun first, and then into the bay with you."

"I need to speak to my servant in private," said Ludovic. "Any objections?"

"Private?" Naseby seemed to find this amusing. "Talk all you likes, your fine lordship. But I'll be listening."

Ludovic turned to Gerald and smiled. He spoke fast and without pause, and he spoke in Latin. "Strangely enough, I believe this man. He's proud of his word being his bond, so I'll be all right. Get to William, and see if he'll cough up a ransom. Naturally I'll pay him back afterwards."

Gerald nodded and replied also in Latin. "I could go to Father."

"There's still the problem of the royal arrest warrant," Ludovic said. "I imagine William would be the safer bet, even though he's presumably still at court. Keep acting the servant and just make sure your own name doesn't get discovered. And that absurd red hair of yours is far too obvious. I suggest a hood. Anyway, there'll be no problem getting to speak to William privately, since whatever ruffians accompany you will never dare set foot inside Westminster Palace."

"They'd be thrown out by the guard," Gerald pointed out. "I could have them arrested on the spot."

"And get yourself arrested too, once you had to explain your story and say who you are. Meanwhile I'd be fed to the fish."

Naseby, losing patience and irritated by a conversation he could not understand, stepped forwards with a grunt and clipped his knife hilt over the side of Ludovic's head. The existing wound broke open, oozing blood. Ludovic winced, wiping the sticky trickle from his forehead. "You's got time all night for blethering your nonsense together," Naseby said. "Now get moving."

They were exceedingly glad to leave the ship. Climbing down the high carvel's sides, walking the perpendicular planks with one hand to a loose hanging rope, made Gerald sick and Ludovic half blind with the headache he had suffered since waking. The rowing boat pulled away immediately they climbed in, four men to the oars, Naseby sitting in the prow, Ludovic and Gerald aft and two others beside them. Within minutes they heaved in to shore, a tiny beach tucked beneath the cliffs. The rowers dragged the small hull up high onto the pebbles and then all nine trudged inland.

First through a scrubby lane shielded by hedges, the land then flattened out, the hedges tangled into thorn and bush, and a sudden twist in the path stopped abruptly at a wide iron gateway. The high studded metal obscured all but peaks of turreted towers touching the low clouds. Naseby produced a key and unlocked the gates. His men shoved the iron spokes open, clanking and reluctant, and immediately the sun flooded back across the land. Beyond was a stone manor, its two towers tall and narrow, the main building squat, and its flanks low and pale in the sunshine. Ludovic and Gerald stared, amazed. "Put 'em in the old barn," Naseby said. "Rope 'em tight. Then come up to the back kitchens. I'm not sure who's at home so watch your step."

Still at some distance from the grand house, Ludovic and Gerald were hauled around the far side where the outbuildings straggled, several barns once housing dairies, breweries and stores. Now they appeared abandoned, but the property was not entirely overgrown. Paths were raked, some hedges nearer the house were clipped, the lower windows gleamed, but the barn where they were dragged had been long closed and smelled of rats. Two straw bales had fallen, scattering into trampled stalk and dust. Ludovic was thrown to the ground on the straw, his wrists tied behind him, the rope looped down to his ankles and tied again. The same was done to Gerald, and then they were left. The group of pirates, muttering and nervously uncomfortable, disappeared. The barn door was pushed shut and a bar could be heard wedged down.

Silence seeped back, ruffled only by the sounds of wind through the bare tree branches outside and the distant boom of the sea. Gerald sighed, leaning back on the broken bales. "Every muscle aches," he said. "It's all night I've been tied up, and now here I am bound again."

"At least the ground beneath us doesn't roll and pitch," said Ludovic, closing his eyes. "And you'll be released in the morning I imagine. I'll probably be kept like this until you return. How long will that take, do you think?"

"Depends on where we are." Gerald shook his head. "Kent perhaps."

"Kent for sure." Ludovic stretched his roped hands down behind him, edging them under his back until he could bend up his knees and hook his feet through. He brought his hands up before him with a sigh. "That's better. Now, what were we saying?"

"That we're somewhere in Kent."

"On the Kentish coast, fairly near Dover. I recognise the lie of the land." Ludovic managed to pull up his wrists to his mouth and began testing the knots with his teeth. "So it won't take you long to get to Westminster. Hopefully Berkhamstead is still there. If he's already left court, then we're in a mess of a fix."

"He'll still be there," said Gerald. "Unless he's been arrested too, of course. It's the start of the Christmas season. No one leaves court now unless they have to."

"I've no idea what the date is," said Ludovic, mouth full of rope. "Could be epiphany for all I know."

Gerald was quiet a moment, silently counting. "It's the twelfth day of December," he said. "At least I think it is. Or is it St. Lucy? Not that it really matters."

Ludovic had loosened but not managed to untie his wrists. He leaned back, resting a moment. "Are we doing the right thing, Gerry? You going straight back into danger like this? Perhaps I'm wrong, and it'd be better to go direct to Father."

"No, you were right. Either Father doesn't even know about the warrant and will resist all attempts to explain. Or royal guards have been sent to surround Sumerford and will still be waiting there for us. At Westminster I can go in disguise and pretend the servant. At Sumerford there's no disguise possible and I'd be known at once. But it's all a guess isn't it? Whatever we choose could be wrong." He was struggling to manoeuvre his own hands to the front, but being far shorter than his brother, the rope uniting wrists to ankles was not as long. "I'd like to get to William as soon as possible. I've an idea I can arrange something. Get the money, come back here and set you free, but have William follow me with a band of men. Attack this place and kill that bastard Naseby."

"At the moment he's only brought seven men here. But he could land half the boat load over the next couple of days." Ludovic reached over to help Gerald, tugging up one booted foot and then the other. "This house could be bristling with fifty pirates by the time you get back. Besides, who has he got in the house already, for it's not been entirely deserted. They must be friends of his, strange though it seems. Someone of reasonable wealth lives here."

Gerald puffed, brought his hands up over his knees, and smiled with satisfaction. "That's a bit more comfortable anyway. Now what?"

"It'll be dark soon. We wait."

Gerald nodded. "And your head, Lu? It's not bleeding anymore but it looks a bit of a mess. Should have been washed at least."

"I doubt pirate's trouble with much doctoring," smiled Ludovic. "Injuries are normal fare, I imagine. The more of them die of wounds and infections the better."

"In terrible agony, I trust," said Gerald cheerfully. He had also managed to loosen the knots on his wrists with his teeth.

Several times they heard voices outside, shouting twice and once the clash of steel on steel. Without windows they could guess time only by the thin crack beneath the door which no longer let in light. Then after some hours an owl hooted very close, the wind dropped and the rats began to scrabble in the straw. His headache still raged and Ludovic was tired. His wrists no longer rubbing, he found some small comfort amongst the straw, shut out the misery of thought and curled, hoping to sleep.

Wide awake, Gerald was gnawing at his ropes, kicking out at a sudden quivering pink snout. "This is ridiculous, Lu," he muttered. "I believe you'd manage to sleep on the scaffold. And where do we aim for afterwards anyway? Back to Somerset? Back to Flanders? Where's your tame captain gone, do you think?"

"London," sighed Ludovic, opening his eyes again. "He still has all my money hidden onboard and will be waiting for me to collect it. Once free from here, we should make for the docks. Then we set sail for Flanders once again, unless we're waylaid in the meantime of course. In which case we can put your theory about the scaffold to the test."

"Stop joking, Lu. It could happen. The axe anyway."

"Go to sleep Gerry," Ludovic complained. "We are certainly both going to need our strength."

A wearisome boredom, the impossibility of walking or even getting to their feet, the apathy of pointless discomfort and the bleak reminders of the probable morrow enclosed them, soon drifting into uneasy dreams. The rats were left in peace, nesting in the straw or nibbling at the new arrivals, their leather boots and their ropes.

It was bitterly cold when both men awoke together, startled back into consciousness. Furious voices had interrupted the silence. Footsteps, someone banging on the barn door as if falling against it. The wind was now gusty and rattled the walls. The rats hid. The arguments were too distant to understand but then someone shouted. Finally a much quieter voice, a little sibilant, cut through the squabble outside. A hushed and educated voice. Ludovic sat up in a hurry.

"You had the temerity to bring prisoners here? A titled man, who might recognise this property? And who, if he does not already know it, soon will. Who might know me?"

"My lord, I beg your pardon." Naseby's voice, apologetic and worried. "I didn't think. But no need for you to be seen, unless you wishes it."

"This creature's name?"

"Seems to be a Lionel Berkhamstead, my lord," Naseby mumbled. "With his brother William being an earl what's staying at court."

A pause. Then the first voice. "I don't know the earl, but have heard of him. He's a nobody, a minor figure with no influence, and I doubt much wealth. I had not heard of any brother, and have no contact with the family. You are lucky, my dear. Had this been a friend of mine, I might have killed you."

"You've always said the gentry was free for sport, my lord," muttered Naseby. "You never said to be careful o' friends before."

"You are absurd. It is not because of friendship," said the quiet voice. "I've no interest in bleating sympathies or the dreary loyalties of acquaintance. A title is the only prisoner to covet after all. What point holding some shepherd's apprentice to ransom? It is the use of my property which disturbs me, for the imprisonment of some creature who might trace its misfortune back to me. You are unutterably brainless Naseby, for all your experience. I sometimes wonder why I chose you to partner."

"Because there's no better, my lord."

Another pause. "Tomorrow, at first light and before my entire estate can be clearly identified, you will remove this Berkhamstead back to the ship and you will keep him there until his ransom is delivered. Throw him in the hold, in the damned bilges if you wish, but well out at sea. I have no need to see him and he must not see me. You will send the servant off to Westminster at the same time. Is this understood?"

Naseby grunted. "How much to ask then?"

"Berkhamstead is not wealthy, but to get his brother back he'll surely stretch his purse. But we cannot wait around for him to raise funds elsewhere."

"'Tis you to decide, my lord, and I'm guided by your word as always," said Naseby. "So if you'll write the demand letter for me now, I'll send Pownsey off first light with four of my men."

"Who?" the quiet voice interrupted, louder suddenly as though startled, and with a hint of menace.

Naseby recognised the menace. He paused before answering, cautious, his voice subdued. "'Tis only Berkhamstead's young servant, my lord," he murmured. "By name of Gerald Pownsey."

With an explosion of fury and astonishment, the quiet man was quiet no longer. "Dear God in Heaven, Jesus Christ and all the saints, what the fuck have you done?" he exclaimed.

It was a voice both Ludovic and Gerald had already most certainly recognised, having been listening in amazement for the past half hour.

CHAPTER THIRTY-EIGHT

T he door crashed open, slamming back against the wall. Naseby and the other man stood, one tall and the other far shorter in the pearly puddled moonlight, the night's thickness behind them. In the house beyond the barns, twenty windows reflected a moon's repeating gleam of silver.

"What remarkably unsavoury friends it seems you have, Naseby," Ludovic said, smiling at the taller man. "But you have interrupted my rest." He sat up a little, turning his attention to the other man. "I admit some element of surprise, big brother. I suspected you of many things. But never, I must confess, of this."

It was a moment before Brice Sumerford found words. He stared down at his two younger brothers. Naseby remained speechless. Gerald scrambled to his feet, then, still part hogtied, tumbled back to the ground.

Brice turned to Naseby. "Untie them at once," he said quietly. "They will probably attempt to kill you. Assuming they don't succeed, bring them both up to the house. If they manage to kill you indeed, I wish them good cheer of it." He turned abruptly and disappeared again into the darkness outside.

Naseby glared at his two prisoners. Gerald spat. "You work for him?"

Naseby shook his head in confusion. "Not as such. Partners we is. You know him then?"

"Let me introduce myself for the third time," smiled Ludovic, "and on this occasion I shall relent and speak the truth. I am Ludovic Sumerford, and this is Gerald Sumerford. We are brothers to your enterprising partner." Ludovic was finally, though faintly, enjoying himself.

Rubbing their wrists, they followed Naseby through the stubbled grass and shadows to the great house. Its doors stood wide, lamplight in a vivid arc illuminating beyond the steps and the approaching path. Ludovic and Gerald entered ahead, Naseby at a discreet distance behind, and marched into the main hall. The boards gleamed, the copper was polished, the mantel dusted, but the furniture was sparse and the atmosphere whispered of abandon. A fire raged huge across the stone hearth however, the chandelier had been lit, other candles flickered from their sconces and Brice sprawled at the great table, cup in hand. He watched his brothers enter.

"It is," he said softly, "an unfortunate mistake for all of us. Why you must stumble into my business in this manner, I cannot tell. But it seems we must exchange excuses."

Ludovic raised an eyebrow. He pulled two pewter cups from their shadowed row centre of the table and filled both from the wine jug. He passed one to Gerald and drained the other, then refilled it. He ignored Naseby, who helped himself. "Is that a form of apology?" Ludovic said, draining the second cup. "I don't offer excuses to pirates and murderers, but I am waiting for yours." He sat facing Brice, and Gerald sat beside him.

Brice nodded. He held a full cup but was not drinking. "Our ancestors were pirates," he said. "The profits are large. The risks are high. I enjoy both."

"As boys we were taught to kill," Gerald glared. "But we were taught chivalry as well, the moral code of decency, ethics and manners, to kill in God's name or in defence of the realm, not for ourselves or for greed. What you do is vile."

Brice smiled. "Hypocritical as always, Gerald my dearest." He leaned back, the vibrancy of his hair flaming in the candle light directly above. "We have an anointed monarch, England's king crowned in God's holy name at His holy altar. But you don't kill in our blessed king's defence. You're a traitor to chivalry. Don't think to judge me, my beloved."

Ludovic drained a third cup of wine. It was an excellent Burgundy and he thought it likely to be a barrel he had once smuggled into England himself. "How long?" he demanded.

Brice shrugged. He wore his usual finery, gleaming in damasks, velvets and furs. His rings reflected the firelight, shrinking the fragility of his small palmed hands and narrow fingers. The luxury of his appearance contrasted with Naseby's slovenly eccentricity, Gerald's coarse broadcloth, and the torn and damaged doublet Ludovic wore, now coatless and cold.

Ludovic smiled. "And are there other skills you practise, my dear? Other forms of subterfuge perhaps? Spying maybe?"

"I distain kings," Brice said, "and work neither for nor against them."

"Merely," Ludovic continued, "that we have recently been informed against, and a warrant is now signed not only for Gerald's arrest, but also for my own. Someone knowing our habits and specific address gave intelligence against us. This was a traitor indeed, without scruples or moral decency. Naturally, my dear, I thought of you."

Brice narrowed his eyes. "Thank you little brother. And you were escaping then, fleeing abroad when my friend Naseby here overtook you?"

"Prudence, not escape," Gerald interrupted. "We left for Flanders. A storm blew us back to the coast. Your foul friend behaved with all the monstrous bestiality and disgusting deviance I'd expect of any pirate. But not of you. Good God, Brice – how could you? How do you?"

"Not having been aboard at the time," Brice pointed out, "I performed no act of deviant monstrosity, my dear. Naseby is his own master. I do not control or command him, except in the taking of prisoners for ransom and the use of my home. I write his ransom demands, since he cannot scribe. He sails my ship. I take his profits."

"You're gone too long from home, my dear, to claim only a passing influence on the business," added Ludovic. "A few times you've come back wounded, so you sail and plunder too. What's more, I've seen you at court recently, so you were there for business, whether it be spying, collecting ransoms perhaps, or selling stolen goods to the highest bidder. So you are amongst the filth of the sea, the dross and shit which slime the waters. Do you know this? Or do you blind yourself with stories of adventure?"

Brice blinked as though stung. "Adventure? I've seen plenty of that, dearest brother, more than any of you with your dullard lives. And I live my life as I wish as do all the Sumerfords. One traitor to the crown running for his life, one smuggler caught up in treason, oh yes, long ago I guessed your game my dear, one simpleton lunatic with a whore for a wife, and both parents as seamed in vitriolic hypocrisy as any of us. What should I learn at the bosom of such a family? What else should I do? Take me to a monastery? But the church is just as seeped in greed and crime, and our most Holy Father in Rome the worst."

Ludovic stood, carried his stool to the great flaming fire and sat, his back to his brothers. He stretched his legs to the blaze and spoke softly to the flames and their dancing shadows. "Simple crime does not disgust me. Cruelty and brutality do," he said. "You will order your men to release the boy who was taken from my ship. He will be brought here to me this night. I leave in the morning."

Brice also stood, scraping back his stool and flinging down his cup. He nodded to Naseby, verifying Ludovic's order. "There are bedchambers above," he said, curt. "I shall not see you again before you leave. You'll carry no tales to father concerning me, and I'll tell him nothing of you, though no doubt the royal guards may already be searching for you at Sumerford. Goodbye little brothers. If we never meet again, I doubt any of us will weep over it."

"For tomorrow we need horses," Ludovic said, not looking up. "And the return of my sword and my purse, coin intact."

Brice did not answer, striding quickly from the hall. Naseby muttered, "I'll arrange that." He left hurriedly, following in Brice's shadow.

Gerald brought his stool and sat beside Ludovic facing the fire's heat. Neither spoke to the other, but watched the flames crackle and leap. It was after the boy from The Fair Rouncie was brought to them, wrapped in a kersey cape, shivering and pale, that they collected candles, climbed the staircase and searched out a bedchamber. Although long closed up, shutters dust ridden and rat droppings scattered deep in the corners, its bed was well clothed in old linen and damp blankets. Gerald broke an old stool leg across his knee and lit the splintered pieces with the candle flame, tossing the burning fragments to the hearth. The room slowly warmed. Ludovic and the boy took to the bed and slept. Gerald sat for long hours beside the little fire, hugging his knees and thinking, allowing the night's depression to wrap him as thick as any quilt.

It was raining in the morning. The dawn misted in a rose and lilac haze through the heavy grey sleet. Two horses from Brice's stables were already saddled and waiting outside the doors, heads hanging, manes and tails dripping. The lord of the house was not present. There seemed to be no staff, but some of Naseby's men, sullen and morose, wandered the corridors, obeying orders. Naseby waited at the doorway.

"Ain't no food for no breakfast, but there's ale," he said. "Have put a flask in the saddle bag, your purse too, intact with naught taken. Both your metal's sheathed ready in the saddle scabbards. You want the skinny lad, then take him up behind. His lordship said just two horses, and there's no more spare."

"I'll take the child up before me," Gerald said, hoisting the boy up into the saddle and quickly mounting himself. The horse stood motionless, dejected by duty to strangers.

Ludovic was frozen, the sleet quickly soaking his shoulders. He stood looking at Naseby, allowing the rain to seep through his torn doublet to his shirt and to his skin. "You still have my coat," he said quietly. "But I will no longer wear something you have defiled. One day I will find you again. Remember me. I want you to know who it is that slits your throat."

Naseby sniffed, returning to swagger. "And fine words from a man wanted by the law hisself," he hissed. "I treated you fair. If you'd not lied about your name, my friend, I'd have known right well who you are, and never taken you on. You and yours would have gone free from the first."

Ludovic shook his head, sending rain drops into small glittering circles. "I won't argue rights and standards with a pirate. You would never understand any explanation of true honesty. One day I'll make my argument with my sword."

"I makes my living by my steel," Naseby glowered. "No man'll take me easy, let alone some pin pricked fart of a lord. I'll have your guts steaming across my deck long afore your blade touches my neck, my fine friend. So remember that, when you comes alooking for Black Baldwin. Brother of his lordship or no, I'll be waiting."

Ludovic, ignoring him, turned on his heel and swung his leg up into the stirrups. Gerald led out of the courtyard, Ludovic to his side. They left the estate, its grand house disappearing quickly into the low clouds behind. The countryside ahead was barely lit by the dawn and the cold shrouded them in the sound of the sleet, diminishing all else.

They rode in a sodden silence. The horses' footsteps squelched, their breathing muffled. The rescued child clung to the front of the saddle. He was barefoot and barely clothed though the thin woollen cape swaddled him. Gerald sat behind, his arms surrounding the boy in warmth, each body protecting the other from wind and cold. Ludovic slumped, letting the horse decide the speed. The sharp slant of the east wind froze the rain on his face turning his expression to ice.

They rode into the hamlet of Ashford as the rain eased. The first building as the narrow unmade road dipped towards the ford across the Stour, was the Carrier's Inn, and brightly welcoming. It was not yet dinner time, but in silent agreement they stopped, called the ostler to stable the horses, and strode immediately into the well-lit tap room. Some hours later they retired to the upper chamber they had paid for, and began to make plans. Gerald regarded the urchin now holding his hands to the brazier. "What the damnation is your name anyway?" Gerald demanded.

"M'lor. 'Tis Ellis, m'lor."

"Then Ellis," said Gerald, refilling three ale cups from the earthenware jug, "we'll first acquire you some warmer clothes, though they'll have to be ready used since there's no time to have anything properly made."

Ellis nodded happily. The pallid misery of his sunken cheeks had now puffed pink with three hours of ale and warmth. "Ain't never had nuffin just once-used afore, m'lor," he said. "'Twill be an honour."

"And shoes too of course," continued Gerald. "We will then attempt to discover a carrier heading for London."

"Will all be headin' for Lonnon from 'ere, m'lor," Ellis pointed out.

"Very well," Gerald said. "We will buy you a place in a cart and send you off to find Captain Kenelm. I hope he'll be waiting at London docks to hear from us."

"He will be," Ludovic interjected from the shadows. "He had better be."

Gerald turned from the boy to Ludovic. "So what should we arrange, Lu? To follow on to the docks once we hear the ship's truly waiting? Or for them to meet us off the coast here somewhere?"

"Unappetising as is the thought of once again going to sea," Ludovic said, "we must. Therefore meeting on the coast will be safer than entering London again. Somewhere at a distance from our dear brother's estate, I think."

Gerald nodded. "Well, that's a subject we've been avoiding, but clearly we have to talk about it one day. A wretched use made of those estates, so proudly bestowed on the family by King Edward after Towton. Now used as a pirate's lair."

"For the moment," said Ludovic, "we need to concentrate on getting safely out of the country. I suggest we follow the Stour up to Margate, and Kenelm can meet us there."

"Good." Gerald smiled at the boy. "Tell your captain we'll be at some hostelry or other in Margate, and to find us as soon as he arrives. You had better sail with him, and pray not to meet any more storms or pirates."

They slept warm that night and the following morning Ellis, dressed in fresh wool, broadcloth, knitted hose, felt hat and thick leather boots, was fed a hot meal and bundled into the back of a carrier's cart, three coins pressed into his excited fist, and ordered not to forget his instructions on pain of being returned to Naseby. Ludovic and Gerald then wandered back into the inn and frowned at each other. There was a considerable amount to discuss.

CHAPTER THIRTY-NINE

Six days later Ellis's tousled tow head once again peeped around their chamber door. It was a different chamber. The Purple Popinjay was a far larger hostelry in the centre of Margate on the north of the village square, and its colourful sign swung in the wind with a squeak as loud as the popinjay it represented. Ludovic and Gerald had taken the best front chamber, sharing a bed wide enough for six, facing a large hearth already blazing with fire, and drinking a superior cabernet. However, although the comfort was considerable, both men were restless and neither appeared content.

Now clothed in practicality, the two younger Sumerford sons had bought the dress of respectable country merchants, good linen, blod and padded Lindsay wool, which they would never have previously worn. Ludovic, stern in dark brunette trimmed in badger and a coat lined in sheepskin, was unrecognisable except for his golden hair. Gerald, his red hair newly cut, now took his blod cape over his arm and stood quickly, head to knee in russet.

"'E's 'ere, m'lors," announced Ellis.

Ludovic and Gerald smiled expansively at the boy. "Thank the good Lord," said Gerald. "The waiting has driven me witless. I am dull as the Exe in flood, and as stiff as an oak in autumn. Let's get moving."

Ludovic paid their bill and they strode out into scattered drizzle. A light wind pulsed in from the sea, the rain no more than a briny mist. A pale sunshine seeped through the cloud and, now just five days before Christmas, the weather seemed mild.

Ludovic sighed as they tramped down to the coast. "A fine sailing day," he said, "no storms in sight, and so it has all been quicker and easier than I'd feared."

Ellis scampered ahead. "Capin's mighty pleased. Fort we was all done for. Proper 'cited when I turns up and gives the news."

"I imagine so," said Ludovic. "I represent his future. At this precise moment however, he represents mine. I am, although too morose to show it, equally 'cited.'"

"An' 'e's still got all the coin them pirates was too stoopid to find," Ellis continued. "Capin' says I've to tell you that, m'lor. All safe and awaitin'."

"Which also most decidedly represents our future," Ludovic nodded, "since we must now make a new life in Flanders."

Gerald laughed. "I've never felt so wealthy. In fact, after selling your fancy doublet and Brice's horses, I feel I can even face storms."

"Yes, considering I paid for all the new clothes and the charges at the inn," said Ludovic. "And you seem remarkably cheerful, Gerry. I do believe you're eager to leave our balmy shores. No regrets at all this time? Abandoning your prince locked up in the Tower for instance, and your Tudor villain still on England's throne?"

Gerald shook his head. "As soon as I put foot to dry land, I'm off to the court at Malines to drum up support for Prince Richard, and see if I can rouse enough interest for an invasion."

"Another war to further subjugate our wretched countrymen."

"Well, they should have had more sense than support Tudor," Gerald objected. "And they won't support the bastard anyway, once there's a suitable alternative and it's explained exactly who Prince Richard really is. Oh, Lu, it'll be a glorious new world."

"It'll be bloodshed and suffering as usual, my dear, and taxing us dry to pay for our own misery," said Ludovic quietly. "At least I shall not be here to see it. But those I love and leave behind will do so."

"We'll come back with the army," Gerald said at once. "Oh, I accept it may take a year or two before I can travel around and rally enough support, but I believe Maximilion will promise Burgundy's and Hapsburg backing, and there's money enough throughout the Holy Roman Empire to fund a dozen wars. Flanders will come to the table of course, and parts of Italy too, though Spain will back Tudor once she's married her princess to Tudor's son. France, naturally, will try and make trouble for everyone, pledge support to both sides, cry off at the last moment, and intercept shipping from every quarter. In any case, don't go thinking we're lost to England for evermore, Lu. Two years at the most, and we'll be back."

Ludovic stared across the little bay to the pier where The Fair Rouncie bobbed complacently at her mooring. "I wonder," he said very softly to himself, "if she might still be waiting after such a time."

Gerald looked up, catching the words on the breeze. "What was that? She? The ship's here already. Who else should be waiting?"

"Nothing," said Ludovic eventually into the pause. "No one. It no longer matters at all."

The gulls wailed, hovering in the colourless sky. Although shortly after midday, the sun was winter low, a hazy luminosity through the cloud. The horizon, flat and empty, gleamed with a grey opaque sheen. The ocean was calm, the breeze wistful, the small cog bumped her rhythmic planks against the quay and Ludovic and Gerald's approach was greeted with an echoing cheer. They climbed aboard, Kenelm beaming at the gunwales and ready with an eager arm. The crew crowded around, hoping for stories of piratical wickedness, dismemberments and heroism, moonlit escapes and vengeance on the high seas. Gerald and Ludovic plodded down to the captain's cabin, the captain himself at their heels, Ellis was sent smirking and proud to his post and the drizzle increased to a light patter of rain across the deck.

Ludovic shrugged out of his damp sheepskin and threw himself on the bed, stretching out his legs and closing his eyes. Gerald sat on the edge of the desk. Kenelm said, "Well, well my lords, and what a blessed relief it is too. I was thinking maybe you was both full dead, and told your noble friend so. Wot a mighty relief it were when I saw that little bugger Ellis turn up, with the story of wot was really happening."

"What noble friend?" demanded Gerald.

"The one you was with, my lord," Kenelm explained. "When you come aboard at St. Katherine's telling of them warrants, and how you must both come to Flanders with me at once. The one as took Lord Ludo's horse. Come back riding the beast, he did, asking for me at the docks to see if all was well."

Gerald grinned. "So William wasn't arrested himself. That's great news."

"Said as how he'd been questioned but his words believed, and was let go without no trouble," said the captain. "When I said as how my lad Ellis had come back that very morning, and followed on with all the news wot the boy'd given, well, your friend sighed a great sigh, said as how he was almost sick with relief. He gave me a letter for you and a purse for helping set up in Flanders." Kenelm handed both letter and purse to Gerald. "Now we must wait till early evening for high tide," he continued, "and then will be off due east, with fine weather and a good moon to guide us safe across the ocean."

Gerald had opened Berkhamstead's letter and was already reading. Ludovic smiled at Kenelm. "Thank you my friend. You'll get the Rouncie careened yet, I promise."

"Three, four hours, and we'll have the sheet slapping full," Kenelm nodded, turning to leave. "I wish your lordships good rest, and will send down the boy to warn you afore we slips our ropes."

The cradled roll of the ship and the faint slap of the waters on wood remained gentle. The little oil lamp swung from the beams, circling its light around the small space. Gerald read the Earl of Berkhamstead's letter and then passed it to Ludovic. "Nothing new Lu. Will wishes us health and good luck and may try and travel over to Flanders to meet up with us next year, but he's as happily wed as a man can expect these days, being cosy at home and hoping for sons to follow. Has had no further contact with the prince but writes that matters remain peaceful, with no plans afoot either good or bad."

Ludovic waved away the letter. "I've had enough of scheming, Gerry. I'm sick to my teeth of this business and its consequences. Brice and his vile pirates sit like stones in my gut, and I carry my own black cloud around my shoulders. I dearly wish myself back home in Sumerford, and my girl in my arms."

"Ah. I'd forgotten about her," said Gerald.

"I try to forget," Ludovic murmured, "but my dreams come back like sour indigestion after a good meal. I thought myself tired of Sumerford but I know nothing of Flanders and have no interest in new shores. So dream your own dreams Gerry and leave me alone until we sail." He turned, facing the wall, eyes closed.

It was shortly after Ellis had brought them supper that everything changed again. Gerald sat at the desk, spooning his cabbage gruel. Ludovic balanced his bowl on his knee. The soup was tepid, thin and bland without salt. The wooden bowls were slightly unclean. Gerald sighed. "And this is while we're at dock. So from now on it will be worse."

"I cannot think," said Ludovic, "all things considered, that the quality of our food is of any major importance. Dream of war instead, my dear, and fill your stomach with the coming glory of a Plantagenet prince again, crowned in bloodshed."

"You know," Gerald said between mouthfuls, "you're becoming damned bad company, Lu. Between your cheerful monologues and this rancid muck, I shan't even notice a little innocent biliousness at sea."

The soup was never finished. The grey drear of the quiet cabin split abruptly into agitated confusion. The marching of heavy feet over the deck above, the jangling and clank of spurs and swords; the shouting and disruption were sudden and ferocious. Gerald's spoon wedged in his mouth, the bowl spinning to the floor as he leapt up with a gulp. Ludovic spun around, swung his legs from the bed and stood, buckling on his steel. "Trouble," said Gerald.

"They've come for us," said Ludovic.

"Impossible." Gerald whispered, cautious, listening. "How could anyone possibly know where we are?"

"Come on," Ludovic said, "we need to find a place below. Kenelm will cover for us if he can."

They heard the demands clearly from above, their own names and titles spoken loud, then orders to search the ship. Boots, ten men perhaps, more voices and Kenelm's plaintive complaints. "I shelter no villains, my good man, nor harbour fugitives. I'm an honest sea captain, awaiting the tide, and I'll have you remember that."

"Seafaring for what business? What trade? And what cargo do you carry?"

There was a pause. "As it happens, I've no cargo onboard as yet. My supplier, a mean bastard he is, has let me down again, and me coming all this way for wool and linen bound for Flanders. But I'm going anyhows, as being expected to pick up the return cargo in Antwerp. And will be late for tide and cargo both," Kenelm warned, "if you keep me on a fool's errand."

"I've no interest in your trade, you imbecile," the louder voice answered. "And if you call this a fool's errand, then the fool is you. No sailor chooses the danger of a crossing without a full hold to cover his costs and his risks. Now, out of my way and let's see who's hidden below."

"No sight nor smell, Sir Jerrid," calling from the prow.

"Nor aft, sir."

But in the deserted cabin a small lamp swung, wasting its oil, and across the floor was spilled soup and a pair of wooden bowls, their spoons discarded. "There's been two men here until moments gone," the guard reported. "Signs in the cabin of supper interrupted, and a cloak tossed on the bed."

"Mine," said Kenelm, growing gruff from complaints. "Can I not sit in my own cabin now, without the king's men accusing me of crime and clandestiny? I was enjoying a hot pottage with my mate when your cursed troops come spoiling my rest, and the last good sup afore I takes the tide."

"Forget the tide," said the guard's captain, "till you produce what I'm after. I've information as to the Sumerford brothers aboard your ship, and will not leave without my quarry. In the meantime, your name will be taken and remembered. Those who work against the king's own majesty are like to suffer for it sooner or later."

Ludovic shoved Gerald into the darkest shadows. They had crept downwards to the depths of the hold, each man with a tight grip on the hilt of his sword. The stench made them reel. First past the sweaty squash of the crew's hammocks slung high in the utter dark, places for others to sleep below amongst the stores, their belongings piled and scattered where they might. The huge trunk of the cog's mast stood mid ship, then on down to the bulk of its foundation. Around this the spare sails and ropes were stacked, lashed tight against the danger of storm, leaking their smells of old adventure, salt and tired damp. With days at anchor making for easy cleaning, the planks had been sluiced and swabbed, but rat urine and human excrement still found their own level and the wet wood still reeked of a thousand nights in rough seas with a groaning crew unable to void bellies or bowels up on deck.

Ludovic crept lower, Gerald keeping close. Deep below the water line, the hull carried ballast instead of cargo; barrels of ale and the weight of ancient untanned sheep hides lying on stone and planks, pieces of an old mast now rotted, and the coils of unwanted rope long since frayed.

"What's that you're holding?" whispered Gerald.

"An axe," Ludovic answered. "Kept for chopping down the mast in case of capsize in the worst storms. Never yet used, I thank the Lord. Perhaps now it will."

"Dear God," murmured Gerald, "are we come to that? And against the king's men? If we're caught, they'll have our heads."

"I know," said Ludovic. "But I shall have theirs first."

Gerald found the end of the shadows and crawled, bent low. "Bloodshed after all, Lu?"

Ludovic crouched into the same dark angle. "Hush, my dear. They're coming."

A sharp voice, too clear and too close. "The buggers came this way. Coils of rope disturbed, look."

"This isn't the king's fleet, fool." Someone held a torch, small wavering flames barely opening the darkness. "They'll not be strict nor shipshape. A loose rope means nothing."

"But footsteps do. Marks in the dirt over there."

"A crew of twenty or more. There'll be dirt and there'll be marks. Don't be a damned fool and report to the captain up above."

"I'm looking around first, like we've been ordered. There's summit amiss. I can smell fear and hear breathing."

"I reckon I'm breathing, idiot, and you too I hopes. As for fear, I'm as shit scared as a good soldier has a right to be in these nasty wet places with a floor as slips from beneath your boots. Let's get back on land quick as we may. There's no ruffians hiding here."

"Ships don't scare me," said the other man. "Did the fishing run over to Brittany many a season when I were a lad. And I'm telling you, there's sommit amiss. You bugger off if you're queasy. I'm following my orders." A large hand probed the shadows. Fingers tested the feel of wood, the ooze of briny water and encrusted salt, then moved on to sturdy broadcloth and the warmth of the man within. "Gotcha," yelled the guard, and grabbed.

Gerald stabbed down with the blade of his knife. The guard yelped and jumped away. Gerald followed him out into the flickering torchlight. Both guards yelled and one stumbled back, his wrist pouring blood. The other cursed, one angry step forwards, his sword slashing straight to Ludovic's neck.

Ludovic swung the axe. Carrying all his pent up frustration and pointless, inescapable misery, the blade reflected the torch flame into sudden blazing light. The guard dropped his sword, gurgled, open mouth filling scarlet, and fell heavy.

"You've killed the bastard," muttered Gerald. "This is it, Lu."

Ludovic nodded and opened his fingers, letting the axe tumble. He stared down at the dead guard at his feet. The man wore chain mail, split across his chest by Ludovic's thrust where the king's colours now hung limp either side of crushed bone. The guard's eyes were open, staring up glazed and blind at the frisking end of a rat's tail disappearing into darkness. Ludovic bent and retrieved the torch, its flame spluttering in the damp. "I should not have killed him. I meant only to silence him."

"Well, you've certainly done that," said Gerald. "An axe will silence most men. So take a deep breath, little brother. We're about to discover the truth about Purgatory."

Yelling once again, a reverberation of fury, more tramping feet and jingling steel. Sir Jarrid strode into the pale light, his sword unsheathed. "So, my lords. It's Gerald and Ludovic Sumerford, no doubt. I've a warrant for your arrest gentleman, and will have the greatest pleasure in fulfilling it."

"I appear to have killed one of your men, sir," said Ludovic. "I apologise. An unfortunate accident."

Sir Jarrid said, "I doubt an accident my lord, but a great mistake without doubt." The nine guards surrounded Ludovic and Gerald, dragging their arms behind them and forcibly roping their wrists. Gerald was thrown to his knees in the dead man's blood. He swore and struggled up but was pushed down again.

Ludovic balanced, braced wide legged against the push of the guards. His hair was in his eyes, every muscle screamed, his shoulders ripped hard back. "It seems this year," he grinned, "Christmas will not be spent at court after all."

"Downriver a little I expect, my lord," the captain of the guards said. "It's the Tower will see your final celebrations, and the executioner's block for Epiphany."

CHAPTER FORTY

The child had been crying all night, first frantic, his screams becoming faint and fitful as dawn crept up beyond the castle turrets. Sweat was slick through the swaddlings, the baby's face was wet and red with suffering and effort, exhausted with voicing pain and securing no release. The downy ginger fluff across the top of his small round head was now flattened over the scalp in damp stripes. The unmistakable smell of dysentery was strong.

The nurse held the little boy tight, rocking him gently and kissing his tiny screwed up lashless eyes. The child whimpered. His flesh had hollowed, cheeks sunken around the small panting mouth. Three days of violent cramps and shitting would have weakened a strong man. The Sumerford infant was only six months old and unlikely to live much longer. He had known his first Christmas and gurgled at his epiphany gift, shaken the ivory rattle in a chubby fist and stuffed the ring into his toothless chuckle. Ten days later he was dying.

Alysson leaned over the nurse's shoulder, gazing down at the child. The nurse shook her head. "I've done all I've been told, Mistress," she said, looking up. Her eyes were pink. "The wet nurse has been sent off and another girl brought in, but the poor mite has not the strength to suckle. Master Penbridge has prescribed the mediks and I've spooned them between the poor little soul's lips, but I doubt he's drunk more than half. Now the apothecary reckons cockerel's blood and Genoa treacle is the best thing for the dysentery but Master Penbridge won't have it and insists on boiled water and earth of alum. But there's naught makes any difference. I knew an old man in the village once, had the diarrhoea real shocking, like to die. But just shit his guts out for a day and a night, then sat down to roast boar and a cup of ale and reckoned it done him good."

"But Master Eddie is just a little baby," whispered Alysson, "and is too young to fight such a terrible illness. Kings have died of it in the past, you know, so I doubt there's a real cure whatever quarrel Master Penbridge and the apothecary get into."

"This babe may not be a king, but like to be an earl," the nurse said. "Lord Humphrey will sob his poor heart out if the little lad dies."

"I shall myself," sighed Alysson. "But I think there's nothing more to be done. Certainly Master Penbridge will be here again within the hour, but it's Father Dorne I believe I ought to be calling."

The nurse shook her head. "Her ladyship will decide. For myself, I wish the poor mite's mamma would come see her son and bring some last comfort."

"I will suggest it again," said Alysson, moving away. "But it's unlikely she'll come. And Lord Eddie barely knows her anyway, and will hardly miss what small comfort she could bring. It's his father will cuddle him at the end."

"Don't be a fool, Alysson," said the Lady Jennine, sitting up in bed. "The child is forbidden to die. After all that monstrous suffering I went through to bring it into the world? It would be appallingly unfair if all that were for nothing. Besides, this is supposed to be a rich and noble household, isn't it? Can't they cure a few passing shits?"

"I don't think so." Alysson sat on the edge of her mistress's bed and stared at her toes. "Perhaps you should go and see the poor child. Comfort him. He's in such distress."

"And risk catching whatever dreadful sickness the brat carries?" Jennine sighed and curled back under the covers. The fire had not yet been lit and the early morning chill was bitter and damp. "How could you suggest such a thing? You've become very irritating lately, my girl. Just because your wretched lover has disappeared yet again, there's no need to take it out on me."

Alysson continued to stare at her toes. "You should go and hold your son," she said quietly. "Not because the child will care very much, or because there's the slightest likelihood of you suffering for the lack of him afterwards if you do not, but simply because this is your child and he's dying." She looked up suddenly. "Perhaps it will bring comfort to someone, even if only to Lord Humphrey. And trying to do the right thing, especially at times of tragedy, is always important. Terribly important, for your own sake. Besides, the dysentery isn't catching. Everyone knows that."

From over the pink feather coverlet tucked up beneath her chin, Jennine glared. "How dare you lecture me, Alysson. The wet nurse has poisoned my child and must be dismissed. And if you aren't careful, my dear, I shall dismiss you too."

"Poor Thomasine has been dismissed. And you can send me away today for all I care." Alysson stood, crossing over to the empty hearth where she kicked at the old ashes and began to lay the fresh twigs brought already by the page and stacked by the grate. "Ilara's back at home with Dulce so I can go and stay there again and be just as comfortable, I assure you."

The lady in the bed sniffed. "Oh yes, living on cabbage water. Honestly Alysson, you're as ungrateful as that child of mine."

Alysson snapped her mouth shut. The fire hissed into small flaming points. Finally she climbed up from her knees and went to the door. "I'm going to see how Eddie is. The doctor will have been again by now."

"That's a pitiful fire," Jennine objected, once again disappearing beneath the bedcovers. "And that damned page should be lighting it anyway, not you."

"Clovis isn't very good at fires," said Alysson. "And he did bring the twigs. Besides, I expect he's now busy stirring medicines somewhere. Have you any message for me to take to the sick room?" She glared back at her mistress. "An announcement that you'll be visiting shortly, for instance?"

Jennine's voice was muffled by blankets. "Don't be beastly, Alysson. And hurry back. I need you. I think I'm catching a cold."

"Since you don't like Clovis, I'll find your own pageboy and send him for wood to build up the fire." Alysson looked back over her shoulder. "I suppose you'd better stay in bed after all. At least it gives me a good excuse for your absence to tell the nurses and everyone else."

Jennine emerged with an explosion. "Don't you dare offer excuses for me to those pathetic nurses, Alysson. Why should I excuse myself to anyone? And don't send Clovis. He's a horrid little boy and I've no idea where he came from. I never asked for him, and he's completely useless as a page."

"Well, that's what he is," said Alysson quickly. "But I'll send Remi with wood as soon as I find him, though he's a nasty spoiled brat and Clovis is much sweeter, even if he's not so experienced at the job. I'll be back myself in a few minutes."

In hot weather the Sumerford castle corridors stayed chill and damp. In mid-January they were mired with ice, and knife draughts discovered every doorway and stairwell. Frost crept along the stone archways and painted the inner window sills white. Alysson hurried down and around the worn and echoing steps of the East Tower, wrapping her hands within her apron skirts for warmth. She bounded into the Nursery and slammed the door against the wind from above. Leaving the freeze without, she entered the sudden swelter. The heat within the great chamber was intimidating, every shutter tight closed and stuffed with rags against draughts. In the fire lit flush, a small crowd had gathered. The baby lay silent. Bending over the crib were the doctor, his assistant, the apothecary, her ladyship the countess, her ladyship's companion and chief maid, two nurses and Humphrey. Alysson whispered. "Is he?"

The younger nurse looked over. "No Mistress, there's change neither for good nor for ill. But the little mite is gone so quiet and the doctor fears the worse."

The countess glanced up. She frowned. "Order that female to

leave," she snapped to the nurse. "She should never be permitted to enter the nursery. Such a shameless character could be a harmful influence. Get rid of her."

For a moment Alysson stood still, one leg hesitating mid-air. Then she swung around and left in a rush, pulling the door behind her. In the sudden cold outside she leaned back against the crumbling stone, blinking back shock and tears. There was, however, no time to be either upset or resentful. Someone was shouting from a distance, then other voices answered. Within a heartbeat Hamnet appeared at great speed, jowls and velvet skirts bouncing.

"My lady." He pushed into the nursery, ignoring the hush of expectation and misery within. "His lordship wishes to see you at once, my lady," Hamnet announced. "It is most urgent. There is terrible news come from London."

The countess looked down her nose. "Hamnet, this is absurd. The situation already threatening us here is far more urgent than any business of king or capital. The next heir lies in danger of his life. What could be worse?"

Hamnet's words trembled. "Forgive me, my lady. I merely obey his lordship's orders." His voice shrank to a whisper. "A messenger has come from his majesty's Chancellor. It is the lords Gerald and Ludovic, my lady. They are to be – executed."

Alysson watched as the Countess of Sumerford hurried from the chamber and followed Hamnet with a rustle of swirling damasks. For some time afterwards Alysson stood quite still in the darkness, staring at nothing but immovable shadow. Then she turned and, once more trudging up the stairs with the whistle of the wind echoing above, slowly returned to the Lady Jennine's apartments.

Jennine was up, sitting close to the newly flaring fire. "Good God, child," she said at once. "You're as white as that damned snow outside. What has happened?"

Alysson shook her head. "It's not the baby. I think Eddie's condition is just the same. It's – something else."

"Well then? Spit it out, foolish girl."

Alysson collapsed on the bed and closed her eyes, addressing the darkness within her own eyelids. "Ludovic," she whispered. "And Gerald. They've been arrested. There is a sentence of – death."

The Earl of Sumerford stood beneath the huge iron portcullis, staring out across the snow spattered moat to the wide road leading away due east. The risen sun was already edging westwards towards the sea. It spangled the flurried snow, sparse flakes and a wistful windless day.

The earl shivered within his furs. He was dressed to impress. The huge shoulders of his surcoat were padded and pricked out in bliaut and sable. Suitable for an elderly man, his doublet was long skirted, his coat swept the turns of his riding boots, and his hat was wider brimmed and his hose thicker than fashion dictated. His gloves were deep cuffed and lined in sable, his sleeves sable trimmed and his shirt woollen. But he was frozen. The world had chilled him beyond reach of fur.

Within the courtyard his men gathered in silence. He would ride amongst forty Sumerford troops fully armoured, ten liveried men of his personal staff, Lord Ludovic's secretary and Lord Gerald's new young squire. On their approach to Westminster Palace, the captain of the guard would ride ahead bearing the Sumerford standard, the arms rich embroidered with dragon and basilisk and twice quartered, argent and gleaming gules.

The stables were in uproar, fifty two horses brought out and saddled and his lordship's own huge charger to be calmed, quickly groomed, caparisoned and bridled in silver. Turvey had already been exercised that morning but, well fed and excited by the noise and turmoil, snorted and rolled his eyes, eager for the sound and smell of his master. The grooms raced, sliding over the sheen of ice on cobbles. The guards claimed their mounts, the bugles sounded, the castle staff ran down to watch.

Two carts were packed high, two sumpters to draw each cart. Supplies for the journey, his lordship's clothes, and generous gifts for the king. His secretary came to the earl, a slight cough to gain attention. "My lord, Turvey is ready waiting and the guards already mounted, awaiting your orders."

The earl turned. "Bring me mulled wine." He turned back to the increasing wind. "And inform my heir that I leave within the half hour. I wish to see him before I go."

"The Lord Humphrey is closeted in the nursery tower, my lord. I shall send a page for him."

"I doubt his son has much further need of him. He may return to the child if he wishes after I have left."

"And her ladyship, my lord?"

"I cannot conceive of any reason to summon that woman now," said the earl. "She may concern herself with her prayers."

The secretary backed away and hurried to the castle. The earl remained staring out across the moat.

Alysson grabbed Clovis. "Have you heard?"

The main hall was deserted. The great fire flared and crackled like a burning forest. Alysson, greatly chilled, was crouching before it, warming her hands. She should not have been there but no one in the castle was now in their rightful place and no one was concerned with protocol. There was stunned silence where there should have been bustle and busy noise, there was consternation where there should have been peace and quiet. Hamnet was outside and the two assistant stewards were busy organising stores to be loaded from the kitchens. Clovis had crept through the long corridors, searching for the woman he had been hired to watch and protect.

He sighed. "Thought I'd lost you. Have searched the whole bloody place twice, I have. An' I've heard all right. If it weren't for wot I promised his lordship, I'd be off to London now to do wot I can to get him out."

Alysson had been crying, but her eyes, red rimmed, were now dry. "His father will get him safely away. He has to."

Clovis sat on the Turkey rug beside her. His eyes reflected the fire, small and demonic. He gazed in misery at Alysson. "Come to London wiv me."

She gulped and shook her head. "I thought of that already. I don't give a damn about the people here and most of them don't like me. There's only Jenny and she's a bitch anyway. I could pretend to be your sister. We could hitch a ride in a carrier's cart. But I don't have a penny. We might barter a ride by helping load and unload, but what would we do in London?"

"So bloody practical," sniffed Clovis. "We'd get by. They does, you know, all them Londoners, and most 'o them ain't got no pennies neither."

"I want so much," said Alysson, "just to be near him. I want to help him. I don't mind not having much to eat, and I don't mind living under The Bridge. At least – I don't think I mind. But I can't make myself believe I'd be the slightest use to him at all. Indeed, it would be the opposite, for as soon as poor Ludovic discovered I was there lurking around the Tower, he'd worry and it might make him feel even worse."

"You females," Clovis declared, "talk such rubbish. Wot's all that romantic shit got to do wiv it? It's bribing guards and sorting escapes we'd be doing."

"Oh dear," said Alysson. "Bribe them with what?"

Within the half hour the earl rode out surrounded by his entourage, the jingling of harness and clanking of weaponry, the creak of wet leather and the snorting of the horses. Turvey tossed his mane, hot breath clouding in the frosty air. The snow had increased to a swirling crystal fantasy, swallowing the troop as they crossed the moat and merged into the white bluster beyond.

Humphrey stood on the drawbridge, hugging himself against the cold. He stood alone. The snowflakes clung to his eyelashes and his beard. He licked them off his moustache, the thick hair reclaiming its rich red through the white sparkles. The first chill shadows spread long across the moat, shuddering into sudden dark as the sun sank westwards behind the turrets. Humphrey tried to remember his father's last words, and wondered, with the bleakness of acknowledged inadequacy, what he should do next. Something inexorably horrible lurked at the back of his consciousness but he could no longer quite remember what it was. He turned, eager to be back in the warm.

It was Hamnet who came, bowing deeply. There were tiny tears in the corners of his eyes. "My lord." The old steward sank to one knee on the rimed cobbles. "Your son, my lord. Her ladyship your mother bids you come quickly."

Humphrey looked down, remembering suddenly the wretched nightmare that he had almost buried for fear of remembering. "My Eddie?"

Hamnet nodded, head low, and cleared his throat. His voice trembled. "I am deeply, deeply sorry, my lord."

CHAPTER FORTY-ONE

L udovic sat across the small table from the man questioning him. He allowed the questions to assimilate slowly, absorbing the words separately before attempting to unite them into form and purpose. Finally, as each question coagulated in his brain, he attempted to formulate an answer. No word, no question and no answer made sense to him and a peculiar feeling of detachment from reality made both listening and speaking unusually difficult. More than anything else, he strained, hoping for enlightenment.

He had been stripped to shirt, hose and boots, and was bitterly cold. He had always thought his own stone house chill, but the Tower iced away memory, its dripping limestone a constant threat to sanity. But it was time which had, more than anything else, become the most treacherous enemy. Hours passed without count and became days without end. Long silent weeks drifted without purpose or hope. The silence of his captivity seeped into his mind like the ooze of the damp, until his thoughts were also frozen and timelessly fragmented.

"You will answer me directly, sir, and you will answer speedily." The narrow lips in the narrow face moved, the words floated on the frost spiked air. To Ludovic, its owner seemed abstract and distant. He nodded, trying to make sense of words and intention. "There is no need to think before answering," the man continued. "With each pause

I know you conjure lies and pretence, which I will not permit. Your responses must be honest and immediate, sir."

Ludovic's tongue felt thick and dry. His throat felt raw. His voice obeyed him only slowly. "Without first thinking," he said carefully, "I cannot remember how to speak. I find it impossible to be immediate, either in response or in comprehension. Everything, including yourself sir, appears to me in the shape of a dream. A nightmare. I have no idea what you ask, or why I am here, or how to answer."

"You will answer with the truth. There are ways of demanding quicker responses. I can show you instant reality, sir, in the shape of the rack. That will facilitate your tongue, I promise you."

Ludovic had been shackled. His hands were free, his fingers balled into fists and frozen, but his ankles were ringed and chained together, each movement grating rust against iron as the chains swung and pulled. The shackles rubbed persistently but had not blooded him, for they encircled his ankles over the soft leather of his riding boots. He was restricted to a slow shuffle and constantly reminded of the humiliation and the nightmare. At first he had also been beaten. Held upright by four men, he had been knocked and pummelled, the guards' knuckles against his face and ribs a hundred times, boots to his shins and knees to his groin. His broken ribs and bruises were now healing, but in the everlasting winter of his tiny room there was little relief from pain. He slept fitfully, hating the solitary and threatening silence and the endlessly long and empty hours, interrupted only rarely by the brief unlocking of the door.

"I have answered as I can," Ludovic replied. "But when you demand to know what plots and treacheries are planned next, the details of foreign letters and conspiracies for invasion and escape, I cannot answer. I know nothing of such things. I have been party to no such business and understand nothing of it. I doubt such plans exist."

The man sitting opposite scowled and bit his lip. Martin Frizzard was a thin man but appeared larger for he was exceedingly warmly dressed. His coat and doublet were plain but they were padded, trimmed in double layers of fox fur and lined in thick wool. He well knew the permanent chill of his official chambers and was clothed against it, for as his prisoners shivered from ice and fear, it was important to sit warm, complacent and comfortable, watching as the pitiful wretches trembled and fell into panic and dejection.

He was, however, not much interested in the prisoner now before him. A minor character, with as yet small proof of intent against him. But if the use of torture was allocated as he expected it would, then his interest would increase immeasurably. Martin Frizzard was intrigued by torture, its methods and its results. Although illegal without explicit authority, its benefits to the state were becoming increasingly appreciated. Authorisation was now more frequently given in cases of high treason where obstinate conspirators refused to divulge their secrets. The continuous problem of the fool and fraud Perkin Warbeck had brought England's lurking traitors into the foreground. The art of successful torture and the employment of those men most particularly experienced in its practice and suitable to its development, had become of major importance to the crown. Master Frizzard was experienced. He was adept at devising new methods and improving and elongating those already much used.

He smiled. "Dissimilation is most unwise, sir," he said. "Information against you has already been laid. Your past involvement in treachery is well known to us. You attended the execution of a known traitor and felon, and visited him beforehand during his custody. You are brother to Sir Gerald Sumerford, a known agitator, also implicated in these plots and conspiracies, a man arrested in the past for the same crime and known as a distributor of treacherous pamphlets. You yourself were arrested while attempting to flee the country, and you were seen to murder a member of his majesty's guard. You are clearly complicit, sir. Your guilt is already proven and your execution is assured. You gain nothing from denial. You must confess."

Ludovic sighed. He was numb both with cold and with confusion. He passed frigid nights in a stumbling puzzle of dream worlds where a small black haired girl curled close in his arms, kissing the wounds on his face and breathing the warming sweetness of her breath against his lips. But throughout the dark hours, he woke constantly to find himself alone and utterly lost.

For two months he had been held in one small chamber in the Salt

Tower. Just above ground level, this overlooked the Thames but no window opened to air or water, and the sharply iced draught was limited to the doorway. There was neither garderobe nor hearth, but a chamber pot and a small brazier stood beside the bed. The mattress was old wool bundled within hessian, grown damp and hard over the years. Ludovic had paid for new sheets and a thin woollen quilt. His own purse brought the limited comforts he was permitted; food, drink and some warmth. The charcoal brazier was refilled twice a week and a small cooked dinner brought each midday, ale and manchet each morning, and hippocras at the wane of each afternoon. The dinner was quite cold by the time it reached him but it warmed him anyway for those few short moments while he ate. He had at first paid for his doctor, ointments and bandages. The doctor had sewed the split above his eyebrow, six neat black stitches, now removed. The tiny holes where the needle and thread had passed still decorated each side of the long pale scar. Now Ludovic bought candles. He bought paper, quill and ink. And he bought news of his brother.

Gerald was kept far distant across the inner ward in the Beauchamp Tower. He was a prisoner of greater importance and proven complicity. Ludovic's purse also paid for his food, his ale and his blankets. In this way, each brother knew the other lived.

Following quickly from Margate back to London, Kenelm had finally been permitted a brief visit with his partner, and immediately handed over the large sum of money which was Ludovic's. Indeed, Kenelm had also parted with his own share of the previous trip's profits; his friend's need being far greater than his own.

"Get to Sumerford as soon as you can," Ludovic asked, "and inform the earl."

It was several months before he knew that Kenelm had also been arrested. While leaving the precincts of the Tower, Kenelm, accompanied by Ellis scurrying in tow, was quickly apprehended and taken to the Marshalsea. They were both accused of aiding and abetting known traitors to the realm, and thrown without questioning into the communal cells. The Fair Rouncie was briefly impounded and they were held for two months before perfunctory pardon without trial. In March the captain paid for his ship's release and the vessel was returned to him, stripped of goods. Kenelm was able to arrange for recaulking and careening at last, but he did not reach Somerset until early in April, nor was able to pre-empt the crown messenger's information regarding the Sumerford sons' incarceration.

It snowed heavily during February and the Thames was under ice above the tidal reaches, but Ludovic saw neither rain nor snow. He did not see the river either in flood or in ebb and forgot the smile of sunshine. Three times he was permitted to remember the colour of the sky and the feel of the wind on his back when he was taken, shackled and stumbling to the whitewashed Keep. There his questioning took place. Sometimes from within his cell, he heard the wail of the gulls through the stone, but he saw no bird or other creature. He saw only his guards. Then spring slipped itself through the flurry of gales and the weather improved but within the walls of the Tower no difference was felt. Icy condensation continued to drip down the stone, turning the walls mossy in slimed stripes from ceiling to floor.

Ludovic was once again taken for questioning. "I have lost track of time," he said.

"Time is not your problem, my lord," Master Frizzard informed him. "If you confess, it is possible you will be pardoned. You may then make time your concern once again."

Ludovic sighed. His wounds had healed and he suspected that two months or more must therefore have passed. But without window or light, he could not even count the days. He had done so at first, scratching a mark into the stone beside his bed as each breakfast ale was delivered. But the confusion of isolation had interrupted consecutive scratches and he had lost all desire to know how many days had passed him by.

"I cannot confess to treachery," Ludovic said. "I've done nothing more than I've already explained. Naturally I was acquainted with my brother's squire Roland Fiddington, and out of human decency visited the man, paid for his food in gaol, and attended his execution as he asked me to. When I heard of the warrant for my own arrest, I believed it farcical and disbelieved the rumour. I therefore did nothing either to avoid arrest or to seek it. My trip to Flanders had long been arranged, and was for business. I trade in dyed wool and fabrics. I killed the king's guard in self-defence, and in the confusion of the moment. I regret my action. I can confess to nothing else."

"I have recently received authorisation to continue questioning you and your brother under duress," smiled Master Frizzard. "Our methods are meticulous and can be prolonged. The storage chambers beneath this Keep await you, sir, if you persist with your lies."

"Torture?" Ludovic said, and nodded. He had expected it for a long time.

"The common word used by the ignorant," smiled the captain. "I prefer the word persuasion. But it is one and the same thing. You will be brought to me again tomorrow. Then you will confess, and put your signature to the document already prepared. Or you will be taken below for – persuasion. The decision is yours, my lord."

"Tell me, sir," Ludovic said softly, "what would you do, should you find yourself in my position, remembering indeed that this frequently happens? It is not unknown for the executioner to be executed, and a man long in royal favour may lose that favour at a moment's notice, and even with no fault of his own. So what would you do, sir, in your innocence? Accused of crimes you have not committed but when threatened with torture, would you confess? Even though you have no knowledge of what you are accused of and could not fully understand your own confession?"

Martin Frizzard leaned forwards, speaking clearly. "I would, sir. I would not willingly commit myself to the methods of persuasion I have at hand, for I know them too well. A confession is simply obedience to the king's wishes. As an obedient servant of his majesty, I would confess and beg his mercy."

"I have not heard," Ludovic said, "that this is a merciful king."

"And I am not a merciful man, for I am dutiful to the king's wishes," said Master Frizzard. "But the rack and the lash await you sir. Think on that as you lie warm in your bed tonight."

"It is a hundred nights since I lay warm," said Ludovic softly. "And the rack often enters my thoughts."

The easy sleep of untroubled youth had deserted Ludovic the first night of his arrest. Instead he watched the faint slime of damp illuminating the darkness within the imagined passing of the hours, eyes open and stinging with dejection and weariness. But he was not always entirely alone.

The voice of his madness accompanied him. The tiny light hovered within the damp chill. "Do you still acknowledge me? Do you come here, because it is where I came long ago?"

"I remember and acknowledge you," Ludovic whispered into the deep black chill. "But I am here against my will. I do not search for you."

"You would not find me," the voice murmured. "I have gone from there. It is a sad place. The echoes remind me of such dismal disillusion. You sleep close to where my hopes died."

"I do not sleep. Nor do I hope," said Ludovic to the shadows.

"Then we are both dead," whispered the voice. "For nor do I sleep and hope is long gone."

"It is true. I believe I am dead," Ludovic said. "Though first there will be pain, and degradation, and the dread of anticipation. I expect to welcome death when it comes." There were long pauses, wandering silences and the unravelling of thought. Ludovic did not know whether both voices were his own, or even if both voices were simply the ghosts of imagination. But if so, the imagination of whom? His own? Or did he exist merely in the thoughts of someone else? He was no longer sure if he was fantasy himself, but he felt the soft damp of his own breath on the air around him and its familiar cloud of faint warmth against his lips. His eyes stung, his limbs ached. Discomfort kept him sane. "If you were once here," he wondered, "then how, if you are who I thought you, did you leave?"

"By river," the voice said, after pause. "Bustle by night and a warm wind in the sails. I was glad to leave. I feared death."

"Then you left here alive?"

"It was arranged for me. I was warned only moments before, and then I breathed brine." The speaker sighed, conjuring sweet memories.

"My servants had told me I would be secretly killed. It was inevitable, they said. They frightened me. Caring, cheerful faces by day. Haunting horrors by night. But they misjudged. I was smuggled out alive, well treated and taken abroad to my aunt."

"Then you are not the child I searched for," murmured Ludovic. "You are not Pagan."

"I am nameless, for they stole my name and my title and my honour." The voice rustled, as if struggling for a lost identity. "And when I died, it was yet another name they gave me, forcing me to hide beneath secrets. I fought for myself but I was not myself when I was killed. I am no longer myself. I have no grave. I have no monument, no marker, no mourners. But in this place where you have come, I begin to remember myself at last."

"This place inspires your memory, but in here I am forgetting myself," Ludovic said. "The cold seeps in where once there was integrity and understanding. I do not know your name after all. Perhaps I do not know my own."

"So do our names make us who we are? Are we judged by names alone?"

"Judgement?" Ludovic sighed. "Judgement is for liars."

"Then we are all lost," whispered the echoes. "But there is someone else nearby. I know him, though I cannot remember who he is. And he knows me, though he struggles to call me by name. But I talk to him in the night just as I speak now with you. And he replies as you do. He is bitterly alone and sometimes I hear him sobbing in the dark. But once he was close to me, and I feel his love like streamers of light in the darkness."

Ludovic shook his head. "I never knew you, nor know you now. So why come to me?"

"You called me," the voice said.

"I was not conscious of it," Ludovic said. "I do not wish to call on the dead."

"Your mind wrapped around me," decided the words. "For a long time, your thoughts surrounded me. Many others have called in the same way. For a long time I knew no peace, being pulled like breezes into other men's minds. But when I answered their calls they were frightened and I was thrust back. You were never frightened. You answered me and gave me comfort, so I came again. I hoped to find myself."

Ludovic lay for some time in silence. When he finally spoke again, he already knew himself alone. "The other man who lies nearby," he whispered, "who sends love and answers when you speak. Is he your brother?"

But there was no movement within. The echoes of his voice fell flat against the wet stone. Ludovic turned, staring out into emptiness. It was a long time before he slept. They came for him in the morning.

CHAPTER FORTY-TWO

They had heard nothing further from London for some time but rumour in Sumerford was busy. The castle staff overheard what they could and imagined the rest. They carried back stories to their families in the village. The butcher told the carpenter and carpenter Berris told his mother. Mistress Berris told the thatcher and the thatcher told his daughter who told her husband who told the innkeeper who told his wife.

Some said the lords Ludovic and Gerald had already been executed, others swore they had heard of pardons. The brewster was quite sure it was the king himself who had been killed while others proclaimed this treason and blasphemy. The countess meanwhile kept to her chambers and no letter arrived from the earl.

Alysson sat with the Lady Jennine as the funeral procession tolled across the moat and down the old beaten roadway towards the village church. The drums thrummed loud and exceedingly slow and the coffin was so tiny it cast no shadow on the catafalque. Black horses drew the cart, lifting their front hooves very high, embraced by circlets of feathers, dyed black. Their manes were plaited, their tails long and twined in black ribbons. The pale sun made their coats gleam, double polished.

The family crypt beneath the Sumerford chapel already held the new marble plaque for Edward Sumerford, rising poignant behind a hundred flickering candles.

Alysson had been crying. "Don't sniff," snapped Jennine from the window enclosure. "And don't pretend it's for my little boy. You're crying for the lover who's abandoned you. You dream of his prick hot between your legs."

Alysson stared back at her. "Don't be a fool, Jenny. You know I dream of him. But not like that. And you know I cry for Eddie too."

Jennine looked away. "I hate the way you talk to me. I wish you wouldn't be so rude. You never used to talk to me that way, Alysson. You make me feel cheap."

Alysson poured wine for them both. "You are cheap, Jenny. Dismiss me if you want to, but then you'll be left with no one to talk sense to at all. Remember I know exactly who you are and what you were, and I'm tired of talking to you as if you're the grand lady and I'm just your maid."

"You are a maid. And I'm a lady now, grand or not." Jennine took the wine and emptied the cup immediately. She held it out for more. "You should be grateful to me even if you don't respect me. I used to think you liked me."

"I did once."

"You still do. You just haven't forgiven me for not seeing little Edward at the end." Jennine drained her second cup of wine. "Why can't you simply understand how much I hate sickness and misery and pain? Why should I be reminded of all that if I don't want to be? There's too much of it in the world. It's better to ignore it and then it doesn't hurt. And the child never missed me anyway. You know that too."

"It doesn't matter," said Alysson. "I'll be honest with you, Jenny. I'm leaving anyway before the end of next month if Ludovic doesn't come back. My nurses have been saving the money Ludovic and I gave them. They've enough to help me travel to London."

Jennine's face changed. She stared. The petulance turned severe. "You will not leave," she said. "I refuse to allow it. I need you."

Alysson smiled. "That's not a compliment."

"It wasn't meant to be," said Jennine. "It's a warning. You won't leave me Alysson. Not until I throw you out."

<hr />

The last days of January spat and sneezed. February strode sinister and threatening across the fields. Snow wove silent curtains, a skyward tapestry, an array of silvered fantasies. The castle slunk and oozed frozen damp. The cobbles were rimed, the limestone iced. The moat froze and snow banked against the towers and their turrets.

In March the snow paled to hail and sleet. Wild flowers peeped, sprigging the slush clogged roadsides and spreading over the hills. The hedges sprouted bird's nests, trees fluffed into blossom, hedgehogs scrambled back into the light, hoping for sunshine. Seabirds crowded the cliffs. The cattle calved and were brought out from their winter byres and the pastures were dotted with new lambs, as pretty as the primroses and buttercups.

After some weeks Clovis discovered a carrier planning to cart his merchandise to London by mid-April, as soon as the rivers were passable and the roads clear. Ilara's savings paid the carter with a further donation made towards the hire of two armed guards. Clovis had no need to announce his departure from the castle. Unknown to all who accepted his small presence and ordered the routine of his days without question, Clovis was not in fact employed as a member of the staff. Ludovic had paid him simply to watch, aid and protect one Alysson Welles, insuring her safety and wellbeing until he might return to care for her himself. Clovis had achieved this for some months. Now he would travel with her to London, attempting to preserve the safety and wellbeing of Lord Ludovic instead. Alysson prepared her departure.

"Won't take more'n four, five days I hopes," Clovis confided. "Calls it spring season, they does, but 'tis bloody cold still. I were bumped eight days coming here when his lordship sent me down last year. Took for bloody ever. An' mighty cold it were then too. Maybe worser."

"Well, we have no horses ourselves," Alysson said, "so we have to go by cart. There's little choice. Besides, I wouldn't like to make that journey on our own. How could we be sure of the way? And what about robbers on the roads, and trying to ford rivers in flood, and getting soaked when it rains and not finding inns with room to take us? Carriers may be slow, but they're far safer and far more comfortable. Hopefully the journey won't take too long."

Clovis scowled. "Better at sea." He thought a moment. "'Cept for storms and pirates and maggoty bacon and sea monsters, that is."

"And the carter won't permit us to take much luggage," Alysson sighed. "I should have liked so much to take my two good gowns so I might dress nicely when I see Ludovic again. But I must be practical for travelling. I would be better staying in my broadcloth livery, but I suppose they'll demand that back from me before I leave."

"They will," Clovis nodded.

"Then I shall have to wear my old tunic from two years ago," Alysson said. "It's such a horrid thing and badly marked. But at least now I have good shoes."

"Wot silly fings females care 'bout," Clovis muttered, backing away. "Startin' a right good adventure we is, and all you talks of is clothes."

It was not clothes Alysson was thinking of. It was soft silken hair against her cheek, penetrating eyes the colour of sunshine on grassed pasture, and a thin lipped mouth tilted into sweet smiling corners. Ludovic's careful hands caressed her through the long cold darkness of her nights, touching secret places where he had never truly touched, whispering words he had never truly spoken. Her dreams warmed and cosseted her, but she woke each morning to cold fear. She did not even know, though clung to hope, whether he lived. It had been nearly six months since she had seen him. There had been no further word of execution, but death in custody was not unknown. She was not sure how such an endless imprisonment could affect even a strong man, and prayed for his safety and his health and his survival. She prayed to find a way to see him, and prayed that eventually, by some skill of her own or through the earl's pleas to the king, Ludovic would come home to her.

Jennine said, "It is the silliest thing, but something's wrong with the cess pit. Her ladyship is furious."

"There's the gong farmer in Sumerford," Alysson said, distracted. She was wondering how to tell the lady she was leaving in three days. "George Wapping. I met him once and he seemed a nice man though his clothes do keep hold of that particular aroma, and sometimes strange things hang around in his beard. But he'll clean out the cess pit and take the muck in cartful's down to the sea."

"I'm sure the countess knows all about that already." Jennine shook her headdress. "But she says there's no reason for the pit to be full already, since it was cleaned right out and re-dug three years ago after they stopped using the moat. It should have lasted without cleaning for several years more. Besides, it smells absolutely horrid and I have to hold my nose going past the privy. Yesterday this shocking yellow sludge came bursting up out of the hole. I was mortified. If the earl was at home, I'm sure he would never have allowed it."

"I don't see how."

"Really Alysson, you're positively boring these days." Jennine sank back against her pillows, reached for her cup and sipped the steaming hippocras. She watched her maid over the brim. Alysson was clearly concentrating on other matters entirely. "Come and sit by me, my dear, and tell me what the problem is."

"Problem?" Alysson whirled around. "How could there be a problem, with life so sweet and so simple? With Ludovic arrested, his execution possible any day. With Gerald also in the Tower facing death. With your baby less than three months in his grave, and Lord Humphrey wailing every morning outside this door until you let him in for comfort. And now the cess pit is overflowing and threatening us all with disease from foul vapours. What a wonderful and fulfilling life we all lead in this great draughty castle. How could there be a problem?"

"Now that's exactly what I mean, Alysson," said the lady. "You've grown sharp tongued and quite rude. I can't imagine why I put up with you."

Alysson sat suddenly on the edge of the bed where Jennine was stretched. She gazed earnestly at her mistress through the afternoon shadows. "You don't need to put up with me anymore, Jenny." She held her breath, and said it in a hurry. "I'm leaving the day after tomorrow."

A deepening silence merged into the shadows, an early twilight as the drizzle fogged the outside the windows, blurring the glass mullions. The Lady Jennine realised her mouth was open, and shut it with a snap. "I forbid it. I told you before. I won't let you leave."

Alysson sighed. "I'm sorry Jenny. But you won't miss me really, you're just cross that someone has the temerity to walk out on you. And I have to go, you must realise that. I love him. I have to go and see if I can help."

Jennine laughed. "Help? How? Climb up the Tower walls and pass him a sword? Fuck all the guards in return for letting him escape?"

"It's hopeless I know." Because that part at least was true. "There's probably nothing I can do. But I have to be there, and see him, and take him food and blankets, and hold him, and promise I'll never sleep until he's free."

"Do they let mistresses crawl into bed with their prisoners?"

Alysson stared. She felt her cheeks growing pink and hot with anger. "Haven't you ever attempted to do something important yourself, Jenny?" she demanded. "Haven't you ever wanted to help anyone else? Haven't you ever believed, desperately, that you had to try? Or have you always just sat around complaining? Always letting other people do everything for you? And then accusing them of being useless and stupid? While really it's you being useless and stupid?" She found herself panting for breath, her fists clenched. "You've done your best to thrust me into Ludovic's bed for a year or more, and even though you know quite well it never actually happened, now you insult me for being a whore. But you're the whore, Jenny, and I've never thrown that in your face before. I've known the truth since you told me yourself at the beginning, so don't look so prissy. Now I wish I had become Ludovic's mistress. He never wanted me to come back and work for you after I was wounded. He wanted to keep me safe in his own house far away, and I was an absolute fool to turn him down. If I ever get him back I'll say yes without any hesitation. But first I have to see him, and kiss him and convince him he'll be saved somehow. I've waited and waited because I know I can't do much to help him, and I prayed for a miracle, but now I can't wait any longer. I have to go to London."

Jennine's eyes stayed cold but her mouth smiled. "Of course, my dear." She patted the bed beside her. "Come and sit closer. I understand, naturally. In fact, I shall help. You may have money, and clothes, and food to take. I shall arrange everything. But perhaps you should wait a little longer. After all, for all we know the dear boy may be on his way home right now. His lordship the earl may have secured his release already."

Alysson shook her head. "The earl would have sent the countess a message. The castle would be in uproar, preparing a celebration for the homecoming."

"Yes, perhaps you're right, my dear." The smile was fixed like plaster to stone. "So I shall arrange horses and an armed guard for your journey. I shall speak to the countess and get permission to borrow a litter. You shall have only the best, my love."

"The countess will never agree. How could you expect her to supply all that just for a lowly maid servant she doesn't even like?" Alysson frowned. There was something wrong. "Besides, I've made my own arrangements. I leave on Wednesday."

"Ah." Jennine continued to smile. "How efficient you are, my dear. Very well, though I admit to being a little disappointed you told me nothing until almost on the point of leaving. Hardly polite to a faithful friend. But I forgive you, of course. Now, let us make plans together."

Alysson ignored the patted counterpane. She wandered over to the window enclosure. "I told you weeks ago," she said. "But the roads were iced in and the rivers too high for the carrier to cross, so I had to wait. Now the paths are clear."

"I see." Jennine's smile seemed to fade, tiny pricks of high colour appearing like glitter in her eyes. "With such determination, my dear, perhaps you'll secure your lover's release after all." She rose and stretched, reaching for the door. She opened it just a little and peered out. She called. A page came puffing up the stairs outside. It was not Clovis, but Remi, her own personal boy. Jennine addressed him quietly, then turned back to Alysson. "Patience, my dear. I shall organise some treats for you. After all, I cannot lose my very dearest friend without thanking her in some special way."

Alysson felt strangely uncomfortable. "I don't want gifts. I know I've upset you, and I'm sorry, but I can't just sit around here thinking about where he is and what terrible things are happening to him. You'll be all right." Alysson tried to smile and found her mouth would not curl. "You have such a wonderful friendship with Humphrey, and he adores you and the countess likes you so much. I expect you'll be with child again by summer. Then you'll be the most important person in the castle again. You won't even remember me by next month."

Footsteps, running, someone small and light and someone else heavy footed. Banging outside, and the door was wrenched open. Alysson stared.

"Her," Jennine pointed.

CHAPTER FORTY-THREE

Ludovic crossed the yard of the inner ward. He squinted at the unaccustomed light, breathing deep. The stench of the Thames floated close, but air, however cold or rank, smelled sweet after months of knowing only the chill vapour of his cell, and natural light, however dull, seemed gloriously alive after peering only through the shadows of enclosure. The ground sparkled as day slid across wet stone. It had rained in the night though through the huge isolation of the walls, Ludovic had heard nothing.

His steps were restricted by the shackles and he was utterly weary. He had slept very little. He was hungry. The food he paid for himself was meagre once delivered, the cauldron already divided between his gaolers while hot, before he received whatever they had left him when cold. The brazier had remained a faint fitful glow, its tiny charcoal warmth sunk and disillusioned by damp. At first Ludovic had pulled it close, holding his hands up against its open ironwork, clinging to the flicker of diminishing flame and the rising warmth of smoke. But through the low light he had watched his hands tremble, too weak and too cold to hold steady. So then he had crept beneath the cover of his bed, pulling the blanket around his shoulders, laid his head on the flat bolster and closed his eyes. When the ghostly whispers echoed in his head, he could not answer, not knowing anymore what was real. It was only contemplation of the rack and Martin Frizzard's smile which had then filled his vision and the clank of his shackles seemed like the clink of metal on metal which he expected from the pulleys of torture. He shivered and could not sleep.

It was mid-April said the guards who came for him. Spring, a bright new hope and a burgeoning of prosperity. Ludovic nodded, discovering no reply, nor the ease of ready answer he had once known. He had no hope, nor interest in prosperity, and the passing of the time depressed him. He had not supposed April to have come so unannounced, when he still felt himself creeping through midwinter.

Master Frizzard was waiting.

"I have your confession ready for signature, sir." Snuggled in fur, the man tapped a finger to the scroll lying before him. "Here, my lord. Read it and sign it. Or it's the rack which waits, with rollers well oiled and the levers ready warmed."

A stool was set and Ludovic sat, thankful to do so. He was twenty six years old and felt ancient. Each bone suffered its own separate and violent ache. He stared at the paper prepared. At first he found it hard to read, his sight red rimmed and blurred. Then he read the words which spoke in his name, admitting to complicity in crimes which, he believed, had never been committed by anyone let alone himself. He knew himself already irredeemable. He looked up at the small narrow mouth over the width of fur trimming in front of him. "But I have had no contact of any kind with the Duchess of Burgundy. I have never been to Malines. I do not know the man Piers Warbeck. I have no knowledge of these other men you name, nor their conspiracies. Written here are admissions of duplicity and crime, matters which confuse and disgust me. How can I sign this document?"

"Again?" Martin Frizzard scowled and pursed his lips. "Have we not discussed this before, sir? His majesty requires you to sign this confession. The king's wishes should be sufficient motive for compliance. Otherwise your refusal leads directly to the rack. The choice is yours, sir."

During those rare occasions under questioning, Ludovic had previously sat straight. He had not shivered, nor trembled, nor bent. Now he relinquished pride. He folded his arms on the table and laid his head down on his wrists. He spoke into the thin grimed linen of his shirt cuffs. "You give me no choices, sir. I cannot sign. As I face execution in either case, at least I will leave my family with the knowledge of my innocence."

Master Frizzard stood, scraping back his chair. "Then you offer me diversion, my lord, and a good few hours of entertainment before dinner. Boiled mutton today I believe, and boiled onions with curd cheese. I shall work up a good appetite." He reached forwards, grabbing a handful of Ludovic's hair and wrenching up his face to look at him. Ludovic blinked, staring up. "If you have paid for your rations this week," Frizzard smiled, "then you will be served boiled mutton and onions yourself sir. Of course, it will be sadly congealed by the time the platter reaches you. But then," he smiled a little wider, "I doubt that will bother you today. You will have no appetite at all I promise, once I have finished with you. You'll not be able to face a single breadcrumb I'm afraid, nor," he grinned, "have the strength in your broken fingers to hold it."

Ludovic laid his head back down on the table. "Do what you will sir," he murmured. "I no longer care."

Beneath the great Keep the chambers were without windows, but natural light slunk down the wide stairwell and many tall candles banked the walls in iron sconces. The cellar was large and dreary and open. There were three racks, each the same. They were long wooden beds, made of dark oak and heavily built. But they were not true beds and the slatted frames bore no mattress. Massive rollers at either end distorted the surrounding shadows. There was the smell of old blood, and shit, and great fear. The wood was stained.

Winding and steep, the ancient stairwell echoed from the chamber of questioning into the cellars of torture. Martin Frizzard trotted briskly ahead. Four guards brought Ludovic down. His boots had been removed and the feet of his hose were soon wet and sticky with the grime of the stones. He stood in the arched entrance, his wrists roped behind him, his ankles in irons. Without his boots, the shackles rubbed at his feet, wearing holes in the worn out wool. Fire and candlelight shifted around him, playing its theatre across the walls and the floor and the busy machinery of the apparatus, painting the old black wood with a lurid gloss.

Far larger than the brazier in Ludovic's cell, a huge charcoal burner was grotesque with flame, illuminating the damp on the walls. It generated considerable heat. No need for the torturer to shiver. The man already stood waiting, stripped to the waist. He sweated, gleaming like liquid metal in the firelight. Ludovic felt real warmth for the first time in four months, but his back stayed in ice. Released immediately from his bonds and shackles, he was pushed forwards towards the rack which sat central and threatening before him. At once he was forced to his knees against the frame. He stumbled, bent relentlessly forwards. Two guards took his arms, the others took his legs. He was thrown flat, the low slats hard beneath his back, his limbs spread and stretched, his arms above his head and his legs wide. The roller to which his wrists were manacled, groaned, creaking as it pulled against his body. His ankles were chained to the roller at the base, and locked tight. Efficient and busy, the four guards secured him and moved away. Martin Frizzard moved forwards. He looked down on Ludovic and smiled.

"The rack is an interesting instrument, my lord," he said with an inflexion of earnest affection. "Being well practised, I and my assistant here can control the amount of pain inflicted to the tiniest degree. Under the right leverage, the rack can stretch your limbs up to the very point of dislocation without breaking the joints or crippling the bones. The pain caused is, of course, exceptional. But no lasting damage need be done. You would not walk away, of course." Frizzard chuckled. "Indeed, it would be some weeks before you walked again. But in time, with a little doctoring and a good deal of patience, you might recover."

Ludovic closed his eyes. He had not struggled. He had allowed the manipulation of his body without resistance or objection. He reserved his strength and concentrated on his breathing. He felt the hot air reach deep into his lungs and then expelled it slowly. The rhythm calmed him and he did not listen to the man speaking, although the

394

words impinged, distantly impelling. Ludovic said nothing now. He was absorbed in controlling the reactions of his body and of prolonging his life.

Martin Frizzard nodded as though he understood what remained unspoken. "During the process you will be given time to confess," he said. "I will stop the levers at several points, the second time just before the knees and wrists are dislocated, and then finally as the hips, elbows and shoulders snap apart." He paused, as though considering before continuing the conversation. "Of course, it's likely you'll lose consciousness at that stage, but we'll bring you round, never fear. I've ways of keeping a man conscious when I want him fully aware. Indeed, we have a long morning before I need be off to take my midday dinner in peace. And afterwards I shall be back again. But I hope not to prolong the business. It would be a shame to see a man of your bearing quite broken and deformed by the rack." He paused again, for affect. "In the end you'll confess anyway of course. They all do. Older, stronger men than you, my lord. I'm a master at my craft you see, and do not tire easily. Naturally it would save you a deal of pain were you to confess at this early stage, but obstinacy goes hand in hand with treachery they say. You give the word, my lord, to set the rollers turning or to set you free and back to your own hot dinner."

He bent over, testing his prisoner's chains. The pressure on Ludovic's arms was already extreme. Stretched high above his head, the elbows were wrenched against their natural pivot and long weakened by freezing and sleepless imprisonment, Ludovic felt his body brittle. He counted his breaths, regulated strict and rhythmic, and kept his eyes shut.

"Sometimes," Martin Frizzard confided, "a man is too much confused by pain. If he leaves his confession too late, I am engrossed in my work and cannot stop. It is a sad end, but I am not myself at liberty to permit any fool to escape his destiny, and will not impede justice by thinking of mercy before the job is done. But I do not condone stretching until death. I will save your life, my lord, confession or not. You will not die at my hand, but be executed afterwards, whether or not you walk to the block. Many a man needs to be dragged. It makes little difference."

The heat had increased. The brazier stood close, its smoke rising uninterrupted to the vaulted stone roof. There was no movement in the chamber to disturb either smoke or flame. The four guards stood back around the walls. Martin Frizzard stood looking down calmly at Ludovic. Ludovic could not move. The light flared rich red against the back of his eyelids.

"But," Frizzard continued, "I will still allow opportunity for confession, even at the very end, for once persuaded to admit the truth then clearly you need no more persuasion. This form of encouragement is the straightest path to justice. The law must discover the truth, but a guilty man avoids admitting his guilt. Thus he impedes both justice and the law. I am adept in guiding a guilty man back towards righteousness. Indeed, this is an exercise you should welcome, sir, for it returns you to the truths you have so long discarded. However, if you don't choose to stop the racking by making your confession, there are other methods I have devised to encourage you beyond the breaking of your joints." Frizzard paused again, biting his lip. Irritated by his prisoner's lack of reaction, he breathed deep and continued. "Recently one man was sadly obstinate. He refused to sign his own confession, even after his knees fell apart. I then abstracted his teeth one by one. There were two left when he tried to speak. But unfortunately his mouth was full of blood and his words were impossible to understand. He simply gurgled, and how was I to know his intention? After pulling the last two teeth, I allowed him to swallow the blood and rest a little. Then he indicated a great desire to confess after all. I permitted it, feeling magnanimous. But he fainted before able to write his signature. A pity. He went to the axe unabsolved."

The wooden slats beneath Ludovic's spine held him rigid, forcing his chest upwards, but his breathing remained steady. He had narrowed his focus and now thought of nothing else. Fear battered at the edges of his consciousness but remained locked outside the concentration of his breath.

"Then, should all else fail," smiled Frizzard, "there is castration. A traitor sentenced to hang may first be castrated, which entertains the crowd and prepares a common man for the greater tortures of hellfire to come. But nobility, executed on the block, escapes such sordid contempt of his masculinity, as is proper." He sighed. "And I should not want to emasculate a fine man like yourself, my lord. But sometimes castration can encourage a little common sense in an uncommon man, where other methods fail. The knife right through the base of the prick as the pincers sever the cods, it's a painful business, sir, and one to avoid I assure you. And I think it would be a great shame if you were to hobble out into the cold without your better parts, should a pardon then be granted by his majesty's mercy after all."

Ludovic felt a large hand fall flat and heavy across his groin. "I could have your codpiece off and the job done in an instant." Frizzard removed his hand after a brisk pat to the relevant area, and smiled. "But the rack first, as is fitting. For the rest, it's up to you, sir. I am experienced in all these matters, and will be busy about my business until the moment you consent to admit your guilt. And my good assistant here who will be pulling the levers and insuring your lordship stays fully awake, this is the faithful Barnaby, my friend and apprentice Luke. You'll get to know him as well as myself I don't doubt, before the end."

Ludovic said nothing. He heard only a nonsense of rigmarole, words drifting from far away. Nothing but his breathing mattered. He held his own life in complete control, sufficient, he believed, even within his power to stop. Should the pain prove unbearable, he planned to die by the voluntary cessation of breathing. He did not know whether he truly had that power, but he intended to try. He might, at the very least, ensure prolonged unconsciousness. He settled, patiently, and counted his breaths.

The first roll of the base pulley was grindingly brutal; a sudden onslaught on all his senses that instantly wrenched Ludovic away from the studied concentration of his breathing and instead flooded him, reeling, into dizzy and overwhelming agony. The roller had moved very little but the chains holding his manacles sprang into full distension, cutting violently into his ankles. A creak of wooden cogs, the tug on the handle, and every joint in his body screamed. His head pounded. His back arched and his spine vibrated, vertebra leaping in

397

flame as if they tore apart. He felt the sweat soak through his shirt and hose and clamp his hair to his neck. The burst of pain stunned him and the extent shocked him. He remained silent, but instantly knew himself lost.

The levers pressed down again and the roller attached to his legs swept back. His knees were on fire as the joints at his hips cracked. In the silence, he heard his own bones suffer.

"A short pause, perhaps," suggested Martin Frizzard, "for his lordship to contemplate. We are, of course, only at the very beginning and have hardly started. But we've given, I believe, a small indication of what will come." Ludovic heard his chuckle. "You've a fine pair of legs, sir. It's a real shame, I believe, to ruin them. And once we start on the roller holding your wrists, well, you'll not be lifting even a feather for a long time after. Will you reconsider the confession now, perhaps? Before too late?"

Ludovic wondered how long it would take them to break him. He no longer believed he could resist until the end. He abandoned entirely the hope of ending his own life by refusing to breathe. It could not be done. His breathing was now stertorous, each breath short and shallow as he gasped for deeper inhalation. There was no question of choosing to die. He could no more hold his breath than move his breaking joints.

In his wavering and desperate silence, both rollers cranked again. Pain shot through him, darting into each muscle and each bone, riveted as though by iron into his shoulders, wrists and hands, concentrating down his back and swarming into the raw nerves of his hips, knees, ankles and feet. His head swam. For one instant, abstracted, he hoped to prove himself far weaker than most and faint immediately.

He did not. His consciousness, tormented by waves of agony through each tendon and every particle of flesh, remained alive. The rollers turned again and for the first time he screamed. He heard the thin, wild sound and did not know that it was himself.

"Another pause, my lord?" Master Frizzard bent over him, took Ludovic's chin in his hand, and peered into his bloodshot eyes.

Frizzard turned to Barnaby. "Throw cold water over the fool. He's growing faint."

Ludovic shut his eyes. The water was icy and he welcomed it, though it stung. In the nightmare of heat and the rivers of suffering, the water seemed to attach him back into reality. He prepared himself for the next turn of the wheel.

Barbaby was calling for more water and a guard came forwards with a bucket. Frizzard loomed over Ludovic once again. "The initial stage is now over, my lord," he told him. "At the next full roll, the first of your joints will snap. Your muscles will begin to tear beyond mending. You will hear the pop, as the stretching causes the first break. Muscles can mend even when pulled beyond their weight, but not once they have torn apart. To save yourself permanent crippling, will you now confess, sir? It is your last chance to remain whole."

Ludovic tried to find his tongue. His mouth was open when the next bowl of cold water sluiced over him. He drank. It was strangely refreshing.

Frizzard pulled up a stool and sat beside the rack. It seemed a casual act, as of a man invited to supper. "I studied abroad, sir," he said. Ludovic kept his eyes closed. He doubted his own waning comprehension, for the words seemed incongruous. Martin Frizzard continued cheerfully, ready for conversation. "It was France where I learned most of my trade and watched in interest as other methods of persuasion were practised. Sadly most of those are not encouraged here. We English have the Duke of Exeter's daughter, as we call the rack which you are enjoying now, my lord, but France knows greater refinements. Of course, the old days of trials against the Templars were already long over when I studied there, though I heard tell of them. It was torture indeed at that time, for the Templars were proved heretics and the kings of France wanted them punished and their vile secrets uncovered. Obtaining confessions was imperative." He sighed, shaking his head. "A civilised race, the French, even if we call them enemies more often than not. One criminal I saw in Paris, a brute accused of vile blasphemy, sodomy and rape, had escaped death twice. First ran from the cell in which he was held, and then after recapture, he ran again, claiming sanctuary, which was naturally denied. To convince him to stay and face his execution, he was sat on a wooden stool awaiting the hangman. His hose were pulled down around his ankles, his legs spread wide and his prick nailed to the seat of the stool. Sat and howled he did, bleeding merrily as though pissing himself. Then when it came to drag him off to the gallows, no one could extract the nail. I tried myself but it was too far embedded. They had to cut his prick off and leave it attached to the seat. It looked exceedingly strange and sadly wizened; left there alone once the man was carried off screaming."

Ludovic heard very little. The story, whether true or invented, held little importance. He knew himself goaded, encouraged into a confession which would cut short his pain but ensure his death. He was once again concentrating on his breathing. Given pause and time to adjust to the extreme stretching of his limbs and to the limits of his endurance, he believed one more pull on the rollers would break both his limbs and his resolve. His joints remained still intact, though held at the final extremity. Each muscle was ready to burst. Thought, though it was increasingly difficult to summon logic, told him one thing. He decided, slowly and with careful intent, to relinquish all he held important in himself and the truth of his whole life, and instead confess.

"I'm a fair man, sir," Frizzard was saying. "I give my prisoners every chance to turn honest, and will not cause pain beyond what they choose themselves with their silence. But you are obstinate sir, which proves your guilt beyond question. Only a guilty man would be so fearful to admit the truth of his actions."

Ludovic's decision was muffled by confusion but determined by the extremity of suffering. He opened his eyes. He looked into Martin Frizzard's face. "I believe you have won," he said very slowly. But he could barely hear his own voice, his tongue was swollen and the mumbled words held no clarity.

Frizzard bent a little lower, his ear to Ludovic's mouth. "You will have to speak up, sir," he said crossly, shaking his head. "I am a patient man, but 'believe one' means nothing to me. Do you ask for a pause? Or a singular chance? Do you state your belief in the one God? Or is it something else you ask for one of? I cannot understand you, my lord, but I must warn you further. If you do not accept this final offer for confession, the rollers will turn again. First there's the pop, pop of the sinews snapping. That loosens the muscles, which tear like parchment. Finally the crack of the bones as they wrench from their sockets. The knees are left to wobble as the bones above and below pull right out. A dismal picture, my lord, I promise you. This is your last opportunity to repent, or you will surely never walk again."

Ludovic tried to clear his throat and struggled to find his voice. He had whispered just one word when he was interrupted.

He did not hear the opening of the door or the entrance of urgent boots, but he saw Martin Frizzard's expression change abruptly before he stood, hurrying away into the far shadows. Beyond Ludovic's limited range of sight, the voices became loud and imperious. "Stop in the name of the king," someone demanded attention.

"It is finished here, and your work done. Release the chains and remove the irons from the pulleys."

The flames of the brazier flared suddenly. Luke Barnaby folded his arms across the sweating bare muscles of his chest, and scowled.

Frizzard's voice echoed dully from some distance. "My lords, there is no impropriety. I have the authority and can show you my orders signed by the Lord Chancellor. My business here is legally sanctioned."

"Not any longer, fool. This abomination is at an end."

CHAPTER FORTY-FOUR

The Earl of Sumerford carried his son from the cellars of the Tower Keep. He was a strong man, honed in warfare and hunting, but he was well past his zenith and into advanced middle age. The youthful body he carried should have weighed heavily, straining his muscles and his back. But he found his son pitifully light.

Ludovic's head rested silent against his shoulder. The earl looked down and sighed. He had not touched the boy for many years, and now found the closeness strangely emotional. He remembered the scampering of children long ago when life had seemed sweet and there was promise of happiness on each horizon. He shook his head, climbed the winding stairs, and entered again into daylight.

The litter he had hired was waiting for them. The Constable of the Tower had offered two good sized chambers within the Tower's upper apartments to house them, promising food would be brought while the doctor was called to attend. But the earl had declined. "My son is unconscious," he had said. "I will not have him regain his wits, still to look upon the walls of this foul place. I am taking him away."

"He should not be moved yet. It is too soon," murmured the Tower physician.

"I am his father and the decision is mine," said the earl curtly. "You have the papers, signed in the king's own hand. My son has been pardoned. Now I will take him to a place of peace and comfort, far away from here."

He took Ludovic to the great house in the Strand which he had been renting for the past three months and more. The earl had not left his son's side since permission had been given to take him from the place of torture. He had nursed him in the litter, cradling his body to lessen the bumps and grinds of the wheels on the cobbles and deep ruts of the roads. The earl had never before in his life travelled in a litter since leaving behind his infant swaddlings. At the age of three years he had ridden his own pony from Sumerford to Exeter. Now, incredulous at the discomfort, he sat enclosed by sweating hessian, sitting on old woollen cushions, the litter pulled by two tired and flatulent horses. And in the privacy of the shadows, he kissed his son's forehead and prayed silently for Ludovic's recovery.

The hired servants at the Strand house had prepared the bedchamber and it was there that the earl carried his youngest son. The wide windows and furnishings were too modern for the earl's taste, but the great bed was grand and spacious. The linen was aired, the drapery clean, the high tester swagged and hung in green, the coverlet tasselled in purple and quilted in rose, and the bolster well stuffed and perfumed with lilac blossom. The doctor and his assistant were already waiting at the bedside. The earl relinquished his burden, laid his son down and sat close to supervise.

They carefully removed Ludovic's shirt, hose and braies so that he lay naked across the feather quilt. His body was streaked in a broken maze of bruises. Like a beggar, half-starved and beaten, there were no longer signs of the knight and warrior, once trained in combat and gleaming in health under the sun. Where his bones protruded through the shrunken flesh; his ribs, pelvis, clavicles and spine, livid grazes scoured each point, running in stripes across the pale skin. His joints were hugely swollen and inflamed. Great purple bruises had formed around his knees, ankles and wrists, and the flesh there was lurid and blackened.

His body was grimed in old dirt, flea bites and the sour sweat of fear and abandonment. His hair clamped to his head, smelling of months unwashed. His face seemed hollow, the flesh drained into sallow exhaustion, and his eye sockets were deeply bruised. But his breathing was steady and his chest rose and fell with the gentle satisfaction of natural sleep.

"My lord," the doctor was examining Ludovic's legs, his fingers nervous over the massive inflammations and discolouration around the knees. "I must warn you, after racking most men will never walk again. But the young lord lives, and that is, of course, what matters most. However, muscles so far stretched will not usually retract, but will stay always loose and useless. And a dislocation of such complicated joints cannot ever be righted. You must be prepared, my lord, for your son will likely be crippled and confined to his bed for life."

The earl sat rigid on his straight backed chair and stared at the small man bending over the bed. "If," he said, "you speak to me again in terms of hopelessness and negativity, I shall dismiss you instantly. I do not intend to escort an ailing, infirm or disabled son back to his home and family. I shall nurse him here, while you will restore him to full health. Is this clear, sir?"

"Indeed it is, my lord." The doctor blushed slightly. "But I am no saint to work miracles upon the broken and diseased. I shall do my best, I assure you."

"Your best, sir," the earl informed him, "must be sufficient. If it is not, I will find a better man whose best will prove superior. I shall accept neither excuses nor mistakes. I am not a man to be crossed, and failure is not an option here. My son will walk again, and you will achieve this to his satisfaction and mine. You will be well paid, but only after complete success." He clasped his hands in his lap and gazed unblinking towards the bed. "I am waiting for you to begin, sir. The sooner you start your doctoring, the sooner the healing will be accomplished."

Ludovic opened his eyes to a paradise of peace. The sounds around him whispered of care and comfort; the busy crackle of flames from the hearth and its accompanying dance of muted light and colour, the swish of silken curtains, the chink of jug against cup and the pouring of liquid. Sounds long associated with comfort and normality, the pleasant traditions of an ordered and unthreatening life.

He moved his head, deep cushioned on fine linen over feathers and duckling down. The firelight was heady, ranging across a wide glowing hearth. Its warmth seemed magnificent. There was no rack, no green slime streaking bare stone walls, no hard bundled pallet, nor the stench of dirt and misery. There was no cause for panic, for terror or for hopelessness. A new life had been born around him.

He turned his head slowly in the other direction, careful to avoid the pain which still cocooned him. He smiled.

An elderly man was pouring wine, bent over the table, pitcher in hand. His back was to the bed. But Ludovic recognised him at once. He opened his mouth to call his father, but found his voice silent. Then the earl turned as he brought the cup to his mouth to drink. But he paused, cup raised

The old man's face, tired and strained, lifted suddenly into a delighted smile, infused with relief. "My dear boy," he said, striding over. "You are awake."

It occurred to Ludovic that he had not seen his father smile for a very long time. Perhaps years. Ludovic's own smile was smaller, though his relief even greater. But the muscles of his face would not respond and the continuous ache of consistent pain strangled pleasure. It was some hours later, after he had slept deep again and the day had passed on into evening, that he was able to speak, and smile, and believe the horror truly over.

"It is more than three months I have waited," the earl said, sitting stiff at his son's bedside. "A messenger was sent to Sumerford from the Lord Chancellor's office in mid-January, informing me of my sons' arrests on the grounds of high treason, and their immediate incarceration in the Tower. I left Somerset the following day and came directly to Westminster. I proceeded to petition the king for my sons' pardons but it was some time before he agreed to see me. Your arrest, I understand, took place on the 20th of December. We are now in late April, the 23rd to be exact, St. George's Day and high spring of the New Year." The earl sighed, his mouth tight. "His majesty has been

405

– let us say, persistently unmoved. Each day I presented myself at court, and each day he denied me. At first he claimed illness. Indeed, I hear he is often ailing. They say the strain of these constant threats to his throne have unnerved him and weakened his mind and health. Although fierce in denial, clearly he greatly fears this Warbeck's true identity, and the strength of his foreign support. The king is not an old man. I am older by several years. But it seems this Tudor monarch does not have the training nor the iron intellect of the Plantagenets. He prefers to work in the dark and unseen, shuffling his papers and scribing endless meticulous lists of his expenses, trusting no one, peering into matters more suited to an apprentice barrister, a grosser or a clerk. The reappearance of old King Edward's sons claiming their right of inheritance has ruined Tudor's nerve. They say he was previously confident in his arrogance, thinking the princes long dead. But now he appears shaken and bent. He fears his own shadow and accuses every man who blinks, of plotting against him. The monarchy of England is in wreckage. Does Tudor suffer from guilt? He clearly knows the truth, though cannot admit it. Denied open battle, he fights with the quill, and dips his nib in malice and propaganda. His eyes are haunted. He fears for his soul, yet cannot abandon avarice and determination, and will hold frantically to what he has so gleefully acquired. The tyrant I once thought him would surely be less destroyed by his own actions. But he is not so destroyed that he permits doubt, or becomes less angry and obdurate. He knows himself disliked by his people, and is determined not to mind. When he eventually received me, I saw his disillusion. But I also saw his fury."

Ludovic remained propped by pillows, leaning back heavily. "I trust," he said softly, "that you have checked whether we might be overheard? You speak terrible treason. Are we safe in this place? Are there spies amongst the servants?"

The earl smiled. "I am not a fool, my boy. I do not intend the arrest of the son to be echoed by that of the father."

Ludovic, his head now calm and the pain lessened, ignored what agony remained throbbing through the misery of his joints. "But in the end," he said, "clearly the king remembered his duty of mercy, for after all this time we are pardoned. You must have been relentless, my lord."

The earl paused before speaking again. "Indeed. I was relentless, my son. I am not known to accept failure, nor do I permit myself retirement before I achieve my aims. I have never yet started something which I have not also finished, as I believe you are aware, Ludovic. Over these past months I have daily battered at the king's doors and when he refused me, I sent endless messages and petitions. I presented him with gifts, with promises, with reminders of past loyalty, with legal argument, and even with veiled threats. I have employed six attorneys and two sergeants-at-law. I have spoken at such length with the Lord Chancellor, that I could count the whiskers on his foul chin."

Ludovic closed his eyes. The chamber rested in shadow, but the huge firelight stung his eyelids. Each sound louder than a rustle, each light brighter than a pale glow, attacked his senses, sending him black pain-clouded and his head reeling. "But you succeeded," he murmured. "Have I yet truly thanked you, sir, for saving my life? Long ago I surrendered hope. It seems still almost unbelievable that I am here, in comfort and assured of safety. Is Gerald here too?"

Once again the earl paused. "I believe Gerald is asleep," he said at last. "And I have spoken enough. You should also sleep."

Ludovic opened his eyes again. "I expected to sleep forever. Now I fear to dream."

The doctors had left for the evening. Ludovic had been sleeping as they left, and their prognostications had been confided to the earl in whispers. They had not yet been able to promise their patient a full recovery and were still unsure whether the young lord would ever walk again. His bones and muscles were much damaged. Until the swellings shrank, a full examination was impossible without causing great pain. But victims of the rack were rarely fortunate in their futures and most broken bodies stripped from the arms of the Duke of Exeter's daughter were likely to remain broken.

The earl had not informed his son of these doubts. "When you are quite recovered, my boy, we will return to Sumerford. But your body has been much abused. We will rest here for some time as is necessary. Weeks perhaps. You will soon learn to trust your dreams again."

"I'll sleep better once I've seen Gerald." Ludovic frowned, gazing across to his father. "Tell me the truth, Father. Is he well? Was he also racked?"

The earl bent his head. "He was," he said softly. "Several days before your own ordeal. He is, however," the earl looked up, staring directly into Ludovic's questioning gaze, "as well as can be expected."

"I'm greatly relieved." Ludovic's face relaxed. "Gerald would be considered a more proven traitor than myself, though they can't hold incontrovertible proof or no confession under torture would have been required." Ludovic sighed. "Gerald's body might have broken quicker, but not his resolve. He'd never have confessed whatever force was used against him." Ludovic sighed again, looking into his father's severe grey eyes. "I was ready to confess, you see, before you came and set me free."

"Then I came in time," said his lordship. "Had you confessed, Ludovic, the pardon would not have sufficed."

Ludovic nodded. "Indeed, I had confessed. In my mind the words were spoken. But no one heard." He smiled slightly. "I'm weaker than Gerald, you see. The confession mentioned inciting rebellion and secret meetings with men whose names I'd never heard before. The words have echoed many times in my mind since, remembering what I was willing to sign in order to escape the pain."

"And yet," said the earl very quietly, "you were involved, I believe, in some small treachery. And Gerald in more."

"What Gerald did or did not do," Ludovic said, "I will leave to him to explain. He is more passionate, more loyal, and an idealist, whereas I prefer pragmatism. I do not love lost causes and I've neither incited rebellion nor actively promoted Tudor's overthrow. I believe Prince Richard's claim to be utterly hopeless. But my opinions have been shared with no one else, sir, and only Gerald knew my sympathies."

"And the person who betrayed you to the king's spies."

Ludovic could still not easily move his shoulders, but he shook his head slightly. "I have no idea who that might be. But I was seen attending the execution of Gerald's squire. I saw him first in Newgate,

I paid for his keep in gaol, and was on the official's list of visitors. I believe that was the only suspicion they had against me."

"You have been exceptionally foolhardy, my son," the earl said. "And careless in more ways than this. But we will speak of sweeter things in the morning. Now you must sleep."

Ludovic looked up. "Already? There seems so much to talk of. All those bitter weeks in prison were wretched for many reasons, but most of all for the silence and the solitary isolation. To speak to no one for months, not to hear the sound of any voice, to have no human contact nor even the illusion of company, is a desperate sort of loneliness which I never thought to experience. Days had no beginning and nights no end. One's own thoughts ramble and become insane. Now your company is as sweet as any I could imagine. And I have so many questions. For instance, you've avoided telling me anything of the doctor's predictions." He stared at his father, challenging. "Before I sleep, tell me one thing. Will I walk again?"

"You are my son," said the earl. "You will walk, and ride, and fight again. You will return to Sumerford in full health. And I will have you know that the discomforts of travelling by horse drawn litter are so abysmal, that I recommend the saddle however weak you may still feel. You will regain your pride and your strength, Ludovic, but you will never again become involved in politics or threaten the power of kings. Do you hear me?"

Ludovic smiled. "I do, my lord. And will obey."

"I am glad to hear it, my boy." The earl nodded, his own smile controlled. "My manner may have weakened during these past days – softened you might say – in face of peril, of losing my sons, and of contemplating their pain. No doubt you have noticed. But the House of Sumerford retains its pride, and I still demand obedience."

The first thorough examination of Ludovic's legs was performed the next afternoon after dinner. He ate little, finding his stomach considerably shrunken. Following months of little food, he desired great feasts but found he could not swallow them. The Burgundy wine made him light headed and sleepy but helped to lessen the incessant pain. As the doctors manipulated his knee sockets, Ludovic gasped, drawing in his breath and clamping his jaw on a moan.

"If," said the earl from the bedside, "you believe I desire my son to act the fool and pretend heroism, then you are greatly mistaken, Ludovic. You may howl like a wolf, my boy. I shall not be disturbed."

"I'm obliged, my lord," Ludovic said, teeth clamped. "But I shall endeavour not to impersonate the animals of the forest. I imagine it would be quite exhausting."

It was several hours before the doctors decided on a verdict. They demanded Ludovic urinate in a cup, and then examined the liquid with considerable interest, dabbling with a fingertip to taste the acidity. They consulted his horoscope, and although his Sun at birth was in Scorpio, which was not at all auspicious, it caused no particular friction with the Taurean bull in the zodiac of the present month. There was therefore a harmonious balance, while Jupiter in Aquarius would pour healing waters on the suffering bones.

"I believe, my lord," said the medik, addressing the earl while Ludovic gazed from one to the other, "that no permanent damage has been sustained. The muscles are much weakened but no joint is dislocated or fractured. It would seem most possible that your son will walk again in time, but only if he is exceedingly patient and makes no attempt to rise from his bed for at least two months. No strain must be put upon the legs, nor weights carried by the arms. He must not wash himself nor dress himself, and I will prescribe a special diet of milks, berries and red meat, with willow bark and poppy in a tincture of garlic and marigold. He appears to be of a sanguine nature and therefore needs to reconstitute the blood, so I do not intend to bleed him at this time. I may decide to do so over the next few days if the humours prove further undermined. I am also tempted to administer an enema in order to purge the past months of poisonous air and damp vapours, but will wait until he is a little stronger. Above all he must not take up exercise or anything strenuous. He must not copulate for at least three months, and must not strain his bowls or his lungs."

Ludovic smiled faintly. "Some of your restrictions, sir, will be comparatively easy to follow. But is the matter so grave that I need stay in bed for quite so long?"

"Indeed, my lord. Or risk shattering both legs, which are already much weakened," insisted the doctor. "I will continue to evaluate the situation each day. Should your recovery be quicker than expected, I shall be able to adjust my prescriptions."

The following day Ludovic was surprised to wake early, and with little immediate pain until he moved, and winced. His father was curled asleep beside him, snoring gently and twitching in his dreams. The heavy shutters enclosed the chamber in darkness and last night's fire was reduced to a scattering of sooty warm ashes. Ludovic could see very little, smelling only smoke and the faint floating sweetness of lilac. He heard a rustle in the roof above, and his father's rhythmic and guttural breathing. He lay silent, staring into the shadows.

At first he expected to hear the small voice of his other companion, the only friend who had spoken to him during his long months in the Tower. But no ghostly whispers reminded him of misery and death. It was his father's voice that came abruptly, though he had not been aware that the sounds of his guttural breathing had ceased.

"Awake, my son? How do you feel?"

"I need to see Gerald," Ludovic said carefully into the darkness. "It occurs to me that you have been persistently at my side, sir. I supposed Gerry to be here in another chamber, but why do you not visit him? You even sleep here beside me, which you have never done before in my life." Ludovic paused, gathering his strength for the truth. "What is wrong with Gerald, Papa?"

The earl remained quiet for some moments. He did not move, but lay quite still. Then he said, very softly, "Your brother confessed, Ludovic. On the rack, he consented to sign his confession, and then did so. His trial followed immediately. Gerald remains in the Tower. His execution will take place in five days' time."

CHAPTER FORTY-FIVE

"If fer his lordship," Ellis insisted, "I'll do it. Anyfing, wotever and wherever. If this is his lordship's lady friend and he wants her, then I'll get her for him, if'n she bloody likes it or no."

"Idiot brat," seethed the captain. "It ain't no abduction I'm planning. The lady is willing, at least, I reckon she must be. Knowing his lordship, wouldn't any plain Miss be ready and right proper willing?"

Ellis shook his head. He distrusted women and their capricious decisions. "Far as I see it, she's done run away. But I shall get her back fer 'is lordship."

Kenelm leaned his elbows on the table and glared over his ale cup. "And the thing is – it's Clovis gone and disappeared too. His mother's right bloody worried, and I'm getting the blame."

Ellis had already finished his ale and was hoping for another. The innkeeper was busy with other customers but Ellis kept him in sight. "That little bugger Clovis," he said, "were always well past the yardarm. You reckon he's the cock's spurs just 'cos he's yer nevvy. Shouldn't never have taken him on, you should'n. I should've bin the Rouncie's cabin boy from the start."

"Less o' yer jealousy," objected Kenelm. "This is a serious situation, and we've got to sort it quick. There's his lordship real sick after just bin pardoned, and wants his lady friend to hear the good news right away. But with her disappeared and Clovis gone too, things look mighty odd."

"Mayhap they've run off together," suggested Ellis. "Never trusted Clovis I didn't. An' don't trust no females neither."

Captain Kenelm regarded his cabin boy with measured dislike. "Is you a moon looned pillicoot, boy? My nevvy has fair on eleven years to his name. The lady in question, not that I've met her, but I reckon she's nigh on eighteen or more from wot Lord Ludo says. Have you taken leave o' yer senses, lad? Wot lady is gonna choose Clovis over his lordship?"

"Fair enuff. Pr'aps she told him no. So Clovis done her in," concluded Ellis.

"I am going to see the countess," Kenelm said with dignity and a scathing disregard for Ellis's suspicions. "I've proper authority and we ain't talking smuggling here. I've news o' his lordship and have a right to see her ladyship. You wait here. I'll be back some time. At least, I hopes I will."

"His lordship and t'other lordship done saved my life," said Ellis, standing at once. "I'm coming wiv you."

Kenelm sighed. "One look at you, they'll have the steward chuck us both out. Do like I says for once in yer miserable life, and stay here. If I don't come back tonight, you go for the sheriff." He smiled faintly at Ellis's look of thunderstruck incredulity. "Yes, yes, I know," he continued. "'Tis against the natural morals of an honest seafaring man, but we're talking real law-abiding folk here, with titles and castles and everything. If I can't do naught, then it's the sheriff we needs." He stood, and then relented, throwing two silver pennies onto the table. "Go on. Fill yersell with beer while yer wait for me like a good boy."

<hr />

The castle page, having answered the door to a stocky and ill-dressed ruffian, and having been unable to persuade the ruffian to remove his foot and take himself off, informed Hamnet. At first inclined to

413

dismiss both the man and his story, the steward finally condescended to question the interloper in person. He stood on the doorstep and surveyed the creature before him. "Beggars and vagrants," he said, in his loftiest voice and with calculated insult, "must go around to the kitchens for begging, where their lordship's remainders from the high table will be allotted to the needy."

Kenelm adjusted his stance, setting his shoulders into a belligerent width, and glared. "I'll have you know," he said loudly, "I'm a respectable ship's captain, and the Lord Ludovic Sumerford's legal partner. I has papers to prove it wot's more, though not on me o'course. Him an' me is owners of a grand little cob together, and a trading business wot I runs for him."

"If you have recent news of Lord Ludovic," Hamnet said at once, "then you must speak to her ladyship, the young lord's mother. I shall enquire whether she will consent to see you. What name shall I give?"

"Captain Kenelm," he announced with pride. "But I've a couple o' questions meself to ast first. Like the whereabouts o' the Missus Alysson Welles wot was staying here. And the young page Clovis, wot his lordship sent to look after her."

Hamnet shook his head. "Such matters are none of your business, my man," he said with careful hauteur. "Nor do I concern myself with the female staff, nor the hire of the castle pages. If this is all you have to say, you must leave. I shall not allow you to pester her ladyship with such demeaning business."

"You let me worry 'bout that," said Kenelm with an unwise wink. "Meantime, I've had word from the master, Lord Ludovic that is, and want to see the countess."

The captain was eventually shown into the great hall where the Countess of Sumerford sat beside the cold and empty hearth, discussing her tapestry stitches with her female companion. She did not ask Kenelm to sit. "Speak up, man," said her ladyship, peering through the gloom. "What news?"

Kenelm bowed low. "If I might introduce myself, yer ladyship." He bowed a second time, hands behind his back. "Captain Kenelm at yer service, and have news o' my business partner Lord Ludovic, straight from Westminster. His pardon were signed by the king hisself on St. George's Day, an' is now a free man in his earlship's care."

The countess sniffed. "I am already perfectly well aware of this," she said, "since my husband's most recent letter was delivered some days back. Is that all you have to say? Have you any information regarding my other son Gerald?"

"Not got nuffin on him, yer ladyship, him not being much known to me personal, and not being mentioned in my message. But I've more on Lord Ludovic to say." Kenelm searched in his memory for other snippets of information. "Fact is, his lordship's done written to me too, yer ladyship, and did ast me special to come here. Says as how his legs is a flea's bite better and can get around a step or two wiv a stick when he has to, like for the privy and suchlike."

"Very well." The countess deigned to smile slightly. "That's good news. If you report to Hamnet, I shall instruct him to pay you a groat for your troubles."

Kenelm frowned. "I's a wealthy man, yer ladyship, and ain't come for no payment. It were a favour to his lordship, wot ast me to see you." He bowed again, conscious of scrutiny. "And wanted especial for me to tell his news to a Mistress Alysson, wot lives here as a maid." He took a deep breath. "Indeed, I've a neat little paper, sealed and scribed, to give into her hand from his lordship. But this Mistress Alysson Welles has gone, proper disappeared, my lady, and 'tis a worry, for his lordship was real urgent on the matter. See my girl Alysson Welles, he says, give her my letter an' tell her everyfing in case she don't know it all yet. An' I got the innkeeper to check on the words too, just in case I got it wrong, seeing as I ain't no expert on the reading of stuff."

"I have no idea what you are gabbling about, my man," said her ladyship. She was rigidly straight backed, and appeared to be both uncomfortable and affronted. "I refuse to listen to prattle about the servants. I thank you for your information regarding my son, but you will now leave at once."

"An' my nevvy Clovis," insisted Kenelm, not moving. "Just a little lad, he is. Lord Ludo sent him here to look after the lady. Mistress Alysson that is. And they's both up and gone."

"I imagine you therefore have your own solution," said her

ladyship, white lipped. She clapped her hands. "Hamnet, see this creature off the premises immediately. Give him a groat and throw him out."

━━◆━━

A slow starting spring moved into a mild May, with blossoms in the breezes and the young fledglings flying their nests. Somerset lay placid under the fitful sunshine, its pastures green between the wild flowers, the hedgerows rustling with burrowing things, and the clouds parting to clear starlit nights.

The sisters Ilara and Dulce were not accustomed to male visitors, but their fears regarding Alysson overcame any other considerations. Kenelm and Ellis were invited in immediately, were asked to sit, served light beer and offered a dish of luxuriously expensive raisins. "It is utterly perplexing," Dulce said, leaning forwards earnestly to face her unexpected visitors.

"And utterly terrifying," Ilara said. "Our dearest Alysson is such an innocent and inexperienced young girl, most gently brought up and quite unused to the ways of the world."

Kenelm regarded the two nervous women, and decided that the ways of the world would mean something quite different to them than they did to him. "It's the Lord Ludovic has ast me to find her," he said with a reassuring smile. "That is, not that he knows she's even bin and gone. But I feel it my responsibility, if you understand me ma'am, since his lordship is so mighty interested in her wellbeing."

"Indeed, the concern appears to be mutual," Ilara admitted. "Dear Alysson was preparing to travel to London nigh on two weeks back, and had already paid for cartage with a local carrier. Young Clovis was to travel with her as escort, masquerading as her brother. It was all set. Alysson was first to arrange her departure from the castle, then come here for the final night to collect the packages and money she would need while staying in the great city."

"But she did not come," sniffed Dulce. "We waited and waited, and the next morning we set off to the castle to enquire. We were told she had left the previous afternoon and not been seen since. We

416

immediately asked for Clovis, since we knew Alysson's plans regarding him. Yet we were informed Clovis had accompanied Alysson when she left, and neither was any longer employed at the castle."

"It was most upsetting," said Ilara. "And we have hardly known what to do since. The carter left without her and we've been to the village many times, walking through the woods searching for them both. Finally we decided to ask the sheriff to assist us. He has promised to do so, but he's a busy man, and we fear he doesn't take us as seriously as we would like."

Dulce sniffed. "Sheriff Simples made some unnecessary remarks about the inconstancy of young women," she said. "Of course, he doesn't wish to cause affront at the castle, and fears to offend the countess. He inferred that Alysson had run away with Clovis."

"Most foolish," murmured Kenelm, sipping his beer. "Only a right silly bugger would think such a thing." Ellis wriggled silently and wiped his nose with the back of his hand.

Ilara nodded. "But what can you do, Captain, that the sheriff cannot? We have no idea where to start."

It was a sunny afternoon as the captain, pink and proud with a sweet faced lady at his side, strolled into the village square. It was not market day and the green was noisy with children. A gaggle of housewives were discussing the butcher's daughter who had recently created a scandal by smiling at the young corvisor. The knife sharpener was wheeling his whetting stone and shouting for business, and the butcher was running out with his knives. A small goose boy was crying in the shadows of the village oak tree because he had lost his clogs in the pond while chasing his geese, and stubbed his toes on the fording slabs. He would have preferred to be playing with the other children kicking a pig's bladder across the scrubby grass, but knew his father would beat him if he did. The geese gathered around him, clacking in apologetic sympathy.

"It's anyone wot works up at the castle we wants," Kenelm informed Ilara. "Someone wiv a bit o' inside knowledge as it were."

"Indeed. Dulce and your young boy will go straight to the tanners out by the forest ditch, and then to the cook's daughter, Beatrice

Shore. She was quite friendly with Alysson once. We should aim for Mistress Barnes." Ilara nodded, pointing along the pathway. "She's the brewster at the castle and a dear soul, but she still lives in the village with her mother and is often home on a Wednesday afternoon to keep her company, for that's when the old woman has her weekly purge. Then there's Mistress Tenby who is a most important personage, being in charge of all the female staff up at the Hall. She'd never deign to confide castle secrets to us I'm afraid, but it's her sister lives in the village. She often picks up a good bit of gossip and is only too happy to pass it on. There's also George Wapping, the gong farmer. Not a man I would normally consider associating with of course, but I hear he's been working at the castle lately for they've had trouble with the cess pit overflowing and the latrines blocked."

"Right then," said Kenelm. "I shall take my lead from you, Missus, seeing as how your head's well set on them shoulders. And I'm mighty obliged for your help and condescension."

Ilara's smile glowed. She was deeply concerned for Alysson, but had never walked closely beside a personable gentleman before, nor received gratitude and compliments from one. She was fully aware that the villagers were staring at them, either openly or surreptitiously. She patted her hood, tucked in a wisp of curl, hid her smile and breathed deep.

But Mistress Barnes was not at home after all. Her ancient mother mumbled toothlessly about wort and mashing malt and seemed to have no interest in life at the Sumerford castle beyond the brewing and the ale, complaining that it was not done as thoroughly as when she was a girl in the same profession, and that now the sieving was bare boulted and the barme too frugal.

From there Kenelm escorted Ilara towards the prim stone house where Mistress Tenby's sister lived. Only the small maid was at home. "My mistress is away, Mistress Ilara," the girl said, wiping her hands on her apron. "She went off to stay with her brother in the north. Meant to go for Easter, she did, but what with spring coming late and the roads still being iced, the trip was delayed three weeks. She's not yet back."

"That leaves the gong farmer," sighed Kenelm. "An' I can't proper see as how a man wot clears the muck from the pits is gonna know about a lady's maid."

"He's a man that likes to know everyone else's business," said Ilara. "So may be quite useful, or I would never even consider speaking to him. We needn't stay long if he has nothing to tell us."

George Wapping's small thatched croft was pretty with dogwood and crab-apples. A red haired, large muscled and amiable man, he was at home and delighted to receive unexpected guests. He offered a cold fusion of herbs and mace spiced with ginger, and invited the captain and Mistress Ilara to sit at the table, hurrying to bring the best stools and wiping them down first with his sleeve.

It was true, he said, that the cess pit at the castle was somehow blocked and would need emptying. He had been up to inspect it more than a week back and had begun excavation almost immediately. However during the course of digging he had unfortunately damaged his wrist and the doctor had expressly forbidden him to work again for a sennight. Her ladyship was not best pleased, but had accepted the inevitable since bringing in another experienced man from the next village of Browny, would take even longer. The steward had kindly and secretly passed him a few pennies to tide him over while unable to work, and he was now sitting it out, counting his rosary beads each morning to plead for a quick recovery before his business was ruined.

"I don't suppose, Master Wapping," Ilara said, leaning forwards across the table, "you ever remember meeting a young maid at the castle, by name of Alysson Welles? She used to live with myself and my sister, and sometimes we came into the village together so you might have noticed her." George squinted, trying to remember. "She is remarkably pretty and quite young," Ilara continued. "Her hair is very black, though of course you would be unlikely to see that beneath her cap, but her eyes are quite unusual, being almost golden with green depths, like the forest in summer. Everyone remarks on her eyes."

"'Tis the young Lord Ludovic has them eyes too," nodded Master Wapping. "I've noted his eyes whenever I've met his lordship, though not being often of course. Is it his young maid you're speaking of then? For they say the two are a match with eyes like that, though he is a great noble gentleman and pale haired, and her just a little servant lass with hair black as charcoal. But the innkeeper reckons his lordship had the lass live in the castle like a proper lady after she were hurt last summer, with her own bedchamber all to herself, and seen private by the castle medik and all."

Ilara nodded eagerly. "Yes, certainly that is my dear Alysson. Now, this is most important, if you will consider carefully. Have you seen or heard of her lately, Master Wapping, within the past two weeks? She has quite disappeared you see, and we are dreadfully perturbed."

Captain Kenelm sipped his mace and ginger. "Seems this innkeeper o' yours knows all the prattle o' the village. Maybe we'd best go see him instead."

"Affleston's a right knowledgeable man," Wapping agreed. "You go talk to him whenever you wants, for he serves a good drop of ale into the bargain. But as it happens, I knows more'n a bit myself." He settled himself more comfortably, elbows to the table. "For instance, I knows the Lord Ludovic's bin pardoned by the king hisself, and will soon be home. He'll be looking for his lady-love, I reckon."

Kenelm sniffed. "Knows that myself, man. T'was me as got a personal letter from his lordship. Proper wax sealed wiv the Sumerford crest, and brought direct by a carrier all the way from Westminster." He patted his doublet. "And here I've another letter from him special, if I ever sees her to pass it over."

"Well now," said Master Wapping. "In my profession, I don't get to see the ladies much, but the young lads up at the castle, I chats to them from time to time. Them pages has more time to themselves, and skives off sometimes, pretending they've messages to bring outside so as not to get caught and beaten by the steward. One lad there was, name of Clovis."

Ilara and Kenelm sat up very straight. "Go on," Kenelm said. "Clovis is my nevvy, and was supposed to look after Mistress Alysson for his lordship. He's gone missing too, nor hair nor heel seen for two weeks."

"The lad told me 'bout Lord Ludovic and his lady-friend a few times, as it happens," nodded George. "I liked to let him ramble on. More savvy than some of them other pages, he were."

"So where is he now?" demanded Kenelm. "Do you know?"

"Ah," said Wapping, "I don't rightly know, not to be sure. But I can tell you this. My brother Vymer, he's always up at the castle, he is. A hard worker and a useful man, and they relies on him. 'Specially the Lord Humphrey, him being a bit simple and needing a strong shoulder at times, and someone to help when he gets all muddled up and bothered. Vymer cares for the Lord Humphrey special like, and they's been close for years. Now my brother, not that he tells me much as a rule, but he mentioned the other day as how I won't be seeing the little lad Clovis to chat to no more. Can be a bit difficult, my brother, and likes to tease. Knew I was fond of the lad. Was maybe a mite jealous, seeing as I don't get on with his own boy, Clovis being brighter and a sight better company that is. Vymer told me how he'd finished the little lad off for good. Not that I believed him at the time, but it's true young Clovis ain't been around ever since. He's not been seen by no one, not me nor others neither, for I've asked."

"Sweet Mother Mary," gasped Ilara.

Kenelm lurched up from his stool, leaning across the table and grabbing at the neck of Wapping's shirt. "Wot is you talking about? You explain and quick about it. Wot's happened to my little nephew?"

George detached himself. He was considerably larger than Kenelm. He shook his head. "No point getting riled up with me," he objected. "I didn't do nothing, and there's no saying it's true anyways. Besides, my brother Vymer, well there's no telling him what to do, nor holding him to task for it afterwards."

"Spit it out," seethed Kenelm. "Wot happened to Clovis?"

"Drowned," sighed Wapping. "Vymer reckoned he drowned the little lad. In the moat."

CHAPTER FORTY-SIX

P ermission had been given. For a few minutes before the prisoner was escorted from his cell to the execution block set on the sward by the Tower chapel, his father and brother would be allowed words with him, immediately after he had made his final confession and received the sacrament of penance.

Ludovic rode the litter from the Strand to the Tower. His father did not sit beside him, but rode his own courser, following across the city behind the two carter's horses. Ludovic lay within the bumping, rolling cart, his eyes closed. It was the first time he had left his sick bed since departing the Tower himself a week previously, and he felt nauseous. Unused to the sweaty sway of the leather canopy and the lurch of the wheels on the broken flagstones, he concentrated, as he had once before, only on his breathing. The focus was controlled, and it worked. He did not allow himself to think of Gerald yet. He could not think of the unthinkable.

He had been carried into the hired litter by the Strand house steward, but he left it on his own feet. Much supported by his father on his right side, and leaning on a thick wooden stick at his left, Ludovic managed the three steps to the doorway leading into his brother's tiny chamber in the Beauchamp Tower. The door was unlocked and opened for them. He stumbled in and a stool was set for him, the guards returning outside. Gerald was sitting slumped, head bowed, on the low bed. The priest was speaking softly to him.

Immediately Ludovic felt the old familiar menace of chill, the seeping damp of utter drear and the bitter threat of hopelessness. He and his father waited in awful silence as the priest concluded his prayer and left, the door pulled shut behind him, the lock grating to the twist of the great iron key.

Gerald sighed and looked up. He was shackled as Ludovic had been, and the small chamber was similar, furnished with the brazier and blankets that Ludovic had paid for months back. One candle glimmered, its light sinking in the gloom. There was no window but ice slipped sibilant beneath the door, whistling low across the old stones.

"I have no regrets," Gerald said abruptly. The words were swallowed by damp stone, and sounded flat and dull and dead of meaning.

"I have many, my boy," said the earl. "But they are all of my own failures, and do not degrade you, or your courage and loyalty. I did not come here to berate or criticise you, only to say goodbye, and give you my blessing for what it may be worth."

Gerald looked away. "I have only one regret. That I failed to secure Prince Richard's rights, or ensure his future. This is a miserable world of injustice and brutality, and I'm glad enough to leave it."

"You attempted to bring justice, of a sort, into this sad country," the earl nodded. "It was an admirable goal, and I do not call it misguided. Your family may not be alone in remembering your virtues and strengths, my son."

Gerald smiled shyly and looked to Ludovic. "Strengths? Not many, I think. I weakened on the rack, and confessed before they broke my bones. You were stronger, little brother."

Ludovic shook his head. "Not at all, Gerry dear. I was ready to admit anything they asked of me. A few minutes more, and I would have confessed. Luck favoured me. Simply that."

"You deserve your luck, my dear, for you are innocent and I am guilty," Gerald said. "The confession they prepared, which I signed, was close enough to the truth. And I've seen Berkhamstead, and asked him to carry on the fight. That's inciting rebellion, isn't it?" He frowned. "William has seen the prince several times, and is furious at his treatment. The poor wretch is shackled too, and quite alone, though his apartment is grand and comfortable, unlike ours. Too many prisoners, the cells all full, and our titles no longer grand enough. But at first Will says the prince went almost mad with loneliness, but it seems he's recently discovered a friend."

Ludovic thought of the whispering ghost in the shadows, and raised an eyebrow. "A friend? In this place?"

"Indeed." Gerald sighed. "It seems poor Edward, the young Earl of Warwick, is housed in the apartment directly above him. Warwick's been imprisoned ever since Tudor forced his way to the throne. They're both kept in the Lanthorn Tower you know, and have discovered a way of speaking through the grills and passing messages up and down through the bars of the windows. Even the prince's guards are sympathetic it seems, and help him keep his sanity that way. No plotting or planning to escape, just two desperate young men eager for friendship. They can't see each other and they can't touch, but they can whisper and write."

"What a vile and miserable end," Ludovic murmured. "Is that all life can offer the innocent?"

The earl interrupted softly, a hand to Ludovic's shoulder, smiling at Gerald. "I honour your cares and intentions, my child, but we have very little time. You must leave this prince of yours to his own devices now, and think of yourself."

"I'm afraid I've been thinking of little else for some days," Gerald said, looking down again at his feet, shifting the rusted iron rings around his ankles and adjusting the weight. "I've made my last testament, and the priest has it in hand, though I've little to leave." He looked back up at his father, his expression suddenly defiant. "What little I have goes to young Edward, Jennine's child, my lord. He won't need it, since eventually he'll inherit everything, the title and Sumerford itself. But I want him to have something of mine, and remember me through that, though he'll never know me in person."

The sudden pause lengthened, each man looking to the other.

Eventually Ludovic said, "Your son?"

Gerald nodded. "Jenny was frightened that poor Humphrey would seed a child like himself. She asked me – just before the wedding – but there was nothing salacious I promise. I'm not ashamed of what I did. Indeed, I'm proud my son will become the earl, and perhaps be a greater man than I have been. And don't blame Jenny, or say anything to any of the others, I beg you. Naturally Humphrey doesn't know. I respected Jenny for insuring a fitting heir, but still insisting the title remain truly within the family."

Ludovic frowned. "It had to be. Without red hair and a family likeness, each one of us would have suspected the child's parentage."

"I think she wanted you at first, Lu." Gerald smiled somewhat ruefully. "I saw the way she looked at you those first days. Well, you're the handsome one among us after all. But you'd have none of her. You've proved yourself stronger than me in many things, little brother."

The earl interrupted again. "My dear child, I promise you I will keep your secrets and respect your choices but I fear the guards will come at any moment. Now, I have something of my own to say." Gerald looked up as the earl leaned over, clasping his hand. "I do not find it easy to speak of love, my son. I have never known the words to express feeling or intimacy. But before I go, I must tell you that I love you. I have always loved you. And I shall continue to do so, even though you will not be present in my life. You have often been absent, and it has never affected the love I feel for you. It will not do so now. You will remain alive in the hearts of your family, of your prince, and of all those who have known you. I have permission to take your body back to Sumerford for consecrated burial, and prayers for your soul will be said daily in the castle chapel. You will never be forgotten, my son, and I shall continue to keep holy remembrance in your name each year until I myself die."

They walked slowly across the inner ward to the Chapel of St. Peter Ad Vincula where the block was set, surrounded by straw. It had been well scrubbed and seemed strangely diminished, insignificant beneath the pale spring sunshine. Ludovic was in considerable pain and needed constant support. He leaned heavily on the earl's shoulder and used his stick to help swing his legs, taking no weight on the joints. After managing to control his breathing, he said quietly, "Did you know of the child, sir?"

The earl sighed. "I did not. I had no reason to question Humphrey's virility. His brain is weak but his body is strong."

"Perhaps," said Ludovic, "it is no bad thing. It is still in the family and the child comes from a better father than I thought."

"It is of no matter," said the earl quietly. "For the child is already dead."

Ludovic bowed his head.

Gerald was escorted by two guards. He could walk very little, for he remained shackled and his knees and ankles were still much affected by the racking, but the guards had only a passing interest in his last remaining agonies. His chains rang as he stumbled. The priest walked ahead, reading aloud from his Bible. Gerald was led to the block.

The watching crowd was small. Some of the castle staff had stopped to witness the death of a traitor, and Ludovic recognised William of Berkhamstead, standing alone and forlorn at the back. It was not a time to wish for company or the greetings of friends. Ludovic did not acknowledge the young earl, nor was acknowledged in return. The sun was warming and gentle, a glitter catching along the white stones of the Keep, sparkling on the spread of the Thames and lighting Gerald's red hair, uncombed, long and unkempt across his shoulders. He wore only shirt and hose, his father had given him coin to pay the executioner, and his boots and doublet would go to his guards. He struggled to stay upright, but on reaching the block and forced to kneel, he moaned. His knees were already much destroyed.

Gerald's final speech was brief, and his voice was too weak for the sound to carry on the breeze. He spoke only of pride in his loyalties, of his belief in the young Prince Richard, true heir to the throne, and of Tudor's shame in dubbing a royal prince with a false name and accusations of trickery. He asked God to have mercy on his soul, and he laid his head down on the block.

The axe man had been well paid and it took only one clean stroke to sever Gerald's head from his body. Ludovic turned away, staring at the small passing clouds as they shrouded the sun. He did not watch, but smelled his brother's blood. He made no attempt to lessen the sting in his eyes or the tears wet on his cheeks. He swayed a little, clinging to the wooden stick that supported him. He did not pray, but heard his father's voice beside him, mumbling the Latin that absolved the soul of his son. Ludovic whispered his own private words of goodbye, and wished his favourite brother Godspeed and a safe journey to the great wide paradise beyond.

There was an interruption. The crowd had enlarged, and someone at the back was pushing to the front. There was sudden anger and a flurry of cursing.

The earl looked up, white lipped at the disrespect for Gerald's passing, but a massing of guards hid the cause. Ludovic raised his eyes and instead looked, unwillingly but impelled, at his brother's remains. The straw surrounding the block was soaked and dark. The head was already taken, carried off by its bright hair, as red as the slashed stump of its neck. The trunk remained, for Gerald had not been sentenced to quartering. When the king had answered the earl's petition with a final pardon for the younger son, he had lessened the older son's death warrant to simple execution, head to be spiked above the gate to the Bridge as all traitors were displayed as a warning to others, but the body to be given to the family for Christian burial. The earl's own servants scurried quickly forwards with sheets, claiming the remains.

There was still shouting behind them, louder now, and a voice strangely familiar, interspersed with the clash of steel. More guards rushed forwards, running from the bastion of the Tower. Someone, just moments after Gerald's death, was to be arrested there before the block.

A darker cloud had now smothered the sun and a pale drizzle misted the air in a sheen of inescapable tears. The earl took Ludovic's arm. "It is time to go, my boy," he said softly. "There is nothing more to be done here."

The rain mingled with Ludovic's misery, eyes blurred, smarting and salty, the bleak tears washed from his face. He leaned back against his father. For a moment he thought he saw William of Berkhamstead running towards the guards, sword unsheathed, but he saw no more. The milling of the troopers closed tight, the cause of the confusion still unseen as the remainder of the crowd dispersed and the noise increased. Helped, hobbling but unconscious of all pain except Gerald's death, Ludovic was taken to the covered litter and carried quickly back to the house in the Strand.

CHAPTER FORTY-SEVEN

"He's dead," said the Lady Jennine. "Executed along with his brother, as you've known for days. Face it. You've driven us all mad with your silly sobbing, so now accept the inevitable, stupid girl, and the solution I offer. With him gone, it is now, after all, the only solution."

Alysson clutched at the knot she had made of her livery apron, soiled now and creased across her lap. She lowered her eyes and shook her head. "It's no solution at all. Merely degradation. You don't even offer me any time for mourning."

Jennine flounced to the settle and sat with a thud, stretching her legs and smoothing out her silks. "Stupid girl. Why mourn anyway? You could have had him, but you turned him down. Now you'll take a different man and be thankful for him."

"I've regretted my past decisions for the last six months," Alysson whispered. "Even back when I thought he would return, and when I still thought you were my friend, I was a fool then. But I'm not a fool now. You can do what you want to me, but I won't do it willingly."

Jennine tittered. "Yes, I'll do exactly what I want with you, and now there's no one to interfere. I'd prefer your co-operation, and I've even offered inducements. But alright, now I'll simply demand obedience. Remember your noble lover's head is spiked on the gate to the Bridge, with those pretty green eyes pecked out by ravens and his tongue all swollen and black. And those lips that kissed you so passionately? They'll be full of fly's eggs and maggots crawling under the skin. The stink of it already makes the travellers gag as they ride beneath. Will the dear earl ride home that way, do you think, and pass through the arch where his two sons' heads are mouldering in the sun?"

"You can't make me feel any worse than I do already." Alysson looked away. "I've thought of all those horrors and I can imagine the worst without your spiteful words. I've cried till I was sick, night after night. But being gone doesn't make Ludovic any less beautiful in my mind, or any less lovable, any more than you can change what I really am even though you try and make me behave like a whore. You're still a whore, Jenny, even though now you're married and a titled lady, and as rich as I'm poor. The person inside doesn't change just because of things that happen. Even a traitor's death."

The three chambers were small, but great efforts had once been made to ensure them comfortable. Limited by the restrictions on space high under the turrets of the eastern tower, each room led to the other, coming back upon themselves in a tight little circle. The dark and narrow steps outside led down to the Lady Jennine's quarters, and up to the windswept stone above, but the doors to freedom were always kept locked. The windows, originally arrow slits, had been glazed some years back, and wooden shutters kept out the baleful moon at night. The damp ooze of the curved walls was hidden behind tapestry arras. The bed was wide, warm and feather filled, the curtains heavy lined and the coverlet thick velvet. There were chairs and a cushioned settle, a table, a wash stand, two large chests and a desk. The cold flagged floor was spread with Turkey rugs, though worn to the weft, and there was a small stone hearth, empty now, but still holding to its ashes.

It was not Jennine, but a strange man who eventually explained many things to Alysson about where she was, and why.

Dragged yelling and scratching from the lady's chambers, with Jennine's personal page scampering ahead to unlock and then lock the doors, the great red beast had bundled Alysson beneath one arm, and with little regard to her kicks and screams, had trundled her up to the small secret apartment at the very top of the tower. Then he had flung her to the bed, punched her heftily in the stomach when she rebounded back to her feet and tried to attack, and then sat hugging his knees on the ground while waiting for her to recover her breath.

She had recognised this man as Humphrey. Winded, shocked and terrified, she had stood gasping, heaving and staring down at him, understanding nothing but bewildered panic. At Jennine's call, it seemed the Lord Humphrey, her own noble husband, had come puffing into the chamber and abducted Alysson by force, dragging her to the prison high in the eastern tower.

It was only after some minutes that Alysson realised it was not Humphrey at all. It was a man of similar size and identical colouring and the likeness was too remarkable for coincidence. He was perhaps somewhat taller than Humphrey, his shoulders wider and his face more rugged. The heavy jaw was hidden beneath beard and moustache as Humphrey's was, but above it the nose was more pugnacious and the forehead higher. It was a larger face than Humphrey's, the eyes less lost and more knowing with a flicker of cleverness, the mouth less loose and wet but firm lipped and determined. The mass of body was all bulk beneath the coarse doublet and shirt, but did not swell with belly fat around the middle, nor puff with soft flesh across the palms and fingers as Humphrey's did. This was a man of muscle and intention. But the colour of him was the same, a rich red as threatening as blood, the hair silky over his head and curling into a fuzz of fire around his face. As she controlled her panic, Alysson knew immediately it had been this man who had attacked her several times in the past, and not Humphrey at all.

Afterwards she was ashamed, remembering how frightened she had been. But for some time it seemed as though the world, already harsh and judgemental enough, was now gone quite mad. Then finally, because it was the only way to understand anything at all, Alysson sat quietly on a small chair and listened.

"Vymer," said the man, watching her as intently as she watched him. "Master Vymer to you, wench. And I reckon you know me well enough, if you use your head and think, though not being a thing females can do as a rule. But I'm your master now, so be careful what you says."

"You work for Jennine? Or for the earl? Or for Humphrey?" she had demanded, struggling to be calm and unclench her fists.

"Their lordships to you, trollop," the man growled. "You'll use respect in my hearing, or answer for it."

Alysson shivered. "So which of their lordships has ordered my captivity?"

"I reckon it's safe to tell you, since you'll not be talking to no one else, not for a long, long time and maybe nor never again." Vymer grinned. "And I reckon I can choose what I says, for I'm a Sumerford myself, I am, though took me ma's name of Wapping seeing as I was born bastard, and not ashamed of it. Born in the village to my ma Mabel Wapping just a week before the Lord Humphrey saw the light, him being heir to the title, firstborn o' the countess, and me being his half-brother. Was his lordship the earl was my father, and acknowledged me, he did, and done me right. Since I was born first by a week, if I'd come of a different mother then I'd be the next earl, and don't you forget that. His lordship my father brought me to the castle when I was a little lad, to be tutored alongside Lord Humphrey, to be his companion and look after him. I was taken on as his page, but was more playmate than servant, and was treated decent by her ladyship from the start. His lordship made sure of that. I was happy then, and had a grand time as a little lad."

Alysson whispered, "So you work for the earl?"

Vymer shook his huge head. "That I do not. Not no more, I don't. I'm my dearest Humphrey's friend, and look after him in every way. He's my beloved brother and not my master, but now I takes my orders from the countess herself and none other, seeing as it's her has the care o' my Humphrey closest to heart."

"That can't be true," Alysson said at once. "The countess would never order me prisoner, though I know she dislikes me. I've no particular liking for her either, but she's a grand lady with a hundred servants or more and no need for another. What reason could she possibly have to lock me up here? There would be no sense in it."

"And what would a stupid trollop like you know of sense?"

Twenty nine years back, the existence of the earl's illegitimate son had been accepted by her ladyship. A common enough situation, she had adjusted, and grown to trust the boy, in looks so alike to her own child. A useful servant and companion for the erratic legitimate heir, Vymer joined the schoolroom and shared some of the tutoring. When Humphrey had merited the lash or the cane, it was Vymer who had been accorded the punishment. And as Humphrey's unexpected disadvantages and weaknesses had become more apparent, so Vymer had been kept closeted with his half-brother, learning to placate and comfort him.

Alysson hung her head. "I know the Lord Humphrey is, I can only say – difficult." She was cautious and careful of her words. "But you speak of him – lovingly."

"Because I loves him," said Vymer simply. "He is my beloved, and I does all I can, in every way, to make my beloved happy."

"I understand," Alysson said, though she did not. "But please – what's any of this to do with me? Why did you attack me before? And why am I imprisoned now?"

"'Tis the Lady Jennine as will answer them questions," Vymer told her. He lurched up and stood, smiling, and preparing to leave. "She'll be up soon, to see you and talk no doubt. But you'll be seeing me again, never fear. And won't be too long afore you gets to know me mighty well indeed. Intimately, you might say. And I shall look forward to that, though I don't reckon you will, nor needs to."

Over past years the small chambers, once used only for storage, had proved useful for another reason. As the Lord Humphrey grew, he developed strange habits. When he was at his most difficult he could be locked away in comfort and kept calm until his moods passed, when he could again resume a normal life. And sometimes, when secrecy was the only diplomacy, Vymer used the same rooms, either alone or in company with his brother.

Now they were Alysson's rooms. She was not permitted to leave them.

⊰◇⊱

433

The first day after Vymer had left, she was left alone. There was time to think herself ragged, imagining everything that frightened her most. She slept in her clothes, fearing to undress. Then in the morning Jennine had come, and Alysson discovered that many of those fears were coming true after all.

Jennine said, "It's amazing how patient I've been. But then of course, there was plenty of time to wait since I had no immediate use for you. Then you and that irritating boy Ludovic spoiled my plans, with all your silly delays and excuses. But I was still content. I decided to keep you around long enough to help me once I needed it." She sighed, spreading her polished hands. "But then, my dear, you plotted to leave. How could I allow it? After all my patient preparations, and just when my real need was closing in. So – this! I had to make sure of you, and now you're mine."

"You're mad." Alysson had crept from the bedclothes once she heard the door unlocked, and sat now, crumpled and bemused, on the quilted cover.

"Very, very sane, my dear." Jennine shook her head. "I know exactly what I'm doing, unlike this castle-full of idiot puzzlers with their muddles of chivalry and greed all mixed together with arrogance and useless pride."

Alysson had been frightened of Vymer but she was not scared of Jennine. "You've locked me in here just because you can't bear anyone to leave you? You can't stand to be flouted? Is that sanity?"

Jennine had laughed. "How naive you are, stupid child." She lounged over to the bed, tilting up Alysson's chin, gazing into her eyes. "No, you're not as beautiful as me, my dear. But you are quite remarkable, and your eyes are almost unique. You're here simply to save my marriage - which means to save me."

For two days Alysson had been brought good food, ale and wine. She had been brought rosewater for washing, a brush for her hair and goose grease to soften the workaday roughness of her servant's hands. She had sat in furious and bitter silence, staring and waiting through the long dreary hours. But then, later the next evening, something wonderful happened, which she had least expected. She was brought company.

As the door unlocked, expecting attack or abuse, Alysson stood, her back to the wall, the empty ale jug gripped tight behind her back for a ready defence. But the door was pushed open and the boy Clovis had been thrust into the chamber. He had crumpled on the stone, bleeding from the nose and mouth. Alysson rushed immediately forward, flinging her arms around him and helping the child to the bed.

He had been beaten but was not badly hurt, and sat up with an angry glare. "Bin bashed afore," he remarked, wiping nose and mouth on the turn of his cuff. "Don't worry me none. But them bastards, they took me from behind, or I'd have shook them off right enuff. I were searching for you. Two days and not a whiff of you, well I knew summit were up. But they knew I were asking around and getting mighty suspicious, so they nobbled me. And here you is all along."

"I am so – incredibly – pleased to see you." Alysson sniffed, resisting the temptation to wipe her own eyes and nose on her sleeve. But neither understood what had really happened, nor why. There was no news yet from London, no return of the earl, and no explanation for the sudden imprisonment. There was only Vymer.

Clovis had seen Vymer before. "His lordship done told me months back," Clovis insisted. "Said as how there were someone looked mighty like his daft brother Humphrey, but wasn't. Most like one o' the earl's bastards from way back, Lord Ludo reckoned, kept secret and paid to keep that loony Humphrey quiet. An' I found the bugger I did, soon after I got 'ere. I'm a good spy and I knows my stuff. But wot the bastard wants us for now, you and me, now that I don't rightly know at all."

"Vymer attacked me before," Alysson said, "though I didn't know it was him until now. I thought it was Lord Humphrey. Perhaps that's why I'm here, though I can't see why Jenny's just handed me over to him. And why are you locked up here as well?"

"Ter shut me up and keep their secrets safe I s'pose," announced Clovis, "And if this bugger comes to get you, I'll have his guts wrapped around his bloody neck I will, like them wrigglers on the gallows gets their bellies slit and their 'testines pulled out afore they dies."

Alysson frowned. "I think," she said, "this man is a little too large and strong for that."

"Reckon you don't know how I was brung up," Clovis shook his head. "Can handle meself, I can. Big buggers – well they fall harder, that's all."

"I imagine this one can handle himself too," sighed Alysson. "But I won't argue with you, and after all, Ludovic must have trusted you very highly to send you here on purpose. And I'm terribly grateful – really I am – for all your loyalty and courage – past and present. But I just wish," she wiped her eyes with the corner of her apron, "that I understood what – and why – and could somehow manage to escape. If only Ludovic would come."

"He might just do that, if we waits," Clovis nodded vigorously. "Never give up heart, that's wot I says. Lord Ludovic, now he's a right enterprising gent he is, never known anovver like him. He'll rescue both of us, you'll see."

Alysson and Clovis slept together like the brother and sister they had once pretended to be. But there was no need of protection. She had expected molestation, even rape, but day after day there was no change, merely Jennine's page bringing food while Vymer stood guard, glowering from the shadows.

Unable to change her clothes or bathe properly, Alysson knew herself more of a slut than when Ludovic had first seen her, when life had been simple, and though miserable, less difficult than now. She was well fed, encouraged to soften her hands with ointments and comb rosewater through her hair, yet was given no chance to brush out her gown or change her linen. She could make sense of nothing.

Then finally the person she had least expected came to visit her.

The Countess of Sumerford swept into the small solar with a swish of damasks and her nose high. Jennine came close behind, then the page bearing a tray with wine. Her ladyship surveyed Alysson, who was curled on a chair in the watery sunshine, her eyes closed. Clovis was clearing out the garderobe. He poked his nose around the corner, glowered at the visitors, and retreated quickly back to his work.

Alysson opened her eyes. She did not scramble up to curtsey, nor hurriedly mumble her apologies as once she would have done. She stayed where she was and stared in angry silence.

The countess said, "I have never liked this girl. She is common and quite rude. But if you assure me that my son wants her, then I am prepared to comply. But why is she not clean? Someone should scrub her."

"She will be, my lady, when the time comes." Jennine sat opposite Alysson and sipped the wine she was handed. Wine was not offered to Alysson. "But she is for Vymer first, and I doubt he'll notice one way or the other. Indeed, I think he likes them rough."

The countess sighed, and sat very carefully on the edge of the settle beside Jennine. "He is certainly rough himself. As long as he doesn't damage the girl irretrievably. My son should not be offered soiled goods. But I imagine you know your business best."

"I do, my lady." Jennine smiled. "It's a business I've been in for many years, and earned my way to the top. And I understand your dearest son and heir very well too, and know exactly what he needs."

"I chose well, when I chose you, my dear." The countess finished her wine and demanded another. Her voice seemed already a little slurred and her cheeks were flushed. "Vymer proved his usefulness as usual when he found you and brought you to me. I've been well satisfied with the bargain, though in the end you stand to gain far more of course. But Humphrey's happiness shall be my most precious reward."

The page Remi stepped forwards to fill her ladyship's cup. As he stepped back again, Alysson noticed his small smirk, his bright blue eyes and his deep madder hair. Jennine said, "Humphrey's happiness is equally important to me, my lady. And in a few weeks, when he is ready and demands her, this girl will ensure it." She nodded towards Alysson. "In the meantime, since Ludovic did not oblige, I shall give her over to Vymer for training. He will not be such a refined tutor, but as Humphrey's tastes are deteriorating somewhat, it will hardly matter. In fact, it may prove more fitting."

The countess blanched slightly. "I've no wish to concern myself with such matters. That is what you were hired for, and I shan't ask questions. Besides, dearest Ludovic might have been more of a disadvantage in many ways, since he became far too fond of the wench for my liking." She looked suddenly and directly at Alysson. "And that would have been disastrous. But under the circumstances, it is no longer a problem."

Alysson had kept quiet. Seething but intimidated, she had waited, hoping to understand. Now she sat forward. "My lady, have you news of him from London?"

The countess became pink. "Normally I would refuse to answer you," she said, eyes cold. She had finished her third cup of wine. "But I have some compassion. So yes, I will tell you that I have received news." She stood abruptly. She did not look at Alysson as she answered, but walked instead, rather unsteadily, to the door. She did not turn around. "My sons have been executed," she said softly from the doorway. "The king has taken their lives. Ludovic is dead."

The page opened the door for her, and when she left, he followed behind and the sound of the key turning echoed back. Jennine stayed. She sat, ankles crossed, hands clasped neatly in her lap, and smiled, watching Alysson. Alysson stared back. Her mind was utterly blank. The shock of the words was like sudden cold water and she could not think or speak.

Jennine nodded. "So now you know, my dear. And you also know my plans. I persistently encouraged you into your chivalrous hero's arms for this reason alone. It should have proved a perfect training as a knight's mistress. And once he discarded you and moved on to some other woman, you would have been left ruined, and ready to listen to your dear and trusted friend Jenny's advice to save your reputation and keep hold of your newly discovered comforts."

"He knew?" Alysson sat with her mouth open and her mind in a panic. She could only whisper, now more afraid than she had ever been before.

Jennine laughed. "Naturally. But he didn't want to force you, and Humphrey was happy with me and didn't need you yet. There was still time."

"And now? Why this?" She found the words stuck in her throat.

"To stop you running off," Jennine said. "You are to stay here and save me. For without this marriage, I'd be back in the brothel, or even

438

back on the streets." She tossed her head, frowning. "Not that I planned any of this from the start you know, and might never have thought of it until Ludovic brought you to me. He's to be commended, for my husband approves of you, and now I know you're the answer to what I need. Humphrey's asked for you a few times already, but I've kept him too interested in me, and he's still fairly tame to my call. Before I ever arrived here he was getting far too difficult and her ladyship had lost almost all control over him, which is why she sent Vymer looking for the perfect woman. Now the countess and I have made a good bargain, and I shall keep to my side. I'm no romantic, and I know if I fail, I'll be discarded. But I'm getting older, and that damned child played havoc with my figure. For a woman with little else to my fortune except my looks and my experience, that's a great risk. In a short time Humphrey will start to stray. And like all stray dogs, he'll become dangerous. I shall need to keep him busy, and in check, which means something new to divert him, with special treats as bribes for bad days. While he had me every night, and the child to play with each day, it was easier and he stayed tame. But now the brat is dead and I'm aging, so he needs – a little more."

"Are you really that – vile?" Alysson paused, horrified. "All that time, I honestly thought you were my friend. But Ludovic knowing – I don't believe it. It can't be true. It's all a hideous, unbelievable nightmare."

Jennine stood with a flounce, and stamped her foot. "Fool. Nightmares are real and all around us. How do you think the brats in London's shitty alleys grow up? How do you think I grew up? In a nightmare, until I scratched my own way out of it. Do you think I enjoyed being a whore? Another nightmare, but at least I got rich. Rich enough to buy my own Stewe House, and employ others off the street. Your nightmare will be comfortable enough. You'll be well fed. You'll have nice clothes. You'll never know the horrors I grew up with. You should be grateful."

Alysson stared. "So what – exactly – will you do with me?"

"In a few weeks Vymer moves in here." She loomed over Alysson, hands on her hips, glaring down. "Not yet, because if I let him have you too soon, he might ruin you. But a week or two before Humphrey needs you, Vymer will start your training. Then, when Vymer and I think you're ready, I'll get you cleaned up and plumped out, and pass you over to Humphrey. My dear husband has special needs as I've told you already. I won't bother to explain them yet, but Vymer knows exactly what they are and he'll teach you. I'll continue your training afterwards, since Humphrey will probably need both of us by then. You'll go on living up here, and Humphrey and Vymer will both stay here with you whenever Humphrey needs particular restraint. You'll obey them both of course, but I shall be your main controller."

"And Clovis?" Alysson whispered.

"He can stay locked up here while he makes himself useful." Jennine turned to go. "But if he misbehaves, then Vymer will get rid of him. So you'd better warn the brat to keep quiet and do as he's told."

Alysson felt the tears slip noiselessly down her face. She tasted the salt. But she was quite unable to speak, her eyes stung and became blurred and she could not think clearly about anything at all. It was when Jennine left, that Alysson collapsed.

Clovis hurried to her, his own cheeks wet and his eyes bloodshot. He gathered her against him, rocking her is if she were a fractious infant. "I don't believe it," he muttered. "Lord Ludo ain't dead. His lordship'll come. I knows it."

Alysson curled over, choking suddenly on her tears. "How can he? He's dead, Clovis, executed by the king. Ludovic will never come – never again."

CHAPTER FORTY-EIGHT

Clovis sat at her feet, his arms folded on her lap, and gazed up at her. "P'raps females is braver than I thought," he conceded. "And you're doing very good at it, being mighty brave that is, and I's proud o' you. But you gotta listen to wot I says now, or we're lost, both of us."

Alysson swallowed hard. "I know. We must rescue ourselves, because there's no hope anymore of rescue – from him."

Clovis was supposed to sleep on the pallet in the small outer chamber, but desperate for comfort, they curled together in the wide bed, like mother and son or brother and sister. Clovis frequently had night terrors, crying out often in his sleep. Alysson had not told him of this, nor of how she woke and wrapped the warmth of her arms around him when he sobbed. She did not want to wound or embarrass him with tales of how she comforted his fears. Her own dreams were terrible and sometimes she wondered if he did the same to her, and if for the same reasons, he never spoke of it.

Now he patted her knee. "So, listen proper now, for I've got it worked. It ain't no good, wotever I'd like to think different, planning to knock off that bastard Vymer. But if your pissing nasty lady Jenny ever comes alone with just her sneaky little bugger of a page, well, we gotta be ready. We can grab 'em, one each, and squeeze the bloody life out of them both."

"I will," said Alysson sitting up straight. "I could easily strangle the vile treacherous creature, I know I could. And that horrid little boy is no patch on you." She nodded. "I never thought of it before of course, but do you think he's another – of them – you know?"

"Reckon so. Could be another of the earl's side-slips. Or even that bugger Vymer's own brat. Remi they calls him. Pig bastard, I calls him."

"We'll wait for the right moment, but it must be before Vymer moves in here," said Alysson. "I couldn't bear – really, really couldn't bear that. I'd die, I'm sure of it, long before I gathered enough strength to retaliate."

"Don't you worry none," Clovis assured her. "You don't know wot I can do yet. Lord Ludo, he didn't send me here for nuffing you know."

"You're very kind," Alysson said softly. "But I wish you wouldn't – talk about him yet. It still hurts – so very much. I shall get over it soon I promise. And then I'll be as strong as you like, and we'll beat our enemies together." She looked away with a sigh. "But Jenny never comes without Vymer standing outside with the keys you know. And there's no point us strangling Jenny and that horrid little child if the door's locked against us, and Vymer waiting. Perhaps we should kill him first after all. I do at least have my own little knife for cutting my meat at dinnertime."

Clovis grinned. "Knew you was a cockproud female all along," he said. "I reckon we'll make a grand pair, and when we's free, I'll take you to my ma in Browny. Her and the captain and me, we'll look after you."

There was little to do throughout the long days. Clovis, trained as a ship's cabin boy and itching for action, was happy to clean and tidy, fussing over the creased linen on the bed and brushing down the hangings. Although also long trained as a servant, Alysson found nothing to do. She asked for paper and quill to teach Clovis numbers and letters, but was refused. She asked for a change of clothes and was also denied. Until, Jennine told her, she was ready and willing to obey orders when she would get clothes aplenty, she could receive no favours. Eventually, as the Lord Humphrey's accepted mistress, she would be presented with fine materials, bed robes and blanchets of muslin and velvet, shifts of the finest linen, stockings and gowns of silk, and slippers of softest leather. In the meantime, she could satisfy herself with her broadcloth livery and keep it as clean as she might.

Although interrupting the stultifying boredom, Jennine's visits were not welcome. Her page would unlock the door but it was always Vymer who stood guard outside, making attack or defence unwise. Waiting turned into slow drudgery and even Ludovic's face in Alysson's dreams became blurred by misery and the aimless drip of hopelessness. Summer came edging through the shutters, a hazy lazy sunshine that dithered across the worn rugs. The silences became sleepy, spoiled only by the irritating drone of flies as trapped as the room's other occupants.

Sweating in her thick gown, Alysson was lying on the bed when Jennine strode in one afternoon, Vymer at her heels. Clovis stayed carefully hidden, watching for opportunity. Vymer was dragging a large and heavy sack, its stains seeping black and putrid, oozing dark slime over the floorboards. Alysson sat up in alarm, her hand across her nose and mouth. Vymer dropped the sack and grinning wide, left the chamber, slamming the door and locking it behind him.

Jennine laughed. "A gift, my dear. You persist in asking for diversions, so I have discovered a special surprise for you. To be honest, it was a surprise for me too. But I thought you would like to see, before I have it burned."

The stench was all invading. "What ghastly thing have you discovered? Why torture me?" demanded Alysson. "I'm already your prisoner."

"But, stupid girl, you refuse to behave. Promise me you'll do exactly what I say, and I can make a fair bargain with you. For instance, I'll take this most delightful gift away, and not trouble you with it at all. I'll get you clothes and a bath tub. Sweetmeats and good wine. Ink, paper, even books, if you want such dull things. Promise me faithfully you'll obey me and behave, and I shall be your friend again my dear."

Alysson blanched, crawling back across the bed, away from the sack of decay lying just inside the doorway. "I can't do anything except behave," she muttered. "What choice do you give me, locked in here? I've done nothing to you at all, except call you the whore you are."

Jennine laughed. "Call me what you like, I certainly don't care," she said. "It's an entirely different behaviour I want from you, and you know it. I need your willing surrender. My dear Humphrey is becoming impatient, and Vymer more so. But if I let Vymer loose on you now, he may break your back. I don't want that. I want you quiet and obedient. Take the training Vymer gives you for a few days, a sennight at the most, and then I'll keep him away from you afterwards. I give you my word on that – a fair bargain for a fair bargain. Now, promise me complete compliance, and I'll take this – thing away – undisclosed."

"Obey that – foul creature? Let Vymer rape me while I lie quiet and do whatever he tells me? Learn about degradation and prostitution at his vile hands? Never!" Alysson sat straight and furious, her back hard up against the bed's headboard. She knew her face was flushed and her gown dark with sweat. She was finding it difficult to breathe. "He'll force me anyway. I know that. I'm expecting it. But I'll never willingly cooperate."

Jennine shook her head. "Little fool. If you try and defend yourself, Vymer will hurt you badly, which is exactly what he likes to do. I believe he can hardly help himself. But that's not what I want."

"You think I want that?"

"Then be a good girl and obey orders," Jennine said. "I've forbidden Vymer to be too rough as long as you're good. But if you fight, how can I stop him fighting you back? He's not an easy man to control. After Vymer has broken you in and taught you the first rules, then I shall bring Humphrey to you. I'll stay with you, don't worry, and help you through, explaining and teaching. But you must be very careful with Humphrey, I warn you. He'll not stand for defiance when he's roused but together we can keep him very happy. And over the next year or so, you'll become his principal amourette. You could grow to enjoy that, I assure you. My husband can be very generous as long as he gets what he wants, and he's really kind and loving at heart."

Alysson shivered. "You mean to keep me locked up here – for years?"

"Not necessarily." Jennine shrugged. "Make me the promises I ask for, and prove yourself utterly trustworthy, and I'll let you go in time. Perhaps you can share my quarters downstairs. Perhaps I'll secure you a cottage in the village. But not yet of course. I shall have to be sure of you first, and that will take some months."

"While I become your own husband's whore?"

"You're ridiculously innocent, silly girl." Jennine shook her head. "Listen to me very carefully. Dear Humphrey has special requirements, which I'm sure everyone in the castle realises including you, but few people know exactly what most of these needs actually are. I do. That was what I was hired for. The countess herself taught me how to impersonate a lady, just sufficient for me to pretend to be a respectable heiress. Well, I'd already learned the refinements necessary to run a high class brothel so it wasn't so hard. It's the countess who paid me, and promised me the position as her heir's wife. Oh yes, our marriage was legal. I'm Lady Jennine Sumerford now, and no one can deny it."

"I don't care about any of that," Alysson said. "I've known where you came from almost since I started as your maid."

"Which is why I trusted you enough to choose you for my future plans. That, and your pretty eyes, and the fact that Humphrey liked you as soon as he saw you in the dairies, when he sent Vymer to get you for him." Jennine chuckled. "So when you came to me as a maid, I was delighted." She sat, also keeping her distance from the leaking sack. The stink of it still pervaded all the room. "Humphrey needs constant pleasure," she continued, searching for her kerchief and holding it to her nose. "I'm afraid it can be hard work thinking of new pleasures to keep him happy. So I needed a younger companion to train for when I get too old. I'm nearly thirty now, and my lifestyle hasn't been kind to my skin. You're what? Eighteen? Nineteen? You've ten years in you, and maybe by then Humphrey might be past caring about such refinements as youth and beauty. He might even be dead himself, for men such as him rarely live into their dotage I believe. I needed a male child to be the heir after Humphrey, and at first everything went according to plan. I gave the countess my word that any child would be a Sumerford of course. In fact, she suggested I couple immediately with one of her other sons, in the hope of insuring the firstborn had none of Humphrey's weaknesses. That I did, but to no avail in the end. I hoped you'd produce a brat with Ludovic, and if he repudiated it as most men do to their bastards, it could have been passed off as Humphrey's and become the second heir. Your foolish cowardice and pride, and that idiot boy's patient chivalry nearly spoiled everything. But now you're trapped my girl. Perhaps you'll have Humphrey's child and I can easily pass it off as my own. Give in with a good grace now and you'll have ten years of hard work it's true, but with luxury and comfort and riches thrown in, and a sweet hearted man-child who cares for you."

"And be cast off once I'm old. And with the horrors you've planned, my God I'd be haggard in no time."

Jennine shook her head. "The countess is a fair minded woman, and she cares for Humphrey. She'd eventually settle you in some village well out of the area I imagine. I'll help you myself, if you're truly hard working and reliable until then."

"I think," said Alysson, "I'm going to be extremely sick." She struggled to keep her voice calm, staring at Jennine across the end of the bed. "That muck you've dragged in here in that sack doesn't seem as disgusting as you are, Jenny," she said. "Whatever it is, couldn't be as vile as you. I used to feel sorry for you with Humphrey as a husband, and I knew some of the suffering you've hinted at from your past. But you're wicked. Truly wicked. You're not a whore because of what you had to do in the past, but because of what you are deep down inside. In spite of what the priests say, I never really believed people could be so evil. Now I know they can."

Jennine sat stiffly and stared back. Two small spots of colour appeared high on her perfect cheekbones. She kept her lavender perfumed kerchief tight to her nose and spoke, a little muffled, through the fine linen. "Then I have no more to say to you," she said. "I shall leave you to examine my gift. Vymer will come in and unwrap it

446

for you and explain exactly what it is. Then you'll be left alone to enjoy it." She stood abruptly, and carefully skirting the wallowing sack, walked to the door. Then she turned, glaring back over her shoulder. "Tomorrow I shall order Vymer to return and remove the thing. And a day or so after, once the floor's been scrubbed clean by your page brat, Vymer'll be back again, but this time to stay. He'll start your education, and I won't bother to keep him under restraint. He can do what he likes to you as far as I'm concerned. I doubt dear Humphrey will mind too much, once Vymer passes you over to him." Jennine knocked briefly on the door, calling to Vymer to let her out. As the door opened for her, she smiled. "So in the meantime Alysson my dear, enjoy your last few nights of innocence. You're about to learn some very interesting lessons."

Vymer was already standing in the doorway as Jennine left in a swirl of petulant silks. He grinned, gap toothed. "Where's that weasely brat?" he demanded.

Alysson's head was reeling and she could not think. "Who? Clovis?"

Vymer nodded, striding forwards. He grabbed the neck of the sack, pulling it open. "Get him in here," he demanded. "The runt's to see this too. I want you both remembering it good and clear, and let it be a warning to both o' yous. For I'll stand for no nonsense when I moves in here in a couple o' days. You heard her ladyship. You're mine soon, trull. And you'll do as I says."

"I'll fight you as long as I've the strength to," Alysson whispered, staring from Vymer's grin to his grip on the yawning sack.

Vymer laughed. "Good," he said. "I like a wench that spits. But I'll knock respect into you, same time as I fuck obedience into you. And like I've told her ladyship, I'm a Sumerford I am, and won't stand for no nonsense. Long as you're docile, I'll keep my word and treat you gentle enough. But if you wants to scratch, well, I can scratch harder, and in places you won't like at all."

Clovis had crept in. From the archway on the far side of the room, he sidled into the bedchamber, gazing in revulsion at the bag Vymer was holding. Clovis had smelled the stench of it and had long been listening from behind the door. He climbed quickly to Alysson's side

447

on the bed, putting his arm around her shoulders. "Don't you worry, lady," he said softly. "I'll look after you."

Vymer ignored the child. He kicked the Turkey rug out of the way and gripping the neck of the sack, hurled it open so that it tipped, emptying in a rush across the floorboards. A slippery black mess slid and rolled with a thud, spreading its ink and rottenness. Vymer stood grinning. Alysson heaved, clutching at her mouth and throat.

"Wot the shit?" demanded Clovis. "You filthy bastard. Wot is it?"

Vymer nodded. "Shit it is, just like you says." He flipped the sack over and let it sink into the decaying and viscous liquid. "It's what was bunging up the cess pit, this is. All them pretty lady's privies blocked with shit they was, and the staff all pissing themselves trying to hurry off to some chamber pot so as not to use the latrines. So they calls for my brother, poor old George. He's a Sumerford too, and ought to have more respect than emptying other folk's shit, but he ain't as smart as me, is George. Content he is, poor bugger, to do the dirty jobs, and happy to dig holes and shift muck."

Alysson wrapped her arms around her middle, bent over and swallowed hard. She tried not to look at the reeking mess on the floor at Vymer's feet. "You mean," she demanded in disgust and seething fury, "you and that vile woman have actually brought a barrow load here out of the cess pit?"

"Not rightly." Vymer was enjoying himself. "Though you're right in a way. This is what were blocking the drains, sure enough. Dug it up this morning, George did. But I knows just what it is, being as how I put it there couple o' years back, and there's a sight more than shit. Not that I meant it to bung up the pit, but I had to get rid of it somewhere. Reckon I should have thrown it all in the moat, but then I'd not have had the please o' showing it to you now, would I?"

"You're all mad," Alysson choked on her words. "They call Humphrey crazy. But he isn't mad at all compared to you and Jenny. You're both quite insane."

"As it happens," Vymer Wapping scratched his bright red head, "you got it wrong again. You see, t'was me as chucked this stuff in the cess pit, but t'was my Humphrey what did it. He killed the little lad after he'd played with him a couple of hours that is, and then cut the

448

body up into handy chunks for the ridding of. You see, Humphrey was a bit irritated back then, seeing as how he seen you once and wanted you but couldn't have you, and meantime was waiting for his bride but still had to wait a bit longer. He asked me nice, and I comes down to get you for him like he wanted, but couldn't get you when you ran off. So he went and took the next best thing."

Alysson was completely white. The day no longer seemed warm and she could smell nothing. Everything had turned to ice. "Explain. Tell me the truth."

"Hard to see the bits and pieces proper," Vymer agreed, kicking at the middle of the black heap where bones had begun to show through as the slime oozed away. "But all the stuff's there if you wants to sort through it. Legs and arms and ribs and that. The skull's easy seen, look, though ain't no flesh left for the recognising of. I never seen the lad all in one piece, not since my brother called me once it were all over. But it was a skinny brat, far as I remember. And here he is, all restored to you, as is proper for a sister to take charge of her little brother."

Alysson had doubled over, sobbing and heaving. Clovis was clutching at her, trying to comfort her. She was choking, unable to hear him or anything except Vymer's voice.

Vymer chuckled. "It's a right jovial thought," he said, "being as for the past year or two living in the castle, whenever you've set your arse on the privy, you've shat all over what's left of your own brother. Quite comical, I reckon. He'll not be thanking you for that, watching from Purgatory. But then, when I moves in here in a couple o' days, you'll have no time to think of him nor nothing else anymore. I shall be keeping you proper busy, that I promise."

CHAPTER FORTY-NINE

"We have been summoned to court," said the earl.

Ludovic lifted an eyebrow. "To thank his gentle majesty on bended knee for my pardon? After he murdered my brother?"

His lordship nodded. "For that exact reason, I imagine," he said. "And we will comply. I trust you realise we have no choice. Your pardon can still be rescinded."

"I know my duty." Ludovic sighed. "And in gratitude to you, my lord, since I thank you for my life and not the bastard king, I should in any case do whatever you ask of me. But it will stick in my craw, and kneeling to him will remind me forcibly of the torture I experienced at his command."

"You have me to thank, but also the king," the earl said. "And you will contrive to remember it, Ludovic. His majesty is, let us say, much shaken by the continuous threats to his power, of this – Peter Warbeck – in particular. He is unwell, both in body and in mind. Like any cornered rat, an irascible man attacks when he imagines disrespect or danger." The earl wandered over to the window, gazing out over the sheen of the peaceful river beyond the sloping greens. "The battle this Henry Tudor so unexpectedly won against our late King Richard was so against all likelihood, it could only have occurred by the will of God," he murmured, his back to his son. "Tudor therefore saw himself as sublimely chosen. He should certainly have died and came within a sword's width of it, and yet instead of lying in his grave, he found himself sitting proud on England's throne. So he believed himself invulnerable, set on high by God, angelically anointed and specifically blessed by the Lord God's own hand. But the resurrection of the Plantagenet princes has shattered his faith in being God's chosen – and has shattered his peace, his mind, and his body too."

"Do you pity the wretch?" Ludovic frowned.

"I do." The earl turned, smiling faintly. "Losing Gerald has changed me, my son. His bloodied head haunts my dreams. Now I've watched your recovery these past weeks, so slow, so bitter, so doubtful. Daily I imagine the pain you must have known. I feared you might be crippled forever, and even now I know how each step you take must hurt you. I pity you, though I know you despise my pity. I pity your mother, who sits and weeps nightly over the sorrow of her loss, and each of the sons she bore now suffering their own agonies." His lordship came back, sitting abruptly on the low settle by the hearth where the sunbeams from the window turned his hair into burnished strands, shot through with flame. "From the first day I met your mother, a few days before our marriage, I disliked her," he said. "I do not care what she thinks of me, but I doubt she thinks of me with affection. Our alliance was arranged by our fathers, and I did not question it. But at the time I did not know of her grandfather, nor her uncle. They both carry the madness of the old French king and his own grandson, our late King Henry VI. There was a relationship to your mother's sires which at the time my father thought admirable, royal lineage being more important than simple sanity. If kings can be lunatic, why not earls? But I blamed her for Humphrey's afflictions. She blames herself. Now I pity her, and I pity Humphrey. So I can see this Tudor king's dilemma, and I pity him also."

"I hate the Tudor court," Ludovic sighed, slumping back within the padding of his cushioned seat. He did not question his father's dislike of his mother. He had always known it. He also knew of the madness inherent within his mother's family, barely matching the unspoken brutality within his father's. "The palace seethes with hatred," Ludovic said. "It's all jealousy and ferments of plotting, each one against the other. And all for royal favour, even though most of them hate the king they fawn over."

"The Plantagenet court was little different," the earl said. "Both previous kings were far better liked, but the courtiers envied each other with the same vengeance, and changed sides as self-interest moved them. It will always be the same."

Ludovic now walked without the crutch, but his recovery had been slow and he still limped and used a stick when tired. He had battled for the return of his health but was as surprised to see summer as it was to see him. He had not expected to walk again in the sunshine. Now there were only the king's demands to obey, and he would be free to return to whatever hope of happiness might still be waiting for him in Sumerford.

But although commanded to appear, they were not granted the crown's indulgence immediately. They were not invited to stay at court, merely ordered to return again and again to await his majesty's pleasure. The days became hot and humid, with the threat of storm hanging sticky over the Abbey. Those out of royal favour were not courted and the palace corridors held few invitations. But those lacking favour one year might be powerful the next, so some stopped to talk, offered company through the long and dreary afternoons, and exchanged gossip. And there was also William of Berkhamstead. Ludovic sought him out.

"She lost the first one," he said, shaking his head. "They often do, you know. But dear Gwennie is carrying again already, and I've great hopes of this one coming to term. Sons, Ludovic! I can hardly wait to tell his majesty my first son and heir is born."

They sat in the small inner courtyard, within hearing of the Abbey's great bell. Ludovic's appointment with the king was scheduled for ten of the clock, and he could not afford to be late. He frowned. "As likely to be a girl."

"What a misery you are Ludovic." William smiled but shook his head. "Though girls have their uses too, especially on the marriage mart of course. But the first must be a boy. I don't usually believe in superstitions, but come now my friend, no need to encourage the evil eye."

Ludovic sighed. "I wish you all the luck in the world." He looked directly into the young earl's soft brown eyes. "But I cannot forget Gerald, nor even the miseries of Prince Richard still imprisoned in the Tower. You seem strangely at home here now Will, talking of the king as a friend and ally. I find it hard enough to be cheerful at any time, and have no reason to think kindly of Henry Tudor. I'm dreading having to see him this morning."

William blushed. "Gerald. Of course. I miss him too you know. I saw you at his execution. That was a terrible day, but I had to be there, and send him what comfort I could. I nearly came over to speak to you and meet your father, but thought you'd sooner be left in peace at such a time. And then there was the unexpected trouble afterwards. I pray that scandal's done with and settled now."

"Scandal?" Ludovic stared. "Gerald's death was certainly a scandal, but not one I'd expect you to call settled."

The early sun flickered over the peaks of the royal gables. The warmth did not yet sink beyond the stone walls into the little paved courtyard with its bench and sundial, still too early for the morning's long shadows to dissipate. The night's dew still hung like rain drops from the buttresses. William's pause was as lengthy as the blackbird's song from the willow sapling, and he sighed with relief as the Abbey bells began to chime ten. "You'll have to run," his lordship said abruptly. "The king won't wait, you know. I'll look for you afterwards, to hear if it all went well."

Henry Tudor, King of England, clung to his throne. The Earl of Sumerford and his youngest son were announced by the royal usher, and walked the length of the great echoing chamber as the courtiers moved back a little, grouping out of earshot but watching carefully and listening where they could. The earl knelt his right knee three times to his king before standing straight backed before the throne. Ludovic, his knee to the boards, felt the familiar twist of pain as his bones struck wood. His knees remembered the rack with every step he walked, and kneeling was an even sharper torture. His ankles, straining as he bent both leg and foot, screamed silently. The bandages remained within his hose, their folds showing through the grip of the knitted silk, but did little to cushion the still swollen joints.

His majesty's eyes remained cold. He said, "Sumerford? Did I call for you?" He never forgot anything. He was sick, but not forgetful.

The earl bowed and looked down his nose. "If it pleases you, majesty, we are here at your grace's summons."

"I have enough traitors and evil wishers around me," the king said, "why should I welcome more?" His words were precise but heavily accented in French with a strong Breton burr, and his voice was prim and colourless, finding its own way between closed lips.

"We have come to humbly thank your majesty," said the earl, his voice as expressionless and his mouth as static. "We are most conscious of your majesty's magnanimity in granting my son a pardon and releasing him from custody. Before returning to the Sumerford lands, we are deeply honoured for the opportunity to express our gratitude."

The king deigned to nod, but raised one finger, indicating a moment's silence. A woman sat beside him. It was not his wife. The king's finger was heavy knuckled and shook a little, like the tentatively wagging tail of a hunting hound past its usefulness. The woman unbent and leaned towards him, whispering something. Tudor nodded again. He looked back to the earl. "We are pleased to accept your gratitude, my lord. But two sons implicated in treachery does no credit to an English nobleman. My lady mother reminds me that you had four sons, two now proven traitors, and another banished in disgrace. What of the fourth, my lord? Is your heir an honest knight at least?"

Ludovic frowned, puzzled, and looked to his father, but kept his mouth shut.

454

The earl bowed again and said, "My eldest son Lord Humphrey is well, sire, but has recently suffered the loss of his firstborn. He is an honest knight of England and utterly loyal to your majesties."

The woman seated beside the king whispered to him again. Dressed in severe black with a headdress closely resembling a nun's, she was elderly, small and remarkably thin. Her eyes, beneath high arched but unplucked brows, stared disdainfully, ignoring all company except the king. Her mouth was tiny and lipless, barely finding voice. The king nodded to her, smiling warmly. "My lady mother," he said, "is pleased to hear that at least one of your family keeps a dutiful heart and a wise head." The earl bowed. The king continued. "My lord, we well remember your particular loyalty at Stoke and Exeter. It was for this we pardoned your son, but he will not again be accepted at court until he proves his own loyalty to his country."

"I beg to point out that my son has never been proven guilty of treachery, sire," the earl replied, unsmiling. "He was not called to trial, and did not confess, even on the rack. After many months confined to the Tower, his questioning was finally interrupted by the issuing of the pardon graciously signed by your majesty's self."

"Ah yes." The king chewed his lip. He looked towards his mother, who gazed balefully and unblinking at the earl. The earl bowed again. "Very well," decided his majesty. "For the sake of your past services, my lord, I shall condescend presumption of your son's innocence. But I advise you both to keep your distance from court until matters here are more ordered, and there is no more possible threat of rebellion." He stared, tapping his fingers on the arms of his great carved chair, and bent forwards a little as though confiding matters not intended for public knowledge. "Unrest continues, and troubles us," he said, low voiced. "I will not suffer traitors any longer, and will not accept those around me who mutter and stir up discontent. So stay within your own lands as the year wanes, sir, and do not approach me again for favours or mercy unless I send for you. While we remain beset by evil and treachery, it would be wise for those under taint of such conspiracies to keep their distance, or be accused themselves."

"I understand, sire. As your majesty wishes."

The king nodded dismissal. He raised one fur cuffed wrist and waved his fingers, turning back at once to his mother's murmurings. The earl and his youngest son bowed low, backing slowly from the throne. His majesty's mother whispered once more. The king bent dutifully towards her, smiling, his court forgotten. The earl and Ludovic Sumerford strode from the hall.

Leaving Westminster without words either to each other or with any other, they rode quickly back along the Strand. The sun, now midday, was high and hot. The Thames shimmered in a sulphur gloss across the deep churning brown beneath. A stray dog was scavenging amongst the dross on the banks, barking to warn away the ravens.

Dismounting at the stables of their own hired premises as the ostler ran to take the horses, Ludovic began to speak at last. The earl shook his head. They were back in their own solar before his lordship said, "From now on, my son, you will be more careful than ever before in your life. There are spies in every corner of the land, and now the king suspects us personally. Everything we do will be watched. What you say in the hearing of others could cost both our lives."

Ludovic frowned, sitting immediately on the low cushioned window seat. His legs were on fire, his back throbbed and his head had begun to ache. He stretched, easing his knee joints. "This dark brooding fear feels close enough to death already. I'm well enough to travel now," he said. "Even the damned doctor admits I'm nearly recovered. The sooner we leave the better I shall like it."

"I needed only the king's permission and official corroboration of the pardon," said the earl. "Tomorrow I shall order preparations for our return to Sumerford." He paced the chamber, hands clasped behind his back. "His majesty hinted at something in particular, though whether he intended to warn me or not, I cannot be sure." He stopped pacing and stood before his son, gazing down into Ludovic's eyes. "But, my disposition not being readily obtuse, I assume, and read his words this way. The king wants the threat of this Plantagenet prince finished forever. He needs to execute the boy. He therefore intends creating a situation of sufficient suspicion to give a direct excuse. He will use whoever is in the vicinity, and will implicate whomever he wishes. Others will devise the details, but the orders will be the king's. Prince Richard will be hanged as Peter Warbeck before the year is out. And you, my son, must not be anywhere near, or you will be too convenient as dupe or scapegoat. All those once implicated in treachery are now in danger, whatever their guilt or innocence. You will not be one of them. Do I make myself sufficiently clear?"

"You appear to understand this Harry Tudor very well, my lord."

"He is both clever and devious," said the earl. "But I do not condemn the skills of manipulation. I have never claimed naïve candour and have no wish to appear an artless simpleton. I believe the king warned me, and I translate his warning as I have told you. You may make your own judgements."

Ludovic nodded. "I judge the king, not you my lord. And he sits his wretched mother on the queen's throne. She looks a sour, malignant creature for all her famed charitable chastity."

"Tudor credits God and his mother, in that order, for putting him on the throne," the earl said. "He is probably right, though I would reverse the order."

Ludovic paused, staring carefully back up at his father. Then he straightened his back and sighed. He was hot, dressed suitably for court and king, now sweating in heavy crimson silk and cream fur trimmings. But he made no attempt to throw off the damask surcoat or loosen his neck lacings. "There is something else, Father, far more important than the wretched king and his mother," Ludovic said. "There's something he said which I did not understand. It was what was hinted, what was implied, and what I now need explained, sir. What is it you have intentionally not told me of Brice?"

The earl nodded. He pulled up a small chair and sat again, looking across the sunbeams at his son. "We are a family who keeps secrets, my boy," he said softly. "I have kept many secrets from you in the past, and will no doubt do so again. But this time my silence was inspired by consideration. You have been exceedingly ill, Ludovic. You are still extremely weak, and could have done nothing whatsoever to help either myself or your brother. Nor did I require your interference. You needed to concentrate only on regaining your strength. Indeed,

Gerald's loss has weakened us both. I therefore chose to keep silent for excellent reasons, as you also have, in the past. I imagine what you knew of Brice you kept to yourself in order to save my feelings and my paternal pride. What has now occurred regarding your brother, I kept to myself for the sake of your recovery."

"I believe," Ludovic said, "you had better tell me now."

CHAPTER FIFTY

The door unlocked. Jennine had brought clothes. The page Remi piled the heap of soft materials on the chest and stood back with a small smirk. Jennine nodded to him. "Off you go now, boy. Tell Vymer to lock the door behind you, and to stand guard outside until I knock for him."

Alysson was curled on the bed, the covers creased up beneath and around her. She wore only her shift for it was hot and humid. A summer storm was gathering high above the castle. Alysson's back was to the door. She did not move, but stayed staring out through the window to the billowing clouds and the calls of the kittiwakes and terns. "What now?" she said, without turning around.

"Rude girl." Jennine flopped down on the nearest chair and glared at her prisoner's back. "Turn around and look what I've brought you. You've been begging endlessly for clean clothes. So I decided to be kind."

Alysson looked briefly back over her shoulder. "I don't care," she said. "I've already seen the quality of your special gifts in the past. And you only want me to dress up for him."

Clovis, knees hugged to his chin, was hunched on the window seat. His eyes were closed. He did not open them. The heat of the sun through the glass clipped the top of his grubby curls, turning the dun thatch bright. He grunted, pretending to snore.

Jennine ignored him. "Alysson, I demand you sit up and take some interest. Have I sent Humphrey to you yet? Have I sent Vymer? No. I've given you a few more days to think about things and see my point of view. You should be thoroughly grateful."

"How could I be anything else, after all your kindness," said Alysson without expression and without moving.

Jennine stamped her foot. "Sarcasm doesn't suit you Alysson. Try thinking instead. I could have you thrashed. I could send Vymer in to beat you, and then tell him to take you to bed and be as rough as he likes. Instead I've treated you with consideration and respect. I've waited and waited. I've been kind, Alysson."

Alysson finally turned. She sat cross legged on the old velvet counterpane, glaring at the other woman through the rising dust dithering and trapped in the sunbeams. "I watched you bring in my little brother's remains and order his poor broken bones tipped over the floor. You knew about Pagan's murder, and you laughed. I'll never forgive you for that, Jenny. Taking me prisoner, keeping me here, threatening me with every vile horror you can think of – I could almost forgive that. Not entirely, but I know about your past, and your childhood, and some of the wretched things you've been forced to do yourself. And I know what contempt you have for respectability, even if you secretly yearn for it. You think I have nothing else to aim for, so why don't I just accept your offer. Prostitution seems natural to you, and you think I'm absurdly squeamish to object. But you're twisted, and cruel, and you don't understand me at all. I could never forgive all your filthy plans and how you plotted to use me from the start. But now, after Pagan, if I believed in curses, I'd damn you to Hell." She paused, and nodded. "In fact, I believe you've cursed yourself, Jenny. You're evil. Hell's waiting for you. Evil people bring evil on themselves."

The spots of high colour had reappeared on Jennine's cheekbones. "Don't you dare speak to me like that, horrid common brat," she snapped. "It's been your own fault from the beginning, if only you'd realise it. If you hadn't been so sneaky and secretive, and planned to leave me after all I'd done for you, I wouldn't have needed to lock you up. You could have stayed free in my service and I'd have kept you in comfort for months before I passed you over to Humphrey. So you brought all this on yourself. And now you simply refuse to co-operate, even though it's clear you've no choice but to do what I tell you. Yet still I'm patient. I didn't kill your nasty little brother and chop him up in bits. That happened even before I was married, and I knew nothing about it until that pathetic turd digger finally dug the pieces up. So don't blame me. And I was simply cross about your stupid stubbornness, or I wouldn't have had all that shit spread under your nose either. So, if you don't want any more unpleasant surprises, sit up and smile and try to please me for once."

Clovis opened one eye. Between the knees he was hugging cramped up beneath his chin, was wedged the small meat knife that he and Alysson shared. He had grabbed and hidden it as soon as the key grated in the lock. With a nod to Alysson, he had taken up position. Now he watched surreptitiously, his breathing deep and even and his twitching fingers unseen.

Jennine stood angrily, kicking away the folds of her hems and marching over to the bed. Her gown was rose pink purpura and her shift was crimson cendal. The two layers of silk clung to the dark sweat in her armpits, collected in her cleavage and trickled sour down her spine. Her back was to Clovis. From his small angle, Clovis looked up. Alysson's nod was imperceptible.

Alysson said, "You are mad, Jenny. Mad and wicked and foolish. And whatever you suffered in the past can't excuse your wickedness now."

Jennine loomed over her, pointing at her in fury. "You know nothing about the misery I experienced before coming here," she spat. "You pride yourself on being a virgin? Nineteen years, and still untouched! I was seven when I was raped the first time, and by someone far worse than Vymer."

Alysson kept her own voice calm and spoke slowly, ensuring Jennine's full attention. As she spoke, she kept her eyes focused and

461

did not watch Clovis creep silently from his seat, approaching Jennine from behind. But she saw the flicker of his shadow and she saw the knife raised, the sun catching the edge of the blade.

"I'm not proud of being a virgin, Jenny," she said. "Actually, I'm ashamed of it. I should have agreed to be Ludovic's mistress from the start. And perhaps he was in on your plots and plans all along, and perhaps he wasn't. I'll never know now, so I prefer to think the best of him. I think he was always suspicious of you and I'm sure he didn't like you, but I believe he never suspected the real truth. No one could guess how disgusting you actually are. I loved Ludovic and I'm still in love with him, and I don't think he was capable of such wickedness, and he didn't ever lead me on. He was always gracious and kind and understanding and he wanted to take me away from you. And I don't think anyone is worse than Vymer. In fact, I think it was him that killed Pagan. Humphrey is odd and simple and childish. He isn't a villain, but Vymer is. I think everything you say is a pack of lies."

Jennine leaned over, one knee on the mattress, and slapped Alysson's face very hard. The corner of her square ruby ring cut into the soft flesh below Alysson's eye. Jennine's cleavage quivered, her breasts bursting from the low neckline. She pressed her nose down to Alysson's and hissed. "You could have had my friendship. You could have become more than the little simpleton you really are, more than just that silly boy's discarded mistress. I'd have made you important. And it's true Vymer can be rough. He's a brutal man, but what he does, he does for love of Humphrey. Then my Humphrey has his own moods – and moments of – raptus." She grabbed Alysson's shoulder, pulling at her shift. "You'll find out in time just what he's capable of. Now I'll inform the countess how mean you are. She'll have you whipped. Then I'll let Vymer loose."

Clovis stabbed. The knife slipped through the pink silk and between Jennine's ribs with barely a pause. The rush of warm blood seemed to sigh as it soaked outwards, staining the pink gown red. Jennine's eyes rolled up and she slumped forwards, crushing Alysson beneath her. But as she fainted, she squealed once. The sound wailed, hung in the air, and stopped on a rattle.

Alysson squeezed herself from under the voluptuous squash of her gaoler's body, and scrambled out. She stared at Clovis. Clovis stared back. He still gripped the little knife, bloody at his side. He shook his head, whispering very quietly. "If Vymer heard that, the bugger'll think it were you. I reckon he won't come a running."

"But we want him in," Alysson whispered back. "Otherwise we can't get out. The door's locked and he's guarding the corridor." She stared down briefly at Jennine. The small black hole in her back just above her waist, was still oozing blood. "Do you think she's - dead?"

"No. The bitch is breathing, look. So we sharpened it fer nigh an hour, but a silly little blade like that ain't gonna to do nobody in for good." He dropped the knife with a sudden clatter. Alysson automatically raised her finger to her lips. Clovis frowned. "Thought we wants the bugger to hear and come in? Besides, the bitch'll come round pretty soon. Only fainted she has. Knock her out quick. We can't take 'em both at once."

"She's losing a lot of blood," whispered Alysson dubiously.

Clovis shook his head. "Not enuff. Get on wiv it."

It had started to rain. The oppression of the waiting storm still hung heavy, the clouds darkened and the first heavy drops of rain pattered against the window panes.

Alysson used the ale pitcher. Thick glazed terracotta, the jug broke over Jennine's head, shattering shards and crumbling red dust on the bed. Jennine grunted and her body jolted once in a sudden spasm. Her headdress had dislodged and her pale hair tumbled from its pins. Her head opened with a vicious cut and began to bleed in a thick sickly trickle. Alysson peered down. "She's still breathing," she said, "but she looks ghastly."

"Kill the bitch," insisted Clovis. "Wot will she do later, when she wakes up if'n she ain't dead? Come and get us an' pissing flay us alive, she will."

"She won't," said Alysson. "Because we'll be far away." She leaned over, both arms beneath her past mistress's prone body. The weight was greater than she expected. She heaved, and the body rolled face up across the bed. Jennine's mouth was open and gulping for air, but the eyes were tight closed, the beautiful blonde lashes thick over her cheeks like small dead spiders. Alysson looked down and saw she now had the woman's blood on her hands and shift. She wiped her palms on the old counterpane.

"You looks a bit of a mess," Clovis conceded. "Better put summit proper on before we runs away, or we'll have the sheriff after us for improper undress. Then we'll be back in the pokey afore we've even had a chance to taste freedom, and then they'll find out wot we done, and that'll mean the swing."

Alysson nodded. She hurried to the pile of clothes Jennine had brought with her. On top was her blue silk gown, worn only for Ludovic in the past. She struggled to put it on, and had to ask for help with the hooks and laces. Clovis, ham fingered, was embarrassed. "I'm sorry," Alysson whispered. "But we must look as respectable as possible. Should I brush my hair, do you think?"

They stood in the middle of the room, staring at each other. There had been no sound from outside, and no sign of the door unlocking. Clovis shook his head again. "You'll do," he whispered. "Now, we knocks for the bugger. I stands behind the door. When it opens, then I runs in and stabs the bastard. You gotta be ready wiv the jug."

"It's broken," Alysson indicated the handle, which was all that remained intact. "I'll find something else."

"So this is it." Clovis shrugged. "Kill or get killed. One last chance."

Alysson took a deep breath. "It's worth all the risks. Or we'll be here forever."

"Is you scared?" Clovis had grabbed up the knife again, wiped its blade on the rug, and taken a good hold of the bone hilt. "You ain't, is you? I reckon yous too much a battler to muck it up now."

She had no clear idea of whether she was afraid. The anger and the desperation were too great. But the terror of failing at the final stage made her ice cold. "I'm all right," she muttered. She held both hands behind her, hidden carefully by the folds of her skirts. One hand gripped the cracked wooden wash bowl, the other held her little mirror, not heavy but with glass that would break and prove sharper than a knife. "Go on. I'm ready. Get behind the door, don't breathe loudly - and knock."

Alysson stood very still. She felt her legs tremble and shook her head, forbidding fear. Then, with a flooding determination, she thought of Ludovic. She thought of his own pain from months in a prison far more terrible than her own, without warmth or comfort, company or decent food. She thought of his cell door grinding open and the gaoler informing him of his death warrant. She thought of his slow steps across the stone slabs in the Tower's great shadow, shackled and led to the block, the priest murmuring at his side. She thought of him kneeling in the sawdust and straw, and laying his head on the stained wood. She heard the swing of the axe slicing air, and she began silently to cry. She was no longer afraid.

Clovis knocked on the inside of the door. Three sharp taps, as Jennine had always done. Alysson looked over at the bed where Jennine still lay unmoving. Her blood was drying in the heat and turning black, pin points of ruby catching the muted light from the window. Alysson's stomach heaved. It had been a thoughtless mistake to leave the woman so visible. She should have been hidden, covered by blankets and pillows. It was now too late. The key was turning and the door was opening.

Vymer slammed the door hard open. Hidden behind, Clovis took the force against his chest and nose, and wheezed. Vymer hearing nothing, marched in, staring only at Alysson. The door remained wide at his back, gaping its shadows. "Well, trollop? Where's my lady?"

Alysson smiled. Her cheeks were wet and her eyes blurred. "In the garderobe. She'll be out in a minute."

Vymer did not look towards the bed, which was across the chamber and partially behind him. He did not see Clovis. Through the coarse linen of his shirt and the thick hide of his skin, the blade hardly penetrated. He barely felt the stabbing knife, but he realised what had happened. Vymer turned in a fury and grabbed Clovis by the arm, wrenching it behind him, almost cracking his elbow. "Wot the fuck, little varmint?"

Alysson hit him first with the bowl. She used all the force she had, reaching up and bringing the base down heavily on top of his skull. Vymer turned from Clovis, shaking his head in puzzlement. His brilliant red hair fell shaggy and matted into his eyes. Through the hair a wide graze oozed beads of blood. He swore, and rushed at Alysson. Clovis immediately stabbed him again, first in the shoulder and then in the hand. Vymer never felt the small wound to his shoulder muscle, but the cut to the back of his hand was long and deep. Immediately he swung backwards, catching Clovis above the ear. Clovis crumpled.

Vymer came at Alysson again. She smashed the mirror against her own raised knee, dropped the frame and grabbed one long splinter of silvered glass. She held it up high before her and stuck it straight into Vymer's chest.

He stared in amazement. His mouth dropped open. Blood pumped up from his throat and collected around the stumps of his teeth. His eyes were wide and red veined. His words stuck against his tongue and became growls. "Filthy bitch. I'll tear you limb from fucking limb. I'll rape you ragged and toss you in the moat." He lunged.

"The bugger ain't dead," Clovis wailed, scrambling up from the ground and rubbing his head. "Hit him again."

Alysson darted sideways, still clutching the broken splinter of mirror. She felt the sting of her own blood as the edges ripped into her palm. She tried to dodge Vymer's grappling fury. His huge hands were reaching wild and erratic, his eyes half blinded. Alysson struck again. The point of glass caught the man's wrist and dragged upwards, tearing all along his forearm. He staggered back, nursing the sudden pain.

Clovis came again from behind. He had time to aim, and stuck the tiny knife hard to the hilt in the back of Vymer's neck. Vymer dropped to his knees, toppled forwards, and crashed face down to the floor. He lay shuddering a moment. Beneath him was the fading stain where the mess of Pagan's remains had sunk into the floorboards. Now there was Vymer's blood.

Alysson stared a moment, then knelt and rummaged inside the man's shirt, pulling it open. The iron key to the door was strung around his neck. Alysson used the shard of glass to cut the string, took the key and beckoned Clovis. They both crept to the door. One look behind. Jennine was stirring. She moved slightly with a guttural sigh, rolling to her side, her eyelids flickering.

Vymer lay still, the blood soaking his clothes, his hair and the ground beside him. "He's dead," muttered Clovis.

Alysson shook her head. "No. His fingers are twitching. We have to get out quick. I'll lock the door behind us."

"Fort my aim were better," Clovis sighed. "But reckon the knife were too little. I musta struck too low." He gazed accusingly at the small stained blade still clutched in his fist.

The door stood wide as Vymer had left it, the hot gloom silent beyond. Clovis ran out, still holding tight to the knife. Alysson dropped the piece of shattered mirror, her blood soaked fingers now clutching the key. As she hauled the great door shut behind them, it swung on rusted hinges and clanged fast. Shaking and barely able to push the key in, she heard it turn with the harsh iron grating she had heard a hundred times over the past three months. She grabbed Clovis's hand and together they ran at once down the little winding stairs.

It was very dark. They could hear the desperation of their own breathless panic, and the patter of their feet echoing on the stone. As they circled downwards, the first halo of light from the landing window loomed up through the shadows. Clovis had Vymer's blood on the soles of his shoes and his feet slid on the worn treads. Alysson's hold on his hand kept him upright.

They were near the bottom. Then the shape of the shadows abruptly changed and something large blocked the incoming light. A body swayed, filling the gap. Then, bending slightly, perplexed at something, the man twisted his head and peered up into the gloom.

Alysson stopped with a gasp, one foot poised in the air. Clovis clutched at her. She stepped back, feeling her way, both hands now to the cold curved wall enclosing the steps at either side. Clovis wriggled in front, ready with the knife. Alysson had left her own small weapon behind, and held nothing but the key to her prison door.

"Who's that? What's going on?"

A voice she knew, but muffled by sudden thunder. The summer storm had burst at last. Beyond the castle turrets, the lightning broke and a torrent of rain slammed against the windows.

Alysson stood very still and did not answer. The peering head bent a little lower, and lit from behind, the face suddenly shone clear white. The casement window on the lower landing became luminous just before the thunder exploded. It lit the man and the long shining sword he carried unsheathed. For one hideous moment, Alysson thought it was somehow Vymer.

CHAPTER FIFTY-ONE

"And you've kept this from me, sir?" Ludovic demanded. "For more than two months?"

"Since St. Edmund's Day, my son. I had no option. You may think what you wish."

Ludovic sighed. "Was I so feeble, you couldn't tell me about my own brother?"

"You had watched one brother die," his father said. "You were nigh dead yourself. Knowing would have hindered, not helped you. There was nothing you could do. And I am not inept, Ludovic. I did everything I considered necessary."

"And before he left the country, he told you about us? The attack at sea? Gerald and I held captive on his own property?"

His lordship nodded. "He told me. And I did not tell you, my son, for a father has a duty to protect all his sons. Your anger might have inspired retaliation. Were it not for the attack at sea, your original escape from the country would likely have proved successful. You would now both have been comfortably settled in Flanders. Gerald would not have died, and you would have been saved many months in prison and never experienced the torture that has almost maimed you. Some desire for vengeance against Brice would therefore have been excusable." He sighed, standing abruptly and walking to the window. He stood, his back to Ludovic, and stared out to the sun dappled river. "There was another consideration that inspired my silence," he continued at last. "Brice was also – let us say – considering a revenge of sorts – after his unexpected arrest at the Tower. Hearing of Gerald's execution, he came at once. But he was recognised, as should not have been, and taken almost immediately by the guards. He believes you laid information against him, accusing him of piracy. He saw no other motive for his arrest, and no other manner in which the Constable would have known of him except by your laying a personal complaint before the authorities." The earl turned suddenly and regarded his son. "Did you do so, Ludovic?"

Ludovic stared up at his father. "No. How could I have? I thought him still in Kent or at sea. I was with you. You never left me. You know I could not have done so."

"You might have," sighed the earl. "While held captive in the Tower, you might have informed the guards, perhaps gaining some credence for yourself by giving information against another. You had every reason for righteous anger."

"I was furious," glowered Ludovic. "But I would have killed him myself, had I wanted him dead. And after Gerald, I did want him dead. But not to give him over to the authorities. Good God, Father, how can you ask?"

The earl shook his head. "I thought not, but could not be sure. For a long time I believed it possible that Brice spied for the crown. Treachery, my son, is inherent in times such as these, and the crown pays well."

"But has never paid me, which should be clear enough. Nor, it now appears, paid Brice. But is a pirate a better man than a traitor?"

"You forget," sighed the earl. "We now live in a land ruled by an anointed Tudor king, and loyalty means different things to different people. In truth, it is Gerald who was the traitor." Ludovic glared and the earl waved a hand vaguely to the ceiling. "Yes, yes, I know. But let us not pretend innocence, my boy. We both support the Plantagenets in our hearts, though only Gerald was prepared to act on his beliefs. So we are all traitors. But a king, however you may dislike him and despise his claims, still represents the land of our birth. We have a

470

duty to king and country. We would not be alone in believing one way, and acting another."

"Though innocence seems no barrier to the rack," Ludovic said, turning away. "Perhaps hypocrisy merits its own punishments. But I hate to think too long on the past. Now I only need know about Brice. He's gone then? To Italy?"

"Officially banished," said his lordship. "And has chosen Venice I believe. La Serenissima has much in common with your brother's ambitions. There his talents will be appreciated. No doubt he will spy both for and against the Doge, and become wealthy. One day he may return here. But he will not return as my son."

"Then he'll have sailed with that filth Naseby," Ludovic snapped. "I hope the damned Cock's Crest sinks, with all onboard lost at sea."

"My dear boy," said the earl, once again taking a seat across from the window, "you assume too much as usual. Your brother and his companion were arrested and taken to the Marshalsea. After some weeks Brice stood his trial and was found guilty of piracy. But because of his birth and title he was freed, to be banished by the king for the term of twenty years. However, the other man, being a commoner and miscreant, did not receive such a lenient sentence. He was found to be the more guilty, and now rots in gaol awaiting death. He will be hanged as a pirate at low tide, as is usual. There is some delay however, while the remainder of his crew is discovered, rounded up, and sentenced to hang with their captain. Naseby is to be kept alive until he can be forced to identify his principal men. He remains in the Marshalsea."

"William of Berkhamstead," Ludovic muttered, more to himself than to his father. "I saw him after Gerald – saw him running, unsheathing his sword. And this morning I spoke to him and he alluded – clearly he knew about Brice. He said very little since he obviously presumed I knew myself. Yet how would he recognise Brice?"

"Your brother accompanied me to court several times in the past, Ludovic," the earl said. "I do not know this Berkhamstead, but it is possible Brice may have. Since I could not take Humphrey to Westminster on the rare occasions I was required to attend, and invariably chose not to take your mother, I sometimes requested your brother's attendance. And upon acceptance at the palace, I believe he returned alone, and was seen there on occasion. He had his own – motives."

Ludovic shook his head. "I saw him there once. I assume his piracy involved others, selling or lending. Collecting ransoms perhaps. Corruption at court is hardly rare and no doubt Brice felt quite at home there. But dammit, I'd like to know what Berkhamstead knows."

"You will not, however, attempt to satisfy your curiosity," the earl continued. "You have been ordered not to return to court by the king himself. He does not like his orders ignored and will not be merciful a second time. I forbid you to return to Westminster to question this person. You have no reason to mourn Brice's departure. Think on Gerald, and let the matter rest."

"Very well. I will not return to Westminster Palace," said Ludovic softly. "But I shall visit the Marshalsea."

The earl stood again and strode back to the window. His face was expressionless, his voice impatient. "You will no doubt do as you wish, as always," he said, "whatever the consequences. Let us hope this excursion brings less severe consequences than the last." He turned again, facing Ludovic. "Since you intend taxing your strength to this extent, I can only presume the matter is of some importance to you. I shall therefore not forbid it. But I insist on some things, my son, and I trust you will comply. You will become embroiled in no private vendetta. And in no place, either here or abroad, will you attempt to trace your brother."

Ludovic's eyes narrowed. "A surprising demand, sir. It makes me wonder –"

"It is quite futile to wonder, my son," remarked the earl. "Nor do I intend explaining myself further. You will simply strive to remember your duty to your father."

—◆—

Ludovic left the next morning for the Marshalsea, but he did not cross the Thames by the Bridge. He rode down to the Strand quay and called for a showte. He then rode his horse onto the boards of the flat bottomed boat, dismounted carefully, and sat there, holding tight to the reins. The horse snorted, rolling its eyes at the sullen flowing water. Ludovic was ferried across river to the quay at Southwark, paid the fourpenny fare, and rode his horse up onto the far bank. He did not look back. Behind him rose the southern entrance to the Bridge and its massive stone arch. The gate had opened two hours back and traffic was intense. And above the raised portcullis were spiked the heads of traitors executed by the crown, paraded as a warning to every man who passed beneath, or saw from afar, or smelled the decaying flesh of the shameful dead. Ludovic slumped his shoulders, breathed shallow, and rode on.

At the stables beyond the prison's rambling two story building he dismounted again, gave his sword from the saddle harness over to the wardens, and asked to see one Baldwin Naseby. A gentleman dressed, in spite of the warm weather, in black and silver damask trimmed in sable, was rarely denied. Ludovic was shown in at once.

The cage was cramped. A bucket stood in the far corner but its slops had overflowed. Yellow slime and mucus trailed across the flagstones. Six men lounged on the ground, eyes closed in apathy. One of the men was Naseby.

The warden poked at him through the bars. "A visitor, you worthless lump of shit. Wake up and mind your manners."

Naseby opened his eyes, but the disappointment was obvious. He had expected someone else. Ludovic smiled. "I am," he said, "quite remarkably content to see you here, Naseby. You, on the other hand, seem less elated. Now I wonder, whom did you think your visitor might be?"

Naseby turned away, not bothering to answer. The warden again reached through the bars with his stick, ramming it hard into Naseby's chest. "Answer the gentleman, or I'll have you thrashed."

"No need for that." Ludovic shook his head. "Indeed, I should be obliged if you leave me to talk to the prisoner alone. There'll be no danger to either of us, I assure you." He untied his purse, passed over a shilling, and waited until the warden had stomped off before turning back to the cage and its occupants. "So, Naseby," he said softly, "where exactly is my brother?"

Naseby looked up and grinned suddenly. His gums were bleeding. Every one of his teeth had been knocked out. His voice was slurred and sibilant. "Worked that one out, have you? Well, I'll be telling naught to the bugger as betrayed his own, and is the cause of me kept in this hell hole and waiting for the gallows."

Ludovic leaned back against the stone wall behind him, regarding the men through the rusted iron of the cage. "It seems my brother also believed this of me," he said thoughtfully. "But since I also once thought it of him, I can hardly pretend outrage. However, the truth is simply that in spite of all provocation I did not lay information or complaint against my brother, nor even against you, my friend. Nor do I have any idea who did. I was arrested almost immediately after leaving your – protection last year. I spent many months in the Tower and then saw my favourite brother executed. I knew nothing of Brice's arrest until yesterday. Now I'm aware he's been officially banished but I suspect he still remains in England. In which case, you will know precisely where he is. And now you will tell me. Otherwise I shall arrange some form of – let us say – inducement."

Naseby grinned again. "Not sure I believes those as claims innocence so easy," he said. "So t'wasn't you as got us done for piracy, you says? Might be true. Might not. Now, with me, like I told you afore, I'm a man as deals honest, for what I says, I does. If I says I done it then I did it, and if I says I done nothing, then it's naught but the truth. But with you high and mighty lordships, there's no telling, is there?" He crawled to his feet, lurching up to the bars to face Ludovic, hands gripping to the irons. In spite of his long incarceration, his boots, old leather bleached with sea water, still held the smell of salt. "But if you wants information o' me," he said, keeping his voice low, "well, I reckon t'would be better to bribe than to threaten."

"First give me your information," Ludovic smiled, "and I'll decide what it's worth. A nobleman also keeps his word, and I give you mine. If you tell me where my brother is, I shall pay you. If I find him where you tell me he is, I shall return and pay more. If I go where you send me and find no one, I shall also return. And I shall also pay, but in another coin."

"I seems to remember you lied plenty when I had you on my ship afore. I can't trust a man as lies. What pledge does you give?"

"None," Ludovic shook his head. "I'm not playing calcio, to chase you through a maze of absurdities. Tell me what you know, and quick."

Naseby sighed. "Being as how my funds is getting mighty low," he muttered, "I'll tell. You give the warden enough for my keep for a sennight, and extra for ale and a blanket, then when you finds his lordship right enough, come back and pay another month. Lest I'm already dangling on the end of the rope, that is. It's a bargain?"

"A bargain. Though I'm surprised your own purse doesn't cover it."

"As it happens," Naseby leaned very close to the bars, his voice little more than a whisper, "was his lordship as had trust of the money chests. Paid up plenty afore the trial and promised more, but there's been nothing for nigh on a month, and I've been waiting a mighty weary time for his coming. Living on black bread don't suit me none. If it weren't for old Pigsnout over there, I'd be bloody hungry by now."

Ludovic gazed at the figure Naseby had indicated. A thin shouldered man in a torn shirt over bare legs lay on the ground in the shadows. If his description fitted the name, it was too dark to tell and remained obscure. "Why would a hungry man choose to share his rations?" Ludovic said. "The creature looks more dead than alive."

"Well, that he is," Naseby nodded more cheerfully. "Bugger's wife paid a month in advance for his supper, and a hot dinner every day with ale. And me with nothing. Too much for me it were. So I wrung the bastard's skinny neck like a hen for the pot. And it's a pot I gets in exchange, for till the warden finds it's a corpse he's feeding, I gets the grub. And there's no stupid shit scared bugger in here will tell on me, not after they seen what I can do when I wants. And I reckon you won't tell neither, not if you wants to find your so noble brother."

Ludovic raised an eyebrow. "Hardly your first murder, and quicker than the gallows perhaps," he said. "So tell me what I want to know, Naseby, and make sure it's not only the truth, but sufficient of the truth to lead me to him."

Ludovic did not inform the earl. Although directly disobeying his father's orders, he had known his parent for long enough to assume that the old man knew exactly what would happen and was happening, but preferred not to be told. The preparations for their return to Sumerford had begun but were of necessity, slow. With consideration for Ludovic's condition, although many weeks of treatment and rest had by now ensured a more than partial recovery, the earl instructed his servants to arrange for a leisurely departure. The sumpters, litters and carts were ordered in advance, the guards and drivers paid ahead. The accompanying Sumerford staff took over from the hired staff at the Strand, and began to scrub out and pack the chests. Clothes were brushed through with Fuller's Earth, leather polished, fur combed. The doctor was called to perform a final examination, and to give his opinion as to the patient's condition and his suitability for lengthy and tedious travel. No attempt was made at haste. His health was the principal consideration but Ludovic suspected the pace was also to give him time; sufficient to discover Brice's hiding place and search him out. That the earl already knew where Brice stayed, Ludovic did not doubt but it remained irrelevant. The Strand house had been hired since late January with six month's rental paid. Nearly all had passed. It was time to go home.

July swept in sultry and wearisome. London's summer stench steamed beneath heaving clouds. Storms rolled up the Thames from the sea, washing the muck of the gutters into the river and saving the raykers their work. The cobbles dried briefly, collecting more excrement for the next downpour.

Having rested two days after the strain of the Marshalsea visit, Ludovic rebound the bandages which still supported his knees and ankles, and planned a second solitary journey. He left a brief message with his secretary, not to be opened unless he failed to return by the following day. He then buckled on his sword, wedged a short handled knife down the cuff of his left boot and a sheathed kidney dagger tucked into his belt. Then he pulled the oiled hood over his long feathered hat, took up the reins and mounted.

It was raining as he set off for Piccadilly Lane and the orchards leading past the convent's garden, before turning north and heading for the heaths and villages. Half a rainbow smeared its pastel colours between sky and grass. Ludovic rode beneath it as though he entered a gateway, seeming a promise of sorts.

CHAPTER FIFTY-TWO

The voice was too indistinct at first to hear words. After some moments, Ludovic knew it was a song. Gradually the melody impinged, becoming clear. It was the morning blessing that a nurse might chant to a waking child, with a pretty tune and simple advice to guide him through his stumbling hours until the night's prayers would take him again to his cot.

It was unexpected and Ludovic smiled. He listened idly, enjoying a brief nostalgia. It seemed to him a very long time since he had remembered his own past life with any pleasure. He was alone and the lanes were deserted, so he said aloud, "Is it you then? And do you sing to yourself, or to me?"

The song faded with a soft Amen. "To both of us," said the disembodied voice, "since we both now face a better future. I see you have discovered your brother. You are on your way to see him. I have discovered myself. And I am waiting to see my brother."

Ludovic nodded. "It's true then. You are Edward."

The rain had stopped, the air was shining and fresh, and the rainbow had completed its arc. Ludovic slowed his horse, leaning back in the saddle. The high sun dazzled his eyes, shimmering across the wet grass and dripping diamonds from the oak leaves. The soft voice murmured directly into his ears. "Yes. Edward. It is good at last to know my name. You should have called me by it before."

"I did not know it." Ludovic's horse ambled, then paused to graze. "At first I believed you were someone else; a child I was searching for. He was the brother of the woman I care for, but his body was never found. I believe he died badly."

"I died badly," said the voice on the breeze. "I died in battle. I remember it clearly now, and the slam of the lance to my shoulder. I fell, blood in my eyes and a sword to my neck. It could have been a hero's death, but I was buried in an unmarked grave amongst the men who fought for me. No one knew me, no one found me. I had already lost my name. I was taught to hide my identity so often over the years, I accepted any name I was given and they called me everything except who I truly was. I died a stranger to the land of my birth, unknown to the people who should have called me king. But most of all I was a stranger to myself."

"You were killed at Stoke?" Ludovic slumped, inert, his spine tired and sore, allowing his horse time to feed, welcoming the sun's new warmth on his back. He eased his joints, loosening control and the strain of the stirrups. "Had I been older, I'd have fought at Stoke," he murmured. "But I'd have followed my father's colours, and fought for Tudor against the Earl of Lincoln." The gentle heat steamed, drying his velvet and feathers. It was a strangely bright and comfortable moment to talk to ghosts. "I'm glad I was never in the battle since it would have been the wrong side. I ask pardon for that."

"The Earl of Lincoln was my cousin. Dear John. As my uncle's heir, he should have claimed the throne for himself, but he chose to fight for me." The voice trailed off, lost in memories. "He was a great man and I was honoured," it continued softly. "He made me proud to be my father's son. At first he encouraged me to use my own name and rally the country behind a royal Plantagenet. I declared myself in Ireland, but Henry Tudor distorted the truth and put out false documents, saying I claimed to be another. It seemed almost unimportant. I had been so long incognito, it became a habit." The voice lapsed, then renewed. "Now my brother should be crowned Richard IV. But he will also die under a false name, as I did. A miserable irony."

Ludovic sighed, tightened his knees and urged his horse on again. "Irony?" He smiled. "You remember a great deal at last. The first time you came to me, you asked only why."

There was another pause, and for some time Ludovic thought his invisible companion gone. He waited at ease in the saddle, enjoying the rest, the gentle sunbeams, and the peculiar satisfaction of speaking to phantoms without either fear of devilry or doubt of his own sanity.

Then the voice came stronger, echoing across the low grasses, louder than the breeze. "Now I know why. I was still a child and awaiting my coronation when witnesses proved me bastard, and I thought myself lost then. But I have no resentment against my uncle. He took my crown but he did only what was forced upon him, and he continued to treat me well. Entrusted to my aunt abroad, I was sorry to hear of my uncle's death in battle. I did not expect the same to happen to me just two years later. After I was slain, the living called out to me and their thoughts dragged me back into the mists of life. But when I answered their calls they were frightened and closed their minds. Some thought me already dead years back, killed in the Tower. Some thought I was my cousin, others thought I was still not dead at all. Then they confused me with some simple child, working in the royal kitchens. I was a warrior and died as a warrior, but confusion surrounded me and my body lay unclaimed. I couldn't find my way onwards into the golden places of the pardoned dead. I was left drifting, faceless and nameless."

Ludovic shook his head. "Do we hold the dead back from their Heaven then, with our memories and our sadness?" But it was not the prince he thought of now. Each night he still saw Gerald's body leaning forward across the executioner's block. He sighed. "Must we let our loved ones go?"

"We can be trapped here if the living need us too desperately," the voice said. "But for me, the living called me without knowing me. And the great battle which should have placed me on my throne, has now been subverted with Tudor naming some child he found to play the part, though never seen at Stoke. A boy paid to take my place and deceive the English people."

"Lambert Simnel," said Ludovic. "Tudor claimed the child was set up by his enemies, to pretend the part of a prince. But of course he was set up by Tudor himself to hide the truth. So Tudor publicly forgave him and took Simnel into his employ."

The floating voice turned harsh and angry. "This usurping king treats his people as fools, and they accept it. They believe his ludicrous stories. A little peasant boy? Ten years of age, or thereabouts? Leading armies? A dupe so absurd, yet supposedly fooled my cousin Lincoln into abandoning his own royal claims in order to fight to the death for a common simpleton? Why do such nonsense tales gain credence?"

"It is wise to believe a vindictive and powerful king."

The voice sank again like an ebbing tide. "My mother was not intimidated. She supported my cause and even though her daughter was queen, she turned away from Tudor and put her faith in me. Would she have done that for a stranger and no relation to herself, a pathetic deceiver and an obvious lie?"

Ludovic shook his head. "And a hundred Irish lords, so foolish they were taken in by an ignorant child bare able to read or speak his name, yet crowned him king in Ireland? Your mother was made to suffer for supporting you. Tudor locked her away in penury. And now we have another supposed peasant boy, this time a foreigner pretending nobility to claim Tudor's throne. But the English lords know the truth. They know, but choose not to say, for few of them will ever again risk their lives or titles for a hopeless cause. I myself chose not to, though was punished for the little I did. Tudor has made himself too powerful."

"He hates the Plantagenets."

"He has reason."

"But perhaps," wondered the voice, "it isn't Tudor who shattered the House of York at all. We undermined our own foundations, like a castle besieged by its own lords. It seems my father was a wilful and indulgent king."

He had been too young for politics, but Ludovic knew the sorrows of the past, told by his father. "All England knows Edward IV was secretly married before he wed the Woodville queen in yet another secret but bigamous union. I doubt Tudor would ever have dared challenge for power had that not happened."

"I was angry when Uncle Richard accepted the crown." The voice wavered a little. "But he saved our lives by sending us to my aunt in Flanders, with money and his friends to keep us safe."

"And to make sure no one raised a rebellion against him in your names."

"That too. He protected himself while protecting us. I blamed him then, but not now."

Ludovic lowered his face over his steed's neck, running his fingers through the long coppery mane. The ambling horse had stopped once more, sensing the lack of direction, pausing to pull at clover through the tangled grass. When Ludovic spoke again, it was a whisper muffled by the low wind, the bees in the wild flowers and the sounds of satisfied chewing. "Yet you stay?" Ludovic wondered. "You have a rightful place, either in Purgatory or in Paradise. Now you know your name. You remember your life. Your uncle, your cousins, your father, and so many of the countrymen who fought for you, they're all dead. Don't they look for you beyond the grave?"

"Yes. And they call to me," the voice whispered back. "I'm ready to go where they call. I wait only for my brother. What happened to me before, now happens to him. He must not give up his name. He must not lose his identity in fear."

"Most men fear death," said Ludovic.

"They should fear life," murmured the voice, clarity fading a little like a leaf carried high off by the breeze. "Death is so easy. Alive, you have a worldly future. But one day all futures stretch backwards instead of forwards. Everything bright turns into the shadows of the past."

Ludovic smiled. "What cheerful company."

"Loving is the only happiness," whispered the voice. "I never had a woman."

"So losing love is the greatest misery?" Ludovic's own words breathed Alysson's face back into his mind so strongly that for a moment, he gasped, as if he might reach out and touch her. Her memory had endlessly warmed him throughout the wretchedness of his imprisonment, even though he had expected only death for himself at the end. But hope of finding her waiting had since lapsed, knowing the long months he had been gone, and how he might return lame and aged and disillusioned. "I've written," he said, "many times, both to the girl I want, and to others who know her. No message comes back. Only silence. And she was never truly mine."

"I cannot be your messenger," sighed the voice. "I know nothing of women. My brother had a wife and he loved her, but she was taken from him. He's coming over soon. Until then I will stay and comfort him, talking to him in his dreams as I talked to you when you were a prisoner in the same cold place. I will be the first light he sees when his eyes close forever. Then I'll take his hand and lead him over."

Ludovic lifted his head. "I believe I'll miss you. Once I tried to help you, but in the end you helped me far more. I shall be sorry not to hear from you again."

"You won't ever hear me," the words floated back, the voice now trailing like clouds. "But I will hear you sometimes. And maybe I'll find a way to watch over you as my uncle once watched over me. But your own trials are almost over. There is very little more you need do now to earn happiness. Your doorways are opening. You don't need me anymore. My little brother needs me now."

"Then I pray for you both," said Ludovic. "And I thank you, and wish you all the blessings of Paradise."

But there was no one there.

For some miles Ludovic rode on without focused thought. The sun was slipping to the west as its warmth spread, replacing the shower with summer's placid expectations. But his reason for coming had dissipated with the whispered reminders of love, and his anger had burned away in the sunbeams. Bitter determination had dissolved into gentle hope and he discovered his mind rambling, recreating the unencumbered voice in his thoughts, pondering the words and sorrows of a dead prince. He thought of the new prisoner in the Tower and his probable fate, and he thought of how loyalty had been destroyed, and whether these dismal memories should be permitted to die as Gerald had, allowing the soul to move on into the sweet plains of the departed. If death was a warm and wholesome destiny, then danger took a different meaning. Most of all, fondly repeating her details into his mind like tapestry stitches, her almost forgotten

483

words and the vibrant touch of her brought back to life, he remembered Alysson.

By the time he remembered Brice, he no longer cared. But now so close, he did not turn his horse. He continued towards the place he had been told his brother now occupied, and wondered briefly what he would find, or whether an otherwise wasted day had at least been vindicated by the last words of a royal ghost. This had been his only companion when he was kept prisoner himself, and now this ghost had promised him – Edward Plantagenet, eldest son of the late King Edward IV, had promised him – that his trials were nearly over. He did not entirely believe it. But happiness promised from beyond Purgatory would surely be worthy of faith, and hold some hope of truth.

Meandering the open meadows, unhedged and unfenced, he had come to a farm house, long, low and thatched, that stood beside a creek. The horse stopped and bent to drink. Ludovic sat loose in the saddle, half thinking, half dreaming. He leaned down, scratching his horse's head between its ears. It tossed its mane, acknowledging affection. A gossamer dragonfly uncurled new born from the surface of the water. A cock crowed in the distance, but no farm animals grazed the land and the muddle of outhouses straddling the fields seemed quite abandoned.

The horse stretched its front legs, hooves in the splashing shallows. Ludovic looked down. He saw both his own rippled reflection, and that of one other man. For a moment, he thought it was another ghost, or perhaps simply a dream. He did not even bother to turn around.

The knife blade against his throat was suddenly cold. "So you came. He said you would never come, but I says as how you would. He's waiting."

The voice was disappointingly familiar. "Then put away your steel and take me to my brother," sighed Ludovic.

CHAPTER FIFTY-THREE

Brice was sitting beneath the window on the long farmhouse bench, scrubbed wood bleached by age and wear. The window panes were broken and the sunshine slanted in across the worn stone pavings, splashing scarlet brilliance over Brice's hair. His clothes were unclean and he was ungroomed. His shirt was open, torn and grimed with sweat. His legs were spread out before him and the wide flat blade of his sword was laid free of its scabbard across his knees. His metal shone, carefully attended, though the rest of him was not. Chickens pecked at the straw beside him and the trivets and iron chains for pots lay on an empty hearth where a deserted rat's nest nestled amongst the cold ashes. Once the fine kitchen of a wealthy farmer, the abandoned room was now as slovenly as its occupant.

Brice smiled. "How kind of you to visit, and at such a time, my dear. Yet in such a pitiful condition I see. You are woefully lame, little brother. It seems his majesty's displeasure proves almost as vengeful as my own."

Careful not to limp, Ludovic ducked into the sun-striped low ceilinged chamber, Naseby at his back. Avoiding the two broken and splintered benches, he pulled a stool from its corner and sat heavily. He smiled back at his brother. "It seems you're not enjoying the pleasure barges of Venice after all, my dear. Surely the Doge has had no time to spit you back yet. Is your fine ship run aground on the sandbanks of Kent, then? Or has pirating simply given you a taste for squalor?"

Brice continued smiling. "Naseby is the pirate, in case you forget, my love. I am a representative of England's noble heritage; the second heir to the earldom of Sumerford, and a knight of the realm." He tapped the hilt of his sword, as if its gilt inlay proved status. "As for squalor," he said, "I bought this property a year back, paid for with the death of its owner, a miserable wretch who owed me too much for too long. I'm selling, but with Tudor's taxes making misers of us all, the present market is beggarly. I'll take my time looking for a higher price, since I need to draw in funds for a new life abroad. I won't be forced to run in penury and I won't be hurried or harried. Which means, little brother, eliminating anyone who might lay information against me, or let the authorities know I'm still in England." Brice leaned forwards suddenly, fingers slipping around the grip of his sword. "And that means you, my dearest. Though you have your uses too." He laughed. "Naseby thanks you for financing his release."

Nasby remained knife in hand in the open doorway. His long shadow filled the room, spreading over the flagstones like spilt ink. The blocked sun filtered its lemon warmth in one thin stripe between his legs.

Ludovic did not bother to turn around. "We choose our friends as we see fit," he said. "But family comes unchosen. I'd never have picked you for brother, but having accepted you as a condition of my birth, I'll not turn traitor against you, and never have." He paused, but Brice said nothing, his eyes narrowing. Ludovic sighed. "I've motive, I agree. Piracy disgusts me. A thief is a vile creature unless starvation prompts him. But larceny at sea means cruelty for pleasure, with vicious greed the only other motive, and you've proved both. Discovering your secret appalled me, and Naseby repels me even more. If you'd not taken my ship and terrorised my crew, I'd have got Gerald safe away to Flanders. Instead I was imprisoned for months and put to the rack. But Gerald lost everything. It's a bitter end, execution for treason, and I trust you'll answer to God for your hand in it." The stool where Ludovic sat was squat to the ground and his knees had begun to throb. Standing strained him, but sitting too low was worse. He stood very slowly, hiding the pain in his joints as he leaned against the wall, gazing down at his elder brother. "I hold you responsible for Gerald's death," he continued. "And I'd do whatever needed if it could bring Gerald back. But I never informed against you, and never considered doing so. Nor would Gerald, since he held loyalty especially dear. So your banishment seems well deserved but I never caused your arrest, nor sought it."

Eyes narrowed and focused, Brice stared back. "Now, whether to believe you, my dear. I think perhaps not."

Ludovic shrugged. "You must have made as many enemies as livings you've stolen and ruined over the years. Why suspect me in particular?"

"Because those enemies are gone. I killed most and of those who lived on, none knew me by name. I remained free all these years until Naseby and you crossed paths, my dear."

"Naseby I mean to kill," Ludovic said. "But I'll do it myself, not send in the law. And I won't threaten you unless you force me to it. At least you came to Gerald's execution when you heard. That's a form of apology."

"Came, and was arrested."

"Not on my word." Ludovic shook his head. "I'll give you my pledge to that and I'll swear my innocence this once, but I'll not plead my case again. I despise you, my dear, and if you want to fight me over a false suspicion, I might welcome the chance. You know I can out-fight you."

Brice sneered. "Not as you are, my beloved. In the past, perhaps yes. But racked and lame? I hardly think so."

"Try me," said Ludovic.

"I will." Naseby marched fully into the room, still waving his knife, his hair dusting the unpainted ceiling beams. Toothless now, and thick tongued, his words were slurred. "I don't give a turd's squelch whether you speak the truth or a god-damned lie, it's all the same to me. I want you dead, be it a crippled bastard or a fit one, and you'll not outfight me neither way. No bugger has. No bugger does."

Ludovic regarded him with faint amusement. "And I thought you were grateful to me for saving you from the Marshalsea cages."

"No fucking gift o' yorn," Naseby objected, wiping dribbled saliva from his mouth onto his sleeve. "Was me had the sense to take your coin and bribe a guard to look t'other way. So I thank myself, not you. And when I called out as how Pigsnout was lying there dead so they comes to drag out the corpse, then I knocks out the two stupid bastards and were free with an open door and a guard paid to be more interested in his arse than his eyes. And since now you finds what I said about your brother were the truth and he's here right enough, I reckons you owes me the next instalment."

Ludovic laughed. "Perhaps I do. Perhaps I'll pay it in steel." He needed to sit again but did not do so, balancing himself against the wall and kept his eye on Naseby, judging his strengths and attitude. He remained ready for the sudden attack.

Brice interrupted. "Then if it's the truth, my beloved brother, that you never stood turncoat against me, will you help me now? I need a full purse or two if I'm to sail for Italy and not live there as a pauper. The Cock's Crest was commandeered and all her treasure taken by the crown. What coin I had safe in Kent was found by the king's men, and taken too. That property still legally belongs to Father, but he refuses to sell it or pay me out. He intends disinheriting me. That should please you, little brother."

"I knew it already. It seems just."

"With Gerald gone and me too, there's a damned fine inheritance coming to you one day, my dearest, unless Humphrey grabs it all." Brice again tapped the blade of his sword. "The misfortune of others is not the misfortune of all, it seems. So pay me now what you'll gain in the future. You're rich enough from all your smuggling, and you've a guarantee I'll not crawl whining to the authorities about your own illegal gains since I won't be here, nor could afford such visibility while I am. And I'll not return to piracy, if that matters to you. Naseby can take his own risks from now on. There's adventure of another kind to be found in Italy."

"Where cruelty and murder are as well practised as the Pope's prick."

"Ah, the unholy diversions of our saintly Alexander Borgia," Brice nodded. "And how typically mundane of you to care, my dear. But I shall study poisons, since the tainted goblet and the poisoned blade are the currency of Venice. Only boredom terrifies me. La Serenissima will suit me very well, but first I need money."

Ludovic pulled back the stool and sat heavily again with a sigh, suspecting his knees of trembling. Disguising pain, he stretched his legs, then loosened the buckle of his belt, bringing the hilt of the hidden knife within easy grasp. He murmured, "You think four months in the Tower left me rich?"

"But you have Father doting at your bedside, you have whatever coin you secreted beforehand, and you've another ship on your horizons. You always had two craft. With my own contacts at sea, I always knew what you were up to. So are both your ships capsized then, to leave you so bereft?"

Ludovic raised an eyebrow. "You know so much? Yet attacked the Fair Rouncie in ignorance that she was mine?"

"Salvami, salvami," Brice sighed. "I knew your ship, my dear, but Naseby, in his haste, did not. He can neither read a ship's name, nor recognise yours, never having seen it before. I would apologise for him, but at present he's all I have. Now give me your trust, little brother, and I shall give you precisely what I know you want, which at the moment only I can promise."

Naseby turned in sudden suspicion. He glared at both men. "You's better not be meaning what I reckons you might be," he growled. "And just remember I looks after myself, as always have."

Ludovic, ignoring Naseby, shook his head, still speaking to Brice. "What little I have remaining to me lies in Somerset. As for Father, he can't be persuaded against his will and you know it. His family pride is turned bitter, and that's something he'll never forgive."

"Family pride? I'm the least of it, my dear. One son executed for high treason, and the other arrested for the same crime. And Father had to swallow his damned pride while kneeling to Tudor anyway, even before the shame of Stoke. And then there's dearest Humphrey, the glorious heir. The next generation will be a proud one indeed."

"Father's already learned to live with Humphrey," said Ludovic.

"He could have chosen to overlook him and put you up as heir from the beginning, but decided not to. As for Gerald and myself, there's no shame to it in his mind, since he secretly supports our beliefs. It's only you tastes sour as ashes on his tongue."

"Piss on him then," muttered Brice.

The sun had brightened, washing the last shadows in glitter as Ludovic took stock. With little trust in his own legs, when attack came, as he knew it would, he planned on using other advantage, noting where the light was strongest, where each stool and bench stood, and how many paces there were to the door. He turned back, and smiled. "You've a poor promised bride left lonely somewhere, I believe? I heard Father arranged some sort of match, an heiress, naturally, to suit the proud Sumerfords. Ask her father to buy you off."

Brice snorted. "A nine years infant, daughter of some fool with more piss than sense up his codpiece. The girl's not even bleeding yet, and no use as a wife for another four or five years. A proxy marriage was to be held this Christmastide. They called it off as soon as they heard of my arrest. I'm hardly heartbroken."

Ludovic was intrigued. "You never met the girl?"

"It was her property, not her flesh I wanted. Sons are obligatory, but apart from that I've little interest in women." Brice shook his head. "Nor in boys, before you ask. I'll sweat for other passions, but not for lust and never for love."

"I believe it. You've no love in you to give." Ludovic resisted the urge to rub his knee joints. He further wondered, once forced to stand and fight, whether he'd fall before he swung his sword.

Brice smiled, as if guessing his brother's mind. "And you, my dearest, are as lame as a dotard, and you're a hypocrite besides. You whine like a querulous vintner about broken loyalties and poor Gerald's fate, but it's not him you miss. It's that common trollop's face in your thoughts, and her you're saving your money for. Let his damned lordship mourn lost family pride if he wishes, but if you bring a servant wench into your bed, I wager he'll throw you both out of it."

Before Ludovic's reply, Naseby interrupted, marching forwards again. "Still bleating over Sumerford honour? I shit on it. Get the silver you want from this snivelling cripple, my lord, and then send him home on his knees. Otherwise, give up your useless begging for I doubt you'll be getting neither purse nor promises out of him. I'll thrash the bugger instead and then cut his foul gullet."

"A sweet natured pair." Ludovic smiled. He slipped his thumbs casually inside his belt, fingers closer to his knife.

Brice nodded. "Indeed. So pay up, my love. Devise a manner of getting your money to me, promised and pledged, or I'll let this cannon loose. He's itching to fight, and you'll never last the distance as you are, even allowing for past expertise. A shame to kill you quick of course but a neat end is better after all, since I'm impatient and Naseby's temper is up. And don't think I'd scruple to fight you two to one, little brother, for I've no interest in any absurd pretence at chivalry."

Ludovic said, "Piracy, it seems, operates also on land, since it appears you've accepted my innocence, yet plan to murder me anyway." His left heel, ankle joint creaking, pivoted, ready to spring.

"Let me at him," Naseby complained. "Let me unarm the bugger at least."

Brice still smiled at Ludovic. "And have I truly accepted your protestations of innocence, my dear? Perhaps. But can I trust you now? When you leave here, if you leave here, whom will you confide in, my love? Can you return home without tumbling into temptation? Can you resist the urge to tell of your banished brother remaining in England, ready to do battle for coin? Can I risk leaving you free to babble at will?"

"Don't be a fool, Brice." Ludovic slid his left elbow back, swinging his coat a little away from the hang of his scabbard. He edged his right elbow forwards, ready to grasp the hilt. He said, "I'll not be threatened by my own brother, nor by any pirate scum. If you mean to kill me, get on with it."

"What impatience, little one." Brice still grasped the hilt of his sword, the fingers of his other hand playing along the blade, tapping against the steel like a woodpecker in the trees. "I've lost one brother to the axe. I've lost my father to his own pride. My mother is a braying jackass, my elder brother a senseless loon. Shall I destroy the only member of my family left to me?"

Ludovic said, "You already lost me, my dear, when I found you in Naseby's company, and at Gerald's death you made me your enemy. You'll never live in England again. You don't need a family. So make your play." He flexed the fingers of both hands and began to breathe deep and even. He felt the dark cold of Naseby's shadow to his right. He judged the distance.

"Culpa mia." Brice leaned back. He felt his power and savoured the taste. "So, life or death? And how to choose?" he smiled. "Which way shall I decide, I wonder?"

Naseby took one abrupt step forwards. Hearing the boot leather creak and the knife swing, Ludovic came up immediately on his left foot, turning to face the falling blade. In the same breath, he drew his sword with his right hand and his kidney dagger with his left.

He threw the dagger, heard the thud of contact, and spun, facing Brice again. Now behind him, Naseby fell heavily to the flagstones, his knife clattering beside him. Ludovic's sword point hovered at Brice's throat, pricking the skin. "Drop your metal," Ludovic said softly. "And tell your pappagallo to stay down, or my sword goes home and you never do."

Brice smiled. "Quick as ever, my love. I'm impressed." He held his hands clear of his own weapon, but did not remove it from his knees. "Though I've an idea your back is breaking. Your muscles are torn, every joint is pulling open and you are about to faint. You cannot fight us both, little brother."

"I'm habituated to pain," Ludovic said. "And your mule is all brute strength and little skill."

He heard Naseby scramble to his feet behind him, reclaiming his fallen knife. In an instant Ludovic slashed down, then hooked Brice's sword hilt, swinging it up high and wide. It hurtled, spinning in an arc of sunshine across the chamber and far out of reach. Brice slumped forwards, breathing fast. A wide cut across both his thighs marked the passage of Ludovic's sword edge. The black knitted hose sprang open, the flesh cut almost to the bone. Blood was pouring across his lap. Brice wheezed, his head reeling, unable to speak. Ludovic turned away, pivoting again, and faced Naseby. Naseby leaped forwards in fury. His shoulder was bleeding but he was otherwise unhurt. His long knife stabbed out and down. Ludovic danced back, his sword firm in his right hand. He parried, keeping light footed.

Naseby's toothless gape spat saliva. "Come on, you puddle of vomit. Come meet your death from a real fighting man as knows his trade. Knights and lords? Just a bilge drip o' ballast with no value nor worth beyond fish bait. They hides behind their armour, but you, you shit, have none. I'll slit you through, prick to teeth."

Ludovic ducked the next lunge and moved easily sideways, sweeping up his own fallen dagger from the ground. Then crossing his blades before his face, he caught Naseby's knife against his own steel and held it trapped. With two steps forwards, he forced Naseby slowly backwards. He knew his strength was limited, but he had judged the direction carefully. Unable to look back, Naseby shook his head and reeled, furious, stumbling away. He fell heavily over the unseen stool immediately behind him.

With his own grunt of pain from all joints, Ludovic knelt over the toppling man's flailing legs, sword slashing straight to Naseby's groin. Naseby gurgled, head rolling, trying to grapple for balance. Ludovic leaned further. He slid the point of his kidney dagger directly into Naseby's open eye. Naseby jerked and screamed once. The steel slid in further, smooth as dawn over the horizon. The knife point hit brain and bone. Ludovic disengaged and staggered quickly backwards. Blood gushed from Naseby's nose and mouth and both eyes as he slid heavy to the ground. The sweet perfumes of sun on damp grass from beyond the open doorway were now doused as Naseby lost control of his bowels and jerked, gargling blood. He was slow in dying.

Ludovic turned away. He could barely breathe. Though unwounded, every joint was inflamed and every bone and muscle screaming. He sat a moment beside the dying man, but looked up at his brother.

Brice stared down at his companion's corpse. "Enough," he whispered. "You have your victory. Now help me."

Ludovic shook his head. "You'll not bleed to death yet," he said, gasping for words. "Your bones aren't broken and your legs aren't

493

sliced right through. Crawl to the corner by the old table. That's where your sword fell. Take it and cut the shirt from your pirate friend. Use that to bind up your legs. Your horse is out back I imagine, and will carry you to some other place of hiding. But I won't help you, Brice. Not anymore."

"You'll leave me to die here?" Brice said. "Then kill me quick."

"I'll not kill you nor help you, though I'll forget you if I can," Ludovic said. He pulled himself partly up, grasping the edge of the hearth, hanging onto the trivet, hands thick in ashes. His coat and hose were already bloodstained but it was not his own blood. "No doubt you'll save yourself and still get to Venice one day," he muttered. "But send no messengers, for you're no longer my brother."

Ludovic wiped his sword blade on the straw at his side and gradually stood straight, discovering balance, strengthening his calf muscles and ignoring pain. He sheathed his blade, leaving his knife wedged tight in Naseby's skull. Then he unbuckled the purse concealed beneath his doublet, and threw it at Brice's feet. It fell heavy and full. He turned, breathing deeply, and strode from the room.

His horse was still tethered outside. Ludovic heaved himself into the saddle, leaned forwards across the animal's neck, and immediately lost consciousness.

CHAPTER FIFTY-FOUR

The earl regarded his youngest son in faint surprise. Since he had long thought his father incapable of surprise, Ludovic smiled with a gentle but incongruous pride. "I believe I've disobeyed you yet again, my lord," he murmured. "But if I don't lie down very soon, I may not live to incur your choice of punishment." He promptly collapsed on the bed, closed his eyes, and fell deeply asleep.

"Not every egg in a brood will prove fertile," the earl said softly to himself, "but if one hatches, fledges and flies strong and high, the falconer must be well enough pleased."

Once in the night Ludovic woke, sweating and lost in nightmare. He thought he saw his father sitting at his bedside, watching him intently through the gloom. Across the room a small fire flared across the hearth, flames dancing distant but seeming virulent as hell's welcome. A smoky airless nausea filled the room. Ludovic flung off the covers that swamped him. The earl shook his head. His long fingered hands carefully smoothed back the quilt. "No, my son. Or your fever will turn to ice."

"Summer," Ludovic murmured, half in dreams. "Too hot. Not wounded."

"The doctor has recommended you sweat out the ill humours, my child. We will comply with his advice. I will not risk your health."

"Not my blood," Ludovic muttered, "pirate's blood," and relapsed again.

Ludovic's dreams were often nightmares, visions of Gerald's execution, Brice crawling legless to Naseby's gutted corpse, the rack, and the chill dark of the Tower. But when his dreams were gentle and harmless, they were always of Alysson. Her face came close each night, her mouth open for kissing, with the warmth of her tangible. But sometimes the two extremes of dream world came together, and Alysson cried out to him for protection. As her brothers had died within the shadows of Sumerford castle, so Alysson was under threat, and Ludovic could not yet struggle forwards to save her. Held back by distance, by briars, by stone and by his own helplessness, he repeatedly failed her and in his dreams, saw her fall.

It was a week he remained in bed, forbidden to rise even for the garderobe, staying naked and sweating beneath a wilful heap of covers. At first he could not hold a spoon and the milk diet the doctor prescribed decorated more blanket than tongue. "Slops! I shall arrive home thin as a scarecrow," he objected.

"Your failing intellect matches your failing health, Ludovic," his parent informed him, holding the bowl of gruel beneath his son's nose. "You will oblige me for once in your life, and attempt some semblance of obedience. No doubt the experience will be sufficiently unique to shock you into some clarity of comprehension."

"Dutiful son," Ludovic mumbled, mouth full of broth. "Remarkably obedient. Always. Well, invariably. At least, often. Sometimes, anyway."

The earl took advantage of the open mouth before him and inserted the spoon once more. "My dear boy, if you believe such manifest absurdities, then you are ill indeed. You have once again put your life at risk against my express wishes, chasing after your brother when I had requested you specifically to leave his whereabouts unsought. When you returned here covered in blood and ashes and bare able to stand, I believed I had lost you. Brice can be – let us say – ruthless in the acquisition of his own desires. Nor are his companions likely to be more compassionate. But your brother was already subject both to the severity of the law and to my own somewhat more practical measures of censure. There was no benefit to be gained in seeking your own personal retaliation."

Ludovic meekly swallowed the gruel. "Not retaliation, sir, since I didn't kill Brice," he said. "Nor ever meant to. I intended killing the pirate Naseby, and did so. But I needed to speak with Brice. He believed I'd turned him in to the crown and I intended exonerating myself. Simple pride perhaps. But more importantly, I wanted him carrying the guilt of Gerald's death."

"Again to exonerate yourself?" The earl raised an eyebrow and held out another spoonful of broth.

Ludovic took it. "Astute as usual, sir. I felt considerable guilt, yes. I still do."

"I imagine it would be pointless to explain how you could never have dissuaded Gerald from his chosen path," said the earl. "Nor did you have the right to do so. He was a grown man, a clever and a loving knight. His decisions were his own and he paid the price he always knew hung there. I shall grieve my son's departure for the rest of my own life, but I am not arrogant enough to hold myself responsible for his death."

Ludovic smiled. "But presumably arrogant enough for everything else?"

"Naturally," said his lordship. "I am a Sumerford."

The fever passed but still Ludovic was forbidden to leave his bed. The liquid diet kept him weak while his aggravated joints calmed, the new swelling and inflammation dissipated and the pain faded into an occasional ache. When he was finally permitted to move around the room, it felt like Epiphany.

In fact it was mid-July and the bright hot morning of St. Everildis that a bumptious and noisy cavalcade left the Strand and set off towards Somerset. Ludovic, after some argument, rode. He felt strong, and the enthusiasm for his own home rebounded in waves as sparkling as the sunshine.

Regular replies had come to the earl's letters, informing him that

Humphrey and her ladyship were both thriving, the farms were prosperous, the property in good repair, the countryside at peace and the weather clement. Eventually a single and laboriously ill-spelled response arrived from Kenelm, finally replying to Ludovic's own frequent letters concerning Alysson. The captain, aided by the inn keeper, informed Ludovic that all was well except that Mistress Alysson Welles had unaccountably left the castle, the village, and the vicinity.

Ludovic was bitterly disappointed but not surprised. He had promised Alysson to return and claim her before midwinter of the previous year, and now past midsummer of the year following, he was still far away. For the past two months of convalescence he had written concerning her each time a messenger had been available, but during the previous months he had been quite incapable of contacting anyone. How much information concerning his own circumstances had ever reached her, he did not know. He doubted whether the Lady Jennine would have considered it convenient to tell Alysson too much, and his own mother would never have deigned to speak to her at all. Some castle gossip at least should have slipped through, but gossip was rarely accurate. Ludovic had long expected Alysson to forget and desert him. That she had left her employment at the castle might in fact be good news, though not to have returned to her nurse Ilara was more alarming. He intended to find her wherever she had gone, since determination might discover anyone, and then, as long as she had not rushed into the loving arms of some other man, he could begin again with a careful but faster courtship. And this time he would be less circumspect, and promise far more.

At first exuberant and then impatient, Ludovic soon found the journey home tedious. The earl insisted on short stages and frequent stops. They rested at only the most renowned and comfortable hostelries, stopping each afternoon and setting off again late the next morning once the sun was high. Some consideration was made for the lumbering speed of the accompanying carts and litters. Most was for Ludovic's health.

"At this rate it'll be winter before I see Sumerford again," Ludovic informed his father over supper. "We'll arrive for All Saint's. In which case I shall be ill again and far too stiff to walk."

The earl leaned back in his chair and regarded his son over the brim of his wine cup. "How lamentably predictable you are, my boy," he sighed. "But I assure you, a woman who does not wait, does not merit the erection."

Ludovic smiled. "If you expect me to blush, sir, you're destined for disappointment. And I look forward to seeing many people and to finding the old comforts I miss, though I admit my girl's by far the most essential anticipation. But I seem to remember your particular disapproval of her in the past."

"I do not now speak of my own approval, but of yours, my boy," murmured the earl. "But even I can become accustomed, given time. I have, naturally, been aware of your studious attempts to trace this female over some weeks. Since you prove so consistent, I might be persuaded to comply, reluctantly of course, with your choice of union." He paused, revolving his cup between his palms. "I assume," he continued, "that you now intend something more than dalliance with a common serving maid for a mistress?"

"She was a serving maid only by my own contrivance," Ludovic said. "She's from a respectable family and her late father was an alderman. You know all this, since I've told you it before, and you tend always to know everything anyway. And yes, I no longer intend taking her to mistress. I mean to marry Alysson Welles." He frowned, shaking his head. "What's more, sir, I'd be grateful in future if you refrained from reading my private letters."

"Sadly, your gratitude is doomed to impotence," said his father, draining his cup and refilling it. "I broke no seals. I have my own methods, and will not alter them to oblige you, my child. But nor do I choose to antagonise or distress you, since I've come to value your life and contentment more than most. Indeed, I shall sanction your wedding. You may marry the girl whenever you wish."

Ludovic gazed at his father with deep suspicion. "You're aware that her ladyship will never agree?"

"That," said the earl, "is a matter of complete indifference to me. But I would prefer to make the acquaintance of this young person beforehand, should you ever discover her again. Has she run away from you, do you think, or from someone else?"

Ludovic sighed. "Since I clearly have no privacy whatsoever, neither concerning the letters I write nor those that return to me, I suppose I might as well admit her disappearance. But Alysson's not run from me. I don't understand what's happened. I've been gone too long. But I'll find her."

"You traced your brother's whereabouts," said the earl. "No doubt you can find one, so I am assured, remarkably innocent and respectable young female."

The weather turned fitful and the journey slowed again. It was late July when they finally came within sight of Sumerford. It was raining. A thunderstorm was mounting behind the castle turrets and the sky was black.

They avoided fording either river or stream for all waterways were swollen and part flooded, the guards instead skirting through the neighbouring townships. But no river could have soaked them more. Ludovic felt already half drowned. He imagined the rich warming seclusion of a fire in his chamber, his bed soft aired and freshly made, and hippocras steaming aromatic by the bedside. He had recently resented the prolonged bedrest imposed upon him but now he welcomed the memory of his mattress, eager to stretch and ease every sore muscle in dry warmth again. His oiled cape covered his head, shoulders and knees, but the ends streamed water into his boots and his sleeves emerged dripping from the swathes of cloak. His riding gloves were sodden, squeaking against the wet leathers of the reins. Forked lightning dazzled through the clouds and the great echoing explosion of thunder shuddered across the cliffs. The rain became heavier, closing in dark steel screens. Ludovic could see nothing ahead except the backs of the other riders, each man sodden, the horse's tails streaming thin and soaked. He smelled wet earth, wet hide, wet sweat, wet breath. Even the clattering, jangling music of the hooves and bridals, the saddles creaking with endless jogging and the tired whinny of the horses, was swallowed by the noise of pelting rain.

Then they came out of the valley and looked up. Here the road was wide and kempt, for it was the responsibility of the castle and tended by the Sumerford retainers. Almost home, they quickened speed. The earl sent no buglers forward, but expected to be seen from the high windows. He expected the castle's doors swung open, the servants to bustle, informing Humphrey and her ladyship, preparing a hot supper and fires lit in all the bedchambers. He expected Humphrey, wide and beaming and ruddy, to hurry out into the rain, not caring about the squelch of mud beneath his indoor shoes, ignoring his mother's squeaks of warning as he ruined his velvets and feathers. He expected Hamnet clapping his hands for hippocras to be served and brought out on the great silver trays to the stable courtyard where the ostlers would be scurrying and the grooms in a sudden flurry. He expected the kitchens to wake, rushing to build up the cooking fires and set the spits turning. He expected what always occurred when he returned home after a long absence, and in foul weather too, demanding attention and comfort and respect.

But the castle stood cold and quiet beneath the storm. Nothing was happening and there was no sign of welcome at all. The great stone walls soared in dripping silence, the streaming sky flinging itself into the moat.

The earl held up one hand, and riding through the clutch of guards and staff around him, made his way to the front of the procession. He sat there a moment, holding his horse steady. With a push of impatient mounts sensing their own warm stalls so close, hands tight on the reins, each man stopped and waited. Ludovic moved to his father's side. "Something is wrong," he said.

The earl nodded. "We've no enemies in these parts, and there's no sign of siege. But you are right. Something bad has happened." He turned to the cluster of men behind him. The carts and litters had pulled in at the farthest end. The sound of the rain muffled his voice, so that those in front murmured back to those behind. "We move forwards slowly and with great caution," commanded the earl. "Dockett, Hardy and Frouste, take the pass and enter by the south tower. Parton and Sweet remain here with the baggage and carriers. If there are signs of difficulty after we enter the main gates, ride for the sheriff at once. The rest of you keep your weapons close and stay behind me."

"Let me lead the way, my lord," Ludovic said softly.

The earl raised an eyebrow. "I thank you for your considerations, my son, but I am hardly flattered. Indeed, I believe my own fitness to be far superior to your own at present, and am unlikely to fall from my saddle for any reason beyond an arrow to the throat. Sadly, I cannot say the same of you. You will therefore oblige me by remembering I am still the Earl of Sumerford and master of my own castle. You will keep behind me Ludovic, and have a care to your own safety and not to mine."

Ludovic smiled. "Yes, my lord. But I presume you don't suspect any particular danger?"

The earl loosened the reins and his horse trotted forwards. Ludovic stayed close beside his father. "I do not," said the earl, "but in these days of uncertainty, an intelligent man is alert for whatever may arise. I do not trust the great powers of this land. We are a rural outpost, and with three sons recently under the extreme displeasure of the king. A greedy enemy strikes when his adversary is weakest."

It was a smaller group which picked its way down the path towards the drawbridge and towering stone beyond. As the riders emerged from the shadows of the forest to their left, they saw the portcullis was raised and the drawbridge down as in times of peace. No signs of any frantic defence were visible but nor of the castle guards, usually lounging half asleep outside the walls. The rain continued to pour, masking any lights from the windows. The moat was a busy grey slime, bouncing with hurtling raindrops. All doors and gates were closed and only the sounds of the storm echoed. The puddles beneath the horse's hooves rebounded, splashing each rider with mud. Far away across the distant ocean, thunder rumbled another warning.

On the banks of the moat they stopped once more. Ludovic gazed to his right and his mother's apartments in the south tower. He thought he saw a flicker of candle light high up. He turned, staring up

502

at the east tower. The lower floors contained the deserted nursery block. Above were the Lady Jennine's quarters, where Alysson had lived. The windows were blank and dark.

Following his father, Ludovic crossed the sleek wet drawbridge, the waters churning to either side. There was still no sign of activity outside nor within the castle, no welcome and no recognition. The earl stopped. Ludovic dismounted at once and strode ahead. The doors, iron hinged and braced, stood fractionally ajar, as though someone had been unsure, or too hurried, either to open or to close the way. Ludovic pushed, and the doors swung open.

CHAPTER FIFTY-FIVE

The bailey and the open stable courtyard stood empty but horses neighed from their stalls, kicking at their doors. The earl clapped his hands, calling for the ostlers, while his men dismounted and began to lead away their own horses. The earl remained mounted. The rain was streaming from his hood down his face. "Only one thing is clear. There has been a disaster," he said quietly.

Ludovic nodded. He stood on the cobbles, gazing up at his father's wretchedness. "Will you stay here, my lord, while I go in to investigate?"

"No." The earl's horse danced, smelling home, looking for groom, warm blankets and hay. Ludovic reached up, taking its bit and calming it, scratching between its ears. "We will go in together," said the earl.

"My lord," someone yelled from across the courtyard. "We've unearthed the grooms, your lordship." The young man hurried across the pavings, dragging a youth by a firm hold to his ear. "The cowards have been hiding in their dormitory, my lord. We've hauled them out and set them back to work. But there's something strange amiss, and I've got neither explanation nor sense out of them."

The earl stared down at the small frightened boy, who quickly dropped to one knee. "Well boy? Tell me quickly."

"I don't rightly know wot to say, my lord." The boy snivelled, knees in the puddles. "None of us know wot happened, truly we doesn't your lordship. There was a right commotion inside, wiv screaming and clashing. Then some of the staff runs out, all awry and yelling. Says there's blood and fighting and their ladyships hurt. The castle guards, they goes straight in wiv their swords flashing. Master Hamnet, he sends Ben and Master Cooper and two of the guards to the village for the sheriff, and then goes back indoors. We was frightened my lord, and hid by our pallets. We heard a load more noise and running and suchlike, and some of the horses was took, wiv folk galloping off out the castle at great speed. A mighty clash o' steel there were, and then silence. Begging your pardon, my lord, but we was scared. So we stayed hid."

Lightning sprang from between the clouds, striking the east tower. The sudden illumination was stark. A bright white echo fizzled over the merlons and then fell again into blackness. The thunder reverberated directly over their heads. The small groom fell flat on his face.

"Get up child," said Ludovic, a hand hoisting up the boy by the neck of his grubby soaked shirt. "Get to the horses and do your job. The animals are wet and tired and hungry. You'll be safe enough now, whatever has happened."

The earl dismounted, handed his reins to the shivering groom and took Ludovic's arm. "Well, my son," he said. "Let us face this together."

The cobbles streamed water. Then suddenly within, the rain was shut out and the gloom closed over. The great hall was deserted and the remains of a fire, lit many hours earlier against the chill of the oncoming storm, had fallen to ashes. The usual smell of smoke and soot lingered. No candles were lit and the shadows hung indistinct, enclosing their secrets. The sounds of the rain were now muted and lost and the silence slipped all around, claiming sovereignty over bustle. Nothing moved, not even the scamper of mice. Ludovic marched to the hearth and kicked the dozing fire into sparks.

"Leave it," said the earl. "There's no need of fire yet. No doubt the staff are hiding either in the kitchens or in their quarters. What we are looking for, will surely be upstairs."

505

Ludovic stared. "And what are we looking for, my lord?"

"Humphrey," said the earl.

They found Hamnet first. The old steward lay sprawled face up on the lower steps of the main staircase. He still grasped a cup, its wine spilled and still wet across the boards as if he had been trying to offer it, attempting to calm someone who faced him. His throat had been cut and his head fell a little sideways, the jaw slack.

"Dear God," Ludovic whispered.

The earl crossed himself, stepped over his dead servant, and continued to climb the stairs. Ludovic leaned down and closed Hamnet's glazed eyes. Then he followed his father.

Immediately to their right the long corridor led in total darkness to the east tower. The doors leading off one side remained closed, locked and silent. The earl and Ludovic entered the stairwell of the tower where the nursery levels led up to the Lady Jennine's apartments above. Her doors lay open to the gloom of wide windows, the plummeting rain outside, and the soft furnishings within. Jennine was curled beneath the archway leading from the solar to her bedchamber. She was quite still, face down in a great pool of blood. Ludovic knelt but did not touch the body or attempt to roll her over. He put his fingertip to the blood. It was dry and black and hard. She had been dead some time. One desultory trapped fly buzzed from the lady's ear to her shoulder to the stickiness which had once been her life. There was no sign of any other person, nor the sound of movement or of breathing. No servants scurried or shrank away, no one living was there at all. Ludovic knew that Alysson was already gone, and for the first time was deeply relieved. Her disappearance had first seemed a disaster, but was now the only blessing.

They left the room and returned quickly to the corridor leading west along the main castle building, fast footsteps and a faint vibration of tread on wood. Directly before them were Humphrey's apartments, the great luxurious chambers allotted to the title's heir. Beyond that stood the north tower, the earl's own. His private staff would be there, barricaded in perhaps, if they had not run. Ludovic kept pace with his father. The cold stone around them smelled of damp and the usual draught sped from the stairs along the boards, finding entrance beneath each doorway. The earl proceeded to his eldest son's quarters and found the first doors shut. He grasped the handles and pushed open.

The large solar was empty. Usually bright with sunshine from the mullioned window, now the corners whispered with gloom. The door from the solar to the inner chambers was also shut. The earl paused a moment before opening it. It swung wide to the sound of the rain. Ludovic and his father went in.

The first of the private rooms, an annex and wardrobe, was also empty but the door beyond was already open to Humphrey's own bedchamber. Between the doorway and the massive bed, was the gleaming wealth of a Turkey rug over the polished boards. It depicted the fall of Jerusalem, Acre and the battles of Saladin. Across the warring armies and the saffron spread of the woven desert, three people sat, part sprawled, two tightly entwined.

The countess sat on the ground, cradling her eldest son. She had been crying. Her headdress was unpinned and her hair was dishevelled, lying lank grey down her face. Humphrey, smiling placidly, was cushioned to her breast, nodding occasionally, as though deeply content. The countess was singing very softly as to a small child, a gentle lullaby with lilting melody and words of sleep and trust. Humphrey had one thumb firm in his mouth. His other hand was tucked busy inside his codpiece. At their feet lay the headless body of a young boy, partly clothed in Sumerford's green livery. The stump of the child's neck was ragged and bloody and a long bladed knife lay beside him. The pattering of the rain outside never wavered, like a tabor keeping rhythm to the song.

The countess watched her husband enter as she continued singing. She cradled one arm around Humphrey, the fingers of her other hand playing in his hair. She appeared quite unhurt, but somehow perplexed.

Humphrey sat up as he saw his father. He stopped sucking his thumb and clasped both hands eagerly before him. "Papa. I'm glad you're home. You can help me fix everything up. Mamma says I've done bad things, and she doesn't know how to put it right. But you can always put everything right, can't you Papa?"

The countess slowly stopped her singing, her voice trailing off as if blown in the wind. "Even your father cannot work miracles, my dearest son," she said softly, patting his shoulder. "This time, Humphrey my love, you have gone just a little too far."

Humphrey looked up at her. "But there's Ludovic too, Mamma, look. Hello Lu. Haven't seen you for such a long time. Much too long, which wasn't fair. Someone said you were dead, but I knew that couldn't be true. You'd never let anyone kill you, would you, Lu? And papa can mend everything, Mamma, can't he? I know I've been bad, but then I can't help being bad sometimes and it always gets put right again. Vymer usually puts things right, or father does, or Jenny does. Except for little Eddie. He went away and no one put him right, which wasn't fair either. And that wasn't my fault. I liked him so much and he was all mine. But perhaps some of these other things are my fault. You don't care, do you Lu? You aren't ever shocked by anything."

Ludovic struggled for words. He was gazing at the small headless boy tumbled disjointed on the ground, one plump hand still grasping helplessly at the countess's skirts. Humphrey's hands were thick with blood. As he clutched his mother, her clothes were smeared and streaked in dark and tired crimson.

The earl went forwards, bending over his wife and son. "I shall put it right, my dear boy," he said, "never fear. You will be safe now and for always." He looked up briefly at her ladyship. "Tell me quickly, without prevarication," he said curtly "How many? And how?"

The countess looked away, avoiding her husband's eyes. She spoke to the wavering shadows across the floor where the light from the window puddled and swam, reflecting the movement of the rain. "How? With a knife of course," she murmured. "Sometimes fast, in temper. Sometimes slow. Six, I think. Jennine. Her maid. Hamnet, poor dear. This page child, lying here. One of the guards, outside. And Vymer, somewhere downstairs. I've seen no one else."

"Six?" breathed Ludovic.

"Have I said six? Were there more? I cannot be sure anymore," the countess mumbled. "My darling can be so fierce, so hard to control. I have tried over the years, and always so alone. This time was so much worse than ever before. It is Jennine's fault of course. She was hired to stop these scenes. She has quite failed in her job."

"I doubt you can blame her for it now, Mamma," Ludovic said, unblinking, barely breathing. "She's past recriminations."

The earl squatted beside his son, gently taking his great blood stained hand in his own. "Has the mood left you now, my boy?" he asked carefully. "How do you feel?"

"Oh, much better, Papa," Humphrey smiled. "I don't mean to hurt people, you know. Hamnet was fussing and I was very naughty to hurt him, but he was so very much in the way and made me cross. The others, well I just wanted to play. No one wants to play anymore. And I have to play sometimes. You do understand, don't you? When I get that funny feeling here." He patted his head, then his belly. "Like being hungry, but not for eggy custards. Then after I play for a little while, it all feels so much better. I'm all right now, thank you Papa. You're not going to spank me like you used to do when I was little, are you? I think I'd like to go to bed now."

Ludovic had moved back and was leaning heavily against the wall. He felt his breathing forced and his brain quite immovable so that he could not think or speak at all. Gazing a little wildly around the room he saw the crumpled blankets on Humphrey's bed had been pulled back. On the feather bolster lay the small bodiless head of a child, tucked as if for sleep.

The earl continued holding Humphrey's hand, nodding comfortingly. "No, I shan't punish you, my boy," he said quietly. "Going to your sleep seems best. You need, I think, to close your eyes in peace, and rest for a very long time. I will not hurt you, my dear, and nor will anyone else. It is time, I think, for you to go beyond pain."

The earl unbent, his hand moving slowly to the pummel of his sword. The countess squinted up at him through her tears. "No," she moaned. "Please, not that."

The earl spoke almost in a whisper. "I have to, my dear. This time I must."

Humphrey smiled cheerfully from one parent to the other. "Come on Mamma, it's no good arguing like you always do. Father always knows best. Men do, you know. I'm always good for papa, aren't I sir?"

"Invariably, my boy," sighed the earl.

"But," Humphrey chattered, "I try to be good for you too, Mamma. Just sometimes the feelings get too strong. But you do understand, don't you? And now I think I've done something else naughty. You won't get cross again, will you?"

The countess breathed deeply, her fingers back amongst Humphrey's curls. "No, my love, I shan't ever be cross with you again. Tell Mamma what you've done."

"I think I've pissed my hose," he said mournfully.

The earl nodded. "I believe I am close to that myself, my boy," he murmured. "You'll feel a great deal more comfortable soon. But first, you must do something important for me, something to make matters right again." He squeezed Humphrey's hand. Humphrey looked up at him nodding eagerly. "You must pray with me, my son," the earl said. "I do not choose to call Father Dorne this time. Indeed, I would prefer him not to be involved. But there are words you must say, my dear, before you go to your rest."

"I always forget my prayers, Papa," Humphrey said. "Mamma usually says the words first and then I say them after her. You've never prayed with me before, Papa. I shall like that. So you say it first, and then I'll repeat it. That's the way I like best."

"You must make your confession first, my child," said the earl. "And I will listen and give you absolution."

Something struck Humphrey and he frowned. "That's not proper, Papa," he objected. "It's the priest I have to say my confession to."

The earl shook his head. "Not this time, my son. This time you will confess to me," he said. "It is quite proper, I assure you."

"Oh well," smiled Humphrey. "If you say so, then it must be right. I forget the words Father Dorne always tries to make me say, but I can do it my own way, can't I Papa?" He sat up straight as though in a confessional and spoke in a gallop without breathing. "Then I'm sorry that I hurt Hamnet, and I wish I hadn't. I like Hamnet. He used to bring me honey cakes and custards when I was little. But he tried to get in the way after he saw what I'd done, so I had to hurt him. First of all I hurt Jenny's maid, but I only wanted to play. Jenny held her tight for me but the girl kept screaming and it gave me a headache so I had to play harder, and then she went all sticky and floppy like they always do. So I confess to that. Then I didn't feel any better at all so I told Jenny I had to play with her instead and she got all squawky, so I hurt her too. Quite a lot I think. I'm sorry about that too, but it was her own fault. She usually understands, but this time she said no and that wasn't fair."

The earl nodded. "Go on, my son."

"Then I wanted to play with one of the page boys," Humphrey said with a confiding smile. "I like them. But the only boy I could find was Remi. That's Vymer's little boy and Vymer got all funny about it and he said no too. I don't like it when people say no to me. Vymer never says no, he always helps me play and brings me people to play with, but this time he was mean and stopped me, so I got angry. So I hurt Vymer. He sort of cried while I was hurting him so I'm sorry about that too. I ought to confess because it was naughty. Then I hurt a guard who tried to grab my arm. I mean, I'll confess to that too if you like Father, but you can't say that was naughty. I'm the Sumerford heir, aren't I? The guards shouldn't try to hold on to me, it isn't right. And then there was lots of screaming and people running around and locking up the kitchens and everything, it was most confusing. And that wasn't my fault either. I would have liked something to eat but Master Shore wouldn't let me in. And then mother came and found me and she sung me songs. And now you're here too Papa, so it's nice and comfy again. And even Ludovic's here, so that's good, just like family dinners all together. For ages and ages I've really missed not having family dinners. So you shouldn't go away again Lu. You've been gone so long and I got lonely."

Ludovic grappled for voice. "You said – Jenny's maid," he said, half strangled. "The girl you – hurt. Where is she? Who was she? Which girl? Do you know her name?"

"Oh yes." Humphrey smiled again, happy to please. "Jenny always called her girl. Just come here girl. You know, that kind of thing. But I asked her name while I was playing with her. I like to be polite. She was making lots of silly noises, but she said her name too because I made her. Helena, she said. I think that's a very nice name."

Ludovic felt the sweat on his back turn to ice. He sank back again against the stone wall. "And Alysson," he whispered, "who used to be Jenny's maid. Black haired and beautiful. Do you remember her, Humphrey? Think hard. I have to know."

"Of course." Humphrey nodded. "That's silly, Lu, thinking I wouldn't remember her. Jenny always said Alysson was going to be my special play partner one day, but I had to be good for ages first before I could have her."

Ludovic's face became white and drawn. He felt overwhelming and utter nausea, his knees too weak to hold him upright. "Tell me what happened," he whispered.

Humphrey shook his head. "I'm not sure," he answered, from smile to frown. "She was kept upstairs for me, getting nice and fat just how I wanted her and Jenny told me lovely stories about what I could do with her one day. Then the funny feelings started after dinner and no one was around to play with so I went upstairs to find my new special play-mate where Jenny had locked her up. But she didn't want to play at all. I found that mean Alysson running away with a little boy. I got quite cross. Well, so would you, if that sort of thing happened after you'd been promised treats and waited and waited and been good and got all excited."

"You never – touched her?" croaked Ludovic.

"No. I couldn't," Humphrey complained. "I tried but she ran away too fast. At least I got the key off her but she kicked me too, which hurt. So I went upstairs and found Jenny and Vymer. They were both groggy and had blood on them which was silly because I never touched them before that. So I shook them and made them get up and come downstairs and help me play. There was lots of thunder and lightning and I don't like storms, they make my head go funny. I shouldn't be left all alone when there's storms, should I Papa? So Vymer and Jenny came downstairs all staggering and peculiar and they didn't seem very well, but they promised to be nice to me and that's when it all started. But that's all right, isn't it, Father? I can't think of anything else to confess except wetting my braies."

Humphrey smiled, looking around and hoping for praise. Heaving from the countess's arms, he scrambled onto his knees but the earl shook his head.

"Not just yet, my child. After confession, you must receive the Lord's absolution." He raised his hand, making the sign of the cross in the sultry air. "I therefore absolve you from all sin, in the name of God the Father, God the Son and God the Holy Spirit. I'm no priest, but I believe the saints will understand, and be kind." He smiled gently, smoothing the sweat streaked hair back from Humphrey's forehead. "I forgive you, my son, for all you've done. Indeed, I barely hold you responsible. I give you my own blessing, and that of our Lord. And now I wish you a deep and refreshing sleep."

Humphrey nodded, again extricating himself from his mother's embrace. "That's good, Papa, because I'm really tired. All that playing around is so exhausting. Even more than hunting. So now I'm specially sleepy."

The earl had withdrawn his sword from its scabbard. Beneath the folds of his damask, still wet from the journey, he kept it firm gripped and hidden. The countess began to cry again, hearty gulps which shuddered against Humphrey's straining ear.

The earl said, "Then you will sleep well, my boy."

"And I won't dream," smiled Humphrey. "I don't like dreaming. My dreams are nasty things, all full of worms, and screaming and shouting and people running away from me. But after I've played, I sleep without dreaming at all. So I'll wake up happy tomorrow. Can we go hunting tomorrow, Papa, now you're home again at last?"

"I shall see, my dear. I shall see." The earl sighed, coming closer to kneel beside his son. He reached out his left hand and gently shifted the body of the slaughtered child from where it lay at the countess's feet. The small boy was fine boned and pale skinned with a scattering of freckles across his shoulders. The headless neck looked thin and fragile. The earl pushed the ruined remains aside. He leaned forwards, smiling into his son's eyes. His sword was poised, its blade still wrapped beneath his coat.

The countess screamed. Humphrey turned, surprised, his mouth open in question. He was interrupted by thunder, shattering reverberations rolling over the cliffs beyond the castle. The sound of the rain increased. Humphrey moved once again into his mother's warmth, clutching at her, pressing against her in panic. The earl paused, the point of his sword no longer finding its aim.

The countess of Sumerford kissed her son's brow, leaned across him and took up the long knife which had been used against the dead child. The blade still lay, still sticky and dark, on the ground amidst its stains. She wrapped her fingers around the plain wooden hilt, twisted her wrist, and then quite noiselessly slipped the steel beneath Humphrey's left breast into the small pulse beating very fast and loud. The knife slid deep through Humphrey's doublet and disappeared silently into his body. Humphrey seemed barely to notice. He spat blood once as if finding it an inconvenience, smiled, and leaned his head on his mother's shoulder. Something rattled in his throat. His head became heavier and his eyes closed for sleep.

CHAPTER FIFTY-SIX

Ludovic swallowed bile. Turning abruptly, he left the room. A frantic disbelief made him dizzy. He shook his head, clearing his mind, concentrating only on urgency. He ran the corridor, hurrying again into the Lady Jennine's quarters and crossing at once to the inner chamber. Jennine's body had stiffened. Ludovic stepped across her and began to search the room beyond.

There were no signs of Alysson. The clothes he remembered her wearing were not visible in any place, nor were any of her belongings. He clearly recollected the little she owned. During the weeks he had visited and nursed her during her convalescence, he had seen each part of the small collection she prized, two gowns apart from her old tunic and her livery, a hair brush, small mirror, blanchet and shoes. The garderobe was badly cleaned and rank. He began to knock on the walls. Humphrey had spoken of going upstairs. There was no upper level that Ludovic knew where a woman could be hidden or locked away and he supposed such a secret prison would have to be in one of the towers. The earl would not countenance such a thing above his own quarters and Ludovic himself inhabited the west tower. The hidden rooms might be sequestered above his mother's apartments in the south tower, but he doubted it. The idea seemed preposterous. Only the east tower might possibly be used for that purpose and he examined everything carefully. But Ludovic found no secret closet there.

He left quickly and began to explore the stone stairs outside. They wound downwards, leading to the nurseries. Then, amongst the chill and damp, he found another way, almost lost in shadows. Through an iron door bare wide enough for his shoulders to pass, narrower steps led steeply upwards. Ludovic took them two at a time and immediately entered the dark space above.

He had never been there, never knew the place existed. He stepped in.

The tower's round peak held three tiny rooms, each leading into the next. Each was open. The doors swung, creaking in the wind. A window pane was cracked and the storm whined through. Rainwater trickled black from the broken casement across the bare boards. Ludovic bent and tested the liquid. It was not blood. He retraced his steps but each room was empty. There was no one there but there were signs of who had been before, and of what had happened to them.

Alysson's blanchet lay strewn across the bed. He recognised her old livery, torn and filthy on the ground. Her working shoes were neat beside a chest, the chest open, and others of her possessions within. Her best blue dress was gone, her good shoes no longer there. He found neither her hairbrush nor her shift, but shards of broken mirror lay scattered on the rug. There was blood both on the ground and on the bed. Not pools, as in Humphrey's room, but old trails streaking the sheets and floor. There was also a boy's shirt, small and very dirty. There was nothing else.

Ludovic explored the entire castle carefully and systematically. It took him a very long time. Most of the staff had locked themselves in the kitchens and outhouses and it was some time before he could convince them to unlock the doors. They had feared a massacre, had seen the old guardsman murdered before their eyes, but could not protect either him or themselves for the wild eyed killer was their own master. They had served Humphrey throughout their lives, though had always been careful around him, knowing him to be odd and his behaviour erratic. Care and respect were due by right to all the noble Sumerfords, but Humphrey was irascible and unpredictable. Many guessed him capable of sudden violence, some had suffered his tempers. No one welcomed the thought of this heir becoming earl, for a man who enjoys whipping his servants is a hard master to serve. But they had never suspected him capable of unnatural slaughter.

They came out, one by one, frightened and staring around. Ludovic spoke to them briefly, telling them little but promising his protection and the safety due them. He set them back to work, to build up the fires and to light the candles. There would soon be a great deal more to do.

Ludovic met up with the guards Dockett, Hardy and Frouste whom the earl had sent to the castle's second entrance, and ordered them to return to the small group still waiting outside, to reassure them and bring them home. He then ordered his father's elderly secretary, waiting patiently at the bottom of the main staircase, to organise the staff in Hamnet's absence. So the small furtive noises of fearful tread again filled the hall and the chambers beyond. Finally Ludovic asked for wine, and quickly drained the cup.

He found his own quarters in the west tower barricaded. The doors were quickly unlocked for him but there was nothing to search there. He reassured his servants and left at once. He carried on to the north tower and his father's domain. Again the personal staff were hiding within. Ludovic explained briefly. The recent problems with the Lord Humphrey had now been resolved, he told them. The earl, now exhausted, would soon retire, so required his chambers warmed and hippocras brought. Ludovic, avoiding passing beyond to Humphrey's own apartments, then returned the way he had come.

He asked constantly after Alysson. No one had seen her and no one knew where she was. She had left months ago, he was told, either dismissed or by choice. Perhaps her aunt had been ill. Perhaps she had been ill herself. Perhaps she had found a better position far away. Too fancy for a maid, they muttered, and was treated too easy by the lady. In any case and whatever the cause, Alysson Welles had disappeared long back and not been heard of again, neither in the castle nor in the village.

Ludovic discovered Mistress Tenby shivering in the servant's quarters, and he sat with her for a minute, patting her hand and comforting her. But she had no news either, and had never traced the lost lady's maid who had left the castle employ with wages owing and no claim put in since. The Lady Jennine had spoken severely of the girl, Mistress Tenby said. In spite of being so well treated, positively cossetted in fact, Mistress Alysson had proved a sad disappointment in the end and the Lady Jennine had admonished her and sent her off. Others had come searching for her once, an old woman and a man, but that had been some time ago and nothing had come of it.

There had been too many problems recently, Mistress Tenby admitted. Of his lordship the heir she was not qualified to speak, nor would permit herself such licence, but disorder had occurred on several occasions during the earl's absence, especially when Master Vymer was suddenly re-introduced back into the castle and given authorisation to order the staff in the Lord Humphrey's name. This had distressed everyone. Vymer Wapping was not liked, not liked at all, and was a common man for all his red hair was so like the Sumerfords'. And then there had been the endless problem of the privies. The cess pit had become blocked and a miasma of foul vapours had invaded the castle as sure as a heathen curse or a plague of serpents. A dreadful sludge had issued from the latrines and as soon as it was cleared then it came again. Vymer's brother, the more likeable George Wapping, had set about digging the pit, which had made him ill, but the trouble was finally solved and some kind of dreadful muck taken away to clear the blockage. The privy was usable again but the stench still lingered in places, and the memory certainly did. The earl himself, bless his lordship's noble heart, had of course been sore missed. As to the latest violence, well Mistress Tenby was unsure of the facts and could not comment. She had locked herself in her chamber at the first signs, hands firm against her ears. She had prayed that all would be well, and now here was proof of God's mercy for the earl and Lord Ludovic were returned safe and sound. The castle could return to order again at last.

It was to the privy that Ludovic went. Two cubicles occupied an angle on the lower stairs leading from the hall to the pantries. Here the seats were built into ledges within the dark corner, wide enough for a man to sit in quiet contemplation. Though without doors to close, the spaces were private enough within their shadows and good manners prescribed that no one would interrupt or speak to anyone seated upon their business. But one cubicle was not empty. With a flush of skirts upturned, a young woman, her upper parts squashed downwards through the circle of wooden seat, had been abandoned there. Her bare legs curled within the flounced hems of her shift, her feet still snug in little tight shoes.

Ludovic threw off his coat and rolled up his doublet cuffs. The girl wore the castle livery. Nothing else of her could be recognised. He put his arms around her waist and brought the body carefully up from its miserable oblivion. Her expression was obscured only by the darkness, the smears from the privy and her own silenced screams. Ludovic laid the small corpse gently down on the cold stone ground, rearranging her skirts to cover her legs and her modesty and the violence done to her. He did not know her. He supposed she was Helena, who had once perhaps been proud to take Alysson's place as Jennine's maid. Her limbs were stiff and distorted so he could not lay her flat, but he gave her what respect he could, and quietly left her there alone.

Father Dorne was discovered crouched sobbing beside his own altar, and Ludovic called him to come and absolve the dead of the sins they could no longer confess. They should receive final absolution now, while their souls still struggled to enter purgatory. Ludovic also discovered Master Pembridge the doctor and young Nobb the apothecary. He sent them scurrying to Humphrey's quarters.

It was the second privy where he himself knelt, swore, and was brutally ill. It was some time since he had eaten, and thanked God for it. He had drunk two cups of wine, and now returned both to the cesspit. He remained slumped there, the smell of his own vomit strong in his nostrils.

It was someone else who found Vymer and came pounding along the passageway to report the discovery.

Skewered with a great meat iron hook, Vymer's body hung upside down in the cold pantry amongst the carcasses. Mutton, venison, beef and pork was suspended, gutted and slit, waiting for the slow spit over the fire and the merriment of castle feasts. Vymer hung silent amongst them. His throat had been cut through, severing his windpipe. His eyes stared down at his own black puddles, and his bright red hair was mired in dried blood, its drips suspended globulous from the long strands. Red hair, red blood, both turning gelatinous and dark in the dry chill, but the body was now strangely white and almost luminous. It took three men to bring him down and lay his body outside the door beside that of the dead guard, ready for collection and Christian burial.

Ludovic was still searching the castle and its outhouses when the sheriff arrived, soaked and breathless, his horse rolling its eyes at the thunder. Ludovic led the man to Humphrey's apartments. He found his father still there, seated on a low chest, Humphrey's smiling corpse lying at his feet. Her ladyship was not visible but her choking sobs echoed, partly stifled, from the far room. Across the chamber the small boy's mutilated body, now reunited with its head, lay beneath a sheet. The earl looked up and nodded. His eyes were bloodshot.

"There is much to be done, Simples, and you will need to call for your assistant," he said without expression. "You've known of my son's personal problems for some time, I believe. His intellectual weakness has never been a secret, but I did not personally suspect him of brutality. Today on my return from Westminster however, I discovered him more distracted than usual. No doubt you have already heard something of the story."

The sheriff was gaping and stuttering.

"The problem," the earl continued, his voice level, "is now solved. Your particular skills will not be required. However your presence is essential. My son suffered an attack of great irregularity this morning during my absence, and was moved to terrible violence. Due to his state of imbalance, I do not hold him personally responsible for his own actions but I regret them deeply. Humphrey was my son and heir but he caused much misery here today, and you will inevitably be shown the results of his – unusual predilections. However, I will not permit this day's wretchedness to be broadcast beyond these walls and I expect your discretion and loyalty in this matter. You will do what needs to be done, and you will keep your mouth shut."

Sheriff Simples already kept his mouth shut. He could not find words, but nodded a little wildly. Ludovic remained standing behind him in the doorway. He also kept his silence.

"My son," the earl proceeded, "realising too late what he had caused, then took his own life. But he will be buried in the family vault on sanctified ground with the full blessings of the church, and I will hear no argument on any count. Is this clear?"

"Indeed, my lord." The sheriff managed to bow low.

"What is more, you will," the earl informed him, "accept the events as I describe them. You will not in any manner question my word. You will not speak to the staff or to my family. This is a time of tragedy for us all, so you will be discreet and keep your distance. This is also quite clear?"

"Indeed, my lord."

"Her ladyship," continued the earl as the sobs from the inner chamber lessened, "will not be consulted on any matter, nor spoken to concerning any of this."

"Certainly, your lordship. I would never think of intruding at such a time."

"Very well." The earl nodded, dismissing him. "I trust your compliance, Simples, and will no doubt have occasion in future to remember your loyalty with gratitude. I shall speak to you again before you leave the castle."

Ludovic watched the man depart hurriedly, his hat clutched under his arm, his head bowed. "Are you all right, sir?" Ludovic asked, regarding his father with some caution. "Can I get you something? Wine? Your manservant?"

The earl continued staring at Humphrey's body. "Don't be a fool, Ludovic," he said quietly.

Ludovic left and returned downstairs. He followed the stone steps deeper, holding his torch high, his footsteps echoing. The cellars were lightless, windowless and musty. Here in the driest chambers the wine was kept. In the lower tunnels many other stores were stacked, kegs, sacks and chests veneered in mildew and mould. Once there had been dungeons, but the old chambers with their low ceilings and dripping walls no longer needed to be locked. The keys were lost, the locks rusted, the requirement forgotten, the seep of the moat outside making them icy and rank. Ludovic hurried through every corner, bringing the sudden flare of torch flame to explore each angle. He called but there was no reply. He heard the rats running, but nothing else moved. He hurried back upstairs.

It was still raining. Ludovic went out into the smaller courtyard which led away from the stables, the drawbridge and the main gateway, to the second entrance where the sounds of the surf pounded loud as the thunder. The lightning tore across the battlements, sparkling vivid reflections over the tiny window high in the east tower where Alysson had once been held captive.

The little courtyard, open to the sky but enclosed on all four sides by the massive castle walls, sheltered the kitchen garden with its rows of beans, herbs and salads. The tufts of greenery lay wilted and sodden beneath the storm. Behind the small plot was a shed, thatched and neat and angled between wall and shrubbery. It was large enough for the tools of gardening and little else, but sometimes the chickens wandered there, finding sacks of grain. It was the only place Ludovic had not yet searched.

She was curled amongst the brooms, with folded hessian as a pillow. She seemed to be asleep. Beside her, wrapped tight, was Clovis. His nose was bloody but there was no sign of deeper hurt to either, no other blood and no stench of pain and death. But the child's eyes were closed as Alysson's were. Ludovic slumped heavily back against the open door, catching his breath. The rain lashed in over his shoulder, soaking the soiled blue hems of Alysson's skirts. Then he knelt quickly beside her, shielding her from the cold, and smoothed his hand across her cheek. He believed her dead. When she blinked and gazed up at him Ludovic thought himself dreaming. He was almost sick again, this time with fear, and hope, and the sour bile of utter disbelief.

"My God," he whispered, and gathered her up into his arms.

She gulped, crushed against him and shivering. Clovis woke with a start and scrambled up, ready for battle. Then he saw his master and stopped, frantic hands still raised and clenched.

Alysson's voice was muffled. Ludovic could hear no words. He steadied himself, standing quickly with her still nestled tight to him, bent his head and kissed her words away. Her mouth responded and her hands crept up around his neck. She was bitterly cold and her clothes were sodden. She rested her wet hair against his chest and sighed.

Ludovic looked down at the startled boy. "Are you hurt?" Clovis shook his head, hair in his eyes, mouth open. "Good," said Ludovic. "Then come with me."

The snuggled body in his arms seemed as fragile as coloured glass. Her natural warmth had begun to dry her silks and he felt her yielding softness, the curve of her shoulder tucked beneath his own, his fingers enclosing her waist and beneath her knees. He touched her heartbeat, quick and uneven, pounding just above his palm. She stopped trembling and closed her eyes again to the world, as though disbelieving her rescue. Ludovic held her as though breakable, and as the most precious thing he had ever known. He marched with her across the dripping courtyard and into the sudden dark seclusion of the castle corridors. Clovis scurried behind.

Ludovic strode directly to his own quarters, not bothering to seek elsewhere. He kicked open the door to his bedchamber, sending the hovering servants into a flurry. There he laid Alysson very carefully on his bed. The rich fur and velvet bedcover cocooned her. She snuggled into warm feathers, breathing deep.

He took her hand and sat beside her, speaking in a whisper. "Open your eyes, my beloved. I swear I shan't leave you again. Everything is safe now, I promise, and always will be. I will always look after you now and stay close forever."

CHAPTER FIFTY-SEVEN

Ellis regarded his rival with disgust. "Thought the little bugger were dead," he muttered.

"You can't speak to me like that," objected Clovis. "I'm a bloody hero, I am. Ain't I, m'lor?"

Ludovic smiled. The smile had recently become persistent. "Indubitably."

"He is a hero," said Alysson. "Clovis has looked after me most wonderfully for all the time you were away, and nearly lost his life for it."

She had been ceremonially removed from Ludovic's quarters and settled once again in the grand chambers she had previously occupied during her convalescence. Aired, warmed, glass newly sparkling and the bed laid with clean pressed linen, the rooms smelled of fresh herbs and the cut flowers clustered in the empty hearths. Now well wrapped within a brand new sarsenet bedrobe trimmed in miniver, Alysson sat in her very own solar, curled on the cushioned settle, legs tucked beneath her, and her own smile as permanent as Ludovic's.

With an imperceptible nod from Ludovic, her guests were leaving. It was Kenelm who accepted the quiet dismissal and quickly ushered the two boys away. "Time we was gone, I reckon my lord," he said with an improper wink. "In fact, I got a lady o' my own to see to now. And I'll sort them little bastards out, don't worry. As fer heroes, well I reckon that's not a matter o' who done what, but more of who didn't have no choice." He bundled the boys from the room, pulling the door shut behind him.

Ludovic stood by the hearth, his elbow to the high mantle, one foot to the iron grating. He looked down on Alysson, his eyes fixed on her smile. He said, "This still seems a miracle to me. I thought you dead."

"I thought you dead." She clasped her hands in her lap, but no attempt at maidenly calm could stop her fingers twitching or disguise her nerves.

It had been just three days. Within those three days everything had happened. Funerals had been arranged, services read, the household reorganised, the castle aired, cleaned and polished. All signs of the great tragedy were carefully and strenuously removed, but a faint stench of fear lingered on. Humphrey's great bulk lay in quiet state in the chapel. Within the lead lined coffin, his head cushioned, he slept. The gash through his heart had closed to a dark hole and had been washed, salved and bandaged as if to alleviate the sufferings of a man still living. He was almost naked, the wallowing belly now slumped and hollow. The cloth across his loins was embroidered with the Sumerford arms, once worked by the countess herself for her eldest son's cradle. Now he smiled a little, as he had within her embrace as she raised the knife and killed him.

The Lady Jennine slept regal beneath the chapel candles, though few came to stand witness and she would be buried without pomp, taking her place once again at her husband's side. That she lay dead at his hand was no longer mentioned.

It was accepted that Humphrey had, in contrition, taken his own life, but Father Dorne obeyed the earl's command and no shame was put upon the corpse. The heir's memory would be forever stained with the fear and horror he had generated, but not sullied with the taint of suicide. He would be buried with some ceremony and take his proper place in hallowed ground. The priest dutifully chanted his prayers for the departed soul beneath the rows of flickering candles, but the staff did not file past the coffin to pay their last respects. The echoes remained muted.

The countess attended neither funerals nor chapel services, but took Mass within her private chambers. She received no visitors there. The earl did not approach her quarters and nor did her remaining son. She refused to open her doors to any except the priest, her female companion and her personal maid. Nothing was seen nor heard of her and it was as if she had ceased to exist. She was consulted on no matter, her opinions were not sought, nor her wishes considered. Only her desire for solitude was adhered to.

The earl was unusually quiet at first. He gave orders in a voice more mellow than before and asked for very little. He barely ate but drank a good deal.

On the third day he called for his son. "Well my boy. You are the heir now. That is one aspect of this foul business which I do not regret. But it will no doubt require a considerable adjustment for you and your intended."

"Intended what?" inquired Ludovic with some suspicion.

The earl smiled faintly, the first smile in three days. "You have grown strangely untrusting recently, Ludovic," he said. "Beware becoming too much like your father, my boy. Indeed, I was not casting aspersions on your future plans, but merely referring to your intended bride. Although you have chosen not to inform me of it, I presume you have asked the lady?"

Ludovic sat down abruptly. "No." He shook his head, staring bleakly up at his father. "Alysson's been imprisoned for months and threatened with appalling abuse by members of this family. I also carry the same bloodline. Marriage with me would seem a – brutal destiny. How can I ask it of her?"

"Your sanity has, as far as I recall, only rarely been in question," sighed the earl. "And whatever your inadequacies, my boy, the female under discussion most certainly needs a husband. She has been singularly compromised in every way. Perhaps this family owes her a more settled future. And incidentally, in spite of certain qualities sadly lacking, I have always considered that you took more after myself both in looks and character."

"With all due respect, sir," Ludovic said while showing very little respect, "your own bloodline seems just as dubious. I prefer not to speak of Brice, but that creature Vymer bore no relationship to my mother but only to yourself, and I question both his appalling character and his sanity."

"Ah. The Wapping girl," nodded the earl. "A vacuous mare, but always dutiful and exceptionally trim. A mistake in fact. But am I to believe you now have your own regrets? You no longer desire the intimate companionship of Alysson Welles?"

Ludovic glowered. "I'll certainly marry her if she'll have me, and desire little else. But she needs time to recover first, and to recognise what risks she takes by accepting me. If she turns me down, I'll set her up wherever she wishes, somewhere away from the scandals here. She has a respectable nurse as chaperone, and I'll buy them a house. I'll buy them anything they want."

"There are few lady's maids – forgive me – daughters of aldermen – given the chance to become a countess. I imagine she'll consent to take you rather than a lonely obscurity."

"She wouldn't –"

The earl raised one hand. "Spare me your protestations, my boy. I am sublimely disinterested in this female's moral character, or indeed in any other. My opinion of the fair sex has been honed over many years and is unlikely to alter, while your own present opinion is undoubtedly ingenuous and utterly biased. I should therefore not believe whatever you say. I should, however, appreciate being kept informed of your imminent plans. I have been daily expecting your collapse, your departure, your marriage, or all three simultaneously. Since my every reasonable expectation has recently been shredded and my hopes for the future of this family ruined, what little remains now seems of more particular interest. I trust you will deign to entrust me with some knowledge of your intentions."

Ludovic came to his father and knelt, taking the earl's hand and bringing it to his lips. "We've both been crushed by what's happened, sir. Your pain must be greater than my own. Whatever I decide to do, I shall tell you first, and ask for your blessing."

The earl nodded. "I believe I shall be proud of my new heir, my boy. Although I regretted his disadvantages and would have wished him other than my firstborn, poor Humphrey was very dear to me. The weak and vulnerable, you know, can touch us more deeply than the strong. But I was blind. I never knew his secrets and never understood his needs. Your mother kept a great deal from me and I was content to let her smother and cosset the boy whom I knew to be her favourite. I was aware he could be brutal while hunting, but so can many of us. What I have seen on the battlefield would horrify those same men if the identical deeds were practised during peacetime. I thought Humphrey excitable and easily unbalanced. Perhaps I chose not to see the truth. And that is a great weakness in a man assuming leadership and power. You will be stronger, my boy, and bring the Sumerfords back into greatness under the Tudors."

"You know I loathe the Tudors, Father."

"Your personal opinion of any crowned king is utterly irrelevant, my boy," the earl said. "You have a duty to accept whosoever is anointed in the good Lord's name, and you have an equal duty to your family. You will have sons by this girl of yours. Will they inherit pride, or only dust and nightmares from the past?"

"If Alysson will have me," nodded Ludovic, "I shall try and deserve her. But I cannot ask her yet." He stood again and crossed to the wide casement window. It was late afternoon and the sun was sinking low, streaming warmth directly into the chamber. All storms had passed and the flooded land was beaming fresh. Ludovic gazed out over the rolling pastures, his back to his father.

"Have I just reflected that your sanity is not in question? Perhaps I was mistaken." The earl smiled, stretched his legs and reached for his wine cup. He found it empty. "Get me some wine, my boy. This business of parental advice to the young and foolish I find quite exhausting." He took the cup Ludovic filled, and drained it. "You and this female have something unexpected in common," he continued. "You have both been locked away from your fellows for some months. This weakens all resolve and undermines all confidence. Under considerable threat and the possibility of facing a violent death, a man – and no doubt a woman – knows himself helpless. He is forced to relinquish control. On release, he remains weak and confused, habituated to self-doubt. Taking up control once again demands a great effort of will and determination, but it must be done. If you are to sire your own heirs, my boy, you must become the lord of your destiny once more. Take this girl and take your life back into your own hands."

Ludovic poured himself wine and drank it quickly. "I'll force no one I love to act against her own best interests."

"I am not suggesting rape, my boy," the earl said with a sigh. "There has been sufficient threat of that already I believe. But your strength has been shattered, first in the Tower, and then by each of your brothers in turn and for different reasons. I am simply suggesting you remember the pride of the Sumerfords and foster your own confidence anew. Since you threw off your swaddlings as an infant, you have always been my favourite son, Ludovic. It is time you proved the accuracy of my opinions."

Ludovic looked at his father in surprise. "I beg your pardon, sir?"

"So you should, my boy," said the earl. "So you should. Now go away and propose to your alderman's daughter."

Already cut and partially stitched for the Lady Jennine, the sarsenet bedrobe was threaded in turquoise over a lining of white velvet. Ludovic requisitioned the half-finished garment from the castle seamstress and ordered it completed within the day. He then presented it to Alysson and promised more gifts to come. She had not yet dared to leave her seclusion. "You can hardly stay here permanently," Ludovic laughed, striding into her open solar, the bedrobe over his arm. "Take this for now – it's a respectable enough cover for use in your own chambers. I'll have gowns made for you over the next few days. Then you must join me at dinner. I want you there."

She shook her head. "The scullions and serving boys would hate to wait on me, you know they would. They still think of me as a servant. And at the moment my blue gown is quite ruined, which only leaves the pink, and that's made of woollen jersey which is stifling in this sultry weather. Besides," she blushed and looked away, "I'd be dreadfully uncomfortable facing her ladyship. Your mother dislikes me so much. And honestly Ludovic, after everything she planned for me, I can't forgive her. I can't imagine how I ever will."

"My wretched mother's in hiding," Ludovic said. "I've not seen her myself since it all happened, and frankly I doubt I can forgive her either. In fact, I've come to doubt her sanity." He sat down beside Alysson, pressing the swathes of soft material into her arms. "Which doesn't say a lot for me, my love. Can you forgive me for being a part of this family?"

He came again the next day and found her wearing the bedrobe. He brought Clovis and Ellis with him, shepherded by the eager Kenelm. The captain was preparing his next voyage and hoping for a necessary replenishment to the coffers, but first relished any excuse to meet up again with the nurse Ilara, now in constant attendance on Alysson. Kenelm also intended taking both cabin boys into shipboard service and hoped to knock out their jealous rivalry which Ludovic found so amusing.

"Hussey's already at sea," Ludovic said, "and making a fair profit in the Middle Sea. Business is building with Spain. Spanish settlements in the New Indies are making her exceedingly rich, so she's ready and open for profitable barter."

"I know it. I'll be catching tomorrow's tide myself, my lord, and beating Hussey's carvel to the portolan. Given a month or two, I'll bring home a right good living for you and for me, and train them boys while I'm at it."

"I've a soft spot for your boys," Ludovic nodded. "And I owe them both a good deal. I'll take them on myself if they've a mind to it instead of going back to sea."

"There's no one in their right mind as would want work on the land 'stead of the waves, my lord," Kenelm said, aghast. "But I'll tell them little buggers afore I leaves, and give them the choice of it."

Alone with Alysson, Ludovic, elbow to the mantel, smiled down at her. "You call Clovis a hero, my love, but you've a better claim to heroism yourself. My father knows it too."

She shook her head. "That's silly. Some things, the terrible business

530

of Pagan of course, are too dreadful to think of. But I was never touched you know and I escaped almost all the things I was threatened with. I can hardly claim heroism and I'm quite sure your father wouldn't think of me that way, if he even thinks of me at all."

Ludovic smiled. "On the contrary. He accepts and is no longer disapproving of your presence here. Won't you consent to meet him one day?"

Alysson stared back. "Everyone in the castle is terrified of your father, Ludovic, and long before this recent trouble. I couldn't possibly face him. And why should I? What good would it do? And what in the world would I say?"

"He's a difficult man, but he's lonely." Ludovic came quickly and sat beside her on the long settle. Her bare toes beneath the bedrobe were tucked inches from his leg. He resisted the urge to caress them. "I've a notion he's hoping to befriend you. And in case I've not already made it obvious, I'm hoping to befriend you too. Since I'm the only remaining heir, my father will have to be at least distantly involved."

Alysson continued staring. "I've no idea what you're talking about. We were friends before, and your father had nothing to do with me then. Why should he? He didn't approve, I know that. None of your family ever liked me except Jenny, and that certainly turned out to be a hideous mistake."

"The idea of friendship with anyone in my family must seem an even more hideous mistake now," Ludovic said softly. "What was done to you and what was planned, was lunacy and wickedness. I've no excuses to offer for any of us. I can only try and put things right."

Alysson sat very straight, holding her breath. "How?" she said.

Ludovic was staring at her toes. They suddenly seemed immensely kissable. He looked away. "Ilara and Dulce. If you prefer to live with them again, I'll procure you a house, a beautiful house, somewhere you'd be unknown and the scandals wouldn't follow. You'd never be called a servant again. You'd be the lady you deserve to be, and I'd make sure you had land and property and funds. I make a reasonable living from investments in trade, and will come into all my father's properties and title one day. I can give you whatever you want."

Alysson's toes twitched. "You haven't asked me what I want."

Ludovic took a deep breath, as if about to enter deep water. He already felt himself drowning. He said, "No. Perhaps I've been fearful of what I expect you to say. So, say it now. What is it, my love, that you want?"

"You ought to know," Alysson said in a rush, her voice growing louder with frustrated. "I've been through utter misery for months, not just because of all the vile things that were happening with Jenny and your mother and Humphrey and Vymer, but because they told me you were dead. That was the meanest of all, because it took away every little bit of hope I had, which is why they said it of course. And now you're alive and the miracle I prayed for came true and it's a wonderful dream instead of a nightmare. Hell went away and heaven came back. So since then I've been sitting here day after day stuck in these rooms – and they're lovely rooms but that's not the point – it's just another prison really because I can't leave. And I've just been waiting and waiting for you to say what I thought you would. Because all the time you were away I regretted so dreadfully having told you no. And now I want to say yes. It's infuriating because it really ought to be you saying it, but you won't ask." Alysson quivered, her fingers entwining in her lap, and her eyes now moist. "So what do I want? Well, it's obvious, isn't it?" she scowled. "I want to be your mistress."

Ludovic gazed at her one moment, then leaned forwards and took her tight into his embrace. His fingers crawled up her neck to her loose curls, his other hand wrapping her against him. Her cheek was wet with tears. He kissed her mouth, no longer trembling but strong and open to his. He felt her response and pressed deeper.

When he pulled back she gasped for breath. Mesmerised, he looked down past the spangles in her eyes to the bruised gleam of her lips where he had kissed her, to the quickened rise and fall of her breasts beneath the bright sarsenet and miniver. He smiled, lingering. "But, my precious beloved," he sighed, "I no longer intend asking you to be my mistress."

Alysson sat up in shock. Her eyes glazed, she straightened her back and she wound her fingers very tightly into the lacings of Ludovic's doublet. "You have to," she glared. "It wouldn't be fair to go off me now. What's wrong with me all of a sudden? I'm not old yet. I'll seduce

532

you. I know how to. Jenny taught me. I might make a fool of myself, but you can just sit there and don't dare laugh at me while I try."

Ludovic caught her wandering fingers and brought both her hands to his lips. "Silly puss," he smiled. "I adore you. How could I laugh? Instead it's likely I'd suffer from a condition I've not known since emerging from puberty." She began to struggle but he restrained her, capturing her again within his arms. "It's no longer a mistress I'm dreaming of, my love," he whispered to her ear, "I want you as my wife. Could you bear that? After everything that's happened I expected you to refuse me. But it seems there's hope. Perhaps you'll consider me worth taking after all."

CHAPTER FIFTY-EIGHT

"I imagine," said the Earl of Sumerford, "that my blessing will serve neither to encourage nor impede your union, my children. But since it is a rare occurrence that I bestow blessings rather than objections, my approval may bring some small and insignificant benefit. I therefore offer approbation, make whatever you will of it, and I shall be pleased to arrange and attend your nuptials."

But without the presence of priest nor marriage ring, nor holy oil nor witnesses, Ludovic and Alysson were united that same night, a full week before the ceremony which the earl attended.

Ludovic had taken her to the north tower and officially presented her to his father as his intended wife. Dressed in a new gown, Alysson had curtsied and kept her eyes lowered. She found the earl gracious but intimidating and was glad to escape. She did not meet the countess. Ludovic made no attempt to speak to his mother on the subject, though later that day he sent a written message. He received no answer. He was quite sure the countess would be horrified, and was both mildly sorry, and mildly pleased.

He then escorted Alysson back to her own rooms where Ilara, Dulce and Clovis waited, all three having taken up residence in her new quarters. The abruptly announced news of her imminent marriage was met with considerable twittering and screeching.

Clovis put his hands over his ears. "Seagulls," he objected. "Women wailing 'n squeaking like them bloody birds. Anyone 'd fink it were a surprise."

Ilara hauled Clovis tight to her generosity of bosom. "Dear boy. You must surely be as excited as we are."

Clovis's reply was muffled. "I were better off at sea after all," he complained. "And don't you dare kiss me again, missus."

"The marriage will be solemnised by the village priest next Wednesday," Ludovic told them. "The following day I intend taking Alysson away from here. The memories cling too close. I'm taking her to my property in Bedfordshire. Naturally, you'll all accompany us." He turned to Ilara with a slight bow. "And I believe Kenelm has been remarkably solicitous in your direction lately madam. But he can visit you in Bedfordshire just as well, and you can both make your future plans as you wish. In the meantime, Alysson will certainly hope for your company."

"Dear Clarence. And my dearest Alysson," murmured Ilara, blushing pink. The twittering increased.

"Well," smiled Alysson, "I couldn't think of leaving any of you behind, could I? You're family."

Ludovic did not relinquish Alysson to her avid entourage. He first took her to the battlements where they had sometimes walked together before. Her hand warm tucked in his, he leaned down and kissed her. The wind was in his hair and over his shoulder the great plains of Somerset and its wild coastline stretched and sparkled beneath the sunshine. When he allowed her breath again, Alysson squinted up at him. "We shouldn't go to Bedfordshire," she said.

He raised an eyebrow. "You've another place in mind, my love?"

"The Bedfordshire property belongs to your mother," she said simply. "And now you're the heir of Sumerford."

He grinned. "You dread the thought of becoming a countess? Or aspire to it?"

"Neither. Because it doesn't seem real, and anyway a countess is just the same person dressed up in ermine instead of rabbit. You told me that once, in different words. But I don't think you've ever run away from anything, Ludovic, and I don't want to be the reason for you doing it now. Besides," her voice shrank to a whisper, "I don't want to be beholden to her."

"You won't be. It doesn't work like that, my love," Ludovic said. "And of course we'll have to come back here one day. My father will need me as he gets older. But by then perhaps your own memories will have faded and you'll be able to face Sumerford again."

She shook her head. "I'm not a coward. What happened won't ever go away. But I've always been good at facing the truth. I've had to. With you beside me, it'll all be so much easier anyway. So different."

"It'll certainly be different. I'll make sure of that." He laughed and pulled her into his arms. "But my mother's dower lands belong to me now. She signed them over and it'll be legal in a few days. My father arranged it. He probably bribed and threatened, but I don't care about that. She never lived there, it was a minor part of her father's properties, and I need a place to take you. Her family are the Clintons and the place is known as Clinton House, but in time I'll change that too. We'll stay a few years I expect. It's a beautiful property. You'll like it."

She sniffed, cuddling in tight to his side. "You wanted to take me there before. I wish I'd agreed. When I was held in the – east tower – for all that time, I kept thinking how I should have said yes to you. Then none of all that horror would have happened." The breezes were threatening Alysson's headdress and she held it on, the flat of her hand on top of her head. "So in a way, it was my fault," she continued in a rush. "Modesty's fault, and timidity's fault. And I'd probably have loved being your mistress, Ludovic. It was only those things Jenny kept saying that frightened me off. Silly really, when she was actually trying to push me into your bed all the time." She gulped. "Because she thought you'd educate me – in the skills of – and ruin me for respectability before getting tired of me – well, you know why."

Ludovic sighed. "You'll like being my wife better, I promise. As for being your fault, the idea's absurd." He pulled her tighter. "You'll be mistress of Clinton House and the Bedfordshire lands, and the education I'll offer will be a sweet one, I swear. It's a grand place for I've been there several times over past years, and refurbished it to my own taste. No one there will know you were ever called servant, nor have heard the latest scandals. They'll know you only as the lady of the house, and as my wife and future countess."

"Gossip spreads. They'll know one day, but I don't care." Alysson peeped up at Ludovic, her fingers curled around his. "And I don't care about being a countess because that's years away. It's being your wife that's exciting, Ludovic. That seems really, really exciting. I may not make a very good lady at first, or a very good wife either since I haven't any idea what I'm supposed to do about it. But I'll learn, really I will. I'm a quick learner."

He laughed. "That wasn't what I had in mind as the education I'm offering."

"Oh. That." Seeing the laugh in his eyes, Alysson avoided his gaze, quickly looking down at her toes and the flurry of her hems caught in the wind.

Ludovic frowned. "Not nervous are you, my love?"

"What should I be nervous about?" Alysson demanded. "You mean about – the wedding night? Do you? I hope you don't expect me to be a frightened little virgin because I won't be."

"I expect only bliss." Ludovic grinned and gathered her closer. The wind had begun to bluster, curling around the battlements and blowing wisps of sea cloud down over the tops of the stone towers. A thin chill haze slipped low. "Time to go back down," he said, "before you catch cold and I have to delay the wedding and spoil that bliss. But I need you to myself. Or do you want your own chambers, my love?"

"If you start being polite and asking my opinion all the time," said Alysson, "I shall think it's you who's ill. And of course I don't want my own rooms. What on earth for? The pleasure of Ilara and Dulce squeezing me half to death again? No thank you. Couldn't we walk in the gardens instead?"

Ludovic shook his head. "The sun's heading west and the wind's increasing." He began to walk with her back to the narrow stone steps. He did not explain himself further but when they reached the deep darkness of the long corridor below, he stopped abruptly and pulled her again into his embrace. The shadows fell suddenly black, the warmth disappeared with the light, and the damp enclosed them. Then he leaned her back to the wall, bent and kissed her hard.

She felt the curl of his lashes against her cheek, the slight roughness of his jaw and the heat of his breath. He held her firm against him but his other hand roamed, discovering the soft silk warmth of her heartbeat. Then his fingers pushed up, sliding over her breast and pressing around her nipple. She gasped, her mouth imprisoned by his, but she made no attempt to pull away. His hands continued to travel, reaching for the yielding flesh above the trimming of her gown. His fingertips smoothed across the curve, savouring her nakedness, then dipping quickly into her cleavage, finding her breast once again. She stood very still, holding her breath. Then he moved back a little, released her from his kissing, and looked down. She caught the glint of his eyes in the darkness.

"I take a woman's silence as permission," he said softly, "but with you, my love, I should beware my own arrogance. Stop me if you will."

Alysson took a deep breath. With her inhalation, her breasts swelled against Ludovic's palm. "I don't want you to stop," she whispered. "I've imagined this for so long. Lying in that miserable place, trying not to think of what might happen, I dreamed of you instead. I dreamed of you making love to me."

He smiled and she felt his fingers tighten on her. "And what did you dream, my precious girl?"

"I wasn't sure." She buried her head against his chest and closed her eyes. "I imagined – lots of things – but I didn't really know, you see. Jenny told me what to do at the start, but she never really – explained everything. Not in a nice way. She made it sound terribly – rude and painful and sordid. But I don't mind it being sordid if it's with you."

She found herself flying. He had gathered her up, feet swept from the ground and knees tucked to his waist. He carried her the few short dark steps towards his own chambers, kicked open the door and marched into the sudden light. The door slammed back against the inside wall with a shuddering crash and the servants hovering within all leapt up in shock. The page who had been sitting cross legged on the rug practising reading his book of psalms, fell flat on his face with a squeak. The two men brushing out Ludovic's clothes in the garderobe came running out white faced.

"Out," said Ludovic and everybody ran.

He strode into the inner chamber where the great bed rose like a curtained throne, the unshuttered window still bright with waning sunlight and the velvets and silks glowing in the late summer glow. He laid Alysson on the bed and sat immediately on the edge, facing her.

"Come to me now," he said.

Alysson felt herself unusually hot. "You want to call the priest? Now?"

Ludovic grinned. "Certainly not. We can do without him." He reached out and took her hand again, more gently this time. "My father has the ring. We should still go through with the ceremony he's arranged at the church, with the banns read and the witnesses present. But I don't need to wait to prove there's nothing sordid in loving. Take me now, if you want me."

"I want you," she breathed.

He sat a little closer, his face bright on one side where the sunshine turned his hair pure gold, the other side etched in shadows below the cheekbone and around the crease of his widening smile. "In my heart, this'll be my wedding night. I give you my hand and my body," he said, "and claim you as mine."

Alysson hiccupped. "I'll be a good wife, Ludovic. I promise I'll try."

"I'll show you how."

She was propped against pillows and bolster, her skirts spread across the furs and velvets of the bedcover. He held her eyes with his smile as he slipped his hands to her ankles beneath her hems, quickly removing both her shoes and tossing them to the floor. His hands returned to her ankles, his palms warm against the thin knitted wool of her stockings, pushing up her skirts to her knees. She trembled slightly.

He bent over her, his eyes bright, his breath in her ear. "Nervous after all, my beloved? Shall I put up the shutters?"

"No. Don't make it dark," she gulped. "I don't think I want to be seen. But I want to see you. I want to see you beautiful and naked and sunlit." The hiccups had come back. "Is that – wrong?"

He laughed. "Wonderfully unexpected." His hands had found the tops of her stockings where the little garters were tied tight around her thighs. Still watching her expression intently, his fingers quickly pulled at the knots and sprang the ribbons loose. He began to roll her stockings down. His hands, deft with a woman's intimate clothing, were warm and brisk.

Alysson sat very still holding her breath. She wondered if she should be doing something herself. "I don't know how to undo a man's lacings," she whispered.

Ludovic laughed again. "I shall show you. But this first." He pulled each stocking from her toes, tossing the little rolled bundles aside to where her shoes lay discarded. At last he removed his intensity from her face and looked down at where his hands were so busy. He had raised her skirts, his palms back to her thighs. Then he leaned forwards and kissed her again. As his tongue pushed deep past her lips, one hand crept up around her shoulders, the other to her waist where he quickly unhooked her stomacher and then the hooks of her gown.

She pulled away a little, blinking up at him, suddenly timid. "Perhaps," she whispered, "the dark would be kinder after all."

Ludovic laughed again and shook his head. "Too late." He reached down and grasping the double swathes of materials at their hems, swept her chemise and gown up together and lifted them high over her head until they fell to the ground beside the bed.

Alysson's curls tumbled around her face as she sat quite naked on his bed. She crossed her arms hurriedly over her breasts, squeezing her legs together and blushing. He watched her for a moment with a curious expression she had never seen before, then gently took her hands in his and uncrossed her arms, bringing them around to his own back. Then he pressed onto her, kissing her eyes and her ears and the corners of her mouth, and down her neck to her shoulders. Finally he kissed her breasts. He felt her quiver, and sat back with a reluctant smile.

"Too fast, my precious? It's been so long. I'm impatient and want you too much."

She tried to smile, though it went lop sided. Without his body wrapped tight to her, she felt suddenly cold. "I've never seen a man naked," she said tentatively. "Only little boys. Is it the same?"

Ludovic smiled down at her and stood, tall and straight beside the bed where the sunbeams spun a halo around him, lighting his back and leaving him in shadow. He began to undress. Alysson watched him unlace his doublet and pull it off, shrug his shirt over his head, and release the points of his hose, braies and codpiece. When he stood quite naked in front of her, he was still smiling.

"Well? Is it the same?" he asked softly.

"Oh no," she whispered. "It isn't the same at all."

CHAPTER FIFTY-NINE

Autumn flecked scarlet and golden across the Bedfordshire countryside. Through the Clifton House parks with their low hedges and angular paths, the sun lit each leaf in gaudy colour, a fluttering of copper willow and saffron beech. The Lady Alysson wandered the grounds of her new home, her hand clutching tightly to her husband's sleeve and creasing his flowing velvets. It was, he remarked, as though she expected him to run away if allowed free, to dissolve perhaps, or melt in the sunshine.

"It could still all be a dream," she nodded. "You could be a phantasm."

Ludovic had almost forgotten the ghost in his life. He had decided he preferred reality after all.

The Countess of Sumerford had not attended her only remaining son's nuptials. A message was sent, excusing herself with explanations of ill health, but it was not written by her own hand. Following soon after the previous heir's funeral with the earl and his entire household officially in mourning, the marriage ceremony had been intended as a small and private affair, the priest officiating at the porch of the little village church. Alysson had at first been amazed when most of the villagers and almost every one of the castle staff had appeared through the trees and across the village green, clustering outside and climbing the churchyard's low wall. They had cheered, and clapped, danced and sung. There was great approval for the new heir, and for his unexpected wife. After the misery of the last weeks, it was a good time to celebrate. The earl, standing a little aside, had smiled quietly. Ludovic had laughed and Alysson had blushed the same colour as her new gown.

They had left for Bedfordshire the next day, taking the journey in easy stages and resting frequently, their lengthy entourage requiring a slow pace. Alysson had first seen her new home glowing mellow brick under the late afternoon sunshine, the long rows of windows reflecting the light and the flutter of the leaf. Huge chimneys peeped up through the surrounding greenery, and oaks and willows stretched to either side, marking the pathway to the stables and outhouses. The parklands were arranged behind, wide and open between clipped hedges, then sloping down to the lake where the fish were kept, and the trees grew thicker again.

But it was the interior that delighted Alysson the most for she could remember no house like it. Larger than anything she had known except Sumerford castle, yet far warmer and more intimate, the furnishings were elaborate and fresh in their sunny silks, and the many large windows welcomed in the light. There was no damp stone nor icy draughts. There was no mildew on worn stair treads, no mould creeping up the bedchamber walls nor moss clinging to the ceiling beams. The grand staircase was a great sweep of dark carved wood, wide enough for four. No narrow stone steps wound steeply up, no towers brooded from their cloud cover, no freezing battlements collected the winter's snow in slippery banks, and no open arrow slits let in the whine of wind or sleet. The sea did not pound through her dreams, nor the wail of gulls, and instead Alysson heard the blackbird announce the dawn before the cockerels crowed and bustle began.

It was still courtship more than marriage, but Alysson learned as she had promised. When she asked questions and Ludovic answered, because I love you, it was not enough.

"I need to understand more than that. Love means lots of things. Vymer loved Humphrey," she whispered one night from the security of Ludovic's embrace. "He idolised him as a brother and a master. Vymer was a terrible man, but he was sad too. And it was sad that Humphrey killed him, who loved him so. And then your mother, who loved Humphrey most of all -"

"Hush my beloved." Ludovic's warm breath tickled her ear. They lay naked together in the gentle sweat after love-making, and his hand was on her breast. "This isn't the same love that we have. I'm bitterly sorry for what my family has done to you, but I swear you'll always be safe with me."

"I won't forgive your mother, but I feel sorry for her too."

"More memories?" Ludovic murmured. "Does it help, or hinder, to speak of them?"

"It helps, now I feel so safe. It tames them," Alysson said. "And I try to make sense of what happened."

"There's no sense to madness."

"Is your mother – just perhaps – a little mad as well?" Alysson sighed. "I don't think so. But now she's lost everything. Oh, she still has your father of course, but they don't like each other at all. Just seeing her seemed to annoy him and he used to hit her. Sometimes she had so many bruises she had to disguise them with lead powder. They could both be so cruel."

"I don't expect you to forgive my parents, little one." Ludovic pulled her closer. "I can only promise never to become like either of them."

Alysson peeped up at him. His hair was in his eyes, his face relaxed and peaceful. "You're very meek these days," she whispered. "But remember, I knew you before. You won't always be like this."

"I've been through my own nightmares, beloved. I've changed. Grown."

"Grown? If you grow any more, my love, I shall have to sleep in separate quarters after all."

He chuckled. "Brat. Go to sleep. I've a long day tomorrow, since I've word that both Kenelm and Hussey are back in dock."

"I'll come to London with you," Alysson said at once. "And Ilara will want to see Kenelem. But I'm glad we don't ever have to go to court, though London will be exciting."

He smiled, eyes closed. "One day the summons will come from the king, and we'll have to attend court, my love. I've a duty as heir to the title and once Tudor decides to forgive and forget, he'll demand our presence. He needs allies. These claims to the throne have rattled him. Now he's old and sick before his time, and his sons still too young for kingship."

"I hate the king after everything he did to you," Alysson said. "I don't care to meet him."

"But he will care about you," Ludovic said, "and will demand fealty."

Alysson sighed. "Sumerford is a title for summer. But last summer was so sad. Now it's autumn. I love the autumn colours, but it means winter's coming. Will a Sumerford winter be bitterly cold?"

"Winter means the coming of spring. Spring is birth. Then comes summer again. We'll have a Sumerford summer together, my sweet. Don't fear the winter. I'll keep you safely warm. We've no more tragedies to threaten us."

The autumn stayed fine as the fruit ripened in the orchards, the wheat waved tall to the cloudless sky, harvests were rich and plentiful, verjuice, cider and perry fermented in their barrels and the countryside bloomed. Clinton House became known as Sumerford House and its halls glowed in autumn warmth as its trees flushed crimson, azurite and madder, a last flamboyance before the fading.

Then finally the cold slipped in between the sunbeams and rains dampened the birdsong. The larks and swallows flocked, massing in dark clouds above the soaring chimney pots before escaping to warmer shores. The breezes turned to sharp biting winds, collecting dead leaves like scavengers on the wing.

It was the last days of their Sumerford autumn when Ludovic woke in the night. An owl was calling, a soft hoot in the starshine. There was no moon and the land was quiet. He lay in darkness for a few moments, then rolled again into the cradle of Alysson's warmth. She slept, curled to the shape of him, her knees tucked beneath his own. He closed his eyes and closed his mind to sleep again, when he heard the words as he had before.

"Do you hear me? Will you listen?" But it was not the same voice.

Ludovic sat up carefully, disentangling Alysson's embrace. She continued to sleep undisturbed. Ludovic left the bed and padded to the window. One of the shutters hung crooked, with a crack of starlight shining between the slats. He was naked, and the sudden chill made him reach for his bedrobe. He shrugged it on, righted the loose shutter, and turned. A faint glow of light had entered the chamber and hung now before him, as if a star had escaped its heaven and come to find him. "What do you want?" Ludovic whispered. "Are you Edward again? Your voice is changed, and you told me you'd not return. Why haven't you stayed with your brother?"

The silence swept cold. Ludovic stood where he was, gazing at the pale light. It flickered, as if trembling. Then the voice said, "I am not my brother Edward. I remember my real name, though I've been given many and some have been forced on me. My true name is Richard and I am the son of a true king. My brother should have been king, but when he was lost and died, I claimed the throne. But I failed, as my brother failed." The voice sighed, like the breeze rustling through fallen leaves.

Ludovic frowned. "Richard? Prince Edward's brother then, the Duke of York? How do you come to me? And why?"

The answer floated a little louder, the voice gaining strength. "Edward sent me. He's taking me on into the light. I've no regrets, not any longer, though I leave the wife and son I loved."

"You leave them? Then you died?" Ludovic leaned back heavily against the tapestried wall, pulling his bedrobe tight around him. "You were a prisoner in the Tower when I was last in London. I've heard no news of your death."

"You will." The pause lengthened, then the voice came softer. "They called me Piers Warbeck, a foreigner, and my own country repudiated me, accusing me of treason. They hung me as a common traitor. But I only wanted their love."

Ludovic nodded. "I'm sorry. My brother loved you and died for you. I regret that beyond anything else, but I regret your death too.

You had my support, but I had other loves in my life to live for. Is purgatory such a hard road, that ghosts choose to linger here? I don't understand why you come to me, as your brother did."

"I come to you because you suffered for me," the voice replied. "My brother sent me. I came to thank you, and ask your forgiveness before I travel on. Now I see no threat nor is there the murk of purgatory, only light and colour and beauty. Edward will take me into the planes of Paradise."

"Then you have my prayers," murmured Ludovic.

"I don't need your prayers anymore," the voice said. "But you have mine. And Edward's. He's grateful for the comfort you gave him, and I'm sorry for the pain I caused you. Your life will be easier now. Your future waits peacefully in your wife's arms and the founding of your own family. No man needs power, only love. I should have learned that before."

The next morning Ludovic rode to Westminster. He travelled alone. It was the first time he had left Alysson in nearly four months, but he would not risk taking her to court unannounced and unsummoned.

It was late November and the leaves had blown. Dark branches flared stark against a pale, snow laden sky. The sleet held off until Ludovic dismounted. The Abbey bells were ringing, muffled behind the sudden downpour. Ludovic strode into the long passages of Westminster Palace and went straight to the chambers he knew. A page announced him but he did not wait to be invited in.

He found the Earl of Berkhamstead sitting over a candle stub, playing chess with himself. William looked up, startled. Ludovic entered quickly and stood, looking down at him. "So, it's finished at last," he said softly.

William's eyes were bloodshot. His face loomed white above the tiny flickering flame. He nodded. "You heard then. Four days ago. A travesty. A tragedy."

Ludovic frowned. "The last time I saw you, you'd become mighty friendly with the king. I imagined you'd changed loyalties. Doesn't the prince's death leave you free to advance your own family fortunes?"

"I loved him." Berkhamstead looked away, his eyes moist. "I tried to speak for him at his trial, but they allowed no one in and no evidence of any kind was given. It was a mockery of justice with the result a foregone conclusion. The prince was condemned as a traitor to the crown. What bitter irony. As the true heir to the throne, he should have worn the crown himself."

"He was tried under the name Piers Warbeck?" Ludovic raised one eyebrow. "As a foreigner then? But how can a foreigner be a traitor to an English monarch? What nonsense was condoned here?"

"De Vere sat as Lord High Steward, and stated simply that Warbeck's actions were sufficient justification, found him guilty and sentenced him to death without a jury." William shook his head, thumping his fist on the low table. The chess pieces jumped and tumbled. "De Vere was always Tudor's pawn. I'm told that the prince stood silent and gazed around him as if bemused. When he heard the sentence of hanging and quartering, he blanched and bowed his head. He offered no defence."

"For pity's sake." Ludovic sat down opposite the young earl, staring across the chess board. "Defence? To what crime? For being himself?"

"They say he plotted to escape from the Tower. The prince and poor miserable Clarence's son Edward of Warwick found a way to correspond. Imprisoned in dreadful isolation, what man wouldn't welcome the friendship of another? But then others, some sympathetic gaolers and hopeful conspirators from outside, both those who hate Tudor and those with their own ambitions, it was said they planned to free the prisoners." Berkhamstead leaned forwards, speaking suddenly in whispers. "I knew of those plans. I encouraged them. The prince deserved to be free again, and young Warwick too. But I kept separate, and spoke of it to no one except Gwen. Then the plots were discovered. Thank the Lord, my own part in it stayed secret."

Ludovic paused a moment. He nodded towards the door. "The page is outside," he said. "Send him for wine."

The boy was called and sent running for hot gingered Malmsey.

Once gone, Berkhampstead leaned forwards again across the table. "You've news of some kind? Something dangerous? Tell me."

"Not news. Suspicions." Ludovic smiled slightly. "But your story first. What of the prince? Bad enough to be hung as a commoner, but surely not eviscerated alive? I've seen that done. It's a torture no criminal deserves, let alone a prince of the realm."

"No, that sentence was passed by the court, but then mitigated. Prince Richard was hung, the wretched murder of a man innocent of everything except claiming his rights. But no other abuse was carried out in the end. I'm told the prince agreed to make no final announcement of his true identity on the scaffold, in exchange for mercy. Mercy indeed! I was there. I saw it from the crowd. I sobbed unashamed. Others did too. But when they behead young Edward of Warwick next week, there'll be an outcry, that I know. Few realised who Prince Richard truly was and took Tudor's word the boy was simply some false pretender from Flanders. But they know exactly who Warwick is, and respect his title and his absolute innocence."

Ludovic sighed. "Tell me the rest. Before I hear it from someone less sympathetic."

"Prince Richard was drawn all the way from the Tower. It was bitterly cold. He wore only a workman's shirt, naked beneath with his legs bare and his head uncovered like a felon. He was roped to the hurdle and dragged through the mud and muck all the cold miles to Tyburn. He was filthy when he arrived at the scaffold, with his feet thick in shit and his face streaked in dirt. But he kept his dignity and said nothing at all. I watched from the crowd but my eyes were so full of tears I could barely see."

"And before his death?" Ludovic said. "He made no accusations?"

"No. It was the price of escaping the quartering," William said. "Tudor ensured all the foreign ambassadors were present, so he wanted a full confession. I don't know if the prince had agreed to make one, but in the end he said very little. Tudor must have been disappointed."

"That's a small consolation."

"Some official was sent up to make a statement of guilt on the prince's behalf, but the prince just stood there, as if broken. He tried hard not to shiver. I could see how desperately he tried to keep his dignity, and act as a prince through the stench and the muck that covered him." Berkhamstead shook his head. He was crying again, the tears filling his eyes and slipping over his cheeks. "They pushed him up the ladder to the noose. I was still terrified they might quarter him alive, but the prince showed no fear, only quiet acceptance. As if he welcomed the end of it all. All that miserable effort come to nothing. All that hope and suffering, the death of hundreds and the prayers of thousands."

"He said nothing?"

"The official said it for him. 'The traitor Piers Warbeck wishes it said that he admits his guilt ----.' I could barely hear. The crowd were clamouring; those calling for blood, and those calling for pity. But he spoke briefly at the end, asking that God and the king and all others whom he had offended, would forgive him. Then they put the noose around his neck and pulled the ladder away. I wept." He was weeping now, and continued in a whisper. "They usually struggle, you know, at the first drop. It's natural perhaps. But the prince hardly moved. He just hung there, so thin and pale and mired by the city's filth. He never kicked, nor cried out. He seemed already broken and so pitiful."

"They die quicker if they struggle," Ludovic murmured.

"It took a long time. The wind blew like ice. I stayed, trying to pray. He just hung there quietly, waiting to die. When they were sure he had died at last, the guards cut him down and took his head to spike on the bridge."

Ludovic looked away. "Is Gerald still there? He'd be proud to share a place beside his prince."

"I daren't pass," William whispered. "So I don't know. But with so many new executions, previous remains are disposed of after a month or two. Besides, there's no recognising the identity after time, the weathering and the ravens. They boil and tar the heads to keep scavengers away, but the scavengers come anyway. Best not think of it."

"I don't." Ludovic stood suddenly and marched across to the window. He turned his back on the other man, and stood, his hands clasped behind him, staring across to the Abbey steeple. "The shame's on Tudor's head," he said softly, "for the murdering of the innocents. And Warwick is to be beheaded? Poor wretched child."

"But you wanted the page sent away," Berkhamstead interrupted. "You spoke of suspicions. What's happened, then?"

"A good deal, but that needn't interest you," Ludovic said. "I've married the girl I've wanted for a long time, and that's keeping me sane and wiping out the memories of Gerald, and the racking and the Tower. But as for suspicions, it was you I suspected." He turned abruptly, staring again at Berkhamstead. "We were betrayed, but there were things only you knew. About where Gerald was and what we had planned. About the inn by the Fleet at first. Then later about our intention to embark at Margate. I know my captain told you that when you visited him. Even the wickedness of my brother Brice, and his friendship with pirates. Kenelm told you about that too, didn't he? Information only you had, Will. I've suspected you for a long time."

"My God." Berkhamstead had gone quite white again. "You thought I'd betrayed you to Tudor? I never would have," he whispered. "Never. I loved Gerald as I loved the prince. Gerald was my dearest friend."

"Perhaps I believe you." Ludovic nodded, tight lipped. "But if it wasn't you, there's only one other person."

William gulped, staring back. "She wouldn't."

"She must have. You told me she was from an old Lancastrian family. She acts the innocent, but she can't be, Will. Can't you see how everything you tell her rebounds on others, yet you stay free? And this latest tragedy? Now there's hangings, beheadings, accusations and attainders by the score, but not against you Will, never against you."

William had jumped up. "She's the mother of my son. The woman I love. If you say that again, I'll kill you."

"You've a lot to thank her for. I imagine she's saved your skin from Tudor's spite a dozen times." Ludovic had walked to the door. "No doubt her family discovered you were under suspicion for involvement in the very first plots. Gerald certainly was. You must have been too. So she went to the king and made a bargain to spy for him if he promised your safety. I believe she caused my imprisonment and Gerald's death, but she did it for you, and your sons. I wish you joy of the results, my friend." And he turned on his heel, wrenched open the door and stalked out.

The page was running breathless with the tray of gingered wine, and nearly hurtled into Ludovic in the long shadows.

"My lord?"

Ludovic nodded, took the brimming cup and drained it. The wine was thick spiced and very hot. It scorched his tongue, calming him. The aromatic steam stung his eyes. He nodded, returned the empty cup to the tray, and strode quickly back outside into the cold.

CHAPTER SIXTY

"Y ou've seemed happy for so long. Now you're sad again." Alysson laid her cheek on his breast, absently kissing the raised nipple nudging her lips. Her hand sought his. "You were away four whole days, but then you come home sad. I missed you so much while you were gone. But it feels like only half of you came back."

Ludovic brought her fingers to his lips. "Do I seem so dismal? How selfish of me. I promise to laugh again tomorrow."

"Silly." She wedged herself up on one elbow, looking down at him. "You don't have to humour me."

He smiled. "Unforgivably patronising?"

"Yes. It is when you try to keep me happy without telling me about your troubles, hiding things from me as if I were a child who wouldn't understand."

"Forgive me, my love," he sighed. "But it seems our Sumerford autumn is over and winter's here at last." He pulled her back down within the feather warmth of the bed, and into the greater warmth of his arms. "I've been reminded of Gerald all over again, and remembering Gerald's death reminds me of what the rest of my family did, and how I've lost nearly all of them within a few months. And now with Prince Richard executed, the time for royal reconciliations is come. We've been summoned to court for the

Christmas season. I'm not important enough to require royal approval for my choice of bride, but my father informed Tudor of our marriage, and the king insists on meeting you."

"Our first celebrations together?" She scowled. "And I have to be on my best behaviour, and not speak out of turn and learn boring protocol and how to address kings and walk backwards and not kiss you whenever I want to? I can't dance very well I'm afraid, and I don't like clarions and pibcorns."

Ludovic caressed her cheek, kissing the curve of her neck beneath her ear. "There's no escape, my sweet. It's a Tudor England from now on, and we must live with the new rules. The king has annihilated every Plantagenet he could get his hands on, and has even set about annihilating their reputations, rewriting history to his own benefit. His power is now unassailable and the lords have been forced to accept it. So must we, my love. Will you hate court so much?"

"Of course I shall. I just want to curl up here with you, and watch our own mummings and mysteries, and kiss you under the mistletoe bough."

"Kiss me now," he said, and kissed her first.

She clung to him. The sweat from across his chest trickled between her breasts, collecting in her navel where his own body flattened against her. His fingers followed its damp snail trail, smoothing wet heat across her belly and into the silky dark curls at her groin. His wandering continued down, caressing her thighs.

A huge fire had been lit earlier that evening, the logs filling the hearth and the blaze hurtling up the chimney in brilliant crackles and sparks. When the ice wind blew back the smoke, it billowed out into the room like a dragon's breath. The chamber wallowed in warmth. Ludovic did not visit his lady's quarters, but had brought her permanently into his own. He would not leave her alone, both for her comfort and for his, so the bile of past memories stayed safe cosseted away. Now the fire was burning low but the hiss of spitting logs still flared and the swelter, trapped all around, remained. Ludovic's bed cocooned them both in curtained shadows, the whispering rustle of the silks and the gentle giving sigh of soft feather mattress and quilt.

Ludovic tossed back the covers. "I want to see you." The light from the fire danced in cinnabar fingers across her body. His own fingers traced the dance.

"I like it when you say that," she whispered. "And I'm not shy anymore. I like seeing you too. I like the smell of you, all sweaty and musky. I don't know what you smell of, as if you've been rolling in something secret and wonderful. You smell of you."

"That's desire." He grinned down at her. "I smell desire on you too. Rosewater, fresh herbs, sweet soap in your hair, and the great and glorious sweat of desire. It's as arousing as touch."

Her palms clutched at his shoulders, drawing him tight. "No. Touch is the best of all," she smiled. "Touching you is almost as wonderful as you touching me. Your muscles are so strong and hard."

"I was little more than rattling bones after those months in the Tower. Now I'm myself again." He had eased his body between her legs, pressing against her so that she lay in his shadow. "Strong enough to protect you, little one. No one will ever dare threaten you again, I promise. Not here. Not at court. Not anywhere."

"I'm not frightened. I'm never frightened now," she said. "There's different sorts of happiness, but this is one I never suspected was possible." He kissed her breasts, pulling like a suckling child on the nipples. His head rested against her collar bone so the bright springing light of his hair was on her lips and tickled her cheek. His bright silk merged with her thick dark waves. "You make me feel powerful as well," she murmured. "I used to pretend to feel powerful, but it wasn't true at all. I used to be frightened about so many things. I lied about that too. I expected to be sad all my life. And I felt so weak. I don't anymore. You've made me into a new person, with a whole new life. Now I know what power really means."

When he came up for air, he cradled her again, smiling and content. His hands crept between her thighs which his own legs had parted. "You are powerful, my beloved. Far more powerful than I am. Especially here, and here, and here."

At her groin her hair curled tight and very dark. His was thicker, but bright and sweat slick. His hands played between the two, black twined to gold, groin to groin, finding her entrance. She trembled and clung to him. He began to whisper, his mouth so close to her ear that she felt he entered her there, as well as below. When he finally pressed deep inside her, she groaned and arched her back.

He moved very slowly, supporting himself on his elbows, smiling down at her as he watched her expression. She blinked, feeling his watchfulness, and opened her eyes. "What do you see?" she whispered.

"The woman I adore."

"Did you expect to discover someone else? I want more than that. Tell me properly."

He grinned, still moving within her, creating an easy, rhythmic pressure. "I like seeing the faces you make when I touch you deeper inside. You screw your nose up and breathe very fast. Then, when you squeeze hard around me, drawing me in, just as you're doing now, your face concentrates as if you're waiting to explode."

"I am. And I do explode. It's like those artificial lights they set off with the St. John bonfires. All sparks and flares."

"Then when I draw out a little, you take a deep breath, waiting for me to push down again. Your expressions echo my movements. I like to watch the pleasure written across your face."

"I'd like to watch you too, but I can't make love with my eyes open," she whispered, closing them tight again. "It lets too much of the world back in. It interrupts the feeling."

"Then feel this, my beloved," he murmured.

He pushed hard and fast, forcing suddenly deeper. Immediately reaching the tightness he sought far within, he stopped moving. The moist heat closed around him and he stayed quite still for one sweltering moment, gripping her to him. She felt his strength pulsating and filling her. He caught his breath, then subsided, shuddering. She gasped, and clung to him.

They collapsed together, close entwined. He wrapped the covers up around her shoulders and kissed her hard and long. When he finally released her, she smiled and whispered, "I feel scorched."

He rolled away a little, his head laid back on the bolster. Finally he closed his eyes. His hair, usually a bright sheen straight cut to his shoulders, was now tangled as if after battle. His laugh sounded tired. "Like branding a heifer?"

She sat up a little, tracing the tiny damp curls across his chest.

"Perhaps it is," she said. "They say wives are just useful as brood mares. Bought like any good breeding stock to produce heirs. And then, like a baker's bonus, to look pretty in church on saints' days."

His eyes snapped open then, as if to reassure himself she was teasing. "So forget being a wife," he smiled. "I need no breeding mare. Be my mistress. Can a man take his own wife as his mistress?"

"I don't see why not. Men usually think they can do anything they want to. And this time I don't need to think about it first. I'm not modest or nervous anymore. I'll say yes, right away."

Ludovic chuckled, one eyebrow raised. "That's mighty helpful to know beforehand. It seems you've become most improper, my love."

Alysson sat up a little straighter, cross legged on the soft mattress, blankets discarded. "Oh, I hope so. I'd like to scandalise the matrons at court. Though I suppose if they know anything about me, they'll be scandalised anyway. So can I wear my gowns cut very, very low, and my headdresses very high? So when I curtsey to the king, I shall almost burst out of my fichu, and make all the dukes stare. And can I flirt?"

"Only with me. And at Westminster, a woman who flirts with her husband will seem the most scandalous of all."

"But you said I'm not going to be your boring sheltered wife anymore, Ludovic. I know tricks I haven't used because I think you'll laugh at me. Jenny taught me ages ago, when I was supposed to snare you. I was so uncomfortable about it then. But now I'm going to be your mistress, so I can be outrageous and amazing and shock you, and I can practise all those strange contortions and special squeezes and other surprising things I learned, just as long as you promise not to snigger. I'll try to be an interesting mistress." She lowered her eyes. "Only you haven't actually asked me yet."

Ludovic's eyes half closed, the lids heavy. His mouth curved up very slowly, the smile sensual, barely tucked. He reached out, caressing her, his hands warm and intimate again on her body. Her breasts responded immediately.

"So be my mistress, beloved. Indeed, it's no longer something I ask of you," he breathed. "I demand it."

Dear Reader,

Ludovic's journey was quite dark at times, I hope it didn't upset you too much? On a slightly brighter note, why not try 'The Deception of Consequences'?

This time we are at Henry VIII's court. A time of excess, intrigue and corruption. Henry's advisor Richard Wolfdonn, is about to enter a web of death and conspiracy...

You'll love meeting this new cast of characters. And what a cast it is, with a pirates eccentric parcel of mistresses lined up to mourn him, Richard struggles to find the truth.

And do remember that when a reader leaves a review, an Author Angel gets their wings!

ABOUT THE AUTHOR

My passion is for late English medieval history and this forms the background for my historical fiction. I also have a love of fantasy and the wild freedom of the imagination, with its haunting threads of sadness and the exploration of evil. Although all my books have romantic undertones, I would not class them purely as romances. We all wish to enjoy some romance in our lives, there is also a yearning for adventure, mystery, suspense, friendship and spontaneous experience. My books include all of this and more, but my greatest loves are the beauty of the written word, and the utter fascination of good characterisation. Bringing my characters to life is my principal aim.

For more information on this and other books, or to subscribe for updates, new releases and free downloads, please visit barbaragaskelldenvil.com